Joseph Alexander Altsheler

THE SCOUTS OF THE VALLEY

THE BORDER WATCH

The Young Trailers Series Vol.3

BOOK SEVEN. THE SCOUTS OF THE VALLEY 1

A story of Wyoming and the Chemung 1

CHAPTER I. THE LONE CANOE 1

CHAPTER II. THE MYSTERIOUS HAND 10

CHAPTER III. THE HUT ON THE ISLET.....................................21

CHAPTER IV. THE RED CHIEFS 29

CHAPTER V. THE IROQUOIS TOWN.. 36

CHAPTER VI. THE EVIL SPIRIT'S WORK................................... 49

CHAPTER VII. CATHARINE MONTOUR 62

CHAPTER VIII. A CHANGE OF TENANTS 71

CHAPTER IX. WYOMING.. 83

CHAPTER X. THE BLOODY ROCK 90

CHAPTER XI. THE MELANCHOLY FLIGHT............................... 100

CHAPTER XII. THE SHADES OF DEATH 111

CHAPTER XIII. A FOREST PAGE...122

CHAPTER XIV. THE PURSUIT ON THE RIVER 134

CHAPTER XV. "THE ALCOVE" 144

CHAPTER XVI. THE FIRST BLOW 151

CHAPTER XVII. THE DESERTED CABIN 168

CHAPTER XVIII. HENRY'S SLIDE..179

CHAPTER XIX. THE SAFE RETURN 191

CHAPTER XX. A GLOOMY COUNCIL.....................................199

CHAPTER XXI. BATTLE OF THE CHEMUNG 204

CHAPTER XXII. LITTLE BEARD'S TOWN 212

CHAPTER XXIII. THE FINAL FIGHT.................................... 223

CHAPTER XXIV. DOWN THE OHIO 234

BOOK EIGHT. THE BORDER WATCH.................................... 236

A STORY OF THE GREAT CHIEF'S LAST STAND..................... 236

PREFACE.. 236

CHAPTER I. THE PASSING FLEET...................................... 237

CHAPTER II. THE SILVER BULLET 248

CHAPTER III. THE HOT SPRING..258

CHAPTER IV. THE SEVEN HERALDS 264

CHAPTER V. THE WYANDOT COUNCIL.................................. 272

CHAPTER VI. THE RUINED VILLAGE 280

CHAPTER VII. THE TAKING OF HENRY 291

CHAPTER VIII. THE NORTHWARD MARCH 303

CHAPTER IX. AT DETROIT.. 312

CHAPTER X. THE LETTER OF THE FOUR 324

CHAPTER XI THE CRY FROM THE FOREST............................336

CHAPTER XII THE CANOE ON THE RIVER 346

CHAPTER XIII. ON THE GREAT LAKE 357

CHAPTER XIV. A TIMELY RESCUE...367

CHAPTER XV. THE PAGES OF A BOOK 379

CHAPTER XVI. THE RIVER FIGHT 394

CHAPTER XVII THE ROAD TO WAREVILLE...........................405

CHAPTER XVIII. THE SHADOWY FIGURE 421

CHAPTER XIX. A HERALD BY WATER 433

CHAPTER XX. THE COUNTER-STROKE 457

CHAPTER XXI. THE BATTLE OF PIQUA................................... 471

CHAPTER XXII. THE LAST STAND 487

BOOK SEVEN.
THE SCOUTS OF THE VALLEY

A STORY OF WYOMING AND THE CHEMUNG

CHAPTER I. THE LONE CANOE

A light canoe of bark, containing a single human figure, moved swiftly up one of the twin streams that form the Ohio. The water, clear and deep, coming through rocky soil, babbled gently at the edges, where it lapped the land, but in the center the full current flowed steadily and without noise.

The thin shadows of early dusk were falling, casting a pallid tint over the world, a tint touched here and there with living fire from the sun, which was gone, though leaving burning embers behind. One glowing shaft, piercing straight through the heavy forest that clothed either bank, fell directly upon the figure in the boat, as a hidden light illuminates a great picture, while the rest is left in shadow. It was no common forest runner who sat in the middle of the red beam. Yet a boy, in nothing but years, he swung the great paddle with an ease and vigor that the strongest man in the West might have envied. His rifle, with the stock carved beautifully, and the long, slender blue barrel of the border, lay by his side. He could bring the paddle into the boat, grasp the rifle, and carry it to his shoulder with a single, continuous movement.

His most remarkable aspect, one that the casual observer even would have noticed, was an extraordinary vitality. He created in the minds of those who saw him a feeling that he lived intensely every moment of his life. Born and-bred in the forest, he was essentially its child, a perfect physical being, trained by the utmost hardship and danger, and with every faculty, mental and physical, in complete coordination. It is only by a singular combination of time and place, and only once in millions of chances, that Nature produces such a being.

The canoe remained a few moments in the center of the red light, and its occupant, with a slight swaying motion of the paddle, held it steady in the current, while he listened. Every feature stood out in the glow, the firm chin, the straight strong nose, the blue eyes, and the thick yellow hair. The red blue, and yellow beads on his dress of beautifully tanned deerskin flashed in the brilliant rays. He was the great picture of fact, not of fancy, a human being animated by a living, dauntless soul.

He gave the paddle a single sweep and shot from the light into the shadow. His canoe did not stop until it grazed the northern shore, where bushes and overhanging boughs made a deep shadow. It would have taken a keen eye now to have seen either the canoe or its occupant, and Henry Ware paddled slowly and without noise in the darkest heart of the shadow.

The sunlight lingered a little longer in the center of the stream. Then the red changed to pink. The pink, in its turn, faded, and the whole surface of the river was somber gray, flowing between two lines of black forest.

The coming of the darkness did not stop the boy. He swung a little farther out into the stream, where the bushes and hanging boughs would not get in his way, and continued his course with some increase of speed.

The great paddle swung swiftly through the water, and the length of stroke was amazing, but the boy's breath did not come faster, and the muscles on his arms and shoulders rippled as if it were the play of a child. Henry was in waters unknown to him. He had nothing more than hearsay upon which to rely, and he used all the wilderness caution that he had acquired through nature and training. He called into use every faculty of his perfect physical being. His trained eyes continually pierced the darkness. At times, he stopped and listened with ears that could hear the footfall of the rabbit, but neither eye nor ear brought report of anything unusual. The river flowed with a soft, sighing sound. Now and then a wild creature stirred in the forest, and once a deer came down to the margin to drink, but this was the ordinary life of the woods, and he passed it by.

He went on, hour after hour. The river narrowed. The banks grew higher and rockier, and the water, deep and silvery under the moon, flowed in a somewhat swifter current. Henry gave a little stronger sweep to the paddle, and the speed of the canoe was maintained. He still kept within the shadow of the northern bank.

He noticed after a while that fleecy vapor was floating before the moon. The night seemed to be darkening, and a rising wind came out of the southwest. The touch of the air on, his face was damp. It was the token of rain, and he felt that it would not be delayed long.

It was no part of his plan to be caught in a storm on the Monongahela. Besides the discomfort, heavy rain and wind might sink his frail canoe, and he looked for a refuge. The river was widening again, and the banks sank down until they were but little above the water. Presently he saw a place that he knew would be suitable, a stretch of thick bushes and weeds growing into the very edge of the water, and extending a hundred yards or more along the shore.

He pushed his canoe far into the undergrowth, and then stopped it in shelter so close that, keen as his own eyes were, he could scarcely see the main stream of the river. The water where he came to rest was not more than a foot deep, but he remained in the canoe, half reclining and wrapping closely around himself and his rifle a beautiful blanket woven of the tightest fiber.

His position, with his head resting on the edge of the canoe and his shoulder pressed against the side, was full of comfort to him, and he awaited calmly whatever might come. Here and there were little spaces among the leaves overhead, and through them he saw a moon, now almost hidden by thick and rolling vapors, and a sky that had grown dark and somber. The last timid star had ceased to twinkle, and the rising wind was wet and cold. He was glad of the blanket, and, skilled forest runner that he was, he never traveled without it. Henry remained perfectly still. The light canoe did not move beneath his weight the fraction of an inch. His upturned eyes saw the little cubes of sky that showed through the leaves grow darker and darker. The bushes about him were now bending before the wind, which blew steadily from the south, and presently drops of rain began to fall lightly on the water.

The boy, alone in the midst of all that vast wilderness, surrounded by danger in its most cruel forms, and with a black midnight sky above him, felt neither fear nor awe. Being what nature and circumstance had made him, he was conscious, instead, of a deep sense of peace and comfort. He was at ease, in a nest for the night, and there was only the remotest possibility that the prying eye of an enemy would see him. The leaves directly over his head were so thick that they formed a canopy, and, as he heard the drops fall upon them, it was like the rain on a roof, that soothes the one beneath its shelter.

Distant lightning flared once or twice, and low thunder rolled along the southern horizon, but both soon ceased, and then a rain, not hard, but cold and persistent, began to fall, coming straight down. Henry saw that it might last all night, but he merely eased himself a little in the canoe, drew the edges of the blanket around his chin, and let his eyelids droop.

The rain was now seeping through the leafy canopy of green, but he did not care. It could not penetrate the close fiber of the blanket, and the fur cap drawn far down on his head met the blanket. Only his face was uncovered, and when a cold drop fell upon it, it was to him, hardened by forest life, cool and pleasant to the touch.

Although the eyelids still drooped, he did not yet feel the tendency to sleep. It was merely a deep, luxurious rest, with the body completely relaxed, but with the senses alert. The wind ceased to blow, and the rain came down straight with an even beat that was not unmusical. No other sound was heard in the forest, as the ripple of the river at the edges was merged into it. Henry began to feel the desire for sleep by and by, and, laying the paddle across the boat in such a way that it sheltered his face, he closed his eyes. In five minutes he would have been sleeping as soundly as a man in a warm bed under a roof, but with a quick motion he suddenly put the paddle aside and raised himself a little in the canoe, while one hand slipped down under the folds of the blanket to the hammer of his rifle.

His ear had told him in time that there was a new sound on the river. He heard it faintly above the even beat of the rain, a soft sound, long and sighing, but regular. He listened, and then he knew it. It was made by oars, many of them swung in unison, keeping admirable time.

Henry did not yet feel fear, although it must be a long boat full of Indian warriors, as it was not likely, that anybody else would be abroad upon these waters at such a time. He made no attempt to move. Where he lay it was black as the darkest cave, and his cool judgment told him that there was no need of flight.

The regular rhythmic beat of the oars came nearer, and presently as he looked through the covert of leaves the dusky outline of a great war canoe came into view. It contained at least twenty warriors, of what tribe he could not tell, but they were wet, and they looked cold and miserable. Soon they were opposite him, and he saw the outline of every figure. Scalp locks drooped in the rain, and he knew that the warriors, hardy as they might be, were suffering.

Henry expected to see the long boat pass on, but it was turned toward a shelving bank fifty or sixty yards below, and they beached it there. Then all sprang out, drew it up on the land, and, after turning it over, propped it up at an angle. When this was done they sat under it in a close group, sheltered from the rain. They were using their great canoe as a roof, after the habit of Shawnees and Wyandots.

The boy watched them for a long time through one of the little openings in the bushes, and he believed that they would remain as they were all night, but presently he saw a movement among them, and a little flash of light. He understood it. They were trying to kindle a fire-with flint and steel, under the shelter of the boat. He continued to watch them 'lazily and without alarm.

Their fire, if they succeeded in making it, would cast no light upon him in the dense covert, but they would be outlined against the flame, and he could see them better, well enough, perhaps, to tell to what tribe they belonged.

He watched under his lowered eyelids while the warriors, gathered in a close group to make a shelter from stray puffs of wind, strove with flint and steel. Sparks sprang up and went out, but Henry at last saw a little blaze rise and cling to life. Then, fed with tinder and bark, it grew under the roof made by the boat until it was ruddy and strong. The boat was tilted farther back, and the fire, continuing to grow, crackled cheerfully, while the flames leaped higher.

By a curious transfer of the senses, Henry, as he lay in the thick blackness felt the influence of the fire, also. Its warmth was upon his face, and it was pleasing to see the red and yellow light victorious against the sodden background of the rain and dripping forest. The figures of the warriors passed and repassed before the fire, and the boy in the boat moved suddenly. His body was not shifted more than an inch, but his surprise was great.

A warrior stood between him and the fire, outlined perfectly against the red light. It was a splendid figure, young, much beyond the average height, the erect and noble head crowned with the defiant scalplock, the strong, slightly curved nose and the massive chin cut as clearly as if they had been carved in copper. The man who had laid aside a wet blanket was bare now to the waist, and Henry could see the powerful muscles play on chest and shoulders as he moved.

The boy knew him. It was Timmendiquas, the great White Lightning of the Wyandots, the youngest, but the boldest and ablest of all the Western chiefs. Henry's pulses leaped a little at the sight of his old foe and almost friend. As always, he felt admiration at the sight of the young chief. It was not likely that he would ever behold such another magnificent specimen of savage manhood.

The presence of Timmendiquas so far east was also full of significance. The great fleet under Adam Colfax, and with Henry and his comrades in the van, had reached Pittsburgh at last. Thence the arms, ammunition, and other supplies were started on the overland journey for the American army, but the five lingered before beginning the return to Kentucky. A rumor came that the Indian alliance was spreading along the entire frontier, both west and north. It was said that Timmendiquas, stung to fiery energy by his defeats, was coming east to form a league with the

Iroquois, the famous Six Nations. These warlike tribes were friendly with the Wyandots, and the league would be a formidable danger to the Colonies, the full strength of which was absorbed already in the great war.

But the report was a new call of battle to Henry, Shif'less Sol, and the others. The return to Kentucky was postponed. They could be of greater service here, and they plunged into the great woods to the north and, east to see what might be stirring among the warriors.

Now Henry, as he looked at Timmendiquas, knew that report had told the truth. The great chief would not be on the fringe of the Iroquois country, if he did not have such a plan, and he had the energy and ability to carry it through. Henry shuddered at the thought of the tomahawk flashing along every mile of a frontier so vast, and defended so thinly. He was glad in every fiber that he and his comrades had remained to hang upon the Indian hordes, and be heralds of their marches. In the forest a warning usually meant the saving of life.

The rain ceased after a while, although water dripped from the trees everywhere. But the big fire made an area of dry earth about it, and the warriors replaced the long boat in the water. Then all but four or five of them lay beside the coals and went to sleep. Timmendiquas was one of those who remained awake, and Henry saw that he was in deep thought. He walked back and forth much like a white man, and now and then he folded his hands behind his back, looking toward the earth, but not seeing it. Henry could guess what was in his mind. He would draw forth the full power of the Six Nations, league them with the Indians of the great valley, and hurl them all in one mass upon the frontier. He was planning now the means to the end.

The chief, in his little walks back and forth, came close to the edge of the bushes in which Henry lay, It was not at all probable that he would conclude to search among them, but some accident, a chance, might happen, and Henry began to feel a little alarm. Certainly, the coming of the day would make his refuge insecure, and he resolved to slip away while it was yet light.

The boy rose a little in the boat, slowly and with the utmost caution, because the slightest sound out of the common might arouse Timmendiquas to the knowledge of a hostile presence. The canoe must make no plash in the water. Gradually he unwrapped the blanket and tied it in a folded square at his back. Then he took thought a few moments. The forest was so silent now that he did not believe he could push the canoe through the bushes without being heard. He would leave it there for use another day and go on foot through the woods to his comrades.

Slowly he put one foot down the side until it rested on the bottom, and then he remained still. The chief had paused in his restless walk back and forth. Could it be possible that he had heard so slight a sound as that of a human foot sinking softly into the water? Henry waited with his rifle ready. If necessary he would fire, and then dart away among the bushes.

Five or six intense moments passed, and the chief resumed his restless pacing. If he had heard, he had passed it by as nothing, and Henry raised the other foot out of the canoe. He was as delicate in his movement as a surgeon mending the human eye, and he had full cause, as not eye alone, but life as well, depended upon his success. Both feet now rested upon the muddy bottom, and he stood there clear of the boat.

The chief did not stop again, and as the fire had burned higher, his features were disclosed more plainly in his restless walk back and forth before the flames. Henry took a final look at the lofty features, contracted now into a frown, then began to wade among the bushes, pushing his way softly. This was the most delicate and difficult task of all. The water must not be allowed to plash around him nor the bushes to rustle as he passed. Forward he went a yard, then two, five, ten, and his feet were about to rest upon solid earth, when a stick submerged in the mud broke under his moccasin with a snap singularly loud in the silence of the night.

Henry sprang at once upon dry land, whence he cast back a single swift glance. He saw the chief standing rigid and gazing in the direction from which the sound had come. Other warriors were just behind him, following his look, aware that there was an unexpected presence in the forest, and resolved to know its nature.

Henry ran northward. So confident was he in his powers and the protecting darkness of the night that he sent back a sharp cry, piercing and defiant, a cry of a quality that could come only from a white throat. The warriors would know it, and he intended for them to know it. Then, holding his rifle almost parallel with his body, he darted swiftly away through the black spaces of the forest. But an answering cry came to his, the Indian yell taking up his challenge, and saying that the night would not check pursuit.

Henry maintained his swift pace for a long time, choosing the more open places that he might make no noise among the bushes and leaves. Now and then water dripped in his face, and his moccasins were wet from the long grass, but his body was warm and dry, and he felt little weariness. The clouds were now all gone, and the stars sprang out, dancing in a sky of dusky blue. Trained eyes could see far in the forest despite the night, and Henry felt that he must be wary. He recalled the skill and tenacity of Timmendiquas. A fugitive could scarcely be trailed in the darkness, but the great chief would spread out his forces like a fan and follow.

He had been running perhaps three hours when he concluded to stop in a thicket, where he lay down on the damp grass, and rested with his head under his arm.

His breath had been coming a little faster, but his heart now resumed its regular beat. Then he heard a soft sound, that of footsteps. He thought at first that some wild animal was prowling near, but second thought convinced him that human beings had come. Gazing through the thicket, he saw an Indian warrior walking among the trees, looking searchingly about him as if he were a scout. Another, coming from a different direction, approached him, and Henry felt sure that they were of the party of Timmendiquas. They had followed him in some manner, perhaps by chance, and it behooved Mm now to lie close.

A third warrior joined them and they began to examine the ground. Henry realized that it was much lighter. Keen eyes under such a starry sky could see much, and they might strike his trail. The fear quickly became fact. One of the warriors, uttering a short cry, raised his head and beckoned to the others. He had seen broken twigs or trampled grass, and Henry, knowing that it was no time to hesitate, sprang from his covert. Two of the warriors caught a glimpse of his dusky figure and fired, the bullets cutting the leaves close to his head, but Henry ran so fast that he was lost to view in an instant.

The boy was conscious that his position contained many elements of danger. He was about to have another example of the tenacity and resource of the great young chief of the Wyandots, and he felt a certain anger. He, did not wish to be disturbed in his plans, he wished to rejoin his comrades and move farther east toward the chosen lands of the Six Nations; instead, he must spend precious moments running for his life.

Henry did not now flee toward the camp of his friends. He was too wise, too unselfish, to bring a horde down upon them, and he curved away in a course that would take him to the south of them. He glanced up and saw that the heavens were lightening yet more. A thin gray color like a mist was appearing in the east. It was the herald of day, and now the Indians would be able to find his trail. But Henry was not afraid. His anger over the loss of time quickly passed, and he ran swiftly on, the fall of his moccasins making scarcely any noise as he passed.

It was no unusual incident. Thousands of such pursuits occurred in the border life of our country, and were lost to the chronicler. For generations they were almost a part of the daily life of the frontier, but the present, while not out of the common in itself, had, uncommon phases. It was the most splendid type of white life in all the wilderness that fled, and the finest type of red life that followed.

It was impossible for Henry to feel anger or hate toward Timmendiquas. In his place he would have done what he was doing. It was hard to give up these great woods and beautiful lakes and rivers, and the wild life that wild men lived and loved. There was so much chivalry in the boy's nature that he could think of all these things while he fled to escape the tomahawk or the stake.

Up came the sun. The gray light turned to silver, and then to red and blazing gold. A long, swelling note, the triumphant cry of the pursuing warriors, rose behind him. Henry turned his head for one look. He saw a group of them poised for a moment on the crest of a low hill and outlined against the broad flame in the east. He saw their scalp locks, the rifles in their hands, and their bare chests shining bronze in the glow. Once more he sent back his defiant cry, now in answer to theirs, and then, calling upon his reserves of strength and endurance, fled with a speed that none of the warriors had ever seen surpassed.

Henry's flight lasted all that day, and he used every device to evade the pursuit, swinging by vines, walking along fallen logs, and wading in brooks. He did not see the warriors again, but instinct warned him that they were yet following. At long intervals he would rest for a quarter of an hour or so among the bushes, and at noon he ate a little of the venison that he always carried. Three hours later he came to the river again, and swimming it he turned on his course, but kept to the southern side. When the twilight was falling once more he sat still in dense covert for a long time. He neither saw nor heard a sign of human presence, and he was sure now that the pursuit had failed. Without an effort he dismissed it from his mind, ate a little more of the venison, and made his bed for the night.

The whole day had been bright, with a light wind blowing, and the forest was dry once more. As far as Henry could see it circled away on every side, a solid dark green, the leaves of oak and beech, maple and elm making a soft, sighing sound as they waved gently in the wind. It told Henry of nothing but peace. He had eluded the pursuit, hence it was no more. This was a great, friendly forest, ready to shelter him, to soothe him, and to receive him into its arms for peaceful sleep.

He found a place among thick trees where the leaves of last year lay deep upon the ground. He drew up enough of them for a soft bed, because now and for the moment he was a forest sybarite. He was wise enough to take his ease when he found it, knowing that it would pay his body to relax.

He lay down upon the leaves, placed the rifle by his side, and spread the blanket over himself and the weapon. The twilight was gone, and the night, dark and without stars, as he wished to see it, rolled up, fold after fold, covering and hiding everything. He looked a little while at a breadth of inky sky showing through the leaves, and then, free from trouble or fear, he fell asleep.

CHAPTER II. THE MYSTERIOUS HAND

Henry slept until a rosy light, filtering through the leaves, fell upon his face. Then he sprang up, folded the blanket once more upon his back, and looked about him. Nothing had come in the night to disturb him, no enemy was near, and the morning sun was bright and beautiful. The venison was exhausted, but he bathed his face in the brook and resumed his journey, traveling with a long, swift stride that carried him at great speed.

The boy was making for a definite point, one that he knew well, although nearly all the rest of this wilderness was strange to him. The country here was rougher than it usually is in the great valley to the west, and as he advanced it became yet more broken, range after range of steep, stony hills, with fertile but narrow little valleys between. He went on without hesitation for at least two hours, and then stopping under a great oak he uttered a long, whining cry, much like the howl of a wolf.

It was not a loud note, but it was singularly penetrating, carrying far through the forest. A sound like an echo came back, but Henry knew that instead of an echo it was a reply to his own signal. Then he advanced boldly and swiftly and came to the edge of a snug little valley set deep among rocks and trees like a bowl. He stopped behind the great trunk of a beech, and looked into the valley with a smile of approval.

Four human figures were seated around a fire of smoldering coals that gave forth no smoke. They appeared to be absorbed in some very pleasant task, and a faint odor that came to Henry's nostrils filled him with agreeable anticipations. He stepped forward boldly and called:

"Jim, save that piece for me!"

Long Jim Hart halted in mid-air the large slice of venison that he had toasted on a stick. Paul Cotter sprang joyfully to his feet, Silent Tom Ross merely looked up, but Shif'less Sol said:

"Thought Henry would be here in time for breakfast."

Henry walked down in the valley, and the shiftless one regarded him keenly.

"I should judge, Henry Ware, that you've been hevin' a foot race," he drawled.

"And why do you think that?" asked Henry.

"I kin see where the briars hev been rakin' across your leggins. Reckon that wouldn't happen, 'less you was in a pow'ful hurry."

"You're right," said Henry. "Now, Jim, you've been holding that venison in the air long enough. Give it to me, and after I've eaten it I'll tell you all that I've been doing, and all that's been done to me."

Long Jim handed him the slice. Henry took a comfortable seat in the circle before the coals, and ate with all the appetite of a powerful human creature whose food had been more than scanty for at least two days.

"Take another piece," said Long Jim, observing him with approval. "Take two pieces, take three, take the whole deer. I always like to see a hungry man eat. It gives him sech satisfaction that I git a kind uv taste uv it myself."

Henry did not offer a word 'of explanation until his breakfast was over. Then lie leaned back, sighing twice with deep content, and said:

"Boys, I've got a lot to tell."

Shif'less Sol moved into an easier position on the leaves.

"I guess it has somethin' to do with them scratches on your leggins."

"It has," continued Henry with emphasis, "and I want to say to you boys that I've seen Timmendiquas, the great White Lightning of the Wyandots."

"Timmendiquas!" exclaimed the others together.

"No less a man than he," resumed Henry. "I've looked upon his very face, I've seen him in camp with warriors, and I've had the honor of being pursued by him and his men more hours than I can tell. That's why you see those briar scratches on my leggins, Sol."

"Then we cannot doubt that he is here to stir the Six Nations to continued war," said Paul Cotter, "and he will succeed. He is a mighty chief, and his fire and eloquence will make them take up the hatchet. I'm glad that we've come. We delayed a league once between the Shawnees and the

Miamis; I don't think we can stop this one, but we may get some people out of the way before the blow falls."

"Who are these Six Nations, whose name sounds so pow'ful big up here?" asked Long Jim.

"Their name is as big as it sounds," replied Henry. "They are the Onondagas, the Mohawks, Oneidas, Senecas, Cayugas, and Tuscaroras. They used to be the Five Nations, but the Tuscaroras came up from the south and fought against them so bravely that they were adopted into the league, as a new and friendly tribe. The Onondagas, so I've heard, formed the league a long, long time ago, and their head chief is the grand sachem or high priest of them all, but the head chief of the Mohawks is the leading war chief."

"I've heard," said Paul, "that the Wyandots are kinsmen of all these tribes, and on that account they will listen with all the more friendliness to Timmendiquas."

"Seems to me," said Tom Ross, "that we've got a most tre-men-je-ous big job ahead."

"Then," said Henry, "we must make a most tremendous big effort."

"That's so," agreed all.

After that they spoke little. The last coals were covered up, and the remainder of the food was put in their pouches. Then they sat on the leaves, and every one meditated until such time as he might have something worth saying. Henry's thoughts traveled on a wide course, but they always came back to one point. They had heard much at Pittsburgh of a famous Mohawk chief called Thayendanegea, but most often known to the Americans as Brant. He was young, able, and filled with intense animosity against the white people, who encroached, every year, more and more upon the Indian hunting grounds. His was a soul full kin to that of Timmendiquas, and if the two met it meant a great council and a greater endeavor for the undoing of the white man. What more likely than that they intended to meet?

"All of you have heard of Thayendanegea, the Mohawk?" said Henry.

They nodded.

"It's my opinion that Timmendiquas is on the way to meet him. I remember hearing a hunter say at Pittsburgh that about a hundred miles to the east of this point was a Long House or Council House of the Six Nations. Timmendiquas is sure to go there, and we must go, too. We must find out where they intend to strike. What do you say?"

"We go there!" exclaimed four voices together.

Seldom has a council of war been followed by action so promptly.

As Henry spoke the last word he rose, and the others rose with him. Saying no more, he led toward the east, and the others followed him, also saying no more. Separately every one of them was strong, brave, and resourceful, but when the five were together they felt that they had the skill and strength of twenty. The long rest at Pittsburgh had restored them after the dangers and hardship of their great voyage from New Orleans.

They carried in horn and pouch ample supplies of powder and bullet, and they did not fear any task.

Their journey continued through hilly country, clothed in heavy forest, but often without undergrowth. They avoided the open spaces, preferring to be seen of men, who were sure to be red men, as little as possible. Their caution was well taken. They saw Indian signs, once a feather that had fallen from a scalp lock, once footprints, and once the bone of a deer recently thrown away by him who had eaten the meat from it. The country seemed to be as wild as that of Kentucky. Small settlements, so they had heard, were scattered at great distances through the forest, but they saw none. There was no cabin smoke, no trail of the plow, just the woods and the hills and the clear streams. Buffalo had never reached this region, but deer were abundant, and they risked a shot to replenish their supplies.

They camped the second night of their march on a little peninsula at the confluence of two creeks, with the deep woods everywhere. Henry judged that they were well within the western range of the Six Nations, and they cooked their deer meat over a smothered fire, nothing more than a few coals among the leaves. When supper was over they arranged soft places for themselves and their blankets, all except Long Jim, whose turn it was to scout among the woods for a possible foe.

"Don't be gone long, Jim," said Henry as he composed himself in a comfortable position. "A circle of a half mile about us will do."

"I'll not be gone more'n an hour," said Long Jim, picking up his rifle confidently, and flitting away among the woods.

"Not likely he'll see anything," said Shif'less Sol, "but I'd shorely like to know what White Lightning is about. He must be terrible stirred up by them beatin's he got down on the Ohio, an' they say that Mohawk, Thayendanegea is a whoppin' big chief, too. They'll shorely make a heap of trouble."

"But both of them are far from here just now," said Henry, "and we won't bother about either."

He was lying on some leaves at the foot of a tree with his arm under his head and his blanket over his body. He had a remarkable capacity for dismissing trouble or apprehension, and just then he was enjoying great physical and mental peace. He looked through half closed eyes at his comrades, who also were enjoying repose, and his fancy could reproduce Long Jim in the forest, slipping from tree to tree and bush to bush, and finding no menace.

"Feels good, doesn't it, Henry?" said the shiftless one. "I like a clean, bold country like this. No more plowin' around in swamps for me."

"Yes," said Henry sleepily, "it's a good country."

The hour slipped smoothly by, and Paul said:

"Time for Long Jim to be back."

"Jim don't do things by halves," said the shiftless one. "Guess he's beatin' up every squar' inch o' the bushes. He'll be here soon."

A quarter of an hour passed, and Long Jim did not return; a half hour, and no sign of him. Henry cast off the blanket and stood up. The night was not very dark and he could see some distance, but he did not see their comrade.

"I wonder why he's so slow," he said with a faint trace of anxiety.

"He'll be 'long directly," said Tom Ross with confidence.

Another quarter of an hour, and no Long Jim. Henry sent forth the low penetrating cry of the wolf that they used so often as a signal.

"He cannot fail to hear that," he said, "and he'll answer."

No answer came. The four looked at one another in alarm. Long Jim had been gone nearly two hours, and he was long overdue. His failure to reply to the signal indicated either that something ominous had happened or that—he had gone much farther than they meant for him to go.

The others had risen to their feet, also, and they stood a little while in silence.

"What do you think it means?" asked Paul.

"It must be all right," said Shif'less Sol. "Mebbe Jim has lost the camp."

Henry shook his head.

"It isn't that," he said. "Jim is too good a woodsman for such a mistake. I don't want to look on the black side, boys, but I think something has happened to Jim."

"Suppose you an' me go an' look for him," said Shif'less Sol, "while Paul and Tom stay here an' keep house."

"We'd better do it," said Henry. "Come, Sol."

The two, rifles in the hollows of their arms, disappeared in the darkness, while Tom and Paul withdrew into the deepest shadow of the trees and waited.

Henry and the shiftless one pursued an anxious quest, going about the camp in a great circle and then in another yet greater. They did not find Jim, and the dusk was so great that they saw no evidences of his trail. Long Jim had disappeared as completely as if he had left the earth for another planet. When they felt that they must abandon the search for the time, Henry and Shif'less Sol looked at each other in a dismay that the dusk could not hide.

"Mebbe be saw some kind uv a sign, an' has followed it," said the shiftless one hopefully. "If anything looked mysterious an' troublesome, Jim would want to hunt it down."

"I hope so," said Henry, "but we've got to go back to the camp now and report failure. Perhaps he'll show up to-morrow, but I don't like it, Sol, I don't like it!"

"No more do I," said Shif'less Sol. "'Tain't like Jim not to come back, ef he could. Mebbe he'll drop in afore day, anyhow."

They returned to the camp, and two inquiring figures rose up out of the darkness.

"You ain't seen him?" said Tom, noting that but two figures had returned.

"Not a trace," replied Henry. "It's a singular thing."

The four talked together a little while, and they were far from cheerful. Then three sought sleep, while Henry stayed on watch, sitting with his back against a tree and his rifle on his knees. All the peace and content that he had felt earlier in the evening were gone. He was oppressed by a sense of danger, mysterious and powerful. It did not seem possible that Long Jim could have gone away in such a noiseless manner, leaving no trace behind. But it was true.

He watched with both ear and eye as much for Long Jim as for an enemy. He was still hopeful that he would see the long, thin figure coming among the bushes, and then hear the old pleasant drawl. But he did not see the figure, nor did he hear the drawl.

Time passed with the usual slow step when one watches. Paul, Sol, and Tom were asleep, but Henry was never wider awake in his life. He tried to put away the feeling of mystery and danger. He assured himself that Long

Jim would soon come, delayed by some trail that he had sought to solve. Nothing could have happened to a man so brave and skillful. His nerves must be growing weak when he allowed himself to be troubled so much by a delayed return.

But the new hours came, one by one, and Long Jim came with none of them. The night remained fairly light, with a good moon, but the light that it threw over the forest was gray and uncanny. Henry's feeling of mystery and danger deepened. Once he thought he heard a rustling in the thicket and, finger on the trigger of his rifle, he stole among the bushes to discover what caused it. He found nothing and, returning to his lonely watch, saw that Paul, Sol, and Tom were still sleeping soundly. But Henry was annoyed greatly by the noise, and yet more by his failure to trace its origin. After an hour's watching he looked a second time. The result was once more in vain, and he resumed his seat upon the leaves, with his back reclining against an oak. Here, despite the fact that the night was growing darker, nothing within range of a rifle shot could escape his eyes.

Nothing stirred. The noise did not come a second time from the thicket. The very silence was oppressive. There was no wind, not even a stray puff, and the bushes never rustled. Henry longed for a noise of some kind to break that terrible, oppressive silence. What he really wished to hear was the soft crunch of Long Jim's moccasins on the grass and leaves.

The night passed, the day came, and Henry awakened his comrades. Long Jim was still missing and their alarm was justified. Whatever trail lie might have struck, he would have returned in the night unless something had happened to him. Henry had vague theories, but nothing definite, and he kept them to himself. Yet they must make a change in their plans. To go on and leave Long Jim to whatever fate might be his was unthinkable. No task could interfere with the duty of the five to one another.

"We are in one of the most dangerous of all the Indian countries," said Henry. "We are on the fringe of the region over which the Six Nations roam, and we know that Timmendiquas and a band of the Wyandots are here also. Perhaps Miamis and Shawnees have come, too."

"We've got to find Long Jim," said Silent Tom briefly.

They went about their task in five minutes. Breakfast consisted of cold venison and a drink from a brook. Then they began to search the forest. They felt sure that such woodsmen as they, with the daylight to help them, would find some trace of Long Jim, but they saw none at all, although they constantly widened their circle, and again tried all their signals. Half the forenoon passed in the vain search, and then they held a council.

16

"I think we'd better scatter," said Shif'less Sol, "an' meet here again when the sun marks noon."

It was agreed, and they took careful note of the place, a little hill crowned with a thick cluster of black oaks, a landmark easy to remember. Henry turned toward the south, and the forest was so dense that in two minutes all his comrades were lost to sight. He went several miles, and his search was most rigid. He was amazed to find that the sense of mystery and danger that he attributed to the darkness of the night did not disappear wholly in the bright daylight. His spirit, usually so optimistic, was oppressed by it, and he had no belief that they would find Long Jim.

At the set time he returned to the little hill crowned with the black oaks, and as he approached it from one side he saw Shif'less Sol coming from another. The shiftless one walked despondently. His gait was loose and shambling-a rare thing with him, and Henry knew that he, too, had failed. He realized now that he had not expected anything else. Shif'less Sol shook his head, sat down on a root and said nothing. Henry sat down, also, and the two exchanged a look of discouragement.

"The others will be here directly," said Henry, "and perhaps Long Jim will be with one of them."

But in his heart he knew that it would not be so, and the shiftless one knew that he had no confidence in his own words.

"If not," said Henry, resolved to see the better side, "we'll stay anyhow until we find him. We can't spare good old Long Jim."

Shif'less Sol did not reply, nor did Henry speak again, until lie saw the bushes moving slightly three or four hundred yards away.

"There comes Tom," he said, after a single comprehensive glance, "and he's alone."

Tom Ross was also a dejected figure. He looked at the two on the hill, and, seeing that the man for whom they were searching was not with them, became more dejected than before.

"Paul's our last chance," he said, as he joined them. "He's gen'rally a lucky boy, an' mebbe it will be so with him to-day."

"I hope so," said Henry fervently. "He ought to be along in a few minutes."

They waited patiently, although they really had no belief that Paul would bring in the missing man, but Paul was late. The noon hour was well past. Henry took a glance at the sun. Noon was gone at least a half hour, and he stirred uneasily.

"Paul couldn't get lost in broad daylight," he said.

"No," said Shif'less Sol, "he couldn't get lost!"

Henry noticed his emphasis on the word "lost," and a sudden fear sprang up in his heart. Some power had taken away Long Jim; could the same power have seized Paul? It was a premonition, and he paled under his brown, turning away lest the others see his face. All three now examined the whole circle of the horizon for a sight of moving bushes that would tell of the boy's coming.

The forest told nothing. The sun blazed brightly over everything, and Paul, like Long Jim, did not come. He was an hour past due, and the three, oppressed already by Long jim's disappearance, were convinced that he would not return. But they gave him a half hour longer. Then Henry said:

"We must hunt for him, but we must not separate. Whatever happens we three must stay together."

"I'm not hankerin' to roam 'roun jest now all by myself," said the shiftless one, with an uneasy laugh.

The three hunted all that afternoon for Paul. Once they saw trace of footsteps, apparently his, in some soft earth, but they were quickly, lost on hard ground, and after that there was nothing. They stopped shortly before sunset at the edge of a narrow but deep creek.

"What do you think of it, Henry?" asked Shif'less Sol.

"I don't know what to think," replied the youth, "but it seems to me that whatever took away Jim has taken away Paul, also."

"Looks like it," said Sol, "an' I guess it follers that we're in the same kind o' danger."

"We three of us could put up a good fight," said Henry, "and I propose that we don't go back to that camp, but spend the night here."

"Yes, an' watch good," said Tom Ross.

Their new camp was made quickly in silence, merely the grass under the low boughs of a tree. Their supper was a little venison, and then they watched the coming of the darkness. It was a heavy hour for the three. Long Jim was gone, and then Paul-Paul, the youngest, and, in a way, the pet of the little band.

"Ef we could only know how it happened," whispered Shif'less Sol, "then we might rise up an' fight the danger an' git Paul an' Jim back. But you can't shoot at somethin' you don't see or hear. In all them fights o' ours, on the Ohio an' Mississippi we knowed what wuz ag'inst us, but here we don't know nothin'."

"It is true, Sol," sighed Henry. "We were making such big plans, too, and before we can even start our force is cut nearly in half. To-morrow we'll begin the hunt again. We'll never desert Paul and Jim, so long as we don't know they're dead."

"It's my watch," said Tom. "You two sleep. We've got to keep our strength."

Henry and the shiftless one acquiesced, and seeking the softest spots under the tree sat down. Tom Ross took his place about ten feet in front of them, sitting on the ground, with his hands clasped around his knees, and his rifle resting on his arm. Henry watched him idly for a little while, thinking all the time of his lost comrades. The night promised to be dark, a good thing for them, as the need of hiding was too evident.

Shif'less Sol soon fell asleep, as Henry, only three feet away, knew by his soft and regular breathing, but the boy himself was still wide-eyed.

The darkness seemed to sink down like a great blanket dropping slowly, and the area of Henry's vision narrowed to a small circle. Within this area the distinctive object was the figure of Tom Ross, sitting with his rifle across his knees. Tom had an infinite capacity for immobility. Henry had never seen another man, not even an Indian, who could remain so long in one position contented and happy. He believed that the silent one could sit as he was all night.

His surmise about Tom began to have a kind of fascination for him. Would he remain absolutely still? He would certainly shift an arm or a leg. Henry's interest in the question kept him awake. He turned silently on the other side, but, no matter how intently he studied the sitting figure of his comrade, he could not see it stir. He did not know how long he had been awake, trying thus to decide a question that should be of no importance at such a time. Although unable to sleep, he fell into a dreamy condition, and continued vaguely to watch the rigid and silent sentinel.

He suddenly saw Tom stir, and he came from his state of languor. The exciting question was solved at last. The man would not sit all night absolutely immovable. There could be no doubt of the fact that he had raised an arm, and that his figure had straightened. Then he stood up, full height, remained motionless for perhaps ten seconds, and then suddenly glided away among the bushes.

Henry knew what this meant. Tom had heard something moving in the thickets, and, like a good sentinel, he had gone to investigate. A rabbit, doubtless, or perhaps a sneaking raccoon. Henry rose to a sitting position, and drew his own rifle across his knees. He would watch while Tom was gone, and then lie would sink quietly back, not letting his comrade know that lie had taken his place.

The faintest of winds began to stir among the thickets. Light clouds drifted before the moon. Henry, sitting with his rifle across his knees, and Shif'less Sol, asleep in the shadows, were invisible, but Henry saw beyond the circle of darkness that enveloped them into the grayish light that fell over the bushes. He marked the particular point at which he expected Tom Ross to appear, a slight opening that held out invitation for the passage of a man.

He waited a long time, ten minutes, twenty, a half hour, and the sentinel did not return. Henry came abruptly out of his dreamy state. He felt with all the terrible thrill of certainty that what happened to Long Jim and Paul had happened also to Silent Tom Ross. He stood erect, a tense, tall figure, alarmed, but not afraid. His eyes searched the thickets, but saw nothing. The slight movement of the bushes was made by the wind, and no other sound reached his ears.

But he might be mistaken after all! The most convincing premonitions were sometimes wrong! He would give Tom ten minutes more, and he sank down in a crouching position, where he would offer the least target for the eye.

The appointed time passed, and neither sight nor sound revealed any sign of Tom Ross. Then Henry awakened Shif'less Sol, and whispered to him all that he had seen.

"Whatever took Jim and Paul has took him," whispered the shiftless one at once.

Henry nodded.

"An' we're bound to look for him right now," continued Shif'less Sol.

"Yes," said Henry, "but we must stay together. If we follow the others, Sol, we must follow 'em together."

"It would be safer," said Sol. "I've an idee that we won't find Tom, an' I want to tell you, Henry, this thing is gittin' on my nerves."

It was certainly on Henry's, also, but without reply he led the way into the bushes, and they sought long and well for Silent Tom, keeping at the same time a thorough watch for any danger that might molest themselves. But no danger showed, nor did they find Tom or his trail. He, too, had vanished into nothingness, and Henry and Sol, despite their mental strength, felt cold shivers. They came back at last, far toward morning, to the bank of the creek. It was here as elsewhere a narrow but deep stream flowing between banks so densely wooded that they were almost like walls.

"It will be daylight soon," said Shif'less Sol, "an' I think we'd better lay low in thicket an' watch. It looks ez ef we couldn't find anything, so we'd better wait an' see what will find us."

"It looks like the best plan to me," said Henry, "but I think we might first hunt a while on the other side of the creek. We haven't looked any over there."

"That's so," replied Shif'less Sol, "but the water is at least seven feet deep here, an' we don't want to make any splash swimmin'. Suppose you go up stream, an' I go down, an' the one that finds a ford first kin give a signal. One uv us ought to strike shallow water in three or four hundred yards."

Henry followed the current toward the south, while Sol moved up the stream. The boy went cautiously through the dense foliage, and the creek soon grew wider and shallower. At a distance of about three hundred yards lie came to a point where it could be waded easily. Then he uttered the low cry that was their signal, and went back to meet Shif'less Sol. He reached the exact point at which they had parted, and waited. The shiftless one did not come. The last of his comrades was gone, and he was alone in the forest.

CHAPTER III. THE HUT ON THE ISLET

Henry Ware waited at least a quarter of an hour by the creek on the exact spot at which he and Solomon Hyde, called the shiftless one, had parted, but he knew all the while that his last comrade was not coming. The same powerful and mysterious hand that swept the others away had taken him, the wary and cunning Shif'less Sol, master of forest lore and with all the five senses developed to the highest pitch. Yet his powers had availed him nothing, and the boy again felt that cold chill running down his spine.

Henry expected the omnipotent force to come against him, also, but his instinctive caution made him turn and creep into the thickest of the forest, continuing until he found a place in the bushes so thoroughly hidden that no one could see him ten feet away. There he lay down and rapidly ran over in his mind the events connected with the four disappearances. They were few, and he had little on which to go, but his duty to seek his four comrades, since he alone must do it, was all the greater. Such a thought as deserting them and fleeing for his own life never entered his mind. He would not only seek them, but he would penetrate the mystery of the power that had taken them.

It was like him now to go about his work with calmness and method. To approach an arduous task right one must possess freshness and vigor, and one could have neither without sleep. His present place of hiding seemed to be as secure as any that could be found. So composing himself he took all chances and sought slumber. Yet it needed a great effort of the will to calm his nerves, and it was a half hour before he began to feel any of the soothing effect that precedes sleep. But fall asleep he did at last, and, despite everything, he slept soundly until the morning.

Henry did not awake to a bright day. The sun had risen, but it was obscured by gray clouds, and the whole heavens were somber. A cold wind began to blow, and with it came drops of rain. He shivered despite the enfolding blanket. The coming of the morning had invariably brought cheerfulness and increase of spirits, but now he felt depression. He foresaw heavy rain again, and it would destroy any but the deepest trail. Moreover, his supplies of food were exhausted and he must replenish them in some manner before proceeding further.

A spirit even as bold and strong as Henry's might well have despaired. He had found his comrades, only to lose them again, and the danger that had threatened them, and the elements as well, now threatened him, too. An acute judge of sky and air, he knew that the rain, cold, insistent, penetrating, would fall all day, and that he must seek shelter if he would keep his strength. The Indians themselves always took to cover at such times.

He wrapped the blanket around himself, covering his body well from neck to ankle, putting his rifle just inside the fold, but with his hand upon it, ready for instant use if it should be needed. Then he started, walking straight ahead until he came to the crown of a little hill. The clouds meanwhile thickened, and the rain, of the kind that he had foreseen and as cold as ice, was blown against him. The grass and bushes were reeking, and his moccasins became sodden. Despite the vigorous walking, lie felt the wet cold entering his system. There come times when the hardiest must yield, and he saw the increasing need of refuge.

He surveyed the country attentively from the low hill. All around was a dull gray horizon from which the icy rain dripped everywhere. There was no open country. All was forest, and the heavy rolling masses of foliage dripped with icy water, too.

Toward the south the land seemed to dip down, and Henry surmised that in a valley he would be more likely to find the shelter that he craved. He needed it badly. As he stood there he shivered again and again from head to foot, despite the folds of the blanket. So he started at once, walking fast, and feeling little fear of a foe. It was not likely that any would be seeking him at such a time. The rain struck him squarely in the face now. Water came from his moccasins every time his foot was pressed against the earth, and, no matter how closely he drew the folds of the blanket, little streams of it, like ice to the touch, flowed down his neck and made their way under his clothing. He could not remember a time when he had felt more miserable.

He came in about an hour to the dip which, as he had surmised, was the edge of a considerable valley. He ran down the slope, and looked all about for some place of shelter, a thick windbreak in the lee of a hill, or an outcropping of stone, but he saw neither, and, as he continued the search, he came to marshy ground. He saw ahead among the weeds and bushes the gleam of standing pools, and he was about to turn back, when he noticed three or four stones, in a row and about a yard from one another, projecting slightly above the black muck. It struck him that the stones would not naturally be in the soft mud, and, his curiosity aroused, he stepped lightly from one stone to another. When he came to the last stone that he had seen from the hard ground he beheld several more that had been hidden from him by the bushes. Sure now that he had happened upon something not created by nature alone, he followed these stones, leading like steps into the very depths of the swamp, which was now deep and dark with ooze all about him. He no longer doubted that the stones, the artificial presence of which might have escaped the keenest eye and most logical mind, were placed there for a purpose, and he was resolved to know its nature.

The stepping stones led him about sixty yards into the swamp, and the last thirty yards were at an angle from the first thirty. Then he came to a bit of hard ground, a tiny islet in the mire, upon which he could stand without sinking at all. He looked back from there, and he could not see his point of departure. Bushes, weeds, and saplings grew out of the swamp to a height of a dozen or fifteen feet, and he was inclosed completely. All the vegetation dripped with cold water, and the place was one of the most dismal that he had ever seen. But he had no thought of turning back.

Henry made a shrewd guess as to whither the path led, but he inferred from the appearance of the stepping stones-chiefly from the fact that an odd one here and there had sunk completely out of sight-that they had not been used in a long time, perhaps for years. He found on the other side of the islet a second line of stones, and they led across a marsh, that was almost like a black liquid, to another and larger island.

Here the ground was quite firm, supporting a thick growth of large trees. It seemed to Henry that this island might be seventy or eighty yards across, and he began at once to explore it. In the center, surrounded so closely by swamp oaks that they almost formed a living wall, he found what he had hoped to find, and his relief was so great that, despite his natural and trained stoicism, he gave a little cry of pleasure when he saw it.

A small lodge, made chiefly of poles and bark after the Iroquois fashion, stood within the circle of the trees, occupying almost the whole of the space. It was apparently abandoned long ago, and time and weather had done it much damage. But the bark walls, although they leaned in places at dangerous angles, still stood. The bark roof was pierced by holes on one side, but on the other it was still solid, and shed all the rain from its slope.

The door was open, but a shutter made of heavy pieces of bark cunningly joined together leaned against the wall, and Henry saw that he could make use of it. He stepped inside. The hut had a bark floor which was dry on one side, where the roof was solid, but dripping on the other. Several old articles of Indian use lay about. In one corner was a basket woven of split willow and still fit for service. There were pieces of thread made of Indian hemp and the inner bark of the elm. There were also a piece of pottery and a large, beautifully carved wooden spoon such as every Iroquois carried. In the corner farthest from the door was a rude fireplace made of large flat stones, although there was no opening for the smoke.

Henry surveyed it all thoughtfully, and he came to the conclusion that it was a hut for hunting, built by some warrior of an inquiring mind who had found this secret place, and who had recognized its possibilities. Here after an expedition for game he could lie hidden from enemies and take his comfort without fear. Doubtless he had sat in this hut on rainy days like the present one and smoked his pipe in the long, patient calm of which the Indian is capable.

Yes, there was the pipe, unnoticed before, trumpet shaped and carved beautifully, lying on a small bark shelf. Henry picked it tip and examined the bowl. It was as dry as a bone, and not a particle of tobacco was left there. He believed that it had not been used for at least a year. Doubtless the Indian who had built this hunting lodge had fallen in some foray, and the secret of it had been lost until Henry Ware, seeking through the cold and rain, had stumbled upon it.

It was nothing but a dilapidated little lodge of poles and bark, all a-leak, but the materials of a house were there, and Henry was strong and skillful. He covered the holes in the roof with fallen pieces of bark, laying heavy pieces of wood across them to hold them in place. Then he lifted the bark shutter into position and closed the door. Some drops of rain still came in through the roof, but they were not many, and he would not mind them for the present. Then he opened the door and began his hardest task.

He intended to build a fire on the flat stones, and, securing fallen wood, he stripped off the bark and cut splinters from the inside. It was slow work and he was very cold, his wet feet sending chills through him, but he persevered, and the little heap of dry splinters grew to a respectable size. Then he cut larger pieces, laying them on one side while he worked with his flint and steel on the splinters.

Flint and steel are not easily handled even by the most skillful, and Henry saw the spark leap up and die out many times before it finally took hold of the end of the tiniest splinter and grew. He watched it as it ran along the little piece of wood and ignited another and then another, the beautiful little red and yellow flames leaping up half a foot in height. Already he felt the grateful warmth and glow, but he would not let himself indulge in premature joy. He fed it with larger and larger pieces until the flames, a deeper and more beautiful red and yellow, rose at least two feet, and big coals began to form. He left the door open a while in order that the smoke might go out, but when the fire had become mostly coals he closed it again, all except a crack of about six inches, which would serve at once to let any stray smoke out, and to let plenty of fresh air in.

Now Henry, all his preparations made, no detail neglected, proceeded to luxuriate. He spread the soaked blanket out on the bark floor, took off the sodden moccasins and placed them at one angle of the fire, while he sat with his bare feet in front. What a glorious warmth it was! It seemed to enter at his toes and proceed upward through his body, seeking out every little nook and cranny, to dry and warm it, and fill it full of new glow and life.

He sat there a long time, his being radiating with physical comfort. The moccasins dried on one side, and he turned the other. Finally they dried all over and all through, and he put them on again. Then he hung the blanket on the bark wall near the fire, and it, too, would be dry in another hour or so. He foresaw a warm and dry place for the night, and sleep. Now if one only had food! But he must do without that for the present.

He rose and tested all his bones and muscles. No stiffness or soreness had come from the rain and cold, and he was satisfied. He was fit for any physical emergency. He looked out through the crevice. Night was coming, and on the little island in the swamp it looked inexpressibly black and gloomy. His stomach complained, but he shrugged his shoulders, acknowledging primitive necessity, and resumed his seat by the fire. There he sat until the blanket had dried, and deep night had fully come.

In the last hour or two Henry did not move. He remained before the fire, crouched slightly forward, while the generous heat fed the flame of life in him. A glowing bar, penetrating the crevice at the door, fell on the earth outside, but it did not pass beyond the close group of circling trees. The rain still fell with uncommon steadiness and persistence, but at times hail was mingled with it. Henry could not remember in his experience a more desolate night. It seemed that the whole world dwelt in perpetual darkness, and that he was the only living being on it. Yet within the four or five feet square of the hut it was warm and bright, and he was not unhappy.

He would forget the pangs of hunger, and, wrapping himself in the dry blanket, he lay down before the bed of coals, having first raked ashes over them, and he slept one of the soundest sleeps of his life. All night long, the dull cold rain fell, and with it, at intervals, came gusts of hail that rattled like bird shot on the bark walls of the hut. Some of the white pellets blew in at the door, and lay for a moment or two on the floor, then melted in the glow of the fire, and were gone.

But neither wind, rain nor hail awoke Henry. He was as safe, for the time, in the hut on the islet, as if he were in the fort at Pittsburgh or behind the palisades at Wareville. Dawn came, the sky still heavy and dark with clouds, and the rain still falling.

Henry, after his first sense of refreshment and pleasure, became conscious of a fierce hunger that no amount of the will could now keep quiet. His was a powerful system, needing much nourishment, and he must eat. That hunger became so great that it was acute physical pain. He was assailed by it at all points, and it could be repelled by only one thing, food. He must go forth, taking all risks, and seek it.

He put on fresh wood, covering it with ashes in order that it might not blaze too high, and left the islet. The stepping stones were slippery with water, and his moccasins soon became soaked again, but he forgot the cold and wet in that ferocious hunger, the attacks of which became more violent every minute. He was hopeful that he might see a deer, or even a squirrel, but the animals themselves were likely to keep under cover in such a rain.

He expected a hard hunt, and it would be attended also by much danger—these woods must be full of Indians—but he thought little of the risk. His hunger was taking complete possession of his mind. He was realizing now that one might want a thing so much that it would drive away all other thoughts.

Rifle in hand, ready for any quick shot, he searched hour after hour through the woods and thickets. He was wet, bedraggled, and as fierce as a famishing panther, but neither skill nor instinct guided him to anything. The rabbit hid in his burrow, the squirrel remained in his hollow tree, and the deer did not leave his covert.

Henry could not well calculate the passage of time, it seemed so fearfully long, and there was no one to tell him, but he judged that it must be about noon, and his temper was becoming that of the famished panther to which he likened himself. He paused and looked around the circle of the dripping woods. He had retained his idea of direction and he knew that he could go straight back to the hut in the swamp. But he had no idea of returning now. A power that neither he nor anyone else could resist was pushing him on his search.

Searching the gloomy horizon again, he saw against the dark sky a thin and darker line that he knew to be smoke. He inferred, also, with certainty, that it came from an Indian camp, and, without hesitation, turned his course toward it. Indian camp though it might be, and containing the deadliest of foes, he was glad to know something lived beside himself in this wilderness.

He approached with great caution, and found his surmise to be correct. Lying full length in a wet thicket he saw a party of about twenty warriors-Mohawks he took them to be-in an oak opening. They had erected bark shelters, they had good fires, and they were cooking. He saw them roasting the strips over the coals-bear meat, venison, squirrel, rabbit, bird-and the odor, so pleasant at other times, assailed his nostrils. But it was now only a taunt and a torment. It aroused every possible pang of hunger, and every one of them stabbed like a knife.

The warriors, so secure in their forest isolation, kept no sentinels, and they were enjoying themselves like men who had everything they wanted. Henry could hear them laughing and talking, and he watched them as they ate strip after strip of the delicate, tender meat with the wonderful appetite that the Indian has after long fasting. A fierce, unreasoning anger and jealousy laid hold of him. He was starving, and they rejoiced in plenty only fifty yards away. He began to form plans for a piratical incursion upon them. Half the body of a deer lay near the edge of the opening, he would rush upon it, seize it, and dart away. It might be possible to escape with such spoil.

Then he recalled his prudence. Such a thing was impossible. The whole band of warriors would be upon him in an instant. The best thing that he could do was to shut out the sight of so much luxury in which he could not share, and he crept away among the bushes wondering what he could do to drive away those terrible pains. His vigorous system was crying louder than ever for the food that would sustain it. His eyes were burning a little too brightly, and his face was touched with fever.

Henry stopped once to catch a last glimpse of the fires and the feasting Indians under the bark shelters. He saw a warrior raise a bone, grasping it in both hands, and bite deep into the tender flesh that clothed it. The sight inflamed him into an anger almost uncontrollable. He clenched his fist and shook it at the warrior, who little suspected the proximity of a hatred so intense. Then he bent his head down and rushed away among the wet bushes which in rebuke at his lack of caution raked him across the face.

Henry walked despondently back toward the islet in the swamp. The aspect of air and sky had not changed. The heavens still dripped icy water, and there was no ray of cheerfulness anywhere. The game remained well hidden.

It was a long journey back, and as he felt that he was growing weak he made no haste. He came to dense clumps of bushes, and plowing his way through them, he saw a dark opening under some trees thrown down by an old hurricane. Having some vague idea that it might be the lair of a wild animal, he thrust the muzzle of his rifle into the darkness. It touched a soft substance. There was a growl, and a black form shot out almost into his face. Henry sprang aside, and in an instant all his powers and faculties returned. He had stirred up a black bear, and before the animal, frightened as much as he was enraged, could run far the boy, careless how many Indians might hear, threw up his rifle and fired.

His aim was good. The bear, shot through the head, fell, and was dead. Henry, transformed, ran up to him. Bear life had been given up to sustain man's. Here was food for many days, and he rejoiced with a great joy. He did not now envy those warriors back there.

The bear, although small, was very fat. Evidently he had fed well on acorns and wild honey, and he would yield up steaks which, to one with Henry's appetite, would be beyond compare. He calculated that it was more than a mile to the swamp, and, after a few preliminaries, he flung the body of the bear over his shoulder. Through some power of the mind over the body his full strength had returned to him miraculously, and when he reached the stepping stones he crossed from one to another lightly and firmly, despite the weight that he carried.

He came to the little bark hut which he now considered his own. The night had fallen again, but some coals still glowed under the ashes, and there was plenty of dry wood. He did everything decently and in order. He took the pelt from the bear, carved the body properly, and then, just as the Indians had done, he broiled strips over the coals. He ate them one after another, slowly, and tasting all the savor, and, intense as was the mere physical pleasure, it was mingled with a deep thankfulness. Not only was the life nourished anew in him, but he would now regain the strength to seek his comrades.

When he had eaten enough he fastened the body of the bear, now in several portions, on hooks high upon the walls, hooks which evidently had been placed there by the former owner of the hut for this very purpose. Then, sure that the savor of the food would draw other wild animals, he brought one of the stepping stones and placed it on the inside of the door. The door could not be pushed aside without arousing him, and, secure in the knowledge, he went to sleep before the coals.

CHAPTER IV. THE RED CHIEFS

Henry awoke only once, and that was about half way between midnight and morning, when his senses, never still entirely, even in sleep, warned him that something was at the door. He rose cautiously upon his arm, saw a dark muzzle at the crevice, and behind it a pair of yellow, gleaming eyes. He knew at once that it was a panther, probably living in the swamp and drawn by the food. It must be very hungry to dare thus the smell of man. Henry's hand moved slowly to the end of a stick, the other end of which was a glowing coal. Then he seized it and hurled it directly at the inquisitive head.

The hot end of the stick struck squarely between the yellow eyes. There was a yelp of pain, and the boy heard the rapid pad of the big cat's feet as it fled into the swamp. Then he turned over on his side, and laughed in genuine pleasure at what was to him a true forest joke. He knew the panther would not come, at least not while he was in the hut, and he calmly closed his eyes once more. The old Henry was himself again.

He awoke in the morning to find that the cold rain was still falling. It seemed to him that it had prepared to rain forever, but he was resolved, nevertheless, now that he had food and the strength that food brings, to begin the search for his comrades. The islet in the swamp would serve as his base-nothing could be better-and he would never cease until he found them or discovered what had become of them.

A little spring of cold water flowed from the edge of the islet to lose itself quickly in the swamp. Henry drank there after his breakfast, and then felt as strong and active as ever. As he knew, the mind may triumph over the body, but the mind cannot save the body without food. Then he made his precious bear meat secure against the prowling panther or others of his kind, tying it on hanging boughs too high for a jump and too slender to support the weight of a large animal. This task finished quickly, he left the swamp and returned toward the spot where lie had seen the Mohawks.

The falling rain and the somber clouds helped Henry, in a way, as the whole forest was enveloped in a sort of gloom, and he was less likely to be seen. But when he had gone about half the distance he heard Indians signaling to one another, and, burying himself as usual in the wet bushes, he saw two small groups of warriors meet and talk. Presently they separated, one party going toward the east and the other toward the west. Henry thought they were out hunting, as the Indians usually took little care of the morrow, eating all their food in a few days, no matter how great the supply might be.

When he drew near the place he saw three more Indians, and these were traveling directly south. He was quite sure now that his theory was correct. They were sending out hunters in every direction, in order that they might beat up the woods thoroughly for game, and his own position anywhere except on the islet was becoming exceedingly precarious. Nevertheless, using all his wonderful skill, he continued the hunt. He had an abiding faith that his four comrades were yet alive, and he meant to prove it.

In the afternoon the clouds moved away a little, and the rain decreased, though it did not cease. The Indian signs multiplied, and Henry felt sure that the forest within a radius of twenty miles of his islet contained more than one camp. Some great gathering must be in progress and the hunters were out to supply it with food. Four times he heard the sound of shots, and thrice more he saw warriors passing through the forest. Once a wounded deer darted past him, and, lying down in the bushes, he saw the Indians following the fleeing animal. As the day grew older the trails multiplied. Certainly a formidable gathering of bands was in progress, and, feeling that he might at any time be caught in a net, he returned to the islet, which had now become a veritable fort for him.

It was not quite dark when he arrived, and he found all as it had been except the tracks of two panthers under the boughs to which he had fastened the big pieces of bear meat. Henry felt a malicious satisfaction at the disappointment of the panthers.

"Come again, and have the same bad luck," he murmured.

At dusk the rain ceased entirely, and he prepared for a journey in the night. He examined his powder carefully to see that no particle of it was wet, counted the bullets in his pouch, and then examined the skies. There was a little moon, not too much, enough to show him the way, but not enough to disclose him to an enemy unless very near. Then he left the islet and went swiftly through the forest, laying his course a third time toward the Indian camp. He was sure now that all the hunters had returned, and he did not expect the necessity of making any stops for the purpose of hiding. His hopes were justified, and as he drew near the camp he became aware that its population had increased greatly. It was proved by many signs. New trails converged upon it, and some of them were very broad, indicating that many warriors had passed. They had passed, too, in perfect confidence, as there was no effort at concealment, and Henry surmised that no white force of any size could be within many days' march of this place. But the very security of the Indians helped his own design. They would not dream that any one of the hated race was daring to come almost within the light of their fires.

Henry had but one fear just now, and that was dogs. If the Indians had any of their mongrel curs with them, they would quickly scent him out and give the alarm with their barking. But he believed that the probabilities were against it. This, so he thought then, was a war or hunting camp, and it was likely that the Indians would leave the dogs at their permanent villages. At any rate he would take the risk, and he drew slowly toward the oak opening, where some Indians stood about. Beyond them, in another dip of the valley, was a wider opening which he had not seen on his first trip, and this contained not only bark shelters, but buildings that indicated a permanent village. The second and larger opening was filled with a great concourse of warriors.

Fortunately the foliage around the opening was very dense, many trees and thickets everywhere. Henry crept to the very rim, where, lying in the blackest of the shadows, and well hidden himself, he could yet see nearly everything in the camp. The men were not eating now, although it was obvious that the hunters had done well. The dressed bodies of deer and bear hung in the bark shelters. Most of the Indians sat about the fires, and it seemed to Henry that they had an air of expectancy. At least two hundred were present, and all of them were in war paint, although there were several styles of paint. There was a difference in appearance, too, in the warriors, and Henry surmised that representatives of all the tribes of the Iroquois were there, coming to the extreme western boundary or fringe of their country.

While Henry watched them a half dozen who seemed by their bearing and manner to be chiefs drew together at a point not far from him and talked together earnestly. Now and then they looked toward the forest, and he was quite sure that they were expecting somebody, a person of importance. He became deeply interested. He was lying in a dense clump of hazel bushes, flat upon his stomach, his face raised but little above the ground. He would have been hidden from the keenest eye only ten feet away, but the faces of the chiefs outlined against the blazing firelight were so clearly visible to him that he could see every change of expression. They were fine-looking men, all of middle age, tall, lean, their noses hooked, features cut clean and strong, and their heads shaved, all except the defiant scalp lock, into which the feather of an eagle was twisted. Their bodies were draped in fine red or blue blankets, and they wore leggins and moccasins of beautifully tanned deerskin.

They ceased talking presently, and Henry heard a distant wailing note from the west. Some one in the camp replied with a cry in kind, and then a silence fell upon them all. The chiefs stood erect, looking toward the west. Henry knew that he whom they expected was at hand.

The cry was repeated, but much nearer, and a warrior leaped into the opening, in the full blaze of the firelight. He was entirely naked save for a breech cloth and moccasins, and he was a wild and savage figure. He stood for a moment or two, then faced the chiefs, and, bowing before them, spoke a few words in the Wyandot tongue-Henry knew already by his paint that he was a Wyandot.

The chiefs inclined their heads gravely, and the herald, turning, leaped back into the forest. In two or three minutes six men, including the herald, emerged from the woods, and Henry moved a little when he saw the first of the six, all of whom were Wyandots. It was Timmendiquas, head chief of the Wyandots, and Henry had never seen him more splendid in manner and bearing than he was as he thus met the representatives of the famous Six Nations. Small though the Wyandot tribe might be, mighty was its valor and fame, and White Lightning met the great Iroquois only as an equal, in his heart a superior.

It was an extraordinary thing, but Henry, at this very moment, burrowing in the earth that he might not lose his life at the hands of either, was an ardent partisan of Timmendiquas. It was the young Wyandot chief whom he wished to be first, to make the greatest impression, and he was pleased when he heard the low hum of admiration go round the circle of two hundred savage warriors. It was seldom, indeed, perhaps never, that the Iroquois had looked upon such a man as Timmendiquas.

Timmendiquas and his companions advanced slowly toward the chiefs, and the Wyandot overtopped all the Iroquois. Henry could tell by the manner of the chiefs that the reputation of the famous White Lightning had preceded him, and that they had already found fact equal to report.

The chiefs, Timmendiquas among them, sat down on logs before the fire, and all the warriors withdrew to a respectful distance, where they stood and watched in silence. The oldest chief took his long pipe, beautifully carved and shaped like a trumpet, and filled it with tobacco which he lighted with a coal from the fire. Then he took two or three whiffs and passed the pipe to Timmendiquas, who did the same. Every chief smoked the pipe, and then they sat still, waiting in silence.

Henry was so much absorbed in this scene, which was at once a spectacle and a drama, that he almost forgot where he was, and that he was an enemy. He wondered now at their silence. If this was a council surely they would discuss whatever question had brought them there! But he was soon enlightened. That low far cry came again, but from the east. It was answered, as before, from the camp, and in three or four minutes a warrior sprang from the forest into the opening. Like the first, he was naked except for the breech cloth and moccasins. The chiefs rose at his coming, received his salute gravely, and returned it as gravely. Then he returned to the forest, and all waited in the splendid calm of the Indian.

Curiosity pricked Henry like a nettle. Who was coming now? It must be some man of great importance, or they would not wait so silently. There was the same air of expectancy that had preceded the arrival of Timmendiquas. All the warriors looked toward the eastern wall of the forest, and Henry looked the same way. Presently the black foliage parted, and a man stepped forth, followed at a little distance by seven or eight others. The stranger, although tall, was not equal in height to Timmendiquas, but he, too, had a lofty and splendid presence, and it was evident to anyone versed at all in forest lore that here was a great chief. He was lean but sinewy, and he moved with great ease and grace. He reminded Henry of a powerful panther. He was dressed, after the manner of famous chiefs, with the utmost care. His short military coat of fine blue cloth bore a silver epaulet on either shoulder. His head was not bare, disclosing the scalp lock, like those of the other Indians; it was covered instead with a small hat of felt, round and laced. Hanging carelessly over one shoulder was a blanket of blue cloth with a red border. At his side, from a belt of blue leather swung a silver-mounted small sword. His leggins were of superfine blue cloth and his moccasins of deerskin. Both were trimmed with small beads of many colors.

The new chief advanced into the opening amid the dead silence that still held all, and Timmendiquas stepped forward to meet him. These two held the gaze of everyone, and what they and they alone did had become of surpassing interest. Each was haughty, fully aware of his own dignity and importance, but they met half way, looked intently for a moment or two into the eyes of each other, and then saluted gravely.

All at once Henry knew the stranger. He had never seen him before, but his impressive reception, and the mixture of military and savage attire revealed him. This could be none other than the great Mohawk war chief, Thayendanegea, the Brant of the white men, terrible name on the border. Henry gazed at him eagerly from his covert, etching his features forever on his memory. His face, lean and strong, was molded much like that of Timmendiquas, and like the Wyandot he was young, under thirty.

Timmendiquas and Thayendanegea-it was truly he-returned to the fire, and once again the trumpet-shaped pipe was smoked by all. The two young chiefs received the seats of favor, and others sat about them. But they were not the only great chiefs present, though all yielded first place to them because of their character and exploits.

Henry was not mistaken in his guess that this was an important council, although its extent exceeded even his surmise. Delegates and head chiefs of all the Six Nations were present to confer with the warlike Wyandots of the west who had come so far east to meet them. Thayendanegea was the great war chief of the Mohawks, but not their titular chief. The latter was an older man, Te-kie-ho-ke (Two Voices), who sat beside the younger. The other chiefs were the Onondaga, Tahtoo-ta-hoo (The Entangled); the Oneida, O-tat-sheh-te (Bearing a Quiver); the Cayuga, Te-ka-ha-hoonk (He Who Looks Both Ways); the Seneca, Kan-ya-tai-jo (Beautiful Lake); and the Tuscarora, Ta-ha-en-te-yahwak-hon (Encircling and Holding Up a Tree). The names were hereditary, and because in a dim past they had formed the great confederacy, the Onondagas were first in the council, and were also the high priests and titular head of the Six Nations. But the Mohawks were first on-the war path.

All the Six Nations were divided into clans, and every clan, camping in its proper place, was represented at this meeting.

Henry had heard much at Pittsburgh of the Six Nations, their wonderful league, and their wonderful history. He knew that according to the legend the league had been formed by Hiawatha, an Onondaga. He was opposed in this plan by Tododaho, then head chief of the Onondagas, but he went to the Mohawks and gained the support of their great chief, Dekanawidah. With his aid the league was formed, and the solemn agreement, never broken, was made at the Onondaga Lake. Now they were a perfect little state, with fifty chiefs, or, including the head chiefs, fifty-six.

Some of these details Henry was to learn later. He was also to learn many of the words that the chiefs said through a source of which he little dreamed at the present. Yet he divined much of it from the meeting of the fiery Wyandots with the highly developed and warlike power of the Six Nations.

Thayendanegea was talking now, and Timmendiquas, silent and grave, was listening. The Mohawk approached his subject indirectly through the trope, allegory, and simile that the Indian loved. He talked of the unseen deities that ruled the life of the Iroquois through mystic dreams. He spoke of the trees, the rocks, and the animals, all of which to the Iroquois had souls. He called on the name of the Great Spirit, which was Aieroski before it became Manitou, the Great Spirit who, in the Iroquois belief, had only the size of a dwarf because his soul was so mighty that he did not need body.

"This land is ours, the land of your people and mine, oh, chief of the brave Wyandots," he said to Timmendiquas. "Once there was no land, only the waters, but Aieroski raised the land of Konspioni above the foam. Then he sowed five handfuls of red seed in it, and from those handfuls grew the Five Nations. Later grew up the Tuscaroras, who have joined us and other tribes of our race, like yours, great chief of the brave Wyandots."

Timmendiquas still said nothing. He did not allow an eyelid to flicker at this assumption of superiority for the Six Nations over all other tribes. A great warrior he was, a great politician also, and he wished to unite the Iroquois in a firm league with the tribes of the Ohio valley. The coals from the great fire glowed and threw out an intense heat. Thayendanegea unbuttoned his military coat and threw it back, revealing a bare bronze chest, upon which was painted the device of the Mohawks, a flint and steel. The chests of the Onondaga, Cayuga, and Seneca head chiefs were also bared to the glow. The device on the chest of the Onondaga was a cabin on top of a hill, the Caytiga's was a great pipe, and the figure of a mountain adorned the Seneca bronze.

"We have had the messages that you have sent to us, Timmendiquas," said Thayendanegea, "and they are good in the eyes of our people, the Rotinonsionni (the Mohawks). They please, too, the ancient tribe, the Kannoseone (the Onondagas), the valiant Hotinonsionni (the Senecas), and all our brethren of the Six Nations. All the land from the salt water to the setting sun was given to the red men by Aieroski, but if we do not defend it we cannot keep it."

"It is so," said Timmendiquas, speaking for the first time. "We have fought them on the Ohio and in Kaintuck-ee, where they come with their rifles and axes. The whole might of the Wyandots, the Shawnees, the Miamis, the Illinois, the Delawares, and the Ottawas has gone forth against them. We have slain many of them, but we have failed to drive them back. Now we have come to ask the Six Nations to press down upon them in the east with all your power, while we do the same in the west. Surely then your Aieroski and our Manitou, who are the same, will not refuse us success."

The eyes of Thayendanegea glistened.

"You speak well, Timmendiquas," he said. "All the red men must unite to fight for the land of Konspioni which Aieroski raised above the sea, and we be two, you and I, Timmendiquas, fit to lead them to battle."

"It is so," said Timmendiquas gravely.

CHAPTER V. THE IROQUOIS TOWN

Henry lay fully an hour in the bushes. He had forgotten about the dogs that he dreaded, but evidently he was right in his surmise that the camp contained none. Nothing disturbed him while he stared at what was passing by the firelight. There could be no doubt that the meeting of Timmendiquas and Thayendanegea portended great things, but he would not be stirred from his task of rescuing his comrades or discovering their fate.

They two, great chiefs, sat long in close converse. Others-older men, chiefs, also-came at times and talked with them. But these two, proud, dominating, both singularly handsome men of the Indian type, were always there. Henry was almost ready to steal away when he saw a new figure approaching the two chiefs. The walk and bearing of the stranger were familiar, and HENRY knew him even before his face was lighted tip by the fire. It was Braxton Wyatt, the renegade, who had escaped the great battles on both the Ohio and the Mississippi, and who was here with the Iroquois, ready to do to his own race all the evil that he could. Henry felt a shudder of repulsion, deeper than any Indian could inspire in him. They fought for their own land and their own people, but Braxton Wyatt had violated everything that an honest man should hold sacred.

Henry, on the whole, was not surprised to see him. Such a chance was sure to draw Braxton Wyatt. Moreover, the war, so far as it pertained to the border, seemed to be sweeping toward the northeast, and it bore many stormy petrels upon its crest.

He watched Wyatt as he walked toward one of the fires. There the renegade sat down and talked with the warriors, apparently on the best of terms. He was presently joined by two more renegades, whom Henry recognized as Blackstaffe and Quarles. Timmendiquas and Thayendanegea rose after a while, and walked toward the center of the camp, where several of the bark shelters had been enclosed entirely. Henry judged that one had been set apart for each, but they were lost from his view when they passed within the circling ring of warriors.

Henry believed that the Iroquois and Wyandots would form a fortified camp here, a place from which they would make sudden and terrible forays upon the settlements. He based his opinion upon the good location and the great number of saplings that had been cut down already. They would build strong lodges and then a palisade around them with the saplings. He was speedily confirmed in this opinion when he saw warriors come to the forest with hatchets and begin to cut down more saplings. He knew then that it was time to go, as a wood chopper might blunder upon him at any time.

He slipped from his covert and was quickly gone in the forest. His limbs were somewhat stiff from lying so long in one position, but that soon wore away, and he was comparatively fresh when he came once more to the islet in the swamp. A good moon was now shining, tipping the forest with a fine silvery gray, and Henry purveyed with the greatest satisfaction the simple little shelter that he had found so opportunely. It was a good house, too, good to such a son of the deepest forest as was Henry. It was made of nothing but bark and poles, but it had kept out all that long, penetrating rain of the last three or four days, and when he lifted the big stone aside and opened the door it seemed as snug a place as he could have wished.

He left the door open a little, lighted a small fire on the flat stones, having no fear that it would be seen through the dense curtain that shut him in, and broiled big bear steaks on the coals. When he had eaten and the fire had died he went out and sat beside the hut. He was well satisfied with the day's work, and he wished now to think with all the concentration that one must put upon a great task if he expects to achieve it. He intended to invade the Indian camp, and he knew full well that it was the most perilous enterprise that he had ever attempted. Yet scouts and hunters had done such things and had escaped with their lives. He must not shrink from the path that others had trodden.

He made up his mind firmly, and partly thought out his plan of operations. Then he rested, and so sanguine was his temperament that he began to regard the deed itself as almost achieved. Decision is always soothing after doubt, and he fell into a pleasant dreamy state. A gentle wind was blowing, the forest was dry and the leaves rustled with the low note that is like the softest chord of a violin. It became penetrating, thrillingly sweet, and hark! it spoke to him in a voice that he knew. It was the same voice that he had heard on the Ohio, mystic, but telling him to be of heart and courage. He would triumph over hardships and dangers, and he would see his friends again.

Henry started up from his vision. The song was gone, and he heard only the wind softly moving the leaves. It had been vague and shadowy as gossamer, light as the substance of a dream, but it was real to him, nevertheless, and the deep glow of certain triumph permeated his being, body and mind. It was not strange that he had in his nature something of the Indian mysticism that personified the winds and the trees and everything about him. The Manitou of the red man and the ancient Aieroski of the Iroquois were the same as his own God. He could not doubt that he had a message. Down on the Ohio he had had the same message more than once, and it had always come true.

He heard a slight rustling among the bushes, and, sitting perfectly still, he saw a black bear emerge into the open. It had gained the islet in some manner, probably floundering through the black mire, and the thought occurred to him that it was the mate of the one he had slain, drawn perhaps by instinct on the trail of a lost comrade. He could have shot the bear as he sat-and he would need fresh supplies of food soon-but he did not have the heart to do it.

The bear sniffed a little at the wind, which was blowing the human odor away from him, and sat back on his haunches. Henry did not believe that the animal had seen him or was yet aware of his presence, although he might suspect. There was something humorous and also pathetic in the visitor, who cocked his head on one side and looked about him. He made a distinct appeal to Henry, who sat absolutely still, so still that the little bear could not be sure at first that he was a human being. A minute passed, and the red eye of the bear rested upon the boy. Henry felt pleasant and sociable, but he knew that he could retain friendly relations only by remaining quiet.

"If I have eaten your comrade, my friend," he said to himself, "it is only because of hard necessity." The bear, little, comic, and yet with that touch of pathos about him, cocked his head a little further over on one side, and as a silver shaft of moonlight fell upon him Henry could see one red eye gleaming. It was a singular fact, but the boy, alone in the wilderness, and the loser of his comrades, felt for the moment a sense of comradeship with the bear, which was also alone, and doubtless the loser of a comrade, also. He uttered a soft growling sound like the satisfied purr of a bear eating its food.

The comical bear rose a little higher on his hind paws, and looked in astonishment at the motionless figure that uttered sounds so familiar. Yet the figure was not familiar. He had never seen a human being before, and the shape and outline were very strange to him. It might be some new kind of animal, and he was disposed to be inquiring, because there was nothing in these forests which the black bear was afraid of until man came.

He advanced a step or two and growled gently. Then he reared up again on his hind paws, and cocked his held to one side in his amusing manner. Henry, still motionless, smiled at him. Here, for an instant at least, was a cheery visitor and companionship. He at least would not break the spell.

"You look almost as if you could talk, old fellow," he said to himself, "and if I knew your language I'd ask you a lot of questions."

The bear, too, was motionless now, torn by doubt and curiosity. It certainly was a singular figure that sat there, fifteen or twenty yards before him, and he had the most intense curiosity to solve the mystery of this creature. But caution held him back.

There was a sudden flaw in the light breeze. It shifted about and brought the dreadful man odor to the nostrils of the honest black bear. It was something entirely new to him, but it contained the quality of fear. That still strange figure was his deadliest foe. Dropping down upon his four paws, he fled among the trees, and then scrambled somehow through the swamp to the mainland.

Henry sighed. Despite his own friendly feeling, the bear, warned by instinct, was afraid of him, and, as he was bound to acknowledge to himself, the bear's instinct was doubtless right. He rose, went into the hut, and slept heavily through the night. In the morning he left the islet once more to scout in the direction of the Indian camp, but he found it a most dangerous task. The woods were full of warriors hunting. As he had judged, the game was abundant, and he heard rifles cracking in several directions. He loitered, therefore, in the thickest of the thickets, willing to wait until night came for his enterprise. It was advisable, moreover, to wait, because he did not see yet just how he was going to succeed. He spent nearly the whole day shifting here and there through the forest, but late in the afternoon, as the Indians yet seemed so numerous in the woods, he concluded to go back toward the islet.

He was about two miles from the swamp when he heard a cry, sharp but distant. It was that of the savages, and Henry instinctively divined the cause. A party of the warriors had come somehow upon his trail, and they would surely follow it. It was a mischance that he had not expected. He waited a minute or two, and then heard the cry again, but nearer. He knew that it would come no more, but it confirmed him in his first opinion.

Henry had little fear of being caught, as the islet was so securely hidden, but he did not wish to take even a remote chance of its discovery. Hence he ran to the eastward of it, intending as the darkness came, hiding his trail, to double back and regain the hut.

He proceeded at a long, easy gait, his mind not troubled by the pursuit. It was to him merely an incident that should be ended as soon as possible, annoying perhaps, but easily cured. So he swung lightly along, stopping at intervals among the bushes to see if any of the warriors had drawn near, but he detected nothing. Now and then he looked up to the sky, willing that night should end this matter quickly and peacefully.

His wish seemed near fulfillment. An uncommonly brilliant sun was setting. The whole west was a sea of red and yellow fire, but in the east the forest was already sinking into the dark. He turned now, and went back toward the west on a line parallel with the pursuit, but much closer to the swamp. The dusk thickened rapidly. The sun dropped over the curve of the world, and the vast complex maze of trunks and boughs melted into a solid black wall. The incident of the pursuit was over and with it its petty annoyances. He directed his course boldly now for the stepping stones, and traveled fast. Soon the first of them would be less than a hundred yards away.

But the incident was not over. Wary and skillful though the young forest runner might be, he had made one miscalculation, and it led to great consequences. As he skirted the edge of the swamp in the darkness, now fully come, a dusky figure suddenly appeared. It was a stray warrior from some small band, wandering about at will. The meeting was probably as little expected by him as it was by Henry, and they were so close together when they saw each other that neither had time to raise his rifle. The warrior, a tall, powerful man, dropping his gun and snatching out a knife, sprang at once upon his enemy.

Henry was borne back by the weight and impact, but, making an immense effort, he recovered himself and, seizing the wrist of the Indian's knife hand, exerted all his great strength. The warrior wished to change the weapon from his right band, but he dared not let go with the other lest he be thrown down at once, and with great violence. His first rush having failed, he was now at a disadvantage, as the Indian is not generally a wrestler. Henry pushed him back, and his hand closed tighter and tighter around the red wrist. He wished to tear the knife from it, but he, too, was afraid to let go with the other hand, and so the two remained locked fast. Neither uttered a cry after the first contact, and the only sounds in the dark were their hard breathing, which turned to a gasp now and then, and the shuffle of their feet over the earth.

Henry felt that it must end soon. One or the other must give way. Their sinews were already strained to the cracking point, and making a supreme effort he bore all his weight upon the warrior, who, unable to sustain himself, went down with the youth upon him. The Indian uttered a groan, and Henry, leaping instantly to his feet, looked down upon his fallen antagonist, who did not stir. He knew the cause. As they fell the point of the knife bad been turned upward, and it had entered the Indian's heart.

Although he had been in peril at his hands, Henry looked at the slain man in a sort of pity. He had not wished to take anyone's life, and, in reality, he had not been the direct cause of it. But it was a stern time and the feeling soon passed. The Wyandot, for such he was by his paint, would never have felt a particle of remorse had the victory been his.

The moon was now coming out, and Henry looked down thoughtfully at the still face. Then the idea came to him, in fact leaped up in his brain, with such an impulse that it carried conviction. He would take this warrior's place and go to the Indian camp. So eager was he, and so full of his plan, that he did not feel any repulsion as he opened the warrior's deerskin shirt and took his totem from a place near his heart. It was a little deerskin bag containing a bunch of red feathers. This was his charm, his magic spell, his bringer of good luck, which had failed him so woefully this time. Henry, not without a touch of the forest belief, put it inside his own hunting shirt, wishing, although he laughed at himself, that if the red man's medicine had any potency it should be on his own side.

Then he found also the little bag in which the Indian carried his war paint and the feather brush with which he put it on. The next hour witnessed a singular transformation. A white youth was turned into a red warrior. He cut his own hair closely, all except a tuft in the center, with his sharp hunting knife. The tuft and the close crop he stained black with the Indian's paint. It was a poor black, but he hoped that it would pass in the night. He drew the tuft into a scalplock, and intertwined it with a feather from the Indian's own tuft. Then he stained his face, neck, hands, and arms with the red paint, and stood forth a powerful young warrior of a western nation.

He hid the Indian's weapons and his own raccoon-skin cap in the brush. Then he took the body of the fallen warrior to the edge of the swamp and dropped it in. His object was not alone concealment, but burial as well. He still felt sorry for the unfortunate Wyandot, and he watched him until he sank completely from sight in the mire. Then he turned away and traveled a straight course toward the great Indian camp.

He stopped once on the way at a clear pool irradiated by the bright moonlight, and looked attentively at his reflection. By night, at least, it was certainly that of an Indian, and, summoning all his confidence, he continued upon his chosen and desperate task.

Henry knew that the chances were against him, even with his disguise, but he was bound to enter the Indian camp, and he was prepared to incur all risks and to endure all penalties. He even felt a certain lightness of heart as he hurried on his way, and at length saw through the forest the flare of light from the Indian camp.

He approached cautiously at first in order that he might take a good look into the camp, and he was surprised at what he saw. In a single day the village had been enlarged much more. It seemed to him that it contained at least twice as many warriors. Women and children, too, had come, and he heard a stray dog barking here and there. Many more fires than usual were burning, and there was a great murmur of voices.

Henry was much taken aback at first. It seemed that he was about to plunge into the midst of the whole Iroquois nation, and at a time, too, when something of extreme importance was going on, but a little reflection showed that he was fortunate. Amid so many people, and so much ferment it was not at all likely that he would be noticed closely. It was his intention, if the necessity came, to pass himself off as a warrior of the Shawnee tribe who had wandered far eastward, but he meant to avoid sedulously the eye of Timmendiquas, who might, through his size and stature, divine his identity.

As Henry lingered at the edge of the camp, in indecision whether to wait a little or plunge boldly into the light of the fires, he became aware that all sounds in the village-for such it was instead of a camp-had ceased suddenly, except the light tread of feet and the sound of many people talking low. He saw through the bushes that all the Iroquois, and with them the detachment of Wyandots under White Lightning, were going toward a large structure in the center, which he surmised to be the Council House. He knew from his experience with the Indians farther west that the Iroquois built such structures.

He could no longer doubt that some ceremony of the greatest importance was about to begin, and, dismissing indecision, he left the bushes and entered the village, going with the crowd toward the great pole building, which was, indeed, the Council House.

But little attention was paid to Henry. He would have drawn none at all, had it not been for his height, and when a warrior or two glanced at him he uttered some words in Shawnee, saying that he had wandered far, and was glad to come to the hospitable Iroquois. One who could speak a little Shawnee bade him welcome, and they went on, satisfied, their minds more intent upon the ceremony than upon a visitor.

The Council House, built of light poles and covered with poles and thatch, was at least sixty feet long and about thirty feet wide, with a large door on the eastern side, and one or two smaller ones on the other sides. As Henry arrived, the great chiefs and sub-chiefs of the Iroquois were entering the building, and about it were grouped many warriors and women, and even children. But all preserved a decorous solemnity, and, knowing the customs of the forest people so well, he was sure that the ceremony, whatever it might be, must be of a highly sacred nature. He himself drew to one side, keeping as much as possible in the shadow, but he was using to its utmost power every faculty of observation that Nature had given him.

Many of the fires were still burning, but the moon had come out with great brightness, throwing a silver light over the whole village, and investing with attributes that savored of the mystic and impressive this ceremony, held by a savage but great race here in the depths of the primeval forest. Henry was about to witness a Condoling Council, which was at once a mourning for chiefs who had fallen in battle farther east with his own people and the election and welcome of their successors.

The chiefs presently came forth from the Council House or, as it was more generally called, the Long House, and, despite the greatness of Thayendanegea, those of the Onondaga tribe, in virtue of their ancient and undisputed place as the political leaders and high priests of the Six Nations, led the way. Among the stately Onondaga chiefs were: Atotarho (The Entangled), Skanawati (Beyond the River), Tehatkahtons (Looking Both Ways), Tehayatkwarayen (Red Wings), and Hahiron (The Scattered). They were men of stature and fine countenance, proud of the titular primacy that belonged to them because it was the Onondaga, Hiawatha, who had formed the great confederacy more than four hundred years before our day, or just about the time Columbus was landing on the shores of the New World.

Next to the Onondagas came the fierce and warlike Mohawks, who lived nearest to Albany, who were called Keepers of the Eastern Gate, and who were fully worthy of their trust. They were content that the Onondagas should lead in council, so long as they were first in battle, and there was no jealousy between them. Among their chiefs were Koswensiroutha (Broad Shoulders) and Satekariwate (Two Things Equal).

Third in rank were the Senecas, and among their chiefs were Kanokarih (The Threatened) and Kanyadariyo (Beautiful Lake).

These three, the Onondagas, Mohawks, and Senecas, were esteemed the three senior nations. After them, in order of precedence, came the chiefs of the three junior nations, the Oneidas, Cayugas, and Tuscaroras. All of the great chiefs had assistant chiefs, usually relatives, who, in case of death, often succeeded to their places. But these assistants now remained in the crowd with other minor chiefs and the mass of the warriors. A little apart stood Timmendiquas and his Wyandots. He, too, was absorbed in the ceremony so sacred to him, an Indian, and he did not notice the tall figure of the strange Shawnee lingering in the deepest of the shadows.

The head chiefs, walking solemnly and never speaking, marched across the clearing, and then through the woods to a glen, where two young warriors had kindled a little fire of sticks as a signal of welcome. The chiefs gathered around the fire and spoke together in low tones. This was Deyuhnyon Kwarakda, which means "The Reception at the Edge of the Wood."

Henry and some others followed, as it was not forbidden to see, and his interest increased. He shared the spiritual feeling which was impressed upon the red faces about him. The bright moonlight, too, added to the effect, giving it the tinge of an old Druidical ceremony.

The chiefs relapsed into silence and sat thus about ten minutes. Then rose the sound of a chant, distant and measured, and a procession of young and inferior chiefs, led by Oneidas, appeared, slowly approaching the fire. Behind them were warriors, and behind the warriors were many women and children. All the women were in their brightest attire, gay with feather headdresses and red, blue, or green blankets from the British posts.

The procession stopped at a distance of about a dozen yards from the chiefs about the council fire, and the Oneida, Kathlahon, formed the men in a line facing the head chiefs, with the women and children grouped in an irregular mass behind them. The singing meanwhile had stopped. The two groups stood facing each other, attentive and listening.

Then Hahiron, the oldest of the Onondagas, walked back and forth in the space between the two groups, chanting a welcome. Like all Indian songs it was monotonous. Every line he uttered with emphasis and a rising inflection, the phrase "Haih-haih" which may be translated "Hail to thee!" or better, "All hail!" Nevertheless, under the moonlight in the wilderness and with rapt faces about him, it was deeply impressive. Henry found it so.

Hahiron finished his round and went back to his place by the fire. Atotarho, head chief of the Onondagas, holding in his hands beautifully beaded strings of Iroquois wampum, came forward and made a speech of condolence, to which Kathlahon responded. Then the head chiefs and the minor chiefs smoked pipes together, after which the head chiefs, followed by the minor chiefs, and these in turn by the crowd, led the way back to the village.

Many hundreds of persons were in this procession, which was still very grave and solemn, every one in it impressed by the sacred nature of this ancient rite. The chief entered the great door of the Long House, and all who could find places not reserved followed. Henry went in with the others, and sat in a corner, making himself as small as possible. Many women, the place of whom was high among the Iroquois, were also in the Long House.

The head chiefs sat on raised seats at the north end of the great room. In front of them, on lower seats, were the minor chiefs of the three older nations on the left, and of the three younger nations on the right. In front of these, but sitting on the bark floor, was a group of warriors. At the east end, on both high and low seats, were warriors, and facing them on the western side were women, also on both high and low seats. The southern side facing the chiefs was divided into sections, each with high and low seats. The one on the left was occupied by men, and the one on the right by women. Two small fires burned in the center of the Long House about fifteen feet apart.

It was the most singular and one of the most impressive scenes that Henry had ever beheld. When all had found their seats there was a deep silence. Henry could hear the slight crackling made by the two fires as they burned, and the light fell faintly across the multitude of dark, eager faces. Not less than five hundred people were in the Long House, and here was the red man at his best, the first of the wild, not the second or third of the civilized, a drop of whose blood in his veins brings to the white man now a sense of pride, and not of shame, as it does when that blood belongs to some other races.

The effect upon Henry was singular. He almost forgot that he was a foe among them on a mission. For the moment he shared in their feelings, and he waited with eagerness for whatever might come.

Thayendanegea, the Mohawk, stood up in his place among the great chiefs. The role he was about to assume belonged to Atotarho, the Onondaga, but the old Onondaga assigned it for the occasion to Thayendanegea, and there was no objection. Thayendanegea was an educated man, he had been in England, he was a member of a Christian church, and he had translated a part of the Bible from English into his own tongue, but now he was all a Mohawk, a son of the forest.

He spoke to the listening crowd of the glories of the Six Nations, how Hah-gweh-di-yu (The Spirit of Good) had inspired Hiawatha to form the Great Confederacy of the Five Nations, afterwards the Six; how they had held their hunting grounds for nearly two centuries against both English and French; and how they would hold them against the Americans. He stopped at moments, and deep murmurs of approval went through the Long House. The eyes of both men and women flashed as the orator spoke of their glory and greatness. Timmendiquas, in a place of honor, nodded approval. If he could he would form such another league in the west.

The air in the Long House, breathed by so many, became heated. It seemed to have in it a touch of fire. The orator's words burned. Swift and deep impressions were left upon the excited brain. The tall figure of the Mohawk towered, gigantic, in the half light, and the spell that he threw over all was complete.

He spoke about half an hour, but when he stopped he did not sit down. Henry knew by the deep breath that ran through the Long House that something more was coming from Thayendanegea. Suddenly the red chief began to sing in a deep, vibrant voice, and this was the song that he sung:

This was the roll of you,
All hail! All hail! All hail!
You that joined in the work,
All hail! All hail! All hail!
You that finished the task,
All hail! All hail! All hail!
The Great League,
All hail! All hail! All hail!

There was the same incessant repetition of "Haih haih!" that Henry had noticed in the chant at the edge of the woods, but it seemed to give a cumulative effect, like the roll of thunder, and at every slight pause that deep breath of approval ran through the crowd in the Long House. The effect of the song was indescribable. Fire ran in the veins of all, men, women, and children. The great pulses in their throats leaped up. They were the mighty nation, the ever-victorious, the League of the Ho-de-no-sau-nee, that had held at bay both the French and the English since first a white man was seen in the land, and that would keep back the Americans now.

Henry glanced at Timmendiquas. The nostrils of the great White Lightning were twitching. The song reached to the very roots of his being, and aroused all his powers. Like Thayendanegea, he was a statesman, and he saw that the Americans were far more formidable to his race than English or French had ever been. The Americans were upon the ground, and incessantly pressed upon the red man, eye to eye. Only powerful leagues like those of the Iroquois could withstand them.

Thayendanegea sat down, and then there was another silence, a period lasting about two minutes. These silences seemed to be a necessary part of all Iroquois rites. When it closed two young warriors stretched an elm bark rope across the room from east to west and near the ceiling, but between the high chiefs and the minor chiefs. Then they hung dressed skins all along it, until the two grades of chiefs were hidden from the view of each other. This was the sign of mourning, and was followed by a silence. The fires in the Long House had died down somewhat, and little was to be seen but the eyes and general outline of the people. Then a slender man of middle years, the best singer in all the Iroquois nation, arose and sang:

To the great chiefs bring we greeting,
All hail! All hail! All hail!
To the dead chiefs, kindred greeting,
All hail! All hail! All hail!
To the strong men 'round him greeting,
All hail! All hail! All hail!
To the mourning women greeting,
All hail! All hail! All hail!
There our grandsires' words repeating,
All hail! All hail! All hail!

The singing voice was sweet, penetrating, and thrilling, and the song was sad. At the pauses deep murmurs of sorrow ran through the crowd in the Long House. Grief for the dead held them all. When he finished, Satekariwate, the Mohawk, holding in his hands three belts of wampum, uttered a long historical chant telling of their glorious deeds, to which they listened patiently. The chant over, he handed the belts to an attendant, who took them to Thayendanegea, who held them for a few moments and looked at them gravely.

One of the wampum belts was black, the sign of mourning; another was purple, the sign of war; and the third was white, the sign of peace. They were beautiful pieces of workmanship, very old.

When Hiawatha left the Onondagas and fled to the Mohawks he crossed a lake supposed to be the Oneida. While paddling along he noticed that man tiny black, purple, and white shells clung to his paddle. Reaching the shore he found such shells in long rows upon the beach, and it occurred to him to use them for the depiction of thought according to color. He strung them on threads of elm bark, and afterward, when the great league was formed, the shells were made to represent five clasped hands. For four hundred years the wampum belts have been sacred among the Iroquois.

Now Thayendanegea gave the wampum belts back to the attendant, who returned them to Satekariwate, the Mohawk. There was a silence once more, and then the chosen singer began the Consoling Song again, but now he did not sing it alone. Two hundred male voices joined him, and the time became faster. Its tone changed from mourning and sorrow to exultation and menace. Everyone thought of war, the tomahawk, and victory. The song sung as it was now became a genuine battle song, rousing and thrilling. The Long House trembled with the mighty chorus, and its volume poured forth into the encircling dark woods.

All the time the song was going on, Satekariwate, the Mohawk, stood holding the belts in his hand, but when it was over he gave them to an attendant, who carried them to another head chief. Thayendanegea now went to the center of the room and, standing between the two fires, asked who were the candidates for the places of the dead chiefs.

The dead chiefs were three, and three tall men, already chosen among their own tribes, came forward to succeed them. Then a fourth came, and Henry was startled. It was Timmendiquas, who, as the bravest chief of the brave Wyandots, was about to become, as a signal tribute, and as a great sign of friendship, an adopted son and honorary chief of the Mohawks, Keepers of the Western Gate, and most warlike of all the Iroquois tribes.

As Timmendiquas stood before Thayendanegea, a murmur of approval deeper than any that had gone before ran through all the crowd in the Long House, and it was deepest on the women's benches, where sat many matrons of the Iroquois, some of whom were chiefs-a woman could be a chief among the Iroquois.

The candidates were adjudged acceptable by the other chiefs, and Thayendanegea addressed them on their duties, while they listened in grave silence. With his address the sacred part of the rite was concluded. Nothing remained now but the great banquet outside—although that was much—and they poured forth to it joyously, Thayendanegea, the Mohawk, and Timmendiquas, the Wyandot, walking side by side, the finest two red chiefs on all the American continent.

CHAPTER VI. THE EVIL SPIRIT'S WORK

Henry slipped forth with the crowd from the Long House, stooping somewhat and shrinking into the smallest possible dimensions. But there was little danger now that any one would notice him, as long as he behaved with prudence, because all grief and solemnity were thrown aside, and a thousand red souls intended to rejoice. A vast banquet was arranged. Great fires leaped up all through the village. At every fire the Indian women, both young and old, were already far forward with the cooking. Deer, bear, squirrel, rabbit, fish, and every other variety of game with which the woods and rivers of western New York and Pennsylvania swarmed were frying or roasting over the coals, and the air was permeated with savory odors. There was a great hum of voices and an incessant chattering. Here in the forest, among themselves, and in complete security, the Indian stoicism was relaxed. According to their customs everybody fell to eating at a prodigious rate, as if they had not tasted anything for a month, and as if they intended to eat enough now to last another month.

It was far into the night, because the ceremonies had lasted a long time, but a brilliant moon shone down upon the feasting crowd, and the flames of the great fires, yellow and blue, leaped and danced. This was an oasis of light and life. Timmendiquas and Thayendanegea sat together before the largest fire, and they ate with more restraint than the others. Even at the banquet they would not relax their dignity as great chiefs. Old Skanawati, the Onondaga, old Atotarho, Onondaga, too, Satekariwate, the Mohawk, Kanokarih, the Seneca, and others, head chiefs though they were of the three senior tribes, did not hesitate to eat as the rich Romans of the Empire ate, swallowing immense quantities of all kinds of meat, and drinking a sort of cider that the women made. Several warriors ate and drank until they fell down in a stupor by the fires. The same warriors on the hunt or the war path would go for days without food, enduring every manner of hardship. Now and then a warrior would leap up and begin a chant telling of some glorious deed of his. Those at his own fire would listen, but elsewhere they took no notice.

In the largest open space a middle-aged Onondaga with a fine face suddenly uttered a sharp cry: "Hehmio!" which he rapidly repeated twice. Two score voices instantly replied, "Heh!" and a rush was made for him. At least a hundred gathered around him, but they stood in a respectful circle, no one nearer than ten feet. He waved his hand, and all sat down on the ground. Then, he, too, sat down, all gazing at him intently and with expectancy.

He was a professional story-teller, an institution great and honored among the tribes of the Iroquois farther back even than Hiawatha. He began at once the story of the warrior who learned to talk with the deer and the bear, carrying it on through many chapters. Now and then a delighted listener would cry "Hah!" but if anyone became bored and fell asleep it was considered an omen of misfortune to the sleeper, and he was chased ignominiously to his tepee. The Iroquois romancer was better protected than the white one is. He could finish some of his stories in one evening, but others were serials. When he arrived at the end of the night's installment he would cry, "Si-ga!" which was equivalent to our "To be continued in our next." Then all would rise, and if tired would seek sleep, but if not they would catch the closing part of some other story-teller's romance.

At three fires Senecas were playing a peculiar little wooden flute of their own invention, that emitted wailing sounds not without a certain sweetness. In a corner a half dozen warriors hurt in battle were bathing their wounds with a soothing lotion made from the sap of the bass wood.

Henry lingered a while in the darkest corners, witnessing the feasting, hearing the flutes and the chants, listening for a space to the story-tellers and the enthusiastic "Hahs!" They were so full of feasting and merrymaking now that one could almost do as he pleased, and he stole toward the southern end of the village, where he had noticed several huts, much more strongly built than the others. Despite all his natural skill and experience his heart beat very fast when he came to the first. He was about to achieve the great exploration upon which he had ventured so much.

Whether he would find anything at the end of the risk he ran, he was soon to see.

The hut, about seven feet square and as many feet in height, was built strongly of poles, with a small entrance closed by a clapboard door fastened stoutly on the outside with withes. The hut was well in the shadow of tepees, and all were still at the feasting and merrymaking. He cut the withes with two sweeps of his sharp hunting knife, opened the door, bent his head, stepped in and then closed the door behind him, in order that no Iroquois might see what had happened.

It was not wholly dark in the hut, as there were cracks between the poles, and bars of moonlight entered, falling upon a floor of bark. They revealed also a figure lying full length on one side of the hut. A great pulse of joy leaped up in Henry's throat, and with it was a deep pity, also. The figure was that of Shif'less Sol, but he was pale and thin, and his arms and legs were securely bound with thongs of deerskin.

Leaning over, Henry cut the thongs of the shiftless one, but he did not stir. Great forester that Shif'less Sol was, and usually so sensitive to the lightest movement, he perceived nothing now, and, had he not found him bound, Henry would have been afraid that he was looking upon his dead comrade. The hands of the shiftless one, when the hands were cut, had fallen limply by his side, and his face looked all the more pallid by contrast with the yellow hair which fell in length about it. But it was his old-time friend, the dauntless Shif'less Sol, the last of the five to vanish so mysteriously.

Henry bent down and pulled him by the shoulder. The captive yawned, stretched himself a little, and lay still again with closed eyes. Henry shook him a second time and more violently. Shif'less Sol sat up quickly, and Henry knew that indignation prompted the movement. Sol held his arms and legs stiffly and seemed to be totally unconscious that they were unbound. He cast one glance upward, and in the dim light saw the tall warrior bending over him.

"I'll never do it, Timmendiquas or White Lightning, whichever name you like better!" he exclaimed. "I won't show you how to surprise the white settlements. You can burn me at the stake or tear me in pieces first. Now go away and let me sleep."

He sank back on the bark, and started to close his eyes again. It was then that he noticed for the first time that his hands were unbound. He held them up before his face, as if they were strange objects wholly unattached to himself, and gazed at them in amazement. He moved his legs and saw that they, too, were unbound. Then he turned his startled gaze upward at the face of the tall warrior who was looking down at him. Shif'less Sol was wholly awake now. Every faculty in him was alive, and he pierced through the Shawnee disguise. He knew who it was. He knew who had come to save him, and he sprang to his feet, exclaiming the one word:

"Henry!"

The hands of the comrades met in the clasp of friendship which only many dangers endured together can give.

"How did you get here?" asked the shiftless one in a whisper.

"I met an Indian in the forest," replied Henry, "and well I am now he."

Shif'less Sol laughed under his breath.

"I see," said he, "but how did you get through the camp? It's a big one, and the Iroquois are watchful. Timmendiquas is here, too, with his Wyandots."

"They are having a great feast," replied Henry, "and I could go about almost unnoticed. Where are the others, Sol?"

"In the cabins close by."

"Then we'll get out of this place. Quick! Tie up your hair! In the darkness you can easily pass for an Indian."

The shiftless one drew his hair into a scalp lock, and the two slipped from the cabin, closing the door behind them and deftly retying the thongs, in order that the discovery of the escape might occur as late as possible. Then they stood a few moments in the shadow of the hut and listened to the sounds of revelry, the monotone of the story-tellers, and the chant of the singers.

"You don't know which huts they are in, do you?" asked Henry, anxiously.

"No, I don't," replied the shiftless one.

"Get back!" exclaimed Henry softly. "Don't you see who's passing out there?"

"Braxton Wyatt," said Sol. "I'd like to get my hands on that scoundrel. I've had to stand a lot from him."

"The score must wait. But first we'll provide you with weapons. See, the Iroquois have stacked some of their rifles here while they're at the feast."

A dozen good rifles had been left leaning against a hut near by, and Henry, still watching lest he be observed, chose the best, with its ammunition, for his comrade, who, owing to his semi-civilized attire, still remained in the shadow of the other hut.

"Why not take four?" whispered the shiftless one. "We'll need them for the other boys."

Henry took four, giving two to his comrade, and then they hastily slipped back to the other side of the hut. A Wyandot and a Mohawk were passing, and they had eyes of hawks. Henry and Sol waited until the formidable pair were gone, and then began to examine the huts, trying to surmise in which their comrades lay.

"I haven't seen 'em a-tall, a-tall," said Sol, "but I reckon from the talk that they are here. I was s'prised in the woods, Henry. A half dozen reds jumped on me so quick I didn't have time to draw a weepin. Timmendiquas was at the head uv 'em an' he just grinned. Well, he is a great chief, if he did truss me up like a fowl. I reckon the same thing happened to the others."

"Come closer, Sol! Come closer!" whispered Henry. "More warriors are walking this way. The feast is breaking up, and they'll spread all through the camp."

A terrible problem was presented to the two. They could no longer search among the strong huts, for their comrades. The opportunity to save had lasted long enough for one only. But border training is stern, and these two had uncommon courage and decision.

"We must go now, Sol," said Henry, "but we'll come back."

"Yes," said the shiftless one, "we'll come back."

Darting between the huts, they gained the southern edge of the forest before the satiated banqueters could suspect the presence of an enemy. Here they felt themselves safe, but they did not pause. Henry led the way, and Shif'less Sol followed at a fair degree of speed.

"You'll have to be patient with me for a little while, Henry," said Sol in a tone of humility. "When I wuz layin' thar in the lodge with my hands an' feet tied I wuz about eighty years old, jest ez stiff ez could be from the long tyin'. When I reached the edge o' the woods the blood wuz flowin' lively enough to make me 'bout sixty. Now I reckon I'm fifty, an' ef things go well I'll be back to my own nateral age in two or three hours."

"You shall have rest before morning," said Henry, "and it will be in a good place, too. I can promise that."

Shif'less Sol looked at him inquiringly, but he did not say anything. Like the rest of the five, Sol had acquired the most implicit confidence in their bold young leader. He had every reason to feel good. That painful soreness was disappearing from his ankles. As they advanced through the woods, weeks dropped from him one by one. Then the months began to roll away, and at last time fell year by year. As they approached the deeps of the forest where the swamp lay, Solomon Hyde, the so called shiftless one, and wholly undeserving of the name, was young again.

"I've got a fine little home for us, Sol," said Henry. "Best we've had since that time we spent a winter on the island in the lake. This is littler, but it's harder to find. It'll be a fine thing to know you're sleeping safe and sound with five hundred Iroquois warriors only a few miles away."

"Then it'll suit me mighty well," said Shif'less Sol, grinning broadly. "That's jest the place fur a lazy man like your humble servant, which is me."

They reached the stepping stones, and Henry paused a moment.

"Do you feel steady enough, Sol, to jump from stone to stone?" he asked.

"I'm feelin' so good I could fly ef I had to," he replied. "Jest you jump on, Henry, an' fur every jump you take you'll find me only one jump behind you!"

Henry, without further ado, sprang from one stone to another, and behind him, stone for stone, came the shiftless one. It was now past midnight, and the moon was obscured. The keenest eyes twenty yards away could not have seen the two dusky figures as they went by leaps into the very heart of the great, black swamp. They reached the solid ground, and then the hut.

"Here, Sol," said Henry, "is my house, and yours, also, and soon, I hope, to be that of Paul, Tom, and Jim, too."

"Henry," said Shif'less Sol, "I'm shorely glad to come."

They went inside, stacked their captured rifles against the wall, and soon were sound asleep.

Meanwhile sleep was laying hold of the Iroquois village, also. They had eaten mightily and they had drunk mightily. Many times had they told the glories of Hode-no-sau-nee, the Great League, and many times had they gladly acknowledged the valor and worth of Timmendiquas and the brave little Wyandot nation. Timmendiquas and Thayendanegea had sat side by side throughout the feast, but often other great chiefs were with them- Skanawati, Atotarho, and Hahiron, the Onondagas; Satekariwate, the Mohawk; Kanokarih and Kanyadoriyo, the Senecas; and many others.

Toward midnight the women and the children left for the lodges, and soon the warriors began to go also, or fell asleep on the ground, wrapped in their blankets. The fires were allowed to sink low, and at last the older chiefs withdrew, leaving only Timmendiquas and Thayendanegea.

"You have seen the power and spirit of the Iroquois," said Thayendanegea. "We can bring many more warriors than are here into the field, and we will strike the white settlements with you."

"The Wyandots are not so many as the warriors of the Great League," said Timmendiquas proudly, "but no one has ever been before them in battle."

"You speak truth, as I have often heard it," said Thayendanegea thoughtfully. Then he showed Timmendiquas to a lodge of honor, the finest in the village, and retired to his own.

The great feast was over, but the chiefs had come to a momentous decision. Still chafing over their defeat at Oriskany, they would make a new and formidable attack upon the white settlements, and Timmendiquas and his fierce Wyandots would help them. All of them, from the oldest to the youngest, rejoiced in the decision, and, not least, the famous Thayendanegea. He hated the Americans most because they were upon the soil, and were always pressing forward against the Indian. The Englishmen were far away, and if they prevailed in the great war, the march of the American would be less rapid. He would strike once more with the Englishmen, and the Iroquois could deliver mighty blows on the American rearguard. He and his Mohawks, proud Keepers of the Western Gate, would lead in the onset. Thayendanegea considered it a good night's work, and he slept peacefully.

The great camp relapsed into silence. The warriors on the ground breathed perhaps a little heavily after so much feasting, and the fires were permitted to smolder down to coals. Wolves and panthers drawn by the scent of food crept through the thickets toward the faint firelight, but they were afraid to draw near. Morning came, and food and drink were taken to the lodges in which four prisoners were held, prisoners of great value, taken by Timmendiquas and the Wyandots, and held at his urgent insistence as hostages.

Three were found as they had been left, and when their bonds were loosened they ate and drank, but the fourth hut was empty. The one who spoke in a slow, drawling way, and the one who seemed to be the most dangerous of them all, was gone. Henry and Sol had taken the severed thongs with them, and there was nothing to show how the prisoner had disappeared, except that the withes fastening the door had been cut.

The news spread through the village, and there was much excitement. Thayendanegea and Timmendiquas came and looked at the empty hut. Timmendiquas may have suspected how Shif'less Sol had gone, but he said nothing. Others believed that it was the work of Hahgweh-da-et-gah (The Spirit of Evil), or perhaps Ga-oh (The Spirit of the Winds) had taken him away.

"It is well to keep a good watch on the others," said Timmendiquas, and Thayendanegea nodded.

That day the chiefs entered the Long House again, and held a great war council. A string of white wampum about a foot in length was passed to every chief, who held it a moment or two before handing it to his neighbors. It was then laid on a table in the center of the room, the ends touching. This signified harmony among the Six Nations. All the chiefs had been summoned to this place by belts of wampum sent to the different tribes by runners appointed by the Onondagas, to whom this honor belonged. All treaties had to be ratified by the exchange of belts, and now this was done by the assembled chiefs.

Timmendiquas, as an honorary chief of the Mohawks, and as the real head of a brave and allied nation, was present throughout the council. His advice was asked often, and when he gave it the others listened with gravity and deference. The next day the village played a great game of lacrosse, which was invented by the Indians, and which had been played by them for centuries before the arrival of the white man. In this case the match was on a grand scale, Mohawks and Cayugas against Onondagas and Senecas.

The game began about nine o'clock in the morning in a great natural meadow surrounded by forest. The rival sides assembled opposite each other and bet heavily. All the stakes, under the law of the game, were laid upon the ground in heaps here, and they consisted of the articles most precious to the Iroquois. In these heaps were rifles, tomahawks, scalping knives, wampum, strips of colored beads, blankets, swords, belts, moccasins, leggins, and a great many things taken as spoil in forays on the white settlements, such is small mirrors, brushes of various kinds, boots, shoes, and other things, the whole making a vast assortment.

These heaps represented great wealth to the Iroquois, and the older chiefs sat beside them in the capacity of stakeholders and judges.

The combatants, ranged in two long rows, numbered at least five hundred on each side, and already they began to show an excitement approaching that which animated them when they would go into battle. Their eyes glowed, and the muscles on their naked backs and chests were tense for the spring. In order to leave their limbs perfectly free for effort they wore no clothing at all, except a little apron reaching from the waist to the knee.

The extent of the playground was marked off by two pair of "byes" like those used in cricket, planted about thirty rods apart. But the goals of each side were only about thirty feet apart.

At a signal from the oldest of the chiefs the contestants arranged themselves in two parallel lines facing each other, inside the area and about ten rods apart. Every man was armed with a strong stick three and a half to four feet in length, and curving toward the end. Upon this curved end was tightly fastened a network of thongs of untanned deerskin, drawn until they were rigid and taut. The ball with which they were to play was made of closely wrapped elastic skins, and was about the size of an ordinary apple.

At the end of the lines, but about midway between them, sat the chiefs, who, besides being judges and stakeholders, were also score keepers. They kept tally of the game by cutting notches upon sticks. Every time one side put the ball through the other's goal it counted one, but there was an unusual power exercised by the chiefs, practically unknown to the games of white men. If one side got too far ahead, its score was cut down at the discretion of the chiefs in order to keep the game more even, and also to protract it sometimes over three or four days. The warriors of the leading side might grumble among one another at the amount of cutting the chiefs did, but they would not dare to make any protest. However, the chiefs would never cut the leading side down to an absolute parity with the other. It was always allowed to retain a margin of the superiority it had won.

The game was now about to begin, and the excitement became intense. Even the old judges leaned forward in their eagerness, while the brown bodies of the warriors shone in the sun, and the taut muscles leaped up under the skin. Fifty players on each side, sticks in hand, advanced to the center of the ground, and arranged themselves somewhat after the fashion of football players, to intercept the passage of the ball toward their goals. Now they awaited the coming of the ball.

There were several young girls, the daughters of chiefs. The most beautiful of these appeared. She was not more than sixteen or seventeen years of age, as slender and graceful as a young deer, and she was dressed in the finest and most richly embroidered deerskin. Her head was crowned with a red coronet, crested with plumes, made of the feathers of the eagle and heron. She wore silver bracelets and a silver necklace.

The girl, bearing in her hand the ball, sprang into the very center of the arena, where, amid shouts from all the warriors, she placed it upon the ground. Then she sprang back and joined the throng of spectators. Two of the players, one from each side, chosen for strength and dexterity, advanced. They hooked the ball together in their united bats and thus raised it aloft, until the bats were absolutely perpendicular. Then with a quick, jerking motion they shot it upward. Much might be gained by this first shot or stroke, but on this occasion the two players were equal, and it shot almost absolutely straight into the air. The nearest groups made a rush for it, and the fray began.

Not all played at once, as the crowd was so great, but usually twenty or thirty on each side struck for the ball, and when they became exhausted or disabled were relieved by similar groups. All eventually came into action.

The game was played with the greatest fire and intensity, assuming sometimes the aspect of a battle. Blows with the formidable sticks were given and received. Brown skins were streaked with blood, heads were cracked, and a Cayuga was killed. Such killings were not unusual in these games, and it was always considered the fault of the man who fell, due to his own awkwardness or unwariness. The body of the dead Cayuga was taken away in disgrace.

All day long the contest was waged with undiminished courage and zeal, party relieving party. The meadow and the surrounding forest resounded with the shouts and yells of combatants and spectators. The old squaws were in a perfect frenzy of excitement, and their shrill screams of applause or condemnation rose above every other sound.

On this occasion, as the contest did not last longer than one day, the chiefs never cut down the score of the leading side. The game closed at sunset, with the Senecas and Onondagas triumphant, and richer by far than they were in the morning. The Mohawks and Cayugas retired, stripped of their goods and crestfallen.

Timmendiquas and Thayendanegea, acting as umpires watched the game closely to its finish, but not so the renegades Braxton Wyatt and Blackstaffe. They and Quarles had wandered eastward with some Delawares, and had afterward joined the band of Wyandots, though Timmendiquas gave them no very warm welcome. Quarles had left on some errand a few days before. They had rejoiced greatly at the trapping of the four, one by one, in the deep bush. But they had felt anger and disappointment when the fifth was not taken, also. Now both were concerned and alarmed over the escape of Shif'less Sol in the night, and they drew apart from the Indians to discuss it.

"I think," said Wyatt, "that Hyde did not manage it himself, all alone. How could he? He was bound both hand and foot; and I've learned, too, Blackstaffe, that four of the best Iroquois rifles have been taken. That means one apiece for Hyde and the three prisoners that are left."

The two exchanged looks of meaning and understanding.

"It must have been the boy Ware who helped Hyde to get away," said Blackstaffe, "and their taking of the rifles means that he and Hyde expect to rescue the other three in the same way. You think so, too?"

"Of course," replied Wyatt. "What makes the Indians, who are so wonderfully alert and watchful most of the time, become so careless when they have a great feast?"

Blackstaffe shrugged his shoulders.

"It is their way," he replied. "You cannot change it. Ware must have noticed what they were about, and he took advantage of it. But I don't think any of the others will go that way."

"The boy Cotter is in here," said Braxton Wyatt, tapping the side of a small hut. "Let's go in and see him."

"Good enough," said Blackstaffe. "But we mustn't let him know that Hyde has escaped."

Paul, also bound hand and foot, was lying on an old wolfskin. He, too, was pale and thin-the strict confinement had told upon him heavily-but Paul's spirit could never be daunted. He looked at the two renegades with hatred and contempt.

"Well, you're in a fine fix," said Wyatt sneeringly. "We just came in to tell you that we took Henry Ware last night."

Paul looked him straight and long in the eye, and he knew that the renegade was lying.

"I know better," he said.

"Then we will get him," said Wyatt, abandoning the lie, "and all of you will die at the stake."

"You, will not get him," said Paul defiantly, "and as for the rest of us dying at the stake, that's to be seen. I know this: Timmendiquas considers us of value, to be traded or exchanged, and he's too smart a man to destroy what he regards as his own property. Besides, we may escape. I don't want to boast, Braxton Wyatt, but you know that we're hard to hold."

Then Paul managed to turn over with his face to the wall, as if he were through with them. They went out, and Braxton Wyatt said sulkily:

"Nothing to be got out of him."

"No," said Blackstaffe, "but we must urge that the strictest kind of guard be kept over the others."

The Iroquois were to remain some time at the village, because all their forces were not yet gathered for the great foray they had in mind. The Onondaga runners were still carrying the wampum belts of purple shells, sign of war, to distant villages of the tribes, and parties of warriors were still coming in. A band of Cayugas arrived that night, and with them they brought a half starved and sick, Lenni-Lenape, whom they had picked up near the camp. The Lenni-Lenape, who looked as if he might have been when in health a strong and agile warrior, said that news had reached him through the Wyandots of the great war to be waged by the Iroquois on the white settlements, and the spirits would not let him rest unless he bore his part in it. He prayed therefore to be accepted among them.

Much food was given to the brave Lenni-Lenape, and he was sent to a lodge to rest. To-morrow he would be well, and he would be welcomed to the ranks of the Cayugas, a Younger nation. But when the morning came, the lodge was empty. The sick Lenni-Lenape was gone, and with him the boy, Paul, the youngest of the prisoners. Guards bad been posted all around the camp, but evidently the two had slipped between. Brave and advanced as were the Iroquois, superstition seized upon them. Hah-gweli-da-et-gah was at work among them, coming in the form of the famished Lenni-Lenape. He had steeped them in a deep sleep, and then he had vanished with the prisoner in Se-oh (The Night). Perhaps lie had taken away the boy, who was one of a hated race, for some sacrifice or mystery of his own. The fears of the Iroquois rose. If the Spirit of Evil was among them, greater harm could be expected.

But the two renegades, Blackstaffe and Wyatt, raged. They did not believe in the interference of either good spirits or bad spirits, and just now their special hatred was a famished Lenni-Lenape warrior.

"Why on earth didn't I think of it?" exclaimed Wyatt. "I'm sure now by his size that it was the fellow Hyde. Of Course he slipped to the lodge, let Cotter out, and they dodged about in the darkness until they escaped in the forest. I'll complain to Timmendiquas."

He was as good as his word, speaking of the laxness of both Iroquois and Wyandots. The great White Lightning regarded him with an icy stare.

"You say that the boy, Cotter, escaped through carelessness?" he asked.

"I do," exclaimed Wyatt.

"Then why did you not prevent it?"

Wyatt trembled a little before the stern gaze of the chief.

"Since when," continued Timmendiquas, "have you, a deserter front your own people, had the right to hold to account the head chief of the Wyandots?" Braxton Wyatt, brave though he undoubtedly was, trembled yet more. He knew that Timmendiquas did not like him, and that the Wyandot chieftain could make his position among the Indians precarious.

"I did not mean to say that it was the fault of anybody in particular," he exclaimed hastily, "but I've been hearing so much talk about the Spirit of Evil having a hand in this that I couldn't keep front saying something. Of course, it was Henry Ware and Hyde who did it!"

"It may be," said Timmendiquas icily, "but neither the Manitou of the Wyandots, nor the Aieroski of the Iroquois has given to me the eyes to see everything that happens in the dark."

Wyatt withdrew still in a rage, but afraid to say more. He and Blackstaffe held many conferences through the day, and they longed for the presence of Simon Girty, who was farther west.

That night an Onondaga runner arrived from one of the farthest villages of the Mohawks, far east toward Albany. He had been sent from a farther village, and was not known personally to the warriors in the great camp, but he bore a wampum belt of purple shells, the sign of war, and he reported directly to Thayendanegea, to whom he brought stirring and satisfactory words. After ample feasting, as became one who had come so far, he lay upon soft deerskins in one of the bark huts and sought sleep.

But Braxton Wyatt, the renegade, could not sleep. His evil spirit warned him to rise and go to the huts, where the two remaining prisoners were kept. It was then about one o'clock in the morning, and as he passed he saw the Onondaga runner at the door of one of the prison lodges. He was about to cry out, but the Onondaga turned and struck him such a violent blow with the butt of a pistol, snatched from under his deerskin tunic, that he fell senseless. When a Mohawk sentinel found and revived him an hour later, the door of the hut was open, and the oldest of the prisoners, the one called Ross, was gone.

Now, indeed, were the Iroquois certain that the Spirit of Evil was among them. When great chiefs like Timmendiquas and Thayendanegea were deceived, how could a common warrior hope to escape its wicked influence!

But Braxton Wyatt, with a sore and aching head, lay all day on a bed of skins, and his friend, Moses Blackstaffe, could give him no comfort.

The following night the camp was swept by a sudden and tremendous storm of thunder and lightning, wind and rain. Many of the lodges were thrown down, and when the storm finally whirled itself away, it was found that the last of the prisoners, he of the long arms and long legs, had gone on the edge of the blast.

Truly the Evil Spirit had been hovering over the Iroquois village.

CHAPTER VII. CATHARINE MONTOUR

The five lay deep in the swamp, reunited once more, and full of content. The great storm in which Long Jim, with the aid of his comrades, had disappeared, was whirling off to the eastward. The lightning was flaring its last on the distant horizon, but the rain still pattered in the great woods.

It was a small hut, but the five could squeeze in it. They were dry, warm, and well armed, and they had no fear of the storm and the wilderness. The four after their imprisonment and privations were recovering their weight and color. Paul, who had suffered the most, had, on the other hand, made the quickest recovery, and their present situation, so fortunate in contrast with their threatened fate a few days before, made a great appeal to his imagination. The door was allowed to stand open six inches, and through the crevice he watched the rain pattering on the dark earth. He felt an immense sense of security and comfort. Paul was hopeful by nature and full of courage, but when he lay bound and alone in a hut in the Iroquois camp it seemed to him that no chance was left. The comrades had been kept separate, and he had supposed the others to be dead. But here he was snatched from the very pit of death, and all the others had been saved from a like fate.

"If I'd known that you were alive and uncaptured, Henry," he said, "I'd never have given up hope. It was a wonderful thing you did to start the chain that drew us all away."

"It's no more than Sol or Tom or any of you would have done," said Henry.

"We might have tried it," said Long Jim Hart, "but I ain't sure that we'd have done it. Likely ez not, ef it had been left to me my scalp would be dryin' somewhat in the breeze that fans a Mohawk village. Say, Sol, how wuz it that you talked Onondaga when you played the part uv that Onondaga runner. Didn't know you knowed that kind uv Injun lingo."

Shif'less Sol drew himself up proudly, and then passed a thoughtful hand once or twice across his forehead.

"Jim," he said, "I've told you often that Paul an' me hez the instincts uv the eddicated. Learnin' always takes a mighty strong hold on me. Ef I'd had the chance, I might be a purfessor, or mebbe I'd be writin' poetry. I ain't told you about it, but when I wuz a young boy, afore I moved with the settlers, I wuz up in these parts an' I learned to talk Iroquois a heap. I never thought it would be the use to me it hez been now. Ain't it funny that sometimes when you put a thing away an' it gits all covered with rust and mold, the time comes when that same forgot little thing is the most vallyble article in the world to you."

"Weren't you scared, Sol," persisted Paul, "to face a man like Brant, an' pass yourself off as an Onondaga?"

"No, I wuzn't," replied the shiftless one thoughtfully, "I've been wuss scared over little things. I guess that when your life depends on jest a motion o' your hand or the turnin' o' a word, Natur' somehow comes to your help an' holds you up. I didn't get good an' skeered till it wuz all over, an' then I had one fit right after another."

"I've been skeered fur a week without stoppin'," said Tom Ross; "jest beginnin' to git over it. I tell you, Henry, it wuz pow'ful lucky fur us you found them steppin' stones, an' this solid little place in the middle uv all that black mud."

"Makes me think uv the time we spent the winter on that island in the lake," said Long Jim. "That waz shorely a nice place an' pow'ful comf'table we wuz thar. But we're a long way from it now. That island uv ours must be seven or eight hundred miles from here, an' I reckon it's nigh to fifteen hundred to New Orleans, whar we wuz once."

"Shet up," said Tom Ross suddenly. "Time fur all uv you to go to sleep, an' I'm goin' to watch."

"I'll watch," said Henry.

"I'm the oldest, an' I'm goin' to have my way this time," said Tom.

"Needn't quarrel with me about it," said Shif'less Sol. "A lazy man like me is always willin' to go to sleep. You kin hev my watch, Tom, every night fur the next five years."

He ranged himself against the wall, and in three minutes was sound asleep. Henry and Paul found room in the line, and they, too, soon slept. Tom sat at the door, one of the captured rifles across his knees, and watched the forest and the swamp. He saw the last flare of the distant lightning, and he listened to the falling of the rain drops until they vanished with the vanishing wind, leaving the forest still and without noise.

Tom was several years older than any of the others, and, although powerful in action, he was singularly chary of speech. Henry was the leader, but somehow Tom looked upon himself as a watcher over the other four, a sort of elder brother. As the moon came out a little in the wake of the retreating clouds, he regarded them affectionately.

"One, two, three, four, five," he murmured to himself. "We're all here, an' Henry come fur us. That is shorely the greatest boy the world hez ever seed. Them fellers Alexander an' Hannibal that Paul talks about couldn't hev been knee high to Henry. Besides, ef them old Greeks an' Romans hed hed to fight Wyandots an' Shawnees an' Iroquois ez we've done, whar'd they hev been?"

Tom Ross uttered a contemptuous little sniff, and on the edge of that sniff Alexander and Hannibal were wafted into oblivion. Then he went outside and walked about the islet, appreciating for the tenth time what a wonderful little refuge it was. He was about to return to the hut when he saw a dozen dark blots along the high bough of a tree. He knew them. They were welcome blots. They were wild turkeys that had found what had seemed to be a secure roosting place in the swamp.

Tom knew that the meat of the little bear was nearly exhausted, and here was more food come to their hand. "We're five pow'ful feeders, an' we'll need you," he murmured, looking up at the turkeys, "but you kin rest thar till nearly mornin'."

He knew that the turkeys would not stir, and he went back to the hut to resume his watch. Just before the first dawn he awoke Henry.

"Henry," he said, "a lot uv foolish wild turkeys hev gone to rest on the limb of a tree not twenty yards from this grand manshun uv ourn. 'Pears to me that wild turkeys wuz made fur hungry fellers like us to eat. Kin we risk a shot or two at 'em, or is it too dangerous?"

"I think we can risk the shots," said Henry, rising and taking his rifle. "We're bound to risk something, and it's not likely that Indians are anywhere near."

They slipped from the cabin, leaving the other three still sound asleep, and stepped noiselessly among the trees. The first pale gray bar that heralded the dawn was just showing in the cast.

"Thar they are," said Tom Ross, pointing at the dozen dark blots on the high bough.

"We'll take good aim, and when I say 'fire!' we'll both pull trigger," said Henry.

He picked out a huge bird near the end of the line, but he noticed when he drew the bead that a second turkey just behind the first was directly in his line of fire. The fact aroused his ambition to kill both with one bullet. It was not a mere desire to slaughter or to display marksmanship, but they needed the extra turkey for food.

"Are you ready, Tom?" he asked. "Then fire."

They pulled triggers, there were two sharp reports terribly loud to both under the circumstances, and three of the biggest and fattest of the turkeys fell heavily to the ground, while the rest flapped their wings, and with frightened gobbles flew away.

Henry was about to rush forward, but Silent Tom held him back.

"Don't show yourself, Henry! Don't show yourself!" he cried in tense tones.

"Why, what's the matter?" asked the boy in surprise.

"Don't you see that three turkeys fell, and we are only two to shoot? An Injun is layin' 'roun' here some whar, an' he drew a bead on one uv them turkeys at the same time we did."

Henry laughed and put away Tom's detaining hand.

"There's no Indian about," he said. "I killed two turkeys with one shot, and I'm mighty proud of it, too. I saw that they were directly in the line of the bullet, and it went through both."

Silent Tom heaved a mighty sigh of relief, drawn up from great depths.

"I'm tre-men-jeous-ly glad uv that, Henry," he said. "Now when I saw that third turkey come tumblin' down I wuz shore that one Injun or mebbe more had got on this snug little place uv ourn in the swamp, an' that we'd hev to go to fightin' ag'in. Thar come times, Henry, when my mind just natchally rises up an' rebels ag'in fightin', 'specially when I want to eat or sleep. Ain't thar anythin' else but fight, fight, fight, 'though I 'low a feller hez got to expect a lot uv it out here in the woods?"

They picked up the three turkeys, two gobblers and a hen, and found them large and fat as butter. More than once the wild turkey had come to their relief, and, in fact, this bird played a great part in the life of the frontier, wherever that frontier might be, as it shifted steadily westward. As they walked back toward the hut they faced three figures, all three with leveled rifles.

"All right, boys," sang out Henry. "It's nobody but Tom and myself, bringing in our breakfast."

The three dropped their rifles.

"That's good," said Shif'less Sol. "When them shots roused us out o' our beauty sleep we thought the whole Iroquois nation, horse, foot, artillery an' baggage wagons, wuz comin' down upon us. So we reckoned we'd better go out an' lick 'em afore it wuz too late.

"But it's you, an' you've got turkeys, nothin' but turkeys. Sho' I reckoned from the peart way Long Jim spoke up that you wuz loaded down with hummin' birds' tongues, ortylans, an' all them other Roman and Rooshian delicacies Paul talks about in a way to make your mouth water. But turkeys! jest turkeys! Nothin' but turkeys!"

"You jest wait till you see me cookin' 'em, Sol Hyde," said Long Jim. "Then your mouth'll water, an' it'll take Henry and Tom both to hold you back."

But Shif'less Sol's mouth was watering already, and his eyes were glued on the turkeys.

"I'm a pow'ful lazy man, ez you know, Saplin'," he said, "but I'm goin' to help you pick them turkeys an' get 'em ready for the coals. The quicker they are cooked the better it'll suit me."

While they were cooking the turkeys, Henry, a little anxious lest the sound of the shots had been heard, crossed on the stepping stones and scouted a bit in the woods. But there was no sign of Indian presence, and, relieved, he returned to the islet just as breakfast was ready.

Long Jim had exerted all his surpassing skill, and it was a contented five that worked on one of the turkeys—the other two being saved for further needs.

"What's goin' to be the next thing in the line of our duty, Henry?" asked Long Jim as they ate.

"We'll have plenty to do, from all that Sol tells us," replied the boy. "It seems that they felt so sure of you, while you were prisoners, that they often talked about their plans where you could hear them. Sol has told me of two or three talks between Timmendiquas and Thayendanegea, and from the last one he gathered that they're intending a raid with a big army against a place called Wyoming, in the valley of a river named the Susquehanna. It's a big settlement, scattered all along the river, and they expect to take a lot of scalps. They're going to be helped by British from Canada and Tories.

Boys, we're a long way from home, but shall we go and tell them in Wyoming what's coming?"

"Of course," said the four together.

"Our bein' a long way from home don't make any difference," said Shif'less Sol. "We're generally a long way from home, an' you know we sent word back from Pittsburgh to Wareville that we wuz stayin' a while here in the east on mighty important business."

"Then we go to the Wyoming Valley as straight and as fast as we can," said Henry. "That's settled. What else did you hear about their plans, Sol?"

"They're to break up the village here soon and then they'll march to a place called Tioga. The white men an' I hear that's to be a lot uv 'em-will join 'em thar or sooner. They've sent chiefs all the way to our Congress at Philydelphy, pretendin' peace, an' then, when they git our people to thinkin' peace, they'll jump on our settlements, the whole ragin' army uv 'em, with tomahawk an' knife. A white man named John Butler is to command 'em."

Paul shuddered.

"I've heard of him," he said. "They called him 'Indian' Butler at Pittsburgh. He helped lead the Indians in that terrible battle of the Oriskany last year. And they say he's got a son, Walter Butler, who is as bad as he is, and there are other white leaders of the Indians, the Johnsons and Claus."

"'Pears ez ef we would be needed," said Tom Ross.

"I don't think we ought to hurry," said Henry. "The more we know about the Indian plans the better it will be for the Wyoming people. We've a safe and comfortable hiding place here, and we can stay and watch the Indian movements."

"Suits me," drawled Shif'less Sol. "My legs an' arms are still stiff from them deerskin thongs an' ez Long Jim is here now to wait on me I guess I'll take a rest from travelin."

"You'll do all your own waitin' on yourself," rejoined Long Jim; "an' I'm afraid you won't be waited on so Pow'ful well, either, but a good deal better than you deserve."

They lay on the islet several days, meanwhile keeping a close watch on the Indian camp. They really had little to fear except from hunting parties, as the region was far from any settled portion of the country, and the Indians were not likely to suspect their continued presence. But the hunters were numerous, and all the squaws in the camp were busy jerking meat. It was obvious that the Indians were preparing for a great campaign, but that they would take their own time. Most of the scouting was done by Henry and Sol, and several times they lay in the thick brushwood and watched, by the light of the fires, what was passing in the Indian camp.

On the fifth night after the rescue of Long Jim, Henry and Shif'less Sol lay in the covert. It was nearly midnight, but the fires still burned in the Indian camp, warriors were polishing their weapons, and the women were cutting up or jerking meat. While they were watching they heard from a point to the north the sound of a voice rising and failing in a kind of chant.

"Another war party comin'," whispered Shif'less Sol, "an' singin' about the victories that they're goin' to win."

"But did you notice that voice?" Henry whispered back. "It's not a man's, it's a woman's."

"Now that you speak of it, you're right," said Shif'less Sol. "It's funny to hear an Injun woman chantin' about battles as she comes into camp. That's the business o' warriors."

"Then this is no ordinary woman," said Henry.

"They'll pass along that trail there within twenty yards of us, Sol, and we want to see her."

"So we do," said Sol, "but I ain't breathin' while they pass."

They flattened themselves against the earth until the keenest eye could not see them in the darkness. All the time the singing was growing louder, and both remained, quite sure that it was the voice of a woman. The trail was but a short distance away, and the moon was bright. The fierce Indian chant swelled, and presently the most singular figure that either had ever seen came into view.

The figure was that of an Indian woman, but lighter in color than most of her kind. She was middle-aged, tall, heavily built, and arrayed in a strange mixture of civilized and barbaric finery, deerskin leggins and moccasins gorgeously ornamented with heads, a red dress of European cloth with a red shawl over it, and her head bare except for bright feathers, thrust in her long black hair, which hung loosely down her back. She held in one hand a large sharp tomahawk, which she swung fiercely in time to her song. Her face had the rapt, terrible expression of one who had taken some fiery and powerful drug, and she looked neither to right nor to left as she strode on, chanting a song of blood, and swinging the keen blade.

Henry and Shif'less Sol shuddered. They had looked upon terrible human figures, but nothing so frightful as this, a woman with the strength of a man and twice his rage and cruelty. There was something weird and awful in the look of that set, savage face, and the tone of that Indian chant. Brave as they were, Henry and the shiftless one felt fear, as perhaps they had never felt it before in their lives. Well they might! They were destined to behold this woman again, under conditions the most awful of which the human mind can conceive, and to witness savagery almost unbelievable in either man or woman. The two did not yet know it, but they were looking upon Catharine Montour, daughter of a French Governor General of Canada and an Indian woman, a chieftainess of the Iroquois, and of a memory infamous forever on the border, where she was known as "Queen Esther."

Shif'less Sol shuddered again, and whispered to Henry:

"I didn't think such women ever lived, even among the Indians."

A dozen warriors followed Queen Esther, stepping in single file, and their manner showed that they acknowledged her their leader in every sense. She was truly an extraordinary woman. Not even the great Thayendanegea himself wielded a stronger influence among the Iroquois. In her youth she had been treated as a white woman, educated and dressed as a white woman, and she had played a part in colonial society at Albany, New York, and Philadelphia. But of her own accord she had turned toward the savage half of herself, had become wholly a savage, had married a savage chief, bad been the mother of savage children, and here she was, at midnight, striding into an Iroquois camp in the wilderness, her head aflame with visions of blood, death, and scalps.

The procession passed with the terrifying female figure still leading, still singing her chant, and the curiosity of Henry and Shif'less Sol was so intense that, taking all risks, they slipped along in the rear to see her entry.

Queen Esther strode into the lighted area of the camp, ceased her chant, and looked around, as if a queen had truly come and was waiting to be welcomed by her subjects. Thayendanegea, who evidently expected her, stepped forward and gave her the Indian salute. It may be that he received her with mild enthusiasm. Timmendiquas, a Wyandot and a guest, though an ally, would not dispute with him his place as real head of the Six Nations, but this terrible woman was his match, and could inflame the Iroquois to almost anything that she wished.

After the arrival of Queen Esther the lights in the Iroquois village died down. It was evident to both Henry and the shiftless one that they had been kept burning solely in the expectation of the coming of this formidable woman and her escort. It was obvious that nothing more was to be seen that night, and they withdrew swiftly through the forest toward their islet. They stopped once in an oak opening, and Shif'less Sol shivered slightly.

"Henry," he said, "I feel all through me that somethin' terrible is comin'. That woman back thar has clean give me the shivers. I'm more afraid of her than I am of Timmendiquas or Thayendanegea. Do you think she is a witch?"

"There are no such things as witches, but she was uncanny. I'm afraid, Sol, that your feeling about something terrible going to happen is right."

It was about two o'clock in the morning when they reached the islet. Tom Ross was awake, but the other two slumbered peacefully on. They told Tom what they had seen, and he told them the identity of the terrible woman.

"I heard about her at Pittsburgh, an' I've heard tell, too, about her afore I went to Kentucky to live. She's got a tre-men-jeous power over the Iroquois. They think she ken throw spells, an' all that sort of thing-an' mebbe she kin."

Two nights later it was Henry and Tom who lay in the thickets, and then they saw other formidable arrivals in the Indian camp. Now they were white men, an entire company in green uniforms, Sir John Johnson's Royal Greens, as Henry afterward learned; and with them was the infamous John Butler, or "Indian" Butler, as he was generally known on the New York and Pennsylvania frontier, middle-aged, short and fat, and insignificant of appearance, but energetic, savage and cruel in nature. He was a descendant of the Duke of Ormond, and had commanded the Indians at the terrible battle of the Oriskany, preceding Burgoyne's capture the year before.

Henry and Tom were distant spectators at an extraordinary council around one of the fires. In this group were Timmendiquas, Thayendanegea, Queen Esther, high chiefs of the distant nations, and the white men, John Butler, Moses Blackstaffe, and the boy, Braxton Wyatt. It seemed to Henry that Timmendiquas, King of the Wyandots, was superior to all the other chiefs present, even to Thayendanegea. His expression was nobler than that of the great Mohawk, and it had less of the Indian cruelty.

Henry and Tom could not hear 'anything that was said, but they felt sure the Iroquois were about to break up their village and march on the great campaign they had planned. The two and their comrades could render no greater service than to watch their march, and then warn those upon whom the blow was to fall.

The five left their hut on the islet early the next morning, well equipped with provisions, and that day they saw the Iroquois dismantle their village, all except the Long House and two or three other of the more solid structures, and begin the march. Henry and his comrades went parallel with them, watching their movements as closely as possible.

CHAPTER VIII. A CHANGE OF TENANTS

The five were engaged upon one of their most dangerous tasks, to keep with the Indian army, and yet to keep out of its hands, to observe what was going on, and to divine what was intended from what they observed. Fortunately it, was early summer, and the weather being very beautiful they could sleep without shelter. Hence they found it convenient to sleep sometimes by daylight, posting a watch always, and to spy upon the Indian camp at night. They saw other reinforcements come for the Indian army, particularly a strong division of Senecas, under two great war chiefs of theirs, Sangerachte and Hiokatoo, and also a body of Tories.

Then they saw them go into their last great camp at Tioga, preparatory to their swift descent upon the Wyoming Valley. About four hundred white men, English Canadians and Tories, were present, and eight hundred picked warriors of the Six Nations under Thayendanegea, besides the little band of Wyandots led by the resolute Timmendiquas. "Indian" Butler was in general command of the whole, and Queen Esther was the high priestess of the Indians, continually making fiery speeches and chanting songs that made the warriors see red. Upon the rear of this extraordinary army hung a band of fierce old squaws, from whom every remnant of mercy and Gentleness had departed.

From a high rock overlooking a valley the five saw "Indian" Butler's force start for its final march upon Wyoming. It was composed of many diverse elements, and perhaps none more bloodthirsty ever trod the soil of America. In some preliminary skirmish a son of Queen Esther had been slain, and now her fury knew no limits. She took her place at the very head of the army, whirling her great tomahawk about her head, and neither "Indian" Butler nor Thayendanegea dared to interfere with her in anything great or small.

Henry and his comrades, as they left their rock and hastened toward the valley of Wyoming, felt that now they were coming into contact with the great war itself. They had looked upon a uniformed enemy for the first time, and they might soon see the colonial buff and blue of the eastern army. Their hearts thrilled high at new scenes and new dangers.

They had gathered at Pittsburgh, and, through the captivity of the four in the Iroquois camp, they had some general idea of the Wyoming Valley and the direction in which it lay, and, taking one last look at the savage army, they sped toward it. The time was the close, of June, and the foliage was still dark green. It was a land of low mountain, hill, rich valley, and clear stream, and it was beautiful to every one of the five. Much of their course lay along the Susquehanna, and soon they saw signs of a more extended cultivation than any that was yet to be witnessed in Kentucky. From the brow of a little hill they beheld a field of green, and in another field a man plowing.

"That's wheat," said Tom Ross.

"But we can't leave the man to plow," said Henry, "or he'll never harvest that wheat. We'll warn him."

The man uttered a cry of alarm as five wild figures burst into his field. He stopped abruptly, and snatched up a rifle that lay across the plow handles. Neither Henry nor his companions realized that their forest garb and long life in the wilderness made them look more like Indians than white men. But Henry threw up a hand as a sign of peace.

"We're white like yourselves," he cried, "and we've come to warn you! The Iroquois and the Tories are marching into the valley!"

The man's face blanched, and he cast a hasty look toward a little wood, where stood a cabin from which smoke was rising. He could not doubt on a near view that these were white like himself, and the words rang true.

"My house is strong," he said, "and I can beat them off. Maybe you will help me."

"We'd help you willingly enough," said Henry, "if this were any ordinary raiding band, but 'Indian' Butler, Brant, and Queen Esther are coming at the head of twelve or fifteen hundred men. How could we hold a house, no matter how thick its walls, against such an army as that? Don't hesitate a moment! Get up what you can and gallop."

The man, a Connecticut settler-Jennings was his name-left his plow in the furrow, galloped on his horse to his house, mounted his wife and children on other horses, and, taking only food and clothing, fled to Stroudsburg, where there was a strong fort. At a later day he gave Henry heartfelt thanks for his warning, as six hours afterward the vanguard of the horde burned his home and raged because its owner and his family were gone with their scalps on their own heads.

The five were now well into the Wyoming Valley, where the Lenni-Lenape, until they were pushed westward by other tribes, had had their village Wy-wa-mieh, which means in their language Wyoming. It was a beautiful valley running twenty miles or more along the Susquehanna, and about three miles broad. On either side rose mountain walls a thousand feet in height, and further away were peaks with mists and vapors around their crests. The valley itself blazed in the summer sunshine, and the river sparkled, now in gold, now in silver, as the light changed and fell.

More cultivated fields, more houses, generally of stout logs, appeared, and to all that they saw the five bore the fiery beacon. Simon Jennings was not the only man who lived to thank them for the warning. Others were incredulous, and soon paid the terrible price of unbelief.

The five hastened on, and as they went they looked about them with wondering eyes-there were so many houses, so many cultivated fields, and so many signs of a numerous population. They had emerged almost for the first time from the wilderness, excepting their memorable visit to New Orleans, although this was a very different region. Long Jim spoke of it.

"I think I like it better here than at New Or-leeyuns," he said. "We found some nice Frenchmen an' Spaniards down thar, but the ground feels firmer under my feet here."

"The ground feels firmer," said Paul, who had some of the prescience of the seer, "but the skies are no brighter. They look red to me sometimes, Jim."

Tom Ross glanced at Paul and shook his head ominously. A woodsman, he had his superstitions, and Paul's words weighed upon his mind. He began to fear a great disaster, and his experienced eye perceived at once the defenseless state of the valley. He remembered the council of the great Indian force in the deep woods, and the terrible face of Queen Esther was again before him.

"These people ought to be in blockhouses, every one uv 'em," he said. "It ain't no time to be plowin' land."

Yet peace seemed to brood still over the valley. It was a fine river, beautiful with changing colors. The soil on either side was as deep and fertile as that of Kentucky, and the line of the mountains cut the sky sharp and clear. Hills and slopes were dark green with foliage.

"It must have been a gran' huntin' ground once," said Shif'less Sol.

The alarm that the five gave spread fast, and other hunters and scouts came in, confirming it. Panic seized the settlers, and they began to crowd toward Forty Fort on the west side of the river. Henry and his comrades themselves arrived there toward the close of evening, just as the sun had set, blood red, behind the mountains. Some report of them had preceded their coming, and as soon as they had eaten they were summoned to the presence of Colonel Zebulon Butler, who commanded the military force in the valley. Singularly enough, he was a cousin of "Indian" Butler, who led the invading army.

The five, dressed in deerskin hunting shirts, leggins, and moccasins, and everyone carrying a rifle, hatchet, and knife, entered a large low room, dimly lighted by some wicks burning in tallow. A man of middle years, with a keen New England face, sat at a little table, and several others of varying ages stood near.

The five knew instinctively that the man at the table was Colonel Butler, and they bowed, but they did not show the faintest trace of subservience. They had caught suspicious glances from some of the officers who stood about the commander, and they stiffened at once. Colonel Butler looked involuntarily at Henry-everybody always took him, without the telling, for leader of the group.

"We have had report of you," he said in cool noncommittal tones, "and you have been telling of great Indian councils that you have seen in the woods. May I ask your name and where you belong?"

"My name," replied Henry with dignity, "is Henry Ware, and I come from Kentucky. My friends here are Paul Cotter, Solomon Hyde, Tom Ross, and Jim Hart. They, too, come from Kentucky."

Several of the men gave the five suspicious glances. Certainly they were wild enough in appearance, and Kentucky was far away. It would seem strange that new settlers in that far land should be here in Pennsylvania. Henry saw clearly that his story was doubted.

"Kentucky, you tell me?" said Colonel Butler. "Do you mean to say you have come all that tremendous distance to warn us of an attack by Indians and Tories?"

Several of the others murmured approval, and Henry flushed a little, but he saw that the commander was not unreasonable. It was a time when men might well question the words of strangers. Remembering this, he replied:

"No, we did not come from Kentucky just to warn you. In fact, we came from a point much farther than that. We came from New Orleans to Pittsburgh with a fleet loaded with supplies for the Continental armies, and commanded by Adam Colfax of New Hampshire."

The face of Colonel Butler brightened.

"What!" he exclaimed, "you were on that expedition? It seems to me that I recall hearing of great services rendered to it by some independent scouts."

"When we reached Pittsburgh," continued Henry, "it was our first intention to go back to Kentucky, but we heard that a great war movement was in progress to the eastward, and we thought that we would see what was going on. Four of us have been captives among the Iroquois. We know much of their plans, and we know, too, that Timmendiquas, the great chief of the Wyandots, whom we fought along the Ohio, has joined them with a hand of his best warriors. We have also seen Thayendanegea, every one of us."

"You have seen Brant?" exclaimed Colonel Butler, calling the great Mohawk by his white name.

"Yes," replied Henry. "We have seen him, and we have also seen the woman they call Queen Esther. She is continually urging the Indians on."

Colonel Butler seemed convinced, and invited them to sit down. He also introduced the officers who were with him, Colonel John Durkee, Colonel Nathan Dennison, Lieutenant Colonel George Dorrance, Major John Garrett, Captain Samuel Ransom, Captain Dethrie Hewitt, and some others.

"Now, gentlemen, tell us all that you saw," continued Colonel Butler courteously. "You will pardon so many questions, but we must be careful. You will see that yourselves. But I am a New England man myself, from Connecticut, and I have met Adam Colfax. I recall now that we have heard of you, also, and we are grateful for your coming. Will you and your comrades tell us all that you have seen and heard?"

The five felt a decided change in the atmosphere. They were no longer possible Tories or renegades, bringing an alarm at one point when it should be dreaded at another. The men drew closely around them, and listened as the tallow wicks sputtered in the dim room. Henry spoke first, and the others in their turn. Every one of them spoke tersely but vividly in the language of the forest. They felt deeply what they had seen, and they drew the same picture for their listeners. Gradually the faces of the Wyoming men became shadowed. This was a formidable tale that they were hearing, and they could not doubt its truth.

"It is worse than I thought it could be," said Colonel Butler at last. "How many men do you say they have, Mr. Ware?"

"Close to fifteen hundred."

"All trained warriors and soldiers. And at the best we cannot raise more than three hundreds including old men and boys, and our men, too, are farmers."

"But we can beat them. Only give us a chance, Colonel!" exclaimed Captain Ransom.

"I'm afraid the chance will come too soon," said Colonel Butler, and then turning to the five: "Help us all you can. We need scouts and riflemen. Come to the fort for any food and ammunition you may need."

The five gave their most earnest assurances that they would stay, and do all in their power. In fact, they had come for that very purpose. Satisfied now that Colonel Butler and his officers had implicit faith in them they went forth to find that, despite the night and the darkness, fugitives were already crossing the river to seek refuge in Forty Fort, bringing with them tales of death and devastation, some of which were exaggerated, but too many true in all their hideous details. Men had been shot and scalped in the fields, houses were burning, women and children were captives for a fate that no one could foretell. Red ruin was already stalking down the valley.

The farmers were bringing their wives and children in canoes and dugouts across the river. Here and there a torch light flickered on the surface of the stream, showing the pale faces of the women and children, too frightened to cry. They had fled in haste, bringing with them only the clothes they wore and maybe a blanket or two. The borderers knew too well what Indian war was, with all its accompaniments of fire and the stake.

Henry and his comrades helped nearly all that night. They secured a large boat and crossed the river again and again, guarding the fugitives with their rifles, and bringing comfort to many a timid heart. Indian bands had penetrated far into the Wyoming Valley, but they felt sure that none were yet in the neighborhood of Forty Fort.

It was about three o'clock in the morning when the last of the fugitives who had yet come was inside Forty Fort, and the labors of the five, had they so chosen, were over for the time. But their nerves were tuned to so high a pitch, and they felt so powerfully the presence of danger, that they could not rest, nor did they have any desire for sleep.

The boat in which they sat was a good one, with two pairs of oars. It had been detailed for their service, and they decided to pull up the river. They thought it possible that they might see the advance of the enemy and bring news worth the telling. Long Jim and Tom Ross took the oars, and their powerful arms sent the boat swiftly along in the shadow of the western bank. Henry and Paul looked back and saw dim lights at the fort and a few on either shore. The valley, the high mountain wall, and everything else were merged in obscurity.

Both the youths were oppressed heavily by the sense of danger, not for themselves, but for others. In that Kentucky of theirs, yet so new, few people lived beyond the palisades, but here were rich and scattered settlements; and men, even in the face of great peril, are always loth to abandon the homes that they have built with so much toil.

Tom Ross and Long Jim continued to pull steadily with the long strokes that did not tire them, and the lights of the fort and houses sank out of sight. Before them lay the somber surface of the rippling river, the shadowy hills, and silence. The world seemed given over to the night save for themselves, but they knew too well to trust to such apparent desertion. At such hours the Indian scouts come, and Henry did not doubt that they were already near, gathering news of their victims for the Indian and Tory horde. Therefore, it was the part of his comrades and himself to use the utmost caution as they passed up the river.

They bugged the western shore, where they were shadowed by banks and bushes, and now they went slowly, Long Jim and Tom Ross drawing their oars so carefully through the water that there was never a plash to tell of their passing. Henry was in the prow of the boat, bent forward a little, eyes searching the surface of the river, and ears intent upon any sound that might pass on the bank. Suddenly he gave a little signal to the rowers and they let their oars rest.

"Bring the boat in closer to the bank," he whispered. "Push it gently among those bushes where we cannot be seen from above."

Tom and Jim obeyed. The boat slid softly among tall bushes that shadowed the water, and was hidden completely. Then Henry stepped out, crept cautiously nearly up the bank, which was here very low, and lay pressed closely against the earth, but supported by the exposed root of a tree. He had heard voices, those of Indians, he believed, and he wished to see. Peering through a fringe of bushes that lined the bank he saw seven warriors and one white face sitting under the boughs of a great oak. The face was that of Braxton Wyatt, who was now in his element, with a better prospect of success than any that he had ever known before. Henry shuddered, and for a moment he regretted that he had spared Wyatt's life when he might have taken it.

But Henry was lying against the bank to hear what these men might be saying, not to slay. Two of the warriors, as he saw by their paint, were Wyandots, and he understood the Wyandot tongue. Moreover, his slight knowledge of Iroquois came into service, and gradually he gathered the drift of their talk. Two miles nearer Forty Fort was a farmhouse one of the

Wyandots had seen it-not yet abandoned by its owner, who believed that his proximity to Forty Fort assured his safety. He lived there with his wife and five children, and Wyatt and the Indians planned to raid the place before daylight and kill them all. Henry had heard enough. He slid back from the bank to the water and crept into the boat.

"Pull back down the river as gently as you can," he whispered, "and then I'll tell you."

The skilled oarsmen carried the boat without a splash several hundred yards down the stream, and then Henry told the others of the fiendish plan that he had heard.

"I know that man," said Shif'less Sol. "His name is Standish. I was there nine or ten hours ago, an' I told him it wuz time to take his family an' run. But he knowed more'n I did. Said he'd stay, he wuzn't afraid, an' now he's got to pay the price."

"No, he mustn't do that," said Henry. "It's too much to pay for just being foolish, when everybody is foolish sometimes. Boys, we can yet save that man an' his wife and children. Aren't you willing to do it?"

"Why, course," said Long Jim. "Like ez not Standish will shoot at us when we knock on his door, but let's try it."

The others nodded assent.

"How far back from the river is the Standish house, Sol?" asked Henry.

"'Bout three hundred yards, I reckon, and' it ain't more'n a mile down."

"Then if we pull with all our might, we won't be too late. Tom, you and Jim give Sol and me the oars now."

Henry and the shiftless one were fresh, and they sent the boat shooting down stream, until they stopped at a point indicated by Sol. They leaped ashore, drew the boat down the bank, and hastened toward a log house that they saw standing in a clump of trees. The enemy had not yet come, but as they swiftly approached the house a dog ran barking at them. The shiftless one swung his rifle butt, and the dog fell unconscious.

"I hated to do it, but I had to," he murmured. The next moment Henry was knocking at the door.

"Up! Up!" he cried, "the Indians are at hand, and you must run for your lives!"

How many a time has that terrible cry been heard on the American border!

The sound of a man's voice, startled and angry, came to their ears, and then they heard him at the door.

"Who are you?" he cried. "Why are you beating on my door at such a time?"

"We are friends, Mr. Standish," cried Henry, "and if you would save your wife and children you must go at once! Open the door! Open, I say!"

The man inside was in a terrible quandary. It was thus that renegades or Indians, speaking the white man's tongue, sometimes bade a door to be opened, in order that they might find an easy path to slaughter. But the voice outside was powerfully insistent, it had the note of truth; his wife and children, roused, too, were crying out, in alarm. Henry knocked again on the door and shouted to him in a voice, always increasing in earnestness, to open and flee. Standish could resist no longer. He took down the bar and flung open the door, springing back, startled at the five figures that stood before him. In the dusk he did not remember Shif'less Sol.

"Mr. Standish," Henry said, speaking rapidly, "we are, as you can see, white. You will be attacked here by Indians and renegades within half an hour. We know that, because we heard them talking from the bushes. We have a boat in the river; you can reach it in five minutes. Take your wife and children, and pull for Forty Fort."

Standish was bewildered.

"How do I know that you are not enemies, renegades, yourselves?" he asked.

"If we had been that you'd be a dead man already," said Shif'less Sol.

It was a grim reply, but it was unanswerable, and Standish recognized the fact. His wife had felt the truth in the tones of the strangers, and was begging him to go. Their children were crying at visions of the tomahawk and scalping knife now so near.

"We'll go," said Standish. "At any rate, it can't do any harm. We'll get a few things together."

"Do not wait for anything!" exclaimed Henry. "You haven't a minute to spare! Here are more blankets! Take them and run for the boat! Sol and Jim, see them on board, and then come back!"

Carried away by such fire and earnestness, Standish and his family ran for the boat. Jim and the shiftless one almost threw them on board, thrust a pair of oars into the bands of Standish, another into the hands of his wife, and then told them to pull with all their might for the fort.

"And you," cried Standish, "what becomes of you?"

Then a singular expression passed over his face-he had guessed Henry's plan.

"Don't you trouble about us," said the shiftless one. "We will come later. Now pull! pull!"

Standish and his wife swung on the oars, and in two minutes the boat and its occupants were lost in the darkness. Tom Ross and Sol did not pause to watch them, but ran swiftly back to the house. Henry was at the door.

"Come in," he said briefly, and they entered. Then he closed the door and dropped the bar into place. Shif'less Sol and Paul were already inside, one sitting on the chair and the other on the edge of the bed. Some coals, almost hidden under ashes, smoldered and cast a faint light in the room, the only one that the house had, although it was divided into two parts by a rough homespun curtain. Henry opened one of the window shutters a little and looked out. The dawn had not yet come, but it was not a dark night, and he looked over across the little clearing to the trees beyond. On that side was a tiny garden, and near the wall of the house some roses were blooming. He could see the glow of pink and red. But no enemy bad yet approached. Searching the clearing carefully with those eyes of his, almost preternaturally keen, he was confident that the Indians were still in the woods. He felt an intense thrill of satisfaction at the success of his plan so far.

He was not cruel, he never rejoiced in bloodshed, but the borderer alone knew what the border suffered, and only those who never saw or felt the torture could turn the other cheek to be smitten. The Standish house had made a sudden and ominous change of tenants.

"It will soon be day," said Henry, "and farmers are early risers. Kindle up that fire a little, will you, Sol? I want some smoke to come out of the chimney."

The shiftless one raked away the ashes, and put on two or three pieces of wood that lay on the hearth. Little flames and smoke arose. Henry looked curiously about the house. It was the usual cabin of the frontier, although somewhat larger. The bed on which Shif'less Sol sat was evidently that of the father and mother, while two large ones behind the curtain were used by the children. On the shelf stood a pail half full of drinking water, and by the side of it a tin cup. Dried herbs hung over the fireplace, and two or three chests stood in the corners. The clothing of the children was scattered about. Unprepared food for breakfast stood on a table. Everything told of a hasty flight and its terrible need. Henry was already resolved, but his heart hardened within him as he saw.

He took the hatchet from his belt and cut one of the hooks for the door bar nearly in two. The others said not a word. They had no need to speak. They understood everything that he did. He opened the window again and looked out. Nothing yet appeared. "The dawn will come in three quarters of an hour," he said, "and we shall not have to wait long for what we want to do."

He sat down facing the door. All the others were sitting, and they, too, faced the door. Everyone had his rifle across his knees, with one hand upon the hammer. The wood on the hearth sputtered as the fire spread, and the flames grew. Beyond a doubt a thin spire of smoke was rising from the chimney, and a watching eye would see this sign of a peaceful and unsuspecting mind.

"I hope Braxton Wyatt will be the first to knock at our door," said Shif'less Sol.

"I wouldn't be sorry," said Henry.

Paul was sitting in a chair near the fire, and he said nothing. He hoped the waiting would be very short. The light was sufficient for him to see the faces of his comrades, and he noticed that they were all very tense. This was no common watch that they kept. Shif'less Sol remained on the bed, Henry sat on another of the chairs, Tom Ross was on one of the chests with his back to the wall. Long Jim was near the curtain. Close by Paul was a home-made cradle. He put down his hand and touched it. He was glad that it was empty now, but the sight of it steeled his heart anew for the task that lay before them.

Ten silent minutes passed, and Henry went to the window again. He did not open it, but there was a crack through which he could see. The others said nothing, but watched his face. When he turned away they knew that the moment was at hand.

"They've just come from the woods," he said, "and in a minute they'll be at the door. Now, boys, take one last look at your rifles."

A minute later there was a sudden sharp knock at the door, but no answer came from within. The knock was repeated, sharper and louder, and Henry, altering his voice as much as possible, exclaimed like one suddenly awakened from sleep:

"Who is it? What do you want?"

Back came a voice which Henry knew to be that of Braxton Wyatt:

"We've come from farther up the valley. We're scouts, we've been up to the Indian country. We're half starved. Open and give us food!"

"I don't believe you," replied Henry. "Honest people don't come to my door at this time in the morning."

Then ensued a few moments of silence, although Paul, with his vivid fancy, thought he heard whispering on the other side of the door.

"Open!" cried Wyatt, "or we'll break your door down!" Henry said nothing, nor did any of the others. They did not stir. The fire crackled a little, but there was no other sound in the Standish house. Presently they heard a slight noise outside, that of light feet.

"They are going for a log with which to break the door in," whispered Henry. "They won't have to look far. The wood pile isn't fifty feet away."

"An' then," said Shif'less Sol, "they won't have much left to do but to take the scalps of women an' little children."

Every figure in the Standish house stiffened at the shiftless one's significant words, and the light in the eyes grew sterner. Henry went to the door, put his ear to the line where it joined the wall, and listened.

"They've got their log," he said, "and in half a minute they'll rush it against the door."

He came back to his old position. Paul's heart began to thump, and his thumb fitted itself over the trigger of his cocked rifle. Then they heard rapid feet, a smash, a crash, and the door flew open. A half dozen Iroquois and a log that they held between them were hurled into the middle of the room. The door had given away so easily and unexpectedly that the warriors could not check themselves, and two or three fell with the log. But they sprang like cats to their feet, and with their comrades uttered a cry that filled the whole cabin with its terrible sound and import.

The Iroquois, keen of eyes and quick of mind, saw the trap at once. The five grim figures, rifle in hand and finger on trigger, all waiting silent and motionless were far different from what they expected. Here could be no scalps, with the long, silky hair of women and children.

There was a moment's pause, and then the Indians rushed at their foes. Five fingers pulled triggers, flame leaped from five muzzles, and in an instant the cabin was filled with smoke and war shouts, but the warriors never had a chance. They could only strike blindly with their tomahawks, and in a half minute three of them, two wounded, rushed through the door and fled to the woods. They had been preceded already by Braxton Wyatt, who had hung back craftily while the Iroquois broke down the door.

CHAPTER IX. WYOMING

The five made no attempt to pursue. In fact, they did not leave the cabin, but stood there a while, looking down at the fallen, hideous with war paint, but now at the end of their last trail. Their tomahawks lay upon the floor, and glittered when the light from the fire fell upon them. Smoke, heavy with the odor of burned gunpowder, drifted about the room.

Henry threw open the two shuttered windows, and fresh currents of air poured into the room. Over the mountains in the east came the first shaft of day. The surface of the river was lightening.

"What shall we do with them?" asked Paul, pointing to the silent forms on the floor.

"Leave them," said Henry. "Butler's army is burning everything before it, and this house and all in it is bound to go. You notice, however, that Braxton Wyatt is not here."

"Trust him to escape every time," said Shif'less Sol. "Of course he stood back while the Indians rushed the house. But ez shore ez we live somebody will get him some day. People like that can't escape always."

They slipped from the house, turning toward the river bank, and not long after it was full daylight they were at Forty Fort again, where they found Standish and his family. Henry replied briefly to the man's questions, but two hours later a scout came in and reported the grim sight that he had seen in the Standish home. No one could ask for further proof of the fealty of the five, who sought a little sleep, but before noon were off again.

They met more fugitives, and it was now too dangerous to go farther up the valley. But not willing to turn back, they ascended the mountains that hem it in, and from the loftiest point that they could find sought a sight of the enemy.

It was an absolutely brilliant day in summer. The blue of the heavens showed no break but the shifting bits of white cloud, and the hills and mountains rolled away, solid masses of rich, dark green. The river, a beautiful river at any time, seemed from this height a great current of quicksilver. Henry pointed to a place far up the stream where black dots appeared on its surface. These dots were moving, and they came on in four lines.

"Boys," he said, "you know what those lines of black dots are?"

"Yes," replied Shif'less Sol, "it's Butler's army of Indians, Tories, Canadians, an' English. They've come from Tioga Point on the river, an' our Colonel Butler kin expect 'em soon."

The sunlight became dazzling, and showed the boats, despite the distance, with startling clearness. The five, watching from their peak, saw them turn in toward the land, where they poured forth a motley stream of red men and white, a stream that was quickly swallowed up in the forest.

"They are coming down through the woods on the fort, said Tom Ross.

"And they're coming fast," said Henry. "It's for us to carry the warning."

They sped back to the Wyoming fort, spreading the alarm as they passed, and once more they were in the council room with Colonel Zebulon Butler and his officers around him.

"So they are at hand, and you have seen them?" said the colonel.

"Yes," replied Henry, the spokesman, "they came down from Tioga Point in boats, but have disembarked and are advancing through the woods. They will be here today."

There was a little silence in the room. The older men understood the danger perhaps better than the younger, who were eager for battle.

"Why should we stay here and wait for them?" exclaimed one of the younger captains at length-some of these captains were mere boys. "Why not go out, meet them, and beat them?"

"They outnumber us about five to one," said Henry. "Brant, if he is still with them, though he may have gone to some other place from Tioga Point, is a great captain. So is Timmendiquas, the Wyandot, and they say that the Tory leader is energetic and capable."

"It is all true!" exclaimed Colonel Butler. "We must stay in the fort! We must not go out to meet them! We are not strong enough!"

A murmur of protest and indignation came from the younger officers.

"And leave the valley to be ravaged! Women and children to be scalped, while we stay behind log walls!" said one of them boldly.

The men in the Wyoming fort were not regular troops, merely militia, farmers gathered hastily for their own defense.

Colonel Butler flushed.

"We have induced as many as we could to seek refuge," he said. "It hurts me as much as you to have the valley ravaged while we sit quiet here. But I know that we have no chance against so large a force, and if we fall what is to become of the hundreds whom we now protect?"

But the murmur of protest grew. All the younger men were indignant. They would not seek shelter for themselves while others were suffering. A young lieutenant saw from a window two fires spring up and burn like torch lights against the sky. They were houses blazing before the Indian brand.

"Look at that!" he cried, pointing with an accusing finger, "and we are here, under cover, doing nothing!"

A deep angry mutter went about the room, but Colonel Butler, although the flush remained on his face, still shook his head. He glanced at Tom Ross, the oldest of the five.

"You know about the Indian force," he exclaimed. "What should we do?"

The face of Tom Ross was very grave, and he spoke slowly, as was his wont.

"It's a hard thing to set here," he exclaimed, "but it will be harder to go out an' meet 'em on their own ground, an' them four or five to one."

"We must not go out," repeated the Colonel, glad of such backing.

The door was thrust open, and an officer entered.

"A rumor has just arrived, saying that the entire Davidson family has been killed and scalped," he said.

A deep, angry cry went up. Colonel Butler and the few who stood with him were overborne. Such things as these could not be endured, and reluctantly the commander gave his consent. They would go out and fight. The fort and its enclosures were soon filled with the sounds of preparation, and the little army was formed rapidly.

"We will fight by your side, of course," said Henry, "but we wish to serve on the flank as an independent band. We can be of more service in that manner."

The colonel thanked them gratefully.

"Act as you think best," he said.

The five stood near one of the gates, while the little force formed in ranks. Almost for the first time they were gloomy upon going into battle. They had seen the strength of that army of Indians, renegades, Tories, Canadians, and English advancing under the banner of England, and they knew the power and fanaticism of the Indian leaders. They believed that the terrible Queen Esther, tomahawk in hand, had continually chanted to them her songs of blood as they came down the river. It was now the third of July, and valley and river were beautiful in the golden sunlight. The foliage showed vivid and deep green on either line of high hills. The summer sun had never shown more kindly over the lovely valley.

The time was now three o'clock. The gates of the fort were thrown open, and the little army marched out, only three hundred, of whom seventy were old men, or boys so young that in our day they would be called children. Yet they marched bravely against the picked warriors of the Iroquois, trained from infancy to the forest and war, and a formidable body of white rovers who wished to destroy the little colony of "rebels," as they called them.

Small though it might be, it was a gallant army. Young and old held their heads high. A banner was flying, and a boy beat a steady insistent roll upon a drum. Henry and his comrades were on the left flank, the river was on the right. The great gates had closed behind them, shutting in the women and the children. The sun blazed down, throwing everything into relief with its intense, vivid light playing upon the brown faces of the borderers, their rifles and their homespun clothes. Colonel Butler and two or three of his officers were on horseback, leading the van. Now that the decision was to fight, the older officers, who had opposed it, were in the very front. Forward they went, and spread out a little, but with the right flank still resting on the river, and the left extended on the plain.

The five were on the edge of the plain, a little detached from the others, searching the forest for a sign of the enemy, who was already so near. Their gloom did not decrease. Neither the rolling of the drum nor the flaunting of the banner had any effect. Brave though the men might be, this was not the way in which they should meet an Indian foe who outnumbered them four or five to one.

"I don't like it," muttered Tom Ross.

"Nor do I," said Henry, "but remember that whatever happens we all stand together."

"We remember!" said the others.

On-they went, and the five moving faster were now ahead of the main force some hundred yards. They swung in a little toward the river. The banks here were highland off to the left was a large swamp. The five now checked speed and moved with great wariness. They saw nothing, and they heard nothing, either, until they went forty or fifty yards farther. Then a low droning sound came to their ears. It was the voice of one yet far away, but they knew it. It was the terrible chant of Queen Esther, in this moment the most ruthless of all the savages, and inflaming them continuously for the combat.

The five threw themselves flat on their faces, and waited a little. The chant grew louder, and then through the foliage they saw the ominous figure approaching. She was much as she had been on that night when they first beheld her. She wore the same dress of barbaric colors, she swung the same great tomahawk about her head, and sang all the time of fire and blood and death.

They saw behind her the figures of chiefs, naked to the breech cloth for battle, their bronze bodies glistening with the war paint, and bright feathers gleaming in their hair. Henry recognized the tall form of Timmendiquas, notable by his height, and around him his little band of Wyandots, ready to prove themselves mighty warriors to their eastern friends the Iroquois. Back of these was a long line of Indians and their white allies, Sir John Johnson's Royal Greens and Butler's Rangers in the center, bearing the flag of England. The warriors, of whom the Senecas were most numerous, were gathered in greatest numbers on their right flank, facing the left flank of the Americans. Sangerachte and Hiokatoo, who had taken two English prisoners at Braddock's defeat, and who had afterwards burned them both alive with his own hand, were the principal leaders of the Senecas. Henry caught a glimpse of "Indian" Butler in the center, with a great blood-red handkerchief tied around his head, and, despite the forest, he noticed with a great sinking of the heart how far the hostile line extended. It could wrap itself like a python around the defense.

"It's a tale that will soon be told," said Paul.

They went back swiftly, and warned Colonel Butler that the enemy was at band. Even as they spoke they heard the loud wailing chant of Queen Esther, and then came the war whoop, pouring from a thousand throats, swelling defiant and fierce like the cry of a wounded beast. The farmers, the boys, and the old men, most of whom had never been in battle, might well tremble at this ominous sound, so great in volume and extending so far into the forest. But they stood firm, drawing themselves into a somewhat more compact body, and still advancing with their banners flying, and the boy beating out that steady roll on the drum.

The enemy now came into full sight, and Colonel Butler deployed his force in line of battle, his right resting on the high bank of the river and his left against the swamp. Forward pressed the motley army of the other Butler, he of sanguinary and cruel fame, and the bulk of his force came into view, the sun shining down on the green uniforms of the English and the naked brown bodies of the Iroquois.

The American commander gave the order to fire. Eager fingers were already on the trigger, and a blaze of light ran along the entire rank. The Royal Greens and Rangers, although replying with their own fire, gave back before the storm of bullets, and the Wyoming men, with a shout of triumph, sprang forward. It was always a characteristic of the border settler, despite many disasters and a knowledge of Indian craft and cunning, to rush straight at his foe whenever he saw him. His, unless a trained forest warrior himself, was a headlong bravery, and now this gallant little force asked for nothing but to come to close grips with the enemy.

The men in the center with "Indian" Butler gave back still more. With cries of victory the Wyoming men pressed forward, firing rapidly, and continuing to drive the mongrel white force. The rifles were cracking rapidly, and smoke arose over the two lines. The wind caught wisps of it and carried them off down the river.

"It goes better than I thought," said Paul as he reloaded his rifle.

"Not yet," said Henry, "we are fighting the white men only. Where are all the Indians, who alone outnumber our men more than two to one?"

"Here they come," said Shif'less Sol, pointing to the depths of the swamp, which was supposed to protect the left flank of the Wyoming force.

The five saw in the spaces, amid the briars and vines, scores of dark figures leaping over the mud, naked to the breech cloth, armed with rifle and tomahawk, and rushing down upon the unprotected side of their foe. The swamp had been but little obstacle to them.

Henry and his comrades gave the alarm at once. As many as possible were called off immediately from the main body, but they were not numerous enough to have any effect. The Indians came through the swamp in hundreds and hundreds, and, as they uttered their triumphant yell, poured a terrible fire into the Wyoming left flank. The defenders were forced to give ground, and the English and Tories came on again.

The fire was now deadly and of great volume. The air was filled with the flashing of the rifles. The cloud of smoke grew heavier, and faces, either from heat or excitement, showed red through it. The air was filled with bullets, and the Wyoming force was being cut down fast, as the fire of more than a thousand rifles converged upon it.

The five at the fringe of the swamp loaded and fired as fast as they could at the Indian horde, but they saw that it was creeping closer and closer, and that the hail of bullets it sent in was cutting away the whole left flank of the defenders. They saw the tall figure of Timmendiquas, a very god of war, leading on the Indians, with his fearless Wyandots in a close cluster around him. Colonel John Durkee, gathering up a force of fifty or sixty, charged straight at the warriors, but he was killed by a withering volley, which drove his men back.

Now occurred a fatal thing, one of those misconceptions which often decide the fate of a battle. The company of Captain Whittlesey, on the extreme left, which was suffering most severely, was ordered to fall back. The entire little army, which was being pressed hard now, seeing the movement of Whittlesey, began to retreat. Even without the mistake it is likely they would have lost in the face of such numbers.

The entire horde of Indians, Tories, Canadians, English, and renegades, uttering a tremendous yell, rushed forward. Colonel Zebulon Butler, seeing the crisis, rode up and down in front of his men, shouting: "Don't leave me, my children! the victory is ours!" Bravely his officers strove to stop the retreat. Every captain who led a company into action was killed. Some of these captains were but boys. The men were falling by dozens.

All the Indians, by far the most formidable part of the invading force, were through the swamp now, and, dashing down their unloaded rifles, threw themselves, tomahawk in hand, upon the defense. Not more than two hundred of the Wyoming men were left standing, and the impact of seven or eight hundred savage warriors was so great that they were hurled back in confusion. A wail of grief and terror came from the other side of the river, where a great body of women and children were watching the fighting.

"The battle's lost," said Shif'less Sol.

"Beyond hope of saving it," said Henry, "but, boys, we five are alive yet, and we'll do our best to help the others protect the retreat."

They kept under cover, fighting as calmly as they could amid such a terrible scene, picking off warrior after warrior, saving more than one soldier ere the tomahawk fell. Shif'less Sol took a shot at "Indian" Butler, but he was too far away, and the bullet missed him.

"I'd give five years of my life if he were fifty yards nearer," exclaimed the shiftless one.

But the invading force came in between and he did not get another shot. There was now a terrible medley, a continuous uproar, the crashing fire of hundreds of rifles, the shouts of the Indians, and the cries of the wounded. Over them all hovered smoke and dust, and the air was heavy, too, with the odor of burnt gunpowder. The division of old men and very young boys stood next, and the Indians were upon them, tomahawk in hand, but in the face of terrible odds all bore themselves with a valor worthy of the best of soldiers. Three fourths of them died that day, before they were driven back on the fort.

The Wyoming force was pushed away from the edge of the swamp, which had been some protection to the left, and they were now assailed from all sides except that of the river. "Indian" Butler raged at the head of his men, who had been driven back at first, and who had been saved by the Indians. Timmendiquas, in the absence of Brant, who was not seen upon this field, became by valor and power of intellect the leader of all the Indians for this moment. The Iroquois, although their own fierce chiefs, I-Tiokatoo, Sangerachte, and the others fought with them, unconsciously obeyed him. Nor did the fierce woman, Queen Esther, shirk the battle. Waving her great tomahawk, she was continually among the warriors, singing her song of war and death.

They were driven steadily back toward the fort, and the little band crumbled away beneath the deadly fire. Soon none would be left unless they ran for their lives. The five drew away toward the forest. They saw that the fort itself could not hold out against such a numerous and victorious foe, and they had no mind to be trapped. But their retreat was slow, and as they went they sent bullet after bullet into the Indian flank. Only a small percentage of the Wyoming force was left, and it now broke. Colonel Butler and Colonel Dennison, who were mounted, reached the fort. Some of the men jumped into the river, swam to the other shore and escaped. Some swam to a little island called Monocacy, and hid, but the Tories and Indians hunted them out and slew them. One Tory found his brother there, and killed him with his own hand, a deed of unspeakable horror that is yet mentioned by the people of that region. A few fled into the forest and entered the fort at night.

CHAPTER X. THE BLOODY ROCK

Seeing that all was lost, the five drew farther away into the woods. They were not wounded, yet their faces were white despite the tan. They had never before looked upon so terrible a scene. The Indians, wild with the excitement of a great triumph and thirsting for blood, were running over the field scalping the dead, killing some of the wounded, and saving others for the worst of tortures. Nor were their white allies one whit behind them. They bore a full part in the merciless war upon the conquered. Timmendiquas, the great Wyandot, was the only one to show nobility.

Several of the wounded he saved from immediate death, and he tried to hold back the frenzied swarm of old squaws who rushed forward and began to practice cruelties at which even the most veteran warrior might shudder. But Queen Esther urged them on, and "Indian" Butler himself and the chiefs were afraid of her.

Henry, despite himself, despite all his experience and powers of self-control, shuddered from head to foot at the cries that came from the lost field, and he was sure that the others were doing the same. The sun was setting, but its dying light, brilliant and intense, tinged the field as if with blood, showing all the yelling horde as the warriors rushed about for scalps, or danced in triumph, whirling their hideous trophies about their heads. Others were firing at men who were escaping to the far bank of the Susquehanna, and others were already seeking the fugitives in their vain hiding places on the little islet.

The five moved farther into the forest, retreating slowly, and sending in a shot now and then to protect the retreat of some fugitive who was seeking the shelter of the woods. The retreat had become a rout and then a massacre. The savages raged up and down in the greatest killing they had known since Braddock's defeat. The lodges of the Iroquois would be full of the scalps of white men.

All the five felt the full horror of the scene, but it made its deepest impress, perhaps, upon Paul. He had taken part in border battles before, but this was the first great defeat. He was not blind to the valor and good qualities of the Indian and his claim upon the wilderness, but he saw the incredible cruelties that he could commit, and he felt a horror of those who used him as an ally, a horror that he could never dismiss from his mind as long as he lived.

"Look!" he exclaimed, "look at that!"

A man of seventy and a boy of fourteen were running for the forest. They might have been grandfather and grandson. Undoubtedly they had fought in the Battalion of the Very Old and the Very Young, and now, when everything else was lost, they were seeking to save their lives in the friendly shelter of the woods. But they were pursued by two groups of Iroquois, four warriors in one, and three in the other, and the Indians were gaining fast.

"I reckon we ought to save them," said Shif'less Sol.

"No doubt of it," said Henry. "Paul, you and Sol move off to the right a little, and take the three, while the rest of us will look out for the four."

The little band separated according to the directions, Paul and Sol having the lighter task, as the others were to meet the group of four Indians at closer range. Paul and Sol were behind some trees, and, turning at an angle, they ran forward to intercept the three Indians. It would have seemed to anyone who was not aware of the presence of friends in the forest that the old man and the boy would surely be overtaken and be tomahawked, but three rifles suddenly flashed among the foliage. Two of the warriors in the group of four fell, and a third uttered a yell of pain. Paul and Shif'less Sol fired at the same time at the group of three. One fell before the deadly rifle of Shif'less Sol, but Paul only grazed his man. Nevertheless, the whole pursuit stopped, and the boy and the old man escaped to the forest, and subsequently to safety at the Moravian towns.

Paul, watching the happy effect of the shots, was about to say something to Shif'less Sol, when an immense force was hurled upon him, and he was thrown to the ground. His comrade was served in the same way, but the shiftless one was uncommonly strong and agile. He managed to writhe half way to his knees, and he shouted in a tremendous voice:

"Run, Henry, run! You can't do anything for us now!"

Braxton Wyatt struck him fiercely across the mouth. The blood came, but the shiftless one merely spat it out, and looked curiously at the renegade.

"I've often wondered about you, Braxton," he said calmly. "I used to think that anybody, no matter how bad, had some good in him, but I reckon you ain't got none."

Wyatt did not answer, but rushed forward in search of the others. But Henry, Silent Tom, and Long Jim had vanished. A powerful party of warriors had stolen upon Shif'less Sol and Paul, while they were absorbed in the chase of the old man and the boy, and now they were prisoners, bound securely. Braxton Wyatt came back from the fruitless search for the three, but his face was full of savage joy as he looked down at the captured two.

"We could have killed you just as easily," he said, "but we didn't want to do that. Our friends here are going to have their fun with you first."

Paul's cheeks whitened a little at the horrible suggestion, but Shif'less Sol faced them boldly. Several white men in uniform had come up, and among them was an elderly one, short and squat, and with a great flame colored handkerchief tied around his bead.

"You may burn us alive, or you may do other things jest ez bad to us, all under the English flag," said Shif'less Sol, "but I'm thinkin' that a lot o' people in England will be ashamed uv it when they hear the news."

"Indian" Butler and his uniformed soldiers turned away, leaving Shif'less Sol and Paul in the hands of the renegade and the Iroquois. The two prisoners were jerked to their feet and told to march.

"Come on, Paul," said Shif'less Sol. "'Tain't wuth while fur us to resist. But don't you quit hopin', Paul. We've escaped from many a tight corner, an' mebbe we're goin' to do it ag'in."

"Shut up!" said Braxton Wyatt savagely. "If you say another word I'll gag you in a way that will make you squirm."

Shif'less Sol looked him squarely in the eye. Solomon Hyde, who was not shiftless at all, had a dauntless soul, and he was not afraid now in the face of death preceded by long torture.

"I had a dog once, Braxton Wyatt," he said, "an' I reckon he wuz the meanest, orniest cur that ever lived. He liked to live on dirt, the dirtier the place he could find the better; he'd rather steal his food than get it honestly; he wuz sech a coward that he wuz afeard o' a rabbit, but ef your back wuz turned to him he'd nip you in the ankle. But bad ez that dog wuz, Braxton, he wuz a gentleman 'longside o' you."

Some of the Indians understood English, and Wyatt knew it. He snatched a pistol from his belt, and was about to strike Sol with the butt of it, but a tall figure suddenly appeared before him, and made a commanding gesture. The gesture said plainly: "Do not strike; put that pistol back!" Braxton Wyatt, whose soul was afraid within him, did not strike, and he put the pistol back.

It was Timmendiquas, the great White Lightning of the Wyandots, who with his little detachment had proved that day how mighty the Wyandot warriors were, full equals of Thayendanegea's Mohawks, the Keepers of the Western Gate. He was bare to the waist. One shoulder was streaked with blood from a slight wound, but his countenance was not on fire with passion for torture and slaughter like those of the others.

"There is no need to strike prisoners," he said in English. "Their fate will be decided later."

Paul thought that he caught a look of pity from the eyes of the great Wyandot, and Shif'less Sol said:

"I'm sorry, Timmendiquas, since I had to be captured, that you didn't capture me yourself. I'm glad to say that you're a great warrior."

Wyatt growled under his breath, but he was still afraid to speak out, although he knew that Timmendiquas was merely a distant and casual ally, and had little authority in that army. Yet he was overawed, and so were the Indians with him.

"We were merely taking the prisoners to Colonel Butler," he said. "That is all."

Timmendiquas stared at him, and the renegade's face fell. But he and the Indians went on with the prisoners, and Timmendiquas looked after them until they were out of sight.

"I believe White Lightning was sorry that we'd been captured," whispered Shif'less Sol.

"I think so, too," Paul whispered back.

They had no chance for further conversation, as they were driven rapidly now to that point of the battlefield which lay nearest to the fort, and here they were thrust into the midst of a gloomy company, fellow captives, all bound tightly, and many wounded. No help, no treatment of any kind was offered for hurts. The Indians and renegades stood about and yelled with delight when the agony of some man's wound wrung from him a groan. The scene was hideous in every respect. The setting sun shone blood red over forest, field, and river. Far off burning houses still smoked like torches. But the mountain wall in the east, was growing dusky with the coming twilight. From the island, where they were massacring the fugitives in their vain hiding places, came the sound of shots and cries, but elsewhere the firing had ceased. All who could escape had done so already, and of the others, those who were dead were fortunate.

The sun sank like a red ball behind the mountains, and darkness swept down over the earth. Fires began to blaze up here and there, some for terrible purpose. The victorious Iroquois; stripped to the waist and painted in glaring colors, joined in a savage dance that would remain forever photographed on the eye of Paul Cotter. As they jumped to and fro, hundreds of them, waving aloft tomahawks and scalping knives, both of which dripped red, they sang their wild chant of war and triumph. White men, too, as savage as they, joined them. Paul shuddered again and again from head to foot at this sight of an orgy such as the mass of mankind escapes, even in dreams.

The darkness thickened, the dance grew wilder. It was like a carnival of demons, but it was to be incited to a yet wilder pitch. A singular figure, one of extraordinary ferocity, was suddenly projected into the midst of the whirling crowd, and a chant, shriller and fiercer, rose above all the others. The figure was that of Queen Esther, like some monstrous creature out of a dim past, her great tomahawk stained with blood, her eyes bloodshot, and stains upon her shoulders. Paul would have covered his eyes had his hands not been tied instead, he turned his head away. He could not bear to see more. But the horrible chant came to his ears, nevertheless, and it was reinforced presently by other sounds still more terrible. Fires sprang up in the forest, and cries came from these fires. The victorious army of "Indian" Butler was beginning to burn the prisoners alive. But at this point we must stop. The details of what happened around those fires that night are not for the ordinary reader. It suffices to say that the darkest deed ever done on the soil of what is now the United States was being enacted.

Shif'less Sol himself, iron of body and soul, was shaken. He could not close his ears, if he would, to the cries that came from the fires, but he shut his eyes to keep out the demon dance. Nevertheless, he opened them again in a moment. The horrible fascination was too great. He saw Queen Esther still shaking her tomahawk, but as he looked she suddenly darted through the circle, warriors willingly giving way before her, and disappeared in the darkness. The scalp dance went on, but it had lost some of its fire and vigor.

Shif'less Sol felt relieved.

"She's gone," he whispered to Paul, and the boy, too, then opened his eyes. The rest of it, the mad whirlings and jumpings of the warriors, was becoming a blur before him, confused and without meaning.

Neither he nor Shif'less Sol knew how long they had been sitting there on the ground, although it had grown yet darker, when Braxton Wyatt thrust a violent foot against the shiftless one and cried:

"Get up! You're wanted!"

A half dozen Seneca warriors were with him, and there was no chance of resistance. The two rose slowly to their feet, and walked where Braxton Wyatt led. The Senecas came on either side, and close behind them, tomahawks in their hands. Paul, the sensitive, who so often felt the impression of coming events from the conditions around him, was sure that they were marching to their fate. Death he did not fear so greatly, although he did not want to die, but when a shriek came to him from one of the fires that convulsive shudder shook him again from head to foot. Unconsciously he strained at his bound arms, not for freedom, but that he might thrust his fingers in his ears and shut out the awful sounds. Shif'less Sol, because he could not use his hands, touched his shoulder gently against Paul's.

"Paul," he whispered, "I ain't sure that we're goin' to die, leastways, I still have hope; but ef we do, remember that we don't have to die but oncet."

"I'll remember, Sol," Paul whispered back.

"Silence, there!" exclaimed Braxton Wyatt. But the two had said all they wanted to say, and fortunately their senses were somewhat dulled. They had passed through so much that they were like those who are under the influence of opiates. The path was now dark, although both torches and fires burned in the distance. Presently they heard that chant with which they had become familiar, the dreadful notes of the hyena woman, and they knew that they were being taken into her presence, for what purpose they could not tell, although they were sure that it was a bitter one. As they approached, the woman's chant rose to an uncommon pitch of frenzy, and Paul felt the blood slowly chilling within him.

"Get up there!" exclaimed Braxton Wyatt, and the Senecas gave them both a push. Other warriors who were standing at the edge of an open space seized them and threw them forward with much violence. When they struggled into a sitting position, they saw Queen Esther standing upon a broad flat rock and whirling in a ghastly dance that had in it something Oriental. She still swung the great war hatchet that seemed always to be in her hand. Her long black hair flew wildly about her head, and her red dress gleamed in the dusk. Surely no more terrible image ever appeared in the American wilderness! In front of her, lying upon the ground, were twenty bound Americans, and back of them were Iroquois in dozens, with a sprinkling of their white allies.

What it all meant, what was about to come to pass, nether Paul nor Shif'less Sol could guess, but Queen Esther sang:

> We have found them, the Yengees
> Who built their houses in the valley,
> They came forth to meet us in battle,
> Our rifles and tomahawks cut them down,
> As the Yengees lay low the forest.
> Victory and glory Aieroski gives to his children,
> The Mighty Six Nations, greatest of men.
> There will be feasting in the lodges of the Iroquois,
> And scalps will hang on the high ridge pole,
> But wolves will roam where the Yengees dwelt
> And will gnaw the bones of them all,
> Of the man, the woman, and the child.
> Victory and glory Aieroski gives to his children,
> The Mighty Six Nations, greatest of men.

Such it sounded to Shif'less Sol, who knew the tongue of the Iroquois, and so it went on, verse after verse, and at the end of each verse came the refrain, in which the warriors joined:

"Victory and glory Aieroski gives to his children. The mighty Six Nations, greatest of men."

"What under the sun is she about?" whispered Shif'less Sol.

96

"It is a fearful face," was Paul's only reply.

Suddenly the woman, without stopping her chant, made a gesture to the warriors. Two powerful Senecas seized one of the bound prisoners, dragged him to his feet, and held him up before her. She uttered a shout, whirled the great tomahawk about her head, its blade glittering in the moonlight, and struck with all her might. The skull of the prisoner was cleft to the chin, and without a cry he fell at the feet of the woman who had killed him. Paul uttered a shout of horror, but it was lost in the joyful yells of the Iroquois, who, at the command of the woman, offered a second victim. Again the tomahawk descended, and again a man fell dead without a sound.

Shif'less Sol and Paul wrenched at their thongs, but they could not move them. Braxton Wyatt laughed aloud. It was strange to see how fast one with a bad nature could fall when the opportunities were spread before him. Now he was as cruel as the Indians themselves. Wilder and shriller grew the chant of the savage queen. She was intoxicated with blood. She saw it everywhere. Her tomahawk clove a third skull, a fourth, a fifth, a sixth, a seventh, and eighth. As fast as they fell the warriors at her command brought up new victims for her weapon. Paul shut his eyes, but he knew by the sounds what was passing. Suddenly a stern voice cried:

"Hold, woman! Enough of this! Will your tomahawk never be satisfied?"

Paul understood it, the meaning, but not the words. He opened his eyes and saw the great figure of Timmendiquas striding forward, his hand upraised in protest.

The woman turned her fierce gaze upon the young chief. "Timmendiquas," she said, "we are the Iroquois, and we are the masters. You are far from your own land, a guest in our lodges, and you cannot tell those who have won the victory how they shall use it. Stand back!"

A loud laugh came from the Iroquois. The fierce old chiefs, Hiokatoo and Sangerachte, and a dozen warriors thrust themselves before Timmendiquas. The woman resumed her chant, and a hundred throats pealed out with her the chorus:

Victory and glory Aieroski gives to his children The mighty Six Nations, greatest of men.

She gave the signal anew. The ninth victim stood before her, and then fell, cloven to the chin; then the tenth, and the eleventh, and the twelfth, and the thirteenth, and the fourteenth, and the fifteenth, and the sixteenth-sixteen bound men killed by one woman in less than fifteen minutes. The four in that group who were left had all the while been straining fearfully at their bonds. Now they had slipped or broken them, and, springing to their feet, driven on by the mightiest of human impulses, they dashed through the ring of Iroquois and into the forest. Two were hunted down by the warriors and killed, but the other two, Joseph Elliott and Lebbeus Hammond, escaped and lived to be old men, feeling that life could never again hold for them anything so dreadful as that scene at "The Bloody Rock."

A great turmoil and confusion arose as the prisoners fled and the Indians pursued. Paul and Shif'less Sol; full of sympathy and pity for the fugitives and having felt all the time that their turn, too, would come under that dreadful tomahawk, struggled to their feet. They did not see a form slip noiselessly behind them, but a sharp knife descended once, then twice, and the bands of both fell free.

"Run! run!" exclaimed the voice of Timmendiquas, low but penetrating. "I would save you from this!"

Amid the darkness and confusion the act of the great Wyandot was not seen by the other Indians and the renegades. Paul flashed him one look of gratitude, and then he and Shif'less Sol darted away, choosing a course that led them from the crowd in pursuit of the other flying fugitives.

At such a time they might have secured a long lead without being noticed, had it not been for the fierce swarm of old squaws who were first in cruelty that night. A shrill wild howl arose, and the pointing fingers of the old women showed to the warriors the two in flight. At the same time several of the squaws darted forward to intercept the fugitives.

"I hate to hit a woman," breathed Shif'less Sol to Paul, "but I'm goin' to do it now."

A hideous figure sprang before them. Sol struck her face with his open hand, and with a shriek she went down. He leaped over her, although she clawed at his feet as he passed, and ran on, with Paul at his side. Shots were now fired at him, but they went wild, but Paul, casting a look backward out of the corner of his eye, saw that a real pursuit, silent and deadly, had begun. Five Mohawk warriors, running swiftly, were only a few hundred yards away. They carried rifle, tomahawk, and knife, and Paul and Shif'less Sol were unarmed. Moreover, they were coming fast, spreading out slightly, and the shiftless one, able even at such a time to weigh the case coolly, saw that the odds were against them. Yet he would not despair. Anything might happen. It was night. There was little organization in the army of the Indians and of their white allies, which was giving itself up to the enjoyment of scalps and torture. Moreover, he and Paul were, animated by the love of life, which is always stronger than the desire to give death.

Their flight led them in a diagonal line toward the mountains. Only once did the pursuers give tongue. Paul tripped over a root, and a triumphant yell came from the Mohawks. But it merely gave him new life. He recovered himself in an instant and ran faster. But it was terribly hard work. He could hear Shif'less Sol's sobbing breath by his side, and he was sure that his own must have the same sound for his comrade.

"At any rate one uv 'em is beat," gasped Shif'less Sol. "Only four are ban-in' on now."

The ground rose a little and became rougher. The lights from the Indian fires had sunk almost out of sight behind them, and a dense thicket lay before them. Something stirred in the thicket, and the eyes of Shif'less Sol caught a glimpse of a human shoulder. His heart sank like a plummet in a pool. The Indians were ahead of them. They would be caught, and would be carried back to become the victims of the terrible tomahawk.

The figure in the bushes rose a little higher, the muzzle of a rifle was projected, and flame leaped from the steel tube.

But it was neither Shif'less Sol nor Paul who fell. They heard a cry behind them, and when Shif'less Sol took a hasty glance backward he saw one of the Mohawks fall. The three who were left hesitated and stopped. When a second shot was fired from the bushes and another Mohawk went down, the remaining two fled.

Shif'less Sol understood now, and he rushed into the bushes, dragging Paul after him. Henry, Tom, and Long Jim rose up to receive them.

"So you wuz watchin' over us!" exclaimed the shiftless one joyously. "It wuz you that clipped off the first Mohawk, an' we didn't even notice the shot."

"Thank God, you were here!" exclaimed Paul. "You don't know what Sol and I have seen!"

Overwrought, he fell forward, but his comrades caught him.

CHAPTER XI. THE MELANCHOLY FLIGHT

Paul revived in a few minutes. They were still lying in the bushes, and when he was able to stand up again, they moved at an angle several hundred yards before they stopped. One pistol was thrust into Paul's hand and another into that of Shif'less Sol.

"Keep those until we can get rifles for you," said Henry. "You may need 'em to-night."

They crouched down in the thicket and looked back toward the Indian camp. The warriors whom they had repulsed were not returning with help, and, for the moment, they seemed to have no enemy to fear, yet they could still see through the woods the faint lights of the Indian camps, and to Paul, at least, came the echoes of distant cries that told of things not to be written.

"We saw you captured, and we heard Sol's warning cry," said Henry. "There was nothing to do but run. Then we hid and waited a chance for rescue."

"It would never have come if it had not been for Timmendiquas," said Paul.

"Timmendiquas!" exclaimed Henry.

"Yes, Timmendiquas," said Paul, and then he told the story of "The Bloody Rock," and how, in the turmoil and excitement attending the flight of the last four, Timmendiquas had cut the bonds of Shif'less Sol and himself.

"I think the mind o' White Lightnin', Injun ez he is," said Shif'less Sol, "jest naterally turned aginst so much slaughter an' torture o' prisoners."

"I'm sure you're right," said Henry.

"'Pears strange to me," said Long Jim Hart, "that Timmendiquas was made an Injun. He's jest the kind uv man who ought to be white, an' he'd be pow'ful useful, too. I don't jest eggzactly understan' it."

"He has certainly saved the lives of at least three of us," said Henry. "I hope we will get a chance to pay him back in full."

"But he's the only one," said Shif'less Sol, thinking of all that he had seen that night. "The Iroquois an' the white men that's allied with 'em won't ever get any mercy from me, ef any uv 'em happen to come under my thumb. I don't think the like o' this day an' night wuz ever done on this continent afore. I'm for revenge, I am, like that place where the Bible says, 'an eye for an eye, an' a tooth for a tooth,' an' I'm goin' to stay in this part o' the country till we git it!"

It was seldom that Shif'less Sol spoke with so much passion and energy.

"We're all going to stay with you, Sol," said Henry. "We're needed here. I think we ought to circle about the fort, slip in if we can, and fight with the defense."

"Yes, we'll do that," said Shif'less Sol, "but the Wyoming fort can't ever hold out. Thar ain't a hundred men left in it fit to fight, an' thar are more than than a thousand howlin' devils outside ready to attack it. Thar may be worse to come than anything we've yet seen."

"Still, we'll go in an' help," said Henry. "Sol, when you an' Paul have rested a little longer we'll make a big loop around in the woods, and come up to the fort on the other side."

They were in full accord, and after an hour in the bushes, where they lay completely hidden, recovering their vitality and energy, they undertook to reach the fort and cabins inclosed by the palisades. Paul was still weak from shock, but Shif'less Sol had fully recovered. Neither bad weapons, but they were sure that the want could be supplied soon. They curved around toward the west, intending to approach the fort from the other side, but they did not wholly lose sight of the fires, and they heard now and then the triumphant war whoop. The victors were still engaged in the pleasant task of burning the prisoners to death. Little did the five, seeing and feeling only their part of it there in the dark woods, dream that the deeds of this day and night would soon shock the whole civilized world, and remain, for generations, a crowning act of infamy. But they certainly felt it deeply enough, and in each heart burned a fierce desire for revenge upon the Iroquois.

It was almost midnight when they secured entrance into the fort, which was filled with grief and wailing. That afternoon more than one hundred and fifty women within those walls had been made widows, and six hundred children had been made orphans. But few men fit to bear arms were left for its defense, and it was certain that the allied British and Indian army would easily take it on the morrow. A demand for its surrender in the name of King George III of England had already been made, and, sitting at a little rough table in the cabin of Thomas Bennett, the room lighted only by a single tallow wick, Colonel Butler and Colonel Dennison were writing an agreement that the fort be surrendered the next day, with what it should contain. But Colonel Butler put his wife on a horse and escaped with her over the mountains.

Stragglers, evading the tomahawk in the darkness, were coming in, only to be surrendered the next day; others were pouring forth in a stream, seeking the shelter of the mountains and the forest, preferring any dangers that might be found there to the mercies of the victors.

When Shif'less Sol learned that the fort was to be given up, he said:

"It looks ez ef we had escaped from the Iroquois jest in time to beg 'em to take us back."

"I reckon I ain't goin' to stay 'roun' here while things are bein' surrendered," said Long Jim Hart.

"I'll do my surrenderin' to Iroquois when they've got my hands an' feet tied, an' six or seven uv 'em are settin' on my back," said Tom Ross.

"We'll leave as soon as we can get arms for Sol and Paul," said Henry. "Of course it would be foolish of us to stay here and be captured again. Besides, we'll be needed badly enough by the women and children that are going."

Good weapons were easily obtained in the fort. It was far better to let Sol and Paul have them than to leave them for the Indians. They were able to select two fine rifles of the Kentucky pattern, long and slender barreled, a tomahawk and knife for each, and also excellent double-barreled pistols. The other three now had double-barreled pistols, too. In addition they resupplied themselves with as much ammunition as scouts and hunters could conveniently carry, and toward morning left the fort.

Sunrise found them some distance from the palisades, and upon the flank of a frightened crowd of fugitives. It was composed of one hundred women and children and a single man, James Carpenter, who was doing his best to guide and protect them. They were intending to flee through the wilderness to the Delaware and Lehigh settlements, chiefly Fort Penn, built by Jacob Stroud, where Stroudsburg now is.

When the five, darkened by weather and looking almost like Indians themselves, approached, Carpenter stepped forward and raised his rifle. A cry of dismay rose from the melancholy line, a cry so intensely bitter that it cut Henry to the very heart. He threw up his hand, and exclaimed in a loud voice:

"We are friends, not Indians or Tories! We fought with you yesterday, and we are ready to fight for you now!"

Carpenter dropped the muzzle of the rifle. He had fought in the battle, too, and he recognized the great youth and his comrades who had been there with him.

"What do you want of us?" asked he.

"Nothing," replied Henry, "except to help you."

Carpenter looked at them with a kind of sad pathos.

"You don't belong here in Wyoming," he said, "and there's nothing to make you stick to us. What are you meaning to do?"

"We will go with you wherever you intend to go," replied Henry; "do fighting for you if you need it, and hunt game for you, which you are certain to need."

The weather-beaten face of the farmer worked.

"I thought God had clean deserted us," he said, "but I'm ready to take it back. I reckon that he has sent you five to help me with all these women and little ones."

It occurred to Henry that perhaps God, indeed, had sent them for this very purpose, but he replied simply:

"You lead on, and we'll stay in the rear and on the sides to watch for the Indians. Draw into the woods, where we'll be hidden."

Carpenter, obscure hero, shouldered his rifle again, and led on toward the woods. The long line of women and children followed. Some of the women carried in their arms children too small to walk. Yet they were more hopeful now when they saw that the five were friends. These lithe, active frontiersmen, so quick, so skillful, and so helpful, raised their courage. Yet it was a most doleful flight. Most of these women had been made widows the day before, some of them had been made widows and childless at the same time, and wondered why they should seek to live longer. But the very mental stupor of many of them was an aid. They ceased to cry out, and some even ceased to be afraid.

Henry, Shif'less Sol, and Tom dropped to the rear. Paul and Long Jim were on either flank, while Carpenter led slowly on toward the mountains.

"'Pears to me," said Tom, "that the thing fur us to do is to hurry 'em up ez much ez possible."

"So the Indians won't see 'em crossing the plain," said Henry. "We couldn't defend them against a large force, and it would merely be a massacre. We must persuade them to walk faster."

Shif'less Sol was invaluable in this crisis. He could talk forever in his-placid way, and, with his gentle encouragement, mild sarcasm, and anecdotes of great feminine walkers that he had known, he soon had them moving faster.

Henry and Tom dropped farther to the rear. They could see ahead of them the long dark line, coiling farther into the woods, but they could also see to right and left towers of smoke rising in the clear morning sunlight. These, they knew, came from burning houses, and they knew, also, that the valley would be ravaged from end to end and from side to side. After the surrender of the fort the Indians would divide into small bands, going everywhere, and nothing could escape them.

The sun rose higher, gilding the earth with glowing light, as if the black tragedy had never happened, but the frontiersmen recognized their greatest danger in this brilliant morning. Objects could be seen at a great distance, and they could be seen vividly.

Keen of sight and trained to know what it was they saw, Henry, Sol, and Tom searched the country with their eyes, on all sides. They caught a distant glimpse of the Susquehanna, a silver spot among some trees, and they saw the sunlight glancing off the opposite mountains, but for the present they saw nothing that seemed hostile.

They allowed the distance between them and the retreating file to grow until it was five or six hundred yards, and they might have let it grow farther, but Henry made a signal, and the three lay down in the grass.

"You see 'em, don't you!" the youth whispered to his comrade.

"Yes, down thar at the foot o' that hillock," replied Shif'less Sol; "two o' em, an' Senecas, I take it."

"They've seen that crowd of women and children," said Henry.

It was obvious that the flying column was discovered. The two Indians stepped upon the hillock and gazed under their hands. It was too far away for the three to see their faces, but they knew the joy that would be shown there. The two could return with a few warriors and massacre them all.

"They must never get back to the other Indians with their news," whispered Henry. "I hate to shoot men from ambush, but it's got to be done. Wait, they're coming a little closer."

The two Senecas advanced about thirty yards, and stopped again.

"S'pose you fire at the one on the right, Henry," said Tom, "an' me an' Sol will take the one to the left."

"All right," said Henry. "Fire!"

They wasted no time, but pulled trigger. The one at whom Henry had aimed fell, but the other, uttering a cry, made off, wounded, but evidently with plenty of strength left.

"We mustn't let him escape! We mustn't let him carry a warning!" cried Henry.

But Shif'less Sol and Tom Ross were already in pursuit, covering the ground with long strides, and reloading as they ran. Under ordinary circumstances no one of the three would have fired at a man running for his life, but here the necessity was vital. If he lived, carrying the tale that he had to tell, a hundred innocent ones might perish. Henry followed his comrades, reloading his own rifle, also, but he stayed behind. The Indian had a good lead, and he was gaining, as the others were compelled to check speed somewhat as they put the powder and bullets in their rifles. But Henry was near enough to Shif'less Sol and Silent Tom to hear them exchange a few words.

"How far away is that savage?" asked Shif'less Sol.

"Hundred and eighty yards," said Tom Ross.

"Well, you take him in the head, and I'll take him in the body."

Henry saw the two rifle barrels go up and two flashes of flame leap from the muzzles. The Indian fell forward and lay still. They went up to him, and found that he was shot through the head and also through the body.

"We may miss once, but we don't twice," said Tom Ross.

The human mind can be influenced so powerfully by events that the three felt no compunction at all at the shooting of this fleeing Indian. It was but a trifle compared with what they had seen the day and night before.

"We'd better take the weapons an' ammunition o' both uv 'em," said Sol. "They may be needed, an' some o' the women in that crowd kin shoot."

They gathered up the arms, powder, and ball, and waited a little to see whether the shots had been heard by any other Indians, but there was no indication of the presence of more warriors, and the rejoined the fugitives. Long Jim had dropped back to the end of the line, and when he saw that his comrades carried two extra rifles, he understood.

"They didn't give no alarm, did they?" he asked in a tone so low that none of the fugitives could hear.

"They didn't have any chance," replied Henry. "We've brought away all their weapons and ammunition, but just say to the women that we found them in an abandoned house."

The rifles and the other arms were given to the boldest and most stalwart of the women, and they promised to use them if the need came. Meanwhile the flight went on, and the farther it went the sadder it became. Children became exhausted, and had to be carried by people so tired that they could scarcely walk themselves. There was nobody in the line who had not lost some beloved one on that fatal river bank, killed in battle, or tortured to death. As they slowly ascended the green slope of the mountain that inclosed a side of the valley, they looked back upon ruin and desolation. The whole black tragedy was being consummated. They could see the houses in flames, and they knew that the Indian war parties were killing and scalping everywhere. They knew, too, that other bodies of fugitives, as stricken as their own, were fleeing into the mountains, they scarcely knew whither.

As they paused a few moments and looked back, a great cry burst from the weakest of the women and children. Then it became a sad and terrible wail, and it was a long time before it ceased. It was an awful sound, so compounded of despair and woe and of longing for what they had lost that Henry choked, and the tears stood in Paul's eyes. But neither the five nor Carpenter made any attempt to check the wailing. They thought it best for them to weep it out, but they hurried the column as much as they could, often carrying some of the smaller children themselves. Paul and Long Jim were the best as comforters. The two knew how, each in his own way, to soothe and encourage. Carpenter, who knew the way to Fort Penn, led doggedly on, scarcely saying a word. Henry, Shif'less Sol, and Tom were the rear guard, which was, in this case, the one of greatest danger and responsibility.

Henry was thankful that it was only early summer the Fourth of July, the second anniversary of the Declaration of Independence-and that the foliage was heavy and green on the slopes of the mountain. In this mass of greenery the desolate column was now completely hidden from any observer in the valley, and he believed that other crowds of fugitives would be hidden in the same manner. He felt sure that no living human being would be left in the valley, that it would be ravaged from end to end and then left to desolation, until new people, protected by American bayonets, should come in and settle it again.

At last they passed the crest of the ridge, and the fires in the valley, those emblems of destruction, were hidden. Between them and Fort Penn, sixty miles away, stretched a wilderness of mountain, forest, and swamp. But the five welcomed the forest. A foe might lie there in ambush, but they could not see the fugitives at a distance. What the latter needed now was obscurity, the green blanket of the forest to hide them. Carpenter led on over a narrow trail; the others followed almost in single file now, while the five scouted in the woods on either flank and at the rear. Henry and Shif'less Sol generally kept together, and they fully realized the overwhelming danger should an Indian band, even as small as ten or a dozen warriors, appear. Should the latter scatter, it would be impossible to protect all the women and children from their tomahawks.

The day was warm, but the forest gave them coolness as well as shelter. Henry and Sol were seldom so far back that they could not see the end of the melancholy line, now moving slowly, overborne by weariness. The shiftless one shook his head sadly.

"No matter what happens, some uv 'em will never get out o' these woods."

His words came true all too soon. Before the afternoon closed, two women, ill before the flight, died of terror and exhaustion, and were buried in shallow graves under the trees. Before dark a halt was made at the suggestion of Henry, and all except Carpenter and the scouts sat in a close, drooping group. Many of the children cried, though the women had all ceased to weep. They had some food with them, taken in the hurried flight, and now the men asked them to eat. Few could do it, and others insisted on saving what little they had for the children. Long Jim found a spring near by, and all drank at it.

The six men decided that, although night had not yet come, it would be best to remain there until the morning. Evidently the fugitives were in no condition, either mental or physical, to go farther that day, and the rest was worth more than the risk.

When this decision was announced to them, most of the women took it apathetically. Soon they lay down upon a blanket, if one was to be had; otherwise, on leaves and branches. Again Henry thanked God that it was summer, and that these were people of the frontier, who could sleep in the open. No fire was needed, and, outside of human enemies, only rain was to be dreaded.

And yet this band, desperate though its case, was more fortunate than some of the others that fled from the Wyoming Valley. It had now to protect it six men Henry and Paul, though boys in years, were men in strength and ability—five of whom were the equals of any frontiersmen on the whole border. Another crowd of women was escorted by a single man throughout its entire flight.

Henry and his comrades distributed themselves in a circle about the group. At times they helped gather whortleberries as food for the others, but they looked for Indians or game, intending to shoot in either case. When Paul and Henry were together they once heard a light sound in a thicket, which at first they were afraid was made by an Indian scout, but it was a deer, and it bounded away too soon for either to get a shot. They could not find other game of any kind, and they came back toward the camp-if a mere stop in the woods, without shelter of any kind, could be called a camp.

The sun was now setting, blood red. It tinged the forest with a fiery mist, reminding the unhappy group of all that they had seen. But the mist was gone in a few moments, and then the blackness of night came with a weird moaning wind that told of desolation. Most of the children, having passed through every phase of exhaustion and terror, had fallen asleep. Some of the women slept, also, and others wept. But the terrible wailing note, which the nerves of no man could stand, was heard no longer.

The five gathered again at a point near by, and Carpenter came to them.

"Men," he said simply, "don't know much about you, though I know you fought well in the battle that we lost, but for what you're doin' now nobody can ever repay you. I knew that I never could get across the mountains with all these weak ones."

The five merely said that any man who was a man would help at such a time. Then they resumed their march in a perpetual circle about the camp.

Some women did not sleep at all that night. It is not easy to conceive what the frontier women of America endured so many thousands of times. They had seen their husbands, brothers, and sons killed in the battle, and they knew that the worst of torture had been practiced in the Indian camp. Many of them really did not want to live any longer. They merely struggled automatically for life. The darkness settled down thicker and thicker; the blackness in the forest was intense, and they could see the faces of one another only at a little distance. The desolate moan of the wind came through the leaves, and, although it was July, the night grew cold. The women crept closer together, trying to cover up and protect the children. The wind, with its inexpressibly mournful note, was exactly fitted to their feelings. Many of them wondered why a Supreme Being had permitted such things. But they ceased to talk. No sound at all came from the group, and any one fifty yards away, not forewarned, could not have told that they were there.

Henry and Paul met again about midnight, and sat a long time on a little hillock. Theirs had been the most dangerous of lives on the most dangerous of frontiers, but they had never been stirred as they were tonight. Even Paul, the mildest of the five, felt something burning within him, a fire that only one thing could quench.

"Henry," said he, "we're trying to get these people to Fort Penn, and we may get some of them there, but I don't think our work will be ended them. I don't think I could ever be happy again if we went straight from Fort Penn to Kentucky."

Henry understood him perfectly.

"No, Paul," he said, "I don't want to go, either, and I know the others don't. Maybe you are not willing to tell why we want to stay, but it is vengeance. I know it's Christian to forgive your enemies, but I can't see what I have seen, and hear what I have heard, and do it."

"When the news of these things spreads," said Paul, "they'll send an army from the east. Sooner or later they'll just have to do it to punish the Iroquois and their white allies, and we've got to be here to join that army."

"I feel that way, too, Paul," said Henry.

They were joined later by the other three, who stayed a little while, and they were in accord with Henry and Paul.

Then they began their circles about the camp again, always looking and always listening. About two o'clock in the morning they heard a scream, but it was only the cry of a panther. Before day there were clouds, a low rumble of distant thunder, and faint far flashes of lightning. Henry was in dread of rain, but the lightning and thunder ceased, and the clouds went away. Then dawn came, rosy and bright, and all but three rose from the earth. The three-one woman and two children-had died in silence in the night, and they were buried, like the others, in shallow graves in the woods. But there was little weeping or external mourning over them. All were now heavy and apathetic, capable of but little more emotion.

Carpenter resumed his position at the head of the column, which now moved slowly over the mountain through a thick forest matted with vines and bushes and without a path. The march was now so painful and difficult that they did not make more than two miles an hour. The stronger of them helped the men to gather more whortleberries, as it was easy to see that the food they had with them would never last until they reached Fort Penn, should they ever reach it.

The condition of the country into which they had entered steadily grew worse. They were well into the mountains, a region exceedingly wild and rough, but little known to the settlers, who had gone around it to build homes in the fertile and beautiful valley of Wyoming. The heavy forest was made all the more difficult by the presence everywhere of almost impassable undergrowth. Now and then a woman lay down under the bushes, and in two cases they died there because the power to live was no longer in them. They grew weaker and weaker. The food that they had brought from the Wyoming fort was almost exhausted, and the wild whortleberries were far from sustaining. Fortunately there was plenty of water flowing tinder the dark woods and along the mountainside. But they were compelled to stop at intervals of an hour or two to rest, and the more timid continually expected Indian ambush.

The five met shortly after noon and took another reckoning of the situation. They still realized to the full the dangers of Indian pursuit, which in this case might be a mere matter of accident. Anybody could follow the broad trail left by the fugitives, but the Iroquois, busy with destruction in the valley, might not follow, even if they saw it. No one could tell. The danger of starvation or of death from exhaustion was more imminent, more pressing, and the five resolved to let scouting alone for the rest of the day and seek game.

"There's bound to be a lot of it in these woods," said Shif'less Sol, "though it's frightened out of the path by our big crowd, but we ought to find it."

Henry and Shif'less Sol went in one direction, and Paul, Tom, and Long Jim in another. But with all their hunting they succeeded in finding only one little deer, which fell to the rifle of Silent Tom. It made small enough portions for the supper and breakfast of nearly a hundred people, but it helped wonderfully, and so did the fires which Henry and his comrades would now have built, even had they not been needed for the cooking. They saw that light and warmth, the light and warmth of glowing coals, would alone rouse life in this desolate band.

They slept the second night on the ground among the trees, and the next morning they entered that gloomy region of terrible memory, the Great Dismal Swamp of the North, known sometimes, to this day, as "The Shades of Death."

CHAPTER XII. THE SHADES OF DEATH

"The Shades of Death" is a marsh on a mountain top, the great, wet, and soggy plain of the Pocono and Broad mountains. When the fugitives from Wyoming entered it, it was covered with a dense growth of pines, growing mostly out of dark, murky water, which in its turn was thick with a growth of moss and aquatic plants. Snakes and all kinds of creeping things swarmed in the ooze. Bear and panther were numerous.

Carpenter did not know any way around this terrible region, and they were compelled to enter it. Henry was again devoutly thankful that it was summer. In such a situation with winter on top of it only the hardiest of men could survive.

But they entered the swamp, Carpenter silent and dogged, still leading. Henry and his comrades kept close to the crowd. One could not scout in such a morass, and it proved to be worse than they had feared. The day turned gray, and it was dark among the trees. The whole place was filled with gloomy shadows. It was often impossible to judge whether fairly solid soil or oozy murk lay before them. Often they went down to their waists. Sometimes the children fell and were dragged up again by the stronger. Now and then rattle snakes coiled and hissed, and the women killed them with sticks. Other serpents slipped away in the slime. Everybody was plastered with mud, and they became mere images of human beings.

In the afternoon they reached a sort of oasis in the terrible swamp, and there they buried two more of their number who had perished from exhaustion. The rest, save a few, lay upon the ground as if dead. On all sides of them stretched the pines and the soft black earth. It looked to the fugitives like a region into which no human beings had ever come, or ever would come again, and, alas! to most of them like a region from which no human being would ever emerge.

Henry sat upon a piece of fallen brushwood near the edge of the morass, and looked at the fugitives, and his heart sank within him. They were hardly in the likeness of his own kind, and they seemed practically lifeless now. Everything was dull, heavy, and dead. The note of the wind among the leaves was somber. A long black snake slipped from the marshy grass near his feet and disappeared soundlessly in the water. He was sick, sick to death at the sight of so much suffering, and the desire for vengeance, slow, cold, and far more lasting than any hot outburst, grew within him. A slight noise, and Shif'less Sol stood beside him.

"Did you hear?" asked the shiftless one, in a significant tone.

"Hear what?" asked Henry, who had been deep in thought.

"The wolf howl, just a very little cry, very far away an' under the horizon, but thar all the same. Listen, thar she goes ag'in!"

Henry bent his ear and distinctly heard the faint, whining note, and then it came a third time.

He looked tip at Shif'less Sol, and his face grew white—but not for himself.

"Yes," said Shif'less Sol. He understood the look. "We are pursued. Them wolves howlin' are the Iroquois. What do you reckon we're goin' to do, Henry?"

"Fight!" replied the youth, with fierce energy. "Beat 'em off!"

"How?"

Henry circled the little oasis with the eye of a general, and his plan came.

"You'll stand here, where the earth gives a footing," he said, "you, Solomon Hyde, as brave a man as I ever saw, and with you will be Paul Cotter, Tom Ross, Jim Hart, and Henry Ware, old friends of yours. Carpenter will at once lead the women and children on ahead, and perhaps they will not hear the battle that is going to be fought here."

A smile of approval, slow, but deep and comprehensive, stole over the face of Solomon Hyde, surnamed, wholly without fitness, the shiftless one. "It seems to me," he said, "that I've heard o' them four fellers you're talkin' about, an' ef I wuz to hunt all over this planet an' them other planets that Paul tells of, I couldn't find four other fellers that I'd ez soon have with me."

"We've got to stand here to the death," said Henry.

"You're shorely right," said Shif'less Sol.

The hands of the two comrades met in a grip of steel.

The other three were called and were told of the plan, which met with their full approval. Then the news was carried to Carpenter, who quickly agreed that their course was the wisest. He urged all the fugitives to their feet, telling them that they must reach another dry place before night, but they were past asking questions now, and, heavy and apathetic, they passed on into the swamp.

Paul watched the last of them disappear among the black bushes and weeds, and turned back to his friends on the oasis. The five lay down behind a big fallen pine, and gave their weapons a last look. They had never been armed better. Their rifles were good, and the fine double-barreled pistols, formidable weapons, would be a great aid, especially at close quarters.

"I take it," said Tom Ross, "that the Iroquois can't get through at all unless they come along this way, an' it's the same ez ef we wuz settin' on solid earth, poppin' em over, while they come sloshin' up to us."

"That's exactly it," said Henry. "We've a natural defense which we can hold against much greater numbers, and the longer we hold 'em off, the nearer our people will be to Fort Penn."

"I never felt more like fightin' in my life," said Tom Ross.

It was a grim utterance, true of them all, although not one among them was bloodthirsty.

"Can any of you hear anything?" asked Henry. "Nothin'," replied Shif'less Sol, after a little wait, "nothin' from the women goin', an' nothin' from the Iroquois comin'."

"We'll just lie close," said Henry. "This hard spot of ground isn't more than thirty or forty feet each way, and nobody can get on it without our knowing it."

The others did not reply. All lay motionless upon their sides, with their shoulders raised a little, in order that they might take instant aim when the time came. Some rays of the sun penetrated the canopy of pines, and fell across the brown, determined faces and the lean brown hands that grasped the long, slender-barreled Kentucky rifles. Another snake slipped from the ground into the black water and swam away. Some water animal made a light splash as he, too, swam from the presence of these strange intruders. Then they beard a sighing sound, as of a foot drawn from mud, and they knew that the Iroquois were approaching, savages in war, whatever they might be otherwise, and expecting an easy prey. Five brown thumbs cocked their rifles, and five brown forefingers rested upon the triggers. The eyes of woodsmen who seldom missed looked down the sights.

The sound of feet in the mud came many times. The enemy was evidently drawing near.

"How many do you think are out thar?" whispered Shif'less Sol to Henry.

"Twenty, at least, it seems to me by the sounds." "I s'pose the best thing for us to do is to shoot at the first head we see."

"Yes, but we mustn't all fire at the same man."

It was suggested that Henry call off the turns of the marksmen, and he agreed to do so. Shif'less Sol was to fire first. The sounds now ceased. The

Iroquois evidently had some feeling or instinct that they were approaching an enemy who was to be feared, not weak and unarmed women and children.

The five were absolutely motionless, finger on trigger. The American wilderness had heroes without number. It was Horatius Cocles five times over, ready to defend the bridge with life. Over the marsh rose the weird cry of an owl, and some water birds called in lonely fashion.

Henry judged that the fugitives were now three quarters of a mile away, out of the sound of rifle shot. He had urged Carpenter to marshal them on as far as he could. But the silence endured yet a while longer. In the dull gray light of the somber day and the waning afternoon the marsh was increasingly dreary and mournful. It seemed that it must always be the abode of dead or dying things.

The wet grass, forty yards away, moved a little, and between the boughs appeared the segment of a hideous dark face, the painted brow, the savage black eyes, and the hooked nose of the Mohawk. Only Henry saw it, but with fierce joy-the tortures at Wyoming leaped up before him-he fired at the painted brow. The Mohawk uttered his death cry and fell back with a splash into the mud and water of the swamp. A half dozen bullets were instantly fired at the base of the smoke that came from Henry's rifle, but the youth and his comrades lay close and were unharmed. Shif'less Sol and Tom were quick enough to catch glimpses of brown forms, at which they fired, and the cries coming back told that they had hit.

"That's something," said Henry. "One or two Iroquois at least will not wear the scalp of white woman or child at their belts."

"Wish they'd try to rush us," said Shif'less Sol. "I never felt so full of fight in my life before."

"They may try it," said Henry. "I understand that at the big battle of the Oriskany, farther up in the North, the Iroquois would wait until a white man behind a tree would fire, then they would rush up and tomahawk him before he could reload."

"They don't know how fast we kin reload," said Long Jim, "an' they don't know that we've got these double-barreled pistols, either."

"No, they don't," said Henry, "and it's a great thing for us to have them. Suppose we spread out a little. So long as we keep them from getting a lodging on the solid earth we hold them at a great disadvantage."

Henry and Paul moved off a little toward the right, and the others toward the left. They still had good cover, as fallen timber was scattered all over the oasis, and they were quite sure that another attack would be made soon. It came in about fifteen minutes. The Iroquois suddenly fired a volley at the logs and brush, and when the five returned the fire, but with more deadly effect, they leaped forward in the mud and attempted to rush the oasis, tomahawk in hand.

But the five reloaded so quickly that they were able to send in a second volley before the foremost of the Iroquois could touch foot on solid earth. Then the double barreled pistols came into play. The bullets sent from short range drove back the savages, who were amazed at such a deadly and continued fire. Henry caught sight of a white face among these assailants, and he knew it to be that of Braxton Wyatt. Singularly enough he was not amazed to see it there. Wyatt, sinking deeper and deeper into savagery and cruelty, was just the one to lead the Iroquois in such a pursuit. He was a fit match for Walter Butler, the infamous son of the Indian leader, who was soon to prove himself worse than the worst of the savages, as Thayendanegea himself has written.

Henry drew a bead once on Braxton Wyatt-he had no scruples now about shooting him-but just as he was about to pull the trigger Wyatt darted behind a bush, and a Seneca instead received the bullet. He also saw the renegade, Blackstaffe, but he was not able to secure a shot at him, either. Nevertheless, the Iroquois attack was beaten back. It was a foregone conclusion that the result would be so, unless the force was in great numbers. It is likely, also, that the Iroquois at first had thought only a single man was with the fugitives, not knowing that the five had joined them later.

Two of the Iroquois were slain at the very edge of the solid ground, but their bodies fell back in the slime, and the others, retreating fast for their lives, could not carry them off. Paul, with a kind of fascinated horror, watched the dead painted bodies sink deeper. Then one was entirely gone. The hand of the other alone was left, and then it, too, was gone. But the five had held the island, and Carpenter was leading the fugitives on toward Fort Penn. They had not only held it, but they believed that they could continue to hold it against anything, and their hearts became exultant. Something, too, to balance against the long score, lay out there in the swamp, and all the five, bitter over Wyoming, were sorry that Braxton Wyatt was not among them.

The stillness came again. The sun did not break through the heavy gray sky, and the somber shadows brooded over "The Shades of Death." They heard again the splash of water animals, and a swimming snake passed on the murky surface. Then they heard the wolf's long cry, and the long cry of wolf replying.

"More Iroquois coming," said Shif'less Sol. "Well, we gave them a pretty warm how d'ye do, an' with our rifles and double-barreled pistols I'm thinkin' that we kin do it ag'in."

"We can, except in one case," said Henry, "if the new party brings their numbers up to fifty or sixty, and they wait for night, they can surround us in the darkness. Perhaps it would be better for us to slip away when twilight comes. Carpenter and the train have a long lead now."

"Yes," said Shif'less Sol, "Now, what in tarnation is that?"

"A white flag," said Paul. A piece of cloth that had once been white had been hoisted on the barrel of a rifle at a point about sixty yards away.

"They want a talk with us," said Henry.

"If it's Braxton Wyatt," said Long Jim, "I'd like to take a shot at him, talk or no talk, an' ef I missed, then take another."

"We'll see what they have to say," said Henry, and he called aloud: "What do you want with us?"

"To talk with you," replied a clear, full voice, not that of Braxton Wyatt.

"Very well," replied Henry, "show yourself and we will not fire upon you."

A tall figure was upraised upon a grassy hummock, and the hands were held aloft in sign of peace. It was a splendid figure, at least six feet four inches in height. At that moment some rays of the setting sun broke through the gray clouds and shone full upon it, lighting up the defiant scalp lock interwoven with the brilliant red feather, the eagle face with the curved Roman beak, and the mighty shoulders and chest of red bronze. It was a genuine king of the wilderness, none other than the mighty Timmendiquas himself, the great White Lightning of the Wyandots.

"Ware," he said, "I would speak with you. Let us talk as one chief to another."

The five were amazed. Timmendiquas there! They were quite sure that he had come up with the second force, and he was certain to prove a far more formidable leader than either Braxton Wyatt or Moses Blackstaffe. But his demand to speak with Henry Ware might mean something.

"Are you going to answer him?" said Shif'less Sol.

"Of course," replied Henry.

"The others, especially Wyatt and Blackstaffe, might shoot."

"Not while Timmendiquas holds the flag of truce; they would not dare."

Henry stood up, raising himself to his full height. The same ruddy sunlight piercing the somber gray of the clouds fell upon another splendid figure, a boy only in years, but far beyond the average height of man, his hair yellow, his eyes a deep, clear blue, his body clothed in buckskin, and his whole attitude that of one without fear. The two, the white and the red, kings of their kind, confronted each other across the marsh.

"What do you wish with me, Timmendiquas?" asked Henry. In the presence of the great Wyandot chief the feeling of hate and revenge that had held his heart vanished. He knew that Paul and Shif'less Sol would have sunk under the ruthless tomahawk of Queen Esther, if it had not been for White Lightning. He himself had owed him his life on another and more distant occasion, and he was not ungrateful. So there was warmth in his tone when he spoke.

"Let us meet at the edge of the solid ground," said Timmendiquas, "I have things to say that are important and that you will be glad to hear."

Henry walked without hesitation to the edge of the swamp, and the young chief, coming forward, met him. Henry held out his hand in white fashion, and the young chief took it. There was no sound either from the swamp or from those who lay behind the logs on the island, but some of the eyes of those hidden in the swamps watched both with burning hatred.

"I wish to tell you, Ware," said Timmendiquas, speaking with the dignity becoming a great chief, "that it was not I who led the pursuit of the white men's women and children. I, and the Wyandots who came with me, fought as best we could in the great battle, and I will slay my enemies when I can. We are warriors, and we are ready to face each other in battle, but we do not seek to kill the squaw in the tepee or the papoose in its birch-bark cradle."

The face of the great chief seemed stirred by some deep emotion, which impressed Henry all the more because the countenance of Timmendiquas was usually a mask.

"I believe that you tell the truth," said Henry gravely.

"I and my Wyandots," continued the chief, "followed a trail through the woods. We found that others, Senecas and Mohawks, led by Wyatt and Blackstaffe, who are of your race, had gone before, and when we came up there had just been a battle. The Mohawks and Senecas had been driven back. It was then we learned that the trail was made by women and little children, save you and your comrades who stayed to fight and protect them."

"You speak true words, Timmendiquas," said Henry.

"The Wyandots have remained in the East to fight men, not to kill squaws and papooses," continued Timmendiquas. "So I say to you, go on with those who flee across the mountains. Our warriors shall not pursue you any longer. We will turn back to the valley from which we come, and those of your race, Blackstaffe and Wyatt, shall go with us."

The great chief spoke quietly, but there was an edge to his tone that told that every word was meant. Henry felt a glow of admiration. The true greatness of Timmendiquas spoke.

"And the Iroquois?" he said, "will they go back with you?"

"They will. They have killed too much. Today all the white people in the valley are killed or driven away. Many scalps have been taken, those of women and children, too, and men have died at the stake. I have felt shame for their deeds, Ware, and it will bring punishment upon my brethren, the Iroquois. It will make so great a noise in the world that many soldiers will come, and the villages of the Iroquois will cease to be."

"I think it is so, Timmendiquas," said Henry. "But you will be far away then in your own land."

The chief drew himself up a little.

"I shall remain with the Iroquois," he said. "I have promised to help them, and I must do so."

"I can't blame you for that," said Henry, "but I am glad that you do not seek the scalps of women and children. We are at once enemies and friends, Timmendiquas."

White Lightning bowed gravely. He and Henry touched hands again, and each withdrew, the chief into the morass, while Henry walked back toward his comrades, holding himself erect, as if no enemy were near.

The four rose up to greet him. They had heard part of what was said, and Henry quickly told them the rest.

"He's shorely a great chief," said Shif'less Sol. "He'll keep his word, too. Them people on ahead ain't got anything more to fear from pursuit."

"He's a statesman, too," said Henry. "He sees what damage the deeds of Wyoming Valley will do to those who have done them. He thinks our people will now send a great army against the Iroquois, and I think so, too."

"No nation can stand a thing like that," said Paul, "and I didn't dream it could happen."

They now left the oasis, and went swiftly along the trail left by the fugitives. All of them had confidence in the word of Timmendiquas. There was a remote chance that some other band had entered the swamp at a different point, but it was remote, indeed, and it did not trouble them much.

Night was now over the great swamp. The sun no longer came through the gray clouds, but here and there were little flashes of flame made by fireflies. Had not the trail been so broad and deep it could easily have been lost, but, being what it was, the skilled eyes of the frontiersmen followed it without trouble.

"Some uv 'em are gittin' pow'ful tired," said Tom Ross, looking at the tracks in the mud. Then he suddenly added: "Here's whar one's quit forever."

A shallow grave, not an hour old, had been made under some bushes, and its length indicated that a woman lay there. They passed it by in silence. Henry now appreciated more fully than ever the mercy of Timmendiquas. The five and Carpenter could not possibly have protected the miserable fugitives against the great chief, with fifty Wyandots and Iroquois at his back. Timmendiquas knew this, and he had done what none of the Indians or white allies around him would have done.

In another hour they saw a man standing among some vines, but watchful, and with his rifle in the hollow of his arm. It was Carpenter, a man whose task was not less than that of the five. They were in the thick of it and could see what was done, but he had to lead on and wait. He counted the dusk figures as they approached him, one, two, three, four, five, and perhaps no man ever felt greater relief. He advanced toward them and said huskily:

"There was no fight! They did not attack!"

"There was a fight," said Henry, "and we beat them back; then a second and a larger force came up, but it was composed chiefly of Wyandots, led by their great chief, Timmendiquas. He came forward and said that they would not pursue women and children, and that we could go in safety."

Carpenter looked incredulous.

"It is true," said Henry, "every word of it."

"It is more than Brant would have done," said Carpenter, "and it saves us, with your help."

"You were first, and the first credit is yours, Mr. Carpenter," said Henry sincerely.

They did not tell the women and children of the fight at the oasis, but they spread the news that there would be no more pursuit, and many drooping spirits revived. They spent another day in the Great Dismal

Swamp, where more lives were lost. On the day after their emergence from the marsh, Henry and his comrades killed two deer, which furnished greatly needed food, and on the day after that, excepting those who had died by the way, they reached Fort Penn, where they were received into shelter and safety.

The night before the fugitives reached Fort Penn, the Iroquois began the celebration of the Thanksgiving Dance for their great victory and the many scalps taken at Wyoming. They could not recall another time when they had secured so many of these hideous trophies, and they were drunk with the joy of victory. Many of the Tories, some in their own clothes, and some painted and dressed like Indians, took part in it.

According to their ancient and honored custom they held a grand council to prepare for it. All the leading chiefs were present, Sangerachte, Hiokatoo, and the others. Braxton Wyatt, Blackstaffe, and other white men were admitted. After their deliberations a great fire was built in the center of the camp, the squaws who had followed the army feeding it with brushwood until it leaped and roared and formed a great red pyramid. Then the chiefs sat down in a solemn circle at some distance, and waited.

Presently the sound of a loud chant was heard, and from the farthest point of the camp emerged a long line of warriors, hundreds and hundreds of them, all painted in red and black with horrible designs. They were naked except the breechcloth and moccasins, and everyone waved aloft a tomahawk as he sang.

Still singing and brandishing the tomahawks, which gleamed in the red light, the long procession entered the open space, and danced and wheeled about the great fire, the flames casting a lurid light upon faces hideous with paint or the intoxication of triumph. The glare of their black eyes was like those of Eastern eaters of hasheesh or opium, and they bounded to and fro as if their muscles were springs of steel. They sang:

> We have met the Bostonians [*] in battle,
> We slew them with our rifles and tomahawks.
> Few there are who escaped our warriors.
> Ever-victorious is the League of the Ho-de-no-sau-nee.
> [* Note: All the Americans were often called Bostonians by
> the Indians as late as the Revolutionary War.]
> Mighty has been our taking of scalps,
> They will fill all the lodges of the Iroquois.
> We have burned the houses of the Bostonians.
> Ever-victorious is the League of the Ho-de-no-sau-nee.
> The wolf will prowl in their corn-fields,
> The grass will grow where their blood has soaked;
> Their bones will lie for the buzzard to pick.
> Ever-victorious is the League of the Ho-de-no-sau-nee.
> We came upon them by river and forest;

As we smote Wyoming we will smite the others,
We will drive the Bostonians back to the sea.
Ever-victorious is the League of the Ho-de-no-sau-nee.

The monotonous chant with the refrain, "Ever-victorious is the League of the Ho-de-no-sau-nee," went on for many verses. Meanwhile the old squaws never ceased to feed the bonfire, and the flames roared, casting a deeper and more vivid light over the distorted faces of the dancers and those of the chiefs, who sat gravely beyond.

Higher and higher leaped the warriors. They seemed unconscious of fatigue, and the glare in their eyes became that of maniacs. Their whole souls were possessed by the orgy. Beads of sweat, not of exhaustion, but of emotional excitement, appeared upon their faces and naked bodies, and the red and black paint streaked together horribly.

For a long time this went on, and then the warriors ceased suddenly to sing, although they continued their dance. A moment later a cry which thrilled every nerve came from a far point in the dark background. It was the scalp yell, the most terrible of all Indian cries, long, high-pitched, and quavering, having in it something of the barking howl of the wolf and the fiendish shriek of a murderous maniac. The warriors instantly took it up, and gave it back in a gigantic chorus.

A ghastly figure bounded into the circle of the firelight. It was that of a woman, middle-aged, tall and powerful, naked to the waist, her body covered with red and black paint, her long black hair hanging in a loose cloud down her back. She held a fresh scalp, taken from a white head, aloft in either band. It was Catharine Montour, and it was she who had first emitted the scalp yell. After her came more warriors, all bearing scalps. The scalp yell was supposed to be uttered for every scalp taken, and, as they had taken more than three hundred, it did not cease for hours, penetrating every part of the forest. All the time Catharine Montour led the dance. None bounded higher than she. None grimaced more horribly.

While they danced, six men, with their hands tied behind them and black caps on their heads, were brought forth and paraded around amid hoots and yells and brandishing of tomahawks in their faces. They were the surviving prisoners, and the black caps meant that they were to be killed and scalped on the morrow. Stupefied by all through which they had gone, they were scarcely conscious now.

Midnight came. The Iroquois still danced and sang, and the calm stars looked down upon the savage and awful scene. Now the dancers began to weary. Many dropped unconscious, and the others danced about them where they lay. After a while all ceased. Then the chiefs brought forth a white dog, which Hiokatoo killed and threw on the embers of the fire. When it was thoroughly roasted, the chiefs cut it in pieces and ate it. Thus closed the Festival of Thanksgiving for the victory of Wyoming.

CHAPTER XIII. A FOREST PAGE

When the survivors of the band of Wyoming fugitives that the five had helped were behind the walls of Fort Penn, securing the food and rest they needed so greatly, Henry Ware and his comrades felt themselves relieved of a great responsibility. They were also aware how much they owed to Timmendiquas, because few of the Indians and renegades would have been so forbearing. Thayendanegea seemed to them inferior to the great Wyandot. Often when Brant could prevent the torture of the prisoners and the slaughter of women and children, he did not do it. The five could never forget these things in after life, when Brant was glorified as a great warrior and leader. Their minds always turned to Timmendiquas as the highest and finest of Indian types.

While they were at Fort Penn two other parties came, in a fearful state of exhaustion, and also having paid the usual toll of death on the way. Other groups reached the Moravian towns, where they were received with all kindness by the German settlers. The five were able to give some help to several of these parties, but the beautiful Wyoming Valley lay utterly in ruins. The ruthless fury of the savages and of many of the Tories, Canadians, and Englishmen, can scarcely be told. Everything was slaughtered or burned. As a habitation of human beings or of anything pertaining to human beings, the valley for a time ceased to be. An entire population was either annihilated or driven out, and finally Butler's army, finding that nothing more was left to be destroyed, gathered in its war parties and marched northward with a vast store of spoils, in which scalps were conspicuous. When they repassed Tioga Point, Timmendiquas and his Wyandots were still with them. Thayendanegea was also with them here, and so was Walter Butler, who was destined shortly to make a reputation equaling that of his father, "Indian" Butler. Nor had the terrible Queen Esther ever left them. She marched at the head of the army, singing, horrid chants of victory, and swinging the great war tomahawk, which did not often leave her hand.

The whole force was re-embarked upon the Susquehanna, and it was still full of the impulse of savage triumph. Wild Indian songs floated along the stream or through the meadows, which were quiet now. They advanced at their ease, knowing that there was nobody to attack them, but they were watched by five woodsmen, two of whom were boys. Meanwhile the story of Wyoming, to an extent that neither Indians nor woodsmen themselves suspected, was spreading from town to town in the East, to invade thence the whole civilized world, and to stir up an indignation and horror that would make the name Wyoming long memorable. Wyoming had been a victory for the flag under which the invaders fought, but it sadly tarnished the cause of that flag, and the consequences were to be seen soon.

Henry Ware, Paul Cotter, Sol Hyde, Tom Ross, and Jim Hart were thinking little of distant consequences, but they were eager for the present punishment of these men who had committed so much cruelty. From the bushes they could easily follow the canoes, and could recognize some of their occupants. In one of the rear boats sat Braxton Wyatt and a young man whom they knew to be Walter Butler, a pallid young man, animated by the most savage ferocity against the patriots. He and Wyatt seemed to be on the best of terms, and faint echoes of their laughter came to the five who were watching among the bushes on the river bank. Certainly Braxton Wyatt and he were a pair well met.

"Henry," said Shif'less Sol longingly, "I think I could jest about reach Braxton Wyatt with a bullet from here. I ain't over fond o' shootin' from ambush, but I done got over all scruples so fur ez he's concerned. Jest one bullet, one little bullet, Henry, an' ef I miss I won't ask fur a second chance."

"No, Sol, it won't do," said Henry. "They'd get off to hunt us. The whole fleet would be stopped, and we want 'em to go on as fast as possible."

"I s'pose you're right, Henry," said the shiftless one sadly, "but I'd jest like to try it once. I'd give a month's good huntin' for that single trial."

After watching the British-Indian fleet passing up the river, they turned back to the site of the Wyoming fort and the houses near it. Here everything had been destroyed. It was about dusk when they approached the battlefield, and they heard a dreadful howling, chiefly that of wolves.

"I think we'd better turn away," said Henry. "We couldn't do anything with so many."

They agreed with him, and, going back, followed the Indians up the Susquehanna. A light rain fell that night, but they slept under a little shed, once attached to a house which had been destroyed by fire. In some way the shed had escaped the flames, and it now came into timely use. The five, cunning in forest practice, drew up brush on the sides, and half-burned timber also, and, spreading their blankets on ashes which had not long been cold, lay well sheltered from the drizzling rain, although they did not sleep for a long time.

It was the hottest period of the year in America, but the night had come on cool, and the rain made it cooler. The five, profiting by experience, often carried with them two light blankets instead of one heavy one. With one blanket beneath the body they could keep warmer in case the weather was cold.

Now they lay in a row against the standing wall of the old outhouse, protected by a six- or seven-foot slant of board roof. They had eaten of a deer that they had shot in the morning, and they had a sense of comfort and rest that none of them had known before in many days. Henry's feelings were much like those that he had experienced when he lay in the bushes in the little canoe, wrapped up from the storm and hidden from the Iroquois. But here there was an important increase of pleasure, the pattering of the rain on the board roof, a pleasant, soothing sound to which millions of boys, many of them afterwards great men, have listened in America.

It grew very dark about them, and the pleasant patter, almost musical in its rhythm, kept up. Not much wind was blowing, and it, too, was melodious. Henry lay with his head on a little heap of ashes, which was covered by his under blanket, and, for the first time since he had brought the warning to Wyoming, he was free from all feeling of danger. The picture itself of the battle, the defeat, the massacre, the torture, and of the savage Queen Esther cleaving the heads of the captives, was at times as vivid as ever, and perhaps would always return now and then in its original true colors, but the periods between, when youth, hope, and strength had their way, grew longer and longer.

Now Henry's eyelids sank lower and lower. Physical comfort and the presence of his comrades caused a deep satisfaction that permeated his whole being. The light wind mingled pleasantly with the soft summer rain. The sound of the two grew strangely melodious, almost piercingly sweet, and then it seemed to be human. They sang together, the wind and rain, among the leaves, and the note that reached his heart, rather than his ear, thrilled him with courage and hope. Once more the invisible voice that had upborne him in the great valley of the Ohio told him, even here in the ruined valley of Wyoming, that what was lost would be regained. The chords ended, and the echoes, amazingly clear, floated far away in the darkness and rain. Henry roused himself, and came from the imaginative borderland. He stirred a little, and said in a quiet voice to Shif'less Sol:

"Did you hear anything, Sol?"

"Nothin' but the wind an' the rain."

Henry knew that such would be the answer.

"I guess you didn't hear anything either, Henry," continued the shiftless one, "'cause it looked to me that you wuz 'bout ez near sleep ez a feller could be without bein' ackshooally so."

"I was drifting away," said Henry.

He was beginning to realize that he had a great power, or rather gift. Paul was the sensitive, imaginative boy, seeing everything in brilliant colors, a great builder of castles, not all of air, but Henry's gift went deeper. It was the power to evoke the actual living picture of the event that bad not yet occurred, something akin in its nature to prophecy, based perhaps upon the wonderful power of observation, inherited doubtless, from countless primitive ancestors. The finest product of the wilderness, he saw in that wilderness many things that others did not see, and unconsciously he drew his conclusions from superior knowledge.

The song had ceased a full ten minutes, and then came another note, a howl almost plaintive, but, nevertheless, weird and full of ferocity. All knew it at once. They had heard the cry of wolves too often in their lives, but this had an uncommon note like the yell of the Indian in victory. Again the cry arose, nearer, haunting, and powerful. The five, used to the darkness, could see one another's faces, and the look that all gave was the same, full of understanding and repulsion.

"It has been a great day for the wolf in this valley," whispered Paul, "and striking our trail they think they are going to find what they have been finding in such plenty before."

"Yes," nodded Henry, "but do you remember that time when in the house we took the place of the man, his wife and children, just before the Indians came?"

"Yes," said Paul.

"We'll treat them wolves the same way," said Shif'less Sol.

"I'm glad of the chance," said Long Jim.

"Me, too," said Tom Ross.

The five rose up to sitting positions against the board wall, and everyone held across his knees a long, slender barreled rifle, with the muzzle pointing toward the forest. All accomplished marksmen, it would only be a matter of a moment for the stock to leap to the shoulder, the eye to glance down the barrel, the finger to pull the trigger, and the unerring bullet to leap forth.

"Henry, you give the word as usual," said Shif'less Sol.

Henry nodded.

Presently in the darkness they heard the pattering of light feet, and they saw many gleaming eyes draw near. There must have been at least thirty of the wolves, and the five figures that they saw reclining, silent and motionless, against the unburned portion of the house might well have been those of the dead and scalped, whom they had found in such numbers everywhere. They drew near in a semicircular group, its concave front extended toward the fire, the greatest wolves at the center. Despite many feastings, the wolves were hungry again. Nothing had opposed them before, but caution was instinctive. The big gray leaders did not mind the night or the wind or the rain, which they had known all their lives, and which they counted as nothing, but they always had involuntary suspicion of human figures, whether living or not, and they approached slowly, wrinkling back their noses and sniffing the wind which blew from them instead of the five figures. But their confidence increased as they advanced. They had found many such burned houses as this, but they had found nothing among the ruins except what they wished.

The big leaders advanced more boldly, glaring straight at the human figures, a slight froth on their lips, the lips themselves curling back farther from the strong white teeth. The outer ends of the concave semicircle also drew in. The whole pack was about to spring upon its unresisting prey, and it is, no doubt, true that many a wolfish pulse beat a little higher in anticipation. With a suddenness as startling figures raised themselves, five long, dark tubes leaped to their shoulders, and with a suddenness that was yet more terrifying, a gush of flame shot from five muzzles. Five of the wolves-and they were the biggest and the boldest, the leaders-fell dead upon the ashes of the charred timbers, and the others, howling their terror to the dark, skies, fled deep into the forest.

Henry strode over and pushed the body of the largest wolf with his foot.

"I suppose we only gratified a kind of sentiment in shooting those wolves," he said, "but I for one am glad we did it."

"So am I," said Paul.

"Me, too," said the other three together.

They went back to their positions near the wall, and one by one fell asleep. No more wolves howled that night anywhere near them.

When the five awakened the next morning the rain had ceased, and a splendid sun was tinting a blue sky with gold. Jim Hart built a fire among the blackened logs, and cooked venison. They had also brought from Fort Penn a little coffee, which Long Jim carried with a small coffee pot in his camp kit, and everyone had a small tin cup. He made coffee for them, an uncommon wilderness luxury, in which they could rarely indulge, and they were heartened and strengthened by it.

Then they went again up the valley, as beautiful as ever, with its silver river in the center, and its green mountain walls on either side. But the beauty was for the eye only. It did not reach the hearts of those who had seen it before. All of the five loved the wilderness, but they felt now how tragic silence and desolation could be where human life and all the daily ways of human life had been.

It was mid-summer, but the wilderness was already reclaiming its own. The game knew that man was gone, and it had come back into the valley. Deer ate what had grown in the fields and gardens, and the wolves were everywhere. The whole black tragedy was written for miles. They were never out of sight of some trace of it, and their anger grew again as they advanced in the blackened path of the victorious Indians.

It was their purpose now to hang on the Indian flank as scouts and skirmishers, until an American army was formed for a campaign against the Iroquois, which they were sure must be conducted sooner or later. Meanwhile they could be of great aid, gathering news of the Indian plans, and, when that army of which they dreamed should finally march, they could help it most of all by warning it of ambush, the Indian's deadliest weapon.

Everyone of the five had already perceived a fact which was manifest in all wars with the Indians along the whole border from North to South, as it steadily shifted farther West. The practical hunter and scout was always more than a match for the Indian, man for man, but, when the raw levies of settlers were hastily gathered to stem invasion, they were invariably at a great disadvantage. They were likely to be caught in ambush by overwhelming numbers, and to be cut down, as had just happened at Wyoming. The same fate might attend an invasion of the Iroquois country, even by a large army of regular troops, and Henry and his comrades resolved upon doing their utmost to prevent it. An army needed eyes, and it could have none better than those five pairs. So they went swiftly up the valley and northward and eastward, into the country of the Iroquois. They had a plan of approaching the upper Mohawk village of Canajoharie, where one account says that Thayendanegea was born, although another credits his birthplace to the upper banks of the Ohio.

They turned now from the valley to the deep woods. The trail showed that the great Indian force, after disembarking again, split into large parties, everyone loaded with spoil and bound for its home village. The five noted several of the trails, but one of them consumed the whole attention of Silent Tom Ross.

He saw in the soft soil near a creek bank the footsteps of about eight Indians, and, mingled with them, other footsteps, which he took to be those of a white woman and of several children, captives, as even a tyro would infer. The soul of Tom, the good, honest, and inarticulate frontiersman, stirred within him. A white woman and her children being carried off to savagery, to be lost forevermore to their kind! Tom, still inarticulate, felt his heart pierced with sadness at the tale that the tracks in the soft mud told so plainly. But despair was not the only emotion in his heart. The silent and brave man meant to act.

"Henry," he said, "see these tracks here in the soft spot by the creek."

The young leader read the forest page, and it told him exactly the same tale that it had told Tom Ross.

"About a day old, I think," he said.

"Just about," said Tom; "an' I reckon, Henry, you know what's in my mind."

"I think I do," said Henry, "and we ought to overtake them by to-morrow night. You tell the others, Tom."

Tom informed Shif'less Sol, Paul, and Long Jim in a few words, receiving from everyone a glad assent, and then the five followed fast on the trail. They knew that the Indians could not go very fast, as their speed must be that of the slowest, namely, that of the children, and it seemed likely that Henry's prediction of overtaking them on the following night would come true.

It was an easy trail. Here and there were tiny fragments of cloth, caught by a bush from the dress of a captive. In one place they saw a fragment of a child's shoe that had been dropped off and abandoned. Paul picked up the worn piece of leather and examined it.

"I think it was worn by a girl," he said, "and, judging from its size, she could not have been more than eight years old. Think of a child like that being made to walk five or six hundred miles through these woods!"

"Younger ones still have had to do it," said Shif'less Sol gravely, "an' them that couldn't-well, the tomahawk."

The trail was leading them toward the Seneca country, and they had no doubt that the Indians were Senecas, who had been more numerous than any others of the Six Nations at the Wyoming battle. They came that afternoon to a camp fire beside which the warriors and captives had slept the night before.

"They ate bar meat an' wild turkey," said Long Jim, looking at some bones on the ground.

"An' here," said Tom Ross, "on this pile uv bushes is whar the women an' children slept, an' on the other side uv the fire is whar the warriors lay anywhars. You can still see how the bodies uv some uv 'cm crushed down the grass an' little bushes."

"An' I'm thinkin'," said Shif'less Sol, as he looked at the trail that led away from the camp fire, "that some o' them little ones wuz gittin' pow'ful tired. Look how these here little trails are wobblin' about."

"Hope we kin come up afore the Injuns begin to draw thar tomahawks," said Tom Ross.

The others were silent, but they knew the dreadful significance of Tom's remark, and Henry glanced at them all, one by one.

"It's the greatest danger to be feared," he said, "and we must overtake them in the night when they are not suspecting. If we attack by day they will tomahawk the captives the very first thing."

"Shorely,', said the shiftless one.

"Then," said Henry, "we don't need to hurry. We'll go on until about midnight, and then sleep until sunrise."

They continued at a fair pace along a trail that frontiersmen far less skillful than they could have followed. But a silent dread was in the heart of every one of them. As they saw the path of the small feet staggering more and more they feared to behold some terrible object beside the path.

"The trail of the littlest child is gone," suddenly announced Paul.

"Yes," said Henry, "but the mother has picked it up and is carrying it. See how her trail has suddenly grown more uneven."

"Poor woman," said Paul. "Henry, we're just bound to overtake that band."

"We'll do it," said Henry.

At the appointed time they sank down among the thickest bushes that they could find, and slept until the first upshot of dawn. Then they resumed the trail, haunted always by that fear of finding something terrible beside it. But it was a trail that continually grew slower. The Indians themselves were tired, or, feeling safe from pursuit, saw no need of hurry. By and by the trail of the smallest child reappeared.

"It feels a lot better now," said Tom Ross. "So do I."

They came to another camp fire, at which the ashes were not yet cold. Feathers were scattered about, indicating that the Indians had taken time for a little side hunt, and had shot some birds.

"They can't be more than two or three hours ahead," said Henry, "and we'll have to go on now very cautiously."

They were in a country of high hills, well covered with forests, a region suited to an ambush, which they feared but little on their own account; but, for the sake of extreme caution, they now advanced slowly. The afternoon was long and warm, but an hour before sunset they looked over a hill into a glade, and saw the warriors making camp for the night.

The sight they beheld made the pulses of the five throb heavily. The Indians had already built their fire, and two of them were cooking venison upon it. Others were lying on the grass, apparently resting, but a little to one side sat a woman, still young and of large, strong figure, though now apparently in the last stages of exhaustion, with her feet showing through the fragments of shoes that she wore. Her head was bare, and her dress was in strips. Four children lay beside her' the youngest two with their heads in her lap. The other two, who might be eleven and thirteen each, had pillowed their heads on their arms, and lay in the dull apathy that comes from the finish of both strength and hope. The woman's face was pitiful. She had more to fear than the children, and she knew it. She was so worn that the skin hung loosely on her face, and her eyes showed despair only. The sad spectacle was almost more than Paul could stand.

"I don't like to shoot from ambush," he said, "but we could cut down half of those warriors at our firs fire and rush in on the rest."

"And those we didn't cut down at our first volley would tomahawk the woman and children in an instant," replied Henry. "We agreed, you know, that it would be sure to happen. We can't do anything until night comes, and then we've got to be mighty cautious."

Paul could not dispute the truth of his words, and they withdrew carefully to the crest of a hill, where they lay in the undergrowth, watching the Indians complete their fire and their preparations for the night. It was evident to Henry that they considered themselves perfectly safe. Certainly they had every reason for thinking so. It was not likely that white enemies were within a hundred miles of them, and, if so, it could only be a wandering hunter or two, who would flee from this fierce band of Senecas who bad taken revenge for the great losses that they' had suffered the year before at the Oriskany.

They kept very little watch and built only a small fire, just enough for broiling deer meat which they carried. They drank at a little spring which ran from under a ledge near them, and gave portions of the meat to the woman and children. After the woman had eaten, they bound her hands, and she lay back on the grass, about twenty feet from the camp fire. Two children lay on either side of her, and they were soon sound asleep. The warriors, as Indians will do when they are free from danger and care, talked a good deal, and showed all the signs of having what was to them a luxurious time. They ate plentifully, lolled on the grass, and looked at some hideous trophies, the scalps that they carried at their belts. The woman could not keep from seeing these, too, but her face did not change from its stony aspect of despair. Then the light of the fire went out, the sun sank behind the mountains, and the five could no longer see the little group of captives and captors.

They still waited, although eagerness and impatience were tugging at the hearts of every one of them. But they must give the Indians time to fall asleep if they would secure rescue, and not merely revenge. They remained in the bushes, saying but little and eating of venison that they carried in their knapsacks.

They let a full three hours pass, and the night remained dark, but with a faint moon showing. Then they descended slowly into the valley, approaching by cautious degrees the spot where they knew the Indian camp lay. This work required at least three quarters of an hour, and they reached a point where they could see the embers of the fire and the dark figures lying about it. The Indians, their suspicions lulled, had put out no sentinels, and all were asleep. But the five knew that, at the first shot, they would be as wide awake as if they had never slept, and as formidable as tigers. Their problem seemed as great as ever. So they lay in the bushes and held a whispered conference.

"It's this," said Henry. "We want to save the woman and the children from the tomahawks, and to do so we must get them out of range of the blade before the battle begins." "How?" said Tom Ross.

"I've got to slip up, release the woman, arm her, tell her to run for the woods with the children, and then you four must do the most of the rest."

"Do you think you can do it, Henry?" asked Shif'less Sol.

"I can, as I will soon show you. I'm going to steal forward to the woman, but the moment you four hear an alarm open with your rifles and pistols. You can come a little nearer without being heard."

All of them moved up close to the Indian camp, and lay hidden in the last fringe of bushes except Henry. He lay almost flat upon the ground, carrying his rifle parallel with his side, and in his right hand. He was undertaking one of the severest and most dangerous tests known to a frontiersman. He meant to crawl into the very midst of a camp of the Iroquois, composed of the most alert woodsmen in the world, men who would spring up at the slightest crackle in the brush. Woodmen who, warned by some sixth sense, would awaken at the mere fact of a strange presence.

The four who remained behind in the bushes could not keep their hearts from beating louder and faster. They knew the tremendous risk undertaken by their comrade, but there was not one of them who would have shirked it, had not all yielded it to the one whom they knew to be the best fitted for the task.

Henry crept forward silently, bringing to his aid all the years of skill that he had acquired in his life in the wilds. His body was like that of a serpent, going forward, coil by coil. He was near enough now to see the embers of the fire not yet quite dead, the dark figures scattered about it, sleeping upon the grass with the long ease of custom, and then the outline of the woman apart from the others with the children about her. Henry now lay entirely flat, and his motions were genuinely those of a serpent. It was by a sort of contraction and relaxation of the body that he moved himself, and his progress was absolutely soundless.

The object of his advance was the woman. He saw by the faint light of the moon that she was not yet asleep. Her face, worn and weather beaten, was upturned to the skies, and the stony look of despair seemed to have settled there forever. She lay upon some pine boughs, and her hands were tied behind her for the night with deerskin.

Henry contorted himself on, inch by inch, for all the world like a great snake. Now he passed the sleeping Senecas, hideous with war paint, and came closer to the woman. She was not paying attention to anything about her, but was merely looking up at the pale, cold stars, as if everything in the world had ceased for her.

Henry crept a little nearer. He made a slight noise, as of a lizard running through the grass, but the woman took no notice. He crept closer, and there he lay flat upon the grass within six feet of her, his figure merely a slightly darker blur against the dark blur of the earth. Then, trusting to the woman's courage and strength of mind, he emitted a hiss very soft and low, like the warning of a serpent, half in fear and half in anger.

The woman moved a little, and looked toward the point from which the sound had come. It might have been the formidable hiss of a coiling rattlesnake that she heard, but she felt no fear. She was too much stunned, too near exhaustion to be alarmed by anything, and she did not look a second time. She merely settled back on the pine boughs, and again looked dully up at the pale, cold stars that cared so little for her or hers.

Henry crept another yard nearer, and then he uttered that low noise, sibilant and warning, which the woman, the product of the border, knew to be made by a human being. She raised herself a little, although it was difficult with her bound hands to sit upright, and saw a dark shadow approaching her. That dark shadow she knew to be the figure of a man. An Indian would not be approaching in such a manner, and she looked again, startled into a sudden acute attention, and into a belief that the incredible, the impossible, was about to happen. A voice came from the figure, and its quality was that of the white voice, not the red.

"Do not move," said that incredible voice out of the unknown. "I have come for your rescue, and others who have come for the same purpose are near. Turn on one side, and I will cut the bonds that hold your arms."

The voice, the white voice, was like the touch of fire to Mary Newton. A sudden fierce desire for life and for the lives of her four children awoke within her just when hope had gone the call to life came. She had never heard before a voice so full of cheer and encouragement. It penetrated her whole being. Exhaustion and despair fled away.

"Turn a little on your side," said the voice.

She turned obediently, and then felt the sharp edge of cold steel as it swept between her wrists and cut the thongs that held them together. Her arms fell apart, and strength permeated every vein of her being.

"We shall attack in a few moments," said the voice, "but at the first shots the Senecas will try to tomahawk you and your children. Hold out your hands."

She held out both hands obediently. The handle of a tomahawk was pressed into one, and the muzzle of a double-barreled pistol into the other. Strength flowed down each hand into her body.

"If the time comes, use them; you are strong, and you know how," said the voice. Then she saw the dark figure creeping away.

CHAPTER XIV. THE PURSUIT ON THE RIVER

The story of the frontier is filled with heroines, from the far days of Hannah Dustin down to the present, and Mary Newton, whom the unknown figure in the dark had just aroused, is one of them. It had seemed to her that God himself had deserted her, but at the last moment he had sent some one. She did not doubt, she could not doubt, because the bonds had been severed, and there she lay with a deadly weapon in either hand. The friendly stranger who had come so silently was gone as he had come, but she was not helpless now. Like many another frontier woman, she was naturally lithe and powerful, and, stirred by a great hope, all her strength had returned for the present.

Nobody who lives in the wilderness can wholly escape superstition, and Mary Newton began to believe that some supernatural creature had intervened in her behalf. She raised herself just a little on one elbow and surveyed the surrounding thicket. She saw only the dead embers of the fire, and the dark forms of the Indians lying upon the bare ground. Had it not been for the knife and pistol in her hand, she could have believed that the voice was only a dream.

There was a slight rustling in the thicket, and a Seneca rose quickly to his knees, grasping his rifle in both hands. The woman's fingers clutched the knife and pistol more tightly, and her whole gaunt figure trembled. The Seneca listened only a moment. Then he gave a sharp cry, and all the other warriors sprang up. But three of them rose only to fall again, as the rifles cracked in the bushes, while two others staggered from wounds.

The triumphant shout of the frontiersmen came from the thicket, and then they rushed upon the camp. Quick as a flash two of the Senecas started toward the woman and children with their tomahawks, but Mary Newton was ready. Her heart had leaped at the shots when the Senecas fell, and she kept her courage. Now she sprang to her full height, and, with the children screaming at her feet, fired one barrel of the pistol directly into the face of the first warrior, and served the second in the same way with the other barrel when he was less than four feet away. Then, tomahawk in hand, she rushed forward. In judging Mary Newton, one must consider time and place.

But happily there was no need for her to use her tomahawk. As the five rushed in, four of them emptied their double-barreled pistols, while Henry swung his clubbed rifle with terrible effect. It was too much for the Senecas. The apparition of the armed woman, whom they had left bound, and the deadly fire from the five figures that sprang upon them, was like a blow from the hand of Aieroski. The unhurt and wounded fled deep into the forest, leaving their dead behind. Mary Newton, her great deed done, collapsed from emotion and weakness. The screams of the children sank in a few moments to frightened whimpers. But the oldest, when they saw the white faces, knew that rescue had come.

Paul brought water from the brook in his cap, and Mary Newton was revived; Jim was reassuring the children, and the other three were in the thickets, watching lest the surviving Senecas return for attack.

"I don't know who you are, but I think the good God himself must have sent you to our rescue," said Mary Newton reverently.

"We don't know," said Paul, "but we are doing the best we can. Do you think you can walk now?"

"Away from the savages? Yes!" she said passionately. She looked down at the dead figures of the Senecas, and she did not feel a single trace of pity for them. Again it is necessary to consider time and place.

"Some of my strength came back while I was lying here," she said, "and much more of it when you drove away the Indians."

"Very well," said Henry, who had returned to the dead camp fire with his comrades, "we must start on the back trail at once. The surviving Senecas, joined by other Iroquois, will certainly pursue, and we need all the start that we can get."

Long Jim picked up one of the two younger children and flung him over his shoulder; Tom Ross did as much for the other, but the older two scorned help. They were full of admiration for the great woodsmen, mighty heroes who had suddenly appeared out of the air, as it were, and who had swept like a tornado over the Seneca band. It did not seem possible now that they, could be retaken.

But Mary Newton, with her strength and courage, had also recovered her forethought.

"Maybe it will not be better to go on the back trail," she said. "One of the Senecas told me to-day that six or seven miles farther on was a river flowing into the Susquehanna, and that they would cross this river on a boat now concealed among bushes on the bank. The crossing was at a sudden drop between high banks. Might not we go on, find the boat, and come back in it down the river and into the Susquehanna?"

"That sounds mighty close to wisdom to me," said Shif'less Sol. "Besides, it's likely to have the advantage o' throwin' the Iroquois off our track. They'll think, o' course, that we've gone straight back, an' we'll pass 'em ez we're going forward."

"It's certainly the best plan," said Henry, "and it's worth our while to try for that hidden boat of the Iroquois. Do you know the general direction?"

"Almost due north."

"Then we'll make a curve to the right, in order to avoid any Iroquois who may be returning to this camp, and push for it."

Henry led the way over hilly, rough ground, and the others followed in a silent file, Long Jim and Tom still carrying the two smallest children, who soon fell asleep on their shoulders. Henry did not believe that the returning Iroquois could follow their trail on such a dark night, and the others agreed with him.

After a while they saw the gleam of water. Henry knew that it must be very near, or it would have been wholly invisible on such a dark night.

"I think, Mrs. Newton," he said, "that this is the river of which you spoke, and the cliffs seem to drop down just as you said they would."

The woman smiled.

"Yes," she said, "you've done well with my poor guess, and the boat must be hidden somewhere near here."

Then she sank down with exhaustion, and the two older children, unable to walk farther, sank down beside her. But the two who slept soundly on the shoulders of Long Jim and Tom Ross did not awaken. Henry motioned to Jim and Tom to remain there, and Shif'less Sol bent upon them a quizzical and approving look.

"Didn't think it was in you, Jim Hart, you old horny-handed galoot," he said, "carryin' a baby that tender. Knew Jim could sling a little black bar 'roun' by the tail, but I didn't think you'd take to nussin' so easy."

"I'd luv you to know, Sol Hyde," said Jim Hart in a tone of high condescension, "that Tom Ross an' me are civilized human bein's. In face uv danger we are ez brave ez forty thousand lions, but with the little an' the weak we're as easy an' kind an' soft ez human bein's are ever made to be."

"You're right, old hoss," said Tom Ross.

"Well," said the shiftless one, "I can't argify with you now, ez the general hez called on his colonel, which is me, an' his major, which is Paul, to find him a nice new boat like one o' them barges o' Clepatry that Paul tells about, all solid silver, with red silk sails an' gold oars, an' we're meanin' to do it."

Fortune was with them, and in a quarter of an hour they discovered, deep among bushes growing in the shallow water, a large, well-made boat with two pairs of oars and with small supplies of parched corn and venison hidden in it.

"Good luck an' bad luck come mixed," said the shift-less one, "an' this is shorely one o' our pieces o' good luck. The woman an' the children are clean tuckered out, an' without this boat we could never hev got them back. Now it's jest a question o' rowin' an' fightin'."

"Paul and I will pull her out to the edge of the clear water," said Henry, "while you can go back and tell the others, Sol."

"That just suits a lazy man," said Sol, and he walked away jauntily. Under his apparent frivolity he concealed his joy at the find, which he knew to be of such vast importance. He approached the dusky group, and his really tender heart was stirred with pity for the rescued captives. Long Jim and Silent Tom held the smaller two on their shoulders, but the older ones and the woman, also, had fallen asleep. Sol, in order to conceal his emotion, strode up rather roughly. Mary Newton awoke.

"Did you find anything?" she asked.

"Find anything?" repeated Shif'less Sol. "Well, Long Jim an' Tom here might never hev found anything, but Henry an' Paul an' me, three eddicated men, scholars, I might say, wuz jest natcherally bound to find it whether it wuz thar or not. Yes, we've unearthed what Paul would call an argosy, the grandest craft that ever floated on this here creek, that I never saw before, an' that I don't know the name uv. She's bein' floated out now, an' I, the Gran' Hidalgo an' Majordomo, hev come to tell the princes and princesses, an' the dukes and dukesses, an' all the other gran' an' mighty passengers, that the barge o' the Dog o' Venice is in the stream, an' the Dog, which is Henry Ware, is waitin', settin' on the Pup to welcome ye."

"Sol," said Long Jim, "you do talk a power uv foolishness, with your Dogs an' Pups."

"It ain't foolishness," rejoined the shiftless one. "I heard Paul read it out o' a book oncet, plain ez day. They've been ruled by Dogs at Venice for more than a thousand years, an' on big 'casions the Dog comes down a canal in a golden barge, settin' on the Pup. I'll admit it 'pears strange to me, too, but who are you an' me, Jim Hart, to question the ways of foreign countries, thousands o' miles on the other side o' the sea?"

"They've found the boat," said Tom Ross, "an' that's enough!"

"Is it really true?" asked Mrs. Newton.

"It is," replied Shif'less Sol, "an' Henry an' Paul are in it, waitin' fur us. We're thinkin', Mrs. Newton, that the roughest part of your trip is over."

In another five minutes all were in the boat, which was a really fine one, and they were delighted. Mary Newton for the first time broke down and wept, and no one disturbed her. The five spread the blankets on the bottom of the boat, where the children soon went to sleep once more, and Tom Ross and Shif'less Sol took the oars.

"Back in a boat ag'in," said the shiftless one exultantly. "Makes me feel like old times. My fav'rite mode o' travelin' when Jim Hart, 'stead o' me, is at the oars."

"Which is most o' the time," said Long Jim.

It was indeed a wonderful change to these people worn by the wilderness. They lay at ease now, while two pairs of powerful arms, with scarcely an effort, propelled the boat along the stream. The woman herself lay down on the blankets and fell asleep with the children. Henry at the prow, Tom Ross at the stern, and Paul amidships watched in silence, but with their rifles across their knees. They knew that the danger was far from over. Other Indians were likely to use this stream, unknown to them, as a highway, and those who survived of their original captors could pick up their trail by daylight. And the Senecas, being mad for revenge, would surely get help and follow. Henry believed that the theory of returning toward the Wyoming Valley was sound. That region had been so thoroughly ravaged now that all the Indians would be going northward. If they could float down a day or so without molestation, they would probably be safe. The creek, or, rather, little river, broadened, flowing with a smooth, fairly swift current. The forest on either side was dense with oak, hickory, maple, and other splendid trees, often with a growth of underbrush. The three riflemen never ceased to watch intently. Henry always looked ahead. It would have been difficult for any ambushed marksman to have escaped his notice. But nothing occurred to disturb them. Once a deer came down to drink, and fled away at sight of the phantom boat gliding almost without noise on the still waters. Once the far scream of a panther came from the woods, but Mary Newton and her children, sleeping soundly, did not hear it. The five themselves knew the nature of the sound, and paid no attention. The boat went steadily on, the three riflemen never changing their position, and soon the day began to come. Little arrows of golden light pierced through the foliage of the trees, and sparkled on the surface of the water. In the cast the red sun was coming from his nightly trip. Henry looked down at the sleepers. They were overpowered by exhaustion, and would not awake of their own accord for a long time.

Shif'less Sol caught his look.

"Why not let 'em sleep on?" he said.

Then he and Jim Hart took the oars, and the shiftless one and Tom Ross resumed their rifles. The day was coming fast, and the whole forest was soon transfused with light.

No one of the five had slept during the night. They did not feel the need of sleep, and they were upborne, too, by a great exaltation. They had saved the prisoners thus far from a horrible fate, and they were firmly resolved to reach, with them, some strong settlement and safety. They felt, too, a sense of exultation over Brant, Sangerachte, Hiokatoo, the Butlers, the Johnsons, Wyatt, and all the crew that had committed such terrible devastation in the Wyoming Valley and elsewhere.

The full day clothed the earth in a light that turned from silver to gold, and the woman and the children still slept. The five chewed some strips of venison, and looked rather lugubriously at the pieces they were saving for Mary Newton and the children.

"We ought to hev more'n that," said Shif'less Sol. "Ef the worst comes to the worst, we've got to land somewhar an' shoot a deer."

"But not yet," said Henry in a whisper, lest he wake the sleepers. "I think we'll come into the Susquehanna pretty soon, and its width will be a good thing for us. I wish we were there now. I don't like this narrow stream. Its narrowness affords too good an ambush."

"Anyway, the creek is broadenin' out fast," said the shiftless one, "an' that is a good sign. What's that you see ahead, Henry—ain't it a river?"

"It surely is," replied Henry, who caught sight of a broad expanse of water, "and it's the Susquehanna. Pull hard, Sol! In five more minutes we'll be in the river."

It was less than five when they turned into the current of the Susquehanna, and less than five more when they heard a shout behind them, and saw at least a dozen canoes following. The canoes were filled with Indians and Tories, and they had spied the fugitives.

"Keep the women and the children down, Paul," cried Henry.

All knew that Henry and Shif'less Sol were the best shots, and, without a word, Long Jim and Tom, both powerful and skilled watermen, swung heavily on the oars, while Henry and Shif'less Sol sat in the rear with their rifles ready. Mary Newton awoke with a cry at the sound of the shots, and started to rise, but Paul pushed her down.

"We're on the Susquehanna now, Mrs. Newton," he said, "and we are pursued. The Indians and Tories have just seen us, but don't be afraid. The two who are watching there are the best shots in the world."

He looked significantly at Henry and Shif'less Sol, crouching in the stern of the boat like great warriors from some mighty past, kings of the forest whom no one could overcome, and her courage came back. The children, too, had awakened with frightened cries, but she and Paul quickly soothed them, and, obedient to commands, the four, and Mary Newton with them, lay flat upon the bottom of the boat, which was now being sent forward rapidly by Jim Hart and Tom. Paul took up his rifle and sat in a waiting attitude, either to relieve one of the men at the oars or to shoot if necessary.

The clear sun made forest and river vivid in its light. The Indians, after their first cry, made no sound, but so powerful were Long Jim and Tom that they were gaining but little, although some of the boats contained six or eight rowers.

As the light grew more intense Henry made out the two white faces in the first boat. One was that of Braxton Wyatt, and the other, he was quite sure, belonged to the infamous Walter Butler. Hot anger swept through all his veins, and the little pulses in his temples began to beat like trip hammers. Now the picture of Wyoming, the battle, the massacre, the torture, and Queen Esther wielding her great tomahawk on the bound captives, grew astonishingly vivid, and it was printed blood red on his brain. The spirit of anger and defiance, of a desire to taunt those who had done such things, leaped up in his heart.

"Are you there, Braxton Wyatt?" he called clearly across the intervening water. "Yes, I see that it is you, murderer of women and children, champion of the fire and stake, as savage as any of the savages. And it is you, too, Walter Butler, wickeder son of a wicked father. Come a little closer, won't you? We've messengers here for both of you!"

He tapped lightly the barrel of his own rifle and that of Shif'less Sol, and repeated his request that they come a little closer.

They understood his words, and they understood, also, the significant gesture when he patted the barrel of the rifles. The hearts of both Butler and Wyatt were for the moment afraid, and their boat dropped back to third place. Henry laughed aloud when he saw. The Viking rage was still upon him. This was the primeval wilderness, and these were no common foes.

"I see that you don't want to receive our little messengers," he cried. "Why have you dropped back to third place in the line, Braxton Wyatt and Walter Butler, when you were first only a moment ago? Are you cowards as well as murderers of women and children?"

"That's pow'ful good talk," said Shif'less Sol admiringly. "Henry, you're a real orator. Give it to 'em, an' mebbe I'll get a chance at one o' them renegades."

It seemed that Henry's words had an effect, because the boat of the renegades pulled up somewhat, although it did not regain first place. Thus the chase proceeded down the Susquehanna.

The Indian fleet was gaining a little, and Shif'less Sol called Henry's attention to it.

"Don't you think I'd better take a shot at one o' them rowers in the first boat?" he said to Henry. "Wyatt an' Butler are a leetle too fur away."

"I think it would give them a good hint, Sol!" said Henry. "Take that fellow on the right who is pulling so hard."

The shiftless one raised his rifle, lingered but a little over his aim, and pulled the trigger. The rower whom Henry had pointed out fell back in the boat, his hands slipping from the handles of his oars. The boat was thrown into confusion, and dropped back in the race. Scattering shots were fired in return, but all fell short, the water spurting up in little jets where they struck.

Henry, who had caught something of the Indian nature in his long stay among them in the northwest, laughed in loud irony.

"That was one of our little messengers, and it found a listener!" he shouted. "And I see that you are afraid, Braxton Wyatt and Walter Butler, murderers of women and children! Why don't you keep your proper places in the front?"

"That's the way to talk to 'em," whispered Shif'less Sol, as he reloaded. "Keep it up, an' mebbe we kin git a chance at Braxton Wyatt hisself. Since Wyoming I'd never think o' missin' sech a chance."

"Nor I, either," said Henry, and he resumed in his powerful tones: "The place of a leader is in front, isn't it? Then why don't you come up?"

Braxton Wyatt and Walter Butler did not come up. They were not lacking in courage, but Wyatt knew what deadly marksmen the fugitive boat contained, and he had also told Butler. So they still hung back, although they raged at Henry Ware's taunts, and permitted the Mohawks and Senecas to take the lead in the chase.

"They're not going to give us a chance," said Henry. "I'm satisfied of that. They'll let redskins receive our bullets, though just now I'd rather it were the two white ones. What do you think, Sol, of that leading boat? Shouldn't we give another hint?"

"I agree with you, Henry," said the shiftless one. "They're comin' much too close fur people that ain't properly interduced to us. This promiskus way o' meetin' up with strangers an' lettin' 'em talk to you jest ez ef they'd knowed you all their lives hez got to be stopped. It's your time, Henry, to give 'em a polite hint, an' I jest suggest that you take the big fellow in the front o' the boat who looks like a Mohawk."

Henry raised his rifle, fired, and the Mohawk would row no more. Again confusion prevailed in the pursuing fleet, and there was a decline of enthusiasm. Braxton Wyatt and Walter Butler raged and swore, but, as they showed no great zeal for the lead themselves, the Iroquois did not gain on the fugitive boat. They, too, were fast learning that the two who crouched there with their rifles ready were among the deadliest marksmen in existence. They fired a dozen shots, perhaps, but their rifles did not have the long range of the Kentucky weapons, and again the bullets fell short, causing little jets of water to spring up.

"They won't come any nearer, at least not for the present," said Henry, "but will hang back just out of rifle range, waiting for some chance to help them."

Shif'less Sol looked the other way, down the Susquehanna, and announced that he could see no danger. There was probably no Indian fleet farther down the river than the one now pursuing them, and the danger was behind them, not before.

Throughout the firing, Silent Tom Ross and Long Jim Hart had not said a word, but they rowed with a steadiness and power that would have carried oarsmen of our day to many a victory. Moreover, they had the inducement not merely of a prize, but of life itself, to row and to row hard. They had rolled up their sleeves, and the mighty muscles on those arms of woven steel rose and fell as they sent the boat swiftly with the silver current of the Susquehanna.

Mary Newton still lay on the bottom of the boat. The children had cried out in fright once or twice at the sound of the firing, but she and Paul bad soothed them and kept them down. Somehow Mary Newton had become possessed of a great faith. She noticed the skill, speed, and success with which the five always worked, and, so long given up to despair, she now went to the other extreme. With such friends as these coming suddenly out of the void, everything must succeed. She had no doubt of it, but lay peacefully on the bottom of the boat, not at all disturbed by the sound of the shots.

Paul and Sol after a while relieved Long Jim and Tom at the oars. The Iroquois thought it a chance to creep up again, but they were driven back by a third bullet, and once more kept their distance. Shif'less Sol, while he pulled as powerfully as Tom Ross, whose place he had taken, nevertheless was not silent.

"I'd like to know the feelin's o' Braxton Wyatt an' that feller Butler," he said. "Must be powerful tantalizin' to them to see us here, almost where they could stretch out their hands an' put 'em on us. Like reachn' fur ripe, rich fruit, an' failin' to git it by half a finger's length."

"They are certainly not pleased," said Henry, "but this must end some way or other, you know."

"I say so, too, now that I'm a-rowin'," rejoined the shiftless one, "but when my turn at the oars is finished I wouldn't care. Ez I've said more'n once before, floatin' down a river with somebody else pullin' at the oars is the life jest suited to me."

Henry looked up. "A summer thunderstorm is coming," he said, "and from the look of things it's going to be pretty black. Then's when we must dodge 'em."

He was a good weather prophet. In a half hour the sky began to darken rapidly. There was a great deal of thunder and lightning, but when the rain came the air was almost as dark as night. Mary Newton and her children were covered as much as possible with the blankets, and then they swung the boat rapidly toward the eastern shore. They had already lost sight of their pursuers in the darkness, and as they coasted along the shore they found a large creek flowing into the river from the east.

They ran up the creek, and were a full mile from its mouth when the rain ceased. Then the sun came out bright and warm, quickly drying everything.

They pulled about ten miles farther, until the creek grew too shallow for them, when they hid the boat among bushes and took to the land. Two days later they arrived at a strong fort and settlement, where Mary Newton and her four children, safe and well, were welcomed by relatives who had mourned them as dead.

CHAPTER XV. "THE ALCOVE"

They arrived at the fort as evening was coming on, and as soon as food was served to them the five sought sleep. The frontiersmen usually slept soundly and for a long time after prodigious exertions, and Henry and his comrades were too wise to make an exception. They secured a single room inside the fort, one given to them gladly, because Mary Newton had already spread the fame of their exploits, and, laying aside their hunting shirts and leggins, prepared for rest.

"Jim," said Shif'less Sol, pointing to a low piece of furniture, flat and broad, in one corner of the room, "that's a bed. Mebbe you don't think it, but people lay on top o' that an' sleep thar."

Long Jim grinned.

"Mebbe you're right, Sol," he said. "I hev seen sech things ez that, an' mebbe I've slep' on 'em, but in all them gran' old tales Paul tells us about I never heard uv no big heroes sleepin' in beds. I guess the ground wuz good 'nough for A-killus, Hector, Richard-Kur-de-Leong, an' all the rest uv that fightin' crowd, an' ez I'm that sort uv a man myself I'll jest roll down here on the floor. Bein' as you're tender, Sol Hyde, an' not used to hard life in the woods, you kin take that bed yourself, an' in the mornin' your wally will be here with hot water in a silver mug an' a razor to shave you, an' he'll dress you in a ruffled red silk shirt an' a blue satin waistcoat, an' green satin breeches jest comin' to the knee, where they meet yellow silk stockin's risin' out uv purple satin slippers, an' then he'll clap on your head a big wig uv snow-white hair, fallin' all about your shoulders an' he'll buckle a silver sword to your side, an' he'll say: 'Gentlemen, him that hez long been known ez Shif'less Sol, an' desarvin' the name, but who in reality is the King o' France, is now before you. Down on your knees an' say your prayers!'"

Shif'less Sol stared in astonishment.

"You say a wally will do all that fur me, Jim? Now, what under the sun is a wally?"

"I heard all about 'em from Paul," replied Long Jim in a tone of intense satisfaction. "A wally is a man what does fur you what you ought to do fur yourself."

"Then I want one," said Shif'less Sol emphatically. "He'd jest suit a lazy man like me. An' ez fur your makin' me the King o' France, mebbe you're more'n half right about that without knowin' it. I hev all the instincts uv a king. I like to be waited on, I like to eat when I'm hungry, I like to drink when I'm thirsty, I like to rest when I'm tired, an' I like to sleep when I'm sleepy. You've heard o' children changed at birth by fairies an' sech like. Mebbe I'm the real King o' France, after all, an' my instincts are handed down to me from a thousand royal ancestors."

"Mebbe it's so," rejoined Long Jim. "I've heard that thar hev been a pow'ful lot uv foolish kings."

With that he put his two blankets upon the floor, lay down upon them, and was sound asleep in five minutes. But Shif'less Sol beat him to slumberland by at least a minute, and the others were not more than two minutes behind Sol.

Henry was the first up the next morning. A strong voice shouted in his ear: "Henry Ware, by all that's glorious," and a hand pressed his fingers together in an iron grasp. Henry beheld the tall, thin figure and smiling brown face of Adam Colfax, with whom he had made that adventurous journey up the Mississippi and Ohio.

"And the others?" was the first question of Adam Colfax.

"They're all here asleep inside. We've been through a lot of things, but we're as sound as ever."

"That's always a safe prediction to make," said Adam Colfax, smiling. "I never saw five other human beings with such a capacity for getting out of danger."

"We were all at Wyoming, and we all still live."

The face of the New Englander darkened.

"Wyoming!" he exclaimed. "I cannot hear of it without every vein growing hot within me."

"We saw things done there," said Henry gravely, "the telling of which few men can bear to hear."

"I know! I know!" exclaimed Adam Colfax. "The news of it has spread everywhere!"

"What we want," said Henry, "is revenge. It is a case in which we must strike back, and strike hard. If this thing goes on, not a white life will be safe on the whole border from the St. Lawrence to the Mississippi."

"It is true," said Adam Colfax, "and we would send an army now against the Iroquois and their allies, but, Henry, my lad, our fortunes are at their lowest there in the East, where the big armies are fighting. That is the reason why nobody has been sent to protect our rear guard, which has suffered so terribly. You may be sure, too, that the Iroquois will strike in this region again as often and as hard as they can. I make more than half a guess that you and your comrades are here because you know this."

He looked shrewdly at the boy.

"Yes," said Henry, "that is so. Somehow we were drawn into it, but being here we are glad to stay. Timmendiquas, the great chief who fought us so fiercely on the Ohio, is with the Iroquois, with a detachment of his Wyandots, and while he, as I know, frowns on the Wyoming massacre, he means to help Thayendanegea to the end."

Adam Colfax looked graver than ever.

"That is bad," he said. "Timmendiquas is a mighty warrior and leader, but there is also another way of looking at it. His presence here will relieve somewhat the pressure on Kentucky. I ought to tell you, Henry, that we got through safely with our supplies to the Continental army, and they could not possibly have been more welcome. They arrived just in time."

The others came forth presently and were greeted with the same warmth by Adam Colfax.

"It is shore mighty good for the eyes to see you, Mr. Colfax," said Shif'less Sol, "an' it's a good sign. Our people won when you were on the Mississippi an' the Ohio'—an' now that you're here, they're goin' to win again."

"I think we are going to win here and everywhere," said Adam Colfax, "but it is not because there is any omen in my presence. It is because our people will not give up, and because our quarrel is just."

The stanch New Englander left on the following day for points farther east, planning and carrying out some new scheme to aid the patriot cause, and the five, on the day after that, received a message written on a piece of paper which was found fastened to a tree on the outskirts of the settlement. It was addressed to "Henry Ware and Those with Him," and it read:

"You need not think because you escaped us at Wyoming and on the Susquehanna that you will ever get back to Kentucky. There is a mighty league now on the whole border between the Indians and the soldiers of the king. You have seen at Wyoming what we can do, and you will see at other places and on a greater scale what we will do. "I find my own position perfect. It is true that Timmendiquas does not like me, but he is not king here. I am the friend of the great Brant; and Hiokatoo, Sangerachte, Hahiron, and the other chiefs esteem me. I am thick with Colonel John Butler, the victor of Wyoming; his son, the valiant and worthy Walter Butler; Sir John Johnson, Colonel Guy Johnson, Colonel Daniel Claus, and many other eminent men and brave soldiers.

"I write these words, Henry Ware, both to you and your comrades, to tell you that our cause will prevail over yours. I do not doubt that when you read this you will try to escape to Kentucky, but when we have destroyed everything along the eastern border, as we have at Wyoming, we shall come to Kentucky, and not a

rebel face will be left there. "I am sending this to tell you that there is no hole in which you can hide where we cannot reach you. With my respects, BRAXTON WYATT."

Henry regarded the letter with contempt.

"A renegade catches something of the Indian nature," he said, "and always likes to threaten and boast."

But Shif'less Sol was highly indignant.

"Sometimes I think," he said, "that the invention o' writin' wuz a mistake. You kin send a man a letter an' call him names an' talk mighty big when he's a hundred miles away, but when you've got to stan' up to him face to face an' say it, wa'al, you change your tune an' sing a pow'ful sight milder. You ain't gen'ally any roarin' lion then."

"I think I'll keep this letter," said Henry, "an' we five will give an answer to it later on."

He tapped the muzzle of his rifle, and every one of the four gravely tapped the muzzle of his own rifle after him. It was a significant action. Nothing more was needed.

The next morning they bade farewell to the grateful Mary Newton and her children, and with fresh supplies of food and ammunition, chiefly ammunition, left the fort, plunging once more into the deep forest. It was their intention to do as much damage as they could to the Iroquois, until some great force, capable of dealing with the whole Six Nations, was assembled. Meanwhile, five redoubtable and determined borderers could achieve something.

It was about the first of August, and they were in the midst of the great heats. But it was a period favoring Indian activity, which was now at its highest pitch. Since Wyoming, loaded with scalps, flushed with victory, and aided by the king's men, they felt equal to anything. Only the strongest of the border settlements could hold them back. The colonists here were so much reduced, and so little help could be sent them from the East, that the Iroquois were able to divide into innumerable small parties and rake the country as with a fine tooth comb. They never missed a lone farmhouse, and rarely was any fugitive in the woods able to evade them. And they were constantly fed from the North with arms, ammunition, rewards for scalps, bounties, and great promises.

But toward the close of August the Iroquois began to hear of a silent and invisible foe, an evil spirit that struck them, and that struck hard. There were battles of small forces in which sometimes not a single Iroquois escaped. Captives were retaken in a half-dozen instances, and the warriors who escaped reported that their assailants were of uncommon size and power. They had all the cunning of the Indian and more, and they carried rifles that slew at a range double that of those served to them at the British posts. It was a certainty that they were guided by the evil spirit, because every attempt to capture them failed miserably. No one could find where they slept, unless it was those who never came back again.

The Iroquois raged, and so did the Butlers and the Johnsons and Braxton Wyatt. This was a flaw in their triumph, and the British and Tories saw, also, that it was beginning to affect the superstitions of their red allies. Braxton Wyatt made a shrewd guess as to the identity of the raiders, but he kept quiet. It is likely, also, that Timmendiquas knew, but be, too, said nothing. So the influence of the raiders grew. While their acts were great, superstition exaggerated them and their powers manifold. And it is true that their deeds were extraordinary. They were heard of on the Susquehanna, then on the Delaware and its branches, on the Chemung and the Chenango, as far south as Lackawaxen Creek, and as far north as Oneida Lake. It is likely that nobody ever accomplished more for a defense than did those five in the waning months of the summer. Late in September the most significant of all these events occurred. A party of eight Tories, who had borne a terrible part in the Wyoming affair, was attacked on the shores of Otsego Lake with such deadly fierceness that only two escaped alive to the camp of Sir John Johnson. Brant sent out six war parties, composed of not less than twenty warriors apiece, to seek revenge, but they found nothing.

Henry and his comrades had found a remarkable camp at the edge of one of the beautiful small lakes in which the region abounds. The cliff at that point was high, but a creek entered into it through a ravine. At the entrance of the creek into the river they found a deep alcove, or, rather, cave in the rock. It ran so far back that it afforded ample shelter from the rain, and that was all they wanted. It was about halfway between the top and bottom of the cliff, and was difficult of approach both from below and above. Unless completely surprised-a very unlikely thing with them-the five could hold it against any force as long as their provisions lasted. They also built a boat large enough for five, which they hid among the bushes at the lake's edge. They were thus provided with a possible means of escape across the water in case of the last emergency.

Jim and Paul, who, as usual, filled the role of housekeepers, took great delight in fitting up this forest home, which the fittingly called "The Alcove." The floor of solid stone was almost smooth, and with the aid of other heavy stones they broke off all projections, until one could walk over it in the dark in perfect comfort. They hung the walls with skins of deer which they killed in the adjacent woods, and these walls furnished many nooks and crannies for the storing of necessities. They also, with much hard effort, brought many loads of firewood, which Long Jim was to use for his cooking. He built his little fireplace of stones so near the mouth of "The Alcove" that the smoke would pass out and be lost in the thick forest all about. If the wind happened to be blowing toward the inside of the cave, the smoke, of course, would come in on them all, but Jim would not be cooking then.

Nor did their operations cease until they had supplied "The Alcove" plentifully with food, chiefly jerked deer meat, although there was no way in which they could store water, and for that they had to take their chances. But their success, the product of skill and everlasting caution, was really remarkable. Three times they were trapped within a few miles of "The Alcove," but the pursuers invariably went astray on the hard, rocky ground, and the pursued would also take the precaution to swim down the creek before climbing up to "The Alcove." Nobody could follow a trail in the face of such difficulties.

It was Henry and Shif'less Sol who were followed the second time, but they easily shook off their pursuers as the twilight was coming, half waded, half swam down the creek, and climbed up to "The Alcove," where the others were waiting for them with cooked food and clear cold water. When they had eaten and were refreshed, Shif'less Sol sat at the mouth of "The Alcove," where a pleasant breeze entered, despite the foliage that hid the entrance. The shiftless one was in an especially happy mood.

"It's a pow'ful comf'table feelin'," he said, "to set up in a nice safe place like this, an' feel that the woods is full o' ragin' heathen, seekin' to devour you, and wonderin' whar you've gone to. Thar's a heap in knowin' how to pick your home. I've thought more than once 'bout that old town, Troy, that Paul tells us 'bout, an' I've 'bout made up my mind that it wuzn't destroyed 'cause Helen eat too many golden apples, but 'cause old King Prime, or whoever built the place, put it down in a plain. That wuz shore a pow'ful foolish thing. Now, ef he'd built it on a mountain, with a steep fall-off on every side, thar wouldn't hev been enough Greeks in all the earth to take it, considerin' the miserable weepins they used in them times. Why, Hector could hev set tight on the walls, laughin' at 'em, 'stead o' goin' out in the plain an' gittin' killed by A-killus, fur which I've always been sorry."

"It's 'cause people nowadays have more sense than they did in them ancient times that Paul tells about," said Long Jim. "Now, thar wuz 'Lyssus, ten or twelve years gittin' home from Troy. Allus runnin' his ship on the rocks, hoppin' into trouble with four-legged giants, one-eyed women, an' sech like. Why didn't he walk home through the woods, killin' game on the way, an' hevin' the best time he ever knowed? Then thar wuz the keerlessness of A-killus' ma, dippin' him in that river so no arrow could enter him, but holdin' him by the heel an' keepin' it out o' the water, which caused his death the very first time Paris shot it off with his little bow an' arrer. Why didn't she hev sense enough to let the heel go under, too. She could hev dragged it out in two seconds an' no harm done 'ceptin', perhaps, a little more yellin' on the part of A-killus."

"I've always thought Paul hez got mixed 'bout that Paris story," said Tom Ross. "I used to think Paris was the name uv a town, not a man, an' I'm beginnin' to think so ag'in, sence I've been in the East, 'cause I know now that's whar the French come from."

"But Paris was the name of a man," persisted Paul. "Maybe the French named their capital after the Paris of the Trojan wars."

"Then they showed mighty poor jedgment," said Shif'less Sol. "Ef I'd named my capital after any them old fellers, I'd have called it Hector."

"You can have danger enough when you're on the tops of hills," said Henry, who was sitting near the mouth of the cave. "Come here, you fellows, and see what's passing down the lake."

They looked out, and in the moonlight saw six large war canoes being rowed slowly down the lake, which, though narrow, was quite long. Each canoe held about a dozen warriors, and Henry believed that one of them contained two white faces, evidently those of Braxton Wyatt and Walter Butler.

"Like ez not they've been lookin' fur us," said Tom Ross.

"Quite likely," said Henry, "and at the same time they may be engaged in some general movement. See, they will pass within fifty feet of the base of the cliff."

The five lay on the cave floor, looking through the vines and foliage, and they felt quite sure that they were in absolute security. The six long war canoes moved slowly. The moonlight came out more brightly, and flooded all the bronze faces of the Iroquois. Henry now saw that he was not mistaken, and that Braxton Wyatt and Walter Butler were really in the first boat. From the cover of the cliff he could have picked off either with a rifle bullet, and the temptation was powerful. But he knew that it would lead to an immediate siege, from which they might not escape, and which at least would check their activities and plans for a long time. Similar impulses flitted through the minds of the other four, but all kept still, although fingers flitted noiselessly along rifle stocks until they touched triggers.

The Iroquois war fleet moved slowly on, the two renegades never dreaming of the danger that had threatened them. An unusually bright ray of moonshine fell full upon Braxton Wyatt's face as he paused, and Henry's finger played with the trigger of his rifle. It was hard, very hard, to let such an opportunity go by, but it must be done.

The fleet moved steadily down the lake, the canoes keeping close together. They turned into mere dots upon the water, became smaller and smaller still, until they vanished in the darkness.

"I'm thinkin'," said Shif'less Sol, "that thar's some kind uv a movement on foot. While they may hev been lookin' fur us, it ain't likely that they'd send sixty warriors or so fur sech a purpose. I heard something three or four days ago from a hunter about an attack upon the Iroquois town of Oghwaga."

"It's most likely true," said Henry, "and it seems to me that it's our business to join that expedition. What do you fellows think?"

"Just as you do," they replied with unanimity.

"Then we leave this place and start in the morning," said Henry.

CHAPTER XVI. THE FIRST BLOW

Summer was now waning, the foliage was taking on its autumn hues, and Indian war parties still surged over the hills and mountains, but the five avoided them all. On one or two occasions they would have been willing to stop and fight, but they had bigger work on hand. They had received from others confirmation of the report that Long Jim had heard from the hunters, and they were quite sure that a strong force was advancing to strike the first blow in revenge for Wyoming. Curiously enough, this body was commanded by a fourth Butler, Colonel William Butler, and according to report it was large and its leaders capable.

When the avenging force lay at the Johnstown settlement on the Delaware, it was joined by the five. They were introduced to the colonel by the celebrated scout and hunter, Tini Murphy, whom they had met several times in the woods, and they were received warmly.

"I've heard of you," said Colonel Butler with much warmth, "both from hunters and scouts, and also from Adam Colfax. Two of you were to have been tomahawked by Queen Esther at Wyoming."

Henry indicated the two.

"What you saw at Wyoming is not likely to decrease your zeal against the Indians and their white allies," continued Colonel Butler.

"Anyone who was there," said Henry, "would feel all his life, the desire to punish those who did it."

"I think so, too, from all that I have heard," continued Colonel Butler. "It is the business of you young men to keep ahead of our column and warn us of what lies before us. I believe you have volunteered for that duty."

The five looked over Colonel Butler's little army, which numbered only two hundred and fifty men, but they were all strong and brave, and it was the best force that could yet be sent to the harassed border. It might, after all, strike a blow for Wyoming if it marched into no ambush, and Henry and his comrades were resolved to guard it from that greatest of all dangers.

When the little column moved from the Johnstown settlement, the five were far ahead, passing through the woods, up the Susquehanna, toward the Indian villages that lay on its banks, though a great distance above Wyoming. The chief of these was Oghwaga, and, knowing that it was the destination of the little army, they were resolved to visit it, or at least come so near it that they could see what manner of place it was.

"If it's a big village," said Colonel Butler, "it will be too strong to attack, but it may be that most of the warriors are absent on expeditions."

They had obtained before starting very careful descriptions of the approaches to the village, and toward the close of an October evening they knew that they were near Oghwaga, the great base of the Iroquois supplies. They considered it very risky and unwise to approach in the daytime, and accordingly they lay in the woods until the dark should come.

The appearance of the wilderness had changed greatly in the three months since Wyoming. All the green was now gone, and it was tinted red and yellow and brown. The skies were a mellow blue, and there was a slight haze over the forest, but the air had the wonderful crispness and freshness of the American autumn. It inspired every one of the five with fresh zeal and energy, because they believed the first blow was about to be struck.

About ten o'clock at night they approached Oghwaga, and the reports of its importance were confirmed. They had not before seen an Indian village with so many signs of permanence. They passed two or three orchards of apple and peach trees, and they saw other indications of cultivation like that of the white farmer.

"It ain't a bad-lookin' town," said Long Jim Hart. "But it'll look wuss," said Shif'less Sol, "onless they've laid an ambush somewhar. I don't like to see houses an' sech like go up in fire an' smoke, but after what wuz done at Wyomin' an' all through that valley, burnin' is a light thing."

"We're bound to strike back with all our might," said Paul, who had the softest heart of them all.

"Now, I wonder who's in this here town," said Tom Ross. "Mebbe Timmendiquas an' Brant an' all them renegades."

"It may be so," said Henry. "This is their base and store of supplies. Oh, if Colonel Butler were only here with all his men, what a rush we could make!"

So great was their eagerness that they crept closer to the village, passing among some thick clusters of grapevines. Henry was in the lead, and he heard a sudden snarl. A large cur of the kind that infest Indian villages leaped straight at him.

The very suddenness of the attack saved Henry and his comrades from the consequences of an alarm. He dropped his rifle instinctively, and seized the dog by the throat with both hands. A bark following the snarl had risen to the animal's throat, but it was cut short there. The hands of the great youth pressed tighter and tighter, and the dog was lifted from the earth. The four stood quietly beside their comrade, knowing that no alarm would be made now.

The dog kicked convulsively, then hung without motion or noise. Henry cast the dead body aside, picked up his rifle, and then all five of them sank softly down in the shelter of the grapevines. About fifteen yards away an Indian warrior was walking cautiously along and looking among the vines. Evidently he had heard the snarl of the dog, and was seeking the cause. But it had been only a single sound, and he would not look far. Yet the hearts of the five beat a little faster as he prowled among the vines, and their nerves were tense for action should the need for it come.

The Indian, a Mohawk, came within ten yards of them, but he did not see the five figures among the vines, blending darkly with the dark growth, and presently, satisfied that the sound he had heard was of no importance, he walked in another direction, and passed out of sight.

The five, not daunted at all by this living proof of risk, crept to the very edge of the clusters of grapevines, and looked upon an open space, beyond which stood some houses made of wood; but their attention was centered upon a figure that stood in the open.

Although the distance was too great and the light too poor to disclose the features, every one of the scouts recognized the figure. It could be none other than that of Timmendiquas, the great White Lightning of the

Wyandots. He was pacing back and forth, somewhat in the fashion of the white man, and his manner implied thought.

"I could bring him down from here with a bullet," said Shif'less Sol, "but I ain't ever goin' to shoot at the chief, Henry."

"No," said Henry, "nor will I. But look, there's another."

A second figure came out of the dark and joined the first. It was also that of a chief, powerful and tall, though not as tall as Timmendiquas. It was Thayendanegea. Then three white figures appeared. One was that of Braxton Wyatt, and the others they took to be those of "Indian" Butler and his son, Walter Butler. After a talk of a minute or two they entered one of the wooden houses.

"It's to be a conference of some kind," whispered Henry. "I wish I could look in on it."

"And I," said the others together.

"Well, we know this much," continued Henry. "No great force of the Iroquois is present, and if Colonel Butler's men come up quickly, we can take the town."

"It's a chance not to be lost," said Paul.

They crept slowly away from the village, not stopping until they reached the crest of a hill, from which they could see the roofs of two or three of the Indian houses.

"I've a feeling in me," said Paul, "that the place is doomed. We'll strike the first blow for Wyoming."

They neither slept nor rested that night, but retraced their trail with the utmost speed toward the marching American force, going in Indian file through the wilderness. Henry, as usual, led; Shif'less Sol followed, then came Paul, and then Long Jim, while Silent Tom was the rear guard. They traveled at great speed, and, some time after daylight, met the advance of the colonial force under Captain William Gray.

William Gray was a gallant young officer, but he was startled a little when five figures as silent as phantoms appeared. But he uttered an exclamation of delight when he recognized the leader, Henry.

"What have you found?" he asked eagerly.

"We've been to Oghwaga," replied the youth, "and we went all about the town. They do not suspect our coming. At least, they did not know when we left. We saw Brant, Timmendiquas, the Butlers, and Wyatt enter the house for a conference."

"And now is our chance," said eager young William Gray. "What if we should take the town, and with it these men, at one blow."

"We can scarcely hope for as much as that," said Henry, who knew that men like Timmendiquas and Thayendanegea were not likely to allow themselves to be seized by so small a force, "but we can hope for a good victory."

The young captain rode quickly back to his comrades with the news, and, led by the five, the whole force pushed forward with all possible haste. William Gray was still sanguine of a surprise, but the young riflemen did not expect it. Indian sentinels were sure to be in the forest between them and Oghwaga. Yet they said nothing to dash this hope. Henry had already seen enough to know the immense value of enthusiasm, and the little army full of zeal would accomplish much if the chance came. Besides the young captain, William Gray, there was a lieutenant named Taylor, who had been in the battle at Wyoming, but who had escaped the massacre. The five had not met him there, but the common share in so great a tragedy proved a tie between them. Taylor's name was Robert, but all the other officers, and some of the men for that matter, who had known him in childhood called him Bob. He was but little older than Henry, and his earlier youth, before removal to Wyoming, had been passed in Connecticut, a country that was to the colonials thickly populated and containing great towns, such as Hartford and New Haven.

A third close friend whom they soon found was a man unlike any other that they had ever seen. His name was Cornelius Heemskerk. Holland was his birthplace, but America was his nation. He was short and extremely fat, but he had an agility that amazed the five when they first saw it displayed. He talked much, and his words sounded like grumbles, but the unctuous tone and the smile that accompanied them indicated to the contrary. He formed for Shif'less Sol an inexhaustible and entertaining study in character.

"I ain't quite seen his like afore," said the shiftless one to Paul. "First time I run acrost him I thought he would tumble down among the first bushes he met. 'Stead o' that, he sailed right through 'em, makin' never a trip an' no noise at all, same ez Long Jim's teeth sinkin' into a juicy venison steak."

"I've heard tell," said Long Jim, who also contemplated the prodigy, "that big, chunky, awkward-lookin' things are sometimes ez spry ez you. They say that the Hipperpotamus kin outrun the giraffe across the sands uv Afriky, an' I know from pussonal experience that the bigger an' clumsier a b'ar is the faster he kin make you scoot fur your life. But he's the real Dutch, ain't he, Paul, one uv them fellers that licked the Spanish under the Duke uv Alivy an' Belisarry?"

"Undoubtedly," replied Paul, who did not consider it necessary to correct Long Jim's history, "and I'm willing to predict to you, Jim Hart, that Heemskerk will be a mighty good man in any fight that we may have."

Heemskerk rolled up to them. He seemed to have a sort of circular motion like that of a revolving tube, but he kept pace with the others, nevertheless, and he showed no signs of exertion.

"Don't you think it a funny thing that I, Cornelius Heemskerk, am here?" he said to Paul.

"Why so, Mr. Heemskerk?" replied Paul politely. "Because I am a Dutchman. I have the soul of an artist and the gentleness of a baby. I, Cornelius Heemskerk, should be in the goot leetle country of Holland in a goot leetle house, by the side of a goot leetle canal, painting beautiful blue china, dishes, plates, cups, saucers, all most beautiful, and here I am running through the woods of this vast America, carrying on my shoulder a rifle that is longer than I am, hunting the red Indian and hunted by him. Is it not most rediculous, Mynheer Paul?"

"I think you are here because you are a brave man, Mr. Heemskerk," replied Paul, "and wish to see punishment inflicted upon those who have committed great crimes."

"Not so! Not so!" replied the Dutchman with energy. "It is because I am one big fool. I am not really a big enough man to be as big a fool as I am, but so it is! so it is!" Shif'less Sol regarded him critically, and then spoke gravely and with deliberation: "It ain't that, Mr. Heemskerk, an' Paul ain't told quite all the truth, either. I've heard that the Dutch was the most powerfullest fightin' leetle nation on the globe; that all you had to do wuz to step on the toe uv a Dutchman's wooden shoe, an' all the men, women, an' children in Holland would jump right on top o' you all at once. Lookin' you up an' lookin' you down, an' sizin' you up, an' sizin you down, all purty careful, an' examinin' the corners O' your eyes oncommon close, an' also lookin' at the way you set your feet when you walk, I'm concludin' that you just natcherally love a fight, an' that you are lookin' fur one."

But Cornelius Heemskerk sighed, and shook his head.

"It is flattery that you give me, and you are trying to make me brave when I am not," he said. "I only say once more that I ought to be in Holland painting blue plates, and not here in the great woods holding on to my scalp, first with one hand and then with the other."

He sighed deeply, but Solomon Hyde, reader of the hearts of men, only laughed.

Colonel Butler's force stopped about three o'clock for food and a little rest, and the five, who had not slept since the night before, caught a few winks. But in less than an hour they were up and away again. The five riflemen were once more well in advance, and with them were Taylor and Heemskerk, the Dutchman, grumbling over their speed, but revolving along, nevertheless, with astonishing ease and without any sign of fatigue. They discovered no indications of Indian scouts or trails, and as the village now was not many miles away, it confirmed Henry in his belief that the Iroquois, with their friends, the Wyandots, would not stay to give battle. If Thayendanegea and Timmendiquas were prepared for a strong resistance, the bullets of the skirmishers would already be whistling through the woods.

The waning evening grew colder, twilight came, and the autumn leaves fell fast before the rising wind. The promise of the night was dark, which was not bad for their design, and once more the five-now the seven approached Oghwaga. From the crest of the very same hill they looked down once more upon the Indian houses.

"It is a great base for the Iroquois," said Henry to Heemskerk, "and whether the Indians have laid an ambush or not, Colonel Butler must attack."

"Ah," said Heemskerk, silently moving his round body to a little higher point for a better view, "now I feel in all its fullness the truth that I should be back in Holland, painting blue plates."

Nevertheless, Cornelius Heemskerk made a very accurate survey of the Iroquois village, considering the distance and the brevity of the time, and when the party went back to Colonel Butler to tell him the way was open, he revolved along as swiftly as any of them. There were also many serious thoughts in the back of his head.

At nine o'clock the little colonial force was within half a mile of Oghwaga, and nothing had yet occurred to disclose whether the Iroquois knew of their advance. Henry and his comrades, well in front, looked down upon the town, but saw nothing. No light came from an Indian chimney, nor did any dog howl. Just behind them were the troops in loose order, Colonel Butler impatiently striking his booted leg with a switch, and William Gray seeking to restrain his ardor, that he might set a good example to the men.

"What do you think, Mr. Ware?" asked Colonel Butler.

"I think we ought to rush the town at once."

"It is so!" exclaimed Heemskerk, forgetting all about painting blue plates.

"The signal is the trumpet; you blow it, Captain Gray, and then we'll charge."

William Gray took the trumpet from one of the men and blew a long, thrilling note. Before its last echo was ended, the little army rushed upon the town. Three or four shots came from the houses, and the soldiers fired a few at random in return, but that was all. Indian scouts had brought warning of the white advance, and the great chiefs, gathering up all the people who were in the village, had fled. A retreating warrior or two had fired the shots, but when the white men entered this important Iroquois stronghold they did not find a single human being. Timmendiquas, the White Lightning of the Wyandots, was gone; Thayendanegea, the real head of the Six Nations, had slipped away; and with them had vanished the renegades. But they had gone in haste. All around them were the evidences. The houses, built of wood, were scores in number, and many of them contained furniture such as a prosperous white man of the border would buy for himself. There were gardens and shade trees about these, and back of them, barns, many of them filled with Indian corn. Farther on were clusters of bark lodges, which had been inhabited by the less progressive of the Iroquois.

Henry stood in the center of the town and looked at the houses misty in the moonlight. The army had not yet made much noise, but he was beginning to hear behind him the ominous word, "Wyoming," repeated more than once. Cornelius Heemskerk had stopped revolving, and, standing beside Henry, wiped his perspiring, red face.

"Now that I am here, I think again of the blue plates of Holland, Mr. Ware," he said. "It is a dark and sanguinary time. The men whose brethren were scalped or burned alive at Wyoming will not now spare the town of those who did it. In this wilderness they give blow for blow, or perish."

Henry knew that it was true, but he felt a certain sadness. His heart had been inflamed against the Iroquois, he could never forget Wyoming or its horrors; but in the destruction of an ancient town the long labor of man perished, and it seemed waste. Doubtless a dozen generations of Iroquois children had played here on the grass. He walked toward the northern end of the village, and saw fields there from which recent corn had been taken, but behind him the cry, "Wyoming!" was repeated louder and oftener now. Then he saw men running here and there with torches, and presently smoke and flame burst from the houses. He examined the fields and forest for a little distance to see if any ambushed foe might still lie among them, but all the while the flame and smoke behind him were rising higher.

Henry turned back and joined his comrades. Oghwaga was perishing. The flames leaped from house to house, and then from lodge to lodge. There was no need to use torches any more. The whole village was wrapped in a mass of fire that grew and swelled until the flames rose above the forest, and were visible in the clear night miles away.

So great was the heat that Colonel Butler and the soldiers and scouts were compelled to withdraw to the edge of the forest. The wind rose and the flames soared. Sparks flew in myriads, and ashes fell dustily on the dry leaves of the trees. Bob Taylor, with his hands clenched tightly, muttered under his breath, "Wyoming! Wyoming!"

"It is the Iroquois who suffer now," said Heemskerk, as he revolved slowly away from a heated point.

Crashes came presently as the houses fell in, and then the sparks would leap higher and the flames roar louder. The barns, too, were falling down, and the grain was destroyed. The grapevines were trampled under foot, and the gardens were ruined. Oghwaga, a great central base of the Six Nations, was vanishing forever. For four hundred years, ever since the days of Hiawatha, the Iroquois had waxed in power. They had ruled over lands larger than great empires. They had built up political and social systems that are the wonder of students. They were invincible in war, because every man had been trained from birth to be a warrior, and now they were receiving their first great blow.

From a point far in the forest, miles away, Thayendanegea, Timmendiquas, Hiokatoo, Sangerachte, "Indian" Butler, Walter Butler, Braxton Wyatt, a low, heavybrowed Tory named Coleman, with whom Wyatt had become very friendly, and about sixty Iroquois and twenty Tories were watching a tower of light to the south that had just appeared above the trees. It was of an intense, fiery color, and every Indian in that gloomy band knew that it was Oghwaga, the great, the inviolate, the sacred, that was burning, and that the men who were doing it were the white frontiersmen, who, his red-coated allies had told him, would soon be swept forever from these woods. And they were forced to stand and see it, not daring to attack so strong and alert a force.

They sat there in the darkness among the trees, and watched the column of fire grow and grow until it seemed to pierce the skies. Timmendiquas never said a word. In his heart, Indian though he was, he felt that the Iroquois had gone too far. In him was the spirit of the farseeing Hiawatha. He could perceive that great cruelty always brought retaliation; but it was not for him, almost an alien, to say these things to Thayendanegea, the mighty war chief of the Mohawks and the living spirit of the Iroquois nation.

Thayendanegea sat on the stump of a tree blown down by winter storms. His arms were folded across his breast, and he looked steadily toward that red threatening light off there in the south. Some such idea as that in the mind of Timmendiquas may have been passing in his own. He was an uncommon Indian, and he had had uncommon advantages. He had not believed that the colonists could make head against so great a kingdom as England, aided by the allied tribes, the Canadians, and the large body of Tories among their own people. But he saw with his own eyes the famous Oghwaga of the Iroquois going down under their torch.

"Tell me, Colonel John Butler," he said bitterly, "where is your great king now? Is his arm long enough to reach from London to save our town of Oghwaga, which is perhaps as much to us as his great city of London is to him?"

The thickset figure of "Indian" Butler moved, and his swart face flushed as much as it could.

"You know as much about the king as I do, Joe Brant," he replied. "We are fighting here for your country as well as his, and you cannot say that Johnson's Greens and Butler's Rangers and the British and Canadians have not done their part."

"It is true," said Thayendanegea, "but it is true, also, that one must fight with wisdom. Perhaps there was too much burning of living men at Wyoming. The pain of the wounded bear makes him fight the harder, and it, is because of Wyoming that Oghwaga yonder burns. Say, is it not so, Colonel John Butler?"

"Indian" Butler made no reply, but sat, sullen and lowering. The Tory, Coleman, whispered to Braxton Wyatt, but Timmendiquas was the only one who spoke aloud.

"Thayendanegea," he said, "I, and the Wyandots who are with me, have come far. We expected to return long ago to the lands on the Ohio, but we were with you in your village, and now, when Manitou has turned his face from you for the time, we will not leave you. We stay and fight by your side."

Thayendanegea stood up, and Timmendiquas stood up, also.

"You are a great chief, White Lightning of the Wyandots," he said, "and you and I are brothers. I shall be proud and happy to have such a mighty leader fighting with me. We will have vengeance for this. The power of the Iroquois is as great as ever."

He raised himself to his full height, pointing to the fire, and the flames of hate and resolve burned in his eyes. Old Hiokatoo, the most savage of all the chiefs, shook his tomahawk, and a murmur passed through the group of Indians.

Braxton Wyatt still talked in whispers to his new friend, Coleman, the Tory, who was more to his liking than the morose and savage Walter Butler, whom he somewhat feared. Wyatt was perhaps the least troubled of all those present. Caring for himself only, the burning of Oghwaga caused him no grief. He suffered neither from the misfortune of friend nor foe. He was able to contemplate the glowing tower of light with curiosity only. Braxton Wyatt knew that the Iroquois and their allies would attempt revenge for the burning of Oghwaga, and he saw profit for himself in such adventures. His horizon had broadened somewhat of late. The renegade, Blackstaffe, had returned to rejoin Simon Girty, but he had found a new friend in Coleman. He was coming now more into touch with the larger forces in the East, nearer to the seat of the great war, and he hoped to profit by it.

"This is a terrible blow to Brant," Coleman whispered to him. "The Iroquois have been able to ravage the whole frontier, while the rebels, occupied with the king's troops, have not been able to send help to their own. But they have managed to strike at last, as you see."

"I do see," said Wyatt, "and on the whole, Coleman, I'm not sorry. Perhaps these chiefs won't be so haughty now, and they'll soon realize that they need likely chaps such as you and me, eh, Coleman."

"You're not far from the truth," said Coleman, laughing a little, and pleased at the penetration of his new friend. They did not talk further, although the agreement between them was well established. Neither did the Indian chiefs or the Tory leaders say any more. They watched the tower of fire a long time, past midnight, until it reached its zenith and then began to sink. They saw its crest go down behind the trees, and they saw the luminous cloud in the south fade and go out entirely, leaving there only the darkness that reined everywhere else.

Then the Indian and Tory leaders rose and silently marched northward. It was nearly dawn when Henry and his comrades lay down for the rest that they needed badly. They spread their blankets at the edge of the open, but well back from the burned area, which was now one great mass of coals and charred timbers, sending up little flame but much smoke. Many of the troops were already asleep, but Henry, before lying down, begged William Gray to keep a strict watch lest the Iroquois attack from ambush. He knew that the rashness and confidence of the borderers, especially when drawn together in masses, had often caused them great losses, and he was resolved to prevent a recurrence at the present time if he could. He had made these urgent requests of Gray, instead of Colonel Butler, because of the latter's youth and willingness to take advice.

"I'll have the forest beat up continually all about the town," he said. "We must not have our triumph spoiled by any afterclap."

Henry and his comrades, wrapped in their blankets, lay in a row almost at the edge of the forest. The heat from the fire was still great, but it would die down after a while, and the October air was nipping. Henry usually fell asleep in a very few minutes, but this time, despite his long exertions and lack of rest, he remained awake when his comrades were sound asleep. Then he fell into a drowsy state, in which he saw the fire rising in great black coils that united far above. It seemed to Henry, half dreaming and forecasting the future, that the Indian spirit was passing in the smoke.

When he fell asleep it was nearly daylight, and in three or four hours he was up again, as the little army intended to march at once upon another Indian town. The hours while he slept had passed in silence, and no Indians had come near. William Gray had seen to that, and his best scout had been one Cornelius Heemskerk, a short, stout man of Dutch birth.

"It was one long, long tramp for me, Mynheer Henry," said Heemskerk, as he revolved slowly up to the camp fire where Henry was eating his breakfast, "and I am now very tired. It was like walking four or five times around Holland, which is such a fine little country, with the canals and the flowers along them, and no great, dark woods filled with the fierce Iroquois."

"Still, I've a notion, Mynheer Heemskerk, that you'd rather be here, and perhaps before the day is over you will get some fighting hot enough to please even you."

Mynheer Heemskerk threw up his hands in dismay, but a half hour later he was eagerly discussing with Henry the possibility of overtaking some large band of retreating Iroquois.

Urged on by all the scouts and by those who had suffered at Wyoming, Colonel Butler gathered his forces and marched swiftly that very morning up the river against another Indian town, Cunahunta. Fortunately for him, a band of riflemen and scouts unsurpassed in skill led the way, and saw to it that the road was safe. In this band were the five, of course, and after them Heemskerk, young Taylor, and several others.

"If the Iroquois do not get in our way, we'll strike Cunahunta before night," said Heemskerk, who knew the way.

"It seems to me that they will certainly try to save their towns," said Henry. "Surely Brant and the Tories will not let us strike so great a blow without a fight."

"Most of their warriors are elsewhere, Mynheer Henry," said Heemskerk, "or they would certainly give us a big battle. We've been lucky in the time of our advance. As it is, I think we'll have something to do."

It was now about noon, the noon of a beautiful October day of the North, the air like life itself, the foliage burning red on the hills, the leaves falling softly from the trees as the wind blew, but bringing with them no hint of decay. None of the vanguard felt fatigue, but when they crossed a low range of hills and saw before them a creek flowing down to the Susquehanna, Henry, who was in the lead, stopped suddenly and dropped down in the grass. The others, knowing without question the significance of the action, also sank down.

"What is it, Henry?" asked Shif'less Sol.

"You see how thick the trees are on the other side of that bank. Look a little to the left of a big oak, and you will see the feathers in the headdress of an Iroquois. Farther on I think I can catch a glimpse of a green coat, and if I am right that coat is worn by one of Johnson's Royal Greens. It's an ambush, Sol, an ambush meant for us."

"But it's not an ambush intended for our main force, Mynheer Henry," said Heemskerk, whose red face began to grow redder with the desire for action. "I, too, see the feather of the Iroquois."

"As good scouts and skirmishers it's our duty, then, to clear this force out of the way, and not wait for the main body to come up, is it not?" asked Henry, with a suggestive look at the Dutchman.

"What a goot head you have, Mynheer Henry!" exclaimed Heemskerk. "Of course we will fight, and fight now!"

"How about them blue plates?" said Shif'less Sol softly. But Heemskerk did not hear him.

They swiftly developed their plan of action. There could be no earthly doubt of the fact that the Iroquois and some Tories were ambushed on the far side of the creek. Possibly Thayendanegea himself, stung by the burning of Oghwaga and the advance on Cunahunta, was there. But they were sure that it was not a large band.

The party of Henry and Heemskerk numbered fourteen, but every one was a veteran, full of courage, tenacity, and all the skill of the woods. They had supreme confidence in their ability to beat the best of the Iroquois, man for man, and they carried the very finest arms known to the time.

It was decided that four of the men should remain on the hill. The others, including the five, Heemskerk, and Taylor, would make a circuit, cross the creek a full mile above, and come down on the flank of the ambushing party. Theirs would be the main attack, but it would be preceded by sharpshooting from the four, intended to absorb the attention of the Iroquois. The chosen ten slipped back down the hill, and as soon as they were sheltered from any possible glimpse by the warriors, they rose and ran rapidly westward. Before they had gone far they heard the crack of a rifle shot, then another, then several from another point, as if in reply.

"It's our sharpshooters," said Henry. "They've begun to disturb the Iroquois, and they'll keep them busy."

"Until we break in on their sport and keep them still busier," exclaimed Heemskerk, revolving swiftly through the bushes, his face blazing red.

It did not take long for such as they to go the mile or so that they intended, and then they crossed the creek, wading in the water breast high, but careful to keep their ammunition dry. Then they turned and rapidly descended the stream on its northern bank. In a few minutes they heard the sound of a rifle shot, and then of another as if replying.

"The Iroquois have been fooled," exclaimed Heemskerk. "Our four good riflemen have made them think that a great force is there, and they have not dared to cross the creek themselves and make an attack."

In a few minutes more, as they ran noiselessly through the forest, they saw a little drifting smoke, and now and then the faint flash of rifles. They were coming somewhere near to the Iroquois band, and they practiced exceeding caution. Presently they caught sight of Indian faces, and now and then one of Johnson's Greens or Butler's Rangers. They stopped and held a council that lasted scarcely more than half a minute. They all agreed there was but one thing to do, and that was to attack in the Indian's own way-that is, by ambush and sharpshooting.

Henry fired the first shot, and an Iroquois, aiming at a foe on the other side of the creek, fell. Heemskerk quickly followed with a shot as good, and the surprised Iroquois turned to face this new foe. But they and the Tories were a strong band, and they retreated only a little. Then they stood firm, and the forest battle began. The Indians numbered not less than thirty, and both Braxton Wyatt and Coleman were with them, but the value of skill was here shown by the smaller party, the one that attacked. The frontiersmen, trained to every trick and wile of the forest, and marksmen such as the Indians were never able to become, continually pressed in and drove the Iroquois from tree to tree. Once or twice the warriors started a rush, but they were quickly driven back by sharpshooting such as they had never faced before. They soon realized that this was no band of border farmers, armed hastily for an emergency, but a foe who knew everything that they knew, and more.

Braxton Wyatt and his friend Coleman fought with the Iroquois, and Wyatt in particular was hot with rage. He suspected that the five who had defeated him so often were among these marksmen, and there might be a chance now to destroy them all. He crept to the side of the fierce old Seneca chief, Hiokatoo, and suggested that a part of their band slip around and enfold the enemy.

Old Hiokatoo, in the thick of battle now, presented his most terrifying aspect. He was naked save the waist cloth, his great body was covered with scars, and, as he bent a little forward, he held cocked and ready in his hands a fine rifle that had been presented to him by his good friend, the king. The Senecas, it may be repeated, had suffered terribly at the Battle of the Oriskany in the preceding year, and throughout these years of border were the most cruel of all the Iroquois. In this respect Hiokatoo led all the Senecas, and now Braxton Wyatt used as he was to savage scenes, was compelled to admit to himself that this was the most terrifying human being whom he had ever beheld. He was old, but age in him seemed merely to add to his strength and ferocity. The path of a deep cut, healed long since, but which the paint even did not hide, lay across his forehead. Others almost as deep adorned his right cheek, his chin, and his neck. He was crouched much like a panther, with his rifle in his hands and the ready tomahawk at his belt. But it was the extraordinary expression of his eyes that made Braxton Wyatt shudder. He read there no mercy for anything, not even for himself, Braxton Wyatt, if he should stand in the way, and it was this last fact that brought the shudder.

Hiokatoo thought it a good plan. Twenty warriors, mostly Senecas and Cayugas, were detailed to execute it at once, and they stole off toward the right. Henry had suspected some such diversion, and, as he had been joined now by the four men from the other side of the creek, he disposed his little force to meet it. Both Shif'less Sol and Heemskerk had caught sight of figures slipping away among the trees, and Henry craftily drew back a little. While two or three men maintained the sharpshooting in the front, he waited for the attack. It came in half an hour, the flanking force making a savage and open rush, but the fire of the white riflemen was so swift and deadly that they were driven back again. But they had come very near, and a Tory rushed directly at young Taylor. The Tory, like Taylor, had come from Wyoming, and he had been one of the most ruthless on that terrible day. When they were less than a dozen feet apart they recognized each other. Henry saw the look that passed between them, and, although he held a loaded rifle in his hand, for some reason he did not use it. The Tory fired a pistol at Taylor, but the bullet missed, and the Wyoming youth, leaping forth, swung his unloaded rifle and brought the stock down with all his force upon the head of his enemy. The man, uttering a single sound, a sort of gasp, fell dead, and Taylor stood over him, still trembling with rage. In an instant Henry seized him and dragged him down, and then a Seneca bullet whistled where he had been.

"He was one of the worst at Wyoming-I saw him!" exclaimed young Taylor, still trembling all over with passion.

"He'll never massacre anybody else. You've seen to that," said Henry, and in a minute or two Taylor was quiet. The sharpshooting continued, but here as elsewhere, the Iroquois had the worst of it. Despite their numbers, they could not pass nor flank that line of deadly marksmen who lay behind trees almost in security, and who never missed. Another Tory and a chief, also, were killed, and Braxton Wyatt was daunted. Nor did he feel any better when old Hiokatoo crept to his side.

"We have failed here," he said. "They shoot too well for us to rush them. We have lost good men." Hiokatoo frowned, and the scars on his face stood out in livid red lines.

"It is so," he said. "These who fight us now are of their best, and while we fight, the army that destroyed Oghwaga is coming up. Come, we will go."

The little white band soon saw that the Indians were gone from their front. They scouted some distance, and, finding no enemy, hurried back to Colonel Butler. The troops were pushed forward, and before night they reached Cunahunta, which they burned also. Some farther advance was made into the Indian country, and more destruction was done, but now the winter was approaching, and many of the men insisted upon returning home to protect their families. Others were to rejoin the main Revolutionary army, and the Iroquois campaign was to stop for the time. The first blow had been struck, and it was a hard one, but the second blow and third and fourth and more, which the five knew were so badly needed, must wait.

Henry and his comrades were deeply disappointed. They had hoped to go far into the Iroquois country, to break the power of the Six Nations, to hunt down the Butlers and the Johnsons and Brant himself, but they could not wholly blame their commander. The rear guard, or, rather, the forest guard of the Revolution, was a slender and small force indeed.

Henry and his comrades said farewell to Colonel Butler with much personal regret, and also to the gallant troops, some of whom were Morgan's riflemen from Virginia. The farewells to William Gray, Bob Taylor, and Cornelius Heemskerk were more intimate.

"I think we'll see more of one another in other campaigns," said Gray.

"We'll be on the battle line, side by side, once more," said Taylor, "and we'll strike another blow for Wyoming."

"I foresee," said Cornelius Heemskerk, "that I, a peaceful man, who ought to be painting blue plates in Holland, will be drawn into danger in the great, dark wilderness again, and that you will be there with me, Mynheer Henry, Mynheer Paul, Mynheer the Wise Solomon, Mynheer the Silent Tom, and Mynheer the Very Long James. I see it clearly. I, a man of peace, am always being pushed in to war."

"We hope it will come true," said the five together.

"Do you go back to Kentucky?" asked William Gray.

"No," replied Henry, speaking for them all, "we have entered upon this task here, and we are going to stay in it until it is finished."

"It is dangerous, the most dangerous thing in the world," said Heemskerk. "I still have my foreknowledge that I shall stand by your side in some great battle to come, but the first thing I shall do when I see you again, my friends, is to look around at you, one, two, three, four, five, and see if you have upon your heads the hair which is now so rich, thick, and flowing."

"Never fear, my friend," said Henry, "we have fought with the warriors all the way from the Susquehanna to New Orleans and not one of us has lost a single lock of hair."

"It is one Dutchman's hope that it will always be so," said Heemskerk, and then he revolved rapidly away lest they see his face express emotion.

The five received great supplies of powder and bullets from Colonel Butler, and then they parted in the forest. Many of the soldiers looked back and saw the five tall figures in a line, leaning upon the muzzles of their long-barreled Kentucky rifles, and regarding them in silence. It seemed to the soldiers that they had left behind them the true sons of the wilderness, who, in spite of all dangers, would be there to welcome them when they returned.

CHAPTER XVII. THE DESERTED CABIN

When the last soldier had disappeared among the trees, Henry turned to the others. "Well, boys," he asked, "what are you thinking about?"

"I?" asked Paul. "I'm thinking about a certain place I know, a sort of alcove or hole in a cliff above a lake."

"An' me?" said Shif'less Sol. "I'm thinkin' how fur that alcove runs back, an' how it could be fitted up with furs an' made warm fur the winter."

"Me?" said Tom Ross. "I'm thinkin' what a snug place that alcove would be when the snow an' hail were drivin' down the creek in front of you."

"An' ez fur me," said Long Jim Hart, "I wuz thinkin' I could run a sort uv flue from the back part uv that alcove out through the front an' let the smoke pass out. I could cook all right. It wouldn't be ez good a place fur cookin' ez the one we hed that time we spent the winter on the island in the lake, but 'twould serve."

"It's strange," said Henry, "but I've been thinking of all the things that all four of you have been thinking about, and, since we are agreed, we are bound to go straight to 'The Alcove' and pass the winter there."

Without another word he led the way, and the others followed. It was apparent to everyone that they must soon find a winter base, because the cold had increased greatly in the last few days. The last leaves had fallen from the trees, and a searching wind howled among the bare branches. Better shelter than blankets would soon be needed.

On their way they passed Oghwaga, a mass of blackened ruins, among which wolves howled, the same spectacle that Wyoming now afforded, although Oghwaga had not been stained by blood.

It was a long journey to "The Alcove," but they did not hurry, seeing no need of it, although they were warned of the wisdom of their decision by the fact that the cold was increasing. The country in which the lake was situated lay high, and, as all of them were quite sure that the cold was going to be great there, they thought it wise to make preparations against it, which they discussed as they walked in, leisurely fashion through the woods. They spoke, also, of greater things. All felt that they had been drawn into a mightier current than any in which they had swam before. They fully appreciated the importance to the Revolution of this great rearguard struggle, and at present they did not have the remotest idea of returning to Kentucky under any circumstances.

"We've got to fight it out with Braxton Wyatt and the Iroquois," said Henry. "I've heard that Braxton is organizing a band of Tories of his own, and that he is likely to be as dangerous as either of the Butlers."

"Some day we'll end him for good an' all," said Shif'less Sol.

It was four or five days before they reached their alcove, and now all the forest was bare and apparently lifeless. They came down the creek, and found their boat unharmed and untouched still among the foliage at the base of the cliff.

"That's one thing safe," said Long Jim, "an' I guess we'll find 'The Alcove' all right, too."

"Unless a wild animal has taken up its abode there," said Paul.

"'Tain't likely," replied Long Jim. "We've left the human smell thar, an' even after all this time it's likely to drive away any prowlin' bear or panther that pokes his nose in."

Long Jim was quite right. Their snug nest, like that of a squirrel in the side of a tree, had not been disturbed. The skins which they had rolled up tightly and placed on the higher shelves of stone were untouched, and several days' hunting increased the supply. The hunting was singularly easy, and, although the five did not know it, the quantity of game was much greater in that region than it had been for years. It had been swept of human beings by the Iroquois and Tory hordes, and deer, bear, and panther seemed to know instinctively that the woods were once more safe for them.

In their hunting they came upon the ruins of charred houses, and more than once they saw something among the coals that caused them to turn away with a shudder. At every place where man had made a little opening the wilderness was quickly reclaiming its own again. Next year the grass and the foliage would cover up the coals and the hideous relics that lay among them.

They jerked great quantities of venison on the trees on the cliff side, and stored it in "The Alcove." They also cured some bear meat, and, having added a further lining of skins, they felt prepared for winter. They had also added to the comfort of the place. They had taken the precaution of bringing with them two axes, and with the heads of these they smoothed out more of the rough places on the floor and sides of "The Alcove." They thought it likely, too, that they would need the axes in other ways later on.

Only once during these arrangements did they pass the trail of Indians, and that was made by a party of about twenty, at least ten miles from "The Alcove." They seemed to be traveling north, and the five made no investigations. Somewhat later they met a white runner in the forest, and he told them of the terrible massacre of Cherry Valley. Walter Butler, emulating his father's exploit at Wyoming, had come down with a mixed horde of Iroquois, Tories, British, and Canadians. He had not been wholly successful, but he had slaughtered half a hundred women and children, and was now returning northward with prisoners. Some said, according to the runner, that Thayendanegea had led the Indians on this occasion, but, as the five learned later, he had not come up until the massacre was over. The runner added another piece of information that interested them deeply. Butler had been accompanied to Cherry Valley by a young Tory or renegade named Wyatt, who had distinguished himself by cunning and cruelty. It was said that Wyatt had built up for himself a semi-independent command, and was becoming a great scourge.

"That's our Braxton," said Henry. "He is rising to his opportunities. He is likely to become fully the equal of Walter Butler."

But they could do nothing at present to find Wyatt, and they went somewhat sadly back to "The Alcove." They had learned also from the runner that Wyatt had a lieutenant, a Tory named Coleman, and this fact increased their belief that Wyatt was undertaking to operate on a large scale.

"We may get a chance at him anyhow," said Henry. "He and his band may go too far away from the main body of the Indians and Tories, and in that case we can strike a blow if we are watchful."

Every one of the five, although none of them knew it, received an additional impulse from this news about Braxton Wyatt. He had grown up with them. Loyalty to the king had nothing to do with his becoming a renegade or a Tory; he could not plead lost lands or exile for taking part in such massacres as Wyoming or Cherry Valley, but, long since an ally of the Indians, he was now at the head of a Tory band that murdered and burned from sheer pleasure.

"Some day we'll get him, as shore as the sun rises an' sets," said Shif'less Sol, repeating Henry's prediction.

But for the present they "holed up," and now their foresight was justified. To such as they, used to the hardships of forest life, "The Alcove" was a cheery nest. From its door they watched the wild fowl streaming south, pigeons, ducks, and others outlined against the dark, wintry skies.

So numerous were these flocks that there was scarcely a time when they did not see one passing toward the warm South.

Shif'less Sol and Paul sat together watching a great flock of wild geese, arrow shaped, and flying at almost incredible speed. A few faint honks came to them, and then the geese grew misty on the horizon. Shif'less Sol followed them with serious eyes.

"Do you ever think, Paul," he said, "that we human bein's ain't so mighty pow'ful ez we think we are. We kin walk on the groun', an' by hard learnin' an' hard work we kin paddle through the water a little. But jest look at them geese flyin' a mile high, right over everything, rivers, forests any mountains, makin' a hundred miles an hour, almost without flappin' a wing. Then they kin come down on the water an' float fur hours without bein' tired, an' they kin waddle along on the groun', too. Did you ever hear of any men who had so many 'complishments? Why, Paul, s'pose you an' me could grow wings all at once, an' go through the air a mile a minute fur a month an' never git tired."

"We'd certainly see some great sights," said Paul, "but do you know, Sol, what would be the first thing I'd do if I had the gift of tireless wings?"

"Fly off to them other continents I've heard you tell about."

"No, I'd swoop along over the forests up here until I picked out all the camps of the Indians and Tories. I'd pick out the Butlers and Braxton Wyatt and Coleman, and see what mischief they were planning. Then I'd fly away to the East and look down at all the armies, ours in buff and blue, and the British redcoats. I'd look into the face of our great commander-in-chief. Then I'd fly away back into the West and South, and I'd hover over Wareville. I'd see our own people, every last little one of them. They might take a shot at me, not knowing who I was, but I'd be so high up in the air no bullet could reach me. Then I'd come soaring back here to you fellows."

"That would shorely be a grand trip, Paul," said Shif'less Sol, "an' I wouldn't mind takin' it in myself. But fur the present we'd better busy our minds with the warnin's the wild fowl are givin' us, though we're well fixed fur a house already. It's cu'rus what good homes a handy man kin find in the wilderness."

The predictions of the wild fowl were true. A few days later heavy clouds rolled up in the southwest, and the five watched them, knowing what they would bring them. They spread to the zenith and then to the other horizon, clothing the whole circle of the earth. The great flakes began to drop down, slowly at first, then faster. Soon all the trees were covered with white, and everything else, too, except the dark surface of the lake, which received the flakes into its bosom as they fell.

It snowed all that day and most of the next, until it lay about two feet on the ground. After that it turned intensely cold, the surface of the snow froze, and ice, nearly a foot thick, covered the lake. It was not possible to travel under such circumstances without artificial help, and now Tom Ross, who had once hunted in the far North, came to their help. He showed them how to make snowshoes, and, although all learned to use them, Henry, with his great strength and peculiar skill, became by far the most expert.

As the snow with its frozen surface lay on the ground for weeks, Henry took many long journeys on the snowshoes. Sometimes be hunted, but oftener his role was that of scout. He cautioned his friends that he might be out-three or four days at a time, and that they need take no alarm about him unless his absence became extremely long. The winter deepened, the snow melted, and another and greater storm came, freezing the surface, again making the snowshoes necessary. Henry decided now to take a scout alone to the northward, and, as the others bad long since grown into the habit of accepting his decisions almost without question, he started at once. He was well equipped with his rifle, double barreled pistol, hatchet, and knife, and he carried in addition a heavy blanket and some jerked venison. He put on his snowshoes at the foot of the cliff, waved a farewell to the four heads thrust from "The Alcove" above, and struck out on the smooth, icy surface of the creek. From this he presently passed into the woods, and for a long time pursued a course almost due north.

It was no vague theory that had drawn Henry forth. In one of his journeyings be had met a hunter who told him of a band of Tories and Indians encamped toward the north, and he had an idea that it was the party led by Braxton Wyatt. Now he meant to see.

His information was very indefinite, and he began to discover signs much earlier than he had expected. Before the end of the first day he saw the traces of other snowshoe runners on the icy snow, and once he came to a place where a deer had been slain and dressed. Then he came to another where the snow had been hollowed out under some pines to make a sleeping place for several men. Clearly he was in the land of the enemy again, and a large and hostile camp might be somewhere near.

Henry felt a thrill of joy when he saw these indications. All the primitive instincts leaped up within him. A child of the forest and of elemental conditions, the warlike instinct was strong within him. He was tired of hunting wild animals, and now there was promise of a' more dangerous foe. For the purposes that he had in view he was glad that he was alone. The wintry forest, with its two feet of snow covered with ice, contained no terrors for him. He moved on his snowshoes almost like a skater, and with all the dexterity of an Indian of the far North, who is practically born on such shoes.

As he stood upon the brow of a little hill, elevated upon his snowshoes, he was, indeed, a wonderful figure. The added height and the white glare from the ice made him tower like a great giant. He was clad completely in soft, warm deerskin, his hands were gloved in the same material, and the fur cap was drawn tightly about his head and ears. The slender-barreled rifle lay across his shoulder, and the blanket and deer meat made a light package on his back. Only his face was uncovered, and that was rosy with the sharp but bracing cold. But the resolute blue eyes seemed to have grown more resolute in the last six months, and the firm jaw was firmer than ever.

It was a steely blue sky, clear, hard, and cold, fitted to the earth of snow and ice that it inclosed. His eyes traveled the circle of the horizon three times, and at the end of the third circle he made out a dim, dark thread against that sheet of blue steel. It was the light of a camp fire, and that camp fire must belong to an enemy. It was not likely that anybody else would be sending forth such a signal in this wintry wilderness.

Henry judged that the fire was several miles away, and apparently in a small valley hemmed in by hills of moderate height. He made up his mind that the band of Braxton Wyatt was there, and he intended to make a thorough scout about it. He advanced until the smoke line became much thicker and broader, and then he stopped in the densest clump of bushes that he could find. He meant to remain there until darkness came, because, with all foliage gone from the forest, it would be impossible to examine the hostile camp by day. The bushes, despite the lack of leaves, were so dense that they hid him well, and, breaking through the crust of ice, he dug a hole. Then, having taken off his snowshoes and wrapped his blanket about his body, he thrust himself into the hole exactly like a rabbit in its burrow. He laid his shoes on the crust of ice beside him. Of course, if found there by a large party of warriors on snowshoes he would have no chance to flee, but he was willing to take what seemed to him a small risk. The dark would not be long in coming, and it was snug and warm in the hole. As he sat, his head rose just above the surrounding ice, but his rifle barrel rose much higher. He ate a little venison for supper, and the weariness in the ankles that comes from long traveling on snowshoes disappeared.

He could not see outside the bushes, but he listened with those uncommonly keen ears of his. No sound at all came. There was not even a wind to rustle the bare boughs. The sun hung a huge red globe in the west, and all that side of the earth was tinged with a red glare, wintry and cold despite its redness. Then, as the earth turned, the sun was lost behind it, and the cold dark came.

Henry found it so comfortable in his burrow that all his muscles were soothed, and he grew sleepy. It would have been very pleasant to doze there, but he brought himself round with an effort of the will, and became as wide awake as ever. He was eager to be off on his expedition, but he knew how much depended on waiting, and he waited. One hour, two hours, three hours, four hours, still and dark, passed in the forest before he roused himself from his covert. Then, warm, strong, and tempered like steel for his purpose, he put on his snowshoes, and advanced toward the point from which the column of smoke had risen.

He had never been more cautious and wary than he was now. He was a formidable figure in the darkness, crouched forward, and moving like some spirit of the wilderness, half walking, half gliding.

Although the night had come out rather clear, with many cold stars twinkling in the blue, the line of smoke was no longer visible. But Henry did not expect it to be, nor did he need it. He had marked its base too clearly in his mind to make any mistake, and he advanced with certainty. He came presently into an open space, and he stopped with amazement. Around him were the stumps of a clearing made recently, and near him were some yards of rough rail fence.

He crouched against the fence, and saw on the far side of the clearing the dim outlines of several buildings, from the chimneys of two of which smoke was rising. It was his first thought that he had come upon a little settlement still held by daring borderers, but second thought told him that it was impossible. Another and more comprehensive look showed many signs of ruin. He saw remains of several burned houses, but clothing all was the atmosphere of desolation and decay that tells when a place is abandoned. The two threads of smoke did not alter this impression.

Henry divined it all. The builders of this tiny village in the wilderness bad been massacred or driven away. A part of the houses had been destroyed, some were left standing, and now there were visitors. He advanced without noise, keeping behind the rail fence, and approaching one of the houses from the chimneys of which the smoke came. Here be crouched a long time, looking and listening attentively; but it seemed that the visitors had no fears. Why should they, when there was nothing that they need fear in this frozen wilderness?

Henry stole a little nearer. It had been a snug, trim little settlement. Perhaps twenty-five or thirty people had lived there, literally hewing a home out of the forest. His heart throbbed with a fierce hatred and, anger against those who had spoiled all this, and his gloved finger crept to the hammer of his rifle.

The night was intensely cold. The mercury was far below zero, and a wind that had begun to rise cut like the edge of a knife. Even the wariest of Indians in such desolate weather might fail to keep a watch. But Henry did not suffer. The fur cap was drawn farther over chin and ears, and the buckskin gloves kept his fingers warm and flexible. Besides, his blood was uncommonly hot in his veins.

His comprehensive eye told him that, while some of the buildings had not been destroyed, they were so ravaged and damaged that they could never be used again, save as a passing shelter, just as they were being used now. He slid cautiously about the desolate place. He crossed a brook, frozen almost solidly in its bed, and he saw two or three large mounds that had been haystacks, now covered with snow.

Then he slid without noise back to the nearest of the houses from which the smoke came. It was rather more pretentious than the others, built of planks instead of logs, and with shingles for a roof. The remains of a small portico formed the approach to the front door. Henry supposed that the house had been set on fire and that perhaps a heavy rain had saved a part of it.

A bar of light falling across the snow attracted his attention. He knew that it was the glow of a fire within coming through a window. A faint sound of voices reached his ears, and he moved forward slowly to the window. It was an oaken shutter originally fastened with a leather strap, but the strap was gone, and now some one had tied it, though not tightly, with a deer tendon. The crack between shutter and wall was at least three inches, and Henry could see within very well.

He pressed his side tightly to the wall and put his eyes to the crevice. What he saw within did not still any of those primitive feelings that had risen so strongly in his breast.

A great fire had been built in the log fireplace, but it was burning somewhat low now, having reached that mellow period of least crackling and greatest heat. The huge bed of coals threw a mass of varied and glowing colors across the floor. Large holes had been burned in the side of the room by the original fire, but Indian blankets had been fastened tightly over them.

In front of the fire sat Braxton Wyatt in a Loyalist uniform, a three-cornered hat cocked proudly on his head, and a small sword by his side. He had grown heavier, and Henry saw that the face had increased much in coarseness and cruelty. It had also increased in satisfaction. He was a great man now, as he saw great men, and both face and figure radiated gratification and pride as he lolled before the fire. At the other corner, sitting upon the floor and also in a Loyalist uniform, was his lieutenant, Levi Coleman, older, heavier, and with a short, uncommonly muscular figure. His face was dark and cruel, with small eyes set close together. A half dozen other white men and more than a dozen Indians were in the room. All these lay upon their blankets on the floor, because all the furniture had been destroyed. Yet they had eaten, and they lay there content in the soothing glow of the fire, like animals that had fed well. Henry was so near that he could hear every word anyone spoke.

"It was well that the Indians led us to this place, eh, Levi?" said Wyatt.

"I'm glad the fire spared a part of it," said Coleman. "Looks as if it was done just for us, to give us a shelter some cold winter night when we come along. I guess the Iroquois Aieroski is watching over us."

Wyatt laughed.

"You're a man that I like, Levi," he said. "You can see to the inside of things. It would be a good idea to use this place as a base and shelter, and make a raid on some of the settlements east of the hills, eh, Levi?"

"It could be done," said Coleman. "But just listen to that wind, will you! On a night like this it must cut like a saber's edge. Even our Iroquois are glad to be under a roof."

Henry still gazed in at the crack with eyes that were lighted up by an angry fire. So here was more talk of destruction and slaughter! His gaze alighted upon an Indian who sat in a corner engaged upon a task. Henry looked more closely, and saw that he was stretching a blonde-haired scalp over a small hoop. A shudder shook his whole frame. Only those who lived amid such scenes could understand the intensity of his feelings. He felt, too, a bitter sense of injustice. The doers of these deeds were here in warmth and comfort, while the innocent were dead or fugitives. He turned away from the window, stepping gently upon the snowshoes. He inferred that the remainder of Wyatt's band were quartered in the other house from which he had seen the smoke rising. It was about twenty rods away, but he did not examine it, because a great idea had been born suddenly in his brain. The attempt to fulfill the idea would be accompanied by extreme danger, but he did not hesitate a moment. He stole gently to one of the half-fallen outhouses and went inside. Here he found what he wanted, a large pine shelf that had been sheltered from rain and that was perfectly dry. He scraped off a large quantity of the dry pine until it formed almost a dust, and he did not cease until he had filled his cap with it. Then he cut off large splinters, until he had accumulated a great number, and after that he gathered smaller pieces of half-burned pine.

He was fully two hours doing this work, and the night advanced far, but he never faltered. His head was bare, but he was protected from the wind by a fragment of the outhouse wall. Every two or three minutes he stopped and listened for the sound of a creaking, sliding footstep on the snow, but, never hearing any, he always resumed his work with the same concentration. All the while the wind rose and moaned through the ruins of the little village. When Henry chanced to raise his head above the sheltering wall, it was like the slash of a knife across his cheek.

Finally he took half of the pine dust in his cap and a lot of the splinters under his arm, and stole back to the house from which the light had shone. He looked again through the crevice at the window. The light had died down much more, and both Wyatt and Coleman were asleep on the floor. But several of the Iroquois were awake, although they sat as silent and motionless as stones against the wall.

Henry moved from the window and selected a sheltered spot beside the plank wall. There he put the pine dust in a little heap on the snow and covered it over with pine splinters, on top of which he put larger pieces of pine. Then he went back for the remainder of the pine dust, and built a similar pyramid against a sheltered side of the second house.

The most delicate part of his task had now come, one that good fortune only could aid him in achieving, but the brave youth, his heart aflame with righteous anger against those inside, still pursued the work. His heart throbbed, but hand and eye were steady.

Now came the kindly stroke of fortune for which he had hoped. The wind rose much higher and roared harder against the house. It would prevent the Iroquois within, keen of ear as they were, from hearing a light sound without. Then he drew forth his flint and steel and struck them together with a hand so strong and swift that sparks quickly leaped forth and set fire to the pine tinder. Henry paused only long enough to see the flame spread to the splinters, and then he ran rapidly to the other house, where the task was repeated-he intended that his job should be thorough.

Pursuing this resolve to make his task complete, he came back to the first house and looked at his fire. It had already spread to the larger pieces of pine, and it could not go out now. The sound made by the flames blended exactly with the roaring of the wind, and another minute or two might pass before the Iroquois detected it.

Now his heart throbbed again, and exultation was mingled with his anger. By the time the Iroquois were aroused to the danger the flames would be so high that the wind would reach them. Then no one could put them out.

It might have been safer for him to flee deep into the forest at once, but that lingering desire to make his task complete and, also, the wish to see the result kept him from doing it. He merely walked across the open space and stood behind a tree at the edge of the forest.

Braxton Wyatt and his Tories and Iroquois were very warm, very snug, in the shelter of the old house with the great bed of coals before them. They may even have been dreaming peaceful and beautiful dreams, when suddenly an Iroquois sprang to his feet and uttered a cry that awoke all the rest.

"I smell smoke!" he exclaimed in his tongue, "and there is fire, too! I hear it crackle outside!"

Braxton Wyatt ran to the window and jerked it open. Flame and smoke blew in his face. He uttered an angry cry, and snatched at the pistol in his belt.

"The whole side of the house is on fire!" he exclaimed. "Whose neglect has done this?"

Coleman, shrewd and observing, was at his elbow.

"The fire was set on the outside," he said. "It was no carelessness of our men. Some enemy has done this!"

"It is true!" exclaimed Wyatt furiously. "Out, everybody! The house burns fast!"

There was a rush for the door. Already ashes and cinders were falling about their heads. Flames leaped high, were caught by the roaring winds, and roared with them. The shell of the house would soon be gone, and when Tories and Iroquois were outside they saw the remainder of their band pouring forth from the other house, which was also in flames.

No means of theirs could stop so great a fire, and they stood in a sort of stupefaction, watching it as it was fanned to greatest heights by the wind.

All the remaining outbuildings caught, also, and in a few moments nothing whatever would be left of the tiny village. Braxton Wyatt and his band must lie in the icy wilderness, and they could never use this place as a basis for attack upon settlements.

"How under the sun could it have happened?" exclaimed Wyatt.

"It didn't happen. It was done," said Coleman. "Somebody set these houses on fire while we slept within. Hark to that!"

An Iroquois some distance from the houses was bending over the snow where it was not yet melted by the heat. He saw there the track of snowshoes, and suddenly, looking toward the forest, whither they led, he saw a dark figure flit away among the trees.

CHAPTER XVIII. HENRY'S SLIDE

Henry Ware, lingering at the edge of the clearing, his body hidden behind one of the great tree trunks, had been watching the scene with a fascinated interest that would not let him go. He knew that his work there was done already. Everything would be utterly destroyed by the flames which, driven by the wind, leaped from one half-ruined building to another. Braxton Wyatt and his band would have enough to do sheltering themselves from the fierce winter, and the settlements could rest for a while at least. Undeniably he felt exultation as he witnessed the destructive work of his hand. The border, with its constant struggle for-life and terrible deeds, bred fierce passions.

In truth, although he did not know it himself, he stayed there to please his eye and heart. A new pulse beat triumphantly every time a timber, burned through, fell in, or a crash came from a falling roof. He laughed inwardly as the flames disclosed the dismay on the faces of the Iroquois and Tories, and it gave him deep satisfaction to see Braxton Wyatt, his gaudy little sword at his thigh, stalking about helpless. It was while he was looking, absorbed in such feelings, that the warrior of the alert eye saw him and gave the warning shout.

Henry turned in an instant, and darted away among the trees, half running, half sliding over the smooth, icy covering of the snow. After him came warriors and some Tories who had put on their snowshoes preparatory to the search through the forest for shelter. Several bullets were fired, but he was too far away for a good aim. He heard one go zip against a tree, and another cut the surface of the ice near him, but none touched him, and he sped easily on his snowshoes through the frozen forest. But Henry was fully aware of one thing that constituted his greatest danger. Many of these Iroquois had been trained all their lives to snowshoes, while he, however powerful and agile, was comparatively a beginner. He glanced back again and saw their dusky figures running among the trees, but they did not seem to be gaining. If one should draw too near, there was his rifle, and no man, white or red, in the northern or southern forests, could use it better. But for the present it was not needed. He pressed it closely, almost lovingly, to his side, this best friend of the scout and frontiersman.

He had chosen his course at the first leap. It was southward, toward the lake, and he did not make the mistake of diverging from his line, knowing that some part of the wide half circle of his pursuers would profit by it.

Henry felt a great upward surge. He had been the victor in what he meant to achieve, and he was sure that he would escape. The cold wind, whistling by, whipped his blood and added new strength to his great muscles. His ankles were not chafed or sore, and he sped forward on the snowshoes, straight and true. Whenever he came to a hill the pursuers would gain as he went up it, but when he went down the other side it was he who gained. He passed brooks, creeks, and once a small river, but they were frozen over, many inches deep, and he did not notice them. Again it was a lake a mile wide, but the smooth surface there merely increased his speed. Always he kept a wary look ahead for thickets through which he could not pass easily, and once he sent back a shout of defiance, which the Iroquois answered with a yell of anger.

He was fully aware that any accident to his snowshoes would prove fatal, the slipping of the thongs on his ankles or the breaking of a runner would end his flight, and in a long chase such an accident might happen. It might happen, too, to one or more of the Iroquois, but plenty of them would be left. Yet Henry had supreme confidence in his snowshoes. He had made them himself, he had seen that every part was good, and every thong had been fastened with care.

The wind which bad been roaring so loudly at the time of the fire sank to nothing. The leafless trees stood up, the branches unmoving. The forest was bare and deserted. All the animals, big and little, had gone into their lairs. Nobody witnessed the great pursuit save pursuers and pursued. Henry kept his direction clear in his mind, and allowed the Iroquois to take no advantage of a curve save once. Then he came to a thicket so large that he was compelled to make a considerable circle to pass it. He turned to the right, hence the Indians on the right gained, and they sent up a yell of delight. He replied defiantly and increased his speed.

But one of the Indians, a flying Mohawk, had come dangerously near-near enough, in fact, to fire a bullet that did not miss the fugitive much. It aroused Henry's anger. He took it as an indignity rather than a danger, and he resolved to avenge it. So far as firing was concerned, he was at a disadvantage. He must stop and turn around for his shot, while the Iroquois, without even checking speed, could fire straight at the flying target, ahead.

Nevertheless, he took the chance. He turned deftly on the snowshoes, fired as quick as lightning at the swift Mohawk, saw him fall, then Whirled and resumed his flight. He had lost ground, but he had inspired respect. A single man could not afford to come too near to a marksman so deadly, and the three or four who led dropped back with the main body.

Now Henry made his greatest effort. He wished to leave the foe far behind, to shake off his pursuit entirely. He bounded over the ice and snow with great leaps, and began to gain. Yet he felt at last the effects of so strenuous a flight. His breath became shorter; despite the intense cold, perspiration stood upon his face, and the straps that fastened the snowshoes were chafing his ankles. An end must come even to such strength as his. Another backward look, and he saw that the foe was sinking into the darkness. If he could only increase his speed again, he might leave the Iroquois now. He made a new call upon the will, and the body responded. For a few minutes his speed became greater. A disappointed shout arose behind him, and several shots were fired. But the bullets fell a hundred yards short, and then, as he passed over a little hill and into a wood beyond, he was hidden from the sight of his pursuers.

Henry knew that the Iroquois could trail him over the snow, but they could not do it at full speed, and he turned sharply off at an angle. Pausing a second or two for fresh breath, he continued on his new course, although not so fast as before. He knew that the Iroquois would rush straight ahead, and would not discover for two or three minutes that they were off the trail. It would take them another two or three minutes to recover, and he would make a gain of at least five minutes. Five minutes had saved the life of many a man on the border.

How precious those five minutes were! He would take them all. He ran forward some distance, stopped where the trees grew thick, and then enjoyed the golden five, minute by minute. He had felt that he was pumping the very lifeblood from his heart. His breath had come painfully, and the thongs of the snowshoes were chafing his ankles terribly. But those minutes were worth a year. Fresh air poured into his lungs, and the muscles became elastic once more. In so brief a space he had recreated himself.

Resuming his flight, he went at a steady pace, resolved not to do his utmost unless the enemy came in sight. About ten minutes later he heard a cry far behind him, and he believed it to be a signal from some Indian to the others that the trail was found again. But with so much advantage he felt sure that he was now quite safe. He ran, although at decreased speed, for about two hours more, and then he sat down on the upthrust root of a great oak. Here he depended most upon his ears. The forest was so silent that he could hear any noise at a great distance, but there was none. Trusting to his ears to warn him, he would remain there a long time for a thorough rest. He even dared to take off his snowshoes that he might rub his sore ankles, but he wrapped his heavy blanket about his body, lest he take deep cold in cooling off in such a temperature after so long a flight.

He sat enjoying a half hour, golden like the five minutes, and then he saw, outlined against the bright, moonlit sky, something that told him he must be on the alert again. It was a single ring of smoke, like that from a cigar, only far greater. It rose steadily, untroubled by wind until it was dissipated. It meant "attention!" and presently it was followed by a column of such rings, one following another beautifully. The column said: "The foe is near." Henry read the Indian signs perfectly. The rings were made by covering a little fire with a blanket for a moment and then allowing the smoke to ascend. On clear days such signals could be seen a distance of thirty miles or more, and he knew that they were full of significance.

Evidently the Iroquois party had divided into two or more bands. One had found his trail, and was signaling to the other. The party sending up the smoke might be a half mile away, but the others, although his trail was yet hidden from them, might be nearer. It was again time for flight.

He swiftly put on the snowshoes, neglecting no thong or lace, folded the blanket on his back again, and, leaving the friendly root, started once more. He ran forward at moderate speed for perhaps a mile, when he suddenly heard triumphant yells on both right and left. A strong party of Iroquois were coming up on either side, and luck had enabled them to catch him in a trap.

They were so near that they fired upon him, and one bullet nicked his glove, but he was hopeful that after his long rest he might again stave them off. He sent back no defiant cry, but, settling into determined silence, ran at his utmost speed. The forest here was of large trees, with no undergrowth, and he noticed that the two parties did not join, but kept on as they had come, one on the right and the other on the left. This fact must have some significance, but he could not fathom it. Neither could he guess whether the Indians were fresh or tired, but apparently they made no effort to come within range of his rifle.

Presently he made a fresh spurt of speed, the forest opened out, and then both bands uttered a yell full of ferocity and joy, the kind that savages utter only when they see their triumph complete.

Before, and far below Henry, stretched a vast, white expanse. He had come to the lake, but at a point where the cliff rose high like a mountain, and steep like a wall. The surface of the lake was so far down that it was misty white like a cloud. Now he understood the policy of the Indian bands in not uniting. They knew that they would soon reach the lofty cliffs of the lake, and if he turned to either right or left there was a band ready to seize him.

Henry's heart leaped up and then sank lower than ever before in his life. It seemed that he could not escape from so complete a trap, and Braxton Wyatt was not one who would spare a prisoner. That was perhaps the bitterest thing of all, to be taken and tortured by Braxton Wyatt. He was there. He could hear his voice in one of the bands, and then the courage that never failed him burst into fire again.

The Iroquois were coming toward him, shutting him out from retreat to either right or left, but not yet closing in because of his deadly rifle. He gave them a single look, put forth his voice in one great cry of defiance, and, rushing toward the edge of the mighty cliff, sprang boldly over.

As Henry plunged downward he heard behind him a shout of amazement and chagrin poured forth from many Iroquois throats, and, taking a single glance backward, he caught a glimpse of dusky faces stamped with awe. But the bold youth had not made a leap to destruction. In the passage of a second he had calculated rapidly and well. While the cliff at first glance seemed perpendicular, it could not be so. There was a slope coated with two feet of snow, and swinging far back on the heels of his snowshoes, he shot downward like one taking a tremendous slide on a toboggan. Faster and faster he went, but deeper and deeper he dug his shoes into the snow, until he lay back almost flat against its surface. This checked his speed somewhat, but it was still very great, and, preserving his self-control perfectly, he prayed aloud to kindly Providence to save him from some great boulder or abrupt drop.

The snow from his runners flew in a continuous shower behind him as he descended. Yet he drew himself compactly together, and held his rifle parallel with his body. Once or twice, as he went over a little ridge, he shot clear of the snow, but he held his body rigid, and the snow beyond saved him from a severe bruise. Then his speed was increased again, and all the time the white surface of the lake below, seen dimly through the night and his flight, seemed miles away.

He might never reach that surface alive, but of one thing lie was sure. None of the Iroquois or Tories had dared to follow. Braxton Wyatt could have no triumph over him. He was alone in his great flight. Once a projection caused him to turn a little to one side. He was in momentary danger of turning entirely, and then of rolling head over heels like a huge snowball, but with a mighty effort he righted himself, and continued the descent on the runners, with the heels plowing into the ice and the snow.

Now that white expanse which had seemed so far away came miles nearer. Presently he would be there. The impossible had become possible, the unattainable was about to be attained. He gave another mighty dig with his shoes, the last reach of the slope passed behind him, and he shot out on the frozen surface of the lake, bruised and breathless, but without a single broken bone.

The lake was covered with ice a foot thick, and over this lay frozen snow, which stopped Henry forty or fifty yards from the cliff. There he lost his balance at last, and fell on his side, where he lay for a few moments, weak, panting, but triumphant.

When he stood upright again he felt his body, but he had suffered nothing save some bruises, that would heal in their own good time. His deerskin clothing was much torn, particularly on the back, where he had leaned upon the ice and snow, but the folded blanket had saved him to a considerable extent. One of his shoes was pulled loose, and presently he discovered that his left ankle was smarting and burning at a great rate. But he did not mind these things at all, so complete was his sense of victory. He looked up at the mighty white wall that stretched above him fifteen hundred feet, and he wondered at his own tremendous exploit. The wall ran away for miles, and the Iroquois could not reach him by any easier path. He tried to make out figures on the brink looking down at him, but it was too far away, and he saw only a black line.

He tightened the loose shoe and struck out across the lake. He was far away from "The Alcove," and he did not intend to go there, lest the Iroquois, by chance, come upon his trail and follow it to the refuge. But as it was no more than two miles across the lake at that point, and the Iroquois would have to make a great curve to reach the other side, he felt perfectly safe. He walked slowly across, conscious all the time of an increasing pain in his left ankle, which must now be badly swollen, and he did not stop until he penetrated some distance among low bills. Here, under an overhanging cliff with thick bushes in front, he found a partial shelter, which he cleared out yet further. Then with infinite patience he built a fire with splinters that he cut from dead boughs, hung his blanket in front of it on two sticks that the flame might not be seen, took off his snowshoes, leggins, and socks, and bared his ankles. Both were swollen, but the left much more badly than the other. He doubted whether he would be able to walk on the following day, but he rubbed them a long time, both with the palms of his hands and with snow, until they felt better. Then he replaced his clothing, leaned back against the faithful snowshoes which had saved his life, however much they had hurt his ankles, and gave himself up to the warmth of the fire.

It was very luxurious, this warmth and this rest, after so long and terrible a flight, and he was conscious of a great relaxation, one which, if he yielded to it completely, would make his muscles so stiff and painful that he could not use them. Hence he stretched his arms and legs many times, rubbed his ankles again, and then, remembering that he had venison, ate several strips.

He knew that he had taken a little risk with the fire, but a fire he was bound to have, and he fed it again until he had a great mass of glowing coals, although there was no blaze. Then he took down the blanket, wrapped himself in it, and was soon asleep before the fire. He slept long and deeply, and although, when he awoke, the day had fully come, the coals were not yet out entirely. He arose, but such a violent pain from his left ankle shot through him that he abruptly sat down again. As he bad feared, it had swollen badly during the night, and he could not walk.

In this emergency Henry displayed no petulance, no striving against unchangeable circumstance. He drew up more wood, which he had stacked against the cliff, and put it on the coals. He hung up the blanket once more in order that it might hide the fire, stretched out his lame leg, and calmly made a breakfast off the last of his venison. He knew he was in a plight that might appall the bravest, but he kept himself in hand. It was likely that the Iroquois thought him dead, crushed into a shapeless mass by his frightful slide of fifteen hundred feet, and he had little fear of them, but to be unable to walk and alone in an icy wilderness without food was sufficient in itself. He calculated that it was at least a dozen miles to "The Alcove," and the chances were a hundred to one against any of his comrades wandering his way. He looked once more at his swollen left ankle, and he made a close calculation. It would be three days, more likely four, before he could walk upon it. Could he endure hunger that long? He could. He would! Crouched in his nest with his back to the cliff, he had defense against any enemy in his rifle and pistol. By faithful watching he might catch sight of some wandering animal, a target for his rifle and then food for his stomach. His wilderness wisdom warned him that there was nothing to do but sit quiet and wait.

He scarcely moved for hours. As long as he was still his ankle troubled him but little. The sun came out, silver bright, but it had no warmth. The surface of the lake was shown only by the smoothness of its expanse; the icy covering was the same everywhere over hills and valleys. Across the lake he saw the steep down which he had slid, looming white and lofty. In the distance it looked perpendicular, and, whatever its terrors, it had, beyond a doubt, saved his life. He glanced down at his swollen ankle, and, despite his helpless situation, he was thankful that he had escaped so well.

About noon he moved enough to throw up the snowbanks higher all around himself in the fashion of an Eskimos house. Then he let the fire die except some coals that gave forth no smoke, stretched the blanket over his head in the manner of a roof, and once more resumed his quiet and stillness. He was now like a crippled animal in its lair, but he was warm, and his wound did not hurt him. But hunger began to trouble him. He was young and so powerful that his frame demanded much sustenance. Now it cried aloud its need! He ate two or three handfuls of snow, and for a few moments it seemed to help him a little, but his hunger soon came back as strong as ever. Then he tightened his belt and sat in grim silence, trying to forget that there was any such thing as food.

The effort of the will was almost a success throughout the afternoon, but before night it failed. He began to have roseate visions of Long Jim trying venison, wild duck, bear, and buffalo steaks over the coals. He could sniff the aroma, so powerful had his imagination become, and, in fancy, his month watered, while its roof was really dry. They were daylight visions, and he knew it well, but they taunted him and made his pain fiercer. He slid forward a little to the mouth of his shelter, and thrust out his rifle in the hope that he would see some wild creature, no matter what; he felt that he could shoot it at any distance, and then he would feast!

He saw nothing living, either on earth or in the air, only motionless white, and beyond, showing but faintly now through the coming twilight, the lofty cliff that had saved him.

He drew back into his lair, and the darkness came down. Despite his hunger, he slept fairly well. In the night a little snow fell at times, but his blanket roof protected him, and he remained dry and warm. The new snow was, in a way, a satisfaction, as it completely hid his trail from the glance of any wandering Indian. He awoke the next morning to a gray, somber day, with piercing winds from the northwest. He did not feel the pangs of hunger until he had been awake about a half hour, and then they came with redoubled force. Moreover, he had become weaker in the night, and, added to the loss of muscular strength, was a decrease in the power of the will. Hunger was eating away his mental as well as his physical fiber. He did not face the situation with quite the same confidence that he felt the day before. The wilderness looked a little more threatening.

His lips felt as if he were suffering from fever, and his shoulders and back were stiff. But he drew his belt tighter again, and then uncovered his left ankle. The swelling had gone down a little, and he could move it with more freedom than on the day before, but he could not yet walk. Once more he made his grim calculation. In two days he could certainly walk and hunt game or make a try for "The Alcove," so far as his ankle was concerned, but would hunger overpower him before that time? Gaining strength in one direction, he was losing it in another.

Now he began to grow angry with himself. The light inroad that famine made upon his will was telling. It seemed incredible that he, so powerful, so skillful, so self reliant, so long used to the wilderness and to every manner of hardship, should be held there in a snowbank by a bruised ankle to die like a crippled rabbit. His comrades could not be more than ten miles away. He could walk. He would walk! He stood upright and stepped out into the snow, but pain, so agonizing that he could scarcely keep from crying out, shot through his whole body, and he sank back into the shelter, sure not to make such an experiment again for another full day.

The day passed much like its predecessor, except that he took down the blanket cover of his snow hut and kindled up his fire again, more for the sake of cheerfulness than for warmth, because he was not suffering from cold. There was a certain life and light about the coals and the bright flame, but the relief did not last long, and by and by he let it go out. Then be devoted himself to watching the heavens and the surface of the snow. Some winter bird, duck or goose, might be flying by, or a wandering deer might be passing. He must not lose any such chance. He was more than ever a fierce creature of prey, sitting at the mouth of his den, the rifle across his knee, his tanned face so thin that the cheek bones showed high and sharp, his eyes bright with fever and the fierce desire for prey, and the long, lean body drawn forward as if it were about to leap.

He thought often of dragging himself down to the lake, breaking a hole in the ice, and trying to fish, but the idea invariably came only to be abandoned. He had neither hook nor bait. In the afternoon he chewed the edge of his buckskin hunting shirt, but it was too thoroughly tanned and dry. It gave back no sustenance. He abandoned the experiment and lay still for a long time.

That night he had a slight touch of frenzy, and began to laugh at himself. It was a huge joke! What would Timmendiquas or Thayendanegea think of him if they knew how he came to his end? They would put him with old squaws or little children. And how Braxton Wyatt and his lieutenant, the squat Tory, would laugh! That was the bitterest thought of all. But the frenzy passed, and he fell into a sleep which was only a succession of bad dreams. He was running the gauntlet again among the Shawnees. Again, kneeling to drink at the clear pool, he saw in the water the shadow of the triumphant warrior holding the tomahawk above him. One after another the most critical periods of his life were lived over again, and then he sank into a deep torpor, from which he did not rouse himself until far into the next day.

Henry was conscious that he was very weak, but he seemed to have regained much of his lost will. He looked once more at the fatal left ankle. It had improved greatly. He could even stand upon it, but when he rose to his feet he felt a singular dizziness. Again, what he had gained in one way he had lost in another. The earth wavered. The smooth surface of the lake seemed to rise swiftly, and then to sink as swiftly. The far slope down which he had shot rose to the height of miles. There was a pale tinge, too, over the world. He sank down, not because of his ankle, but because he was afraid his dizzy head would make him fall.

The power of will slipped away again for a minute or two. He was ashamed of such extraordinary weakness. He looked at one of his hands. It was thin, like the band of a man wasted with fever, and the blue veins stood out on the back of it. He could scarcely believe that the hand was his own. But after the first spasm of weakness was over, the precious will returned. He could walk. Strength enough to permit him to hobble along had returned to the ankle at last, and mind must control the rest of his nervous system, however weakened it might be. He must seek food.

He withdrew into the farthest recess of his covert, wrapped the blanket tightly about his body, and lay still for a long time. He was preparing both mind and body for the supreme effort. He knew that everything hung now on the surviving remnants of his skill and courage.

Weakened by shock and several days of fasting, he had no great reserve now except the mental, and he used that to the utmost. It was proof of his youthful greatness that it stood the last test. As he lay there, the final ounce of will and courage came. Strength which was of the mind rather than of the body flowed back into his veins; he felt able to dare and to do; the pale aspect of the world went away, and once more he was Henry Ware, alert, skillful, and always triumphant.

Then he rose again, folded the blanket, and fastened it on his shoulders. He looked at the snowshoes, but decided that his left ankle, despite its great improvement, would not stand the strain. He must break his way through the snow, which was a full three feet in depth. Fortunately the crust had softened somewhat in the last two or three days, and he did not have a covering of ice to meet.

He pushed his way for the first time from the lair under the cliff, his rifle held in his ready hands, in order that he might miss no chance at game. To an ordinary observer there would have been no such chance at all. It was merely a grim white wilderness that might have been without anything living from the beginning. But Henry, the forest runner, knew better. Somewhere in the snow were lairs much like the one that he had left, and in these lairs were wild animals. To any such wild animal, whether panther or bear, the hunter would now have been a fearsome object, with his hollow cheeks, his sunken fiery eyes, and his thin lips opening now and then, and disclosing the two rows of strong white teeth.

Henry advanced about a rod, and then he stopped, breathing hard, because it was desperate work for one in his condition to break his way through snow so deep. But his ankle stood the strain well, and his courage increased rather than diminished. He was no longer a cripple confined to one spot. While he stood resting, he noticed a clump of bushes about half a rod to his left, and a hopeful idea came to him.

He broke his way slowly to the bushes, and then he searched carefully among them. The snow was not nearly so thick there, and under the thickest clump, where the shelter was best, he saw a small round opening. In an instant all his old vigorous life, all the abounding hope which was such a strong characteristic of his nature, came back to him. Already he had triumphed over Indians, Tories, the mighty slope, snow, ice, crippling, and starvation.

He laid the rifle on the snow and took the ramrod in his right hand. He thrust his left hand into the hole, and when the rabbit leaped for life from his warm nest a smart blow of the ramrod stretched him dead at the feet of the hunter. Henry picked up the rabbit. It was large and yet fat. Here was food for two meals. In the race between the ankle and starvation, the ankle had won.

He did not give way to any unseemly elation. He even felt a momentary sorrow that a life must perish to save his own, because all these wild things were his kindred now. He returned by the path that he had broken, kindled his fire anew, dexterously skinned and cleaned his rabbit, then cooked it and ate half, although he ate slowly and with intervals between each piece. How delicious it tasted, and how his physical being longed to leap upon it and devour it, but the power of the mind was still supreme. He knew what was good for himself, and he did it. Everything was done in order and with sobriety. Then he put the rest of the rabbit carefully in his food pouch, wrapped the blanket about his body, leaned back, and stretched his feet to the coals.

What an extraordinary change had come over the world in an hour! He had not noticed before the great beauty of the lake, the lofty cliffs on the farther shore, and the forest clothed in white and hanging with icicles.

The winter sunshine was molten silver, pouring down in a flood.

It was not will now, but actuality, that made him feel the strength returning to his frame. He knew that the blood in his veins had begun to sparkle, and that his vitality was rising fast. He could have gone to sleep peacefully, but instead he went forth and hunted again. He knew that where the rabbit had been, others were likely to be near, and before he returned he had secured two more. Both of these he cleaned and cooked at once. When this was done night had come, but he ate again, and then, securing all his treasures about him, fell into the best sleep that he had enjoyed since his flight.

He felt very strong the next morning, and he might have started then, but he was prudent. There was still a chance of meeting the Iroquois, and the ankle might not stand so severe a test. He would rest in his nest for another day, and then he would be equal to anything. Few could lie a whole day in one place with but little to do and with nothing passing before the eyes, but it was a part of Henry's wilderness training, and he showed all the patience of the forester. He knew, too, as the hours went by, that his strength was rising all the while. To-morrow almost the last soreness would be gone from his ankle and then he could glide swiftly over the snow, back to his comrades. He was content. He had, in fact, a sense of great triumph because he had overcome so much, and here was new food in this example for future efforts of the mind, for future victories of the will over the body. The wintry sun came to the zenith, then passed slowly down the curve, but all the time the boy scarcely stirred. Once there was a flight of small birds across the heavens, and he watched them vaguely, but apparently he took no interest. Toward night he stood up in his recess and flexed and tuned his muscles for a long time, driving out any stiffness that might come through long lack of motion. Then he ate and lay down, but he did not yet sleep.

The night was clear, and he looked away toward the point where he knew "The Alcove" lay. A good moon was now shining, and stars by the score were springing out. Suddenly at a point on that far shore a spark of red light appeared and twinkled. Most persons would have taken it for some low star, but Henry knew better. It was fire put there by human hand for a purpose, doubtless a signal, and as he looked a second spark appeared by the first, then a third, then a fourth. He uttered a great sigh of pleasure. It was his four friends signaling to him somewhere in the vast unknown that they were alive and well, and beckoning him to come. The lights burned for fifteen or twenty minutes, and then all went out together. Henry turned over on his side and fell sound asleep. In the morning he put on his snowshoes and started.

CHAPTER XIX. THE SAFE RETURN

The surface of the snow had frozen again in the night, and Henry found good footing for his shoes. For a while he leaned most on the right ankle, but, as his left developed no signs of soreness, he used them equally, and sped forward, his spirits rising at every step. The air was cold, and there was but little breeze, but his own motion made a wind that whipped his face. The hollows were mostly gone from his cheeks, and his eyes no longer had the fierce, questing look of the famishing wild animal in search of prey. A fine red color was suffused through the brown of his face. He had chosen his course with due precaution. The broad surface, smooth, white, and glittering, tempted, but he put the temptation away. He did not wish to run any chance whatever of another Iroquois pursuit, and he kept in the forest that ran down close to the water's edge. It was tougher traveling there, but he persisted.

But all thought of weariness and trouble was lost in his glorious freedom. With his crippled ankle he had been really like a prisoner in his cell, with a ball and chain to his foot. Now he flew along, while the cold wind whipped his blood, and felt what a delight it was merely to live. He went on thus for hours, skirting down toward the cliffs that contained "The Alcove." He rested a while in the afternoon and ate the last of his rabbit, but before twilight he reached the creek, and stood at the hidden path that led up to their home.

Henry sat down behind thick bushes and took off his snowshoes. To one who had never come before, the whole place would have seemed absolutely desolate, and even to one not a stranger no sign of life would have been visible had he not possessed uncommonly keen eyes. But Henry had such eyes. He saw the faintest wisp of smoke stealing away against the surface of the cliff, and he felt confident that all four were there. He resolved to surprise them.

Laying the shoes aside, he crept so carefully up the path that he dislodged no snow and made no noise of any kind. As he gradually approached "The Alcove" he beard the murmur of voices, and presently, as he turned an angle in the path, he saw a beam of glorious mellow light falling on the snow.

But the murmur of the voices sent a great thrill of delight through him. Low and indistinct as they were, they had a familiar sound. He knew all those tones. They were the voices of his faithful comrades, the four who had gone with him through so many perils and hardships, the little band who with himself were ready to die at any time, one for another.

He crept a little closer, and then a little closer still. Lying almost flat on the steep path, and drawing himself forward, he looked into "The Alcove." A fire of deep, red coals glowed in one corner, and disposed about it were the four. Paul lay on his elbow on a deerskin, and was gazing into the coals. Tom Ross was working on a pair of moccasins, Long Jim was making some kind of kitchen implement, and Shif'less Sol was talking. Henry could hear the words distinctly, and they were about himself.

"Henry will turn up all right," he was saying. "Hasn't he always done it afore? Then ef he's always done it afore he's shorely not goin' to break his rule now. I tell you, boys, thar ain't enough Injuns an' Tories between Canady an' New Orleans, an' the Mississippi an' the Atlantic, to ketch Henry. I bet I could guess what he's doin' right at this moment."

"What is he doing, Sol?" asked Paul.

"When I shet my eyes ez I'm doin' now I kin see him," said the shiftless one. "He's away off thar toward the north, skirtin' around an Injun village,

Mohawk most likely, lookin' an' listenin' an' gatherin' talk about their plans."

"He ain't doin' any sech thing," broke in Long Jim.

"I've sleet my eyes, too, Sol Hyde, jest ez tight ez you've shet yours, an' I see him, too, but he ain't doin' any uv the things that you're talkin' about."

"What is he doing, Jim?" asked Paul.

"Henry's away off to the south, not to the north," replied the long one, "an' he's in the Iroquois village that we burned. One house has been left standin', an' he's been occupyin' it while the big snow's on the groun'. A whole deer is hangin' from the wall, an' he's been settin' thar fur days, eatin' so much an' hevin' such a good time that the fat's hangin' down over his cheeks, an' his whole body is threatenin' to bust right out uv his huntin' shirt."

Paul moved a little on his elbow and turned the other side of his face to the fire. Then he glanced at the silent worker with the moccasins.

"Sol and Jim don't seem to agree much in their second sight," he said. "Can you have any vision, too, Tom?"

"Yes," replied Tom Ross, "I kin. I shet my eyes, but I don't see like either Sol or Jim, 'cause both uv 'em see wrong. I see Henry, an' I see him plain. He's had a pow'ful tough time. He ain't threatenin' to bust with fat out uv no huntin' shirt, his cheeks ain't so full that they are fallin' down over his jaws. It's t'other way roun'; them cheeks are sunk a mite, he don't fill out his clothes, an' when he crawls along he drags his left leg a leetle, though he hides it from hisself. He ain't spyin' on no Injun village, an' he ain't in no snug camp with a dressed deer hangin' by the side uv him. It's t'other way 'roan'. He's layin' almost flat on his face not twenty feet from us, lookin' right in at us, an' I wuz the first to see him."

All the others sprang to their feet in astonishment, and Henry likewise sprang to his feet. Three leaps, and he was in the mellow glow.

"And so you saw me, Tom," he exclaimed, as he joyously grasped one hand after another. "I might have known that, while I could stalk some of you, I could not stalk all of you."

"I caught the glimpse uv you," said Silent Tom, "while Sol an' Jim wuz talkin' the foolish talk that they most always talk, an' when Paul called on me, I thought I would give 'em a dream that 'wuz true, an' worth tellin'."

"You're right," said Henry. "I've not been having any easy time, and for a while, boys, it looked as if I never would come back. Sit down, and I will tell you all about it."

They gave him the warmest place by the fire, brought him the tenderest food, and he told the long and thrilling tale.

"I don't believe anybody else but you would have tried it, Henry," said Paul, when they heard of the fearful slide.

"Any one of you would have done it," said Henry, modestly.

"I'm pow'ful glad that you done it for two reasons," said Shif'less Sol. "One, 'cause it helped you to git away, an' the other, 'cause that scoundrel, Braxton Wyatt, didn't take you. 'Twould hurt my pride tre-men-jeous for any uv us to be took by Braxton Wyatt."

"You speak for us all there, Sol," said Paul.

"What have all of you been doing?" asked Henry.

"Not much of anything," replied Shif'less Sol. "We've been scoutin' several times, lookin' fur you, though we knowed you'd come in some time or other, but mostly we've been workin' 'roun' the place here, fixin' it up warmer an' storin' away food."

"We'll have to continue at that for some time, I'm afraid," said Henry, "unless this snow breaks up. Have any of you heard if any movement is yet on foot against the Iroquois?"

"Tom ran across some scouts from the militia," replied Paul, "and they said nothing could be done until warm weather came. Then a real army would march."

"I hope so," said Henry earnestly.

But for the present the five could achieve little. The snow lasted a long time, but it was finally swept away by big rains. It poured for two days and nights, and even when the rain ceased the snow continued to melt under the warmer air. The water rushed in great torrents down the cliffs, and would have entered "The Alcove" had not the five made provision to turn it away. As it was, they sat snug and dry, listening to the gush of the water, the sign of falling snow, and the talk of one another. Yet the time dragged.

"Man wuz never made to be a caged animile," said Shif'less Sol. "The longer I stay shet up in one place, the weaker I become. My temper don't improve, neither, an' I ain't happy."

"Guess it's the same with all uv us," said Tom Ross.

But when the earth came from beneath the snow, although it was still cold weather, they began again to range the forest far in every direction, and they found that the Indians, and the Tories also, were becoming active. There were more burnings, more slaughters, and more scalpings. The whole border was still appalled at the massacres of Wyoming and Cherry

Valley, and the savages were continually spreading over a wider area. Braxton Wyatt at the head of his band, and with the aid of his Tory lieutenant, Levi Coleman, had made for himself a name equal to that of Walter Butler. As for "Indian" Butler and his men, no men were hated more thoroughly than they.

The five continued to do the best they could, which was much, carrying many a warning, and saving some who would otherwise have been victims. While they devoted themselves to their strenuous task, great events in which they were to take a part were preparing. The rear guard of the Revolution was about to become for the time the main guard. A great eye had been turned upon the ravaged and bleeding border, and a great mind, which could bear misfortune-even disaster-without complaint, was preparing to send help to those farther away. So mighty a cry of distress had risen, that the power of the Iroquois must be destroyed. As the warm weather came, the soldiers began to march.

Rumors that a formidable foe was about to advance reached the Iroquois and their allies, the Tories, the English, and the Canadians. There was a great stirring among the leaders, Thayendanegea, Hiokatoo, Sangerachte, the Johnsons, the Butlers, Claus, and the rest. Haldimand, the king's representative in Canada, sent forth an urgent call to all the Iroquois to meet the enemy. The Tories were' extremely active. Promises were made to the tribes that they should have other victories even greater than those of Wyoming and Cherry Valley, and again the terrible Queen Esther went among them, swinging her great war tomahawk over her head and chanting her song of death. She, more than any other, inflamed the Iroquois, and they were eager for the coming contest.

Timmendiquas had gone back to the Ohio country in the winter, but, faithful to his promise to give Thayendanegea help to the last, he returned in the spring with a hundred chosen warriors of the Wyandot nation, a reenforcement the value of which could not be estimated too highly.

Henry and his comrades felt the stir as they roamed through the forest, and they thrilled at the thought that the crisis was approaching. Then they set out for Lake Otsego, where the army was gathering for the great campaign. They were equipped thoroughly, and they were now so well known in the region that they knew they would be welcome.

They traveled several days, and were preparing to encamp for the last night within about fifteen miles of the lake when Henry, scouting as usual to see if an enemy were near, heard a footstep in the forest. He wheeled instantly to cover behind the body of a great beech tree, and the stranger sought to do likewise, only he had no convenient tree that was so large. It was about the twelfth hour, but Henry could see a portion of a body protruding beyond a slim oak, and he believed that he recognized it. As he held the advantage he would, at any rate, hail the stranger.

"Ho, Cornelius Heemskerk, Dutchman, fat man, great scout and woodsman, what are you doing in my wilderness? Stand forth at once and give an account of yourself, or I will shoot off the part of your body that sticks beyond that oak tree!"

The answer was instantaneous. A round, plump body revolved from the partial shelter of the tree and stood upright in the open, rifle in hand and cap thrown back from a broad ruddy brow.

"Ho, Mynheer Henry Ware," replied Cornelius Heemskerk in a loud, clear tone, "I am in your woods on perhaps the same errand that you are. Come from behind that beech and let us see which has the stronger grip."

Henry stood forth, and the two clasped hands in a grip so powerful that both winced. Then they released hands simultaneously, and Heemskerk asked:

"And the other four mynheers? Am I wrong to say that they are near, somewhere?"

"You are not wrong," replied Henry. "They are alive, well and hungry, not a mile from here. There is one man whom they would be very glad to see, and his name is Cornelius Heemskerk, who is roaming in our woods without a permit."

The round, ruddy face of the Dutchman glowed. It was obvious that he felt as much delight in seeing Henry as Henry felt in seeing him.

"My heart swells," he said. "I feared that you might have been killed or scalped, or, at the best, have gone back to that far land of Kentucky."

"We have wintered well," said Henry, "in a place of which I shall not tell you now, and we are here to see the campaign through."

"I come, too, for the same purpose," said Heemskerk. "We shall be together. It is goot." "Meanwhile," said Henry, "our camp fire is lighted. Jim Hart, whom you have known of old, is cooking strips of meat over the coals, and, although it is a mile away, the odor of them is very pleasant in my nostrils. I wish to go back there, and it will be all the more delightful to me, and to those who wait, if I can bring with me such a welcome guest."

"Lead on, mynheer," said Cornelius Heemskerk sententiously.

He received an equally emphatic welcome from the others, and then they ate and talked. Heemskerk was sanguine.

"Something will be done this time," he said. "Word has come from the great commander that the Iroquois must be crushed. The thousands who have fallen must be avenged, and this great fire along our border must be stopped. If it cannot be done, then we perish. We have old tales in my own country of the cruel deeds that the Spaniards did long, long ago, but they were not worse than have been done here."

The five made no response, but the mind of every one of them traveled back to Wyoming and all that they had seen there, and the scars and traces of many more tragedies.

They reached the camp on Lake Otsego the next day, and Henry saw that all they had heard was true. The most formidable force that they had ever seen was gathering. There were many companies in the Continental buff and blue, epauletted officers, bayonets and cannon. The camp was full of life, energy, and hope, and the five at once felt the influence of it. They found here old friends whom they had known in the march on Oghwaga, William Gray, young Taylor, and others, and they were made very welcome. They were presented to General James Clinton, then in charge, received roving commissions as scouts and hunters, and with Heemskerk and the two celebrated borderers, Timothy Murphy and David Elerson, they roamed the forest in a great circle about the lake, bringing much valuable information about the movements of the enemy, who in their turn were gathering in force, while the royal authorities were dispatching both Indians and white men from Canada to help them.

These great scouting expeditions saved the five from much impatience. It takes a long time for an army to gather and then to equip itself for the march, and they were so used to swift motion that it was now a part of their nature. At last the army was ready, and it left the lake. Then it proceeded in boats down the Tioga flooded to a sufficient depth by an artificial dam built with immense labor, to its confluence with the larger river. Here were more men, and the five saw a new commander, General James Sullivan, take charge of the united force. Then the army, late in August, began its march upon the Iroquois.

The five were now in the van, miles ahead of the main guard. They knew that no important movement of so large a force could escape the notice of the enemy, but they, with other scouts, made it their duty to see that the Americans marched into no trap.

It was now the waning summer. The leaves were lightly touched with brown, and the grass had begun to wither. Berries were ripening on the vines, and the quantity of game had increased, the wild animals returning to the land from which civilized man had disappeared. The desolation seemed even more complete than in the autumn before. In the winter and spring the Iroquois and Tories had destroyed the few remnants of houses that were left. Braxton Wyatt and his band had been particularly active in this work, and many tales had come of his cruelty and that of his swart Tory lieutenant, Coleman. Henry was sure, too, that Wyatt's band, which numbered perhaps fifty Indians and Tories, was now in front of them.

He, his comrades, Heemskerk, Elerson, Murphy, and four others, twelve brave forest runners all told, went into camp one night about ten miles ahead of the army. They lighted no fire, and, even had it been cold, they would not have done so, as the region was far too dangerous for any light. Yet the little band felt no fear. They were only twelve, it is true, but such a twelve! No chance would either Indians or Tories have to surprise them.

They merely lay down in the thick brushwood, three intending to keep watch while the others slept. Henry, Shif'less Sol, and Heemskerk were the sentinels. It was very late, nearly midnight; the sky was clear, and presently they saw smoke rings ascending from high hills to their right, to be answered soon by other rings of smoke to their left. The three watched them with but little comment, and read every signal in turn. They said: "The enemy is still advancing," "He is too strong for us...... We must retreat and await our brethren."

"It means that there will be no battle to-morrow, at least," whispered Heemskerk. "Brant is probably ahead of us in command, and he will avoid us until he receives the fresh forces from Canada."

"I take it that you're right," Henry whispered back. "Timmendiquas also is with him, and the two great chiefs are too cunning to fight until they can bring their last man into action."

"An' then," said the shiftless one, "we'll see what happens."

"Yes," said Henry very gravely, "we'll see what happens. The Iroquois are a powerful confederacy. They've ruled in these woods for hundreds of years. They're led by great chiefs, and they're helped by our white enemies. You can't tell what would happen even to an army like ours in an ambush."

Shif'less Sol nodded, and they said no more until an hour later, when they heard footsteps. They awakened the others, and the twelve, crawling to the edge of the brushwood, lay almost flat upon their faces, with their hands upon the triggers of their rifles.

Braxton Wyatt and his band of nearly threescore, Indians and Tories in about equal numbers, were passing. Wyatt walked at the head. Despite his youth, he had acquired an air of command, and he seemed a fit leader for such a crew. He wore a faded royal uniform, and, while a small sword hung at his side, he also carried a rifle on his shoulder. Close behind him was the swart and squat Tory, Coleman, and then came Indians and Tories together.

The watchful eyes of Henry saw three fresh scalps hanging from as many belts, and the finger that lay upon the trigger of his rifle fairly ached to press it. What an opportunity this would be if the twelve were only forty, or even thirty! With the advantage of surprise they might hope to annihilate this band which had won such hate for itself on the border. But twelve were not enough and twelve such lives could not be spared at a time when the army needed them most.

Henry pressed his teeth firmly together in order to keep down his disappointment by a mere physical act if possible. He happened to look at Shif'less Sol, and saw that his teeth were pressed together in the same manner. It is probable that like feelings swayed every one of the twelve, but they were so still in the brushwood that no Iroquois heard grass or leaf rustle. Thus the twelve watched the sixty pass, and after they were gone, Henry, Shif'less Sol, and Tim Murphy followed for several miles. They saw Wyatt proceed toward the Chemung River, and as they approached the stream they beheld signs of fortifications. It was now nearly daylight, and, as Indians were everywhere, they turned back. But they were convinced that the enemy meant to fight on the Chemung.

CHAPTER XX. A GLOOMY COUNCIL

The next night after Henry Ware and his comrades lay in the brushwood and saw Braxton Wyatt and his band pass, a number of men, famous or infamous in their day, were gathered around a low camp fire on the crest of a small hill. The most distinguished of them all in looks was a young Indian chief of great height and magnificent build, with a noble and impressive countenance. He wore nothing of civilized attire, the nearest approach to it being the rich dark-blue blanket that was flung gracefully over his right shoulder. It was none other than the great Wyandot chief, Timmendiquas, saying little, and listening without expression to the words of the others.

Near Timmendiquas sat Thayendanegea, dressed as usual in his mixture of savage and civilized costume, and about him were other famous Indian chiefs, The Corn Planter, Red jacket, Hiokatoo, Sangerachte, Little Beard, a young Seneca renowned for ferocity, and others.

On the other side of the fire sat the white men: the young Sir John Johnson, who, a prisoner to the Colonials, had broken his oath of neutrality, the condition of his release, and then, fleeing to Canada, had returned to wage bloody war on the settlements; his brother-in-law, Colonel Guy Johnson; the swart and squat John Butler of Wyoming infamy; his son, Walter Butler, of the pallid face, thin lips, and cruel heart; the Canadian Captain MacDonald; Braxton Wyatt; his lieutenant, the dark Tory, Coleman; and some others who had helped to ravage their former land.

Sir John Johnson, a tall man with blue eyes set close together, wore the handsome uniform of his Royal Greens; he had committed many dark deeds or permitted them to be done by men under his command, and he had secured the opportunity only through his broken oath, but he had lost greatly. The vast estates of his father, Sir William Johnson, were being torn from him, and perhaps he saw, even then, that in return for what he had done he would lose all and become an exile from the country in which he was born.

It was not a cheerful council. There was no exultation as after Wyoming and Cherry Valley and the Minisink and other places. Sir John bit his lip uneasily, and his brother-in-law, resting his hand on his knee, stared gloomily at the fire. The two Butlers were silent, and the dark face of Thayendanegea was overcast.

A little distance before these men was a breastwork about half a mile long, connecting with a bend of the river in such a manner that an enemy could attack only in front and on one flank, that flank itself being approached only by the ascent of a steep ridge which ran parallel to the river. The ground about the camp was covered with pine and scrub oaks. Many others had been cut down and added to the breastwork. A deep brook ran at the foot of the hill on which the leaders sat. About the slopes of this hill and another, a little distance away, sat hundreds of Indian warriors, all in their war paint, and other hundreds of their white allies, conspicuous among them Johnson's Royal Greens and Butler's Rangers. These men made but little noise now. They were resting and waiting.

Thayendanegea was the first to break the silence in the group at the fire. He turned his dark face to Sir John Johnson and said in his excellent English: "The king promised us that if we would take up arms for him against the Yankees, he would send a great army, many thousands, to help us. We believed him, and we took up the hatchet for him. We fought in the dark and the storm with Herkimer at the Oriskany, and many of our warriors fell. But we did not sulk in our lodges. We have ravaged and driven in the whole American border along a line of hundreds of miles. Now the Congress sends an army to attack us, to avenge what we have done, and the great forces of the king are not here. I have been across the sea; I have seen the mighty city of London and its people as numerous as the blades of grass. Why has not the king kept his promise and sent men enough to save the Iroquois?"

Sir John Johnson and Thayendanegea were good friends, but the soul of the great Mohawk chief was deeply stirred. His penetrating mind saw the uplifted hand about to strike-and the target was his own people. His tone became bitterly sarcastic as he spoke, and when he ceased he looked directly at the baronet in a manner that showed a reply must be given. Sir John moved uneasily, but he spoke at last.

"Much that you say is true, Thayendanegea," he admitted, "but the king has many things to do. The war is spread over a vast area, and he must keep his largest armies in the East. But the Royal Greens, the Rangers, and all others whom we can raise, even in Canada, are here to help you. In the coming battle your fortunes are our fortunes."

Thayendanegea nodded, but he was not yet appeased. His glance fell upon the two Butlers, father and son, and he frowned.

"There are many in England itself," he said, "who wish us harm, and who perhaps have kept us from receiving some of the help that we ought to have. They speak of Wyoming and Cherry Valley, of the torture and of the slaughter of women and children, and they say that war must not be carried on in such a way. But there are some among us who are more savage than the savages themselves, as they call us. It was you, John Butler, who led at Wyoming, and it was you, Walter Butler, who allowed the women and children to be killed at Cherry Valley, and more would have been slain there had I not, come up in time."

The dark face of "Indian" Butler grew darker, and the pallid face of his son grew more pallid. Both were angry, and at the same time a little afraid.

"We won at Wyoming in fair battle," said the elder Butler.

"But afterwards?" said Thayendanegea.

The man was silent.

"It is these two places that have so aroused the Bostonians against us," continued Thayendanegea. "It is because of them that the commander of the Bostonians has sent a great army, and the Long House is threatened with destruction."

"My son and I have fought for our common cause," said "Indian" Butler, the blood flushing through his swarthy face.

Sir John Johnson interfered.

"We have admitted, Joseph, the danger to the Iroquois," he said, calling the chieftain familiarly by his first Christian name, "but I and my brother-in-law and Colonel Butler and Captain Butler have already lost though we may regain. And with this strong position and the aid of ambush it is likely that we can defeat the rebels."

The eyes of Thayendanegea brightened as he looked at the long embankment, the trees, and the dark forms of the warriors scattered numerously here and there.

"You may be right, Sir John," he said; "yes, I think you are right, and by all the gods, red and white, we shall see. I wish to fight here, because this is the best place in which to meet the Bostonians. What say you, Timmendiquas, sworn brother of mine, great warrior and great chief of the Wyandots, the bravest of all the western nations?"

The eye of Timmendiquas expressed little, but his voice was sonorous, and his words were such as Thayendanegea wished to hear.

"If we fight—and we must fight—this is the place in which to meet the white army," he said. "The Wyandots are here to help the Iroquois, as the Iroquois would go to help them. The Manitou of the Wyandots, the Aieroski of the Iroquois, alone knows the end."

He spoke with the utmost gravity, and after his brief reply he said no more. All regarded him with respect and admiration. Even Braxton Wyatt felt that it was a noble deed to remain and face destruction for the sake of tribes not his own.

Sir John Johnson turned to Braxton Wyatt, who had sat all the while in silence.

"You have examined the evening's advance, Wyatt," he said. "What further information can you give us?"

"We shall certainly be attacked to-morrow," replied Wyatt, "and the American army is advancing cautiously. It has out strong flanking parties, and it is preceded by the scouts, those Kentuckians whom I know and have met often, Murphy, Elerson, Heemskerk, and the others."

"If we could only lead them into an ambush," said Sir John. "Any kind of troops, even the best of regulars, will give way before an unseen foe pouring a deadly fire upon them from the deep woods. Then they magnify the enemy tenfold."

"It is so," said the fierce old Seneca chief, Hiokatoo. "When we killed Braddock and all his men, they thought that ten warriors stood in the moccasins of only one."

Sir John frowned. He did not like this allusion to the time when the Iroquois fought against the English, and inflicted on them a great defeat. But he feared to rebuke the old chief. Hiokatoo and the Senecas were too important.

"There ought to be a chance yet for an ambuscade," he said. "The foliage is still thick and heavy, and Sullivan, their general, is not used to forest warfare. What say you to this, Wyatt?"

Wyatt shook his head. He knew the caliber of the five from Kentucky, and he had little hope of such good fortune.

"They have learned from many lessons," he replied, "and their scouts are the best. Moreover, they will attempt anything."

They relapsed into silence again, and the sharp eyes of the renegade roved about the dark circle of trees and warriors that inclosed them. Presently he saw something that caused him to rise and walk a little distance from the fire. Although his eye suspected and his mind confirmed, Braxton Wyatt could not believe that it was true. It was incredible. No one, be he ever so daring, would dare such a thing. But the figure down there among the trees, passing about among the warriors, many of whom did not know one another, certainly looked familiar, despite the Indian paint and garb. Only that of Timmendiquas could rival it in height and nobility. These were facts that could not be hidden by any disguise.

"What is it, Wyatt?" asked Sir John. "What do you see? Why do you look so startled?"

Wyatt sought to reply calmly.

"There is a warrior among those trees over there whom I have not seen here before," he replied, "he is as tall and as powerful as Timmendiquas, and there is only one such. There is a spy among us, and it is Henry Ware."

He snatched a pistol from his belt, ran forward, and fired at the flitting figure, which was gone in an instant among the trees and the warriors.

"What do you say?" exclaimed Thayendanegea, as he ran forward, "a spy, and you know him to be such!"

"Yes, he is the worst of them all," replied Wyatt. "I know him. I could not mistake him. But he has dared too much. He cannot get away."

The great camp was now in an uproar. The tall figure was seen here and there, always to vanish quickly. Twenty shots were fired at it. None hit.

Many more would have been fired, but the camp was too much crowded to take such a risk. Every moment the tumult and confusion increased, but Thayendanegea quickly posted warriors on the embankment and the flanks, to prevent the escape of the fugitive in any of those directions.

But the tall figure did not appear at either embankment or flank. It was next seen near the river, when a young warrior, striving to strike with a tomahawk, was dashed to the earth with great force. The next instant the figure leaped far out into the stream. The moonlight glimmered an instant on the bare head, while bullets the next moment pattered on the water where it had been. Then, with a few powerful strokes, the stranger reclaimed the land, sprang upon the shore, and darted into the woods with more vain bullets flying about him. But he sent back a shout of irony and triumph that made the chiefs and Tories standing on the bank bite their lips in anger.

CHAPTER XXI. BATTLE OF THE CHEMUNG

Paul had been sleeping heavily, and the sharp, pealing notes of a trumpet awoke him at the sunburst of a brilliant morning. Henry was standing beside him, showing no fatigue from the night's excitement, danger, and escape, but his face was flushed and his eyes sparkled.

"Up, Paul! Up!" he cried. "We know the enemy's position, and we will be in battle before another sun sets."

Paul was awake in an instant, and the second instant he was on his feet, rifle in hand, and heart thrilling for the great attack. He, like all the others, had slept on such a night fully dressed. Shif'less Sol, Long Jim, Silent Tom, Heemskerk, and the rest were by the side of him, and all about them rose the sounds of an army going into battle, commands sharp and short, the rolling of cannon wheels, the metallic rattle of bayonets, the clink of bullets poured into the pouches, and the hum of men talking in half-finished sentences.

It was to all the five a vast and stirring scene. It was the first time that they had ever beheld a large and regular army going into action, and they were a part of it, a part by no means unimportant. It was Henry, with his consummate skill and daring, who had uncovered the position of the enemy, and now, without snatching a moment's sleep, he was ready to lead where the fray might be thickest.

The brief breakfast finished, the trumpet pealed forth again, and the army began to move through the thick forest. A light wind, crisp with the air of early autumn, blew, and the leaves rustled. The sun, swinging upward in the east, poured down a flood of brilliant rays that lighted up everything, the buff and blue uniforms, the cannon, the rifles, the bayonets, and the forest, still heavy with foliage.

"Now! now!" thought every one of the five, "we begin the vengeance for Wyoming!"

The scouts were well in front, searching everywhere among the thickets for the Indian sharpshooters, who could scorch so terribly. As Braxton Wyatt had truly said, these scouts were the best in the world. Nothing could escape the trained eyes of Henry Ware and his comrades, and those of Murphy, Ellerson, and the others, while off on either flank of the army heavy detachments guarded against any surprise or turning movement. They saw no Indian sign in the woods. There was yet a deep silence in front of them, and the sun, rising higher, poured its golden light down upon the army in such an intense, vivid flood that rifle barrels and bayonets gave back a metallic gleam. All around them the deep woods swayed and rustled before the light breeze, and now and then they caught glimpses of the river, its surface now gold, then silver, under the shining sun.

Henry's heart swelled as he advanced. He was not revengeful, but he had seen so much of savage atrocity in the last year that he could not keep down the desire to see punishment. It is only those in sheltered homes who can forgive the tomahawk and the stake. Now he was the very first of the scouts, although his comrades and a dozen others were close behind him.

The scouts went so far forward that the army was hidden from them by the forest, although they could yet hear the clank of arms and the sound of commands.

Henry knew the ground thoroughly. He knew where the embankment ran, and he knew, too, that the Iroquois had dug pits, marked by timber. They were not far ahead, and the scouts now proceeded very slowly, examining every tree and clump of bushes to see whether a lurking enemy was hidden there. The silence endured longer than he had thought. Nothing could be seen in front save the waving forest.

Henry stopped suddenly. He caught a glimpse of a brown shoulder's edge showing from behind a tree, and at his signal all the scouts sank to the ground.

The savage fired, but the bullet, the first of the battle, whistled over their heads. The sharp crack, sounding triply loud at such a time, came back from the forest in many echoes, and a light puff of smoke arose. Quick as a flash, before the brown shoulder and body exposed to take aim could be withdrawn, Tom Ross fired, and the Mohawk fell, uttering his death yell. The Iroquois in the woods took up the cry, pouring forth a war whoop, fierce, long drawn, the most terrible of human sounds, and before it died, their brethren behind the embankment repeated it in tremendous volume from hundreds of throats. It was a shout that had often appalled the bravest, but the little band of scouts were not afraid. When its last echo died they sent forth a fierce, defiant note of their own, and, crawling forward, began to send in their bullets.

The woods in front of them swarmed with the Indian skirmishers, who replied to the scouts, and the fire ran along a long line through the undergrowth. Flashes of flames appeared, puffs of smoke arose and, uniting, hung over the trees. Bullets hissed. Twigs and bark fell, and now and then a man, as they fought from tree to tree. Henry caught one glimpse of a face that was white, that of Braxton Wyatt, and he sought a shot at the renegade leader, but he could not get it. But the scouts pushed on, and the Indian and Tory skirmishers dropped back. Then on the flanks they began to hear the rattle of rifle fire. The wings of the army were in action, but the main body still advanced without firing a shot.

The scouts could now see through the trees the embankments and rifle pits, and they could also see the last of the Iroquois and Tory skirmishers leaping over the earthworks and taking refuge with their army. Then they turned back and saw the long line of their own army steadily advancing, while the sounds of heavy firing still continued on both flanks. Henry looked proudly at the unbroken array, the front of steel, and the cannon. He felt prouder still when the general turned to him and said:

"You have done well, Mr. Ware; you have shown us exactly where the enemy lies, and that will save us many men. Now bigger voices than those of the rifles shall talk."

The army stopped. The Indian position could be plainly seen. The crest of the earthwork was lined with fierce, dark faces, and here and there among the brown Iroquois were the green uniforms of the Royalists.

Henry saw both Thayendanegea and Timmendiquas, the plumes in their hair waving aloft, and he felt sure that wherever they stood the battle would be thickest.

The Americans were now pushing forward their cannon, six three-pounders and two howitzers, the howitzers, firing five-and-a-half-inch shells, new and terrifying missiles to the Indians. The guns were wheeled into position, and the first howitzer was fired. It sent its great shell in a curving line at and over the embankment, where it burst with a crash, followed by a shout of mingled pain and awe. Then the second howitzer, aimed well like the first, sent a shell almost to the same point, and a like cry came back.

Shif'less Sol, watching the shots, jumped up and down in delight.

"That's the medicine!" he cried. "I wonder how you like that, you Butlers an' Johnsons an' Wyatts an' Mohawks an' all the rest o' your scalp-taking crew! Ah, thar goes another! This ain't any Wyomin'!"

The three-pounders also opened fire, and sent their balls squarely into the rifle pits and the Indian camp. The Iroquois replied with a shower of rifle bullets and a defiant war whoop, but the bullets fell short, and the whoop hurt no one.

The artillery, eight pieces, was served with rapidity and precision, while the riflemen, except on their flanks, where they were more closely engaged, were ordered to hold their fire. The spectacle was to Henry and his comrades panoramic in its effect. They watched the flashes of fire from the mouths of the cannon, the flight of the great shells, and the bank of smoke which soon began to lower like a cloud over the field. They could picture to themselves what was going on beyond the earthwork, the dead falling, the wounded limping away, earth and trees torn by shell and shot. They even fancied that they could hear the voices of the great chiefs, Thayendanegea and Timmendiquas, encouraging their men, and striving to keep them in line against a fire not as deadly as rifle bullets at close quarters, but more terrifying.

Presently a cloud of skirmishers issued once more from the Indian camp, creeping among the trees and bushes, and seeking a chance to shoot down the men at the guns. But sharp eyes were watching them.

"Come, boys," exclaimed Henry. "Here's work for us now."

He led the scouts and the best of the riflemen against the skirmishers, who were soon driven in again. The artillery fire had never ceased for a moment, the shells and balls passing over their heads. Their work done, the sharpshooters fell back again, the gunners worked faster for a while, and then at a command they ceased suddenly. Henry, Paul, and all the others knew instinctively what was going to happen. They felt it in every bone of them. The silence so sudden was full of meaning.

"Now!" Henry found himself exclaiming. Even at that moment the order was given, and the whole army rushed forward, the smoke floating away for the moment and the sun flashing off the bayonets. The five sprang up and rushed on ahead. A sheet of flame burst from the embankment, and the rifle pits sprang into fire. The five beard the bullets whizzing past them, and the sudden cries of the wounded behind them, but they never ceased to rush straight for the embankment.

It seemed to Henry that he ran forward through living fire. There was one continuous flash from the earthwork, and a continuous flash replied. The rifles were at work now, thousands of them, and they kept up an incessant crash, while above them rose the unbroken thunder of the cannon. The volume of smoke deepened, and it was shot through with the sharp, pungent odor of burned gunpowder.

Henry fired his rifle and pistol, almost unconsciously reloaded, and fired again, as he ran, and then noticed that the advance had never ceased. It had not been checked even for a moment, and the bayonets of one of the regiments glittered in the sun a straight line of steel.

Henry kept his gaze fixed upon a point where the earthwork was lowest. He saw there the plumed head of Thayendanegea, and he intended to strike if he could. He saw the Mohawk gesticulating and shouting to his men to stand fast and drive back the charge. He believed even then, and he knew later, that Thayendanegea and Timmendiquas were showing courage superior to that of the Johnsons and Butters or any of their British and Canadian allies. The two great chiefs still held their men in line, and the Iroquois did not cease to send a stream of bullets from the earthwork.

Henry saw the brown faces and the embankment coming closer and closer. He saw the face of Braxton Wyatt appear a moment, and he snapped his empty pistol at it. But it was hidden the next instant behind others, and then they were at the embankment. He saw the glowing faces of his comrades at his side, the singular figure of Heemskerk revolving swiftly, and behind them the line of bayonets closing in with the grimness of fate.

Henry leaped upon the earthwork. An Indian fired at him point blank, and he swung heavily with his clubbed rifle. Then his comrades were by his side, and they leaped down into the Indian camp. After them came the riflemen, and then the line of bayonets. Even then the great Mohawk and the great Wyandot shouted to their men to stand fast, although the Royal Greens and the Rangers had begun to run, and the Johnsons, the Butlers, McDonald, Wyatt, and the other white men were running with them.

Henry, with the memory of Wyoming and all the other dreadful things that had come before his eyes, saw red. He was conscious of a terrible melee, of striking again and again with his clubbed rifle, of fierce brown faces before him, and of Timmendiquas and Thayedanegea rushing here and there, shouting to their warriors, encouraging them, and exclaiming that the battle was not lost. Beyond he saw the vanishing forms of the Royal

Greens and the Rangers in full flight. But the Wyandots and the best of the Iroquois still stood fast until the pressure upon them became overwhelming. When the line of bayonets approached their breasts they fell back. Skilled in every detail of ambush, and a wonderful forest fighter, the Indian could never stand the bayonet. Reluctantly Timmendiquas, Thayendanegea and the Mohawks, Senecas, and Wyandots, who were most strenuous in the conflict, gave ground. Yet the battlefield, with its numerous trees, stumps, and inequalities, still favored them. They retreated slowly, firing from every covert, sending a shower of bullets, and now and then tittering the war whoop.

Henry heard a panting breath by his side. He looked around and saw the face of Heemskerk, glowing red with zeal and exertion.

"The victory is won already!" said he. "Now to drive it home!"

"Come on," cried Henry in return, "and we'll lead!"

A single glance showed him that none of his comrades had fallen. Long Jim and Tom Ross had suffered slight wounds that they scarcely noticed, and they and the whole group of scouts were just behind Henry. But they now took breath, reloaded their rifles, and, throwing themselves down in Indian fashion, opened a deadly fire upon their antagonists. Their bullets searched all the thickets, drove out the Iroquois, and compelled them to retreat anew.

The attack was now pressed with fresh vigor. In truth, with so much that the bravest of the Indians at last yielded to panic. Thayendanegea and Timmendiquas were carried away in the rush, and the white leaders of their allies were already out of sight. On all sides the allied red and white force was dissolving. Precipitate flight was saving the fugitives from a greater loss in killed and wounded-it was usually Indian tactics to flee with great speed when the battle began to go against them-but the people of the Long House had suffered the greatest overthrow in their history, and bitterness and despair were in the hearts of the Iroquois chiefs as they fled.

The American army not only carried the center of the Indian camp, but the heavy flanking parties closed in also, and the whole Indian army was driven in at every point. The retreat was becoming a rout. A great, confused conflict was going on. The rapid crackle of rifles mingled with the shouts and war whoops of the combatants. Smoke floated everywhere. The victorious army, animated by the memory of the countless cruelties that had been practiced on the border, pushed harder and harder. The Iroquois were driven back along the Chemung. It seemed that they might be hemmed in against the river, but in their flight they came to a ford.

Uttering their cry of despair, "Oonali! Oonali!" a wail for a battle lost, they sprang into the stream, many of them throwing away their rifles, tomahawks, and blankets, and rushed for the other shore. But the Scouts and a body of riflemen were after them.

Braxton Wyatt and his band appeared in the woods on the far shore, and opened fire on the pursuers now in the stream. He alone among the white men had the courage, or the desperation, to throw himself and his men in the path of the pursuit. The riflemen in the water felt the bullets pattering around them, and some were struck, but they did not stop. They kept on for the bank, and their own men behind them opened a covering fire over their heads.

Henry felt a great pulse leap in his throat at the sight of Braxton Wyatt again. Nothing could have turned him back now. Shouting to the riflemen, he led the charge through the water, and the bank's defenders were driven back. Yet Wyatt, with his usual dexterity and prudence, escaped among the thickets.

The battle now became only a series of detached combats. Little groups seeking to make a stand here and there were soon swept away. Thayendanegea and Timmendiquas raged and sought to gather together enough men for an ambush, for anything that would sting the victors, but they were pushed too hard and fast. A rally was always destroyed in the beginning, and the chiefs themselves at last ran for their lives. The pursuit was continued for a long time, not only by the vanguard, but the army itself moved forward over the battlefield and deep into the forest on the trail of the flying Iroquois.

The scouts continued the pursuit the longest, keeping a close watch, nevertheless, against an ambush. Now and then they exchanged shots with a band, but the Indians always fled quickly, and at last they stopped because they could no longer find any resistance. They had been in action or pursuit for many hours, and they were black with smoke, dust, and sweat, but they were not yet conscious of any weariness. Heemskerk drew a great red silk handkerchief from his pocket, and wiped his glowing face, which was as red as the handkerchief.

"It's the best job that's been done in these parts for many a year," he said. "The Iroquois have always thought they were invincible, and now the spell's been broke. If we only follow it up."

"That's sure to be done," said Henry. "I heard General Sullivan himself say that his orders were to root up the whole Iroquois power."

They returned slowly toward the main force, retracing their steps over the path of battle. It was easy enough to follow it. They beheld a dead warrior at every step, and at intervals were rifles, tomahawks, scalping knives, blankets, and an occasional shot pouch or powder horn. Presently they reached the main army, which was going into camp for the night. Many camp fires were built, and the soldiers, happy in their victory, were getting ready for supper. But there was no disorder. They had been told already that they were to march again in the morning.

Henry, Paul, Tom, Jim, and Shif'less Sol went back over the field of battle, where many of the dead still lay. Twilight was now coming, and it was a somber sight. The earthwork, the thickets, and the trees were torn by cannon balls. Some tents raised by the Tories lay in ruins, and the earth was stained with many dark splotches. But the army had passed on, and it was silent and desolate where so many men had fought. The twilight drew swiftly on to night, and out of the forest came grewsome sounds. The wolves, thick now in a region which the Iroquois had done so much to turn into a wilderness, were learning welcome news, and they were telling it to one another. By and by, as the night deepened, the five saw fiery eyes in the thickets, and the long howls came again.

"It sounds like the dirge of the people of the Long House," said Paul, upon whose sensitive mind the scene made a deep impression.

The others nodded. At that moment they did not feel the flush of victory in its full force. It was not in their nature to rejoice over a fallen foe. Yet they knew the full value of the victory, and none of them could wish any part of it undone. They returned slowly to the camp, and once more they heard behind them the howl of the wolves as they invaded the battlefield.

They were glad when they saw the cheerful lights of the camp fires twinkling through the forest, and heard the voices of many men talking. Heemskerk welcomed them there.

"Come, lads," he said. "You must eat-you won't find out until you begin, how hungry you are-and then you must sleep, because we march early tomorrow, and we march fast."

The Dutchman's words were true. They had not tasted food since morning; they had never thought of it, but now, with the relaxation from battle, they found themselves voraciously hungry.

"It's mighty good," said Shif'less Sol, as they sat by a fire and ate bread and meat and drank coffee, "but I'll say this for you, you old ornery, long-legged Jim Hart, it ain't any better than the venison an' bulffaler steaks that you've cooked fur us many a time."

"An' that I'm likely to cook fur you many a time more," said Long Jim complacently.

"But it will be months before you have any chance at buffalo again, Jim," said Henry. "We are going on a long campaign through the Iroquois country."

"An' it's shore to be a dangerous one," said Shif'less Sol. "Men like warriors o' the Iroquois ain't goin' to give up with one fight. They'll be hangin' on our flanks like wasps."

"That's true," said Henry, "but in my opinion the Iroquois are overthrown forever. One defeat means more to them than a half dozen to us."

They said little more, but by and by lay down to sleep before the fires. They had toiled so long and so faithfully that the work of watching and scouting that night could be intrusted to others. Yet Henry could not sleep for a long time. The noises of the night interested him. He watched the men going about, and the sentinels pacing back and forth around the camp. The sounds died gradually as the men lay down and sank to sleep. The fires which had formed a great core of light also sank, and the shadows crept toward the camp. The figures of the pacing sentinels, rifle on shoulder, gradually grew dusky. Henry's nerves, attuned so long to great effort, slowly relaxed. Deep peace came over him, and his eyelids drooped, the sounds in the camp sank to the lowest murmur, but just as he was falling asleep there came from the battlefield behind then the far, faint howl of a wolf, the dirge of the Iroquois.

CHAPTER XXII. LITTLE BEARD'S TOWN

The trumpets called early the next morning, and the five rose, refreshed, ready for new labors. The fires were already lighted, and breakfast was cooking. Savory odors permeated the forest. But as soon as all had eaten, the army marched, going northward and westward, intending to cut through the very center of the Iroquois country. Orders had come from the great commander that the power of the Six Nations, which had been so long such a terrible scourge on the American frontier, must be annihilated. They must be made strangers in their own country. Women and children were not to be molested, but their towns must perish.

As Thayendanegea had said the night before the Battle of the Chemung, the power beyond the seas that had urged the Iroquois to war on the border did not save them. It could not. British and Tories alike had promised them certain victory, and for a while it had seemed that the promises would come true. But the tide had turned, and the Iroquois were fugitives in their own country.

The army continued its march through the wilderness, the scouts in front and heavy parties of riflemen on either flank. There was no chance for a surprise. Henry and his comrades were aware that Indian bands still lurked in the forest, and they had several narrow escapes from the bullets of ambushed foes, but the progress of the army was irresistible. Nothing could check it for a moment, however much the Indian and Tory chiefs might plan.

They camped again that night in the forest, with a thorough ring of sentinels posted against surprise, although there was little danger of the latter, as the enemy could not, for the present at least, bring a sufficient force into the field. But after the moon had risen, the five, with Heemskerk, went ahead through the forest. The Iroquois town of Kanawaholla lay just ahead, and the army would reach it on the morrow. It was the intention of the scouts to see if it was still occupied.

It was near midnight when the little party drew near to Kanawaholla and watched it from the shelter of the forest. Like most other Iroquois towns, it contained wooden houses, and cultivated fields were about it. No smoke rose from any of the chimneys, but the sharp eyes of the scouts saw loaded figures departing through a great field of ripe and waving corn. It was the last of the inhabitants, fleeing with what they could carry. Two or three warriors might have been in that group of fugitives, but the scouts made no attempt to pursue. They could not restrain a little feeling of sympathy and pity, although a just retribution was coming.

"If the Iroquois had only stood neutral at the beginning of the war, as we asked them," said Heemskerk, "how much might have been spared to both sides! Look! Those people are stopping for a moment."

The burdened figures, perhaps a dozen, halted at the far edge of the corn field. Henry and Paul readily imagined that they were taking a last look at their town, and the feeling of pity and sympathy deepened, despite Wyoming, Cherry Valley, and all the rest. But that feeling never extended to the white allies of the Iroquois, whom Thayendanegea characterized in word and in writing as "more savage than the savages themselves."

The scouts waited an hour, and then entered the town. Not a soul was in Kanawaholla. Some of the lighter things had been taken away, but that was all. Most of the houses were in disorder, showing the signs of hasty flight, but the town lay wholly at the mercy of the advancing army. Henry and his comrades withdrew with the news, and the next day, when the troops advanced, Kanawaholla was put to the torch. In an hour it was smoking ruins, and then the crops and fruit trees were destroyed.

Leaving ruin behind, the army continued its march, treading the Iroquois power under foot and laying waste the country. One after another the Indian towns were destroyed, Catherinetown, Kendaia, Kanadesaga, Shenanwaga, Skoiyase, Kanandaigua, Honeyoye, Kanaghsawa, Gathtsewarohare, and others, forming a long roll, bearing the sounding Iroquois names. Villages around Cayuga and other lakes were burned by detachments. The smoke of perishing towns arose everywhere in the Iroquois country, while the Iroquois themselves fled before the advancing army. They sent appeal after appeal for help from those to whom they had given so much help, but none came.

It was now deep autumn, and the nights grew cold. The forests blazed with brilliant colors. The winds blew, leaves rustled and fell. The winter would soon be at hand, and the Iroquois, so proud of what they had achieved, would have to find what shelter they could in the forests or at the British posts on the Canadian frontier. Thayendanegea was destined to come again with bands of red men and white and inflict great loss, but the power of the Six Nations was overthrown forever, after four centuries of victory and glory. Henry, Paul, and the rest were all the time in the thick of it. The army, as the autumn advanced, marched into the Genesee Valley, destroying everything. Henry and Paul, as they lay on their blankets one night, counted fires in three different directions, and every one of the three marked a perishing Indian village. It was not a work in which they took any delight; on the contrary, it often saddened them, but they felt that it had to be done, and they could not shirk the task.

In October, Henry, despite his youth, took command of a body of scouts and riflemen which beat up the ways, and skirmished in advance of the army. It was a democratic little band, everyone saying what he pleased, but yielding in the end to the authority of the leader. They were now far up the Genesee toward the Great Lakes, and Henry formed the plan of advancing ahead of the army on the great Seneca village known variously as the Seneca Castle and Little Beard's Town, after its chief, a full match in cruelty for the older Seneca chief, Hiokatoo. Several causes led to this decision. It was reported that Thayendanegea, Timmendiquas, all the Butlers and Johnsons, and Braxton Wyatt were there. While not likely to be true about all, it was probably true about some of them, and a bold stroke might effect much.

It is probable that Henry had Braxton Wyatt most in mind. The renegade was in his element among the Indians and Tories, and he had developed great abilities as a partisan, being skillfully seconded by the squat Tory, Coleman. His reputation now was equal at least to that of Walter Butler, and he had skirmished more than once with the vanguard of the army. Growing in Henry's heart was a strong desire to match forces with him, and it was quite probable that a swift advance might find him at the Seneca Castle.

The riflemen took up their march on a brisk morning in late autumn. The night had been clear and cold, with a touch of winter in it, and the brilliant colors of the foliage had now turned to a solid brown. Whenever the wind blew, the leaves fell in showers. The sky was a fleecy blue, but over hills, valley, and forest hung a fine misty veil that is the mark of Indian summer. The land was nowhere inhabited. They saw the cabin of neither white man nor Indian. A desolation and a silence, brought by the great struggle, hung over everything. Many discerning eyes among the riflemen noted the beauty and fertility of the country, with its noble forests and rich meadows. At times they caught glimpses of the river, a clear stream sparkling under the sun.

"Makes me think o' some o' the country 'way down thar in Kentucky," said Shif'less Sol, "an' it seems to me I like one about ez well ez t'other. Say, Henry, do you think we'll ever go back home? 'Pears to me that we're always goin' farther an' farther away."

Henry laughed.

"It's because circumstances have taken us by the hand and led us away, Sol," he replied.

"Then," said the shiftless one with a resigned air, "I hope them same circumstances will take me by both hands, an' lead me gently, but strongly, back to a place whar thar is peace an' rest fur a lazy an' tired man like me."

"I think you'll have to endure a lot, until next spring at least," said Henry.

The shiftless one heaved a deep sigh, but his next words were wholly irrelevant.

"S'pose we'll light on that thar Seneca Castle by tomorrow night?" he asked.

"It seems to me that for a lazy and tired man you're extremely anxious for a fight," Henry replied.

"I try to be resigned," said Shif'less Sol. But his eyes were sparkling with the light of battle.

They went into camp that night in a dense forest, with the Seneca Castle about ten miles ahead. Henry was quite sure that the Senecas to whom it belonged had not yet abandoned it, and with the aid of the other tribes might make a stand there. It was more than likely, too, that the Senecas had sharpshooters and sentinels well to the south of their town, and it behooved the riflemen to be extremely careful lest they run into a hornet's nest. Hence they lighted no fires, despite a cold night wind that searched them through until they wrapped themselves in their blankets.

The night settled down thick and dark, and the band lay close in the thickets. Shif'less Sol was within a yard of Henry. He had observed his young leader's face closely that day, and he had a mind of uncommon penetration.

"Henry," he whispered, "you're hopin' that you'll find Braxton Wyatt an' his band at Little Beard's town?"

"That among other things," replied Henry in a similar whisper.

"That first, and the others afterwards," persisted the shiftless one.

"It may be so," admitted Henry.

"I feel the same way you do," said Shif'less Sol. "You see, we've knowed Braxton Wyatt a long time, an' it seems strange that one who started out a boy with you an' Paul could turn so black. An' think uv all the cruel things that he's done an' helped to do. I ain't hidin' my feelin's. I'm jest itchin' to git at him."

"Yes," said Henry, "I'd like for our band to have it out with his."

Henry and Shif'less Sol, and in fact all of the five, slept that night, because Henry wished to be strong and vigorous for the following night, in view of an enterprise that he had in mind. The rosy Dutchman, Heemskerk, was in command of the guard, and he revolved continually about the camp with amazing ease, and with a footstep so light that it made no sound whatever. Now and then he came back in the thicket and looked down at the faces of the sleeping five from Kentucky. "Goot boys," he murmured to himself. "Brave boys, to stay here and help. May they go through all our battles and take no harm. The goot and great God often watches over the brave."

Mynheer Cornelius Heemskerk, native of Holland, but devoted to the new nation of which he had made himself a part, was a devout man, despite a life of danger and hardship. The people of the woods do not lose faith, and he looked up at the dark skies as if he found encouragement there. Then he resumed his circle about the camp. He heard various noises-the hoot of an owl, the long whine of a wolf, and twice the footsteps of deer going down to the river to drink. But the sounds were all natural, made by the animals to which they belonged, and Heemskerk knew it. Once or twice he went farther into the forest, but he found nothing to indicate the presence of a foe, and while he watched thus, and beat up the woods, the night passed, eventless, away.

They went the next day much nearer to the Seneca Castle, and saw sure indications that it was still inhabited, as the Iroquois evidently were not aware of the swift advance of the riflemen. Henry had learned that this was one of the largest and strongest of all the Iroquois towns, containing between a hundred and two hundred wooden houses, and with a population likely to be swollen greatly by fugitives from the Iroquois towns already destroyed. The need of caution—great caution—was borne in upon him, and he paid good heed.

The riflemen sought another covert in the deep forest, now about three miles from Little Beard's Town, and lay there, while Henry, according to his plan, went forth at night with Shif'less Sol and Tom Ross. He was resolved to find out more about this important town, and his enterprise was in full accord with his duties, chief among which was to save the vanguard of the army from ambush.

When the complete darkness of night had come, the three left the covert, and, after traveling a short distance through the forest, turned in toward the river. As the town lay on or near the river, Henry thought they might see some signs of Indian life on the stream, and from this they could proceed to discoveries.

But when they first saw the river it was desolate. Not a canoe was moving on its surface, and the three, keeping well in the undergrowth, followed the bank toward the town. But the forest soon ceased, and they came upon a great field, where the Senecas had raised corn, and where stalks, stripped of their ears and browned by the autumn cold, were still standing. But all the work of planting, tending, and reaping this great field, like all the other work in all the Iroquois fields, had been done by the Iroquois women, not by the warriors.

Beyond the field they saw fruit trees, and beyond these, faint lines of smoke, indicating the position of the great Seneca Castle. The dry cornstalks rustled mournfully as the wind blew across the field.

"The stalks will make a little shelter," said Henry, "and we must cross the field. We want to keep near the river."

"Lead on," said Shif'less Sol.

They took a diagonal course, walking swiftly among the stalks and bearing back toward the river. They crossed the field without being observed, and came into a thick fringe of trees and undergrowth along the river. They moved cautiously in this shelter for a rod or two, and then the three, without word from any one of them, stopped simultaneously. They heard in the water the unmistakable ripple made by a paddle, and then the sound of several more. They crept to the edge of the bank and crouched down among the bushes. Then they saw a singular procession.

A half-dozen Iroquois canoes were moving slowly up the stream. They were in single file, and the first canoe was the largest. But the aspect of the little fleet was wholly different from that of an ordinary group of Iroquois war canoes. It was dark, somber, and funereal, and in every canoe, between the feet of the paddlers, lay a figure, stiff and impassive, the body of a chief slain in battle. It had all the appearance of a funeral procession, but the eyes of the three, as they roved over it, fastened on a figure in the first canoe, and, used as they were to the strange and curious, every one of them gave a start.

The figure was that of a woman, a wild and terrible creature, who half sat, half crouched in the canoe, looking steadily downward. Her long black hair fell in disordered masses from her uncovered head. She wore a brilliant red dress with savage adornments, but it was stained and torn. The woman's whole attitude expressed grief, anger, and despair.

"Queen Esther!" whispered Henry. The other two nodded.

So horrifying had been the impression made upon him by this woman at Wyoming that he could not feel any pity for her now. The picture of the great war tomahawk cleaving the heads of bound prisoners was still too vivid. She had several sons, one or two of whom were slain in battle with the colonists, and the body that lay in the boat may have been one of them. Henry always believed that it was-but he still felt no pity.

As the file came nearer they heard her chanting a low song, and now she raised her face and tore at her black hair.

"They're goin' to land," whispered Shif'less Sol.

The head of the file was turned toward the shore, and, as it approached, a group of warriors, led by Little Beard, the Seneca chief, appeared among the trees, coming forward to meet them. The three in their covert crouched closer, interested so intensely that they were prepared to brave the danger in order to remain. But the absorption of the Iroquois in what they were about to do favored the three scouts.

As the canoes touched the bank, Catharine Montour rose from her crouching position and uttered a long, piercing wail, so full of grief, rage, and despair that the three in the bushes shuddered. It was fiercer than the cry of a wolf, and it came back from the dark forest in terrifying echoes.

"It's not a woman, but a fiend," whispered Henry; and, as before, his comrades nodded in assent.

The woman stood erect, a tall and stalwart figure, but the beauty that had once caused her to be received in colonial capitals was long since gone. Her white half of blood had been submerged years ago in her Indian half, and there was nothing now about her to remind one of civilization or of the French Governor General of Canada who was said to have been her father.

The Iroquois stood respectfully before her. It was evident that she had lost none of her power among the Six Nations, a power proceeding partly from her force and partly from superstition. As the bodies were brought ashore, one by one, and laid upon the ground, she uttered the long wailing cry again and again, and the others repeated it in a sort of chorus.

When the bodies-and Henry was sure that they must all be those of chiefs-were laid out, she tore her hair, sank down upon the ground, and began a chant, which Tom Ross was afterwards able to interpret roughly to the others. She sang:

> The white men have come with the cannon and bayonet,
> Numerous as forest leaves the army has come.
> Our warriors are driven like deer by the hunter,
> Fallen is the League of the Ho-de-no-sau-nee!
> Our towns are burned and our fields uprooted,
> Our people flee through the forest for their lives,
> The king who promised to help us comes not.
> Fallen is the League of the Ho-de-no-sau-nee!
> The great chiefs are slain and their bodies lie here.
> No longer will they lead the warriors in battle;
> No more will they drive the foe from the thicket.
> Fallen is the League of the Ho-de-no-sau-nee!
> Scalps we have taken from all who hated us;
> None, but feared us in the days of our glory.
> But the cannon and bayonet have taken our country;
> Fallen is the League of the Ho-de-no-sau-nee!

She chanted many verses, but these were all that Tom Ross could ever remember or translate. But every verse ended with the melancholy refrain: "Fallen is the League of the Ho-de-no-sau-nee!" which the others also repeated in chorus. Then the warriors lifted up the bodies, and they moved in procession toward the town. The three watched them, but they did not rise until the funeral train had reached the fruit trees. Then they stood up, looked at one another, and breathed sighs of relief.

"I don't care ef I never see that woman ag'in," said Shif'less Sol. "She gives me the creeps. She must be a witch huntin' for blood. She is shore to stir up the Iroquois in this town."

"That's true," said Henry, "but I mean to go nearer."

"Wa'al," said Tom Ross, "I reckon that if you mean it we mean it, too."

"There are certainly Tories in the town," said Henry, "and if we are seen we can probably pass for them. I'm bound to find out what's here."

"Still huntin' fur Braxton Wyatt," said Shif'less Sol.

"I mean to know if he's here," said Henry.

"Lead on," said the shiftless one.

They followed in the path of the procession, which was now out of sight, and entered the orchard. From that point they saw the houses and great numbers of Indians, including squaws and children, gathered in the open spaces, where the funeral train was passing. Queen Esther still stalked at its head, but her chant was now taken up by many scores of voices, and the volume of sound penetrated far in the night. Henry yet relied upon the absorption of the Iroquois in this ceremonial to give him a chance for a good look through the town, and he and his comrades advanced with boldness.

They passed by many of the houses, all empty, as their occupants had gone to join in the funeral lament, but they soon saw white men-a few of the Royal Greens, and some of the Rangers, and other Tories, who were dressed much like Henry and his comrades. One of them spoke to Shif'less Sol, who nodded carelessly and passed by. The Tory seemed satisfied and went his way.

"Takes us fur some o' the crowd that's come runnin' in here ahead o' the army," said the shiftless one.

Henry was noting with a careful eye the condition of the town. He saw that no preparations for defense had been made, and there was no evidence that any would be made. All was confusion and despair. Already some of the squaws were fleeing, carrying heavy burdens. The three coupled caution with boldness. If they met a Tory they merely exchanged a word or two, and passed swiftly on. Henry, although he had seen enough to know that the army could advance without hesitation, still pursued the quest. Shif'less Sol was right. At the bottom of Henry's heart was a desire to know whether Braxton Wyatt was in Little Beard's Town, a desire soon satisfied, as they reached the great Council House, turned a corner of it, and met the renegade face to face.

Wyatt was with his lieutenant, the squat Tory, Coleman, and he uttered a cry when he saw the tall figure of the great youth. There was no light but that of the moon, but he knew his foe in an instant.

"Henry Ware!" he cried, and snatched his pistol from his belt.

They were so close together that Henry did not have time to use a weapon. Instinctively he struck out with his fist, catching Wyatt on the jaw, and sending him down as if he had been shot. Shif'less Sol and Tom Ross ran bodily over Coleman, hurling him down, and leaping across his prostrate figure. Then they ran their utmost, knowing that their lives depended on speed and skill.

They quickly put the Council House between them and their pursuers, and darted away among the houses. Braxton Wyatt was stunned, but he speedily regained his wits and his feet.

"It was the fellow Ware, spying among us again!" he cried to his lieutenant, who, half dazed, was also struggling up. "Come, men! After them! After them!"

A dozen men came at his call, and, led by the renegade, they began a search among the houses. But it was hard to find the fugitives. The light was not good, many flitting figures were about, and the frantic search developed confusion. Other Tories were often mistaken for the three scouts, and were overhauled, much to their disgust and that of the overhaulers. Iroquois, drawn from the funeral ceremony, began to join in the hunt, but Wyatt could give them little information. He had merely seen an enemy, and then the enemy had gone. It was quite certain that this enemy, or, rather, three of them, was still in the town.

Henry and his comrades were crafty. Trained by ambush and escape, flight and pursuit, they practiced many wiles to deceive their pursuers. When Wyatt and Coleman were hurled down they ran around the Council House, a large and solid structure, and, finding a door on the opposite side and no one there or in sight from that point, they entered it, closing the door behind them.

They stood in almost complete darkness, although at length they made out the log wall of the great, single room which constituted the Council House. After that, with more accustomed eyes, they saw on the wall arms, pipes, wampum, and hideous trophies, some with long hair and some with short. The hair was usually blonde, and most of the scalps had been stretched tight over little hoops. Henry clenched his fist in the darkness.

"Mebbe we're walkin' into a trap here," said Shif'less Sol.

"I don't think so," said Henry. "At any rate they'd find us if we were rushing about the village. Here we at least have a chance."

At the far end of the Council House hung mats, woven of rushes, and the three sat down behind them in the very heart of the Iroquois sanctuary. Should anyone casually enter the Council House they would still be hidden. They sat in Turkish fashion on the floor, close together and with their rifles lying across their knees. A thin light filtered through a window and threw pallid streaks on the floor, which they could see when they peeped around the edge of the mats. But outside they heard very clearly the clamor of the hunt as it swung to and fro in the village. Shif'less Sol chuckled. It was very low, but it was a chuckle, nevertheless, and the others heard.

"It's sorter takin' an advantage uv 'em," said the shiftless one, "layin' here in thar own church, so to speak, while they're ragin' an' tearin' up the earth everywhar else lookin' fur us. Gives me a mighty snug feelin', though, like the one you have when you're safe in a big log house, an' the wind an' the hail an' the snow are beatin' outside."

"You're shorely right, Sol," said Tom Ross.

"Seems to me," continued the irrepressible Sol, "that you did git in a good lick at Braxton Wyatt, after all. Ain't he unhappy now, bitin' his fingers an' pawin' the earth an' findin' nothin'? I feel real sorry, I do, fur Braxton. It's hard fur a nice young feller to have to suffer sech disappointments."

Shif'less Sol chuckled again, and Henry was forced to smile in the darkness. Shif'less Sol was not wholly wrong. It would be a bitter blow to Braxton Wyatt. Moreover, it was pleasant where they sat. A hard floor was soft to them, and as they leaned against the wall they could relax and rest.

"What will our fellows out thar in the woods think?" asked Tom Ross.

"They won't have to think," replied Henry. "They'll sit quiet as we're doing and wait."

The noise of the hunt went on for a long time outside. War whoops came from different points of the village. There were shrill cries of women and children, and the sound of many running feet. After a while it began to sink, and soon after that they heard no more noises than those of people preparing for flight. Henry felt sure that the town would be abandoned on the morrow, but his desire to come to close quarters with Braxton Wyatt was as strong as ever. It was certain that the army could not overtake Wyatt's band, but he might match his own against it. He was thinking of making the attempt to steal from the place when, to their great amazement, they heard the door of the Council House open and shut, and then footsteps inside.

Henry looked under the edge of the hanging mat and saw two dusky figures near the window.

CHAPTER XXIII. THE FINAL FIGHT

Shif'less Sol and Tom Ross were also looking under the mats, and the three would have recognized those figures anywhere. The taller was Timmendiquas, the other Thayendanegea. The thin light from the window fell upon their faces, and Henry saw that both were sad. Haughty and proud they were still, but each bore the look that comes only from continued defeat and great disappointment. It is truth to say that the concealed three watched them with a curiosity so intense that all thought of their own risk was forgotten. To Henry, as well as his comrades, these two were the greatest of all Indian chiefs.

The White Lightning of the Wyandots and the Joseph Brant of the Mohawks stood for a space side by side, gazing out of the window, taking a last look at the great Seneca Castle. It was Thayendanegea who spoke first, using Wyandot, which Henry understood.

"Farewell, my brother, great chief of the Wyandots," he said. "You have come far with your warriors, and you have been by our side in battle. The Six Nations owe you much. You have helped us in victory, and you have not deserted us in defeat. You are the greatest of warriors, the boldest in battle, and the most skillful."

Timmendiquas made a deprecatory gesture, but Thayendanegea went on:

"I speak but the truth, great chief of the Wyandots. We owe you much, and some day we may repay. Here the Bostonians crowd us hard, and the Mohawks may yet fight by your side to save your own hunting grounds."

"It is true," said Timmendiquas. "There, too, we' must fight the Americans."

"Victory was long with us here," said Thayendanegea, "but the rebels have at last brought an army against us, and the king who persuaded us to make war upon the Americans adds nothing to the help that he has given us already. Our white allies were the first to run at the Chemung, and now the Iroquois country, so large and so beautiful, is at the mercy of the invader. We perish. In all the valleys our towns lie in ashes. The American army will come to-morrow, and this, the great Seneca Castle, the last of our strongholds, will also sink under the flames. I know not how our people will live through the Winter that is yet to come. Aieroski has turned his face from us."

But Timmendiquas spoke words of courage and hope.

"The Six Nations will regain their country," he said. "The great League of the Ho-de-no-sau-nee, which has been victorious for so many generations, cannot be destroyed. All the tribes from here to the Mississippi will help, and will press down upon the settlements. I will return to stir them anew, and the British posts will give us arms and ammunition."

The light of defiance shone once more in the eyes of Thayendanegea.

"You raise my spirits again," he said. "We flee now, but we shall come back again. The Ho-de-no-saunee can never submit. We will ravage all their settlements, and burn and destroy. We will make a wilderness where they have been. The king and his men will yet give us more help."

Part of his words came true, and the name of the raiding Thayendanegea was long a terror, but the Iroquois, who had refused the requested neutrality, had lost their Country forever, save such portions as the victor in the end chose to offer to them.

"And now, as you and your Wyandots depart within the half hour, I give you a last farewell," said Thayendanegea.

The hands of the two great chiefs met in a clasp like that of the white man, and then Timmendiquas abruptly left the Council House, shutting the door behind him. Thayendanegea lingered a while at the window, and the look of sadness returned to his face. Henry could read many of the thoughts that were passing through the Mohawk's proud mind.

Thayendanegea was thinking of his great journey to London, of the power and magnificence that he had seen, of the pride and glory of the Iroquois, of the strong and numerous Tory faction led by Sir John Johnson, the half brother of the children of Molly Brant, Thayendanegea's own sister, of the Butlers and all the others who had said that the rebels would be easy to conquer. He knew better now, he had long known better, ever since that dreadful battle in the dark defile of the Oriskany, when the Palatine Germans, with old Herkimer at their head, beat the Tories, the English, and the Iroquois, and made the taking of Burgoyne possible. The Indian chieftain was a statesman, and it may be that from this moment he saw that the cause of both the Iroquois and their white allies was doomed. Presently Thayendanegea left the window, walking slowly toward the door. He paused there a moment or two, and then went out, closing it behind him, as Timmendiquas had done. The three did not speak until several minutes after he had gone.

"I don't believe," said Henry, "that either of them thinks, despite their brave words, that the Iroquois can ever win back again."

"Serves 'em right," said Tom Ross. "I remember what I saw at Wyoming."

"Whether they kin do it or not," said the practical Sol, "it's time for us to git out o' here, an' go back to our men."

"True words, Sol," said Henry, "and we'll go."

Examining first at the window and then through the door, opened slightly, they saw that the Iroquois village bad become quiet. The preparations for departure had probably ceased until morning. Forth stole the three, passing swiftly among the houses, going, with silent foot toward the orchard. An old squaw, carrying a bundle from a house, saw them, looked sharply into their faces, and knew them to be white. She threw down her bundle with a fierce, shrill scream, and ran, repeating the scream as she ran.

Indians rushed out, and with them Braxton Wyatt and his band. Wyatt caught a glimpse of a tall figure, with two others, one on each side, running toward the orchard, and he knew it. Hate and the hope to capture or kill swelled afresh. He put a whistle to his lip and blew shrilly. It was a signal to his band, and they came from every point, leading the pursuit.

Henry heard the whistle, and he was quite sure that it was Wyatt who had made the sound. A single glance backward confirmed him. He knew Wyatt's figure as well as Wyatt knew his, and the dark mass with him was certainly composed of his own men. The other Indians and Tories, in all likelihood, would turn back soon, and that fact would give him the chance he wished.

They were clear of the town now, running lightly through the orchard, and Shif'less Sol suggested that they enter the woods at once.

"We can soon dodge 'em thar in the dark," he said.

"We don't want to dodge 'em," said Henry.

The shiftless one was surprised, but when he glanced at Henry's face he understood.

"You want to lead 'em on an' to a fight?" he said.

Henry nodded.

"Glad you thought uv it," said Shif'less Sol.

They crossed the very corn field through which they had come, Braxton Wyatt and his band in full cry after them. Several shots were fired, but the three kept too far ahead for any sort of marksmanship, and they were not touched. When they finally entered the woods they curved a little, and then, keeping just far enough ahead to be within sight, but not close enough for the bullets, Henry led them straight toward the camp of the riflemen. As he approached, he fired his own rifle, and uttered the long shout of the forest runner. He shouted a second time, and now Shif'less Sol and Tom Ross joined in the chorus, their great cry penetrating far through the woods.

Whether Braxton Wyatt or any of his mixed band of Indians and Tories suspected the meaning of those great shouts Henry never knew, but the pursuit came on with undiminished speed. There was a good silver moon now, shedding much light, and he saw Wyatt still in the van, with his Tory lieutenant close behind, and after them red men and white, spreading out like a fan to inclose the fugitives in a trap. The blood leaped in his veins. It was a tide of fierce joy. He had achieved both of the purposes for which he had come. He had thoroughly scouted the Seneca Castle, and he was about to come to close quarters with Braxton Wyatt and the band which he had made such a terror through the valleys.

Shif'less Sol saw the face of his young comrade, and he was startled. He had never before beheld it so stern, so resolute, and so pitiless. He seemed to remember as one single, fearful picture all the ruthless and terrible scenes of the last year. Henry uttered again that cry which was at once a defiance and a signal, and from the forest ahead of him it was answered, signal for signal. The riflemen were coming, Paul, Long Jim, and Heemskerk at their head. They uttered a mighty cheer as they saw the flying three, and their ranks opened to receive them. From the Indians and Tories came the long whoop of challenge, and every one in either band knew that the issue was now about to be settled by battle, and by battle alone. They used all the tactics of the forest. Both sides instantly dropped down among the trees and undergrowth, three or four hundred yards apart, and for a few moments there was no sound save heavy breathing, heard only by those who lay close by. Not a single human being would have been visible to an ordinary eye there in the moonlight, which tipped boughs and bushes with ghostly silver. Yet no area so small ever held a greater store of resolution and deadly animosity. On one side were the riflemen, nearly every one of whom had slaughtered kin to mourn, often wives and little children, and on the other the Tories and Iroquois, about to lose their country, and swayed by the utmost passions of hate and revenge.

"Spread out," whispered Henry. "Don't give them a chance to flank us. You, Sol, take ten men and go to the right, and you, Heemskerk, take ten and go to the left."

"It is well," whispered Heemskerk. "You have a great head, Mynheer Henry."

Each promptly obeyed, but the larger number of the riflemen remained in the center, where Henry knelt, with Paul and Long Jim on one side of him, and Silent Tom on the other. When he thought that the two flanking parties had reached the right position, he uttered a low whistle, and back came two low whistles, signals that all was ready. Then the line began its slow advance, creeping forward from tree to tree and from bush to bush. Henry raised himself up a little, but he could not yet see anything where the hostile force lay hidden. They went a little farther, and then all lay down again to look.

Tom Ross had not spoken a word, but none was more eager than he. He was almost flat upon the ground, and he had been pulling himself along by a sort of muscular action of his whole body. Now he was so still that he did not seem to breathe. Yet his eyes, uncommonly eager now, were searching the thickets ahead. They rested at last on a spot of brown showing through some bushes, and, raising his rifle, he fired with sure aim. The Iroquois uttered his death cry, sprang up convulsively, and then fell back prone. Shots were fired in return, and a dozen riflemen replied to them. The battle was joined.

They heard Braxton Wyatt's whistle, the challenging war cry of the Iroquois, and then they fought in silence, save for the crack of the rifles. The riflemen continued to advance in slow, creeping fashion, always pressing the enemy. Every time they caught sight of a hostile face or body they sent a bullet at it, and Wyatt's men did the same. The two lines came closer, and all along each there were many sharp little jets of fire and smoke. Some of the riflemen were wounded, and two were slain, dying quietly and without interrupting their comrades, who continued to press the combat, Henry always leading in the center, and Shif'less Sol and Heemskerk on the flanks.

This battle so strange, in which faces were seen only for a moment, and which was now without the sound of voices, continued without a moment's cessation in the dark forest. The fury of the combatants increased as the time went on, and neither side was yet victorious. Closer and closer came the lines. Meanwhile dark clouds were piling in a bank in the southwest. Slow thunder rumbled far away, and the sky was cut at intervals by lightning. But the combatants did not notice the heralds of storm. Their attention was only for each other.

It seemed to Henry that emotions and impulses in him had culminated. Before him were the worst of all their foes, and his pitiless resolve was not relaxed a particle. The thunder and the lightning, although he did not notice them, seemed to act upon him as an incitement, and with low words he continually urged those about him to push the battle.

Drops of rain fell, showing in the moonshine like beads of silver on boughs and twigs, but by and by the smoke from the rifle fire, pressed down by the heavy atmosphere, gathered among the trees, and the moon was partly hidden. But file combat did not relax because of the obscurity. Wandering Indians, hearing the firing, came to Wyatt's relief, but, despite their aid, he was compelled to give ground. His were the most desperate and hardened men, red and white, in all the allied forces, but they were faced by sharpshooters better than themselves. Many of them were already killed, others were wounded, and, although Wyatt and Coleman raged and strove to hold them, they began to give back, and so hard pressed were they that the Iroquois could not perform the sacred duty of carrying off their dead. No one sought to carry away the Tories, who lay with the rain, that had now begun to fall, beating upon them.

So much had the riflemen advanced that they came to the point where bodies of their enemies lay. Again that fierce joy surged up in Henry's heart. His friends and he were winning. But he wished to do more than win. This band, if left alone, would merely flee from the Seneca Castle before the advance of the army, and would still exist to ravage and slay elsewhere.

"Keep on, Tom! Keep on!" he cried to Ross and the others. "Never let them rest!"

"We won't! We ain't dreamin' o' doin' sech a thing," replied the redoubtable one as he loaded and fired. "Thar, I got another!"

The Iroquois, yielding slowly at first, began now to give way faster. Some sought to dart away to right or left, and bury themselves in the forest, but they were caught by the flanking parties of Shif'less Sol and Heemskerk, and driven back on the center. They could not retreat except straight on the town, and the riflemen followed them step for step. The moan of the distant thunder went on, and the soft rain fell, but the deadly crackle of the rifles formed a sharper, insistent note that claimed the whole attention of both combatants.

It was now the turn of the riflemen to receive help. Twenty or more scouts and others abroad in the forest were called by the rifle fire, and went at once into the battle. Then Wyatt was helped a second time by a band of Senecas and Mohawks, but, despite all the aid, they could not withstand the riflemen. Wyatt, black with fury and despair, shouted to them and sometimes cursed or even struck at them, but the retreat could not be stopped. Men fell fast. Every one of the riflemen was a sharpshooter, and few bullets missed.

Wyatt was driven out of the forest and into the very corn field through which Henry had passed. Here the retreat became faster, and, with shouts of triumph, the riflemen followed after. Wyatt lost some men in the flight through the field, but when he came to the orchard, having the advantage of cover, he made another desperate stand.

But Shif'less Sol and Heemskerk took the band on the flanks, pouring in a destructive fire, and Wyatt, Coleman, and a fourth of his band, all that survived, broke into a run for the town.

The riflemen uttered shout after shout of triumph, and it was impossible to restrain their pursuit. Henry would have stopped here, knowing the danger of following into the town, especially when the army was near at band with an irresistible force, but he could not stay them. He decided then that if they would charge it must be done with the utmost fire and spirit.

"On, men! On!" he cried. "Give them no chance to take cover."

Shif'less Sol and Heemskerk wheeled in with the flanking parties, and the riflemen, a solid mass now, increased the speed of pursuit. Wyatt and his men had no chance to turn and fire, or even to reload. Bullets beat upon them as they fled, and here perished nearly all of that savage band. Wyatt, Coleman, and only a half dozen made good the town, where a portion of the Iroquois who had not yet fled received them. But the exultant riflemen did not stop even there. They were hot on the heels of Wyatt and the fugitives, and attacked at once the Iroquois who came to their relief. So fierce was their rush that these new forces were driven back at once. Braxton Wyatt, Coleman, and a dozen more, seeing no other escape, fled to a large log house used as a granary, threw themselves into it, barred the doors heavily, and began to fire from the upper windows, small openings usually closed with boards. Other Indians from the covert of house, tepee, or tree, fired upon the assailants, and a fresh battle began in the town.

The riflemen, directed by their leaders, met the new situation promptly. Fired upon from all sides, at least twenty rushed into a house some forty yards from that of Braxton Wyatt. Others seized another house, while the rest remained outside, sheltered by little outhouses, trees, or inequalities of the earth, and maintained rapid sharpshooting in reply to the Iroquois in the town or to Braxton Wyatt's men in the house. Now the combat became fiercer than ever. The warriors uttered yells, and Wyatt's men in the house sent forth defiant shouts. From another part of the town came shrill cries of old squaws, urging on their fighting men.

It was now about four o'clock in the morning. The thunder and lightning had ceased, but the soft rain was still falling. The Indians had lighted fires some distance away. Several carried torches. Helped by these, and, used so long to the night, the combatants saw distinctly. The five lay behind a low embankment, and they paid their whole attention to the big house that sheltered Wyatt and his men. On the sides and behind they were protected by Heemskerk and others, who faced a coming swarm.

"Keep low, Paul," said Henry, restraining his eager comrade. "Those fellows in the house can shoot, and we don't want to lose you. There, didn't I tell you!"

A bullet fired from the window passed through the top of Paul's cap, but clipped only his hair. Before the flash from the window passed, Long Jim fired in return, and something fell back inside. Bullets came from other windows. Shif'less Sol fired, and a Seneca fell forward banging half out of the window, his naked body a glistening brown in the firelight. But he hung only a few seconds. Then he fell to the ground and lay still. The five crouched low again, waiting a new opportunity. Behind them, and on either side, they heard the crash of the new battle and challenging cries.

Braxton Wyatt, Coleman, four more Tories, and six Indians were still alive in the strong log house. Two or three were wounded, but they scarcely noticed it in the passion of conflict. The house was a veritable fortress, and the renegade's hopes rose high as he heard the rifle fire from different parts of the town. His own band had been annihilated by the riflemen, led by Henry Ware, but he had a sanguine hope now that his enemies had rushed into a trap. The Iroquois would turn back and destroy them.

Wyatt and his comrades presented a repellent sight as they crouched in the room and fired from the two little windows. His clothes and those of the white men had been torn by bushes and briars in their flight, and their faces had been raked, too, until they bled, but they had paid no attention to such wounds, and the blood was mingled with sweat and powder smoke. The Indians, naked to the waist, daubed with vermilion, and streaked, too, with blood, crouched upon the floor, with the muz'zles of their rifles at the windows, seeking something human to kill. One and all, red and white, they were now raging savages, There was not one among them who did not have some foul murder of woman or child to his credit.

Wyatt himself was mad for revenge. Every evil passion in him was up and leaping. His eyes, more like those of a wild animal than a human being, blazed out of a face, a mottled red and black. By the side of him the dark Tory, Coleman, was driven by impulses fully as fierce.

"To think of it!" exclaimed Wyatt. "He led us directly into a trap, that Ware! And here our band is destroyed! All the good men that we gathered together, except these few, are killed!"

"But we may pay them back," said Coleman. "We were in their trap, but now they are in ours! Listen to that firing and the war whoop! There are enough Iroquois yet in the town to kill every one of those rebels!"

"I hope so! I believe so!" exclaimed Wyatt. "Look out, Coleman! Ah, he's pinked you! That's the one they call Shif'less Sol, and he's the best sharpshooter of them all except Ware!"

Coleman had leaned forward a little in his anxiety to secure a good aim at something. He had disclosed only a little of his face, but in an instant a bullet had seared his forehead like the flaming stroke of a sword, passing on and burying itself in the wall. Fresh blood dripped down over his face. He tore a strip from the inside of his coat, bound it about his head, and went on with the defense.

A Mohawk, frightfully painted, fired from the other window. Like a flash came the return shot, and the Indian fell back in the room, stone dead, with a bullet through his bead.

"That was Ware himself," said Wyatt. "I told you he was the best shot of them all. I give him that credit. But they're all good. Look out! There goes another of our men! It was Ross who did that! I tell you, be careful! Be careful!"

It was an Onondaga who fell this time, and he lay with his head on the window sill until another Indian pulled him inside. A minute later a Tory, who peeped guardedly for a shot, received a bullet through his head, and sank down on the floor. A sort of terror spread among the others. What could they do in the face of such terrible sharpshooting? It was uncanny, almost superhuman, and they looked stupidly at one another. Smoke from their own firing had gathered in the room, and it formed a ghastly veil about their faces. They heard the crash of the rifles outside from every point, but no help came to them.

"We're bound to do something!" exclaimed Wyatt. "Here you, Jones, stick up the edge of your cap, and when they fire at it I'll put a bullet in the man who pulls the trigger."

Jones thrust up his cap, but they knew too much out there to be taken in by an old trick. The cap remained unhurt, but when Jones in his eagerness thrust it higher until he exposed his arm, his wrist was smashed in an instant by a bullet, and he fell back with a howl of pain. Wyatt swore and bit his lips savagely. He and all of them began to fear that they were in another and tighter trap, one from which there was no escape unless the Iroquois outside drove off the riflemen, and of that they could as yet see no sign. The sharpshooters held their place behind the embankment and the little outhouse, and so little as a finger, even, at the windows became a sure mark for their terrible bullets. A Seneca, seeking a new trial for a shot, received a bullet through the shoulder, and a Tory who followed him in the effort was slain outright.

The light hitherto had been from the fires, but now the dawn was coming. Pale gray beams fell over the town, and then deepened into red and yellow. The beams reached the room where the beleaguered remains of Wyatt's band fought, but, mingling with the smoke, they gave a new and more ghastly tint to the desperate faces.

"We've got to fight!" exclaimed Wyatt. "We can't sit here and be taken like beasts in a trap! Suppose we unbar the doors below and make a rush for it?"

Coleman shook his head. "Every one of us would be killed within twenty yards," he said.

"Then the Iroquois must come back," cried Wyatt. "Where is Joe Brant? Where is Timmendiquas, and where is that coward, Sir John Johnson? Will they come?"

"They won't come," said Coleman.

They lay still awhile, listening to the firing in the town, which swayed hither and thither. The smoke in the room thinned somewhat, and the daylight broadened and deepened. As a desperate resort they resumed fire from the windows, but three more of their number were slain, and, bitter with chagrin, they crouched once more on the floor out of range. Wyatt looked at the figures of the living and the dead. Savage despair tore at his heart again, and his hatred of those who bad done this increased. It was being served out to him and his band as they had served it out to many a defenseless family in the beautiful valleys of the border. Despite the sharpshooters, he took another look at the window, but kept so far back that there was no chance for a shot.

"Two of them are slipping away," he exclaimed. "They are Ross and the one they call Long Jim! I wish I dared a shot! Now they're gone!"

They lay again in silence for a time. There was still firing in the town, and now and then they heard shouts. Wyatt looked at his lieutenant, and his lieutenant looked at him.

"Yours is the ugliest face I ever saw," said Wyatt.

"I can say the same of yours-as I can't see mine," said Coleman.

The two gazed once more at the hideous, streaked, and grimed faces of each other, and then laughed wildly. A wounded Seneca sitting with his back against the wall began to chant a low, wailing death song.

"Shut up! Stop that infernal noise!" exclaimed Wyatt savagely.

The Seneca stared at him with fixed, glassy eyes and continued his chant. Wyatt turned away, but that song was upon his nerves. He knew that everything was lost. The main force of the Iroquois would not come back to his help, and Henry Ware would triumph. He sat down on the floor, and muttered fierce words under his breath.

"Hark!" suddenly exclaimed Coleman. "What is that?"

A low crackling sound came to their ears, and both recognized it instantly. It was the sound of flames eating rapidly into wood, and of that wood was built the house they now held. Even as they listened they could hear the flames leap and roar into new and larger life.

"This is, what those two, Ross and Hart, were up to!" exclaimed Wyatt. "We're not only trapped, but we're to be burned alive in our trap!"

"Not I," said Coleman, "I'm goin' to make a rush for it."

"It's the only thing to be done," said Wyatt. "Come, all of you that are left!"

The scanty survivors gathered around him, all but the wounded Seneca, who sat unmoved against the wall and continued to chant his death chant. Wyatt glanced at him, but said nothing. Then he and the others rushed down the stairs.

The lower room was filled with smoke, and outside the flames were roaring. They unbarred the door and sprang into the open air. A shower of bullets met them. The Tory, Coleman, uttered a choking cry, threw up his arms, and fell back in the doorway. Braxton Wyatt seized one of the smaller men, and, holding him a moment or two before him to receive the fire of his foe, dashed for the corner of the blazing building. The man whom he held was slain, and his own shoulder was grazed twice, but he made the corner. In an instant he put the burning building between him and his pursuers, and ran as he had never run before in all his life, deadly fear putting wings on his heels. As he ran he heard the dull boom of a cannon, and he knew that the American army was entering the Seneca Castle. Ahead of him he saw the last of the Indians fleeing for the woods, and behind him the burning house crashed and fell in amid leaping flames and sparks in myriads. He alone had escaped from the house.

CHAPTER XXIV. DOWN THE OHIO

"We didn't get Wyatt," said Henry, "but we did pretty well, nevertheless."

"That's so," said Shif'less Sol. "Thar's nothin' left o' his band but hisself, an' I ain't feelin' any sorrow 'cause I helped to do it. I guess we've saved the lives of a good many innocent people with this morning's work."

"Never a doubt of it," said Henry, "and here's the army now finishing up the task."

The soldiers were setting fire to the town in many places, and in two hours the great Seneca Castle was wholly destroyed. The five took no part in this, but rested after their battles and labors. One or two had been grazed by bullets, but the wounds were too trifling to be noticed. As they rested, they watched the fire, which was an immense one, fed by so much material. The blaze could be seen for many miles, and the ashes drifted over all the forest beyond the fields.

All the while the Iroquois were fleeing through the wilderness to the British posts and the country beyond the lakes, whence their allies had already preceded them. The coals of Little Beard's Town smoldered for two or three days, and then the army turned back, retracing its steps down the Genesee.

Henry and his comrades felt that their work in the East was finished. Kentucky was calling to them. They had no doubt that Braxton Wyatt, now that his band was destroyed, would return there, and he would surely be plotting more danger. It was their part to meet and defeat him. They wished, too, to see again the valley, the river, and the village in which their people had made their home, and they wished yet more to look upon the faces of these people.

They left the army, went southward with Heemskerk and some others of the riflemen, but at the Susquehanna parted with the gallant Dutchman and his comrades.

"It is good to me to have known you, my brave friends," said Heemskerk, "and I say good-by with sorrow to you, Mynheer Henry; to you, Mynheer Paul; to you, Mynheer Sol; to you, Mynheer Tom; and to you, Mynheer Jim."

He wrung their hands one by one, and then revolved swiftly away to hide his emotion.

The five, rifles on their shoulders, started through the forest. When they looked back they saw Cornelius Heemskerk waving his hand to them. They waved in return, and then disappeared in the forest. It was a long journey to Pittsburgh, but they found it a pleasant one. It was yet deep autumn on the Pennsylvania hills, and the forest was glowing with scarlet and gold. The air was the very wine of life, and when they needed game it was there to be shot. As the cold weather hung off, they did not hurry, and they enjoyed the peace of the forest. They realized now that after their vast labors, hardships, and dangers, they needed a great rest, and they took it. It was singular, and perhaps not so singular, how their minds turned from battle, pursuit, and escape, to gentle things. A little brook or fountain pleased them. They admired the magnificent colors of the foliage, and lingered over the views from the low mountains. Doe and fawn fled from them, but without cause. At night they built splendid fires, and sat before them, while everyone in his turn told tales according to his nature or experience.

They bought at Pittsburgh a strong boat partly covered, and at the point where the Allegheny and the Monongahela unite they set sail down the Ohio. It was winter now, but in their stout caravel they did not care. They had ample supplies of all kinds, including ammunition, and their hearts were light when they swung into the middle of the Ohio and moved with its current.

"Now for a great voyage," said Paul, looking at the clear stream with sparkling eyes.

"I wonder what it will bring to us," said Shif'less Sol.

"We shall see," said Henry.

THE END

BOOK EIGHT.
THE BORDER WATCH

A STORY OF THE GREAT CHIEF'S LAST STAND

PREFACE

"The Border Watch" closes the series which began with "The Young Trailers," and which was continued successively in "The Forest Runners," "The Keepers of the Trail," "The Eyes of the Woods," "The Free Rangers," "The Riflemen of the Ohio," and "The Scouts of the Valley." All the eight volumes deal with the fortunes and adventures of two boys, Henry Ware and Paul Cotter, and their friends Shif'less Sol Hyde, Silent Tom Ross and Long Jim Hart, in the early days of Kentucky. The action moves over a wide area, from New Orleans in the South to Lake Superior in the North, and from the Great Plains in the West to the land of the Iroquois in the East.

It has been the aim of the author to present a picture of frontier life, and to show the immense hardships and dangers endured by our people, as they passed through the wilderness from ocean to ocean. So much of it occurred in the shadow of the forest, and so much more of it was taken as a matter of course that we, their descendants, are likely to forget the magnitude of their achievement. The conquest of the North American continent at a vast expense of life and suffering is in reality one of the world's great epics.

The author has sought to verify every statement that touches upon historical events. He has read or examined nearly all the books and pamphlets and many of the magazine articles formerly in the Astor and Lenox, now in the New York Public Library, dealing with Indian wars and customs. In numerous cases, narratives written by observers and participants have been available. He believes that all the border battles are described correctly, and the Indian songs, dances and customs are taken from the relations of witnesses.

But the great mass of material dealing with the frontier furnishes another striking illustration of the old saying that truth is stranger than fiction. No Indian story has ever told of danger and escape more marvelous than those that happened hundreds of times. The Indian character, as revealed in numerous accounts, is also a complex and interesting study. The same Indian was capable of noble actions and of unparalleled cruelty.

As a forest warrior he has never been excelled. In the woods, fighting according to his ancient methods, he was the equal alike of Frenchman, Englishman and American, and often their superior. Many of the Indian chiefs were great men. They had the minds of statesmen and generals, and they prolonged, for generations, a fight that was doomed, from the beginning.

We lost more people in our Indian wars than in all the others combined, except the Civil War. More American soldiers fell at St. Clair's defeat by the Northwestern Indians than in any other battle we had ever fought until Bull Run. The British dead at Braddock's disaster in the American wilderness outnumbered the British dead at Trafalgar nearly two to one. So valiant a race has always appealed to youth, at least, as a fit subject of romance.

The long struggle with the brave and wary red men bred a type of white foresters who became fully their equals in the craft and lore of the wilderness. Such as these stood as a shield between the infant settlements and the fierce tribes, and, in this class, the author has placed his heroes.

CHAPTER I. THE PASSING FLEET

A late sun, red and vivid, cast beams of light over a dark river, flowing slowly. The stream was a full half mile from shore to shore, and the great weight of water moved on in silent majesty. Both banks were lined with heavy forest, dark green by day, but fused now into solid blackness by the approach of night.

The scene was wild and primordial. To an eye looking down it would have seemed that man had never come there, and that this was the dawn of time. The deep waters lapped the silent shore until a gentle sighing sound arose, a sound that may have gone on unheard for ages. Close to the water a file of wild ducks flew like an arrow to the north, and, in a little cove where the current came in shallow waves, a stag bent his head to drink.

The sun lingered in the west and then sank behind the vast wall of forest. The beams of red and gold lasted for a little space on the surface of the river, and then faded into the universal night. Under the great cloak of the dark, the surface of the river showed but dimly, and the rising wind blew through the forest with a chill and uncanny sound.

The ordinary soul would have been appalled by the mighty isolation of the wilderness, yet the river itself was not without the presence of human life. Close to the northern shore, where the shadow of the tall forest lay deepest, floated a long boat, containing five figures that rested easily. Two of the crew were boys, but as tall and strong as men. The other three were somewhat older. The boat carried four pairs of oars, but only one man rowed, and he merely pulled on an oar from time to time to give direction, while the current did the work. His comrades leaned comfortably against the sides of the boat, and with keen eyes, trained to the darkness, watched for a break in the black battlement of the trees.

It was Henry Ware who first saw the opening. It was nearly always he who was the first to see, and he pointed to the place where the dark line made a loop towards the north.

"It's a wide break," he said a moment or two later. "It must be the mouth of the river."

"You're shorely right, Henry," said Shif'less Sol, who sat just behind him, "an' from the looks o' the break thar, it's a good, big river, too. S'pose we pull up in it a spell afore we make a landin'."

"It seems a good idea to me," replied Henry. "What say you, Paul?"

"I'm for it," replied Paul Cotter. "I'd like to see this new river coming down from the north, and it's pretty sure, too, that we'd be safer camping on it for the night than on the Ohio."

Jim Hart had been guiding with a single oar. Now he took the pair in his hands and rowed into the mouth of the tributary stream. The smaller river, smaller only by contrast, poured a dark flood into the Ohio, and, seeing that the current was strong, the others took oars and rowed also, all except Paul, who was at the helm. Driven by powerful arms, the boat went swiftly up the new river. Henry in the prow watched with all the interest that he had for new things, and with all the need for watching that one always had in the great forests of the Ohio Valley.

The banks of this river were higher than those of the Ohio, but were clothed also in dense forests, which, from the surface of the stream no human eye could penetrate in the darkness of the night. They rowed in silence for a full hour, seeing no good place for an anchorage, and then, at a sign from Henry, came to rest on the stream. Shif'less Sol, strong of eye and mind, saw an unusual expression on the face of the leader.

"What is it, Henry?" he whispered.

"I thought I heard the sound of an incautious paddle, one that splashed water, but I'm not sure."

"Ah," said the shiftless one, "then we'll listen a little longer."

The others heard the words also, but, saying nothing, they, too, listened. Very soon all heard the splashing of the single paddle and then the swishing sound of many moved steadily in the waters by strong and practiced hands.

"It's a fleet behind us," said Henry, "and a fleet on this river can mean only Indians. Shall we pull ahead with all our might?"

"No," said Shif'less Sol. "Look how thick the bushes grow at the water's edge. We can run our boat in among them and in all this darkness, the Indians, whether Wyandot, Miami or Shawnee, will not know that we are thar. Besides, curiosity is gnawin' at me hard. I want to see what's in this Indian fleet."

"So do I," said Silent Tom Ross, speaking for the first time, and the others also gave their assent. The boat shot diagonally across the stream towards the dark mass of bushes, into which it was pushed slowly and without noise by the guiding arms of the rowers. Here it came to rest, completely hidden in the dense covert of leaves and twigs, while its occupants could see anything that passed on the surface of the river.

"They'll come soon," said Henry, as the sound of the paddles grew louder, "and I should judge that they are many."

"Maybe a hundred boats and canoes," said Shif'less Sol. "It's my guess that it's a big war party of some kind or other."

"The allied Indian nations, no doubt," said Henry thoughtfully. "Despite their defeats in the East, they are yet almost supreme here in the valley, and they hang together."

"Which means," said Shif'less Sol, a warlike tone coming into his voice, "that ef some big movement is afoot, it's our task to find out what it is an' beat it if we kin."

"Certainly," Henry whispered back. "It's what we've been doing, Sol, for the last two or three years, and we won't stop until the work is done."

The tone of the great youth was low, but it was marked by the resolution that he always showed in times of danger. He and his comrades were on the return journey to Wareville, after taking part in the campaigns of Wyoming and the Chemung, but it was scarcely the thought of any one of the five that they would travel the vast distance without interruption. Henry, as he sat in the boat in the darkness, felt that once more they were on the verge of great events. Used so long to the life of the wilderness and its countless dangers, the sudden throb of his heart told not of fear, but rather of exultation. It was the spirit rising to meet what lay before it. The same strength of soul animated his comrades, but everyone took his resolution in silence.

The boat, hidden deep in the mass of foliage, lay parallel with the current of the stream, and it tipped a little on one side, as the five leaned forward and watched eagerlyfor the fleet that was coming up the river. The regular and rhythmic sound of oars and paddles grew louder, and then the head of the fleet, trailing itself like a long serpent, came into view. A great canoe with many men at the paddles appeared first, and behind it, in lines of four, followed the other canoes, at least a hundred in number, bearing perhaps five hundred warriors.

The five thrilled at the sight, which was ominous and full of majesty. The moon was now coming out, and the surface of the dark stream turned to melted silver. But the high banks were still in darkness, and only the savage fleet was thrown into relief.

The paddles rose and fell in unison, and the steady swishing sound was musical. The moonlight deepened and poured its stream of silver over hundreds of savage faces, illuminating the straight black hair, the high cheek bones, and the broad chests, naked, save for the war paint. None of them spoke, but their silence made the passing of this savage array in the night all the more formidable.

Henry's attention was soon caught by a figure in the large boat that led. It was that of a man who did not use the paddle, but who sat near the prow with folded arms. The upper half of his body was so rigidly upright that in another place he might have posed for a figurehead of some old Roman galley. He was of magnificent build. Like the others, he was naked to the waist, and the moonlight showed the great muscles upon his powerful shoulders and chest. The pose of the head expressed pride that nothing could quench.

Henry recognized the man at once. Had he not seen the face, the figure and attitude alone were sufficient to tell him that this was Timmendiquas, the great White Lightning of the Wyandots, returning from the East, where he had helped the Indians in vain, but at the head of a great force, once more in his own country.

Henry put his hand upon that of Shif'less Sol.

"I see," whispered his comrade very low. "It is Timmendiquas, an' whar he comes, big things come, too."

Henry knew in his heart that the shiftless one was right. The coming of Timmendiquas with so large an army meant great events, and it was good fortune that had placed himself and his comrades there that night that they might see. His old feeling of admiration for the chief was as strong as ever, and he felt a certain sympathy, too. Here was a man who had failed despite courage, energy and genius. His help had not been able to save the Iroquois, and his own people might some day meet the same fate.

The long line of the fleet passed on in silence, save for the musical swishing of the paddles. That sound, too, soon died away. Then all the canoes blended together like a long arrow of glittering silver, and the five in the bushes watched the arrow until it faded quite away on the surface of the stream.

Henry and his comrades did not yet come forth from their covert, but they talked frankly.

"What do you think it means?" asked the young leader.

"Another raid on Kentucky," said Tom Ross.

"But not jest yet," said the shrewd and far-seeing Shif'less Sol. "Timmendiquas will go North to gather all the warriors in the valley if he kin. He may even get help in Canada."

"I think so, too," said Paul.

"'Pears likely to me," said Long Jim.

"That being the case," said Henry, "I think we ought to follow. Do you agree with me?"

"We do," said the four together, speaking with the greatest emphasis.

The decision made, nothing more was said upon the point, but they remained fully an hour longer in the covert. It would not be wise to follow yet, because a canoe or two might drop behind to serve as a rear guard. Nor was there any need to hurry.

The five were in splendid shape for a new campaign. They had enjoyed a long rest, as they floated down the Ohio, rarely using the oars. They carried a large supply of ammunition and some extra rifles and other weapons, and, used to success, they were ready to dare anything. When they thought the Indian fleet was several miles ahead, they pulled their boat from the covert and followed. But they did not take the middle of the stream. Theirs was not a large force which could move rapidly, fearing nothing. Instead, they clung close to the eastern shore, in the shadow of the bank and trees, and rowed forward at an even pace, which they slackened only at the curves, lest they plunge suddenly into a hostile force.

About midnight they heard faintly the splash of the paddles, and then they drew in again among the bushes at the bank, where they decided to remain for the rest of the night. Henry was to watch about three hours and

Shif'less Sol would be on guard afterward. The four wrapped themselves in their blankets, lay down in the bottom of the boat, and were sound asleep in a few minutes. Henry, rifle across his knees, crouched in the stern. Now that he did not have the exercise of the oars, the night felt cold, and he drew his own blankets over his shoulders.

Henry expected no danger, but he watched closely, nevertheless. Nothing could have passed on the stream unnoticed by him, and every sound on the bank above would have attracted his attention at once. Despite the fact that they were about to embark upon a new task attended by many dangers, the boy felt a great peace. In the perilous life of the wilderness he had learned how to enjoy the safety and physical comfort of the moment. He looked down at his comrades and smiled to himself. They were merely dark blurs on the bottom of the boat, sleeping soundly in their blankets. What glorious comrades they were! Surely no one ever had better.

Henry himself did not move for a long time. He leaned against the side of the boat, and the blanket remained drawn up about his neck and shoulders. The rifle across his knee was draped by the same blanket, all except the steel muzzle. Only his face was uncovered, but his eyes never ceased to watch. The wind was blowing lightly through the trees and bushes, and the current of the river murmured beside the boat, all these gentle sounds merging into one note, the song of the forest that he sometimes heard when he alone was awake—he and everything else being still.

Henry's mind was peaceful, imaginative, attentive to all the wonders of the forest, beholding wonders that others could not see, and the song went on, the gentle murmur of the river fusing and melting into the wind among the leaves. While he watched and listened, nothing escaping him, his mind traveled far, down the great rivers, through the many battles in which he had borne his share, and up to those mighty lakes of which he had often heard, but which he had never seen.

The moonlight brightened again, clothing all the forest and river in a veil of silver gauze. It was inexpressibly beautiful to Henry who, like the Indians, beheld with awe and admiration the work of Manitou.

A light sound, not in unison with the note of the forest, came from the bank above. It was very faint, nothing more than the momentary displacement of a bough, but the crouching figure in the boat moved ever so slightly, and then was still. The sound was repeated once and no more, but Henry's mind ceased to roam afar. The great river that he had seen and the great lakes that he had not seen were forgotten. With all the power of his marvelous gift he was concentrating his faculties upon the point from which the discord had come once, twice and then no more. Eye, ear and something greater—divination, almost—were bent upon it.

He listened several minutes, but the sound did not come a third time. Forest and river were singing together again, but Henry was not satisfied. He rose to his feet, laid the blanket softly in the boat, and then with a glance at the river to see that nothing was passing there, leaped lightly to the land.

The bank rose above him to a height of thirty feet, but the bushes were thick along its face, and the active youth climbed easily and without noise. Before he reached the crest he flattened himself against the earth and listened. He was quite confident that someone had been passing and was, perhaps, very near. He was too good a forester to ignore the event. He heard nothing and then drew himself up cautiously over the edge of the cliff.

He saw before him thick forest, so heavy and dark that the moon did not light it up. An ordinary scout or sentinel would have turned back, satisfied that nothing was to be found, but Henry entered the woods and proceeded carefully in the direction from which the sound had come. He soon saw faint signs of a trail, evidently running parallel with the river, and, used from time to time, by the Indians. Now Henry was satisfied that his senses had not deceived him, and he would discover who had passed. He judged by the difference between the first and second sounds that the journey was leading northward, and he followed along the trail. He had an idea that it would soon lead him to a camp, and he reckoned right, because in a few minutes he saw a red bead of light to his right.

Henry knew that the light betokened a camp-fire, and he was sure that he would find beside it the cause of the noise that he had heard. He approached with care, the woods offering an ample covert. He soon saw that the fire was of good size, and that there were at least a dozen figures around it.

"More warriors," he said to himself, "probably bound for the same place as the fleet."

But as he drew yet nearer he saw that not all the men around the camp-fire were warriors. Three, despite their faces, browned by wind and rain, belonged to the white race, and in the one nearest to him, Henry, with a leap of the heart, recognized his old enemy, Braxton Wyatt.

Wyatt, like Timmendiquas, had come back to the scene of his earlier exploits and this conjunction confirmed Henry in his belief that some great movement was intended.

Wyatt was on the far side of the fire, where the flames lighted up his face, and Henry was startled by the savagery manifested there. The renegade's face, despite his youth, was worn and lined. His black hair fell in dark locks upon his temples. He still wore the British uniform that he had adopted in the East, but sun and rain had left little of its original color. Wyatt had returned to the West unsuccessful, and Henry knew that he was in his most evil mind.

The short, thick man sitting by Wyatt was Simon Girty, the most famous of all the renegades, and just beyond him was Blackstaffe. The Indians were Shawnees.

The three white men were deep in conversation and now and then they pointed towards the north. Henry would have given much to have heard what they said, but they did not speak loudly enough. He was tempted to take a shot at the villain, Simon Girty. A single bullet would remove a scourge from the border and save hundreds of lives. The bullet sent, he might easily escape in the darkness. But he could not pull the trigger. He could not fire upon anyone from ambush, and watching a little while longer, he crept back through the forest to the boat, which he regained without trouble.

Henry awakened his comrades and told them all that he had seen. They agreed with him that it was of the utmost importance. Wyatt and Girty were, no doubt, coöperating with Timmendiquas, and somewhere to the north the great Wyandot intended to rally his forces for a supreme effort.

"This leaves us without the shadow of a pretext for going on to Wareville," said Henry.

"It shorely does," said Shif'less Sol. "It's now our business to follow the Indians an' the renegades all the way to the Great Lakes ef they go that fur."

"I hope they will," said Paul. "I'd like to see those lakes. They say you can sail on them there for days and days and keep out of sight of land. They're one of the wonders of the world."

"The trail may lead us that far," said Henry. "Who knows! But since the enemy is on both land and water, I think we'll have to hide our boat and take to the forest."

The truth of his words was obvious to them. The renegades or Indians in the woods would certainly see their boat if they continued that method of progress, but on land they could choose their way and hide whenever they wished. Reluctantly they abandoned their boat, which was staunch and strong, but they hid it as well as possible among bushes and reeds. In such a vast wilderness, the chances were twenty to one that it would remain where they had put it until they returned to claim their own. Too wise to burden themselves, they buried all their extra weapons and stores at the base of a great oak, marked well the place, and then, everyone with a blanket and light pack, started forward through the forest. They intended to go ahead of the renegades, observe the anchorage of the boats, and then withdrawing some distance from the river, let Wyatt, Girty and their friends pass them.

Although it was yet several hours until daylight, they resumed their journey along the eastern bank of the stream, Henry leading and Silent Tom Ross bringing up the rear. In this manner they advanced rapidly and just when the first beams of dawn were appearing, they saw the Indian fleet at anchor on the west shore.

They examined them at their leisure from the dense covert of the thickets, and saw that their estimate of five hundred warriors, made the night before, was correct. They also saw Timmendiquas more than once and it was evident that he was in complete command. Respect and attention followed wherever he went. Paint and dress indicated that warriors of all the tribes inhabiting the Ohio Valley were there.

The Indians seemed to be in no hurry, as they lighted fires on the bank, and cooked buffalo and deer meat, which they ate in great quantities. Many, when they had finished their breakfast, lay down on the grass and slept again. Others slept in the larger canoes.

"They are waiting for more of their friends to come up," whispered Henry to his comrades. A few minutes later, Wyatt, Girty and their party hailed the great war band from the east bank. Canoes were sent over for them, and they were taken into the Indian camp, but without much sign of rejoicing.

"We know that Timmendiquas does not like Wyatt," said Henry, "and I don't believe that he really likes any of the renegades, not even Girty."

"Red man ought to stick to red man, an' white man to white," said Shif'less Sol, sententiously. "I think that's the way Timmendiquas looks at it, an' I'd like to stan' ez high ez a white man, ez he does ez a red man."

"I kin smell that cookin' buffler an' venison all the way across the river," said Jim Hart, "an' it's makin' me pow'ful hungry."

"It'll have to be cold meat for us this time, Jim," said Henry.

They had been so engrossed in the spectacle passing before them that they had forgotten food until the savory odors came across the stream and recalled it to Jim Hart's attention. Now they took out strips of dried venison with which they were always provided, and ate it slowly. It was not particularly delicious to the taste, but it furnished sustenance and strength. All the while they were lying in a dense thicket, and the sun was steadily climbing to the zenith, touching the vast green forest with bright gold.

A shout came from a point far down the river. It was faint, but the five in the covert heard it. Someone in the fleet of Timmendiquas sent back an answering cry, a shrill piercing whoop that rose to an extraordinary pitch of intensity, and then sank away gradually in a dying note. Then the first cry came again, not so remote now, and once more it was answered in a similar way from the fleet of Timmendiquas.

"Another fleet or detachment is comm'," said Shif'less Sol, "an' its expected. That's the reason why White Lightnin' has been lingerin' here, ez ef time didn't hev no meanin' at all."

Many of the Indians, and with them Girty, Wyatt and Blackstaffe were looking down the stream. The eyes of the five followed theirs and presently they saw a fleet of thirty or forty canoes emerge into view, welcomed with loud shouts by the men of Timmendiquas. When the re-enforcement was fused into the main fleet, all took their place in line and once more started northward, the five following in the woods on shore.

Henry and his comrades kept up this odd pursuit for a week, curving back and forth, but in the main keeping a northern course. Sometimes they left the river several miles away to the left, and saved distance by making a straight line between curves, but they knew that they would always come back to the stream. Thus it was easytraveling for such capable woodsmen as they. They saw the fleet joined by three more detachments, two by water and one by land. One came on a small tributary stream flowing from the West, and the total force was now increased to nearly a thousand warriors.

On the sixth night of the parallel pursuit the five discussed it sitting in a thicket.

"We must be drawing near to a village," said Henry.

"I believe with you," said Shif'less Sol, "an' I think it likely that it's a Wyandot town."

"It's probable," said Paul, "and now for what purpose is such a great Indian force gathering? Do they mean to go South against Kentucky? Do they mean to go East against New York and Pennsylvania, or do they mean to go northward to join the British in Canada?"

"That's what we've got to find out," said Long Jim tersely.

"That's just it," said Henry. "We've got to stick to 'em until we learn what they mean to try. Then we must follow again. It's my opinion that they intend to go further northward or they wouldn't be gathering at a point two or three hundred miles above the Ohio."

"Reckon you are right, Henry," said Shif'less Sol. "Ez for me I don't care how fur north this chase takes us, even ef we come right spang up ag'in' the Great Lakes. I want to see them five wonders o' the world that Paul talks about."

"We may go to them," said Henry, "but it seems probable to me that we'll reach a big Wyandot village first."

The Indians resumed their voyage in the usual leisurely fashion the next morning, and the five on shore followed at a convenient distance. They observed that the water of the river was now shallowing fast. The Indian boats were of light draft, but they could not go much further, and the village must be near.

That evening just before sunset long cries were heard in the forest, and those in the boat replied with similar signals. Then the fleet swung to the bank, and all the warriors disembarked. Other warriors came through the woods to meet them, and leaving a guard with the boats the whole army marched away through the forest.

The five were observers of all that passed, and they knew that the Indian village was at hand—perhaps not more than three or four miles away. Still keeping their distance, they followed. The sun was now gone, and only a band of red light lingered on the horizon in the West. It, too, faded quickly as they marched through the woods, and the night came down, enveloping the forest in darkness. The five were glad that the landing had occurred at such a time, as it made their own pursuit much safer and easier.

The Indians, feeling perfectly safe, carried torches and talked and laughed with great freedom. The five in the covert had both the light and the noise to guide them, and they followed silently.

They passed over a gently rolling country, heavily wooded, and in a half hour they saw lights ahead, but yet at some distance. The lights, though scattered, were numerous, and seemed to extend along an arc of half a mile. The five knew that the Indian village now lay before them.

CHAPTER II. THE SILVER BULLET

The village, the largest belonging to the Wyandots, the smallest, but most warlike of the valley tribes, lay in a warm hollow, and it did not consist of more than a hundred and fifty skin tepees and log cabins. But it was intended to be of a permanent nature, else a part of its houses would not have been of wood. There was also about it a considerable area of cleared land where the squaws raised corn and pumpkins. A fine creek flowed at the eastern edge of the clearing. Henry and his comrades paused, where the line of forest met the open, and watched the progress of the army across the cleared ground. Everybody in the village, it seemed, was coming forward to meet the chief, the warriors first and then the old men, squaws and children, all alive with interest.

Timmendiquas strode ahead, his tall figure seeming taller in the light of the torches. But it was no triumphant return for him. Suddenly he uttered a long quavering cry which was taken up by those who followed him. Then the people in the village joined in the wail, and it came over and over again from the multitude. It was inexpressibly mournful and the dark forest gave it back in weird echoes. The procession poured on in a great horde toward the village, but the cry, full of grief and lament still came back.

"They are mournin' for the warriors lost in the East," said Tom Ross. "I reckon that after Wyomin' an' Chemung, Timmendiquas wasn't able to bring back more than half his men."

"If the Wyandots lost so many in trying to help the Iroquois, won't that fact be likely to break up the big Indian league?" asked Paul.

Tom Ross shook his head, but Henry answered in words:

"No, the Indians, especially the chiefs, are inflamed more than ever by their losses. Moreover, as Timmendiquas has seen how the allied Six Nations themselves could not hold back the white power, he will be all the more anxious to strike us hard in the valley."

"I've a notion," said Shif'less Sol, "that bands o' the Iroquois, 'specially the Mohawks, may come out here, an' try to do fur Timmendiquas what he tried to do fur them. The savages used to fight ag'in' one another, but I think they are now united ag'in' us, on an' off, all the way from the Atlantic to the Great Plains."

"Guess you're right, Sol," said Long Jim, "but ez fur me, jest now I want to sleep. We had a purty hard march to-day. Besides walkin' we had to be watchin' always to see that our scalps were still on our heads, an' that's a purty wearyin' combination."

"I speak for all, and all are with you," said Paul, so briskly that the others laughed.

"Any snug place that is well hid will do," said Henry, "and as the forest is so thick I don't think it will take us long to find it."

They turned southward, and went at least three miles through heavy woods and dense thickets. All they wanted was a fairly smooth spot with the bushes growing high above them, and, as Henry had predicted, they quickly found it—a small depression well grown with bushes and weeds, but with an open space in the center where some great animal, probably a buffalo had wallowed. They lay down in this dry sandy spot, rolled in their blankets, and felt so secure that they sought sleep without leaving anyone to watch.

Henry was the first to awake. The dawn was cold and he shivered a little when he unrolled himself from his blanket. The sun showed golden in the east, but the west was still dusky. He looked for a moment or two at his four friends, lying as still as if they were dead. Then he stretched his muscles, and beat his arms across his chest to drive away the frost of the morning that had crept into his blood. Shif'less Sol yawned and awoke and the others did likewise, one by one.

"Cold mornin' fur this time o' year," said Shif'less Sol. "Jim, light the fire an' cook breakfast an' the fust thing I want is a good hot cup o' coffee."

"Wish I could light a fire," said Long Jim, "an' then I could give you a cup shore 'nuff. I've got a little pot an' a tin cup inside an' three pounds o' ground coffee in my pack. I brought it from the boat, thinkin' you fellers would want it afore long."

"What do you say, Henry?" asked Shif'less Sol. "Coffee would be pow'ful warmin'. None o' us hez tasted anything but cold vittles for more'n a day now. Let's take the chances on it."

Henry hesitated but the chill was still in his blood and he yielded. Besides the risk was not great.

"All right," he said; "gather dead wood and we'll be as quick about it as we can."

The wood was ready in a minute. Tom Ross whittled off shavings with his knife. Shif'less Sol set fire to them with flint and steel. In a few minutes something was bubbling inside Jim Hart's coffee pot, and sending out a glorious odor.

Shif'less Sol sniffed the odor.

"I'm growin' younger," he said. "I'm at least two years younger than I wuz when I woke up. I wish to return thanks right now to the old Greek feller who invented fire. What did you say his name was, Paul?"

"Prometheus. He didn't invent fire, Sol, but according to the story he brought it down from the heavens."

"It's all the same," said the shiftless one as he looked attentively at the steaming coffee pot. "I guess it wuz about the most useful trip Promethy ever made when he brought that fire down."

Everyone in turn drank from the cup. They also heated their dried venison over the coals, and, as they ate and drank, they felt fresh strength pouring into every vein. When the pot was empty Jim put it on the ground to cool, and as he scattered the coals of fire with a kick, Henry, who was sitting about a yard away suddenly lay flat and put his ear to the earth.

"Do you hear anything, Henry?" asked Shif'less Sol, who knew the meaning of the action.

"I thought I heard the bark of a dog," replied Henry, "but I was not sure before I put my ear to the ground that it was not imagination. Now I know it's truth. I can hear the barking distinctly, and it is coming this way."

"Some o' them ornery yellow curs hev picked up our trail," said Shif'less Sol, "an' o' course the warriors will follow."

"Which, I take it, means that it is time for us to move from our present abode," said Paul.

Long Jim hastily thrust the coffee pot, not yet cold, and the cup back into his pack, and they went towards the South at a gait that was half a run and half a walk, easy but swift.

"This ain't a flight," said Shif'less Sol. "It's just a masterly retreat. But I'll tell you, boys, I don't like to run away from dogs. It humiliates me to run from a brute, an' an inferior. Hark to their barkin'."

They now heard the baying of the dogs distinctly, a long wailing cry like the howling of hounds. The note of it was most ominous to Paul's sensitive mind. In the mythology that he had read, dogs played a great rôle, nearly always as the enemy of man. There were Cerberus and the others, and flitting visions of them passed through his mind now. He was aware, too, that the reality was not greatly inferior to his fancies. The dogs could follow them anywhere, and the accidental picking-up of their trail might destroy them all.

The five went on in silence, so far as they were concerned, for a long time, but the baying behind them never ceased. It also grew louder, and Henry, glancing hastily back, expected that the dogs would soon come into sight.

"Judging from their barking, the Wyandots must love dogs of uncommon size and fierceness," he said.

"'Pears likely to me," said Shif'less Sol. "We're good runners, all five o' us. We've shaken the warriors off, but not the dogs."

"It's just as you say," said Henry. "We can't run on forever, so we must shoot the trailers—that is—the dogs. Listen to them. They are not more than a couple of hundred yards away now."

They crossed a little open space, leaped a brook and then entered the woods again. But at a signal from Henry, they stopped a few yards further on.

"Now, boys," he said, "be ready with your rifles. We must stop these dogs. How many do you think they are, Tom?"

"'Bout four, I reckon."

"Then the moment they come into the open space, Tom, you and Paul and Jim shoot at those on the left, and Sol and I will take the right."

The Indian dogs sprang into the open space and five rifles cracked together. Three of them—they were four in number, as Tom had said—were killed instantly, but the fourth sprang aside into the bushes, where he remained. The five at once reloaded their rifles as they ran. Now they increased their speed, hoping to shake off their pursuers. Behind them rose a long, fierce howl, like a note of grief and revenge.

"That's the dog we did not kill," said Paul, "and he's going to hang on."

"I've heard tell," said Tom Ross, "that 'cordin' to the Indian belief, the souls o' dead warriors sometimes get into dogs an' other animals, an' it ain't fur me to say that it ain't true. Mebbe it's really a dead Injun, 'stead o' a live dog that's leadin' the warriors on."

Paul shuddered. Tom's weird theory chimed in with his own feelings. The fourth dog, the one that had hid from the bullets, was a phantom, leading the savages on to vengeance for his dead comrades. Now and then he still bayed as he kept the trail, but the fleeing five sought in vain to make him a target for their bullets. Seemingly, he had profited by the death of his comrades, as his body never showed once among the foliage. Search as they would with the sharpest of eyes, none of the five could catch the faintest glimpse of him.

"He's a ghost, shore," said Tom Ross. "No real, ordinary dog would keep under cover that way. I reckon we couldn't kill him if we hit him, 'less we had a silver bullet."

The savages themselves uttered the war cry only two or three times, but it was enough to show that with the aid of the dog they followed relentlessly. The situation of the five had become alarming to the last degree. They had intended to pursue, not to be pursued. Now they were fleeing for their lives, and there would be no escape, unless they could shake off the most terrible of all that followed—the dog. And at least one of their number, Silent Tom Ross, was convinced thoroughly that the dog could not be killed, unless they had the unobtainable—a silver bullet. In moments of danger, superstition can take a strong hold, and Paul too, felt a cold chill at his heart.

Their course now took them through a rolling country, clad heavily in forest, but without much undergrowth, and they made good speed. They came to numerous brooks, and sometimes they waded in them a little distance, but they did not have much confidence in this familiar device. It might shake off the warriors for a while, but not that terrible dog which, directed by the Indians, would run along the bank and pick up the trail again in a few seconds. Yet hope rose once. For a long time they heard neither bark nor war cry, and they paused under the branches of a great oak. They were not really tired, as they had run at an easy gait, but they were too wise to let pass a chance for rest. Henry was hopeful that in some manner they had shaken off the dog, but there was no such belief in the heart of the silent one. Tom Ross had taken out his hunting knife and with his back to the others was cutting at something. Henry gave him a quick glance, but he did not deem it wise to ask him anything. The next moment, all thought of Tom was put out of his mind by the deep baying of the dog coming down through the forest.

The single sound, rising and swelling after the long silence was uncanny and terrifying. The face of Tom Ross turned absolutely pale through the tan of many years. Henry himself could not repress a shudder.

"We must run for it again," he said. "We could stay and fight, of course, but it's likely that the Indians are in large numbers."

"If we could only shake off the hound," muttered Tom Ross. "Did you pay 'tention to his voice then, Henry? Did you notice how deep it was? I tell you that ain't no common dog."

Henry nodded and they swung once more into flight. But he and Shif'less Sol, the best two marksmen on the border, dropped to the rear.

252

"We must get a shot at that dog," whispered Henry. "Very likely it's a big wolf hound."

"I think so," said Shif'less Sol, "but I tell you, Henry, I don't like to hear it bayin'. It sounds to me jest ez ef it wuz sayin': 'I've got you! I've got you! I've got you!' Do you reckon there kin be anything in what Tom says?"

"Of course not. Of course not," replied Henry. "Tom's been picking up too much Indian superstition."

At that moment the deep baying note so unlike the ordinary bark of an Indian dog came again, and Henry, despite himself, felt the cold chill at his heart once more. Involuntarily he and the shiftless one glanced at each other, and each read the same in the other's eyes.

"We're bound to get that dog, hound, cur, or whatever he may be!" exclaimed Henry almost angrily.

Shif'less Sol said nothing, but he cast many backward glances at the bushes. Often he saw them move slightly in a direction contrary to the course of the wind, but he could not catch a glimpse of the body that caused them to move. Nor could Henry. Twice more they heard the war cry of the savages, coming apparently from at least a score of throats, and not more than three or four hundred yards away. Henry knew that they were depending entirely upon the dog, and his eagerness for a shot increased. He could not keep his finger away from the trigger. He longed for a shot.

"We must kill that dog," he said to Shif'less Sol; "we can't run on forever."

"No, we can't, but we kin run jest as long as the Injuns kin," returned the shiftless one, "an' while we're runnin' we may get the chance we want at the dog."

The pursuit went on for a long time. The Indians never came into view, but the occasional baying of the hound told the fleeing five that they were still there. It was not an unbroken flight. They stopped now and then for rest, but, when the voice of the hound came near again, they would resume their easy run toward the South. At every stop Tom Ross would turn his back to the others, take out his hunting knife and begin to whittle at something. But when they started again the hunting knife was back in its sheath once more, and Tom's appearance was as usual.

The sun passed slowly up the arch of the heavens. The morning coolness had gone long since from the air, but the foliage of the great forest protected them. Often, when the shade was not so dense they ran over smooth, springy turf, and they were even deliberate enough, as the hours passed, to eat a little food from their packs. Twice they knelt and drank at the brooks.

They made no attempt to conceal their trail, knowing that it was useless, but Henry and Shif'less Sol, their rifles always lying in the hollows of their arms, never failed to seek a glimpse of the relentless hound. It was fully noon when the character of the country began to change slightly. The hills were a little higher and there was more underbrush. Just as they reached a crest Henry looked back. In the far bushes, he saw a long dark form and a pointed gray head with glittering eyes. He knew that it was the great dog, a wolf hound; he was sure now, and, quick as a flash, he raised his rifle and fired at a point directly between the glittering eyes. The dog dropped out of sight and the five ran on.

"Do you think you killed him, Henry?" asked Shif'less Sol breathlessly.

"I don't know; I hope so."

Behind them rose a deep bay, the trailing note of the great dog, but now it seemed more ferocious and uncanny than ever. Shif'less Sol shuddered. Tom Ross' faceturned not pale, but actually white, through its many layers of tan.

"Henry," said Shif'less Sol, "I never knowed you to miss at that range afore."

The eyes of the two met again and each asked a question of the other.

"I think I was careless, Sol," said Henry. His voice shook a little.

"I hope so," said Shif'less Sol, whose mind was veering more and more toward the belief of Tom Ross, "but I'd like pow'ful well to put a bullet through that animal myself. Them awful wolf howls o' his hit on my nerves, they do."

The chance of the shiftless one came presently. He, too, saw among the bushes the long dark body, the massive pointed head and the glittering eyes. He fired as quickly as Henry had done. Then came that silence, followed in a few minutes by the deep and sinister baying note of the great hound.

"I reckon I fired too quick, too," said Shif'less Sol. But the hands that grasped his rifle were damp and cold.

"'Tain't no use," said Tom Ross in a tone of absolute conviction. "I've seen you and Henry fire afore at harder targets than that, an' hit 'em every time. You hit this one, too."

"Then why didn't we kill the brute?" exclaimed Henry.

"'Cause lead wuzn't meant to kill him. Your bullets went right through him an' never hurt him."

Henry forced a laugh.

"Pshaw, Tom," he said. "Don't talk such foolishness.'"

"I never talked solider sense in my life," said Ross.

Henry and Shif'less Sol reloaded their rifles as they ran, and both were deeply troubled. In all their experience of every kind of danger they had met nothing so sinister as this, nothing so likely to turn the courage of a brave man. Twice sharpshooters who never missed had missed a good target. Or could there be anything in the words of Tom Ross?

They left the warriors some distance behind again and paused for another rest, until the terrible hound should once more bring the pursuers near. All five were much shaken, but Tom Ross as usual in these intervals turned his back upon the others, and began to work with his hunting knife. Henry, as he drew deep breaths of fresh air into his lungs, noticed that the sun was obscured. Many clouds were coming up from the southwest, and there was a damp touch in the air. The wind was rising.

"Looks as if a storm was coming," he said. "It ought to help us."

But Tom Ross solemnly shook his head.

"It might throw off the warriors," he said, "but not the dog. Hark, don't you hear him again?"

They did hear. The deep booming note, sinister to the last degree, came clearly to their ears.

"It's time to go ag'in," said Shif'less Sol, with a wry smile. "Seems to me this is about the longest footrace I ever run. Sometimes I like to run, but I like to run only when I like it, and when I don't like it I don't like for anybody to make me do it. But here goes, anyhow. I'll keep on runnin' I don't know whar."

Sol's quaint remarks cheered them a little, and their feet became somewhat lighter. But one among them was thinking with the utmost concentration. Tom Ross, convinced that something was a fact, was preparing to meet it. He would soon be ready. Meanwhile the darkness increased and the wind roared, but there was no rain. The country grew rougher. The underbrush at times was very dense, and one sharp little stony hill succeeded another. The running was hard.

Henry was growing angry. He resented this tenacious pursuit. It had been so unexpected, and the uncanny dog had been so great a weapon against them. He began to feel now that they had run long enough. They must make a stand and the difficult country would help them.

"Boys," he said, "we've run enough. I'm in favor of dropping down behind these rocks and fighting them off. What do you say?"

All were for it, and in a moment they took shelter. The heavy clouds and the forest about them made the air dim, but their eyes were so used to it that they could see anyone who approached them, and they were glad now that they had decided to put the issue to the test of battle. They lay close together, watching in front and also for a flank movement, but for a while they saw nothing. The hound had ceased to bay, but, after a while, both Henry and Sol saw a rustling among the bushes, and they knew that the savages were at hand.

But of all the watchers at that moment Silent Tom Ross was the keenest. He also occupied himself busily for a minute or so in drawing the bullet from his rifle. Henry did not notice him until this task was almost finished.

"Why, in the name of goodness, Tom," he exclaimed, "are you unloading your rifle at such a time?"

Tom looked up. The veteran scout's eyes shone with grim fire.

"I know what I'm doin'," he said. "Mebbe I'm the only one in this crowd who knows what ought to be did. I'm not unloadin' my rifle, Henry. I'm jest takin' out one bullet an' puttin' in another in its place. See this?"

He held up a small disc that gleamed in the dim light.

"That," said Tom, "is a silver bullet. It's flat an' it ain't shaped like a bullet, but it's a bullet all the same. I've been cuttin' it out uv a silver sixpence, an' now it exactly fits my rifle. You an' Sol—an' I ain't sayin' anything ag'in' your marksmanship—could shoot at that dog all day without hurtin' him, but I'm goin' to kill him with this silver bullet."

"Don't talk foolishness, Tom," said Henry.

"You'll see," said the veteran in a tone of such absolute conviction that the others could not help being impressed. Tom curled himself up behind one rock, and in front of another. Then he watched with the full intensity that the danger and his excitement demanded. He felt that all depended upon him, his own life and the lives of those four comrades so dear to him.

Tom Ross, silent, reserved, fairly poured his soul into his task. Nothing among the bushes and trees in front of them escaped his attention. Once he saw a red feather move, but he knew that it was stuck in the hair of an Indian and he was looking for different game. He became so eager that he flattened his face against the rock and thrust forward the rifle barrel that he might lose no chance however fleeting.

Silent Tom's figure and face were so tense and eager that Henry stopped watching the bushes a moment or two to look at him. But Tom continued to search for his target. He missed nothing that human eye could see among those bushes, trees and rocks. He saw an eagle feather again, but it did not interest him. Then he heard the baying of a hound, and he quivered from head to foot, but the sound stopped in a moment, and he could not locate the long dark figure for which he looked. But he never ceased to watch, and his eagerness and intensity did not diminish a particle.

The air darkened yet more, and the moan of the wind rose in the forest. But there was no rain. The five behind the rocks scarcely moved, and there was silence in the bushes in front of them. Tom Ross, intent as ever, saw a bush move slightly and then another. His eyes fastened upon the spot. So eager was he that he seemed fairly to double his power of sight. He saw a third bush move, and then a patch of something dark appear where nothing had been before. Tom's heart beat fast. He thought of the comrades so dear to him, and he thought of the silver bullet in his rifle. The dark patch grew a little larger. He quivered all over, but the next instant he was rigid. He was watching while the dark patch still grew. He felt that he would have but a single chance, and that if ever in his life he must seize the passing moment it was now.

Tom was staring so intently that his gaze pierced the shadows, and now he saw the full figure of a huge hound stealing forward among the bushes. He saw the massive pointed head and glittering eyes, and his rifle muzzle shifted until he looked down the barrel upon a spot directly between those cruel eyes. He prayed to the God of the white man and the Manitou of the red man, who are the same, to make him steady of eye and hand in this, their moment of great need. Then he pulled the trigger.

The great dog uttered a fierce howl of pain, leaped high into the air, and fell back among the bushes. But even as he fell Tom saw that he was stiffening into death, and he exclaimed to his comrades:

"It got him! The silver bullet got him! He'll never follow us any more."

"I believe you're right," said Henry, awed for the moment despite his clear and powerful mind, "and since he's dead we'll shake off the warriors. Come, we'll run for it again."

CHAPTER III. THE HOT SPRING

Bending low, they ran again swiftly forward toward the south. A great cry rose behind them, the whoop of the warriors, a yell of rage and disappointment. A dozen shots were fired, but the bullets either flew over their heads or dropped short. The five did not take the trouble to reply. Confidence had returned to them with amazing quickness, and the most confident and joyous of all was Tom Ross.

"I had the big medicine that time," he exclaimed exultantly. "It's lucky I found the silver sixpence in my pocket, or that hound would have had the savages trailing us forever."

Henry was cooler now, but he did not argue with him about it. In fact, none of them ever did. Both he and Sol were now noting the heavens which had become more overcast. The clouds spread from the horizon to the zenith. Not a ray of sunlight showed. The wind was dropping, but far into the southwest the earth sighed.

"It's the rain," said Henry. "Let it come. It and all this blackness will help our escape."

Low thunder muttered along the western horizon. There were three or four flashes of lightning but when the rain came presently with a sweep, both thunder and lightning ceased, and they ran on clothed in a mantle of darkness.

"Let's stay close together," said Henry, "and after awhile we'll turn to the east and bear back toward the village. Nobody on earth can trail us in all this gloom, with the rain, too, washing out every trace of our footsteps."

Henry's judgment was good. Now that the hound was gone they shook off the savages with ease. The rain was coming down in a steady pour, and, as the twilight also was at hand, they were invisible to anyone fifty yards away. Hence their speed dropped to a walk, and, in accordance with their plan, they turned to the right. They walked on through dark woods, and came to a smoother country, troubled little by rocks and underbrush. The night was fully come, and the rain, that was still pouring out of a black sky, was cold. They had paid no attention to it before except for its concealment, but, as their figures relaxed after long effort, chill struck into the bone. They had kept their rifles dry with their hunting shirts, but now they took their blankets from the packs and wrapped them about their shoulders. The blankets did not bring them warmth. Their soaked clothing chilled them more and more.

They had become inured long since to all kinds of hardships, but one cannot stand everything. Now and then a spurt of hail came with the rain, and it beat in their faces, slipped between the blankets and down their necks, making them shiver. Their weariness after so much exertion made them all susceptible to the rain and cold. Finally Henry called a halt.

"We must find shelter somewhere," he said. "If we don't, we'll be so stiff in the morning we can't walk, and we'll be lucky to escape chills and pneumonia, or something of that kind."

"That's right," said Shif'less Sol. "So we'll jest go into the inn, which ain't more'n a hundred yards further on, git dry clothing, eat a big supper, have a steaming hot drink apiece of something strong an' then crawl in on feather beds with warm dry blankets over us. Oh, I'll sleep good an' long! Don't you worry about that!"

"Solomon Hyde," said Long Jim Hart indignantly, "ef you don't stop talkin' that way I'll hit you over the head with the barrel uv my rifle. I'm cold enough an' wet enough already without you conjurin' up happy dreams an' things that ain't. Them contrasts make me miserabler than ever, an' I'm likely to get wickeder too. I give you fair warnin'."

"All right," replied Shif'less Sol resignedly. "I wuz jest tryin' to cheer you up, Jim, but a good man never gits any reward in this world, jest kicks. How I wish that rain would stop! I never knowed such a cold rain afore at this time o' the year."

"We must certainly find some sort of shelter," Henry repeated.

They searched for a long time, hoping for an alcove among the rocks or perhaps a thick cluster of trees, but they found nothing. Several hours passed. The rain grew lighter, and ceased, although the clouds remained, hiding the moon. But the whole forest was soaked. Water dripped from every twig and leaf, and the five steadily grew colder and more miserable. It was nearly midnight when Henry spied the gleam of water among the tree trunks.

"Another spring," he said. "What a delightful thing to see more water. I've been fairly longing for something wet."

"Yes, and the spring has been rained on so much that the steam is rising from it," said Paul.

"That's so," said Jim Hart. "Shore ez you live thar's a mist like a smoke."

But Henry looked more closely and his tone was joyous as he spoke.

"Boys," he said, "I believe we're in luck, great luck. I think that's a hot spring."

"So do I," said Shif'less Sol in the same joyous tone, "an' ef it is a hot spring, an' it ain't too almighty hot, why, we'll all take pleasant hot baths in it, go to bed an' sleep same ez ef we wuz really on them feather beds in that inn that ain't."

Sol approached and put his hand in the water which he found warm, but not too hot.

"It's all that we hoped, boys," he exclaimed joyfully. "So I'm goin' to enjoy these baths of Lucully right away. After my bath I'll wrap myself in my blanket, an' ez the rain hez stopped I'll hang out my clothes to dry."

It was really a hot spring of the kind sometimes found in the West. The water from the base of a hill formed a large pool, with a smooth bottom of stone, and then flowed away in a little brook under the trees.

It was, indeed, a great piece of luck that they should find this hot bath at a time when it was so badly needed. The teeth of both Paul and Sol were chattering, and they were the first to throw off their clothes and spring into the pool.

"Come right in and be b'iled," exclaimed the shiftless one. "Paul has bragged of the baths o' Caracally but this beats 'em."

There were three splashes as the other three hit the water at once. Then they came out, rolled themselves lightly in the warm blankets, and felt the stiffness and soreness, caused by the rain and cold, departing from their bodies. A light wind was blowing, and their clothes, hung on boughs, were beginning already to dry. An extraordinary sense of peace and ease, even of luxury, stole over them all. The contrast with what they had been suffering put them in a physical heaven.

"I didn't think I could ever be so happy, a-layin' 'roun' in the woods wrapped up in nothin' but a blanket," said Shif'less Sol. "I guess the baths o' Rome that Paul tells about wuz good in their day, which wuz a mighty long time ago, but not needin' 'em ez bad ez we did, mebbe, them Roman fellers didn't enjoy 'em ez much. What do you say to that, Paul, you champion o' the ancient times which hev gone forever?"

The only answer was a long regular breathing. Paul had fallen asleep.

"Good boy," said Shif'less Sol, sympathetically, "I hope he'll enjoy his nap."

"Hope the same fur me," said Long Jim, "'cause I'm goin' to foller him in less than two minutes."

Jim Hart made good his words. Within the prescribed time a snore, not loud nor disagreeable, but gentle and persistent, rose on the night air. One by one the others also fell asleep, all except Henry, who forced himself to keep awake, and who was also pondering the question of Timmendiquas. What were the great chief's plans? What vast scheme had been evolved from the cunning brain of that master Indian? And how were the five—only five—to defeat it, even should they discover its nature?

The light wind blew through all the rest of the night. The foliage became dry, but the earth had been soaked so thoroughly with water that it remained heavy with damp. The night was bright enough for him to observe the faces of his comrades. They were sleeping soundly and everyone was ruddy with health.

"That was certainly a wonderful hot bath," said Henry to himself, as he looked at the pool. He moved a little in his blanket, tested his muscles and found them all flexible. Then he watched until the first tinge of gray appeared in the east, keeping his eyes upon it, until it turned to silver and then to rose and gold, as the bright sun came. The day would be clear and warm, and, after waiting a little longer, he awakened the others.

"I think you'd better dress for breakfast," he said.

Their clothing was now thoroughly dry, and they clothed themselves anew, but breakfast was wholly lacking. They had eaten all the venison, and every man had an aching void.

"The country hez lots o' deer, o' course," said Shif'less Sol, "but jest when you want one most it's pretty shore that you can't find it."

"I'm not so certain about that," said Henry. "When you find a hot spring you are pretty likely to find a mineral spring or two, also, especially one of salt."

"And if it's salt," finished Paul, "we'll see the deer coming there to drink."

"Sound reasonin'," said Tom Ross.

They began the search. About a hundred yards east of the hot spring they found one of sulphur water, and, two hundred yards further, one of salt. Innumerable tracks beside it showed that it was well patronized by the wilderness people, and the five, hiding in a clump of bushes at a point where the wind would not betray them, bided their time. Some small animals came down to drink at the healing salt spring, but the five did not pull a trigger. This was not the game they wanted, and they never killed wantonly. They were waiting for a fine fat deer, and they felt sure that he would come. A great yellow panther padded down to the spring, frightening everything else away and lapped the water greedily, stopping now and then for suspicious looks at the forest. They longed to take a shot at the evil brute, and, under the circumstances, everyone of the five would have pulled the trigger, but now none did so. The panther took his time, but finally he slunk back into the forest, leaving the salt spring to better wilderness people than himself.

At last the sacrifice came, a fat and splendid stag, walking proudly and boldly down to the pool. He sniffed the morning air, but the wind was not blowing from the firetoward him, and, with no feeling of danger, he bent down his regal head to drink. The five felt regret that so noble an animal must give his life for others, but hunger was hunger and in the wilderness there was no other way. By common consent they nodded towards Henry, who was the best shot, and he raised his rifle. It reminded him of the time far back, when, under the tutelage of Tom Ross, he had shot his first stag. But now, although he did not say it to himself or even think of it, he was Tom Ross' master in all the arts of hunting, and in mind as well.

Henry pulled the trigger. The stag leaped high into the air, ran a few yards, fell and was still. They dressed his body quickly, and in a half hour Long Jim Hart, with all the skill and soul of a culinary artist was frying strips of deer meat over the coals that Shif'less Sol had kindled. There was danger of Indians, of course, but they kept a sharp watch, and as they ate, they neither saw nor heard any sign.

"It is pretty sure," said Henry, "that no savage was lingering about when I fired the rifle, because we would have heard something from him by this time."

"You are shorely right," said Shif'less Sol. "Jim, give me another strip. My appetite hez took a fresh hold ez I'm eatin' now with a free mind."

"Here you are, Sol," said Long Jim. "It's a pow'ful pleasure to me to see you eat my cookin'. The health an strength uv a lazy man like you who hez been nourished by my hand is livin' proof that I'm the best cook in the woods."

"We all give you that credit, Jim," said Shif'less Sol contentedly.

After breakfast they took with them as large a supply of the meat as they could carry with convenience and regretfully left the rest to the wolves and panthers. Then they began their journey toward the Wyandot village. Their misadventure and their long flight from the terrible hound had not discouraged them in the least. They would return directly to the storm center and keep watch, as well as they could, upon the movements of Timmendiquas and his allies.

But they chose another and more easterly course now and traveled all day through beautiful sunshine and a dry forest. Their precautions of the night before had served them well, as the rain and cold left no trace of ill, and their spirits rose to heights.

"But thar's one thing we've got to guard ag'in'," said Shif'less Sol. "I don't want to be tracked by any more dogs. Besides bein' dangerous, it gives you a creepy uncomf'table feelin'."

"We'll keep a good watch for them," said Henry.

As they saw no reason for haste, they slept in the woods another night, and the next night thereafter they approached the Indian village. They hung about it a long time, and, at great risk, discovered that a new movement was on foot. Timmendiquas would soon depart for a journey further into the North. With him would go the famous chiefs, Yellow Panther of the Miamis, and Red Eagle of the Shawnees, and the renegades, Simon Girty, Braxton Wyatt and Blackstaffe. They would have a retinue of a hundred warriors, chosen from the different tribes, but with precedence allotted to the Wyandots. These warriors, however, were picked men of the valley nations, splendidly built, tall, lean and full of courage and ferocity. They were all armed with improved rifles, and every man carried a tomahawk and hunting knife. They were also amply supplied with ammunition and provisions.

The five having watched these preparations by night when they could come close to the village, considered them carefully as they lay in a dense covert. So far they had not been able to discover anything that would indicate the intention of Timmendiquas, except that he would march northward, and there were many guesses.

"I'm thinking that he will go to Detroit," said Henry. "That's the strongest British post in the West. The Indians get their arms and ammunition there, and most of the raids on Kentucky have been made from that point."

"Looks ez likely ez anything to me," said Shif'less Sol, "but I'm guessin' that ef Timmendiquas goes to Detroit he won't stop there. He's a big man an' he may then go westward to raise all the tribes o' the Great Lakes."

"It may be so," said Henry.

CHAPTER IV. THE SEVEN HERALDS

Henry, late the next night, was near the Wyandot village, watching it alone. They had decided to divide their work as the border watch. Part of them would sleep in the covert, while the others would scout about the village. That night it was the turn of Shif'less Sol and himself, but they had separated in order to see more. The shiftless one was now on the other side of the town, perhaps a mile away.

Henry was in a thick clump of bushes that lay to the north of the house and tepees. Dogs might stray that way or they might not. If they did, a rifle shot would silence the first that gave tongue, and he knew that alone he was too swift in flight to be overtaken by any Indian force.

Although past midnight the heavens were a fine silky blue, shot with a myriad of stars, and a full rich moon hanging low. Henry, lying almost flat upon his stomach, with his rifle by his side, was able to see far into the village. He noted that, despite the lateness of the hour, fires were burning there, and that warriors, carrying torches, were passing about. This was unusual. It was always characteristic of his mind not only to see, but to ask where, when and, above all, why? Now he was repeatedly asking why of himself, but while asking he never failed to observe the slightest movement in the village.

Presently he saw Timmendiquas walk from a large lodge and stop by one of the fires. Standing in the rays of the moon, light from above and firelight from his side falling upon him the figure of the chief was like that of some legendary Titan who had fought with the gods. A red blanket hung over his shoulder, and a single red feather rose aloft in the defiant scalp lock.

Henry saw the renegade, Simon Girty, approach, and talk with the chief for a few moments, but he was much too far away to hear what they said. Then six warriors, one of them, by his dress, a sub-chief, came from the lodges and stood before Timmendiquas, where they were joined, an instant later, by the renegade Blackstaffe. The chief took from beneath his blanket four magnificent belts of wampum, two of which he handed to the sub-chief and two to the renegade. Timmendiquas said a few words to every one of them, and, instantly leaving the village they traveled northward at the swift running walk of the Indian. They passed near Henry in single file, the sub-chief at the head and Blackstaffe in the rear, and he noticed then that they carried supplies as if for a long journey. Their faces were turned toward the Northwest.

Timmendiquas and Girty stood for a moment, watching the men, then turned back and were lost among the lodges. But Henry rose from his covert and, hidden among the bushes, came to a rapid conclusion. He knew the significance of wampum belts and he could guess why these seven men had departed so swiftly. They were heralds of war. They were on their way to the far northwest tribes, in order that they might bring them to the gathering of the savage clans for the invasion of Kentucky.

Henry felt a powerful impulse, an impulse that speedily became a conviction. Every delay and every reduction of force was a help to the white men and white women and children down below the Ohio. A week of time, or the difference of twenty warriors might be their salvation. He must turn back the messengers, and he must do it with his single hand. How he longed for the help of the brave and resourceful Shif'less Sol. But he was a mile away, somewhere in the dark woods and Henry could not delay. The seven heralds were speeding toward the Northwest, at a pace that would soon take them far beyond his reach, unless he followed at once.

Dropping his rifle in the hollow of his arm he swung in behind them. One could not pick up a trail in dense woods at night, but he had observed their general direction, and he followed them so swiftly that within a half hour he saw them, still traveling in Indian file, the chief as before at the head of the line and Blackstaffe at the rear. The moon had now faded a little, and the light over the forest turned from silver to gray. Many of the stars had withdrawn, but on sped the ghostly procession of seven. No, not of seven only, but of eight, because behind them at a distance of two hundred yards always followed a youth of great build, and of wilderness instinct and powers that none of them could equal.

Chaska, the sub-chief, the Shawnee who led, was an eager and zealous man, filled with hatred of the white people who had invaded the hunting grounds of his race. He was anxious to bring as many warriors as he could to their mighty gathering, even if he had to travel as far as the farthest and greatest of the Great Lakes. Moreover he was swift of foot, and he did not spare himself or the others that night. He led them through bushes and weeds and grass and across the little brooks. Always the others followed, and no sound whatever came from the file of seven which was really the file of eight.

The seven heralds traveled all night and all of the next day, always through forest, and at no time was the eighth figure in the file more than four hundred yards behind them.

The Indian, through centuries of forest life, had gifts of insight and of physical faculties amounting to a sixth sense, yet the keenest among them never suspected, for an instant, that they were eight and not seven. At noon they sat down in the dry grass of a tiny prairie and ate dried deer meat. Henry, in the edge of the woods a quarter of a mile away, also ate dried deer meat. When the seven finished their food and resumed the march the eighth at the same time finished his food and resumed the march. Nothing told the seven that the eighth was there, no voice of the wood, no whisper from Manitou.

The stop had not lasted more than half an hour and the journey led on through great forests, broken only by tiny prairies. Game abounded everywhere, and Henry judged that the Indians, according to the custom among some of the more advanced tribes, had not hunted over it for several seasons, in order that it might have plenty when they came again. Ten or a dozen buffaloes were grazing on nearly every little prairie, splendid deer were in the open and in the woods, but the seven and also the eighth stopped for none of these, although they would have been sorely tempted at any other time.

Their speed was undiminished throughout the afternoon, but Henry knew that they must camp that night. They could not go on forever, and he could secure, too, the rest that he needed. It might also give him the chance to do what he wished to do. At least he would have time to plan.

In the late afternoon the character of the day changed. The sun set in a mackerel sky. A soft wind came moaning out of the Southwest, and drops of rain were borne on its edge. Darkness shut down close and heavy. No moon and no stars came out. The rain fell gently, softly, almost as if it were ashamed, and the voice of the wind was humble and low.

Chaska, Blackstaffe and their men stopped under the interlacing boughs of two giant oaks, and began to collect firewood. Henry, who had been able to come much nearer in the dark, knew then that they would remain there a long time, probably all night, and he was ready to prepare for his own rest. But he did not do anything until the seven had finished their task.

He kept at a safe distance, shifting his position from time to time, until the Indians had gathered all the firewood they needed and were sitting in a group around the heap. Chaska used the flint and steel and Henry saw the fire at last blaze up. The seven warmed their food over the fire and then sat around it in a close and silent circle, with their blankets drawn over their bodies, and their rifles covered up in their laps. Sitting thus,

Blackstaffe looked like the others and no one would have known him from an Indian.

Henry had with him, carried usually in a small pack on his back, two blankets, light in weight but of closely woven fiber, shedding rain, and very warm. He crouched in a dense growth of bushes, three or four hundred yards from the Indian fire. Then he put one blanket on the ground, sat upon it, after the Indian fashion, and put the other blanket over his head and shoulders, just as the warriors had done. He locked his hands across his knees, while the barrel of the rifle which rested between his legs protruded over his shoulder and against the blanket. Some of the stronger and heavier bushes behind him supported his weight. He felt perfectly comfortable, and he knew that he would remain so, unless the rain increased greatly, and of that there was no sign.

Henry, though powerful by nature, and inured to great exertions, was tired. The seven, including the eighth, had been traveling at a great pace for more than twenty hours. While the Indians ate their food, warmed over the fire, he ate his cold from his pocket. Then the great figure began to relax. His back rested easily against the bushes. The tenseness and strain were gone from his nerves and muscles. He had not felt so comfortable, so much at peace in a long time, and yet not three hundred yards away burned a fire around which sat seven men, any one of whom would gladly have taken his life.

The clouds moved continually across the sky, blotting out the moon and every star. The soft, light rain fell without ceasing and its faint drip, drip in the woods was musical. It took the last particle of strain and anxiety from Henry's mind and muscles. This voice of the rain was like the voice of his dreams which sometimes sang to him out of the leaves. He would triumph in his present task. He was bound to do so, although he did not yet know the way.

He watched the fire with sleepy eyes. He saw it sink lower and lower. He saw the seven figures sitting around it become dim and then dimmer, until they seemed to merge into one solid circle.

As long as he looked at them he did not see a single figure move, and he knew that they were asleep. He knew that he too would soon be sleeping and he was willing. But he was resolved not to do so until the darkness was complete, that is, not until the fire had gone entirely out. He watched it until it seemed only a single spark in the night. Then it winked and was gone. At the same time the darkness blotted out the ring of seven figures.

Henry's eyelids drooped and closed. He raised them weakly once or twice, but the delicate voice of the light rain in the forest was so soothing that they stayed down, after the second attempt, and he floated peacefully to unknown shores, hidden as safely as if he were a thousand miles from the seven seated and silent figures.

He awoke about midnight and found himself a little stiff from his crouching position, but dry and rested. The rain was still falling in gentle, persistent fashion. He rolledup the blanket that had lain under him but kept the other around his shoulders. All was dark where the fire and the ring of seven had been, but he knew instinctively that they were there, bent forward with the blankets about their heads and shoulders.

He stole forward until he could see them. He was right. Not one in the circle was missing and not one had moved. Then he passed around them, and, picking his way in the darkness, went ahead. He had a plan, vague somewhat, but one which he might use, if the ground developed as he thought it would. He had noticed that, despite inequalities, the general trend of the earth was downward. The brooks also ran northward, and he believed that a river lay across their path not far ahead.

Now he prayed that the rain would cease and that the clouds would go away so that he might see, and his prayers were answered. A titanic hand dragged all the clouds off to the eastward, and dim grayish light came once more over the dripping forest. He saw forty or fifty yards ahead, and he advanced much faster. The ground continued to drop down, and his belief came true. At a point four or five miles north of the Indian camp he reached a narrow but deep river that he could cross only by swimming. But it was likely a ford could be found near and he looked swiftly for it.

He went a mile down the stream, without finding shallow water, and, then coming back, discovered the ford only a hundred yards above his original point of departure. The water here ran over rocks, and, for a space of ten or fifteen yards, it was not more than four feet deep. The Indians undoubtedly knew of this ford, and here they would attempt to cross.

He waded to the other side, rolled up the second blanket, crouched behind rocks among dense bushes, ate more cold food, and waited. His rifle lay across his knees, and, at all times, he watched the woods on the far shore. He was the hunter now, the hunter of men, the most dangerous figure in the forest, all of his wonderful five senses attuned to the utmost.

The darkness faded away, as the dawn came up, silver and then gold. Golden light poured down in a torrent on river, forest and hills. Every leaf and stem sprang out clear and sharp in the yellow blaze. The waiting youth never stirred. From his covert in the thicket behind the rocks he saw everything. He saw a bush stir, when there was no wind, and then he saw the face of the Indian chief Chaska, appear beside the bush. After him came the remainder of the seven and they advanced toward the ford.

Henry raised his rifle and aimed at Chaska. He picked a spot on the broad and naked chest, where he could make his bullet strike with absolute certainty. Then he lowered it. He could not fire thus upon an unsuspecting enemy, although he knew that Chaska would have no such scruples about him. Pursing his lips he uttered a loud sharp whistle, a whistle full of warning and menace.

The seven sprang back among the bushes. The eighth on the other side of the river lay quite still for a little while. Then a sudden puff of wind blew aside some of the bushes and disclosed a portion of his cap. Chaska who was the farthest forward of the seven saw the cap and fired. The Indian is not usually a good marksman, and his bullet cut the bushes, but Henry, who now had no scruples, was a sharpshooter beyond compare. Chaska had raised up a little to take aim, and, before the smoke from his own weapon rose, the rifle on the other side of the river cracked. Chaska threw up his hands and died as he would have wished to die, on the field of battle, and with his face to the foe. The others shrank farther back among the bushes, daunted by the deadly shot, and the hidden foe who held the ford.

Henry reloaded quietly, and then lay very close among the bushes. Not only did he watch the forest on the other shore, but all his senses were keenly alert. For a distance of a full half mile none of the Indians could cross the river unseen by him, but, in case they went farther and made the passage he relied upon his ears to warn him of their approach.

For a time nothing stirred. Boughs, bushes and leaves were motionless and the gold on the surface of the river grew deeper under the rising sun. Blackstaffe, after the fall of Chaska, was now commander of the seven heralds, who were but six, and at his word the Indians too were lying close, for the soul of Blackstaffe, the renegade, was disturbed. The bullet that had slain Chaska had come from the rifle of a sharpshooter. Chaska had exposed himself for only an instant and yet he had been slain. Blackstaffe knew that few could fire with such swift and deadly aim, but, before this, he had come into unpleasantly close contact with some who could. His mind leaped at once to the conclusion that the famous five were in front of him, and he was much afraid.

An hour passed. The beauty of the morning deepened. The river flowed, an untarnished sheet, now of silver, now of gold as the light fell. Henry crept some distance to the right, and then an equal distance to left. He could not hear the movement of any enemy in front of him, and he believed that they were all yet in the bushes on the other side of the river. He returned to his old position and the duel of patience went on. His eyes finally fixed themselves upon a large bush, the leaves of which were moving. He took the pistol from his belt, cocked it, and put it upon the rock in front of him. Then he slowly pushed forward the muzzle of his long and beautiful Kentucky rifle.

It was certainly a duel to the death. No other name described it, and hundreds of such have been fought and forgotten in the great forests of North America. The Indian behind the bush was crafty and cunning, one of the most skillful among the Shawnees. He had marked the spot where an enemy lay, and was rising a little higher for a better look.

Henry had marked him, too, or rather the movement that was the precursor of his coming, and when the Shawnee rose in the bush he raised a little and fired. There was a terrific yell, a figure leaped up convulsively, and then falling, disappeared. Five shots were fired at Henry, or rather at the flame from his rifle, but he merely sank back a little, snatched up the pistol, and sent a second bullet, striking a brown figure which retreated with a cry to the woods. The remainder, Blackstaffe first among them, also sprang to cover.

The renegade and the four remaining Indians, one of whom was severely wounded, conferred as they lay among the trees. Blackstaffe was no coward, yet his heart was as water within him. He was absolutely sure now that the terrible five were before them. Two shots had been fired, but the others were only waiting their chance. His own force was but five now, only four of whom were effective. He was outnumbered, and he did not know what to do. The Indians would want to carry out the important orders of Timmendiquas, but there was the river, and they did not dare to attempt the crossing.

Henry, in his old position, awaited the result with serene confidence. The seven heralds were now but five, really four, and not only the stars, but the sun, the day, time, circumstance and everything were working for him. He had reloaded his weapons, and he was quite sure now that Blackstaffe and the Indians would stay together. None of them nor any two of them would dare to go far upstream or down stream, cross and attempt to stalk him. Nevertheless he did not relax his vigilance. He was as much the hunter as ever. Every sense was keenly alert, and that superior sense or instinct, which may be the essence and flower of the five was most alert of all.

The duel of patience, which was but a phase of the duel of death, was resumed. On went the sun up the great concave arch of the heavens, pouring its beams upon the beautiful earth, but on either side of the river nothing stirred. The nerves of Blackstaffe, the renegade, were the first to yield to the strain. He began to believe that the five had gone away, and, creeping forward to see, he incautiously exposed one hand. It was only for an instant, but a bullet from the other side of the river cut a furrow all the way across the back of the hand, stinging and burning as if a red hot bar had been laid upon it.

Blackstaffe dropped almost flat upon the ground, and looked at his hand from which the blood was oozing. He knew that it was not hurt seriously, but the wound stung horribly and tears of mingled pain and mortification rose to his eyes. He suggested to the warriors that they go back, but they shook their heads. They feared the wrath of Timmendiquas and the scorn of their comrades. So Blackstaffe waited, but he was without hope. He had been miserably trapped by his belief that the five had gone. They were there, always watching, deadlier sharpshooters than ever.

It was noon now, and a Wyandot, the most zealous of the remaining Indians, lying flat on his stomach, crept almost to the water's edge, where he lay among the grass and reeds. Yet he never crept back again. He stirred the grass and weeds too much, and a bullet, fired by calculation of his movements, and not by any sight of his figure, slew him where he lay.

Then a great and terrible fear seized upon the Indians as well as Blackstaffe. Such deadly shooting as this was beyond their comprehension. The bullets from the rifles of the unseen marksmen were guided by the hand of Manitou. The Great Spirit had turned his face away from them, and helping their wounded comrade, they fled southward as fast as they could. Blackstaffe, his blazed hand burning like fire, went with them gladly.

In that journey of twenty hours' northward the seven heralds had traveled far from the Wyandot village and it was equally as far back to it. Going northward they had zeal and energy to drive them on, and going southward they had terror and superstition to drive them back. They returned as fast as they had gone, and all the time they felt that the same mysterious and deadly enemy was behind them. Once a bullet, cutting the leaves near them, hastened their footsteps. The renegade wished to abandon the wounded man, but the Indians, more humane, would not allow it.

Henry could have reduced the number of the heralds still further, but his mind rebelled at useless bloodshed and he was satisfied to let terror and superstition do their work. He followed them until they were in sight of the village, guessing the surprise and consternation that their news would cause. Then he turned aside to find his comrades in the covert and to tell them what he had done. They admired, but they were not surprised, knowing him so well.

Meanwhile they waited.

CHAPTER V. THE WYANDOT COUNCIL

Henry and his comrades, spying anew from the woods and seeing the village full of stir, thought Timmendiquas and his warriors would depart that day, but they soon gathered that some important ceremonial was at hand, and would be celebrated first. It reminded Henry of the great gathering of the Iroquois before the advance on Wyoming. He was as eager now as then to enter the village and see the rites, which it was quite evident were going to be held at night. Already the dangers of his adventure with the seven heralds were forgotten and he was ready for new risks.

"If I only had a little paint for my face and body," he said, "I could go into the place without much danger, and I'd learn a lot that would be of use to us."

No one answered, but Shif'less Sol, who had been listening attentively, stole away. The sun was then about an hour high, and, a little after twilight, the shiftless one returned with a package wrapped in a piece of deerskin. He held it aloft, and his face was triumphant.

"What have you been doing, Sol?" exclaimed Henry.

"Me? I've been stealin'. An' I tell you I've been a good thief, too, fur a lazy man. You said you wanted paint, Henry. Well, here it is an' the little brushes an' feathers with which you put it on, too. The people are all driftin' toward the center o' the village, an' without any partic'lar trouble to myself or anybody else I entered an outlyin'—an' fur the time empty—lodge an' took away this vallyble paintin' outfit."

"Good," said Henry with delight. "Now you shall paint me, Sol, and in an hour I'll be among the Wyandots. Let's see the paint."

But Shif'less Sol firmly retained his precious package.

"Takin's are keepings," he said. "These paints are mine, an' I 'low you to make use o' them on one condition only."

"What is that?"

"When I paint you, you paint me, an' then we'll go into this mighty Injun metropolis together. Mebbe you'll need me, Henry, an' I'm goin' with you anyway. You've got to agree to it."

Henry and the shiftless one looked each other squarely in the face. Henry read resolve, and also an anxious affection in the gaze of his comrade.

"All right, Sol," he said, "it's agreed. Now let's see which is the better painter."

While the others stood by and gave advice Sol painted Henry. The great youth bared himself to the skin, and Sol, with a deft hand, laid on the Wyandot colors over chest, shoulders, arms, face and hands. Then Henry painted the shiftless one in the same fashion. They also, but with more difficulty, colored their hair black. It was artistic work, and when all was done the two stood forth in the perfect likeness of two splendid Wyandot warriors.

"I think," said Henry, "that if we keep away from Timmendiquas, Wyatt, Girty and those who know us so well, nobody will suspect us."

"But don't run any unnecessary risks," said Paul anxiously. "You know how hard it will be on us waiting out here in the woods, an' if you were captured it's not likely we could save you."

"We'll take every precaution, Paul," said Henry, "and we'll rejoin you here in the morning."

"All right," said Paul, "we'll wait at this point."

They were in an exceedingly dense part of the forest about two miles from the Indian village, and Tom Ross, the phlegmatic, was already selecting a place for his blanket. The moon was not yet out and the light over the forest was dim, but Paul, Long Jim and Silent Tom could see very distinctly the two magnificent young Wyandots who stood near them, bare to the waist, painted wondrously and armed with rifle, tomahawk and knife.

"Henry," said Long Jim, "ef I didn't see your face I could swear that you wuz Timmendiquas his very self. I see Timmendiquas—his shoulders an' the way he carries himself."

"An' I guess you see somethin' gran' an' wonderful in me, too, don't you, Saplin'?" said Shif'less Sol in his most ingratiating tone.

Long Jim gazed at him in his most scornful manner, before he deigned to reply.

"No, I don't see no great chief in you, Sol Hyde," he replied. "I see nothin' but an ornery Wyandot, who's so lazy he has to be fed by squaws, an' who ef he saw a white man would run so fast he'd never stop until he hit Lake Superior an' got beyond his depth."

Shif'less Sol laughed and held out his hand.

"Put 'er thar," he said. "You wouldn't abuse me ef you didn't like me, an' ef I never come back I guess a tear or two would run down that brown face o' yours."

Long Jim returned in kind the iron grasp of his friend.

"Them words o' yours is mighty near to the truth," he said.

Both Henry and Sol said all their good-byes, and then they slid away through the thickets toward the town. As they came to its edge they saw a multitude of lights, fires burning here and there, and many torches held aloft by women and children. There was also the chatter of hundreds of voices, melting into a pleasant river of sound andthe two, not even finding the Indian dogs suspicious, advanced boldly across the maize fields. Henry, remembering his size, which was the chief danger, now stooped and held himself in a shrunken position as much as possible. Thus they came to the town, and they saw that all its inhabitants were converging upon the common in the center.

Both Henry and Sol looked anxiously at the village, which was of a permanent character, containing both single and communal wigwams. The permanent wigwams were of an oblong form, built of poles interwoven with bark. Many were, as Shif'less Sol called them, double-barreled—that is, in two sections, a family to each section, but with a common hall in which the fire was built, each family sitting on its side of the fire. But all these were empty now, as men, women and children had gone to the open space in the center of the village. The communal lodges were much larger, often holding six or seven families, but with entirely distinct partitions for every family. Here in the woods was a rude germ of the modern apartment house.

Henry and Sol drew near to the common, keeping concealed within the shadow of the lodges. The open space was blazing with light from big fires and many squaws carried torches also. Within this space were grouped the guests of the Wyandots, the Shawnees and the Miamis, with their chiefs at their head. They were painted heavily, and were in the finest attire of the savage, embroidered leggings and moccasins, and red or blue blankets. From every head rose a bright feather twined in the defiant scalp lock. But the Shawnees and Miamis stood motionless, every man resting the stock of his rifle upon the ground and his hands upon the muzzle. They were guests. They were not to take any part in the ceremony, but they were deeply interested in the great rites of an allied and friendly nation, the great little tribe of the Wyandots, the woman-ruled nation, terrible in battle, the bravest of the brave the finest savage fighters the North American continent ever produced, the Mohawks not excepted. And the fact remains that they were ruled by women.

The Wyandot warriors had not yet entered the open, which was a great circular grassy space. But as Henry and Shif'less Sol leaned in the shadow of a lodge, a tall warrior painted in many colors came forth into the light of the fires, and uttered a loud cry, which he repeated twice at short intervals. Meanwhile the torches among the women and children had ceased to waver, and the Shawnees and Miamis stood immovable, their hands resting on the muzzles of their rifles. The great fires blazed up, and cast a deep red light over the whole scene. A minute or so elapsed after the last cry, and Henry and Shif'less Sol noticed the expectant hush.

Then at the far side of the circle appeared the Wyandot warriors, six abreast coming between the lodges. They were naked except for the breech cloth and moccasins, but their bodies were gorgeously painted in many colors. Mighty men were they. Few among them were less than six feet in height, and all were splendidly built for strength, skill and endurance. They held their heads high, too, and their eyes flashed with the haughty pride of those who considered themselves first. Not in vain were the woman-ruled Wyandots the bravest of the brave.

The Wyandot people advanced and waited on the outer rim of the circle in the order of their gentes or clans. Their rank like that of all the leading North American tribes was perfect and was never violated. There were eleven clans with the following names in their language: The Bear, the Deer, the Highland Striped Turtle, the Highland Black Turtle, the Mud Turtle, the Large Smooth Turtle, the Hawk, the Beaver, the Wolf, the Snake, and the Porcupine. The rank of the sachem of the nation wasinherent in the clan of the Bear, and the rank of military chief had always belonged hitherto to the clan of the Porcupine, but now the right was about to be waived and for an ample reason.

The Wyandot warriors continued to march steadily into the circle until all were there, and then a deep murmur of approval came from the watching Shawnees and Miamis.

The flower of the Wyandot nation here in its own home was all that wilderness fame had made it. At the head of the first clan, that of the Bear, stood Timmendiquas, and Henry and Shif'less Sol had never seen him appear more commanding. Many tall men were there, but he over-topped them all, and his eyes shone with a deep, bright light, half triumph and half expectancy.

Now all the Wyandots were within the circle, standing as they always camped when on the war path or the hunt. They were arranged in the form of a horseshoe. The head was on the left and the clans ran to the right in this way: The Bear, the Deer, the Highland Striped Turtle, the Highland Black Turtle, the Mud Turtle, the Large Smooth Turtle, the Hawk, the Beaver, the Wolf, the Snake and the Porcupine. These clans were also incorporated into four phratries, or larger divisions. The first phratry included the Bear, the Deer, and the Highland Striped Turtle; the second, the Highland Black Turtle, the Mud Turtle, and the Large Smooth Turtle; the third, the Hawk, the Beaver, and the Wolf, and the fourth, the Snake, and the Porcupine.

Every clan was ruled by a council of five, and of those five, four were women. The fifth, the man, was chosen by the four women from the men of their clan. The four women of the Board of Council had been selected previously by the married women or heads of families of the clans. The wife, not the husband, was the head of the family, nor did he own anything in their home except his clothes and weapons. He was merely a hunter and warrior. All property and rank descended through the female line. The lands of the village which were communal were partitioned for cultivation by the women. The clan council of five was called the Zu-wai-yu-wa, and the lone man was always deferential in the presence of the four women who had elected him. The men councilors, however, had some privilege. When it became necessary to choose the Grand Sachem of the whole nation, they alone did it. But they were compelled to heed the voices of the women who constituted the whole voting population, and who also owned all the property. There was, too, a separate military council of men who chose the military chief. Every clan had a distinctive way of painting the face, and the four women councilors and their man comrade wore on state occasions distinctive chaplets of wild flowers, leaves and grass.

Much of this lore Henry and Shif'less Sol knew already and more they learned later. Now as they watched the impressive ceremonies they often divined what was to come.

After the horseshoe was formed, forty-four women and eleven men in a compact body advanced to the inside of the circle. The women were mostly middle-aged, and they were better looking than the women of other tribes. Seen in the firelight they had primitive dignity and a wilderness majesty, that was brightened by the savage richness of their dress. They wore their hair in long dark braids, adorned by shells and small red and blue feathers. Their tunics, which fell nearly to the knee, were made of the finest dressed deerskin, fastened at the waist with belts of the same material, dyed red or blue. As they watched, the little beads on their leggings and moccasins tinkled and gave forth the colors of the firelight. The expression of all was one of great gravity and dignity. Here was the real senatorial body of the nation. Though they might not fight nor lead in war, they were the lawmakers of the Wyandots. Great deference was paid to them as they passed.

Henry and Shif'less Sol, flattened in the dark against the side of a tepee, watched everything with eager interest. Henry, a keen observer and quick to draw inferences, had seen other but somewhat similar ceremonies among the Iroquois. Women had taken a part there also and some of them had the rank of chieftainess, but they were not predominant as they were among the Wyandots.

The council of the eleven clans stopped in the center of the circle, and a silence, broken only by the crackling of the fires and the sputtering of the torches, came once more over the great assembly. But a thousand eager faces were turned toward them. The Shawnees and Miamis apparently had not yet moved, still standing in rows, every face an impenetrable bronze mask.

The tall warrior of the clan of the Wolf who had made the signal for the ceremony now came forward again. His name was Atuetes (Long Claws) and he was at once the herald and sheriff of the nation. He superintended the erection of the Council House, and had charge of it afterwards. He called the council which met regularly on the night of the full moon, and at such other times as the Grand Sachem might direct. The present was an unusual meeting summoned for an unusual purpose, and owing to the uncommon interest in it, it was held in the open instead of in the Council House.

Timmendiquas, already by common consent and in action the Grand Sachem of the Wyandots, was now about to be formally invested with the double power of Grand Sachem and military chief. The clan of the Porcupine in which the military chieftainship was hereditary had willingly yielded it to Timmendiquas, whose surpassing fitness to meet the coming of the white man was so obvious to everybody.

Atuetes, the herald, advanced to the very center of the ring and shouted three times in loud, piercing tones:

"Timmendiquas! Timmendiquas! Timmendiquas!"

Then the whole nation, with their guests the Shawnees and Miamis, uttered the name in one great cry. After that the deep breathless silence came again and the eager brown faces were bent yet further forward. Timmendiquas standing motionless hitherto at the head of his clan, the Bear, now walked forth alone. The shout suddenly rose again, and then died as quickly as before.

Timmendiquas had thrown aside his magnificent blue blanket, and he stood bare to the waist. The totem of the bear tattooed upon his chest shone in the firelight. His figure seemed to grow in height and to broaden. Never before in all the history and legends of the Wyandots had so mighty an honor been conferred upon so young a warrior. It was all the more amazing because his predominance was so great that none challenged it, and other great warriors were there.

Among the famous chiefs who stood with the councilors or the clan were Dewatire (Lean Deer), Shayantsawat (Hard Skull), Harouyu (The Prowler), Tucae (Slow Walker), and Tadino (Always Hungry).

Timmendiquas continued to walk slowly forward to the point, where the long row of the chieftainesses stood. He would not have been human had he not felt exaltation, and an immense pride as he faced the women, with the hundreds and hundreds of admiring eyes looking on. He came presently within a few feet of them and stopped. Then Ayajinta (Spotted Fawn), the tallest and most majestic of the women, stepped forward, holding in both hands a woven chaplet of flowers and grass. The entire circle was now lighted brilliantly by the fires and torches, and Henry and Shif'less Sol, although at a distance, saw well.

Ayajinta, holding the chaplet in her outstretched hands, stood directly before Timmendiquas. She was a tall woman, but the chief towered nearly a head above her. Nevertheless her dignity was the equal of his and there was also much admiration in her looks.

"Timmendiquas," she said, in tones so clearly that everyone could hear, "you have proved yourself both a great chief and a mighty warrior. For many moons now you have led the Wyandots on the war trail, and you have also been first among them in the Council House. You have gone with our warriors far toward the rising sun and by the side of the great kindred nation, the Iroquois, you have fought with your warriors against the Long Knives. After victory the Iroquois have seen their houses destroyed, but you and your warriors fought valiantly to defend them.

"We, the women of the Wyandots, chosen to the council by the other women, the heads of the families, look upon you and admire you for your strength, your courage and your wisdom. Seldom does Manitou give so much to a single warrior, and, when he does give, then it is not so much for him as it is for the sake of his tribe."

Ayajinta paused and the multitude uttered a deep "Hah!" which signified interest and approval. But Timmendiquas stood upright, unchanging eyes looking at her from the impenetrable brown mask.

"So," she said, "O Timmendiquas, thou hast been chosen Grand Sachem of the Wyandots, and also the leader of the war chiefs. We give you the double crown. Wear it for your own glory, and yet more for the glory of the Wyandot nation."

Timmendiquas bent his lofty head and she put upon it the great flowery crown. Then as he raised his crowned head and looked proudly around the circle, a tremendous shout burst from the multitude. Once more they cried:

"Timmendiquas! Timmendiquas! Timmendiquas!"

Before the third utterance of the name had died, fifty young girls, the fairest of the tribe, dressed in tanned deerskin adorned with beads and feathers, streamed into the inner circle and began to dance before the great chief. Meanwhile they sang:—

Behold the great Timmendiquas!Mightiest of great chiefs,Wisest of all in council,He leads the warriors to battle,He teaches the old men wisdom,Timmendiquas, first of men.

Behold the great Timmendiquas!As strong as the oak on the mountain,As cunning as the wolf of the valley,He has fought beside the great Iroquois,The Yengees flee at the sound of his name,Timmendiquas, first of men.

Then they joined hands and circled about him to a tune played by four men on whistles, made from the bones of eagles. The song died, and the girls flitted away so quickly through the outer ring that they were gone like shadows.

Responsive as they were to wilderness life, the scene was making a mighty impression upon Henry and Shif'less Sol. With the firelight about him and the moonlight above him, the figure of Timmendiquas was magnified in every way. Recognized long since as the most redoubtable of red champions, he showed himself more formidable than ever.

The crowd slowly dispersed, but Atuetes of the clan of the Hawk called a military council in the Council House. Timmendiquas, as became his rank, led the way, and the renegades, Simon Girty, Braxton Wyatt, and Moses Blackstaffe were admitted. Inside the Council House, which was hung with skins and which much resembled those of the Iroquois, the chiefs, after being called to order by Atuetes, the herald and sheriff, sat down in a circle, with Timmendiquas a little further forward than the others.

Atuetes took a great trumpet-shaped pipe, lighted it with a coal that was burning in a small fire in a corner, and inhaled two whiffs of smoke. He breathed out the first whiff toward the heavens and the second toward the earth. He handed the pipe to Timmendiquas, who inhaled the smoke until his mouth was filled. Then, turning from left to right, he slowly puffed out the smoke over the heads of all the chiefs. When the circle was complete, he handed the pipe to the next chief on his left, who puffed out the smoke in the same manner. This was done gravely and in turn by every chief. Then the Grand Sachem, Timmendiquas, announced the great military subject for which they were called together, and they proceeded to discuss it.

CHAPTER VI. THE RUINED VILLAGE

The military council, presided over by Timmendiquas, sat long in the Council House, and about the moment it had concluded its labors, which was some time after midnight, Henry and Shif'less Sol skipped away from the village. Wyandot warriors had passed them several times in the darkness, but they had escaped close notice. Nevertheless, they were glad when they were once more among the trees. The forest had many dangers, but it also offered much shelter.

They rejoined their comrades, slept heavily until daylight, and when they scouted again near the Wyandot village they found that Timmendiquas and his force were gone, probably having started at the dawn and marching swiftly. But they knew that they would have no trouble in finding so large a trail, and as long as they were in proximity of the village they traveled with great care. It was nearly night when they found the broad trail through the woods, leading north slightly by east. All five were now of the belief that the destination of the savages was Detroit, the British post, which, as a depot of supplies and a rallying point for the Indians, served the same purpose as Niagara and Oswego in the East. To Detroit, Wyandots, Shawnees, Miamis, and all the others turned for weapons and ammunition. There went the renegades and there many Kentuckians, who had escaped the tomahawk or the stake, had been taken captive, including such famous men as Boone and Kenton. It was a name that inspired dread and hate on the border, but the five were full of eagerness to see it, and they hoped that the march of Timmendiquas would take them thither.

"I hear they've got big forts thar," said Shif'less Sol, "but ef we don't lose our cunnin', an' I don't think we will, we five kin spy among 'em an' read thar secrets."

"There are many white men at Detroit," said Henry, "and I've no doubt that we can slip in among them without being detected. Tories and renegades who are strangers to the British officers at Detroit must be continually arriving there. In that lies our chance."

Later in the night they approached the Wyandot camp, but they did not dare to go very close, as they saw that it was everywhere guarded carefully and that but few lights were burning. They slept in the woods two or three miles away, and the next day they followed the trail as before. Thus the northward march went on for several days, the great White Lightning of the Wyandots and his warriors moving swiftly, and Henry and his comrades keeping the same pace six or seven miles in the rear.

They advanced through country that none of the five had ever seen before, but it was a beautiful land that appealed alike to the eye and ear of the forest runner. It was not inferior to Kentucky, and in addition it had many beautiful little lakes. Game, however, was not abundant as here were the villages of the Indian tribes, and the forests were hunted more. But the five found deer and buffalo sufficient for their needs, although they took great risks when they fired. Once the shot was heard by a detachment of the Shawnees who also were after game, and they were trailed for a long time, but when night came they shook them off, and the next morning they followed Timmendiquas, as usual, though at a much greater distance.

Their escape in this instance had been so easy that they took enjoyment from it, but they prudently resolved to retain their present great distance in the rear. The trail could not be lost and the danger would be less. The course that Timmendiquas maintained also led steadily on toward Detroit, and they felt so sure now of his destination that they even debated the advisability of passing ahead of the column, in order to reach the neighborhood of Detroit before him. But they decided finally in the negative, and maintained their safe distance in the rear.

As they continued northward the Indian signs increased. Twice they crossed the trails of Indian hunting parties, and at last they came to a deserted village. Either it had been abandoned because of warfare or to escape an unhealthy location, but the five examined it with great curiosity. Many of the lodges built of either poles or birch bark were still standing, with fragments of useless and abandoned household goods here and there. Paul found in one of the lodges a dried scalp with long straight hair, but, obeying a sensitive impulse he hid it from the others, thrusting it between two folds of the birch bark.

They also found fragments of arrows and broken bows. The path leading down to a fine spring was not yet overgrown with grass, and they inferred from it that the Indians had not been gone many months. There was also an open space showing signs of cultivation. Evidently maize and melons had grown there.

"I wonder why they went away?" said Long Jim to Shif'less Sol. "You've made two guesses—unhealthiness or danger from Injuns. Now this site looks purty good to me, an' the Injun tribes up here are generally friendly with one another."

"Them's only guesses," said Sol, "an' we'll never know why. But I take it that Delawares lived here. This is just about thar country. Mebbe they've gone North to be near Detroit, whar the arms an' supplies are."

"Likely enough," said Henry, "but suppose we populate this village for to-night. It looks as if rain were coming on, and none of us is fond of sleeping out in the wet."

"You're talkin' wisdom," said Shif'less Sol, "an' I think we kin find a place in the big wigwam over thar that looks like a Council House."

He pointed to a rough structure of bark and poles, with a dilapidated roof and walls, but in better state of preservation than any of the wigwams, probably because it had been built stronger. They entered it and found that it originally had a floor of bark, some portions of which remained, and there was enough area of sound roof and walls to shelter them from the rain. They were content and with dry bark beneath them and on all sides of them they disposed themselves for the night.

It yet lacked an hour or so of sunset, but the heavy clouds already created a twilight, and the wind began to moan through the forest, bringing with it a cold rain that made a monotonous and desolate patter on leaves and grass. The comrades were glad enough now of their shelter in the abandoned Council House. They had made at Pittsburg a purchase which conduced greatly to their comfort, that is, a pair of exceedingly light but warm blankets for everyone—something of very high quality. They always slept between these, the under blankets fending off the cold that rose from the ground.

Now they lay, dry and warm against the wall of the old Council House, and listened to the steady drip, drip of the rain on the roof, and through the holes in the roof upon the floor. But it did not reach them. They were not sleepy, and they talked of many things, but as the twilight came on and the thick clouds still hovered, the abandoned village took on a ghostly appearance. Nearly all the wall opposite that against which they lay was gone, and, as it faced the larger part of the village, they could see the ruined wigwams and the skeleton frames that had been used for drying game. Out of the forest came the long lonesome howl of a wolf, some ragged, desolate creature that had not yet found shelter with his kind. The effect upon everyone was instantaneous and the same. This flight from the Indians and the slaying of the great hound by Tom Ross with his silver bullet came back in vivid colors.

But the howl was not repeated and the steady drip of the cold rain remained unbroken. It gathered finally in little puddles on the floor not far from them, but their own corner remained dry and impervious. They noticed these things little, however, as the mystic and ghostly effect of the village was deepening. Seen through the twilight and the rain it was now but a phantom. Henry's mind, always so sensitive to the things of the forest, repeopled it. From under his drooping lids he saw the warriors coming in from the hunt or the chase, the women tanning skins or curing game, and the little Indian boys practicing with bows and arrows. He felt a sort of sympathy for them in this wild life, a life that he knew so well and that he had lived himself. But he came quickly out of his waking dream, because his acute ear had heard something not normal moving in the forest. He straightened up and his hand slid to the breech of his rifle. He listened for a few minutes and then glanced at Shif'less Sol.

"Someone comes our way," said Henry.

"Yes," said Shif'less Sol, "but it ain't more'n two or three. Thar, you kin hear the footsteps ag'in, an' their bodies brushing ag'in' the wet bushes."

"Three at the utmost," said Henry, "so we'll sit here and wait."

It was not necessary to tell them to be ready with their weapons. That was a matter of course with every borderer in such moments. So the five remained perfectly still in a sitting position, every one with his back pressed against the bark wall, a blanket wrapped around his figure, and a cocked rifle resting upon his knees. They were so quick that in the darkness and falling rain they might have passed for so many Indian mummies, had it not been for the long slender-barreled rifles and their threatening muzzles.

Yet nobody could have been more alert than they. Five pairs of trained ears listened for every sound that rose above the steady drip of the rain, five pairs of eyes, uncommonly keen in their keenness, watched the bushes whence the first faint signals of approach had come. Now they heard more distinctly that brushing of clothing against the bushes, and then a muttered oath or two. Evidently the strangers were white men, perhaps daring hunters who were not afraid to enter the very heart of the Indian country. Nevertheless the hands still remained on their rifles and the muzzles still bore on the point whence the sounds came.

Three white men, dripping with rain, emerged from the forest. They were clad in garb, half civilized and half that of the hunter. All were well armed and deeply tanned by exposure, but the attention of the five was instantly concentrated upon the first of the strangers, a young man of medium height, but of the most extraordinary ugliness. His skin, even without the tan, would have been very dark. His eyes, narrow and oblique, were almost Oriental in cast and his face was disfigured by a hideous harelip. The whole effect was sinister to the last degree, but Henry and his comrades were fair enough to credit it to a deformity of nature and not to a wicked soul behind. The two with him were a little older. They were short, thickly built, and without anything unusual in their appearance.

The three strangers were dripping with water and when they came into the abandoned village they stood for a few moments talking together. Then their eyes began to roam around in search of shelter.

"They'll be coming this way soon," whispered Henry to Paul, "because it's about the only place large enough to keep three men dry."

"Of course they'll come here," Paul whispered back; "now I wonder who and what they are."

Henry did not reply and the five remained as motionless as ever, five dusky figures in a row, sitting on the bark floor, and leaning against the bark wall. But every sense in them was acutely alive, and they watched the strangers look into one ruined lodge after another. None offered sufficient shelter and gradually they came toward the Council House. Always the man with the harelip and ugly face led. Henry watched him closely. The twilight and the rain did not allow any very clear view of him, just enough to disclose that his face was hideous and sinister. But Henry had a singularly clear mind and he tried to trace the malignant impression to the fact of physical ugliness, unwilling to do injury, even in thought merely, to anyone.

At last the eyes of the three alighted upon the old Council House, and they came forward quickly toward the open end. They were about to enter, but they saw the five figures against the wall and stopped abruptly. The man with the harelip bent forward and gazed at them. Henry soon saw by the expression of his face that he knew they were no mummies. He now thrust his rifle forward and his hand slipped down toward the trigger. Then Henry spoke.

"Come in," he said quickly; "we are white like yourselves, and we claim no exclusive rights to this Council House, which is about the only real shelter left in the Indian town. We are hunters and scouts."

"So are we," said the man with the harelip, speaking grammatically and with a fair degree of courtesy. "We are hardened to the wilderness, but we are thankful for the shelter which you seem to have found before us."

"There is room for all," said Henry. "You will observe the large dry place at the south end. The bark floor there is solid and no matter how the wind blows the rain cannot reach you."

"We'll use it," said the ugly man, and now his teeth began to chatter, "but I confess that I need more than mere shelter. The rain and cold have entered my system, and I shall suffer severely unless we have a fire. Is it not possible to build one here near the center of the Council House? The dry bark will feed it, until it is strong enough to take hold of the wet wood."

"It is the Indian country," said Henry, and yet he pitied him of the harelip.

"I know," replied the man, "I know too that all the tribes are on the war path, and that they are exceedingly bitter against us. My name is Holdsworth, and I am from Connecticut. These are my men, Fowler and Perley, also from the East. We're not altogether hunters, as we have seen service in the Eastern army, and we are now scouting toward Detroit with the intention of carrying back news about the British and Indian power there. But I feel that I must light the fire, despite all Indian danger."

He shook violently and Henry again felt sorry for him. So did the rest of the five. These three had become their comrades for the night, and it would not be fair to prevent the fire that the man so evidently needed.

"We can see that what you say is true," said Henry, "and we'll help you kindle a blaze. These friends of mine are Tom Ross, Jim Hart, Solomon Hyde, and Paul Cotter. My own name is Henry Ware."

He saw the ugly man start a little, and then smile in a way that made his disfigured lip more hideous than ever.

"I've heard the names," said the stranger. "The woods are immense, but there are not many of us, and those of marked qualities soon become known. It seems to me that I've heard you were at Wyoming and the Chemung."

"Yes," said Henry, "we were at both places. But since we're going to have a fire, it's best that we have it as soon as possible."

They fell to work with flint and steel on the dry bark. The two men, Fowler and Perley, had said nothing.

"Not especially bright," said Holdsworth to Henry in a whisper, as he nodded toward them, "but excellent foresters and very useful in the work that I have to do."

"You can't always tell a man by his looks," replied Henry in the same tone.

It was not a difficult matter to light the fire. They scraped off the inside of the bark until they accumulated a little heap of tinder. It was ignited with a few sparks of the flint and steel, and then the bark too caught fire. After that they had nothing to do but feed the flames which grew and grew, casting a luminous red glare in every corner of the old Council House. Then it was so strong that it readily burned the wet bark from the dismantled lodges near by.

The cold rain still came down steadily and the night, thick and dark, had settled over the forest. Henry and his comrades were bound to confess that the fire was a vivid core of cheer and comfort. It thrust out a grateful heat, the high flames danced, and the coals, red and yellow, fell into a great glowing heap. Holdsworth, Fowler and Perley took off nearly all their clothing, dried their bodies, and then their wet garments. Holdsworth ceased to shiver, and while Fowler and Perley still fed the fire, the five resumed their places against the wall, their rifles again lying across their knees, a forest precaution so customary that no one could take exception to it. Apparentlythey dozed, but they were nevertheless wide awake. Holdsworth and his men reclothed themselves in their dry raiment, and when they finished the task, Henry said:

"We've three kinds of dried meat, venison, bear and buffalo, and you can take your choice, one kind, two kinds, or all kinds."

"I thank you, sir," said Holdsworth, "but we also carry a plentiful supply of provisions in our knapsacks, and we have partaken freely of them. We are now dry, and there is nothing else for us to do but sleep."

"Then we had better put out the fire," said Henry. "As we agreed before, we're in the heart of the Indian country, and we do not wish to send up a beacon that will bring the savages down upon us."

But Holdsworth demurred.

"The Indians themselves would not be abroad on such a night," he said. "There can be no possible danger of an attack by them, and I suggest that we keep it burning. Then we will be all the stronger and warmer in the morning."

Henry was about to say something, but he changed his mind and said something else.

"Let it burn, then," he acquiesced. "The flame is hidden on three sides anyhow and, as you say, the savages themselves will keep under cover now. Perhaps, Mr. Holdsworth, as you have come from the East since we have, you can tell us about our future there."

"Not a great deal," replied the man, "but I fear that we are not prospering greatly. Our armies are weak. Although their country is ruined, war parties under Brant came down from the British forts, and ravaged the Mohawk valley anew. 'Tis said by many that the Americans cannot hold out much longer against the forces of the king."

"Your words coming from a great patriot are discouraging," said Henry.

"It is because I cannot make them otherwise," replied Holdsworth.

Henry, from under the edge of his cap, again examined him critically. Holdsworth and his men were reclining against the bark wall in the second largest dry spot, not more than ten feet away. The man was ugly, extremely ugly beyond a doubt, and in the glow of the firelight he seemed more sinister than ever. Yet the young forest runner tried once more to be fair. He recalled all of Holdsworth's good points. The man had spoken in a tone of sincerity, and he had been courteous. He had not said or done anything offensive. If he was discouraged over the patriot cause, it was because he could not help it.

While Henry studied him, there was a silence for a little space. Meantime the rain increased in volume, but it came straight down, making a steady, droning sound that was not unpleasant. The heavy darkness moved up to the very door of the old Council House, and, despite the fire, the forest beyond was invisible. Holdsworth was still awake, but the two men with him seemed to doze. Shif'less Sol was also watching Holdsworth with keen and anxious eyes, but he left the talk to his young comrade, their acknowledged leader.

"You know," said Henry at length, "that some great movement among the Indians is on foot."

Holdsworth stirred a little against the bark wall, and it seemed to Henry that a new eagerness came into his eyes. But he replied:

"No, I have not heard of it yet. You are ahead of me there. But the Indians and British at Detroit are always plotting something against us. What particular news do you have?"

"That Timmendiquas, the Wyandot, the greatest of the western chiefs, accompanied by the head chiefs of the Shawnees and Miamis, and a body of chosen warriors ismarching to Detroit. We have been following them, and they are now not more than twenty-five or thirty miles ahead of us. I take it that there will be a great council at Detroit, composed of the British, the Tories, the Western Indians with Timmendiquas at their head, and perhaps also the Iroquois and other Eastern Indians with Thayendanegea leading them. The point of attack will be the settlements in Kentucky. If the allied forces are successful the tomahawk and the scalping knife will spare none. Doesn't the prospect fill you with horror, Mr. Holdsworth?"

Holdsworth shaded his face with his hand, and replied slowly:

"It does inspire fear, but perhaps the English and Indian leaders will be merciful. These are great matters of which you tell me, Mr. Ware. I had heard some vague reports, but yours are the first details to reach me. Perhaps if we work together we can obtain information that will be of great service to the settlements."

"Perhaps," said Henry, and then he relapsed into silence. Holdsworth remained silent too and gazed into the fire, but Henry saw that his thoughts were elsewhere. A long time passed and no one spoke. The fire had certainly added much to the warmth and comfort of the old house. They were all tired with long marches, and the steady droning sound of the rain, which could not reach them, was wonderfully soothing. The figures against the bark walls relaxed, and, as far as the human eye could see, they dropped asleep one by one, the five on one side and the three on the other.

The fire, well fed in the beginning, burned for two or three hours, but after awhile it begun to smolder, and sent up a long thin column of smoke. The rain came lighter and then ceased entirely. The clouds parted in the center as if they had been slashed across by a sword blade, and then rolled away to left and right. The heavens became a silky blue, and the stars sprang out in sparkling groups.

It was past midnight when Holdsworth moved slightly, like one half awakening from a deep sleep. But his elbow touched the man Fowler, and he said a few words to him in a whisper. Then he sank back into his relaxed position, and apparently was asleep again. Fowler himself did not move for at least ten minutes. Then he arose, slipped out of the Council House, and returned with a great armful of wet leaves, which he put gently upon the fire. Quickly and quietly he sank back into his old position by the wall.

Dense smoke came from the coals and heap of leaves, but it rose in a strong spire and passed out through the broken part of the roof, the great hole there creating a draught. It rose high and in the night, now clear and beautiful, it could be seen afar. Yet all the eight—five on one side and three on the other—seemed to be sound asleep once more.

The column of smoke thickened and rose higher into the sky, and presently the man Fowler was at work again. Rising and stepping, with wonderful lightness for a thick-set heavy man, he spread his open blanket over the smoke, and then quickly drew it away. He repeated the operation at least twenty times and at least twenty great coiling rings of smoke arose, sailing far up into the blue sky, and then drifting away over the forest, until they were lost in the distance.

Fowler folded the blanket again, but he did not resume his place against the wall. Holdsworth and Perley rose lightly and joined him. Then the three gazed intently at the five figures on the other side of the smoke. Not one of them stirred. So far as the three could see, the five were buried in the most profound slumber.

Holdsworth made a signal and the three, their rifles in the hollows of their arms, glided from the Council House and into the forest.

As soon as they were lost in the darkness, Henry Ware sprang to his feet, alive in every nerve and fiber, and tingling with eagerness.

"Up; up, boys!" he cried. "Those three men are Tories or English, and they are coming back with the savages. The rings of smoke made the signal to their friends. But we'll beat them at their own trick."

All were on their feet in an instant—in fact, only Jim Hart and Paul had fallen asleep—and they ran silently into the forest in a direction opposite to that which the three had chosen. But they did not go far. At Henry's whispered signal, they sank down among some dense bushes where they could lie hidden, and yet see all that passed at the Council House. The water from the bushes that they had moved dropped upon them, but they did not notice it. Nor did they care either that the spire of smoke still rose through the roof of the old Council House. Five pairs of uncommonly keen eyes were watching the forest to see their enemies come forth.

"I saw the fellow make the big smoke," said Shif'less Sol, "but I knowed that you saw, too. So I jest waited till you give the word, Henry."

"I wanted them to go through to the end with it," replied Henry. "If we had stopped the man when he was bringing in the leaves he might have made some sort of excuse, and we should have had no proof at all against them."

"Them's false names they gave o' course."

"Of course. It is likely that the man who called himself Holdsworth is somebody of importance. His manner indicated it. How ugly that harelipped fellow was!"

"How long do you think it will be before they come back?" asked Shif'less Sol.

"Not long. The Indian force could not have been more than a mile or so away, or they would not have relied on smoke signals in the night. It will be only a short wait, Sol, until we see something interesting. Now I wish I knew that harelipped man!"

Henry and his comrades could have slipped away easily in the darkness, but they had no mind to do so. Theirs was a journey of discovery, and, since here was an opportunity to do what they wished, they would not avoid it, no matter how great the risk. So they waited patiently. The forest still dripped water, but they had seldom seen the skies a brighter blue at night. The spire of smoke showed against it sharp and clear, as if it had been day. In the brilliant moonlight the ruined village assumed another ghostly phase. All the rugged outlines of half-fallen tepees were silvered and softened. Henry, with that extraordinary sensitiveness of his to nature and the wilderness, felt again the mysticism and unreality of this place, once inhabited by man and now given back to the forest. In another season or two the last remnant of bark would disappear, the footpaths would be grown up with bushes, and the wild animals would roam there unafraid.

All these thoughts passed like a succession of mental flashes through the mind of the forest dreamer—and a dreamer he was, a poet of the woods—as he waited there for what might be, and what probably would be, a tragedy. But as these visions flitted past there was no relaxation of his vigilance. It was he who first heard the slight swishing sound of the bushes on the far side of the Council House; it was he who first heard the light tread of an approaching moccasin, and it was he who first saw the ugly harelipped face of a white man appear at the forest edge. Then all saw, and slow, cold anger rose in five breasts at the treacherous trick.

Behind the harelipped man appeared Perley and Fowler, and six savage warriors, armed fully, and coated thickly with war paint. Now Henry knew that the sinister effect of Holdsworth's face was not due wholly to his harelip, and the ugliness of all his features. He was glad in a way because he had not done the man injustice.

The three white men and the six Indians waited a long time at the edge of the woods. They were using both eye and ear to tell if the five in the old Council House slept soundly. The fire now gave forth nothing but smoke, and they could not see clearly into the depths. They must come nearer if they would make sure of their victims. They advanced slowly across the open, their weapons ready. All the idealist was gone from Henry now. They had taken these three men into what was then their house; they had been warmed and dried by their fire, and now they came back to kill. He watched them slip across the open space, and he saw in the moonlight that their faces were murderous, the white as bad as the red.

The band reached the end of the Council House and looked in, uttering low cries of disappointment when they saw nothing there. None of the five ever knew whether they had waited there for the purpose of giving battle to the raiding band, but at this moment Paul moved a little in order to get a better view, and a bush rustled under his incautious moccasin. One of the savages heard it, gave a warning cry, and in an instant the whole party threw themselves flat upon the earth, with the wall of the Council House between themselves and that point in the forest from which the sound had come. Silence and invisibility followed, yet the forest battle was on.

CHAPTER VII. THE TAKING OF HENRY

"I'm sorry my foot slipped," whispered Paul.

"Don't you worry, Paul," Henry whispered back. "We're as anxious to meet them as they are to meet us. If they are willing to stay and have the argument out, we're willing to give them something to think about."

"An' I'd like to get a shot at that harelipped villain," interjected Shif'less Sol. "I'd give him somethin' he wouldn't furgit."

"Suppose we move a little to the right," said Henry. "They've noted the direction from which the sound came, and they may send a bullet into the bushes here."

They crept quietly to the right, a distance of perhaps ten yards; and they soon found the precaution to be a wise one, as a crack came from the forest, and a bullet cut the twigs where they had lately been. Shif'less Sol sent a return bullet at the flash of the rifle and they heard a suppressed cry.

"It doesn't do to be too keerless," said the shiftless one in a contented tone as he reloaded his rifle. "Whoever fired that shot ought to hev known that something would come back to him."

Several more bullets came from the forest, and now they cut the bushes close by, but the comrades lay flat upon the ground and all passed over their heads.

After Shif'less Sol's single shot they did not return the fire for the present, but continued to move slowly to the right. Thus a full half hour passed without a sign fromeither side. Meanwhile a wind, slowly rising, was blowing so steadily that all the trees and bushes were drying fast.

Neither Henry nor his comrades could now tell just where their enemies were, but they believed that the hostile band had also been circling about the open space in which the ruined village stood. They felt sure that the Indians and the three white men would not go away. The Indians were never keener for scalps than they were that year, and with a force of nearly two to one they would not decline a combat, even if it were not the surprise that they had expected.

"We may stay here until daylight," whispered Henry. "They are now sure we're not going to run away, and with the sunrise they may think that they will have a better chance at us."

"If the daylight finds them here, it will find us too," said Shif'less Sol. They shifted around a little further, and presently another shot was fired from a point opposite them in the forest. Henry sent a bullet in return, but there was nothing to indicate whether it had struck a foe. Then ensued another long silence which was broken at last by a shot from the interior of the old Council House. It was sent at random into the bushes, but the bullet cut the leaves within an inch of Henry's face, and they grew exceedingly cautious. Another bullet soon whistled near them, and they recognized the fact that the Indians who had succeeded in creeping into the Council House had secured an advantage.

But they succeeded in keeping themselves covered sufficiently to escape any wounds, and, turning a thought over in his mind, Henry said:

"Sol, don't you think that this wind which has been blowing for hours has dried things out a good deal?"

"It shorely has," answered Sol.

"And you have noticed, too, Sol, that we are now at a point where the old village touches the forest? You can reach out your hand and put it on that ruined wigwam, can't you?"

"I kin shorely do it, Henry."

"You have noticed also, Sol, that the wind, already pretty fair, is rising, and that it is blowing directly from us against the old Council House in which some of the savages are, and across to the forest at the point where we are certain that the rest of the enemy lie."

"Sounds like good and true reasonin' to me, an eddicated man, Henry."

"Then you and I will get to work with our flint and steel and set this old wigwam afire. It's still high enough to shelter ourselves behind it, and I think we ought to do the task in two or three minutes. Tom, you and Paul and Jim cover us with your rifles."

"Henry, you shorely hev a great head," said Sol, "an' this looks to me like payin' back to a man what belongs to him. That harelipped scoundrel and his fellows warmed by our fire in the Council House, and now we'll jest give 'em notice that thar's another warmin'."

Lying almost flat upon their faces they worked hard with the flint and steel, and in a minute or two a little spark of light leaped up. It laid hold of the thin, dry bark at the edge of the old wigwam and blazed up with extraordinary rapidity. Then the flames sprang to the next wigwam. It, too, was quickly enveloped, and the bark cracked as they ate into it. Not even the soaking given by the rain offered any effective resistance.

Henry and Shif'less Sol put away their flint and steel and quickly slipped into the bushes whence they looked with admiration at the work of their hands. The lodges were burning far faster than they had expected. All the old Indian village would soon go, and now they watched attentively the Council House where the sharpshooters lay. Meanwhile several shots were fired from the forest without effect and the five merely lay close, biding their time.

The flames made a great leap and caught the Council House. It burned so fast that it seemed to be enveloped all at once, and three men, two red and one white burst from it, rushing toward the forest. Henry and his comrades could easily have shot down all three, but Silent Tom Ross was the only one who pulled a trigger and he picked the white man. At the crack of his rifle the fugitive fell. By the flare of the flames Henry caught a glimpse of his face and saw that it was Perley. He fell just at the edge of the forest, but where the fire would not reach him.

The village was now a mass of flames. The whole open space was lighted up brilliantly, and the sparks flew in myriads. Ashes and burning fragments carried by the wind fell thickly through the forest. The vivid flare penetrated the forest itself and the five men saw their foes crouching in the bushes. They advanced, using all the skill of those to whom the wilderness is second nature and a battle from tree to tree ensued. The five were more than a match for the eight who were now against them. The man who had passed as Fowler was quickly wounded in the shoulder, the harelipped leader himself had his cap shot from his head, and one of the Indians was slain. Then they took to flight, and, after a pursuit of some distance, the five returned toward the village, where the flames were now dying down.

Paul had been flicked across the hand by a bullet and Jim Hart shook two bullets out of his clothing, but they were practically unhurt and it was their object now to see the man Perley, who had been left at the edge of the forest. By the time they reached the open where the village had stood, the day was fully come. The Council House had fallen in and the poles and fragments of bark smoked on the ground. Nothing was left of the wigwam but ashes which the wind picked up and whirled about. The wounded man lay on his side and it was quite evident that his hurt was mortal, but his look became one of terror when the five came up.

"We do not mean to hurt you," said Henry; "we will make it as easy for you as we can."

"And the others," gasped the man. "You have beaten them in the battle, and they have fled, the Colonel with them."

"Yes," replied Henry, "they are gone, and with them Colonel—?"

The man looked up and smiled faintly. At the edge of death he read Henry's mind. He knew that he wished to obtain the name of the harelipped man and, sincere enemy of his own people though Perley was, he no longer had any objection to telling.

"Prop me up against that tree trunk," he gasped.

Henry did so, and Paul brought some water from the spring in his cap. The man drank and seemed a little stronger.

"You're better to me perhaps than I'd have been to you if it had been the other way round," he said, "an' I might as well tell you that the man with the harelip was Colonel Bird, a British officer, who is most active against your settlements, and who has become a great leader among the Indians. He's arranging now with the people at Detroit to strike you somewhere."

"Then I'm sorry my bullet didn't find him instead of you," said Tom Ross.

"So am I," said the man with a faint attempt at humor.

Paul, who had been trying to remember, suddenly spoke up.

"I heard of that man when we were in the East," he said. "He fell in love with a girl at Oswego or some other of the British posts, and she rejected him because he was so ugly and had a hare lip. Then he seemed to have a sort of madness and ever since he's been leading expeditions of the Indians against our settlements."

"It's true," said Perley, "he's the man that you're talking about and he's mad about shedding blood. He's drumming up the Indian forces everywhere. His—"

Perley stopped suddenly and coughed. His face became ghastly pale, and then his head fell over sideways on his shoulders.

"He's dead," said Shif'less Sol, "an' I'm sorry, too, Tom, that your bullet didn't hit Colonel Bird 'stead o' him."

"Do you think," asked Paul, "that they are likely to come back and attack us?"

"No," replied Henry, "they've had enough. Besides they can't attack us in broad daylight. Look how open the forest is. We'd be sure to see them long before they could get within rifle shot."

"Then," said Paul, "let's bury Perley before we go on. I don't like to think of a white man lying here in the forest to be devoured by wild beasts, even if he did try to kill us."

Shif'less Sol heartily seconded Paul's suggestion, and soon it was done. They had no spades with which to dig a grave for Perley's body, but they built over him a little cairn of fallen timber, sufficient to protect him from the wolves and bears, and then prepared to march anew.

But they took a last look at the large open space in which the abandoned Indian village had stood. Nothing was left there but ashes and dying coals. Not a fragment of the place was standing. But they felt that it was better for it to be so. If man had left, then the forest should resume its complete sway. The grass and the bushes would now cover it up all the more quickly. Then they shouldered their rifles and went ahead, never looking back once.

The morning was quite cool. It was only the second week in April, the spring having come out early bringing the buds and the foliage with it, but in the variable climate of the great valley they might yet have freezing and snow. They had left Pittsburg in the winter, but they were long on the way, making stops at two or three settlements on the southern shore of the Ohio, and also going on long hunts. At another time they had been stopped two weeks by the great cold which froze the surface of the river from bank to bank. Thus it was the edge of spring and the forests were green, when they turned up the tributary river, and followed in the trail of Timmendiquas.

Now they noticed this morning as they advanced that it was growing quite cold again. They had also come so much further North that the spring was less advanced than on the Ohio. Before noon a little snow was flying, but they did not mind it. It merely whipped their blood and seemed to give them new strength for their dangerous venture. But Henry was troubled. He was sorry that they had not seen an enemy in the man Bird whose name was to become an evil one on the border. But how were they to know? It is true that he could now, with the aid of the dead man's story recall something about Bird and his love affair, his disappointment which seemed to have given him a perfect mania for bloodshed. But again how were they to know?

They pressed on with increased speed, as they knew that Timmendiquas, owing to their delay at the abandoned village must now be far ahead. The broad trail was found easily, and they also kept a sharp watch for that of Bird and his band which they felt sure would join it soon. But when night came there was no sign of Bird and his men. Doubtless they had taken another course, with another object in view. Henry was greatly perplexed. He feared that Bird meant deep mischief, and he should have liked to have followed him, but the main task was to follow Timmendiquas, and they could not turn aside from it.

They would have traveled all that night, but the loss of sleep the night before, and the strain of the combat compelled them to take rest about the twilight hour. The night winds were sharp with chill, and they missed the bark shelter that the ruined Council House had given them. As they crouched in the bushes with their blankets about them and ate cold venison, they were bound to regret what they had lost.

"Still I like this country," said Jim Hart. "It looks kinder firm an' strong ez ef you could rely on it. Then I want to see the big lakes. We come pretty nigh to one uv them that time we went up the Genesee Valley an' burned the Iroquois towns, but we didn't quite git thar. Cur'us so much fresh water should be put here in a string uv big lakes on our continent."

"And the Canadian *voyageurs* say there are big lakes, too, away up in Canada that no white man has ever seen, but of which they hear from the Indians," said Paul.

"I reckon it's true," said Jim Hart, "'cause this is an almighty big continent, an' an almighty fine one. I ain't s'prised at nothin' now. I didn't believe thar wuz any river ez big ez the Missip, until I saw it, an' thar ain't no tellin' what thar is out beyond the Missip, all the thousands uv miles to the Pacific. I'd shorely like to live a thousand years with you fellers an' tramp 'roun' and see it all. It would be almighty fine."

"But I wouldn't like to be spendin' all that thousan' years tryin' to keep my scalp on top o' my head," said Shif'less Sol. "It would be pow'ful wearin' on a lazy man like me."

Thus they talked as the twilight deepened into the night. The feel of the North was in them all. Their minds kindled at the thought of the vast lakes that lay beyond and of the great forest, stretching, for all they knew, thousands of miles to the great ocean. The bushes and their blankets protected them from the cold winds, and it was so dark that no enemy could trail them to their lair. Moreover the five were there, intact, and they had the company of one another to cheer.

"I imagine," said Paul, "that Timmendiquas and the officers at Detroit will make this the biggest raid that they have ever yet planned against Kentucky."

"By surprise an' numbers they may win victories here an' thar," said Shif'less Sol, "but they'll never beat us. When people git rooted in the ground you jest can't drive 'em away or kill 'em out. Our people will take root here, too, an' everywhar the Injuns, the British an' the Tories will have to go."

"An' as our people ain't come up here yet, we've got to look out for our scalps before the rootin' season comes," said Tom Ross.

"An' that's as true as Gospel," said Shif'less Sol, thoughtfully.

After that they spoke little more, but they drew and matted the thick bushes over their heads in such manner that the chill winds were turned aside. Beneath were the dry leaves of last year which they had raked up into couches, and thus, every man with a blanket beneath and another above him, they did not care how the wind blew. They were as snug as bears in their lairs, but despite the darkness of the night and the exceeding improbability of anyone finding them both Henry and Tom Ross lay awake and watched. The others slept peacefully, and the two sentinels could hear their easy breathing only a few feet away.

In the night Henry began to grow uneasy. Once or twice he thought he heard cries like the hoot of the owl or the howl of the wolf, but they were so far away that he was uncertain. Both hoot and howl might be a product of the imagination. He was so alive to the wilderness, it was so full of meaning to him that his mind could create sounds when none existed. He whispered to Tom, but Ross, listening as hard as he could, heard nothing but the rustling of the leaves and twigs before the wind.

Henry was sure now that what he had heard was the product of a too vivid fancy, but a little later he was not so sure. It must be the faint cry of a wolf that he now heard or its echo. He had the keenest ear of them all, and that Tom Ross did not hear the sound, was no proof. A vivid imagination often means a prompt and powerful man of action, and Henry acted at once.

"Tom," he whispered, "I'm going to scout in the distance from which I thought the sounds came. Don't wake the boys; I'll be back before morning."

Tom Ross nodded. He did not believe that Henry had really heard anything, and he would have remonstrated with him, but he knew that it was useless. He merely drew his blanket a little closer, and resolved that one pair of eyes should watch as well as two had watched before.

Henry folded his blankets, put them in his little pack, and in a minute was gone. It was dark, but not so dark that one used to the night could not see. The sounds that he had seemed to hear came from the southwest, and the road in the direction was easy, grown up with forest but comparatively free from undergrowth. He walked swiftly about a mile, then he heard the cry of the wolf again. Now, the last doubt was gone from his mind. It was a real sound, and it was made by Indian calling to Indian.

He corrected his course a little, and went swiftly on. He heard the cry once more, now much nearer, and, in another mile, he saw a glow among the trees. He wentnearer and saw detached cones of light. Then he knew that it was a camp fire, and a camp fire built there boldly in that region, so dangerous to the Kentuckian, indicated that it was surely the Indians themselves and their allies. He did not believe that it was the force of Timmendiquas which could only have reached this spot by turning from its course, but he intended to solve the doubt.

The camp was in one of the little prairies so numerous in the old Northwest, and evidently had been pitched there in order to secure room for the fires. Henry concluded at once that it must be a large force, and his eagerness to know increased. As he crept nearer and nearer, he was amazed by the number of the fires. This was a much larger band than the one led by Timmendiquas. He also heard the sound of many voices and of footsteps. From his place among the trees he saw dark figures passing and repassing. He also caught now and then a metallic glitter from something not a rifle or a tomahawk, but which he could not clearly make out in the dark.

This was a formidable force bent upon some great errand, and his curiosity was intense. The instinct that had sent him upon the journey through the woods was not wrong, and he did not mean to go away until he knew for what purpose this army was gathered. He lay upon the ground in the thickest shadow of the woods, and crept forward a little closer. Then he saw that the camp contained at least five hundred warriors. As nearly as he could make out they were mostly Shawnees, probably from the most easterly villages, but there seemed to be a sprinkling of Delawares and Miamis. White men, Tories, Canadians and English, fifty or sixty in number were present also and a few of them were in red uniform.

All the Indians were in war paint, and they sat in great groups around the fires feasting. Evidently the hunters had brought in plenty of game and they were atoning for a fast. They ate prodigiously of buffalo, deer, bear and wild turkey, throwing the bones behind them when they had gnawed them clean. Meanwhile they sang in the Shawnee tongue a wild chant:

To the South we, the great warriors, goTo the far, fair land of Kaintuckee;We carry death for the Yengees,Our hands are strong, our hearts are fierce;None of the white face can escape us.

We cross the river and steal through the woods;In the night's dark hour the tomahawk falls,The burning houses send flames to the sky,The scalps of the Yengees hang at our belts;None of the white face can escape us.

Henry's heart began to pump heavily. Little specks danced before his eyes. Here was a great war party, one that he had not foreseen, one that was going to march against Kentucky. Evidently this enterprise was distinct from that of Timmendiquas. In his eagerness to see, Henry crept nearer and nearer to the utmost verge of the danger line, lying in a clump of bushes where the warriors were passing, not twenty feet away. Suddenly he started a little, as a new figure came into the light, thrown into distinct relief by the blazing background of the fires.

He recognized at once the harelipped man, Bird, now in the uniform of a Colonel in the King's army. His ugliness was in no whit redeemed by his military attire. But Henry saw that deference was paid him by white men and red men alike, and he had the walk and manner of one who commanded. The youth was sorry now that they had not hunted down this man and slain him. He felt instinctively that he would do great harm to those struggling settlers south of the Ohio.

While Henry waited three loud shouts were heard, uttered at the far end of the camp. Instantly the eating ceased, and all the warriors rose to their feet. Then they moved with one accord toward the point from which the shouts proceeded. Henry knew that someone of importance was coming, and he crept along the edge of the forest to see.

Colonel Bird, several subordinate officers, and some chiefs gathered in front of the mass of warriors and stood expectant. Forth from the forest came a figure more magnificent than any in that group, a great savage, naked to the waist, brilliantly painted, head erect and with the air of a king of men. It was Timmendiquas, and Henry realized, the moment he appeared, that he was not surprised to see him there. Behind him came Red Eagle and Yellow Panther, Simon Girty, Braxton Wyatt and Blackstaffe. Bird went forward, eager to meet them, and held out his hand in white man's fashion to Timmendiquas. The great Wyandot took it, held it only a moment, and then dropped it, as if the touch were hateful to him. Henry had noticed before that Timmendiquas never seemed to care for the white allies of the Indians, whether English, Canadian or Tory. He used them, but he preferred, if victory were won, that it should be won by men of his own race. The manner of the chief seemed to him to indicate repulsion, but Wyatt, Girty and the others greeted the Colonel with great warmth. They were birds of a feather, and it pleased them to flock together there in the great forest.

Timmendiquas and his chiefs walked toward the larger and central fire, whither Bird and his men showed the way. Then pipes were lighted and smoked by all who were high enough in rank to sit in the Council, while the mass of the warriors gathered at a respectful distance. But the fires were replenished, and they blazed up, filling all the camp with ruddy light. Then Henry found the meaning of the metallic gleam that he had seen from the forest. Near the center of the camp and standing in a row were six cannon, fine, bronze guns of large caliber, their dark muzzles, as if by some sinister chance, pointing toward the South. Then full knowledge came in all its gloomy truth. This was an expedition against Kentucky more formidable than any of the many that had yet gone. It carried a battery of large cannon, and plenty of white gunners to man them. The wooden palisades of the new settlements could not stand five minutes before great guns.

In his eagerness to see more of these hateful cannon, Henry, for the first time in years, forgot his customary caution. He made a bush rustle and he did not notice it. A scouting Indian passed near, and he did not hear him. But the scouting Indian, a Shawnee, alert and suspicious, heard the rustling of the bush. He dropped down, crept near and saw the long figure among the bushes. Then he crept away and signaled to his comrades.

Henry was straining forward for a better view of the cannon, when there was a sudden sound behind him. He drew his body quickly together like a powerful animal about to spring, but before he could reach his feet a half dozen warriors hurled themselves upon him.

He fell under the impact of so great a weight and the rifle which he could not use at close quarters was torn from his hands. The warriors uttered a triumphant shout which caused all those sitting by the fire to spring to their feet.

Henry was at the very summit of his youthful strength. There was no one in the forest who matched him in either height or muscular strength, save, possibly Timmendiquas, and with a tremendous effort he rose to his feet, the whole yelling pack clinging to him, one on each arm, one at each leg, and two at his shoulders and waist. He hurled loose the one on his right arm and snatched at a pistol in his belt, but quick as a flash, two others loosing their hold elsewhere, seized the arm. Then they pressed all their weight upon him again, seeking to throw him. Evidently they wished to take him a captive. But Henry remained erect despite the immense weight pulling at him. He was bent slightly forward, and, for a few moments, his efforts exactly balanced the strength of the six who sought to pull him down. In that brief space they remained immovable. The sweat broke out on his forehead in great beads. Then with an effort, convulsive and gigantic, he threw them all from him, standing clear for one brief instant. His hand was on the pistol butt, but the yelling pack were back too quick, leaping at him like wolves. He was dragged to his knees, but once more he struggled to his feet, drenched in perspiration, his heart beating loudly as he made his mighty efforts.

In their struggle they came free of the woods, and out into the open where the light from the fires cast a red glow over the tall figure of the white youth, and the six naked and sinewy brown forms that tore at him. The chief and the white men in the camp rushed forward.

Braxton Wyatt cried exultingly: "It is Ware!" and drew his pistol, but Timmendiquas struck down his arm.

"It is not for you to shoot," he said; "let him be taken alive."

Bird was commander in that camp, and the Wyandot was only a visitor there, but the tone of Timmendiquas was so strong and masterful that Bird himself recognized his predominance, and did not resist it.

And there were others among the Indians who looked with admiration upon the tall youth as he made his magnificent struggle for life and liberty. A deep hum ran through the great circle that had formed about the fighters. Excitement, the joy of a supreme sport, showed upon their savage faces. One or two started forward to help the six, but Timmendiquas waved them back. Then the circle pressed a little closer, and other rows of dark faces behind peered over brown shoulders. Henry was scarcely conscious that hundreds looked on. The pulses in temples and throat were beating heavily, and there was a mist before his eyes. Nobody was present for him, save the six who strove to pull him down. His soul swelled with fierce anger and he hurled off one after another to find them springing back like the rebound of a rubber ball.

His anger increased. These men annoyed him terribly. He was bathed in perspiration and nearly all the clothing was torn from his body, but he still fought against his opponents. The ring had come in closer and closer, and now the savages uttered low cries of admiration as he sent some one of his antagonists spinning. They admired, too, his massive figure, the powerful neck, the white shoulders now bare and the great muscles which bunched up as he put forth supreme efforts.

"Verily, this is a man," said the old chief, Yellow Panther.

Timmendiquas nodded, but he never took his absorbed eyes from the contest. He, too, uttered a low cry as Henry suddenly caught one of the warriors with his fist and sent him like a shot to the earth. But this warrior, a Wyandot, was tough. He sprang up again, the dark blood flowing from his face, but was caught and sent down a second time, to lay where he had fallen, until some of the watchers took him by the legs and dragged him out of the way of the struggle. Henry was rid of one of his opponents for the time, and the five who were left did not dare use their weapons in face of the command from Timmendiquas to take him alive. Yet they rushed in as full of zeal as ever. It may be that they enjoyed the struggle in their savage way, particularly when the prize to be won was so splendid.

Henry's successful blow with his fist reminded him that he might use it again. In the fury of the sudden struggle he had not thought before to fight by this method. A savage had him by the left shoulder. He struck the up-turned face with his right fist and the warrior went down unconscious.

Only four now! The hands of another were seeking his throat. He tore the hands loose, seized the warrior in his arms, and hurled him ten feet away, where he fell with a sprained ankle. A deep cry, and following it, a long-drawn sigh of admiration, came from the crowd.

Only three now! He tripped and threw one so heavily that he could not renew the combat, and the terrible fist sent down the fifth. Once more came that cry and long-drawn sigh from the multitude! A single opponent was left, but he was a powerful fellow, a Wyandot, with long thick arms and a mighty chest. His comrades had been much in his way in the struggle, and, now comparatively fresh and full of confidence, he closed with his white antagonist.

Henry had time to draw a breath or two, and he summoned his last reserve of will and strength. He grasped the Wyandot as he ran in, pinned his arms to his sides, tripped his feet from under him, and, seizing him by shoulders and waist, lifted him high above his head. He held him poised there for a moment while the multitude gazed, tense and awed. Then, hurling him far out, he turned, faced the Wyandot chief, and said:

"To you, Timmendiquas, I surrender myself."

CHAPTER VIII. THE NORTHWARD MARCH

The great Wyandot chief inclined his head slightly, and received the pistol, hatchet, and knife which Henry drew from his belt. Then he said in the grave Wyandot tongue:

"It is the second time that Ware has become my prisoner, and I am proud. He is truly a great warrior. Never have I seen such a fight as that which he has just made, the strength of one against six, and the one was triumphant."

A murmur of approval from the warriors followed his words. Like the old Greeks, the Indians admired size, symmetry and strength, qualities so necessary to them in their daily lives, and Henry, as he stood there, wet with perspiration and breathing heavily, exemplified all that they considered best in man. Few of these savage warriors had any intention of sparing him. They would have burned him at the stake with delight, and, with equal delight, they would have praised him had he never uttered a groan—it would only be another proof of his greatness.

Braxton Wyatt pressed nearer. There was joy in his evil heart over the capture of his enemy, but it was not unalloyed. He knew the friendship that Timmendiquas bore for Henry, and he feared that through it the prisoner might escape the usual fate of captives. It was his part to prevent any such disaster and he had thought already of a method. He dreaded the power of Timmendiquas, but he was bold and he proposed to dare it nevertheless.

"Will you take the prisoner South with you," he said to Colonel Bird.

"I have surrendered to Timmendiquas," said Henry.

"This is the camp of Colonel Bird," said Wyatt in as mild a tone as he could assume, "and of course anyone taken here is his prisoner."

"That is true," said Simon Girty, whose influence was great among the Indians, particularly the Shawnees.

Timmendiquas said not a word, nor did Henry. Both saw the appeal to the pride of Bird who pulled his mustache, while his ugly face grew uglier.

"Yes, it is so," he said at last. "The prisoner is mine, since he was taken in my camp."

Then Timmendiquas spoke very quietly, but, underlying every word, was a menace, which Wyatt, Girty and Bird alike felt and heeded.

"The prisoner surrendered to me," he said. "The Wyandot warriors helped in his capture—their bruises prove it. Colonel Bird even now marches south against Kaintuckee, and he has no need of prisoners. The words of Wyatt are nothing. Girty has become one of our chiefs, but it is not for him to judge in this case. When the council is finished and Timmendiquas resumes his march to Detroit, Ware goes with him as a captive, the prize of his warriors."

His fierce eyes roamed around the circle, challenging one by one those who opposed him. Braxton Wyatt's own eyes dropped, and fear was in his soul. He, a renegade, an enemy to his own people could not afford to lose the favor of the Indians. Girty, also, evaded. Full of craft, it was no part of his policy to quarrel with Timmendiquas. Bird alone was disposed to accept the gage. It was intolerable that he, a colonel in the British army, should be spoken to in such a manner by an Indian. He wrinkled his ugly hare lip and said stubbornly:

"The prisoner was taken in my camp, and he is mine."

But Girty said low in his ear:

"Let Timmendiquas have him. It is not well to alienate the Wyandots. We need them in our attack on Kentucky, and already they are dissatisfied with their heavy losses there. We can do nothing for the king without the Indians."

Bird was not without suppleness. He spoke to Timmendiquas, as if he were continuing his former words:

"But I give up my claim to you, White Lightning of the Wyandots. Take the prisoner and do with him as you choose."

Timmendiquas smiled slightly. He understood perfectly. Braxton Wyatt retired, almost sick with rage. Timmendiquas motioned to two of his warriors who bound Henry's arms securely, though not painfully, and led him away to one of the smaller fires. Here he sat down between his guards who adjusted his torn attire, but did not annoy him, and waited while the council went on.

After the glow of physical triumph had passed, Henry felt a deep depression. It seemed to him that he could never forgive himself when so much depended upon him. He had full knowledge that this expedition was marching southward, and now he could send no warning. Had he returned to his comrades with the news, they might have solved the problem by dividing their force. Two could have hurried to Kentucky ahead of Bird's army, and three might have gone to Detroit to watch what preparations were made there. He condemned himself over and over again, and it is only just to say that he did not think then of his personal danger. He thought instead of those whom he might have saved, but who now would probably fall beneath the Indian tomahawk, with no one to warn them.

But he permitted none of his chagrin and grief to show in his face. He would not allow any Indian or renegade to see him in despair or in anything bordering upon it. He merely sat motionless, staring into the fire, his face without expression. Henry had escaped once from the Wyandots. Perhaps it was a feat that could not be repeated a second time—indeed all the chances were against it—but in spite of everything his courage came back. He had far too much strength, vitality and youth to remain in despair, and gradually new resolutions formed almost unconsciously in his mind. Under all circumstances, fate would present at least a bare chance to do what one wished, and courage gradually became confidence.

Then Henry, remembering that there was nothing he could do at present, lay down on his side before the fire. It was not altogether an assumed manner to impress his guard, because he was really very tired, and, now that his nerves were relaxing, he believed he could go to sleep.

He closed his eyes, and, although he opened them now and then, the lids were heavier at every successive opening. He saw the camp dimly, the dark figures of the warriors becoming shadowy now, the murmur of voices sinking to a whisper that could scarcely be heard, and then, in spite of his bound arms and precarious future, he slept.

Henry's two guards, both Wyandots, regarded him with admiration, as he slept peacefully with the low firelight flickering across his tanned face. Great in body, he was also great in mind, and whatever torture the chief, Timmendiquas, intended for him he would endure it magnificently.

Braxton Wyatt and Simon Girty also came to look at him, and whispered to each other.

"It would have been better if they had made an end of him in the fight for his capture," said Wyatt.

"That is true," said Girty thoughtfully. "As long as he's alive, he's dangerous. Timmendiquas cannot tie him so tight that there is no possibility of escape, and there arethese friends of his whom you have such cause to remember, Braxton."

"I wish they were all tied up as he is," said Wyatt venomously.

Girty laughed softly.

"You show the right spirit, Braxton," he said. "To live among the Indians and fight against one's own white race one must hate well. You need not flush, man. I have found it so myself, and I am older in this business and more experienced than you."

Wyatt choked down words that were leaping to his lips, and presently he and Girty rejoined the white men, who were camped around Bird, their commander. But neither of them felt like sleeping and after a little while there, they went to look at the cannon, six fine guns in a row, constituting together the most formidable weapon that had ever been brought into the western forest. When they looked at them, the spirit of Wyatt and Girty sprang high. They exulted in the prospect of victory. The Kentucky sharpshooters behind their light palisades had been able hitherto to defeat any number of Indians. But what about the big guns? Twelve pound cannon balls would sweep down the palisades like a hurricane among saplings. As there is no zeal like that of the convert, so there is no hate like that of the renegade and they foresaw the easy capture of settlement after settlement by Bird's numerous and irresistible army.

Henry, meanwhile, slept without dreams. It was a splendid tribute to his nerves that he could do so. When he awoke the sun was an hour above the horizon and the camp was active with the preparations of Bird's army to resume its march southward. Timmendiquas stood beside him, and, at his order, one of the Wyandot guards cut the thongs that bound his arms. Henry stretched out his wrists and rubbed them, one after the other, until the impeded circulation was restored. Then he uttered his thanks to the chief.

"I am grateful to you, Timmendiquas," he said, "for insisting last night that I was your prisoner, and should go with you to Detroit. As you have seen, the renegades, Girty and Wyatt do not love me, and whatever I may receive at your hands, it is not as bad as that which they would have incited the warriors to do, had I remained in the power of Bird."

"Neither do I care for Girty or Wyatt," said Timmendiquas, as he smiled slightly, "but they help us and we need all the allies we can get. So we permit them in our lodges. I may tell you now that they debated last night whether to go South with Bird, or to continue to Detroit with me. They go to Detroit."

"I do not care for their company," said Henry, "but I am glad that they are not going to Kentucky."

"I have also to tell you now, Ware," continued Timmendiquas, "that parties were sent out last night to search for your comrades, the four who are always with you."

Henry moved a little and then looked inquiringly at Timmendiquas. The chief's face expressed nothing.

"They did not find them?" he said.

"No," he replied. "The friends of Ware were wary, but we are proud to have taken the leader. Here is food; you can eat, and then we march."

They brought him an abundance of good food, and fresh water in a gourd, and he ate and drank heartily. The morning had become clear and crisp again, and with it came all the freshness and courage that belong to youth. Time was everything, and certainly nothing would be done to him until they reached Detroit. Moreover, his four comrades would discover why he did not return and they would follow. Even if one were helpless himself, he must never despair with such friends free and near at hand.

After he had eaten, his hands were bound again. He made no resistance, knowing that under the Indian code he had no right to ask anything further of Timmendiquas, and he began the march northward in the center of the Wyandot force. At the same time, Bird and his army resumed their southern advance. Henry heard twigs and dead boughs cracking under the wheels of the cannon, and the sound was a menacing one that he did not forget for a long time. He looked back, but the savage army disappeared with amazing quickness in the forest.

They marched all day without interruption, eating their food as they marched. Timmendiquas was at the head of the column, and he did not speak again with Henry. The renegades, probably fearing the wrath of the chief, also kept away. The country, hilly hitherto, now became level and frequently swampy. Here the travelling was difficult. Often their feet sank in the soft mud above the ankles, Briars reached out and scratched them, and, in these damp solitudes, the air was dark and heavy. Yet the Indians went on without complaint, and Henry, despite his bound arms, could keep his balance and pace with the rest, stride for stride.

They marched several days and nights without interruption through a comparatively level country, still swampy at times, thickly grown with forest, and with many streams and little lakes. Most of the lakes were dotted with wild fowl, and often they saw deer in the shallow portions. Two or three of the deer were shot, but the Indians devoted little time to the hunting of game, as they were well provided with food.

Henry, who understood both Wyandot and Shawnee, gathered from the talk of those about him that they were at last drawing near to Detroit, the great Northwestern fort of the British and Indians. They would arrive there to-morrow, and they spent that last night by camp fires, the Indians relaxing greatly from their usual taciturnity and caution, and eating as if at a banquet.

Henry sat on a log in the middle of the camp. His arms were unbound and he could eat with the others as much as he chose. Since they were not to burn him or torture him otherwise, they would treat him well for the present. But warriors, Shawnees, Miamis and Wyandots, were all about him. They took good care that such a prisoner should not have a chance to escape. He might overthrow two or three, even four or five, but a score more would be on him at once. Henry knew this well and bore himself more as if he were a member of the band than a captive. It was a part of his policy to appear cheerful and contented. No Indian should surpass him in careless and apparent indifference, but to-night he felt gloomier than at any time since the moments that immediately followed his capture. He had relied upon the faithful four, but days had passed without a sign from them. There had been no chance, of course, for them to rescue him. He had not expected that, but what he had expected was a sign. They were skillful, masters of wilderness knowledge, but accidents might happen—one had happened to him—and they might have fallen into the hands of some other band.

Waiting is a hard test, and Henry's mind, despite his will, began to imagine dire things. Suppose he should never see his comrades again. A thousand mischances could befall, and the neighborhood of Detroit was the most dangerous part of all the Indian country. Besides the villages pitched near, bands were continually passing, either coming to the fort for supplies, or going away, equipped for a fresh raid upon the settlements.

The laughter and talk among the Indians went on for a long time, but Henry, having eaten all that he wanted, sat in silence. Besides the noise of the camp, he heard the usual murmur of the night wind among the trees. He listened to it as one would to a soft low monotone that called and soothed. He had an uncommonly acute ear and his power of singleness and concentration enabled him to listen to the sound that he wished to hear, to the exclusion of all others. The noises in the camp, although they were as great as ever, seemed to die. Instead, he heard the rustling of the young leaves far away, and then another sound came—a faint, whining cry, the far howl of a wolf, so far that it was no more than a whisper, a mere undernote to the wind. It stopped, but, in a moment or two, was repeated. Henry's heart leaped, but his figure never moved; nor was there any change in the expression of his face, which had been dreamy and sad.

But he knew. Just when he wished to hear a voice out of the dark, that voice came. It was the first part of a signal that he and his comrades often used, and as he listened, the second part was completed. He longed to send back a reply, but it was impossible and he knew that it would not be expected. Joy was under the mask of his sad and dreaming face. He rejoiced, not only for himself, but for two other things; because they were safe and because they were near, following zealously and seeking every chance. He looked around at the Indians. None of them had heard the cry of the wolf, and he knew if it had reached them, they would not have taken it for a signal. They were going on with their feasting, but while Henry sat, still silent, Timmendiquas came to him and said:

"To-morrow we reach Detroit, the great post of the soldiers of the king. We go there to confer with the commander, de Peyster, and to receive many rifles and much ammunition. It is likely, as you already know, that we shall march against your people."

"I know it, Timmendiquas," said Henry, "but I would that it were not so. Why could we not dwell in peace in Kentucky, while the Wyandots, the Shawnees, the Miamis and others ranged their vast hunting grounds in the same peace on this side of the Ohio?"

A spark of fire shot from the dark eyes of Timmendiquas.

"Ware," he said, "I like you and I do not believe that your heart contains hatred towards me. Yet, there cannot be any peace between our races. Peace means that you will push us back, always push us back. Have I not been in the East, where the white men are many and where the mighty confederation of the Six Nations, with their great chief, Thayendanegea, at their head, fight against them in vain? Have I not seen the rich villages of the Indians go up in smoke? The Indians themselves still fight. They strike down many of the Yengees and sometimes they burn a village of the white people, but unless the king prevails in the great war, they will surely lose. Their Aieroski, who is the Manitou of the Wyandots, and your God, merely looks on, and permits the stronger to be the victor."

"Then," said Henry, "why not make peace with us here in the West, lest your tribes meet the same fate?"

The nostrils of Timmendiquas dilated.

"Because in the end we should be eaten up in the same way. Here in the West you are few and your villages are tiny. The seed is not planted so deep that it cannot be uprooted."

Henry sighed.

"I can see the question from your side as well as from mine, White Lightning," he replied. "It seems as you say, that the white men and the red men cannot dwell together. Yet I could wish that we were friends in the field as well as at heart."

Timmendiquas shook his head and replied in a tone tinged with a certain sadness:

"I, too, could wish it, but you were born of one race and I of another. It is our destiny to fight to the end."

He strode away through the camp. Henry watched the tall and splendid figure, with the single small scarlet feather set in the waving scalp lock, and once more he readily acknowledged that he was a forest king, a lofty and mighty spirit, born to rule in the wilderness. Then he took the two blankets which had been left him, enfolded himself between them, and, despite the noises around him, slept soundly all through the night. Early the next morning they began the last stretch of the march to Detroit.

It was with a deep and peculiar interest that they approached Detroit, then a famous British and Indian post, now a great American city. Founded by the French, who lost it to the British, who, in turn, were destined to lose it to the Americans, it has probably sent forth more scalping parties of Indians than any other place on the North American continent. Here the warlike tribes constantly came for rifles, ammunition, blankets and other supplies, and here the agents of the king incited them with every means in their power to fresh raids on the young settlements in the South. Here the renegades, Girty, Blackstaffe and their kind came to confer, and here Boone, Kenton and other famous borderers had been brought as prisoners.

The Indians in the party of Timmendiquas already showed great jubilation. In return for the war that they had made and should make, they expected large gifts from the king, and with such great chiefs as White

Lightning, Red Eagle and Yellow Panther at their head, it was not likely that they would be disappointed.

As they drew near, they passed several Indian camps, containing parties from the Northwest, Sacs, Winnebagoes and others, including even some Chippewas from the far shores of the greatest of all lakes. Many of these looked admiringly at the prisoner whom Timmendiquas had brought, and were sorry that they had not secured such a trophy. At the last of these camps, where they stopped for a little while, a short, thick man approached Henry and regarded him with great curiosity.

The man was as dark as an Indian, but he had a fierce black mustache that curled up at the ends. His hair was black and long and his eyes, too, were black. His dress differed but little from that of a warrior, but his features were unmistakably Caucasian.

"Another renegade," thought Henry, and his detestation was so thorough that he scorned to take further notice of the fellow. But he was conscious that the stranger was eyeing him from head to foot in the most scrutinizing manner, just as one looks at an interesting picture. Henry felt his anger rise, but he still simulated the most profound indifference.

"You are the prisoner of Timmendiquas, *mon petit garcon, mais oui*?"

Henry looked up at the French words and the French accent that he did not understand. But the tone was friendly, and the man, although he might be an enemy, was no renegade.

"Yes," he replied. "I am the prisoner of Timmendiquas, and I am going with him and his men to Detroit. Do you belong in Detroit?"

The man grinned, showing two magnificent rows of strong white teeth.

"I belong to Detroit?" he replied. "Nevaire! I belong to no place. I am ze Frenchman; le Canadien; voyageur, coureur du bois, l'homme of ze wind ovair ze mountains an' ze plain. I am Pierre Louis Lajeunais, who was born at Trois Rivières in ze Province of Quebec, which is a long way from here."

The twinkle in his eye was infectious. Henry knew that he was a man of good heart and he liked him. Perhaps also he might find here a friend.

"Since you have given me your name," he replied, "I will give you mine. I am Henry Ware, and I am from Kentucky. I was captured by Timmendiquas and his warriors a few days ago. They're taking me to Detroit, but I do not know what they intend to do with me there. I suppose that you, of course, are among our enemies."

No Indian was within hearing then, and Lajeunais replied:

"W'y should I wish you harm? I go to Detroit. I sell furs to ze commandaire for powder and bullets. I travel an' hunt wit' mes amis, ze Indians, but I do not love ze Anglais. When I was a boy, I fight wit' ze great Montcalm at Quebec against Wolfe an' les Anglais. We lose an' ze Bourbon lilies are gone; ze rouge flag of les Anglais take its place. Why should I fight for him who conquers me? I love better ze woods an' ze rivière an' ze lakes where I hunt and fish."

"I am glad that you are no enemy of ours, Mr. Lajeunais," said Henry, "and I am certain that my people are no enemies of the French in Canada. Perhaps we shall meet in Detroit."

"Eet ees likely, mon brav," said Lajeunais, "I come into the town in four days an' I inquire for ze great boy named Ware."

Timmendiquas gave the signal and in another hour they were in Detroit.

CHAPTER IX. AT DETROIT

Henry missed nothing as he went on with the warriors. He saw many lodges of Indians, and some cabins occupied by French-Canadians. In places the forest had been cleared away to make fields for Indian corn, wheat and pumpkins. Many columns of smoke rose in the clear spring air, and directly ahead, where he saw a cluster of such columns, Henry knew the fort to be. Timmendiquas kept straight on, and the walls of the fort came into view.

Detroit was the most formidable fortress that Henry had yet seen. Its walls, recently enlarged, were of oak pickets, rising twenty-five feet above the ground and six inches in diameter at the smaller end. It had bastions at every corner, and four gates, over three of which were built strong blockhouses for observation and defense. The gates faced the four cardinal points of the compass, and it was the one looking towards the south that was without a blockhouse. There was a picket beside every gate. The gates were opened at sunrise and closed at sunset, but the wickets were left open until 9 o'clock at night.

This fortification, so formidable in the wilderness, was armed in a manner fitting its strength. Every blockhouse contained four six-pounders and two batteries of six large guns each, faced the river, which was only forty feet away and with very steep banks. Inside the great palisade were barracks for five hundred men, a brick store, a guard house, a hospital, a governor's house, and many other buildings. At the time of Henry's arrival about four hundred British troops were present, and many hundreds of Indian warriors. The fort was thoroughly stocked with ammunition and other supplies, and there were also many English and Canadian traders both inside and outside the palisade.

The British had begun the erection of another fort, equally powerful, at some distance from the present one, but they were not far advanced with it at that time. The increase in protective measures was due to a message that they had received from the redoubtable George Rogers Clark, the victor of Vincennes and Kaskaskia, the man who delivered the heaviest of all blows against the British, Indian and Tory power in the Northwest. He had said that he was coming to attack them.

Henry asked no questions, but he watched everything with the most intense curiosity. The warriors of Timmendiquas stopped about three hundred yards from the palisade, and, without a word to anyone, began to light their camp fires and erect lodges for their chiefs. Girty, Blackstaffe, and Wyatt went away toward the fort, but Henry knew well that Timmendiquas would not enter until messengers came to receive him. Henry himself sat down by one of the fires and waited as calmly as if he had been one of the band. While he was sitting there, Timmendiquas came to him.

"Ware," he said, "we are now at the great post of the King, and you will be held a prisoner inside. I have treated you as well as I could. Is there anything of which you wish to complain?"

"There is nothing," replied Henry. "Timmendiquas is a chief, great alike of heart and hand."

The Wyandot smiled slightly. It seemed that he was anxious for the good opinion of his most formidable antagonist. Henry noticed, too, that he was in his finest attire. A splendid blue blanket hung from his shoulders, and his leggings and moccasins of the finest tanned deerskin were also blue. Red Eagle and Yellow Panther, who stood not far away, were likewise arrayed in their savage best.

"We are now about to go into the fort," said Timmendiquas, "and you are to go with us, Ware."

Four British officers were approaching. Their leader was a stocky man of middle age in the uniform of a colonel. It would have been apparent to anyone that the Wyandot chief was the leader of the band, and the officers saluted him.

"I am speaking to Timmendiquas, the great White Lightning of the Wyandots, am I not?" he asked.

"I am Timmendiquas of the Wyandots, known in your language as White Lightning," replied the chief gravely.

"I am Colonel William Caldwell of the King's army," said the chief, "and I am sent by Colonel de Peyster, the commandant at Detroit, to bid you welcome, and to ask you and your fellow chiefs to meet him within the walls. My brother officers and I are to be your escort of honor, and we are proud of such a service."

Henry saw at once that Caldwell was a man of abundant experience with the Indians. He knew their intense pride, and he was going to see that Timmendiquas and the other chiefs were received in a manner befitting their station among their own people.

"It is well," said Timmendiquas. "We will go with you and Ware will go with us."

"Who is Ware?" asked Caldwell, as Henry stood up. At the same time the Englishman's eyes expressed admiration. The height and splendid figure of the youth impressed him.

"Ware, though young, is the greatest of all the white warriors," replied Timmendiquas. "He is my prisoner and I keep him with me until Manitou tells me what I shall do with him."

His tone was final. Caldwell was a clever man, skilled in forest diplomacy. He saw that nothing was to be gained, and that much might be lost by opposing the will of Timmendiquas.

"Of course he comes with you if you wish it, White Lightning," he said. "Now may we go? Colonel de Peyster awaits us to do you honor."

Timmendiquas inclined his head and he, with nine other chiefs, including Yellow Panther and Red Eagle, and with Henry in the center, started toward the fort. The British officers went with Colonel Caldwell, marching by the side of Timmendiquas. They approached the western gate, and, when they were within a few yards of it, a soldier on top of the palisade began to play a military air on a bugle. It was an inspiring tune, mellow and sweet in the clear spring air, and Caldwell looked up proudly. The chiefs said not a word, but Henry knew that they were pleased. Then the great gate was thrown open and they passed between two files of soldiers, who held their rifles at attention. The music of the bugle ceased, the great gate closed behind them, and the Indians and their escort marched on towards an open square, where a corps of honor, with the commander himself at their head, was drawn up to receive them.

Henry's gaze turned at once towards the commander, whose name filled him with horror and detestation. Arent Schuyler de Peyster had succeeded to Hamilton, the "hair buyer," captured by George Rogers Clark and sent in chains to Virginia. He had shown great activity in arming and inciting the Indians against the settlers in Kentucky, and Henry hated him all the more because he was an American and not an Englishman. He could not understand how an American, Tory though he might be, could send his own people to fire and the stake, and doom women and little children to a horrible death.

Arent Schuyler de Peyster, born in the city of New York, was now a man of middle years, strongly built, haughty in manner, proud of his family and of his rank in the army of the King. He was confident that the royal arms would triumph ultimately, and, meanwhile he was doing his best to curb the young settlements beyond the Ohio, and to prevent the rebel extension to the West. Now the expedition of Bird had gone forth from Detroit against Kentucky and he was anxious to send another and greater one which should have as its core the Wyandots, the bravest and most daring of all the western tribes. He had never seen Timmendiquas before, but he was familiar with his name, and, after a single glance, it was impossible to mistake him. His roving eye also saw the tall white youth, and, for the present, he wondered, but his mind soon turned to his welcome to the warlike chief.

A salute of four guns was fired from one of the batteries in the bastion. Then Colonel de Peyster greeted Timmendiquas and after him, the other chiefs one by one. He complimented them all upon their bravery and their loyalty to the King, their great white father across the ocean. He rejoiced to hear of their great deeds against the rebels, and promised them splendid rewards for the new deeds they would achieve. Then, saying that they had marched far and must be hungry and tired, he invited them to a feast which he had prepared, having been warned by a runner of their coming.

Timmendiquas, Red Eagle, and Yellow Panther heard him in silence and without a change of countenance, but the eyes of the other chiefs sparkled. They loved blankets of brilliant colors, beads, and the many gaudy trinkets that were sold or given away at the post. New rifles and fresh ammunition, also, would be acceptable, and, in order to deserve than in increasing quantities, they resolved that the next quest for scalps should be most zealous.

Having finished his address, which had been studied carefully, de Peyster nodded toward Henry.

"A new recruit, I suppose," he said. "One who has seen the light. Truly, he is of an admirable figure, and might do great service in our cause. But he bears no arms."

Henry himself answered before Timmendiquas could say a word, and he answered all the more promptly, because he knew that the renegades, Girty, Wyatt and Blackstaffe had drawn near and were listening.

"I am no recruit," he said. "I don't want to die, but I'd sooner do it than make war upon my own people as you and your friends are doing, Colonel de Peyster, and be responsible for the murder of women and children, as you and your friends are. I was at Wyoming and I saw the terrible deeds done there. I am no renegade and I never can be one."

The face of the well-fed Colonel flushed an apoplectic purple, and Braxton Wyatt thrust his hand to the butt of the pistol in his belt, but Girty, inured to everything, laughed and said:

"Don't take it so hard, young man."

"Then tell us who you are!" exclaimed Colonel de Peyster angrily.

Now it was Timmendiquas who replied.

"He is my prisoner," he said. "He is the most valiant of all the Kentuckians. We took him after a great struggle in which he overthrew many of our young men. I have brought him as a present to you at Detroit."

Did the words of Timmendiquas contain some subtle irony? De Peyster looked at him sharply, but the coppery face of the great chief expressed nothing. Then the diplomacy which he was compelled to practice incessantly with his red allies came to his aid.

"I accept the present," he replied, "because he is obviously a fine specimen of the *genus* rebel, and we may be able to put him to use. May I ask your name, young sir?"

"Ware—Henry Ware."

"Very well, Master Ware, since you are here with us, you can join in the little banquet that we have prepared, and see what a happy family the King's officers and the great chiefs make."

Now it was de Peyster who was ironical. The words of Henry about renegades and Wyoming and the slaying of women and children had stung him, but he would not show the sting to a boy; instead, he would let him see how small and weak the Kentuckians were, and how the King's men and the tribes would be able to encompass their complete destruction.

"Timmendiquas has given you to me as my prisoner," he said, "but for an hour or two you shall be my guest."

Henry bowed. He was not at all averse. His was an inquiring mind, and if de Peyster had anything of importance to show, he wished to see it.

"Lead the way, Catesby," said the commandant to a young officer, evidently an aide.

Catesby proceeded to a large house near the north end of the court. Colonel de Peyster and Timmendiquas, side by side, followed him. The others came in a group.

Catesby led them into a great room, evidently intended as a public banquet hall, as it had a long and wide table running down its center. But several large windows were opened wide and Henry conjectured that this effect—half out of doors—was created purposely. Thus it would be a place where the Indian chiefs could be entertained without feeling shut in.

Colonel de Peyster evidently had prepared well. Huge metal dishes held bear meat, buffalo meat and venison, beef and fish. Bread and all the other articles of frontier food were abundant. Four soldiers stood by as waiters. De Peyster sat at the head of the table with Timmendiquas on his right and Simon Girty on his left. Henry had a seat almost at the foot, and directly across the table from him was the frowning face of Braxton Wyatt. Colonel Caldwell sat at the foot of the table and several other British or Tory officers also were present. The food was served bountifully, and, as the chiefs had come a long distance and were hungry, they ate with sharp appetites. Many of them, scorning knives and forks, cracked the bones with their hands. For a long time the Indians preserved the calm of the woods, but Colonel de Peyster was bland and beaming. He talked of the success of the King's army and of the Indian armies. He told how the settlements had been destroyed throughout Western New York and Pennsylvania, and he told how those of Kentucky would soon share the same fate. A singular spirit seemed to possess him. The Americans, patriots or rebels, as they were variously called, always hated the Tories more bitterly than they hated the English, and this hatred was returned in full measure.

Now it seemed to Henry that de Peyster intended his remarks largely for him. He would justify himself to the captive youth, and at the same time show him the power of the allied Indians, Tories, and English. He talked quite freely of the great expedition of Bird and of the cannon that he carried with him.

"I don't think that your palisades will stand before heavy cannon balls, will they, Ware?"

"I fear not," replied Henry, "and it is likely that many of our people will suffer, but you must bear in mind, Colonel de Peyster, that whenever a man falls in Kentucky another comes to take his place. We are fighting for the land on which we stand, and you are fighting for an alien ruler, thousands of miles away. No matter how many defeats we may suffer, we shall win in the end."

De Peyster frowned.

"You do not know the strength of Britain," he said, "nor do you know the power of the warriors. You say that you were at Wyoming. Well, you have seen what we could do."

Girty broke into a sneering laugh at Henry and then seconded the words of his chief.

"All we want is union and organization," he said. "Soon our own troops and the red warriors will form one army along the whole line of the war. The rebel cause is already sinking in the East, and in another year the King will be triumphant everywhere."

Girty was a crafty man, something of a forest statesman. He had given the Indians much help on many occasions and they usually deferred to him. Now he turned to them.

"When Colonel Bird achieves his victories south of the Ohio, as he is sure to do," he said, "and when Timmendiquas and his great force marches to destroy all that is left, then you, O chiefs, will have back your hunting grounds for your villages and your people. The deer and the buffalo will be as numerous as ever. Fire will destroy the houses and the forests will grow where they have been. Their cornfields will disappear, and not a single one of the Yengees will be found in your great forests beyond the Beautiful River."

The nostrils of the chiefs dilated. A savage fire, the desire for scalps, began to sparkle in the dark eyes of the wilderness children. At this crucial moment of excitement Colonel de Peyster caused cups to be brought and wine to be passed. All drank, except Henry and the great chief, the White Lightning of the Wyandots. De Peyster himself felt the effect of the strong liquor, and Girty and Wyatt did not seek to hide it.

"There is fire in your veins, my children," exclaimed de Peyster. "You will fight for the King. You will clear the woods of the rebels, and he will send you great rewards. As a proof of what he will do he gives you many presents now."

He made a signal and the soldiers began to bring in gifts for the chiefs, gifts that seemed to them beautiful and of great value. There were silver-mounted rifles for Timmendiquas, Red Eagle, Yellow Panther, and also for another Shawnee chief of uncommon ferocity, Moluntha. Their eyes sparkled as they received them, and all uttered thanks except Timmendiquas, who still did not say a word. Then came knives, hatchets, blankets—always of bright colors—beads and many little mirrors. The Indians were excited with the wine and the variety and splendor of the presents. A young chief, Yahnundasis, a Shawnee, sprang from the table and burst into a triumphant chant:

The great chief beyond the seasSends us the rifle and the knife;He bids us destroy the hated Yengees,And the day of our wrath has come.

We search the forest for white scalps;The cannon, the great guns will help us,Not a foe in Kentucky will be left,None can escape the rage of the warriors.

He sang other verses in the Shawnee tongue, and all the while he was growing more excited with his chant and leapings. He drew his tomahawk and swung it in a glittering circle above his head. The red and black paint upon his face, moistened by his own perspiration, dripped slowly upon his shoulders. He was a wild and terrible figure, a true exponent of primitive savagery, but no one interfered with him. In the minds of the renegades he awoke corresponding emotions.

Caldwell at the foot of the table looked inquiringly at de Peyster at the head of it, but de Peyster raised neither hand nor voice to stay dance and song. It may be that the wine and the intoxication of so wild a scene had gone to his own head. He listened attentively to the song, and watched the feet of the dancer, while he drummed upon the table with his forefingers. One of the chiefs took from his robe a small whistle made of the bone of an eagle, and began to blow upon it a shrill monotonous tune. This inflamed the dancer still further, and he grew wilder and wilder. The note of the whistle, while varying but little, was fierce, piercing, and abundant. It thrilled the blood of red men and white, all save Timmendiquas, who sat, face and figure alike unmoving.

Yahnundasis now began to gaze steadily at Henry. However he gyrated, he did not take his eyes from those of the captive youth. Henry's blood chilled, and for a moment stopped its circulation. Then it flowed in its wonted tide, but he understood. Yahnundasis was seeing red. Like the Malay he was amuck. At any moment he might throw the glittering hatchet at the prisoner. Henry recognized the imminence of his danger, but he steeled his nerves. He saw, too, that much depended upon himself, upon the power of the spirit that radiated from his eyes. Hence, he, too, looked steadily into the eyes of Yahnundasis. He poured all his nervous strength and force into the gaze.

He felt that he was holding the dancing chief in a sort of a spell by the power of a spirit greater than that of Yahnundasis. Yet it could not last; in a minute or two the chief must break the charm, and then, unless someone interfered, he would cast the tomahawk. Obviously the interference should come from de Peyster. But would he do it? Henry did not dare take his eyes from those of Yahnundasis in order to look at the Tory Colonel.

The savage now was maddened completely with his song, the dance, and the wine that he had drunk. Faster and faster whirled the hatchet, but with his powerful gaze deep into the eyes of the other, Henry still sought to restrain the hand that would hurl the deadly weapon. It became a pain, both physical and mental, to strain so. He wanted to look aside, to see the others, and to know why they did not stop so wild a scene. He was conscious of a great silence, save for the singing and dancing of the Indian and the beating of his own heart. He felt convinced now that no one was going to interfere, and his hand stole towards one of the large knives that had been used for cutting meat.

The voice of Yahnundasis rose to a shriek and he leaped like a snake-dancer. Henry felt sure that the tomahawk was going to come, but while he yet stared at the savage he caught a glimpse of a tall, splendidly arrayed figure springing suddenly upright. It was Timmendiquas and he, too, drew a tomahawk. Then with startling quickness he struck Yahnundasis with the flat of the blade. Yahnundasis fell as if he had been slain. The tomahawk flew wildly from his hand, and dark blood from his broken crown mingled with the red and black paint on his face. Timmendiquas stood up, holding his own tomahawk threateningly, an angry look darting from his eyes.

"Take him away," he said, indicating Yahnundasis, in a contemptuous tone. "To-morrow let him nurse his bruised head and reflect that it is not well to be a fool. It is not meet that a warrior, even be he a chief, should threaten a prisoner, when we come to a feast to talk of great things."

As a murmur of assent came from the chiefs about him, he resumed his seat in dignified silence. Henry said nothing, nor did he allow his countenance to change, but deep in his heart he felt that he owed another debt to the Wyandot chieftain. De Peyster and Caldwell exchanged glances. Both knew that they had allowed the affair to go too far, but both alike resented the stern rebuke contained in the words of Timmendiquas. Yet each glance said the same, that it was wise to dissimulate and take no offense.

"You have spoken well, as usual, Timmendiquas," said Colonel de Peyster. "Now as you and the other chiefs are rested after your long march we will talk at once of the great things that we have in mind, since time is of value. Colonel Bird with the cannon has gone against Kentucky. As I have already said we wish to send another force which will seek out and destroy every station, no matter how small, and which will not even leave a single lone cabin unburned. Colonel Caldwell will command the white men, but you, Timmendiquas, and the allied tribes will have the greater task and the greater glory. The King will equip you amply for the work. He will present a rifle, much ammunition and a fine blanket to every warrior who goes. Rifles, blankets and ammunition are all in our storehouses here in Detroit, and they will be distributed the moment the expedition starts."

The renegades clapped their hands. Most of the chiefs uttered cries of approval and shook their tomahawks in exultation, but Timmendiquas remained silent.

"Does it not appeal to you, Timmendiquas?" said de Peyster. "You have been the most zealous of all the chiefs. You have led great attacks against the settlers, and you have been most eager in battle."

Timmendiquas rose very deliberately and speaking in Wyandot, which nearly all present understood, he said:

"What the Colonel of the King says is true. I have fought many times with the Kentuckians, and they are brave men. Sometimes we have beaten them, and sometimes they have beaten us. They have great warriors, Clark, Boone, Kenton, Harrod and the tall youth who sits here, my captive. Let not the colonel of the King forget that with Clark at their head they crossed the Ohio, took Vincennes and Kaskaskia and him who was then the commander of Detroit, Hamilton, now held prisoner in a far land beyond the mountains."

De Peyster's face flushed darkly, and the other white men moved uneasily.

"The things you tell are true, Timmendiquas," said de Peyster, "but what bearing do they have upon our expedition?"

"I wish to speak of many things," resumed the chief. "I am for war to the end against those who have invaded our hunting grounds. But let not Colonel de Peyster and Caldwell and Girty forget that the villages of the Indians lie between Kaintuckee and Detroit."

"What of it?" said de Peyster. "The Kentuckians reduced so low will not dare to come against them."

"That we do not know," said Timmendiquas. "When we destroy the men in Kaintuckee others come to take their places. It is the duty of the Wyandots and all the allied tribes to look into the future. Listen, O Colonel of the King. I was at Wyoming in the East when the Indians and their white friends won a great victory. Never before had I seen such a taking of scalps. There was much joy and feasting, dancing and singing. It was the Iroquois, the great Six Nations who won the victory, and they thought that their Aieroski, who is our Manitou, would never forsake them. They swept the whole valley of Wyoming and many other valleys. They left the country as bare as my hand. But it was not the end."

Timmendiquas seemed to grow in stature, and he looked fiercely into the eyes of the English officers. Despite themselves de Peyster and Caldwell quailed.

"It was not the end," continued Timmendiquas, and his tone was severe and accusing. "The Iroquois had destroyed the rear of the Yengees and great were the thanks of the King's men. The mighty Thayendanegea, the Mohawk, was called the first of all warriors, but the great chief of the Long Knives far away in the East did not forget. By and by a great army came against the Iroquois. Where were the King's men then? Few came to help. Thayendanegea had to fight his battle almost alone. He was beaten, his army was scattered like sand before the wind, and the army of the Long Knives trod out the Iroquois country. Their great villages went up in flames, their Council Houses were destroyed, the orchards that had been planted by their grandfathers were cut down, their fields were deserted, the whole Iroquois country was ruined, and the Six Nations, never before conquered, now huddle by the British posts at Niagara and Oswego for shelter."

"It is a great misfortune, but the brave Iroquois will repair it," said de Peyster. "Why do you tell of it, Timmendiquas?"

"For this reason," replied the chief. "The Iroquois would not have been without a country, if the King's men had helped them as they had helped the King's men. Shall we, in the West, the Wyandots, the Shawnees, the Miamis and the others meet the same fate? Shall we go against Kaintuckee, destroy the settlements there, and then, when an avenging army comes against our villages, lose our country, because the King's men who should help us are far away, as the Iroquois lost theirs?"

He folded his arms across his broad chest and, stern and accusing, awaited the answer. De Peyster quailed again, but he quickly recovered. He was a flexible man skilled in diplomacy, and he saw that he must promise, promise much and promise it in convincing tones. He noticed moreover the deep murmur of approval that the chiefs gave to the words of White

Lightning. Then he in turn rose also and assuming his most imposing manner said:

"On behalf of the King, Timmendiquas, I promise you the help of his full strength. It is not likely that the Kentuckians will ever be able to come against your villages, but if they do I will march forth with all my force to your help. Nay, I will send East for others, to Niagara and Oswego and to Canada. It shall never be said of us that we deserted the tribes in their hour of need, if such an hour should come. I myself would gladly march now against these intruders if my duty did not hold me here."

He looked around the table and his eye encountered Caldwell's. The officer instantly saw his cue and springing to his feet he cried:

"What our brave commander says is true, Timmendiquas. I myself and some of our best men, we will fight beside you."

Now the chiefs murmured approval of the words of de Peyster and Caldwell, as they had approved those of Timmendiquas. The great Wyandot himself seemed to be convinced, and said that it was well. Henry had listened to it all in silence, but now de Peyster turned his attention to him.

"I think that we have given enough of our hospitality to this prisoner," he said, "and since you have turned him over to me, Timmendiquas, I will send him to a place which will hold him for a while."

Henry rose at once.

"I am willing to go," he said. "I thank you for your food and drink, but I think I shall feel more at home in any prison that you may have than here among those who are planning the destruction of my people."

Girty was about to speak, but de Peyster waved his hand, and the words stopped unsaid.

"Take him to the jail, Holderness," he said to one of the younger officers. "He can wait there. We shall have plenty of time to decide concerning his fate."

Henry walked by the side of the officer across the court. Holderness was quite young, ruddy, and evidently not long in America. He looked with admiration at Henry's height and magnificent shoulders.

"You are from that far land they call Kaintuckee?" he said.

"Yes."

"One of the best of the countries belonging to the Indians?"

"It is a good country, but I do not know that it ever belonged to the Indians. No doubt they have hunted there and fought there for hundreds of years, but so far as I know, they've never lived there."

"Then it belongs to the King," said Holderness.

Henry smiled. He rather liked this ingenuous young man who was not much older than himself.

"A country like Kentucky," he replied, "belongs to those who can hold it. Once the French King claimed it, but how could he enforce a claim to a country separated from him by thousands of miles of sea and wilderness? Now the English King makes the same claim, and perhaps he has a better chance, but still that chance is not good enough."

The young officer sighed a little.

"I'm sorry we have to fight you," he said. "I've heard ugly tales since I came about the savages and the white men, too."

"You're likely to hear more," said Henry. "But this I take it is our jail."

"It is. I'll go in and see that you're as comfortable as possible."

CHAPTER X. THE LETTER OF THE FOUR

The building into which Henry was taken was built of brick and rough stone, two stories in height, massive and very strong. The door which closed the entrance was of thick oak, with heavy crosspieces, and the two rows of small windows, one above the other, were fortified with iron bars, so close together that a man could not pass between. Henry's quick eye noticed it all, as they entered between the British guards at the door. The house inside was divided into several rooms, none containing more than a rude pallet bed, a small pine table, a tin pitcher, a cup of water, and a pine stool.

Henry followed Holderness into one of these rooms, and promptly sat on the pine stool by the window. Holderness looked at him with a mixture of admiration and pity.

"I'm sorry, old chap," he said, "that I have to lock you up here. Come now, do be reasonable. These rebels are bound to lose, and, if you can't join us, take a parole and go somewhere into Canada until all the trouble is over."

Henry laughed lightly, but his heart warmed again toward young Holderness who had come from some easy and sheltered spot in England, and who knew nothing of the wilderness and its hardships and terrors.

"Don't you be sorry for me," he said. "As for this room, it's better than anything that I've been used to for years. And so far as giving a parole and going into Canada, I wouldn't dream of such a thing. It would interfere with my plans. I'm going back into the South to fight against your people and the Indians."

"But you're a prisoner!"

"For the present, yes, but I shall not remain so."

"You can't escape."

"I always escape. It's true I was never before in so strong a prison, but I shall go. I am willing to tell you, Lieutenant Holderness, because others will tell you anyhow, that I have outside four very faithful and skillful friends. Nothing would induce them to desert me, and among us we will secure my escape."

Into the look of mingled admiration and pity with which Holderness had regarded Henry crept a touch of defiance.

"You're deucedly confident, old chap," he said. "You don't seem to think that we amount to much here, and yet Colonel de Peyster has undoubtedly saved you from the Indians. You should be grateful to him for that much."

Henry laughed. This ingenuous youth now amused him.

"What makes you think it was Colonel de Peyster or any other English or Tory officer who saved me from the Indians? Well, it wasn't. If Colonel Bird and your other white friends had had their way when I was taken I should have been burned at the stake long before this. It was the Wyandot chief, Timmendiquas, known in our language as White Lightning, who saved me."

The young officer's red face flushed deeper red.

"I knew that we had been charged with such cruelties," he said, "but I had hoped that they were not true. Now, I must leave you here, and, upon my soul, I do not wish you any harm."

He went out and Henry felt a heavy key turn in the lock. A minute or two after he had gone the prisoner tried the door, and found that it was made of heavy oak, with strong crosspieces of the same material. He exerted all his great strength, and, as he expected, he could not shake it. Then he went back to the pine stool, which he drew up near a barred window, and sitting there watched as well as he could what was passing in the great court.

Henry had too much natural wisdom and experience to beat his head uselessly against bars. He would remain quiet, preserving the strength of both body and mind, until the time for action came. Meanwhile he was using his eyes. He saw some of the chiefs pass, always accompanied by white officers. But he saw officers alone, and now and then women, both red and white. He also saw the swarthy faces of woods runners, and among them, one whose face and figure were familiar, that same Pierre Louis Lajeunais, whom he had met outside the fort.

Lajeunais carried his rifle on one shoulder and a pack of furs on the other. It was a heavy pack, probably beaver skins, but he moved easily, and Henry saw that he was very strong. Henry regarded him thoughtfully. This man had been friendly, he had access to the fort, and he might be induced to give him aid. He did not see just then how Lajeunais could be of help to him, but he stored the idea in the back of his head, ready for use if there should be occasion.

He presently saw Timmendiquas go by with Colonel de Peyster on one side of him and Colonel Caldwell on the other. Henry smiled. Evidently they were paying assiduous court to the Wyandot, and well they might. Without the aid of the powerful Indian tribes the British at Detroit could do nothing. In a few moments they were gone and then the twilight began to come over the great western post. From his window Henry caught a view of a distant reach of the broad river, glittering gold in the western sun. It came ultimately from one great lake and would empty into another. Paul's words returned to him. Those mysterious and mighty great lakes! would he live to see them with his comrades? Once in his early captivity with the Indians he had wandered to the shores of the farthest and greatest of them all, and he remembered the awe with which he had looked upon the vast expanse of waters like the sea itself. He wished to go there again. Hundreds of stories and legends about the mighty chain had come from the Indians and this view of the river that flowed from the upper group stirred again all his old curiosity. Then he remembered his position and with a low laugh resumed his seat on the pine stool.

Yet he watched the advance of the night. It seemed that the vast wilderness was coming down on Detroit and would blot it out completely, fortress, soldiers, village and all. In a little while the darkness covered everything save a few flickering lights here and there. Henry sat at the window a while, gazing absently at the lights. But his mind was away with his comrades, Paul, Shif'less Sol, Long Jim and Silent Tom, the faithful four with whom he had passed through a world of dangers. Where were they now? He had no doubt that they were near Detroit. It was no idle boast that he made to Colonel de Peyster when he said they would help rescue him. He awaited the result with absolute confidence. He was in truth so lacking in nervous apprehension that when he lay down on the rude pallet he was asleep in two minutes.

He was awakened the next morning by Lieutenant Holderness who informed him that in the daytime, for the present at least, he would be allowed the liberty of the court. He could also eat outside.

"I'm grateful," said Henry. "I wish to thank Colonel de Peyster, or whoever the man may be who has given me this much liberty."

"It is Colonel de Peyster, of course," said the ruddy one.

But Henry shrewdly suspected that his modicum of liberty was due to Timmendiquas, or rather the fear of de Peyster that he would offend Timmendiquas, and weaken the league, if he ill treated the prisoner.

Henry went outside and bathed his face at a water barrel. Then at the invitation of Holderness he joined some soldiers and Canadian Frenchmen who were cooking breakfast together beside a great fire. They made room readily at the lieutenant's request and Henry began to eat. He noticed across the fire the brown face of Lajeunais, and he nodded in a friendly manner. Lajeunais nodded in return and his black eyes twinkled. Henry thought that he saw some significance in the twinkle, but when he looked again Lajeunais was busy with his own breakfast. Then the incident passed out of his mind and he quickly found himself on good terms with both soldiers and woods runners.

"You give your parole," said Lajeunais, "an' go North wiz me on the great huntin' an' trappin'. We will go North, North, North, beyon' the Great Lakes, an' to other lakes almost as great, a thousan', two thousan' miles beyon' the home of white men to trap the silver fox, the pine marten an' the other furs which bring much gold. Ah, le bon Dieu, but it is gran'! an' you have ze great figure an' ze great strength to stan' ze great cold. Then come wiz me. Ze great lakes an' woods of ze far North is better zan to fret your life out here in ze prison. You come?"

He spoke entreatingly, but Henry smiled and replied in a tone full of good humor:

"It's a tempting offer, and it's very kind of you, Monsieur Lajeunais, but I cannot accept it. Neither am I going to fret my life out within these walls. I'm going to escape."

All the soldiers and woods runners laughed together except Lajeunais. Henry's calm assurance seemed a great joke to them, but the Frenchman watched him shrewdly. He was familiar with men of the woods, and it seemed to him that the great youth was not boasting, merely stating a fact.

"Confidence is ze gran' thing," he said, "but these walls are high an' the ears are many."

While Henry sat there with the men, Colonel de Peyster passed. The commander was in an especially good humor that morning. He was convinced that his negotiations with the Indian were going well. He had sworn to Timmendiquas again that if the Western tribes would fight for the King, the King would help them in return should their villages be attacked. More presents had been distributed judiciously among the chiefs. The renegades also were at work. All of Girty's influence, and it was large, had been brought to bear in favor of the invasion, and it seemed to de Peyster that everything was now settled. He saw Henry sitting by the fire, gave him an ironical look, and, as he passed, sang clearly enough for the captive to hear a song of his own composition. He called it "The Drill Sergeant," written to the tune of "The Happy Beggars," and the first verse ran:

Come, stand well to your order,Make not the least false motion;Eyes to the right,Thumb, muzzle height;Lads, you have the true notion.Here and there,EverywhereThat the King's boys may be found,Fight and die,Be the cry,'Ere in battle to give ground.

De Peyster was not only a soldier, but being born in New York and having grown up there he prided himself upon being a man of the world with accomplishments literary and otherwise. The privilege of humming one's own poetry is great and exalting, and the commander's spirits, already high, rose yet higher. The destruction of Kentucky was not only going to be accomplished, it was in fact accomplished already. He would extirpate the impudent settlers west of the mountains, and, when the King's authority was reestablished everywhere and the time came for rewards, he would ask and receive a great one.

As Colonel de Peyster walked toward the western gate a Tory soldier, with bruises and excitement upon his face, and a torn uniform upon his body, hurried toward him, accompanied by Lieutenant Holderness.

"This is Private Doran, sir," said Holderness, "and he has an important letter for you."

Colonel de Peyster looked critically at Private Doran.

"You seem to have been manhandled," he said.

"I was set upon by a band of cutthroats," said Private Doran, the memory of his wrongs becoming very bitter, "and they commanded me upon pain of death to deliver this letter to you."

He held out a dirty sheet of folded paper.

Colonel de Peyster felt instinctively that it was something that was going to be of great interest, and, before he opened it, he tapped it with a thoughtful forefinger.

"Where did you get this?"

"About five o'clock this morning," replied Private Doran with hesitation and in an apologetic tone, "I was on guard on the western side of the village, near the woods. I was watching as well as I could with my eyes open, and listening too, but I neither heard nor saw anything when four men suddenly threw themselves upon me. I fought, but how could I overcome four? I suffered many bruises, as you can see. I thought they were going to kill me, but they bound me, and then the youngest of 'em wrote this note which they told me to give to you, saying that they would send a rifle bullet through my head some dark night, if I disobeyed 'em, and I believe, sir, they would do it."

"Report to your sergeant," said de Peyster, and Private Doran gladly went away. Then the commander opened the letter and as he read it his face turned a deep red with anger. He read it over again to see that he made no mistake, but the deep red of anger remained.

"What do you think of such impertinence as this, Holderness?" he exclaimed, and then he read:

"To Colonel Arent Schuyler de Peyster, Commander of the King's forces at Detroit:

"*Sir*:

"You have a prisoner in your fort, one Henry Ware, our comrade. We warn you that if he is subjected to any ill-treatment whatever, you and your men shall suffer punishment. This is not an idle threat. We are able to make good our promises.

"SOLOMON	HYDE.
"PAUL	COTTER.
"THOMAS	ROSS.
"JAMES HART."	

"It's impertinence and mummery," repeated de Peyster, "I'll have that man Doran tied to a cannon and lashed on his bare back!"

But Lieutenant Holderness was young and impressionable.

"It's impertinent, of course, Colonel," he said, "and it sounds wild, too, but I believe the signers of this paper mean what they say. Wouldn't it be a good idea to treat this prisoner well, and set such a good watch that we can capture his friends, too? They'll be hanging about."

"I don't know," said de Peyster. "No, I think I have a better plan. Suppose we answer the letter of these fellows. I have had no intention of treating Ware badly. I expected to exchange him or use him profitably as a hostage, but I'll tell his friends that we are going to subject him to severe punishment, and then we'll draw them into our net, too."

"I've heard from Girty and Wyatt that they do wonderful things," said Holderness. "Suppose they should rescue Ware after all?"

De Peyster laughed incredulously.

"Take him away from us!" he said. "Why, he's as safely caged here as if he were in a stone prison in England. Just to show him what I think of their threat I'll let him read this letter."

He approached Henry, who was still sitting by the fire and handed him the sheet of paper.

"A letter from some friends of yours; the four most delightful humorists that these woods can furnish, I take it."

Henry thrilled with delight when he read the paper, but he did not permit his face to show his joy. Like de Peyster he read it over twice, and then he handed it back to the Colonel.

"Well," said de Peyster, "what do you think of it?"

"It speaks for itself," replied Henry. "They mean exactly what they say."

De Peyster chose to adopt a light, ironical tone.

"Do you mean to tell me, my good fellow," he asked, "that four beggarly rebels, hiding for their lives in the wilderness, can punish me for anything that I may do to you?"

"I do not merely tell you so, I know it."

"Very well; it is a game, a play and we shall see what comes of it. I am going to send an answer to their letter, but I shall not tell you the nature of that answer, or what comes of it."

"I've no doubt that I'll learn in time," said Henry quietly.

The boy's calmness annoyed de Peyster, and he left him abruptly, followed by Holderness. While his temper was still warm, he wrote a letter to the four stating that Henry Ware would be delivered to the savages for them to do with as they chose,—the implication being torture and death— and that unless the four gave Detroit a very wide berth they would soon be treated in the same way. Then he called the miserable Doran before him, and told him, when he took the late watch again the next night, to hook the letter on the twig of a tree near where he had been attacked before, and then watch and see what would occur. Doran promised strictly to obey, and, since he was not called upon to fight the terrific four, some of his apprehension disappeared.

Henry meanwhile had left the fire beside which he had eaten breakfast, and—though closely guarded—strolled about the great enclosure. He felt an uncommon lightness of heart. It was almost as if he were the jailer and not the jailed. That letter from his four comrades was a message to him as well as to de Peyster. He knew that the soldiers of de Peyster and the Indians would make every effort to take them, but the woods about Detroit were dense and they would be on guard every second. There was no certainty, either, that all the French-Canadians were warmly attached to the King's cause. Why should they be? Why should they fight so zealously for the country that had conquered them not many years before? He saw once more in the afternoon the square, strong figure of Lajeunais, crossing the court. When the Frenchman noticed him he stopped and came back, smiling and showing his great white teeth.

"Ah, mon brav," he said, "doesn't the great North yet call to you?"

"No," replied Henry, with an answering smile. "As I told you, I am going to escape."

"You may," said Lajeunais, suddenly lowering his voice. "I met one of your friends in the forest. I cannot help, but I will not hinder. C'est une pitie that a garcon so gran' an' magnificent as you should pine an' die within prison walls."

Then he was gone before Henry could thank him. Toward nightfall he was notified that he must return to his prison and now he felt the full weight of confinement when the heavy walls closed about him. But Holderness came with the soldier who brought his supper and remained to talk. Henry saw that Holderness, not long from England, was lonesome and did not like his work. It was true also that the young Englishman was appalled by the wilderness, not in the sense of physical fear, but the endless dark forest filled him with the feeling of desolation as it has many another man. He had found in Henry, prisoner though he was, the most congenial soul, that he had yet met in the woods. As he lingered while Henry ate the hard-tack and coffee, it was evident that he wanted to talk.

"These friends of yours," he said. "They promise wonderful things. Do you really think they will rescue you, or did you merely say so to impress

Colonel de Peyster? I ask, as man to man, and forgetting for the time that we are on opposing sides."

Henry liked him. Here, undoubtedly, was an honest and truthful heart. He was sorry that they were official enemies, but he was glad that it did not keep them from being real friends.

"I meant it just as I said it," he replied. "My friends will keep their words. If I am harmed some of your people here at Detroit will suffer. This no doubt sounds amazing to you, but strange things occur out here in the woods."

"I'm very curious to see," said Holderness. "Colonel de Peyster has sent them a message, telling them in effect that no attention will be paid to their warning, and that he will do with you as he chooses."

"I am curious about it too," said Henry, "and if there is nothing in your duty forbidding it, I ask you to let me know the result."

"I think it's likely that I can tell if there is anything to be told. Well, good night to you, Mr. Ware. I wish you a pleasant sleep."

"Thank you. I always sleep well."

The night was no exception to Henry's statement, but he was awake early the next morning. Colonel de Peyster also rose early, because he wished to hear quickly from Private Doran. But Private Doran did not come at the usual hour of reporting from duty, nor did he return the next hour, nor at any hour. De Peyster, furious with anger, sent a detachment which found his letter gone and another there. It said that as proof of their power they had taken his sentinel and they warned him again not to harm the prisoner.

De Peyster raged for several reasons. It hurt his personal pride, and it injured his prestige with the Indians. Timmendiquas was still troublesome. He was demanding further guarantees that the King's officers help the Indians with many men and with cannon, in case a return attack should be delivered against their villages, and the White Lightning of the Wyandots was not a chief with whom one could trifle.

Timmendiquas had returned to the camp of his warriors outside the walls and de Peyster at once visited him there. He found the chief in a fine lodge of buffalo skin that the Wyandots had erected for him, polishing the beautiful new rifle that had been presented to him as coming from the King. He looked up when he saw de Peyster enter, and his smile showed the faintest trace of irony. But he laid aside the rifle and arose with the courtesy befitting a red chief who was about to receive a white one.

"Be seated, Timmendiquas," said de Peyster with as gracious a manner as he could summon. "I have come to consult with you about a matter of importance. It seems to me that you alone are of sufficient judgment and experience to give me advice in this case."

Timmendiquas bowed gravely.

De Peyster then told him of the threatening letter from the four, and of the disappearance of Private Doran. The nostrils of Timmendiquas dilated.

"They are great warriors," he said, "but the white youth, Ware, whom you hold, is the greatest of them all. It was well done."

De Peyster frowned. In his praise of the woodsmen Timmendiquas seemed to reflect upon the skill of his own troops. But he persisted in his plan to flatter and to appeal to the pride of Timmendiquas.

"White Lightning," he said, "you know the forest as the bird knows its nest. What would you advise me to do?"

The soothing words appealed to Timmendiquas and he replied:

"I will send some of my warriors to trail them from the spot where your man was taken, and do you send soldiers also to take them when they are found. It is my business to make war upon these rangers from Kentucky, and I will help you all I can."

De Peyster, who felt that his honor was involved, left the lodge much more hopeful. It was intolerable that he, a soldier and a poet, should be insulted in such a manner by four wild woodsmen, and he selected ten good men who, following two Wyandot trailers, would certainly avenge him.

Henry heard the details of Private Doran's misadventure from Lieutenant Holderness, who did not fail to do it full justice.

"I should not have believed it," said the young Englishman, "if the facts were not so clear. Private Doran is not a small man. He must weigh at least one hundred and eighty, but he is gone as completely as if the earth had opened and swallowed him up."

Henry smiled and pretended to take it lightly. At heart he was hugely delighted at this new proof of the prowess of his friends.

"I told you what they were," he said. "They are keeping their promises, are they not?"

"So far they have, but they will reach the end very soon. The Chief Timmendiquas, the tall one, who thinks he is as good as the King of England, has furnished two Wyandot trailers—they say the beggars can come pretty near following the trail left by the flight of a bird through the air—and they will take a detachment of ten good men against these four friends of yours."

The prisoner's eyes sparkled. It did not seem to Holderness that he was at all cast down as he should be.

"Shif'less Sol will lead them a glorious chase," said Henry. "The Wyandots are fine trailers, but they are no better than he, maybe not as good, and no detachment of heavy-footed soldiers can surprise him in the woods."

"But if overtaken they will certainly be defeated. All of them will be slain or captured," said Holderness. "There can be no doubt of it."

"It is to be seen," said Henry, "and we must wait patiently for the result."

Henry was allowed to go in the court again that day. He knew that strong influences were working for his good treatment, and with the impossibility of escape in broad daylight under scores of watchful eyes there was no reason why he should be confined in the big jail. He hoped to see Timmendiquas there, but the chief still stayed outside with his Wyandot warriors. Instead he met another who was not so welcome. As he turned a corner of a large log building he came face to face with Braxton Wyatt. Henry turned abruptly away, indicating that he would avoid the young renegade as he would a snake. But Wyatt called to him:

"Henry, I've got a few words to say to you. You know that you and I were boys together down there in Wareville, and if I've done you any harm it seems that the score is about even between us. I've helped to make war on the rebels in the East. I had gathered together a fine band there. I was leader of it and a man of importance, but that band was destroyed and you were the chief instrument of its destruction."

"Why do you say all this?" asked Henry shortly.

"To show you that I am in the right, and that I am now a Loyalist not for profit, but in face of the fact that I suffer for it."

Henry looked at him in amazement. Why should Braxton Wyatt say these things to him whom he hated most? Then he suddenly knew the reason. Deep down in the heart of everyone, no matter how perverted he may become, is some desire for the good opinion of others. The renegade was seeking to justify himself in the eyes of the youth who had been for a while a childhood comrade. He felt a sort of pity, but he knew that nothing good could come of any further talk between Braxton Wyatt and himself.

"Of course you are entitled to your opinion, Braxton," he said, "but it can never be mine. Your hands are red with the blood of your people, our people, and there can never be any friendship between us."

He saw the angry light coming into Wyatt's eyes, and he turned away. He felt that under the circumstances he could not quarrel with him, and he knew that if they were in the forest again they would be as bitter enemies as ever. It was a relief to him to meet Holderness and another young officer, Desmond, also a recent arrival from England, and quite as ignorant as Holderness of wilderness ways and warfare. He found them fair and generous opponents and, in his heart, he absolved them from blame for the terrible consequences following upon the British alliance with the Indians.

They took Henry on the entire inside circuit of the walls, and he, as well as they, was specially interested in the outlook over the river. A platform four feet wide was built against the palisade the same distance from the top. It was reached at intervals by flights of narrow steps, and here in case of attack the riflemen would crouch and fire from their hidden breastwork. Close by and under the high bank flowed the river, a broad, deep stream, bearing the discharge from those mighty inland seas, the upper chain of the Great Lakes. The current of the river, deep, blue and placid and the forests beyond, massive, dark, and green, made Henry realize how bitter it was to be a prisoner. Here separated from him by only a few feet was freedom, the great forest with its sparkling waters that he loved. In spite of himself, he sighed, and both Holderness and Desmond, understanding, were silent.

Near them was a sort of trestle work that ran out toward the river, although it did not reach it by many feet.

"What is that?" asked Henry, as he looked at it curiously.

"It was intended to be a pier or wharf for loading or unloading boats," replied Holderness. "They tell me that Colonel Hamilton started it, in the belief that it would be useful in an emergency, but when Colonel de Peyster succeeded to the command he stopped the work there, thinking that it might be of as much service to an enemy as to a friend."

Henry took little more notice of the unfinished pier, and they descended from the platform to the ground, their attention being attracted by a noise at the most distant gate. When they took a second look at the cause of the tumult, they hurried forward.

CHAPTER XI
THE CRY FROM THE FOREST

The spectacle that met the eyes of Henry and his English friends was one likely to excite curiosity and interest. The party of ten soldiers and two Wyandots that had gone forth to take the youth's four comrades was returning, but they brought with them no prisoners, nor any trophies from the slain. Instead, one of the Wyandots carried an arm in a rude sling, one soldier was missing, and four others bore wounds.

Henry laughed inwardly, and it was a laugh full of satisfaction and triumph. The party had found the four, but his prevision had not failed him. Shif'less Sol and the others were on watch. They had been found, because they permitted themselves to be found, and evidently they had fought with all the advantage of ambush and skill. He felt instinctively that they had not suffered any serious harm.

"They do not bring your friends," said Holderness.

"No," said Henry, "nor do they bring back all of themselves. I do not wish to boast, gentlemen, but I warned you that my comrades would be hard to take."

Henry saw Colonel de Peyster join the group and he saw, too, that his face expressed much chagrin. So, not wishing to exult openly, he deemed it wise to turn aside.

"If you don't mind," he said to the young officers, "I'm willing to go into my cell, and, if you care to tell me later about what has happened, you know I shall be glad to hear it."

"It might be advisable," said Holderness, and accordingly they locked him in, where he waited patiently. He heard the noise of many voices outside, but those to whom the voices belonged did not come within the range of his window, and he waited, alive with curiosity. He did not hear until nearly night, when Holderness came in with the soldier who brought him his supper. Holderness seemed somewhat chagrined at the discomfiture of de Peyster's party, and he sat a little while in silence. Henry, knowing that the young Englishman must have a certain feeling for his own, waited until he should choose to speak.

"I'm bound to confess, old chap," said Holderness at last, "that you were right all the way through. I didn't believe you, but you knew your own friends. It was a facer for us and, 'pon my word, I don't see how they did it. The Wyandots, it seems, found the trail very soon, and it led a long distance through the woods until they came to a deep creek. Our men could wade the creek by holding their rifles and muskets above their heads, which they undertook to do, but a man standing in water up to his neck is not ready for a fight. At that point fire was opened upon them, and they were compelled to beat as hasty a retreat as they could. You must admit, Mr. Ware, that they were taken at a disadvantage."

"I admit it freely enough," said Henry. "It's a dangerous thing to try to cross a deep stream in the face of a bold enemy who knows how to shoot. And of course it was an ambush, too. That is what one has to beware of in these woods."

"It's a truth that I'm learning every day," said Holderness, who left, wishing the prisoner, since he would not give a parole and go into Canada, a speedy exchange with the Americans for some British captive of importance. Henry was not sorry to be left alone as he was trying to fathom through their characters the plan of his comrades.Paul would seek speedy action, Jim Hart would agree with him, but the crafty Shif'less Sol, with a patience equaling that of any Indian, would risk nothing, until the time was ripe, and he would be seconded by the cautious temperament of Silent Tom. Undoubtedly Shif'less Sol would have his way. It behooved him also to show extreme patience; a quality that he had learned long since, and he disposed himself comfortably on his pallet for his night's rest.

The second exploit of his comrades had encouraged him wonderfully. He was not talking folly, when he had said to more than one that he would escape. The five had become long since a beautiful machine that worked with great precision and power, and it was their first principles that, when one was in trouble, all the rest should risk everything for him.

He fell asleep, but awoke some time before midnight. A bright moon was shining in at his window and the little village within the walls was very quiet and peaceful. He turned over and closed his eyes in order that he might go to sleep again, but he was restless and sleep would not come. Then he got up and stood by the window, looking at the part of the court that lay within range. Nothing stirred. There were sentinels, of course, but they did not pass over the area commanded by his window. The silence was very deep, but presently he heard a sound very faint and very distant. It was the weird cry of the owl that goes so far on a still night. No wilderness note could have been more characteristic, but it was repeated a certain number of times and with certain intonations, and a little shiver ran down Henry's back. He knew that cry. It was the signal. His friends were speaking to him, while others slept, sending a voice across the woods and waters, telling him that they were there to help.

Then, a strange, capricious idea occurred to him. He would reply. The second window on the side of the river, too narrow for a man to pass through, was open, and putting his face to it, he sent back the answering cry, the long, weird, wailing note. He waited a little and again he heard a voice from the far shore of the river, the exact rejoinder to his own, and he knew that the four out there understood. The chain of communication had been established. Now he went back to his pallet, fell asleep with ease, and slept peacefully until morning.

The next day, superstition assailed the French-Canadians in the village, and many of the Indians. A second private who had a late beat near the forest had been carried off. There were signs of a struggle. No blood had been shed, but Private Myers had vanished as completely as his predecessor. To many of the people who sat about the lodges or cabins it seemed uncanny, but it filled the heart of de Peyster with rage. He visited Timmendiquas a second time in his lodge of skins and spoke with some heat.

"You have great warriors," he said, "men who can trail anything through the forest. Why is it that they cannot find this petty little band of marauders, only four?"

"They did find them," returned Timmendiquas gravely; "they took your soldiers, but your soldiers returned without them. Now they hold two of your men captive, but it is no fault of the Wyandots or their brethren of the allied tribes. We wait here in peace, while the other presents that you have promised us come from Niagara."

De Peyster bit his lip. He had rashly promised more and greater gifts for which he would have to send to Niagara, and Timmendiquas had announced calmly that the warriors would remain at Detroit until they came. This had made another long delay and de Peyster raged internally, although he strove to hide it. Now he made the same effort at self-command, and replied pacifically:

"I keep all my promises, Timmendiquas, and yet I confess to you that this affair annoys me greatly. As a malignant rebel and one of the most troublesome of our enemies, I would subject Ware to close confinement, but two of my men are in the power of his friends, and they can take revenge."

"De Peyster speaks wisely," said Timmendiquas. "It is well to choose one's time when to strike."

Getting no satisfaction there, de Peyster returned to the court, where he saw Henry walking back and forth very placidly. The sight filled him with rage. This prisoner had caused him too much annoyance, and he had no business to look so contented. He began to attribute the delay in the negotiations to Henry. He, or at least his comrades, were making him appear ignorant and foolish before the chiefs. He could not refrain from a burst of anger. Striding up to Henry he put his hand violently upon his shoulder. The great youth was surprised but he calmly lifted the hand away and said:

"What do you wish, Colonel de Peyster?"

"I wish many things, but what I especially don't wish just now is to see you walking about here, apparently as free as ourselves!"

"I am in your hands," said Henry.

"You can stay in the prison," said de Peyster. "You'll be out of the way and you'll be much safer there."

"You're in command here."

"I know it," said de Peyster grimly, "and into the prison you go."

Henry accordingly was placed in close confinement, where he remained for days without seeing anybody except the soldier who brought him his food and water, and from whom he could obtain no news at all. But he would make no complaint to this soldier, although the imprisonment was terribly irksome. He had been an entire week within walls. Such a thing had never happened before in his life, and often he felt as if he were choking. It seemed also at times that the great body which made him remarkable was shrinking. He knew that it was only the effect of imagination, but it preyed upon him, and he understood now how one could wither away from mere loneliness and inaction.

His mind traveled over the countless scenes of tense activity that had been crowded into the last three or four years of his life. He had been many times in great and imminent danger, but it was always better than lying here between four walls that seemed to come closer every day. He recalled the deep woods, the trees that he loved, the sparkling waters, lakes, rivers and brooks; he recalled the pursuit of the big game, the deer and the buffalo; he recalled the faces of his comrades, how they jested with one another and fought side by side, and once more he understood what a terrible thing it is for a man to have his comings and goings limited to a space a few feet square. But he resolved that he would not complain, that he would ask no favor of de Peyster or Caldwell or any of them.

Once he saw Braxton Wyatt come to a window and gaze in. The look of the renegade was full of unholy triumph, and Henry knew that he was there for the special purpose of exultation. He sat calm and motionless while the renegade stared at him. Wyatt remained at the window a full half hour, seeking some sign of suffering, or at least an acknowledgment of his presence, but he obtained neither, and he went on, leaving the silent figure full of rage.

On the tenth day Holderness came in with the soldier. Henry knew by his face that he had something to say, but he waited for the lieutenant to speak first. Holderness fidgeted and did not approach the real subject for a little while. He spoke with sympathy of Henry's imprisonment and remarked on the loss of his tan.

"It's hard to be shut up like this, I know," he said, "but it is the fortune of war. Now I suppose if I were taken by the Americans they would do to me what Colonel de Peyster has done to you."

"I don't know," replied Henry, truthfully.

"Neither do I, but we'll suppose it, because I think it's likely. Now I'm willing to tell you, that we're going to let you out again. Some of us rather admire your courage and the fact that you have made no complaint. In addition there has been another letter from those impudent friends of yours."

"Ah!" said Henry, and now he showed great interest.

"Yes, another letter. It came yesterday. It seems that there must be some collusion—with the French-Canadians, I suppose. Woodsmen, I'm sure, do not usually carry around with them paper on which to write notes. Nor could they have known that you were locked up in here unless someone told them. But to come back to the point. Those impudent rascals say in their letter that they have heard of your close imprisonment and that they are retaliating on Privates Doran and Myers."

Henry turned his face away a little to hide a smile. He knew that none of his comrades would torture anybody.

"They have drawn quite a dreadful picture, 'pon honor," continued Lieutenant Holderness, "and most of us have been moved by the sufferings of Doran and Myers. We have interceded with Colonel de Peyster, we have sought to convince him that your confinement within these four walls is useless anyhow, and he has acceded to our request. To-morrow you go outside and walk upon the grass, which I believe will feel good to your feet."

"Lieutenant Holderness, I thank you," said Henry in such a tone of emphatic gratitude that Holderness flushed with pleasure.

"I have learned," continued Henry, "what a wonderful thing it is to walk on a little grass and to breathe air that I haven't breathed before."

"I understand," said Lieutenant Holderness, looking at the narrow walls, "and by Jove, I'm hoping that your people will never capture me."

"If they do, and they lock you up and I'm there, I shall do my best to get you out into the air, even as you have done it for me."

"By Jove, I think you would," said Holderness.

The hands of the two official enemies met in a hearty clasp. They were young and generous. The delights of life even as a prisoner now came in a swelling tide upon Henry. He had not known before that air could be so pure and keen, such a delight and such a source of strength to the lungs. The figure that had seemed to shrink within the narrow walls suddenly expanded and felt capable of anything. Strength flowed back in renewed volume into every muscle. Before him beyond the walls curved the dark green world, vital, intense, full of everything that he loved. It was there that he meant to go, and his confidence that he would escape rose higher than ever.

A swart figure passed him and a low voice said in his ear: "Watch the river! Always watch the river!"

It was Lajeunais who had spoken, and already he was twenty feet away, taking no notice of either Henry or Holderness, hurrying upon some errand, connected with his business of trapping and trading. But Henry knew that his words were full of meaning. Doubtless he had communicated in some manner with the four, and they were using him as a messenger. It looked probable. Lajeunais, like many of his race, had no love for the conquerors. He had given the word to watch the river, and Henry meant to do so as well as he could.

He waited some time in order to arouse no suspicion, and then he suggested to Holderness that they walk again upon the platform of the palisade. The lieutenant consented willingly enough, and presently they stood there, looking far up and down the river and across at the forests of Canada. There were canoes upon the stream, most of them small, containing a single occupant, but all of these occupants were Indians. Some of the savages had come from the shores of the Northern waters. Chippewas or Blackfeet, who were armed with bows and arrows and whose blankets were of skins. But they had heard of Detroit, and they brought furs. They would go back with bright blankets and rifles or muskets. Henry watched them with interest. He was trying to read some significance for him into this river and its passengers. But if the text was there it was unintelligible. He saw only the great shining current, breaking now and then into crumbling little waves under the gentle wind, and the Indian canoes, with their silent occupants reflected vividly upon its surface, like pictures in a burnished mirror. Again he strained with eye and mind. He examined every canoe. He forced his brain to construct ingenious theories that might mean something, but all came to naught.

"Strange people," said Holderness, who thought that Henry was watching the Indians with a curiosity like his own, merely that of one who sees an alien race.

"Yes, they're strange," replied Henry. "We must always consider the difference. In some things like the knowledge of nature and the wilderness, they are an old, old race far advanced. In most others they are but little children. Once I was a captive among them for a long time."

"Tell me about it," said Holderness eagerly.

Henry was willing for a double reason. He had no objection to telling about his captivity, and he wished to keep Holderness there on the palisade, where he could watch the river. While his eyes watched his tongue told a good tale. He had the power of description, because he felt intensely what he was saying. He told of the great forests and rivers of the West, of the vast plains beyond, of the huge buffalo herds that were a day in passing, and of the terrible storms that sometimes came thundering out of the endless depths of the plains. Holderness listened without interruption, and at the end he drew a long breath.

"Ah! that was to have lived!" he said. "One could never forget such a life, such adventures, but it would take a frame of steel to stand it!"

"I suppose one must be born to it," said Henry. "I've known no life but that of the wilderness, but my friend Paul, who has read books, often tells me of the world of cities beyond."

"Wouldn't you like to go there?" asked Holderness.

"To see it, yes, perhaps," replied Henry thoughtfully, "but not to stay long. I've nothing against people. I've some of the best friends that a man ever had, and we have great men in Kentucky, too, Boone, Kenton, Harrod, Logan, and the others, but think what a glorious thing it is to roam hundreds of miles just as you please, to enter regions that you've never seen before, to find new rivers, and new lakes, and to feel that with your rifle you can always defend yourself—that suits me. I suppose the time will come when such a life can't be lived, but it can be lived now and I'm happy that this is my time."

Holderness was quiet. He still felt the spell of the wilderness that Henry had cast over him, but, after a moment or two, it began to pass. His nature was wholly different. In his veins flowed the blood of generations that had lived in the soft and protected English lands, and the vast forests and the silence, brave man though he was, inspired him with awe.

Henry, meanwhile, still watched the passing canoes. The last of them was now far down the river, and he and Holderness looked at it, while it became a dot on the water, and then, like the others, sank from sight. Then he and his English friend walked out from the palisade upon the unfinished pier, and watched the twilight come over the great forest. This setting of the sun and the slow red light falling over the branches of the trees always appealed to Henry, but it impressed Holderness, not yet used to it, with the sense of mystery and awe.

"I think," said he, "that it is the silence which affects me most. When I stand here and look upon that unbroken forest I seem face to face with a primeval world into which man has not yet come. One in fancy almost could see the mammoth or great sabre tooth tiger drinking at the far edge of the river."

"You can see a deer drinking," said Henry, pointing with a long forefinger. Holderness was less keen-eyed, but he was able at length to make out the figure of the animal. The two watched, but soon the deepening twilight hid the graceful form, and then darkness fell over the stream which now flowed in a slow gray current. Behind them they heard the usual noises in the fort, but nothing came from the great forest in front of them.

"Still the same silence," said Holderness. "It grows more uncanny."

The last words had scarcely left his lips when out of that forest came a low and long wailing cry, inexpressibly sad, and yet with a decisive touch of ferocity. It sounded as if the first life, lonely and fierce, had just entered this primitive world. Holderness shivered, without knowing just why.

"It is the cry of a wolf," said Henry, "perhaps that of some outcast from the pack. He is probably both hungry and lonesome, and he is telling the world about it. Hark to him again!"

Henry was leaning forward, listening, and young Holderness did not notice his intense eagerness. The cry was repeated, and the wolf gave it inflections like a scale in music.

"It is almost musical," said Holderness. "That wolf must be singing a kind of song."

"He is," said Henry, "and, as you notice, it is almost a human sound. It is one of the easiest of the animal cries to imitate. It did not take me long to learn to do it."

"Can you really repeat that cry?" asked Holderness with incredulity.

Henry laughed lightly.

"I can repeat it so clearly that you cannot tell the difference," he said. "All the money I have is one silver shilling and I'll wager it with you that I succeed, you yourself to be the judge."

"Done," said Holderness, "and I must say that you show a spirit of confidence when you let me, one of the wagerers, decide."

Henry crouched a little on the timbers, almost in the manner of a wolf, and then there came forth not three feet from Holderness a long whining cry so fierce and sibilant that, despite his natural bravery, a convulsive shudder swept over the young lieutenant. The cry, although the whining note was never lost, rose and swelled until it swept over the river and penetrated into the great Canadian forest. Then it died slowly, but that ferocious under note remained in it to the last.

"By Jove!" was all that Holderness could say, but, in an instant, the cry rose again beside him, and now it had many modulations and inflections. It expressed hunger, anger and loneliness. It was an almost human cry, and, for a moment, Holderness felt an awe of the strange youth beside him. When the last variation of the cry was gone and the echo had died away, the lieutenant gravely took a shining shilling from his pocket and handed it to Henry.

"You win with ease," he said. "Listen, you do it so well that the real wolf himself is fooled."

An answering cry came from the wolf in the Canadian woods, and then the deep silence fell again over forest and river.

"Yes, I fooled him," said Henry carelessly, as he put the shilling in his pocket. "I told you it was one of the easiest of the animal cries to imitate."

But he was compelled to turn his face away again in order that Holderness might not see his shining eyes. They were there, the faithful four. Doubtless they had signaled many times before, but they had never given up hope, they had persisted until the answering cry came.

"Shall we go in?" he said to Holderness.

"I'm willing," replied the lieutenant. "You mustn't think any the less of me, will you, if I confess that I am still a little bit afraid of the wilderness at night? I've never been used to it, and to-night in particular that wolf's howl makes it all the more uncanny to me."

The night had come on, uncommonly chill for the period of the year, and Henry also was willing to go. But when he returned to his little room it seemed littler than ever. This was not a fit place to be a home for a human being. The air lay heavy on his lungs, and he felt that he no longer had the patience to wait. The signal of his comrades had set every pulse in his veins to leaping.

But he forced himself to sit down calmly and think it over. Lajeunais had told him to watch the river; he had watched and from that point the first sign had come. Then Lajeunais beyond a doubt meant him well, and he must watch there whenever he could, because, at any time, a second sign might come.

The next day and several days thereafter he was held in prison by order of Colonel de Peyster. The commander seemed to be in a vacillating mood. Now he was despondent, and then he had spells of courage and energy. Henry heard through Holderness that the negotiations with Timmendiquas were not yet concluded, but that they were growing more favorable. A fresh supply of presents, numerous and costly, had arrived from Niagara. The Shawnees and Miamis were eager to go at once against Kentucky. Only the Wyandots still demurred, demanding oaths from the King's commanders at Montreal and Quebec that all the tribes should be aided in case of a return attack by the Kentuckians.

"But I think that in a week or so—two weeks at the furthest—Timmendiquas will be on the march," said Holderness. "A few of our soldiers will go with them and the whole party will be nominally under the command of Colonel William Caldwell, but Timmendiquas, of course, will be the real leader."

"Are you going with them?" asked Henry.

"No, I remain here."

"I am very glad of that."

"Why?"

"Because you do not really know what an Indian raid is."

Henry's tone was so significant that Holderness flushed deeply, but he remained silent. In a little while he left, and Henry was again a prey to most dismal thoughts. Bird, with his army and his cannon, doubtless had reached Kentucky by this time and was doing destruction. Timmendiquas would surely start very soon—he believed the words of Holderness—and perhaps not a single settlement would escape him. It was a most terrible fate to be laid by the heels at such a time. Before, he had always had the power to struggle.

CHAPTER XII
THE CANOE ON THE RIVER

Two more weeks passed and de Peyster's conduct in regard to Henry was regulated again by fits and starts. Sometimes he was allowed to walk in the great court within the palisade. On the fourth night he heard the signal cry once more from the Canadian woods. Now, as on the first night, it was the voice of the owl, and he answered it from the window.

On the sixth day he was allowed to go outside, and, as before, Holderness was his escort. He noticed at once an unusual bustle and all the signs of extensive preparations. Many Indians of the various tribes were passing, and from the large brick building, used as a storehouse of arms and ammunition, they were receiving supplies. Despite their usual reserve all of them showed expectancy and delight and Henry knew at once that the great expedition under Timmendiquas, Caldwell and Girty was about to depart. If he had not known, there was one at hand who took a pleasure in enlightening him. Braxton Wyatt, in a royal uniform, stood at his elbow and said:

"Sorry to bid you good-by, Henry, because the stay at Detroit has been pleasant, but we go to-morrow, and I don't think much will be left of Kentucky when we get through. Pity that you should have to spend the time here while it is all going on. Timmendiquas himself leads us and you know what a man he is."

Lieutenant Holderness, who was with Henry, eyed Wyatt with strong disfavor.

"I do not think it fitting, Captain Wyatt, that you should speak in such a manner to a prisoner," he said.

But Wyatt, at home in the woods and sure of his place, had all the advantage. He rejoined insolently:

"You must realize, Lieutenant Holderness, that war in the American woods is somewhat different from war in the open fields of Europe. Moreover, as a lieutenant it is hardly your place to rebuke a captain."

Holderness flushed deeply and was about to speak, but Henry put his hand on his arm.

"Don't pay any attention to him, Lieutenant," he said. "He's a sort of mad dog, ready to bite anything that gets in his way. Come on, let's take another look at the river."

Holderness hesitated a moment, and then went with Henry. Wyatt's face was black with anger, but he did not dare to follow them and create a scene. While they were in the court the tumult was increased by an unexpected arrival at the western gate. Private Doran, unarmed, his hands bound behind him, his eyes bandaged, but otherwise undamaged, had suddenly appeared in the village, and was at once taken to the fort. Now, surrounded by a curious crowd, he seemed to be dazed, and to be frightened also. Henry saw at once that his fear was of his officers, and that it had not been caused by any suffering in captivity. In truth, Private Doran looked very well, having suffered no diminution of either girth or ruddiness. His fears in regard to his officers were justified, as he was taken at once before Colonel de Peyster, who examined him with the greatest severity.

But Private Doran's apprehensions gave him ready and clear answers. He had been taken, it was true, but it was by men of superhuman skill and intelligence. Then, blindfolded and arms bound, he had been driven away in the woods. How far he traveled he did not know, but when a camp was made it was in a dense forest. Nor did he have any idea in what direction it lay from Detroit. He was joined there by Private Myers who had been abducted in the same way. Their four captors had told them that they were held as hostages, and had many terrible threats, but they had not really suffered anything. One man called Shif'less Sol by the others had been menacing them with strange punishments of which they had never heard before, but with the juice of some herb he cured Private Myers of a bruise that he had received in the struggle when he was captured.

This examination was held in public in the court and Henry heard it all. He smiled at the mention of Shif'less Sol, knowing his flow of language, and his genuine aversion to all forms of cruelty. Finally, according to the continuation of Doran's tale, they had decided that the hostages were no longer necessary. Evidently they believed their friend had suffered no ill treatment, or some important movement was pending. Accordingly he was blindfolded, his arms bound, and he was led away in the night by the two men called Long Jim and Silent Tom. They left him toward morning, saying that the other captive would be delivered on the day following. When curs began to snap at his ankles he knew that he was near the village outside Detroit, and he shouted for help. The rest told itself.

Doran, after a severe rating, was sent about his business. Henry was very thoughtful. Private Doran had not told of crossing any river and hence the camp of his comrades must be on this side of the Detroit. But all the signals had come from the far shore. Doubtless Shif'less Sol had crossed over there to utter the cries and they must possess a boat, a supposition that chimed in well with the warning to him to watch the river. Reflection only deepened his conviction, and he resolved if possible to avoid the anger of de Peyster, as to be shut up again might ruin everything. He felt that the time to act, although he did not know just how and where, was coming soon.

A strong watch was set about both fort and village in order to trap the four the following night, when they came to deliver Private Myers. Both Girty and Blackstaffe told Colonel de Peyster that the forest runners would keep their promise, and the commander was exceedingly anxious to take the impudent rovers who had annoyed him so much. Henry heard something of it from Holderness and, for a moment, he felt apprehension, but he recalled all the skill and craft of his comrades. They would never walk into a trap.

The night turned quite dark with fleeting showers of rain. There was no moon and the stars were hidden. But about two hours before daylight there was a great outcry, and the sentinels, running to the spot, found a white man blindfolded and hands bound, tied in a thicket of briers. It was Private Myers, and his tale was practically the same as that of Private Doran. He had been led in the night, he knew not whither. Then, one of his captors, which one he could not say, as he was blindfolded, gave him a little push and he neither saw nor heard them any more. He had tried to come in the direction in which he thought Detroit lay, but he had become tangled among the briers, and then he had shouted at the top of his voice.

Colonel de Peyster was deeply disgusted. He addressed stern reproofs to the wretched private, who was not to blame, and bade him join his comrade in disgrace. The best Indian trackers were sent to seek the trail of the forest runners, which they found and followed only to end against the wide and deep river. The Indian trailers concurred in Henry's belief that the four had secured a boat, and they felt that it was useless to search on the other side.

Henry heard of it all very early, and that day during his hours of liberty in the court he kept a close watch on the river, but nothing occurred. Evidently the hour had not come for his friends to make whatever attempt they had in mind. He was convinced of it when from the palisade he saw that de Peyster had instituted a patrol on the river. Several Indian canoes, containing warriors, were constantly moving up and down. Henry's heart sank at the sight. He had felt sure all the time that his line of escape lay that way. Meanwhile Timmendiquas, the renegades and their powerful force were marching southward to destroy what Bird had left. He was seized with a terrible impatience that became a real torture. He learned that the patrol on the river had been established as a guard against the dreaded George Rogers Clark, who had made the threats against Detroit. Clark was so crafty that he might circle above the town and come down by the river, but in a week or so the alarm passed.

Henry spent the period of alarm in his prison, but when de Peyster's fears relaxed he was allowed the liberty of the court again. Neither Holderness nor Desmond was visible and he walked back and forth for a long time. He had grown thinner during his imprisonment, and much of the tan was gone from his face, but he did not feel any decrease of strength. As he walked he tested his muscles, and rejoiced that they were still flexible and powerful like woven wire. That morning he heard the call of the wolf from the Canadian shore, but he did not dare reply. A half hour later Colonel de Peyster himself accosted him.

"Well," said the commander in a tone of irony, "I see, young Mr. Ware, that you have not yet escaped."

"Not yet," replied Henry, "but I shall certainly do so."

Colonel de Peyster laughed. He was in great good humor with himself. Why should he not be? He had smoothed away the doubts of Timmendiquas and now that formidable chieftain was gone with a great force against Kentucky. The settlements would be destroyed, men, women and children, and de Peyster would have the credit of it.

"You are surely a confident youth," he said. "This boast of yours was made some time ago, and I do not see that you have made any progress. I'm afraid that you're a great talker and a small performer."

Henry was stung by his words, but he did not show any chagrin.

"I'm going to escape," he said, "and it will not be long, now, until I do so."

Colonel de Peyster laughed again and more loudly than before.

"Well, that's a proper spirit," he said, "and when you've gone you shall tell your friends that on the whole I have not treated you badly."

"I make no complaint," said Henry.

"And now, to show my generous feeling toward you," continued de Peyster, in whom the spirit of humor was growing, "you shall have luncheon with me in honor of your coming escape."

"I'm willing," said Henry, adapting himself to his mood. A life such as his and wonderful natural perception had endowed him with a sort of sixth sense. He began to have a premonition that what de Peyster intended as a joke would be the truth, and it made him all the more willing to join in what the commander intended should be a mockery.

De Peyster led the way to the room in which the first banquet with the Indian chiefs had been held, but now only Henry and he were present, except a soldier who brought food from the kitchen and who waited upon them.

"Sit down, Mr. Ware," said de Peyster with a flourish of both hand and voice. Henry quietly took the seat indicated on the opposite side of the table, and then the commander took his own also, while the attendant brought the food and drink. Henry saw that de Peyster was in an uncommon mood, and he resolved to humor it to the full.

"I regret more than ever that you're not one of us, my young friend," said the commander, surveying his prisoner's splendid proportions. "Expert as you are in the woods, you could soon rise to high command."

"Having started in on one side," said Henry lightly, "I cannot change to the other."

"Wyatt, who I understand was a youthful comrade of yours, has done it."

"Pray do not ask me to imitate any example furnished by Braxton Wyatt."

Colonel de Peyster laughed again.

"He is not an attractive youth, I confess," he said, "but you would count for much more than Braxton Wyatt with us."

"I shall never count at all," replied Henry. "I am for my own people always."

Colonel de Peyster, the Tory, flushed, but he continued:

"Think of the rewards under the King. This is a vast and fertile continent, and those who hold it for him will surely receive vast estates. Any one of us may be as great a feudal lord as Sir William Johnson has been."

"If you triumph," said Henry, although he spoke purposely in a light tone.

"There is no 'if'; we are bound to succeed, and now, sir, as we have eaten we shall drink to your escape."

The attendant poured two glasses of wine and Colonel de Peyster raised his, looking for a minute or two at the little bubbles as they broke.

"Here's to your escape," he said, casting an ironical glance over the edge.

"Here's to my escape," said Henry, meeting his gaze firmly and earnestly.

Then they drank.

"Upon my word, I believe that you mean what you say."

"Certainly."

De Peyster looked curiously at Henry.

"Come," he said, "we'll go outside. I think I'll keep my own eye on you for a little while."

When they emerged from the house a long plaintive howl came from the Canadian forest. A sort of shiver, as if he were looking into the future, ran through Henry's veins. All his premonitions were coming true.

"Did you hear that wolf?" asked de Peyster. "It is but a wilderness after all, and this is merely a point in it like a lighthouse in the sea. Come, we'll walk that way; it's about the only view we have."

Again that strange quiver ran through Henry's veins. Colonel de Peyster himself was leading exactly where the captive wished to go.

"I have often noticed you walking on the palisade with Lieutenant Holderness," said Colonel de Peyster; "now you can go there with me."

"I thank you for the invitation," said Henry, as the two climbed up one of the little ladders and stood side by side on the palisade. "Does not this view of the great river and the limitless forest beyond appeal to you, Colonel?"

"At times," replied Colonel de Peyster in a somewhat discontented tone. "It is the edge of a magnificent empire that we see before us, and I like the active service that I have been able to do for the King, but there are times when I wish that I could be back in New York, where I was born, and which the royal troops occupy. It is a trim city, with wealth and fashion, and one can enjoy life there. Now I wonder if that is one of the Indians whom I have had on watch on the river."

A light canoe containing a single warrior put out from the farther shore, where evidently it had been lying among the dense foliage on the bank. No particular purpose seemed to animate the warrior who sat in it. Both Colonel de Peyster and Henry could see that he was a powerful fellow, evidently a Wyandot. With easy, apparently careless strokes of the paddle, he brought his canoe in a diagonal course to a point near the middle of the stream. Then he began to play with the canoe, sending it hither and thither in long, gliding reaches, or bringing it up with a sharp jerk that would have caused it to overturn in hands less skillful. But so keen was the judgment and so delicate the touch of the warrior that it never once shipped water.

"Wonderful fellows, those Indians," said Colonel de Peyster. "How they do handle a canoe! It is almost like magic! I verily believe the fellow is showing off for our benefit."

"Maybe," said Henry.

"And it is a good show, too. Ah, I thought he would go that time; but look how quickly and delicately he righted himself. Such skill is truly marvelous!"

"It is," said Henry, who was watching the canoe and its occupant with an interest even greater than that of de Peyster. Up at the far corner of the palisade a sentinel was walking back and forth, his rifle on his shoulder, and at the other end another was doing likewise. Three or four officers off duty had also mounted the palisade and were watching the Indian's exhibition of skill.

Suddenly the warrior turned the canoe in toward the palisade at the point where the unfinished pier ran out toward the river. Raising himself on the canoe he uttered the long weird cry of the wolf, the same that had come more than once from the depths of the Canadian woods.

Then an extraordinary thing occurred. De Peyster was standing on the platform nearest the unfinished pier. Henry suddenly seized him by the shoulders, thrust himdown as if he were shot, ran along the platform and down the unfinished pier at his utmost speed. De Peyster was on his feet in an instant, and both sentinels on the alert, raised their rifles to take aim.

Henry did not check his speed for a second. A marvelous power, born of great strength and a great spirit, infused his whole frame. He rushed to the end of the pier, and concentrating his whole strength in one mighty effort, he leaped.

Never before had Detroit seen such a leap. The long body shot outward, the arms thrown parallel with the head, pointing toward the water. It was many feet from the head of the unfinished pier to the river, a leap that seemed superhuman, but Henry had the advantage of the run down the incline and the bracing of every nerve for the supreme effort. After he sprang, and for the few brief moments that he was cutting the air, he was scarcely conscious of what was passing, but he heard the crack of a rifle, and a bullet whizzing by him zip-zipped upon the surface of the water. One of the sentinels, exceeding alert, had fired instantly, but the other, finger on trigger, waited. Colonel de Peyster also drew a pistol and waited. Low cries, half of admiration, came from most of those on the battlements. The warrior in the canoe shot his little craft nearer in shore and then dropped gently over the far side. The canoe moved slowly down stream but its recent occupant was invisible.

Henry, flying like an arrow taking its downward slope, fell into the deep water. The tremendous leap was accomplished. He was dazed for a few moments and he was conscious of nothing except that his body was cutting through the current of the river. Then strength and memory came back, and he knew that the marksmen were watching. Turning slightly on his side he swam down stream but bearing toward the farther shore as fast as he could. The crack of that rifle shot, by some sort of mental reproduction roared in his ears, and the waters sang there also, but he was swimming for his life, and he still swam, while head and chest seemed ready to burst. Suddenly he saw a dark shape above him and at first he thought it was some huge fish. Then he saw that it was the body of a man hanging from another dark shape that seemed to rest upon the surface of the river.

Light came to him in an instant. It was the warrior in the canoe who had given him the signal. It could be none other than the incomparable Shif'less Sol. He shot upward, panting for air, and rose directly by the man and the canoe.

"Keep your head low, Henry," exclaimed the undoubted voice of the shiftless one. "So long as they can't see us behind the canoe they can't take certain aim, and we've more than a chance."

Henry held lightly to the side of the canoe and panted.

"That wuz shorely a mighty jump o' yourn," continued Shif'less Sol. "I don't think anybody else could hev done it, an' you come true ez a bullet when I give the signal. We've won, Henry! We've won ag'in' all the odds. Look out! Duck! that second fellow's goin' to shoot!"

The second sentinel had fired with good aim, so far as the canoe was concerned, as his bullet went through the upper part of it, but he could catch only glimpses of the figures behind it, and they were untouched. Colonel de Peyster also fired his pistol, but the bullet fell short. Two or three others on the battlements had rifles and they also took shots, without avail. The canoe was going very fast now, and always it bore steadily toward the further shore.

Henry felt the great tension relax. Glancing over the canoe he saw figures running up and down the palisade, but he knew that they were out of range. Blessed freedom! Once more before him lay the wilderness that he loved, and in which he was free to roam as he pleased. He had told de

Peyster that he would escape and he had kept his word. He looked now at Shif'less Sol, his faithful comrade, and, despite himself, he laughed. The water had washed most of the paint off the face of the shiftless one, leaving only stripes and bars.

"Sol," he said, "you're the best and smartest friend a man ever had, but just now you don't look like either an Indian or a white man."

"O' course not," replied Shif'less Sol readily, "an' fur the minute I ain't either. I'm a water dog, trampin' 'roun' in the Detroit River, an' enjoyin' myself. Ain't you happy, too, Henry?"

"I was never more so in my life," replied Henry emphatically, "and I can say, too, that this is about the finest swim I ever took. Are the others all right, Sol?"

"They shorely are. They're settin' over thar in the bushes waitin' for our boy Henry, who hez been out late, to come back home. I reckon, too, that they've seen everything that hez happened, includin' that everlastin' mighty big jump o' yourn."

"When a fellow jumps for his life he is apt to jump well," said Henry.

"I know I would," said Shif'less Sol. "Look, Henry, we're goin' to be pursued."

Henry glanced back toward the palisade, and saw troops and Indians at the water's edge, jumping into two boats. The Indians were especially quick, and, in a few moments, a boat under the influence of many paddles, shot far out into the stream. The Detroit is a wide river, and Henry glanced anxiously at the farther shore. Shif'less Sol noticed the look and he said:

"Tom an' Jim an' Paul haven't forgot how to shoot. Besides, my rifle is lyin' in the canoe, an' ez them fellers are comin' within range I think I'll give 'em a hint."

Henry held the boat steady with one hand and maintained their diagonal course toward the farther shore. Sol lifted his rifle from the canoe, and holding it across the gunwale with a single arm took aim and fired. One of the paddlers in the pursuing boat sprang up convulsively, then fell over the side and disappeared. But the boat came steadily on, the paddlers probably knowing that it would be a matter of great difficulty for the marksman to reload while in the water. The second boat containing the soldiers was also now coming fast.

But the shiftless one made no attempt to reload. He took another look at the Canadian shore and said to Henry:

"Both o' them boats will soon be in the range o' three fellers who are settin' on somethin' that don't move, an' who won't miss when they shoot."

He put his unloaded rifle back in the canoe, and the two, still keeping the little boat between them and their pursuers, swam with all their might. But the big boats filled with rowers or paddlers were gaining fast, when a crack came from the Canadian shore, and a warrior fell in the boat. A second shot wounded another in the shoulder. The boat hesitated, and when a third bullet found a mark, it stopped. The second boat stopped also. Henry and Sol made another great spurt, and in ten seconds their feet touched the earth.

"Quick, in here among the bushes!" cried the voice of Tom Ross.

Shif'less Sol, first taking his rifle from it, gave the canoe a push that sent it floating with the current, then he and Henry ran through the shallow water and up among the bushes and trees, just as bullets fired from both boats fell in the water behind them. Strong hands grasped Henry's and again the same strong hands pounded him on the back. Paul, Long Jim and Silent Tom welcomed him jubilantly.

"We thought it a risky scheme, but it's gone through," said Paul.

"So it has," said Shif'less Sol, "an' now we won't waste any time waitin' here for Injuns, Tories an' British to come an' take us."

He led the way into the deep forest, which closed completely about them after the first three or four steps, and Henry followed. Little streams of water ran from them as if they were young water gods, but Henry thought only of that most precious of all gifts, his recovered freedom, and, drawing deep breaths of delight, ran at Shif'less Sol's heels. Paul was just behind him, Long Jim followed Paul, and Tom Ross covered the rear.

Thus they continued for a long time. They had little fear of pursuit by the soldiers, but they knew the Indians might pick up the trail and follow. Yet it would be a hard thing to do, as Shif'less Sol led across brooks and through thickets and deep wood. He did not stop for a full hour, when they all sat down on fallen logs, and drew deep breaths. Henry did not notice until then that Long Jim carried an extra rifle. Shif'less Sol observed Henry's glance and he laughed with quiet satisfaction.

"It's fur you, Henry," he said. "We took it from one o' them soldiers we captured. He had no business with a good Kentucky rifle, which must hev been took from some o' our own people, an' so we saved it fur you. Paul has a double-barreled pistol fur you which we got from a Frenchman, Tom has an extra hatchet an' knife, an' among us we hev plenty o' ammunition fur both rifle an' pistol."

They passed over the complete equipment and again Henry rejoiced. He had not only escaped, but once more he was fully armed, ready to dare anything, and able to do anything.

"What a good lot of fellows you are!" he said to his comrades.

"But we couldn't hev done anything ef you hadn't been such a terrible long jumper," said Shif'less Sol with a grin.

"Do you hear any sounds of pursuit?" asked Paul.

None could detect anything, and Tom went back a little space on their trail, returning in a few minutes with the news that there were no indications of a hostile presence. Hence they rested a while longer and the clothing of Henry and Shif'less Sol dried in the sunshine. When they renewed their flight they proceeded at ease, all the while through a densely wooded country, and Paul gave Henry a brief account of the doings of the four.

"We could tell by the signs just how you were captured," he said, "and we followed close. We came to the very walls of Detroit and we secretly made friends with some of the French in the town."

"There was one Pierre Louis Lajeunais, was there not?"

"Yes, and he was the most valuable. We took the two sentinels, because we did not know what de Peyster would do with you, and, as we wrote, we wanted hostages against ill-treatment. When we found at last that you were to be held only as a prisoner we sent them back, and, for the rest, we trusted to luck, skill and the chance that you might see the warrior in the canoe on the river and understand."

"Fortune seemed to favor us through everything," said Henry, "and now I suppose we had better keep on until we are absolutely sure the Indians will not pick up our trail and give us a fight. As you boys probably know, we have no time to waste."

"We know," said Paul. "Kentucky is calling to us and we are going there as fast as we can."

The night found them far from Detroit. When the twilight turned into the night they were in woods so dense that it seemed as if man had never been there before. There was no turf under the close, spreading branches, but the ground was densely covered with the fallen leaves of last year. Everywhere they lay, a soft, dry carpet, and the five sank down upon them luxuriously.

"Here we rest," said Paul.

"Yes, here we rest, all except one who will watch," said Shif'less Sol, who for the present was in command. "Now we'll eat a little, an' then I think sleep will be the most welcome thing in the world to us."

Nobody said no, and the dried venison was brought from their packs. They also gave further proofs of their foresight for Henry by producing a pair of fine blankets from Tom's roll.

"It was Lajeunais who got those for us," said Tom. "That wuz shorely a fine Frenchman. I hope that some day I'll go huntin' an' trappin' with him."

It was arranged that Tom should keep the first watch and Jim the second, and the others disposed themselves in silence between their blankets. It was summer now, but the nights were cool and they were very snug within the blankets.

Henry, as he relaxed mentally and physically, felt a deep sense of gratitude. It seemed to him in this life of his in the wilderness, engaged in a cause surrounded by dangers, that a protecting hand was constantly stretched out in his behalf. He saw through a narrow opening in the leaves the blue sky and the great stars sailing high. The intense feeling, half religious and half poetic, that often swayed woodsmen, both red and white, stirred him now. Surely there was a divinity in the skies, the God of the white man, the Aieroski of the Mohawk, the Manitou of the Wyandot, one and the same! Never would he despair when that mighty hand could stretch itself forth from the infinite and save him. Thinking thus, he fell asleep and slept peacefully all through the night.

CHAPTER XIII. ON THE GREAT LAKE

When Henry awoke at dawn, all the weariness from his great efforts was gone, and he looked upon a world full of beauty. The unbroken forest of deep green bore a luminous tint, light and golden, from the early sunshine. Free of body and soul, it was the brilliant world that he had known so long, and he was ready once more for any task that might lie before them. Long Jim had already prepared breakfast, and he turned a benevolent gaze upon Henry.

"Ain't it fine," he said, "to have all the family reunited ag'in?"

"It certainly is," said Henry joyously, "and you surely stuck by the missing member in masterly fashion."

"Wa'al, you've stuck by us jest ez hard many a time," said Long Jim meditatively. "Paul, what wuz the name uv the feller that stuck by the other feller, the only big one, that got away from Troy after the Greeks rode into the town inside a hoss?"

"You're thinking of the faithful Achates, Jim," replied Paul, "and Æneas was the name of the big one to whom he was faithful."

"Yes, that's the feller. Henry, you're our Æneas, an' I'm an Achates; Paul's another, Tom's another and Sol's another. Uv course we couldn't go away without our Æneas, an' while I'm talkin' I want to say, Paul, that the tale about the takin' uv Troy is the tallest hoss story ever told. Ef it wuzn't writ in the books I wouldn't believe it. Think uv your fightin' off a hull army fur ten years or so, an' then draggin' that army into your town inside a wooden hoss. It can't be so. I've knowed some pow'ful liars myself, but the tribe must hev gone down hill a lot since the days uv them ancients."

Paul merely laughed and took another bite out of his venison steak.

"Anyway, Henry," said Shif'less Sol, "ef you've been Æneas you're goin' to be the wandering 'Lysses fur a while, an' we're goin' to be fightin' Greeks, sailin' right along with you."

"What do you mean?" asked Henry in astonishment.

"Tell him, Paul," said the shiftless one. "Saplin' hez cooked so well, an' I'm so busy eatin' I can't spare time fur talk."

"We felt sure we'd rescue Henry," said Paul, "and we arranged everything so we could get back South as fast as we could. Knowing that the woods were full of warriors and that we didn't want to be interrupted in our travels, we took a big boat one night from Detroit—I suppose we stole it, but you have a right to steal from an enemy in war—and carried it off down the river, hiding it among thick bushes at the mouth of a creek, where we're sure it's now resting securely, say five or six miles from this spot. We also gathered a lot of stores, food and such things, and put them on the boat. It was another risk, but we took that also, and I'm confident that our good genius will save the boat and stores for us. If they're there waiting for us all right we're going down the river and then across Lake Erie. It will save us a lot of time."

"Fine! fine!" exclaimed Henry with enthusiasm. "You've done well. It will be a lot easier and faster for us going so far by boat."

"An' we'll see one uv the big lakes, too," said Long Jim.

"We shorely will," said Shif'less Sol.

In a few minutes they were on the march again, and found the boat undisturbed at the mouth of the creek. It was a stout craft with a sail, and lockers for stores. Doubtless Colonel de Peyster had attributed its disappearance to some of his own Indians who could not always be trusted, but in the press of military preparations he had found no time to seek it.

"Now," said Shif'less Sol, "we'll take to the river. We may meet enemies thar, but it won't be ez long a trip ez the one we took down the Missip. Besides, ef we do meet enemies they ain't likely to be in big force ez most all the warriors seem to be drawed off fur the expeditions ag'inst Kentucky."

"At any rate we'll risk it, as we have risked many other things," said Henry.

The five embarked, and set sail fearlessly upon the river. Nevertheless, they did not neglect caution. They kept close to the Canadian shore, where they were in the shadow of the dense forest, and at least three were always on the watch with ready rifles across their knees. Yet they saw no enemy. This was the heart of the Indian country and the canoes of the warlike Northwestern tribes often floated on these waters, but to-day the five had the river to themselves. Peace was everywhere. Birds sang in the neighboring woods. Now and then a fish leaped from the water and sank back in a mass of bubbles. The broad river was a sheet of gold, and then a sheet of silver as the sun shifted.

Henry appreciated all this rest and ease. He admired still more the foresight and daring of his comrades which enabled them to travel in such a luxurious way and so far. He examined carefully the weapons they had secured for him and saw that they were all of the first class. He also opened the various lockers and found them filled with venison, jerked buffalo meat, such luxuries as bread and coffee, and large quantities of powder and lead.

"We found part of these in the boat," said Paul, "and it was your friend Lajeunais, who helped us to get the remainder. We do not go to sea unprovided."

"You've all done so well," said Henry lazily, "that I'm not going to bother myself about anything."

He put his double blankets under his head as a pillow and lay back luxuriously. Their good boat moved steadily on, the sail doing the work, while one of their number steered.

"I hope the wind will continue to blow," said Jim Hart, gazing admiringly at Henry, "'cause ef it don't we'll then hev to git our oars an' row. An' it would spoil the purtiest picture uv a lazy feller I ever saw. Why, I never saw Shif'less Sol hisself look lazier or happier."

Henry laughed. He knew that Jim Hart would have died in his defense.

"I am lazy, Jim," he admitted. "I never felt so lazy in my life before. I like to lie here and look at the river and the country."

"It's a fine big river," said Shif'less Sol, "but we can't see much of the country because of the trees, which shoot up so thick an' close on either bank, but I've heard that it ain't really a river, jest the stream o' water pourin' out o' them mighty lakes to the north into them lakes to the south, which ain't so mighty as the others, but which are mighty anyhow."

"It's true," said Paul. "All of this is lake water which runs through the other lakes, too, and then out by a tremendous big river, hundreds of miles to the Atlantic Ocean."

"When God made this chain uv lakes an' rivers he done one uv his biggest an' finest jobs," said Tom Ross reverentially.

They moved on their course slowly but steadily. Once they saw a canoe near the further shore, containing a lone occupant.

"It's a squaw," said Shif'less Sol, "an' she's pulled in near the land so she kin jump an' run ef we make for her."

"Like ez not she thinks we're hunters or French from the fort," said Long Jim.

"At any rate, we'll soon leave her far behind," said Henry.

The breeze stiffened and she quickly dropped out of sight. Nor did they see any other human being that day. At night they anchored close inshore, among bushes and reeds, where they remained undisturbed until the morning. The remainder of the journey down the river passed in the same peace and ease, and then Paul, who was in the prow, caught a glimpse of a broad expanse which looked silvery white in the distance.

"The lake! the lake!" he cried eagerly.

They swept triumphantly over the last reach of the river and out upon the broad bosom of Lake Erie. In their earlier voyage down the Mississippi they had learned how to use a sail, and now when they were about a mile from land they took in the sail and looked about them.

The great inland fresh water seas of North America aroused the greatest interest, even awe, among the earlier explorers, and there was not one among the five who did not look with eager eyes upon the ocean of waters. They were better informed, too, than the average woodsman concerning the size and shape of this mighty chain.

"You look west and you look south an' you don't see nothin' but water," said Long Jim.

"And they say that the whole grand chain is fifteen hundred miles long," said Paul, "and that Lake Superior reaches a width of three hundred miles."

"It's a lot o' water," said Shif'less Sol, trailing his hand over the side, "an' while I'd like to explore it, I guess that the sooner we cross it the better it will be for what we're tryin' to do."

"You're right," said Henry. "We'll set the sail again and tack as fast as we can to the south."

The sail was set, and the boat, heeling over under a good breeze, moved rapidly. Paul and Henry watched with pleasure the white water foaming away on either side of the prow, and Long Jim also watched the trailing wake at the stern. Used to rivers but not to lakes, they did not really appreciate what dangers might await them on the bosom of Erie. Meanwhile the lake presented to them a most smiling surface. The waters rippling before the wind lay blue under a blue sky. The wind with its touch of damp was fresh and inspiring. Behind them the shore, with its great wall of green, sank lower and lower, until at last it passed out of sight. Long Jim, who sat in the stern watching, then spoke.

"Boys," he said, "fur the fust time in the life uv any uv us thar ain't no land. Look to the east an' look to the west, look to the north an' look to the south an' thar ain't nothin' but water. The world uv land hez left us."

There was a certain awe in Jim's tone that impressed them as they looked and saw that he spoke the truth. Their world was now one of water, and they felt how small was the boat that lay between them and the tremendous power of the lake.

It was now somewhat past midday and the sun was uncommonly bright. The wind began to die, and the little waves no longer chased one another over the surface of the lake. No air gathered in the sail and presently the boat stopped.

"Now wouldn't this make you mad?" exclaimed Shif'less Sol. "We can't move at all unless we git out the oars an' row, an' a lazy man like me ain't fond o' rowin' seventy or eighty miles across a big lake."

Nor was the prospect pleasant to any of them. A little while ago they were moving swiftly at ease; now they rocked slightly in the swell, but did not go forward an inch. Hopeful that the wind would soon rise again they did not yet take to the oars. Meanwhile it was growing warmer. The reflection of the sun upon the water was dazzling, and they spread the sail again, not to catch the wind but as an awning to protect them from the burning rays.

They also used the interval for food and drink, and as the wind still did not rise they were thinking of taking to the oars as a last resort when Henry called their attention to the southwest.

"See that black spot down there," he said. "It seems to be only a few inches either way, but it doesn't look natural."

"I'd call it a cloud," said Tom Ross judicially.

"An' clouds ain't what we're wantin' jest now," said Jim Hart.

Henry rose from his luxurious reclining position and gazed long and with great care at the black spot. He knew as well as Jim Hart that it was a cloud and he saw that it was growing. But a few inches across the horizon before, it stretched to feet and then to yards. Meanwhile not a breath of air stirred, the deep waters were waveless and the air hung hot and heavy about them. Henry had heard that dangerous storms came up very fast on the great lakes, and, although with no experience as a sailor except on rivers, he believed that one would soon be upon them.

"Boys," he said, "look how that cloud grows. I believe we're in for a big wind and storm. We'd better take down our mast, make everything tight and strong, and get ready with the oars."

All at once Henry resumed command, and the others instantly accepted it as the most natural and proper thing in the world. The mast was unshipped, it and the sail were lashed down, everything that was loose was put in the lockers, or was tied securely. Meanwhile the cloud grew with amazing rapidity. While the east and north were yet full of blazing light the south and west were darkening. A draught of cold wind came. The waters, motionless hitherto, suddenly heaved convulsively. Low thunder rolled, and the lightning flashed across the troubled waters. The five felt awe. They were familiar with great storms, but never before had they been in one with no land in sight. The little boat, which alone lay between them and the depths of the lake, became smaller and smaller. But the five, although they felt more tremors than when going into battle, sat with their oars in the thwarts, ready to fight as best they could the storm which would soon rush down upon them.

The cold wind came in raw gusts, and there was rain on its edge which cut like hail. The boat rose and fell with the increasing waves. Henry took the helm, and, with the others at the oars, strove to keep the boat as steady as possible. With the usual foresight of borderers, they had already covered up their rifles, pistols and ammunition. Even on the water they would not neglect this precaution. Now the darkness spread to the entire heavens, the thunder crashed heavily, like invisible batteries firing, the lightning flared two or three times, showing the surface of the lake far and wide tinted a ghastly gray, and then, with a shriek and a roar, the wind struck them.

The boat heeled over so far on its side that Henry thought at first they were gone, but after hanging for a moment or two, seemingly undecided, it righted itself, and the five uttered simultaneous sighs of relief. Yet the boat had shipped water which Paul began to bail out with his cap, while the others strove at the oars, seeking to meet and ride the waves which followed one another swiftly. The rain meanwhile was driving hard, and they were drenched, but they had no time to think of such things. Every effort was bent towards keeping afloat the boat, which was rushing before the wind they knew not whither.

"There's a pail in that little locker," shouted Henry to Paul, "you can do better with that than with your cap."

Paul opened the locker, and took out the pail. Then with great difficulty he closed the locker again, and set to work keeping the boat clear of water. He made much better progress with the pail, but now and then wind, rain and the rocking of the boat together threw him to his knees. His comrades were working full as hard. They made up for lack of experience with strength, intuitive quickness and courage. Often the boat seemed to be submerged by the crest of a great wave, but every time it emerged right side up with the industrious Paul still bailing.

Meantime the wind kept up a continuous screaming, almost like that of a wild animal, a fearful sound which got upon the nerves of them all. Except when the lightning flared they were surrounded by a darkness like that of night. Suddenly Tom Ross shouted in a voice that could be heard above the whistling of the wind:

"Jim, you're seein' the Great Lakes at last!"

Then he bent grimly to his oar.

Luckily the boat they had taken was a strong one, built partly for the storms which sometimes drive with such force across Erie, the shallowest of the five Great Lakes, and with the aid of the strong arms at the helm and oars she managed to ride every wave and swell. But it was a long time before the wind began to abate and they were half dead with exhaustion. Moreover they were covered with bruises where they had been hurled against the sides of the boat, and now and then they were almost blinded by the water dashing into their faces. Shif'less Sol afterward said that he felt as if some strong-armed man were slapping his cheek every minute or two.

Yet hope began to return. They had kept afloat so long that they felt sure of keeping afloat all the time. There came a moment when the water from the lake ceased to enter the boat, although the rain still drenched them. The darkness lightened somewhat and Henry looked anxiously about them. He was trying to reckon in what direction they had come, but there was nothing that would enable him to tell. He saw nothing but the waste of waters. He knew that the wind had changed its course and they might now be driving back toward Detroit. He longed for light that might show them whence they had come.

Now the storm, after declining, suddenly acquired new strength. The darkness closed in again thicker than ever and the hearts of the five sank. They were so tired that they felt they could not repel a second attack. Yet they summoned their courage anew and strove even more desperately than before. Another hour passed and Henry, who was looking ahead, suddenly saw a dark mass. He recognized it instantly and gave the sharp cry:

"Land!"

The three who were straining at the oars looked up, and Paul in his surprise let drop his tin pail. Henry had made no mistake. They could see that it was land despite the darkness and the driving rain. There was a low shore, with trees growing almost to the water's edge, and they thought at first that it was the western coast of the lake, but as they swiftly drove nearer Henry saw water both to right and left, and he knew that it was a little island. If they kept a straight course they would strike upon it, but with such violence that shipwreck was inevitable. Strong and agile as they were they might possibly escape with their lives.

"Boys!" cried Henry, above the shouting of the wind, "we must make that island or we'll surely be lost in the storm!"

"It's so!" Shif'less Sol shouted back, "but how are we to do it?"

"Paul, you take the helm," said Henry, "and steer to the left of the island. The wind is blowing straight ahead and if we can come in behind the land we may strike a little stretch of comparatively smooth water."

Paul took the helm and Henry seized a pair of oars. Paul could steer well, but Henry's strength would be needed now. On they drove, the rain beating hard on their backs, and the surf from the lake also driving into the boat. Paul steered steadily and the four bent powerfully on the oars, driving the boat in a wide curve to the left, where it would avoid possible rocks and shoals.

Yet it was hard to bring the boat even diagonally against the wind. The waves turned it on its side and it trembled violently. The four labored at the oars until every pulse in their temples throbbed. Now the low shore and the green forest were coming very near, and Henry glanced at them from time to time. He was afraid that the wind and the waves would bring them back again and dash them upon the island, despite all their efforts. But the boat shot past fifty yards to the left, ran for a quarter of a mile along the edge of a low green island, and then with a mighty effort they brought it in behind the land.

Here in a little space where the wind was beating itself to pieces against the trees in front of it, the sea was comparatively calm, and Paul deftly swung the boat about. His sharp eyes noticed a little cove, and, the four at the oars pulled for it with all their might. A minute, two minutes and they were in the cove and in safety. They had entered it by a channel not more than a dozen feet wide, and Paul's steering had been delicate and beautiful. Now the four drew in their oars and they swung in waters as quiet as those of a pond ruffled only by a little breeze. It it was an inlet not more than twenty yards across and it was sheltered about by mighty trees. The rain still poured upon them, but there was no longer any danger of shipwreck.

The momentum had carried the boat to the far edge of the pool, and Henry sprang out. His muscles were so stiff and sore that, for a moment or two, he reeled, but he seized a bough and held fast. Then Tom tossed him a rope from the locker and in a minute the boat was secured head and stern to the trees. Then they stood upon land, wet but solid land, and in every heart was devout thankfulness.

"The land for me every time," said Long Jim. "I like to feel something under my feet that I don't sink into. Ef an accident happens on land, thar you are, but ef an accident happens on the water, whar are you?"

"What I need most is a pair o' kid gloves," said Shif'less Sol. "I've got purty tough hands, but I think them oars hez took all the skin off the inside o' 'em."

"What we all need most," said Henry, "is shelter. We are soaked through and through, and we are stiff with bruises and exertion. Suppose we bail out the boat and try to use the sail as a sort of roof or cover."

They were wedged in so closely among the trees that together with the boughs and the mast, which they set in place again, they managed to fasten the sail in such a manner that it caught most of the rain as it drove towards them. Everyone also gave up one of his pair of blankets for the same purpose, and then they were protected fairly. Still fearing colds and stiffness of the muscles they took off all their wet clothing and rubbed their bodies long and thoroughly. While they were at this work the rain decreased, and after a while ceased. The wind still blew and they heard branches crashing down from the trees, but none fell over them. They did not reclothe themselves but hung their soaked garments on boughs, and then everyone wrapped himself about with the dry blanket that he had left from his pair, the other still doing duty as a rain shield. Although the air was quite cool after the heavy rain, the blankets protected them and they began to feel a pleasant warmth. Their spirits indeed were improved so much that they could jest.

"One would scarcely expect to see five Roman senators in their togas cast away on this little island in Lake Erie," said Paul, "but here we are."

Long Jim with his bare legs as far as his knees protruding from his blanket was prowling among the lockers.

"What's the noble senator lookin' fur?" asked Shif'less Sol.

"I'm lookin' fur somethin' to help you an' all uv us," replied Long Jim, "while you're settin' thar lazy an' wuthless. We didn't search this boat very well when we took it, hevin' other pow'ful important matters on hand, but them that owned it wuz men uv sense. Lots uv useful things are hid away in these little lockers. Ah, look at this! Shorely it's industry an' enterprise that gits the rewards!"

He drew triumphantly from the corner of a locker an iron coffee pot and a large package of ground coffee.

"Now I've got the coffee an' the coffee pot," he said, "an' ef the rest uv you hev got sense enough to build a fire I'll hev you feelin' like kings ten minutes after that fire is built. Thar are two pewter cups in that locker also, so nothin' is lackin'."

"You've certainly done your part, Jim," said Henry, "an' now we'll try to do ours, although it won't be any easy job."

They had not been woodsmen all their lives for nothing. The ground under the trees was covered more than a foot deep with leaves, the accumulation of many years. It is difficult for water to penetrate all the way through such a carpet, and turning them over they found here and there some leaves fairly dry, which they put in a heap. They also cut off all the wet outside from some dead boughs with their strong hunting knives, and then shaved off dry splinters which they put with the leaves.

The four gathered in a group about the little heap, looking very odd in their blankets, with their bare ankles and shoulders projecting, and Henry began work with the flint and steel. After many efforts he set fire to the finer of the splinters, and then the flames spread to the leaves and larger pieces of wood. They had succeeded, and as Shif'less Sol fed the fire, he said triumphantly to Long Jim:

"Now, Jim, everything's ready fur you. Bring on your coffee an' b'il it. I want fourteen cups myself."

Jim set to work at once, showing with pride his skill in such a task. The flames were not permitted to rise high, but they burned rapidly, making a fine bed of coals, and within ten minutes the coffee was ready. Then they drank, warming themselves through and through, and receiving new life. They also warmed some of the deer and buffalo steaks over the coals, and ate real bread from the lockers.

"All things must come to an end," said Shif'less Sol, with a sigh, when he could eat no more. "It's on sech 'casions ez this that I realize it. I wish I wuz ez hungry ez I wuz a little while ago, an' could eat all over ag'in."

"We've been in big luck," said Henry. "If it hadn't been for this little island I believe we would have been wrecked. It's true, too, that we'll have to go around in our blankets for a while yet, because I don't believe those clothes of ours will dry before morning."

"Suits me," said Jim Hart, as with proverbial caution he put out the fire after finishing cooking. "I wouldn't mind goin' 'roun' in a blanket in summer. Injuns do it an' they find it pow'ful healthy. Now the wind is dyin' an' the clouds are passin' away, but it's goin' to be dark anyhow. Jedgin' from the looks uv things the night is right here."

The wind undoubtedly was sinking fast. The great storm was blowing itself away as rapidly as it had blown up. The trees ceased to shake and moan, and looking down the channel whence they had entered, the five saw that the high waves no longer rolled across the surface of the lake. In a few minutes more the last breath of the wind whistled off to eastward. A cold twilight fell over the little isle of safety and the great lake, of whose rage they had been such vivid witnesses.

CHAPTER XIV. A TIMELY RESCUE

Jim Hart sat down in the boat, drew his legs up under his blanket, shivered as he took a long look down the channel at the cold gray lake, and said:

"Boys, you know how I wanted to see one of the great lakes; well, I hev saw, an' hevin' saw I think the look will last me a long time. I think Injuns wuz right when they put pow'ful spirits on these lakes, ready to make an end of anybody that come foolin' with thar region. The land fur me hereafter. Why, I wuz so skeered an' I had to work so hard I didn't hev time to git seasick."

"But we have to go on the lake again, Jim," said Henry. "This is an island."

Jim sighed.

Henry looked at the dense forest that enclosed the cove, and he thought once of exploring the islet even if it were in the night, but the woods were so thick and they still dripped so heavily with the rain, although the latter had ceased some time ago, that he resolved to remain by the boat. Besides it was only an islet anyway, and there was no probability that it was inhabited.

"I think," he said, "that we'd better fasten our clothes so tightly that they won't blow away, and sleep in the boat. Two will keep watch, and as I have had the most rest I'll be sentinel until about one in the morning, and then Tom can take my place."

The agreement was quickly made. They took down the sail and the wet blankets, spread them out to dry, while the four, disposing themselves as best they could, quickly went to sleep. Henry sat in the prow, rifle across his knees, and thought that, despite dangers passed and dangers to come, Providence had been very kind to them.

The darkness thinned by and by and a fine moon came out. Beads of water still stood upon the leaves and boughs, and the moonshine turned them to silver. The bit of forest seemed to sparkle and in the blue heavens the great stars sprang out in clusters. The contrast between the night and the day was startling. Now everything seemed to breathe of peace, and of peace only. A light wind rose and then the silver beads disappeared from leaf and bough. But it was a friendly wind and it sang most pleasantly among the trees. Under its influence the garments of the five would dry fast, and as Henry looked at them and then down at his comrades, wrapped in their "togas" he felt an inclination to laugh. But this desire to laugh was only proof of his mental relaxation, of the ease and confidence that he felt after great dangers passed.

Certainly his comrades were sleeping well. Not one of them moved, and he saw the blankets across their chests rising and falling with regularity. Once he stepped out of the boat and walked down to the entrance of the channel, whence he looked out upon the surface of the lake. Save for the islet he saw land nowhere, north, south, east or west. The great lake stretched away before them apparently as vast as the sea, not gray now, but running away in little liquid waves of silver in the moonlight. Henry felt its majesty as he had already felt its might. He had never before appreciated so keenly the power of nature and the elements. Chance alone had put in their way this little island that had saved their lives.

He walked slowly back and resumed his place in the boat. That fine drying wind was still singing among the trees, making the leaves rustle softly together and filling Henry's mind with good thoughts. But these gave way after a while to feelings of suspicion. His was an exceedingly sensitive temperament. It often seemed to the others—and the wilderness begets such beliefs—that he received warnings through the air itself. He could not tell why his nerves were affected in this manner, but he resolved that he would not relax his vigilance a particle, and when the time came for him to awaken Tom Ross he decided to continue on guard with him.

"'Tain't wuth while, Henry," remonstrated Ross. "Nothin's goin' to happen here on an islan' that ain't got no people but ourselves on it."

"Tom," replied Henry, "I've got a feeling that I'd like to explore this island."

"Mornin' will be time enough."

"No, I think I'll do it now. I ought to go all over it in an hour. Don't take me for an Indian when I'm coming back and shoot at me."

"I'd never mistake a Roman senator in his togy for an Injun," replied Tom Ross grinning.

Henry looked at his clothes, but despite the drying wind they were still wet.

"I'll have to go as a Roman after all," he said.

He fastened the blanket tightly about his body in the Indian fashion, secured his belt with pistol, tomahawk and knife around his waist, and then, rifle in hand, he stepped from the boat into the forest.

"Watch good, Tom," he said. "I may be gone some time."

"You'll find nothin'."

"Maybe so; maybe not."

The woods through which Henry now passed were yet wet, and every time he touched a bough or a sapling showers of little drops fell upon him. The patch of forest was dense and the trees large. The trees also grew straight upward, and Henry concluded at once that he would find a little distance ahead a ridge that sheltered this portion of the island from the cruel north and northwest winds.

His belief was verified as the rise began within three hundred yards. It ascended rather abruptly, having a total height of seventy or eighty feet, and seeming to cross the island from east to west. Standing under the shadow of a great oak Henry looked down upon the northern half of the island, which was quite different in its characteristics from the southern half. A portion of it was covered with dwarfed vegetation, but the rest was bare rock and sand. There were two or three inlets or landing places on the low shore. As the moonlight was now good, Henry saw all over this portion of the island, but he could not detect any sign of human habitation.

"I suppose Tom is right," he said to himself, "and that there is nothing to be seen."

But he had no idea of going back without exploring thoroughly, and he descended the slope toward the north. The way led for a little distance among the shrub bushes from which the raindrops still fell upon him as he passed, and then he came into an open space almost circular in shape and perhaps thirty yards in diameter. Almost in the center of the rock a spring spouted and flowed away through a narrow channel to the lake. On the far side of the spring rose four upright stakes in a row about six feet apart. Henry wondered what they meant and he approached cautiously, knowing that they had been put there by human hands.

Some drifting clouds now passed and the moonlight shone with a sudden burst of splendor. Henry was close to the stakes and suddenly he shuddered in every vein. They were about as high as a man's head, firmly fastened in the ground, and all of them were blackened and charred somewhat by fire, although their strength was not impaired. At the base of every one lay hideous relics. Henry shivered again. He knew. Here Indians brought their captives and burned them to death, partly for the sake of their own vengeance and partly to propitiate the mighty spirits that had their abode in the depths of the great lakes. He was sure that his comrades and he had landed upon a sacrificial island, and he resolved that they should depart at the very first light in the morning.

This island which had seemed so fine and beautiful to him suddenly became ghastly and repellent, but his second thought told him that they had nothing to fear at present. It was not inhabited. The warriors merely came here for the burnings, and then it was quite likely that they departed at once.

Henry examined further. On the bushes beyond the stakes he found amulets and charms of bone or wood, evidently hung there to ward off evil spirits, and among these bushes he saw more bones of victims. Then he noticed two paths leading away from the place, each to a small inlet, where the boats landed. Calculating by the moon and stars he could now obtain a general idea of the direction in which they had come and he was sure that the nearest part of the mainland lay to the west. He saw a dark line there, and he could not tell whether it was the shore or a low bank of mist.

Then he made a diligent exploration of all this part of the island, assuring himself further that it had never been occupied permanently. He saw at one place the ruins of a temporary brush shelter, used probably during a period of storm like that of the night before, and on the beach he found the shattered remains of a large canoe. Henry looked down at the broken canoe thoughtfully. It may have been wrecked while on its way with a victim for the stake, and if the warriors had perished it might have been due to the wrath of the Great Spirit.

He walked slowly back over the ridge through the forest and down to the boat. Tom saw him coming but said nothing until he stepped into the boat beside him.

"You stayed a long time," he said, "but I see you've brought nothing back with you."

"It's true that I've brought nothing with me, but I've found a lot."

"What did you find, Henry?"

"I found many bones, the bones of human beings."

"Men's bones?"

"Yes. I'm sure that it is an island to which Indiana come to burn their prisoners, and although none are here now—I've looked it all over—I don't like it. There's something uncanny about it."

"An' yet it's a pretty little islan', too," said Tom Ross, thoughtfully, "an' mighty glad we wuz to see it yes'day, when we wuz druv before that howlin' an' roarin' storm, with but one chance in a hundred uv livin'."

"That's so," said Henry. "We owe the island a debt of gratitude if others don't. I've no doubt that if it were not for this little piece of land we should have been drowned. Still, the sooner we get away the better. How have the others been getting on, Tom?"

"Sleepin' ez reg'lar an' steady ez clocks. It's wuth while to see fellers snoozin' away so happy."

Henry smiled. The three, as they lay in the boat, breathing deeply and unconscious of everything, were certainly a picture of rest.

"How long do you calculate it is to daylight?" asked Henry.

"Not more'n two hours, an' it's goin' to come bright an' clear, an' with a steady wind that will take us to the south."

"That's good, and I think that you and I, Tom, ought to be getting ready. This drying wind has been blowing for a long time, and our clothes should be in condition again. Anyway I'm going to see."

He took down the garments from the bushes, and found that all were quite dry. Then he and Tom reclothed themselves and laid the apparel for the other three by their sides, ready for them when they should awake. Tom puckered up his lips and blew out a deep breath of pleasure.

"It may be mighty fine to be a Roman senator in a togy," he said, "but not in these parts. Give me my good old huntin' shirt an' leggings. Besides, I feel a sight more respectable."

Shortly, it was dawn, and the three sleepers awoke, glad to have their clothes dry again, and interested greatly in Henry's exploration of the island.

"Jim, you do a little more cooking," said Henry, "and Sol, Tom and I will go over to the other end of the island again. When we come back we'll hoist our sail, have breakfast, and be off."

They followed the path that Henry had taken during the night, leaving Paul and Jim busy with the cooking utensils. The little patch of forest was now entirely dry, and a great sun was rising from the eastern waters, tingeing the deep green of the trees with luminous gold. The lake was once more as smooth and peaceful as if no storm had ever passed over its surface.

They stopped at the crest of the transverse ridge and saw in the west the dark line, the nature of which Henry had been unable to decipher by moonlight. Now they saw that it was land, and they saw, too, another sight that startled them. Two large canoes were approaching the island swiftly, and they were already so near that Henry and Shif'less Sol could see the features of their occupants. Neither of the boats had a sail. Both were propelled wholly by paddlers—six paddlers to each canoe— stalwart,painted Indians, bare of shoulders and chest. But in the center of the first canoe sat a man with arms bound.

"It's a victim whom they are bringing for the stake and the sacrifice," said Henry.

"He must be from some tribe in the far North," said Shif'less Sol, "'cause all the Indian nations in the valley are allied."

"He is not from any tribe at all," said Henry. "The prisoner is a white man."

"A white man!" exclaimed Shif'less Sol, "an' you an' me, Henry, know that most o' the prisoners who are brought to these parts are captured in Kentucky."

"It's so, and I don't think we ought to go away in such a hurry."

"Meanin' we might be o' help?"

"Meaning we might be of help."

Henry watched the boats a minute or two longer, and saw that they were coming directly for one of the little inlets on the north end of the island. Moreover, they were coming fast under the long sweep of the paddles swung by brown and sinewy arms.

"Tom," he said to Ross, "you go back for Paul. Tell Jim to have the sail up and ready for us when we come, and meanwhile to guard the boat. That's a white man and they intend to burn him as a sacrifice to Manitou or the spirits of the lake. We've got to rescue him."

The others nodded assent and Tom hurried away after Paul, while Henry and Sol continued to watch the oncoming boats. They crept down the slope to the very fringe of the trees and lay close there, although they had little fear of discovery, unless it was caused by their own lack of caution.

The boats reached the inlet, and, for a few moments, they were hidden from the two watchers, by the bushes and rocks, but they heard the Indians talking, and Henry was confirmed in his opinion that they did not dream of any presence besides their own on the island. At length they emerged into view again, the prisoner walking between two warriors in front, and Henry gave a start of horror.

"Sol," he said in a whisper, "don't you recognize that gray head?"

"I think I do."

"Don't you know that tall, slender figure?"

"I'm shore I do."

"Tom, that can be nobody but Mr. Silas Pennypacker, to whom Paul and I went to school in Kentucky."

"It's the teacher, ez shore ez you're born."

Henry's thrill of horror came again. Mr. Pennypacker lived at Wareville, the home of his own family and Paul's. What had happened? There was the expedition of the harelipped Bird with his powerful force and with cannon! Could it be possible that he had swept Wareville away and that the teacher had been given to the Indians for sacrifice? A terrible anger seized him and Shif'less Sol, by his side, was swayed by the same emotion.

"It is he, Sol! It is he!" he whispered in intense excitement.

"Yes, Henry," replied the shiftless one, "it's the teacher."

"Do you think his presence here means Wareville has been destroyed by Bird?"

"I'm hopin' that it doesn't, Henry."

Shif'less Sol spoke steadily, but Henry could read the fear in his mind, and the reply made his own fears all the stronger.

"They are going to sacrifice that good old man, Sol," he said.

"They mean to do it, but people sometimes mean to do things that they don't do."

They remained in silence until Tom returned with Paul, who was excited greatly when he learned that Mr. Pennypacker was there a prisoner.

"Lie perfectly still, all of you, until the time comes," said Henry. "We've got to save him, and we can only do it by means of a surprise and a rush."

The Indians and their prisoner were now not more than a hundred yards away, having come into the center of the open circle used for the sacrifice, and they stood there a little while talking. Mr. Pennypacker's arms were bound, but he held himself erect. His face was turned toward the South, his home, and it seemed to Henry and Paul—although it was fancy, the distance being too great to see—that his expression was rapt and noble as if he already saw beyond this life into the future. They loved and respected him. Paul had been his favorite pupil, and now tears came into the eyes of the boy as he watched. The old man certainly had seen the stakes, and doubtless he had surmised their purpose.

"What's your plan, Henry?" whispered Shif'less Sol.

"I think they're going to eat. Probably they've been rowing all the morning and are tired and hungry. They mean after that to go ahead with their main purpose, but we'll take 'em while they're eating. I hate to fire on anybody from ambush, but it's got to be done. There's no other way. We'll all lie close together here, and when the time comes to fire, I'll give the word."

The Indians sat on the ground after their fashion and began to eat cold food. Apparently they paid little attention to their prisoner, who stood near, and to whom they offered nothing. Why should he eat? He would never be hungry again. Nor need they watch him closely now. They had left a man with each of the boats, and even if he should run he could not escape them on the island.

Henry and Paul saw Mr. Pennypacker walk forward a few steps and look intently at the posts. Then he bowed his gray head and stood quite still. Both believed that he was praying. Water again rose in Paul's eyes and Henry's too were damp.

"Boys," whispered Henry, "I think the time has come. Take aim. We'll pick the four on the left, Sol the first on the end, the second for me, Tom the third and Paul the fourth. Now, boys, cock your rifles, and take aim, the best aim that you ever took in your life, and when I say 'Fire!' pull the trigger."

Every man from the covert did as he was directed. When Henry looked down the sights and picked out the right place on the broad chest of a warrior, he shuddered a little. He repeated to himself that he did not like it, this firing from ambush, but there was the old man, whom they loved, doomed to torture and the sacrifice. His heart hardened like flint and he cried "Fire!"

Four rifles flashed in the thicket. Two warriors fell without a sound. Two more leaped away, wounded, and all the others sprang to their feet with cries of surprise and alarm.

"Up and at 'em!" cried Henry in a tremendous voice. "Cut them to pieces!"

Drawing their pistols they rushed into the open space and charged upon the warriors, firing as they came.

The Indians were Wyandots, men who knew little of fear, but the surprise and the deadly nature of the attack was too much for them. Perhaps superstition also mingled with their emotions. Doubtless the spirits of the lake were angry with them for some cause, and the best thing they could do was to leave it as soon as they could. But one as he ran did not forget to poise his hatchet for a cast at the prisoner. The Reverend Silas Pennypacker would have seen his last sun that day had not Henry noticed the movement and quickly fired his pistol at the uplifted hand. The bullet pierced the Indian's palm, the tomahawk was dashed from his hand, and with a howl of pain he sped after the others who were flying for the boats.

Henry and his comrades did not pursue. They knew that they must act with all speed, as the Wyandots would quickly recover from their panic, and come back in a force that was still two to one. A single sweep of his knife and his old schoolmaster's arms were free. Then he shouted in the dazed man's ears:

"Come, Mr. Pennypacker, we must run for it! Don't you see who we are? Here's Paul Cotter, and I'm Henry Ware, and these are Sol Hyde and Tom Ross! We've got a boat on the other side of the island and the sooner we get there the better!"

He snatched up a rifle, powder horn and bullet pouch from one of the fallen warriors and thrust them in the old man's hands. Mr. Pennypacker was still staring at them in a dazed manner, but at last the light broke through.

"Oh, my boys! my brave boys!" he cried. "It is really you, and you have saved me at the eleventh hour! I had given up all hope, but lo! the miracle is done!"

Henry took him by the arm, and obeying the impulse he ran with them through the wood. Already Henry heard shouts which indicated to him that the Wyandots had turned, and, despite his anxiety about Wareville, he asked nothing of Mr. Pennypacker for the present.

"You lead the way, Paul," he cried. "Jim, of course, has the boat ready with the sail up and the oars in place. We'll be out on the lake in a few minutes, Mr. Pennypacker. There, do you hear that? The Wyandots are now in full pursuit!"

A long piercing cry came from the woods behind them. It was the Wyandot leader encouraging his warriors. Henry knew that they would come fast, and Mr. Pennypacker, old and not used to the ways of the wilderness, could go but slowly. Although Long Jim was sure to be ready, the embarkation would be dangerous. It was evident that Mr. Pennypacker, extremely gaunt and thin, was exhausted already by a long march and other hardships. Now he labored heavily, drawing long breaths.

"Those fellows will be on us in a minute or two, Sol," Henry whispered to the shiftless one, "unless we burn their faces."

"I reckon we're able to do the burnin'," replied Shif'less Sol.

Henry, Tom and Sol dropped to a walk, and in a few moments stopped altogether. Paul, with Mr. Pennypacker by his side, kept on for the boat as fast as the old man's strength would allow. Henry caught a glimpse of a figure running low in the thicket and fired. A cry came back, but he could not tell whether the wound was mortal. Shif'less Sol fired with a similar result. Two or three bullets were sent back at them, but none touched. Then the three, keeping themselves hidden resumed their flight. They reckoned that the check to the Wyandots would give Paul, with Mr. Pennypacker, time to reach the boat before the warriors could come within range of the latter.

The three now ran very swiftly, and, in a few minutes, were at the edge of the inlet, where the boat lay, just in time to see Paul pick up the old schoolmaster, who had fallen with exhaustion, and lift him into the boat. The three sprang in after them.

"We'll watch with the rifles, Sol," exclaimed Henry. "The rest of you row until we're outside, when the sail can do most of the pulling."

It was quick work now and skillful. Mr. Pennypacker, scarcely able to draw a breath, lay like a log in the bottom of the boat, but in less than a half minute after the three leaped on board they were gliding down the inlet. Before they reached the open lake the Indians appeared among the trees and began to shout and fire. But they were in such haste that nothing was struck except the boat, which did not mind. Silent Tom, who had restrained his fire, now sent a bullet that struck the mark and the warriors rushed to cover. Then they were out of the inlet, the fine wind filled the sail, and away they sped toward the south.

The warriors appeared at the edge of the water while the boat's crew were still within range, but when Henry and the shiftless one raised their rifles they shrank back. They had tested already the quality of their foes, and they did not like it. When they reappeared from the shelter of the trees the boat was out of range. Nevertheless they fired two or three shots that spattered on the water, waved their tomahawks and shouted in anger. Shif'less Sol stood up in the boat and shouted back at them:

"Keep cool, my red brethren, keep cool! We have escaped and you see that we have! So do not waste good bullets which you may need another time! And above all keep your tempers! Wise men always do! Farewell!"

It is not likely that they understood the words of the shiftless one, but certainly the derisive gestures that he made as he sat down were not lost upon them.

"Sol, can't you ever be serious?" said Henry to his comrade.

"Be serious? O' course I kin at the right time," replied the shiftless one, "but what's the use o' bein' serious now? Haven't we rescued ourselves an' the schoolmaster, too? Ain't we in a boat with a sail that kin leave the two boats o' them warriors far behind, an' ain't we got a bee-yu-ti-ful day to sail over a bee-yu-ti-ful lake? So what's the use o' bein' serious? The time fur that wuz ten minutes ago."

It was evident that the Wyandots considered pursuit useless or that they feared the Kentucky rifles, as they gathered in a group on the beach and watched the flying boat recede.

"Didn't I tell you it wuzn't wuth while to be serious now, Henry?" said Shif'less Sol. "We're hevin' the easiest kind o' a time an' them warriors standin' thar on the shore look too funny for anything. I wish I could see their faces. I know they would look jest like the faces o' wolves, when somethin' good had slipped from between their teeth."

Paul and Henry were busy reviving Mr. Pennypacker. They threw fresh water from the lake over his face and poured more down his throat. As they worked with him they noted his emaciated figure. He was only a skeleton, and his fainting even in so short a flight was no cause for wonder. Gradually he revived, coughed and sat up.

"I fell," he said. "It was because I was so weak. What has happened? Are we not moving?"

His eyes were yet dim, and he was not more than half conscious.

"You are with us, your friends. You remember?" said Henry. "We rescued you at the place of the stakes, and we all got away unhurt. We are in a boat now sailing over Lake Erie."

"And I saved you a rifle and ammunition," said Paul. "Here they are, ready for you when you land."

Mr. Pennypacker's dim eyes cleared, and he gazed at the two youths in wonder and affection.

"It is a miracle—a miracle!" he said. Then he added, after a moment's pause: "To escape thus after all the terrible things that I have seen!"

Henry shivered a little, and then he asked the fateful questions.

"And what of Wareville, Mr. Pennypacker? Has it been destroyed? Do Paul's people and mine still live? Have they been taken away as captives? Why were you a prisoner?"

The questions came fast, then they stopped suddenly, and he and Paul waited with white faces for the answers.

"Wareville is not destroyed," replied Mr. Pennypacker. "An English officer named Bird, a harelipped man, came with a great force of Indians, some white men and cannon. They easily took Martin's and Ruddle's stations and all the people in them, but they did not go against Wareville and other places. I think they feared the power of the gathering Kentuckians. I was at Martin's Station on a visit to an old friend when I was captured with the others. Bird and his army then retreated North with the prisoners, more than three hundred in number, mostly women and children."

The old man paused a moment and put his hands over his face.

"I have seen many terrible things," he resumed, "and I cannot forget them. They said that we would be taken to Detroit and be held as prisoners there, but it has been a long and terrible march, many hundreds of miles through the wilderness, and the weak ones—they were many—could not stand it. They died in the wilderness, often under the Indian tomahawk, and I think that less than half of them will reach Detroit."

The old schoolmaster paused, his voice choked with emotion, and every one of the five muttered something deep and wrathful under his breath.

"I did the best I could," he resumed. "I helped whenever they let me, but the hardships were so great and they permitted us so little rest that I wasted away. I had no more than the strength of a little child. At last the warriors whom you saw took me from the others and turned to the east. We went through the woods until we came to the great lake. A terrible storm came up, but when it died we embarked in two boats and went to the island on which you found me. I did not know the purpose for which I was intended until I saw the stakes with those ghastly relics about them. Then I made up my mind to bear it as best I could."

"You were to be made a burnt offering to the spirits of the lakes," said Henry. "Thank God we came in time. We go now to warn of another and greater expedition, led by Timmendiquas, the famous chief of the Wyandots."

CHAPTER XV. THE PAGES OF A BOOK

None of the five knew how far they were down the lake, but they were able to guide their course by the sun, and, keeping the low bank of forest far beyond gunshot on their right, they moved before a favoring wind. The schoolmaster regained his strength fast. He was old, but a temperate life in the open air reënforced by plenty of exercise, had kept him wiry and strong. Now he sat up and listened to the long tale of the adventures of the five, whom he had not seen for many months previous to their great journey to New Orleans.

"You have done well—you have done more than well," he said. "You have performed magnificent deeds. It is a beautiful land for which we fight, and, although our enemies are many and terrible and we suffer much, we shall surely triumph in the end. Bird with his cannon was compelled to go back. He could have battered down the palisade walls of any of the stations, but he feared the gathering of the white hunters and fighters. Above all he feared the coming of George Rogers Clark, the shield of the border."

Henry's heart throbbed at the name of Clark, renowned victor of Vincennes and Kaskaskia.

"Clark!" he exclaimed. "Is he in Kentucky?"

"There or to the northward. It is said that he is gathering a force to attack the Indian villages."

"If it could only be true!" said Paul.

The others echoed the wish.

Henry remained silent, but for a long time he was very thoughtful. The news that Wareville was untouched by the raid had relieved him immensely, and he was very hopeful also that George Rogers Clark was coming again to the rescue. The name of Clark was one with which to conjure. It would draw all the best men of the border and moreover it would cause Timmendiquas, Caldwell and their great force to turn aside. Once more hope was in the ascendant. Meanwhile, the sparkling breeze blew them southward, and the eyes of all grew brighter. Fresh life poured into the veins of the schoolmaster, and he sat up, looking with pleasure at the rippling surface of the lake.

"It reminds me in a way of the time when we fled from the place of the giant bones," he said, "and I hope and believe that our flight will end as happily."

"That looks like a long time ago, Mr. Pennypacker," said Tom Ross, "an' we hev traveled a mighty lot since. I reckon that we've been to places that I never heard uv until Paul told about 'em, Troy and Rome an' Alexander—"

"Tom," broke in Shif'less Sol, "you're gettin' mixed. Troy's dead, an' we may hev got close to Rome, but we never did ackshally reach the town. An' ez fur Alexander, that wuz a man an' not a city."

"It don't make no difference," replied Tom, not at all abashed. "What do all them old names amount to anyhow? Like ez not the people that lived in 'em got mixed about 'em themselves."

Mr. Pennypacker smiled.

"It doesn't make any difference about Rome and Troy," he said. "You've been all the way down to New Orleans and you've fought in the East with the Continental troops. Your adventures have been fully as wonderful as those of Ulysses, and you have traveled a greater distance."

They sailed on all through the day, still seeing that low shore almost like a cloud bank on their right, but nothing save water ahead of them. Henry was sure that it was not above sixty miles across the lake, but he calculated that they had been blown about a great deal in the storm, and for all they knew the island might have been far out of their course.

It was evident that they could not reach the south shore before dusk, and they turned in toward the land. Shif'less Sol hailed the turning of the boat's course with delight.

"Boats are all right fur travelin'," he said, "when the wind's blowin' an' you've a sail. A lazy man like me never wants nothin' better, but when the night comes on an' you need to sleep, I want the land. I never feel the land heavin' an' pitchin' under me, an' it gives me more of a safe an' home feelin'."

"Watch, everybody, for a landing place," said Henry, "and Paul, you steer."

The green shore began to rise, showing a long unbroken wall of forest, but the dusk was coming too, and all of them were anxious to make land. Presently, they were only three or four hundred yards from the coast and they skimmed rapidly along it, looking for an anchorage. It was full night before Henry's sharp eyes saw the mouth of a creek almost hidden by tall grass, and, taking down the sail, they pulled the boat into it. They tied their craft securely to a tree, and the night passed without alarm.

They resumed the voyage early the next morning, and that day reached the southern coast of the lake. Here they reluctantly left the boat. They might have found a river emptying into the lake down which they could have gone a hundred or more miles further, but they were not sufficiently acquainted with this part of the country to spend their time in hunting for it. They drew their good little craft as far as they could among the weeds and bushes that grew at the water's edge.

"That's two good boats we've got hid on the water ways," said Shif'less Sol, "besides a half dozen canoes scattered here an' thar, an' mebbe we'll find 'em an' use 'em some day."

"This cost us nothin'," said Jim Hart, "so I reckon we ain't got any right to grieve, 'cause we're givin' up what we never paid fur."

They took out of the boat all the supplies that they could conveniently carry, and then started toward the southwest. The course to Kentucky now led through the heart of the Indian country. Between them and the Ohio lay the great Indian villages of Chillicothe, Piqua and many others, and the journey in any event would be dangerous. But the presence of the old schoolmaster was likely to make it more so, since he could not travel with any approach to the speed and skill of the others. Yet no one thought, for a moment, of blaming him. They were happy to have rescued him, and, moreover, he had brought them the good news that Wareville was untouched by the Bird invasion. Yet speed was vital. The scattered stations must be warned against the second and greater expedition under Caldwell and Timmendiquas. Mr. Pennypacker himself perceived the fact and he urged them to go on and leave him. He felt sure that with a rifle and plenty of ammunition he could reach Wareville in safety.

"You can give me a lot of food," he said, "and doubtless I shall be able to shoot some game. Now go ahead and leave me. Many lives may depend upon it."

They only laughed, but Shif'less Sol and Henry, who had been whispering together, announced a plan.

"This here expedition is goin' to split," said the shiftless one. "Henry is the fastest runner an' the best woodsman of us all. I hate to admit that he's better than me, but he is, an' he's goin' on ahead. Now you needn't say anything, Mr. Pennypacker, about your makin' trouble, 'cause you don't. We'd make Henry run on afore, even ef you wuzn't with us. That boy needs trainin' down, an' we intend to see that he gits the trainin'."

There was nothing more to be said and the rest was done very quietly and quickly. A brief farewell, a handshake for everyone, and he was gone.

Henry had never been in finer physical condition, and the feeling of responsibility seemed to strengthen him also in both body and mind. In one way he was sorry to leave his comrades and in another he was glad. Alone he would travel faster, and in the wilderness he never feared the loneliness and the silence. A sense, dead or atrophied in the ordinary human being, came out more strongly in him. It seemed to be a sort of divination or prescience, as if messages reached him through the air, like the modern wireless.

He went southward at a long walk half a run for an hour or two before he stopped. Then he stood on the crest of a little hill and saw the deep woods all about him. There was no sign of his comrades whom he had left far behind, nor was there any indication of human life save himself. Yet he had seldom seen anything that appealed to him more than this bit of the wilderness. The trees, oak, beech and elm, were magnificent. Great coiling grape vines now and then connected a cluster of trees, but there was little undergrowth. Overhead, birds chattered and sang among the leaves, and far up in the sky a pair of eagles were speeding like black specks toward the lake. Henry inhaled deep breaths. The odors of the woods came to him and were sweet in his nostrils. All the wilderness filled him with delight. A black bear passed and climbed a tree in search of honey. Two deer came in sight, but the human odor reached them and they fled swiftly away, although they were in no danger from Henry.

Then he, too, resumed his journey, and sped swiftly toward the south through the unbroken forest. He came after a while to marshy country, half choked with fallen wood from old storms. He showed his wonderful agility and strength. He leaped rapidly from one fallen log to another and his speed was scarcely diminished. Now and then he saw wide black pools, and once he crossed a deep creek on a fallen tree. Night found him yet in this marshy region, but he was not sorry as he had left no trail behind, and, after looking around some time, he found a little oasis of dry land with a mighty oak tree growing in the center. Here he felt absolutely secure, and, making his supper of dried venison, he lay down under the boughs of the oak, with one blanket beneath him and another above him and was soon in a deep and dreamless sleep.

He awoke about midnight to find a gorgeous parade of the moon and all the stars, and he lay for a while watching them through the leaves of the oak. Powerful are nature and habit, and Henry's life was in accordance with both. Lying alone at midnight on that little knoll in the midst of a great marsh in the country of wary and cruel enemies, he was thankful that it had been given to him to be there, and that his lot had been cast among the conditions that surrounded him.

He heard a slight noise to the left of him, but he knew that it was only another hungry bear stealing about. There was a light splash in the pool at the foot of the knoll, but it was only a large fish leaping up and making a noise as it fell back. Far to the south something gleamed fitfully among the trees, but it was only marsh fire. None of these things disturbed him, and knowing that the wilderness was at peace he laid his head back on the turf and fell asleep again. At break of day he was up and away, and until afternoon he sped toward the south in the long running walk which frontiersmen and Indians could maintain for hours with ease. About 4 o'clock in the afternoon, he stopped as suddenly as if he had come to a river's brink. He had struck a great trail, not a path made by three or four persons but by hundreds. He could see their road a hundred yards wide. Here so many feet had trodden that the grass was yet thinner than elsewhere; there lay the bones of deer, eaten clean and thrown away. Further on was a feather trimmed and dyed that had fallen from a scalp lock, and beyond that, a blanket discarded as too old and ragged lay rotting.

These were signs that spoke to Henry as plainly as if the words themselves were uttered. A great wilderness army had passed that way and for a while he was in doubt. Was it the force of Bird coming back to the

North? But it was undoubtedly a trail several weeks old. Everything indicated it. The bones had been bleached by the sun, the feather was beaten partly into the earth by rain, and the tattered old blanket had been pawed and torn still further by wolves. But none of these things told what army it might be. He hunted, instead, for some low place that might have been soft and marshy when the warriors passed, and which, when it dried, would preserve the outline of a footstep. He advanced a full mile, following the broad trail which was like an open road to him until he came to such a place. Then he kneeled and examined it critically. In a half dozen places he saw held in the hard earth the outline of footsteps. They would have been traces of footsteps to most people and nothing more, but he knew that every one of them pointed to the south. A mile further on and in another low place he had full verification of that, which, in fact, he already knew. Here the prints were numerous. Chance had brought him upon the trail of Timmendiquas, and he resolved, for the present, to follow it.

Henry came to this determination because it was extremely important to know the location and plans of the invading army. More news of an attack would not be nearly so valuable as the time and place at which the attack was to be delivered. The course seemed plain to him and he followed the broad trail with speed and ardor, noting all along the indications that the army took no care to conceal itself or hide its trail. Why should it? There was nothing in these woods powerful enough to meet the Anglo-Indian combination.

For four days and for a part of every night he followed without a break. He saw the trail grow fresher, and he judged that he was moving at least twice as fast as the army. He could see where English or Tory boots had crushed down the grass and he saw also the lighter imprints of moccasins. He passed numerous camps marked by ashes, bones of deer, buffalo, bear and smaller animals, and fragments of old worn-out garments, such as an army casts away as it goes along. He read in these things unlimited confidence on the part of both Indians and white men.

An unusually large camp had been made at one place and some bark shelters had been thrown up. Henry inferred that the army had spent two or three days here, and he could account for the fact only on the ground that some division of counsels had occurred. Perhaps the weather had been stormy meanwhile, and the bark shelters had been constructed for the officers and chiefs.

He spent a night in this camp and used one of the shelters, as it began to rain heavily just after dark. It was a little place, but it kept him dry and he watched with interest as the wind and rain drove across the opening and through the forest. He was as close and snug as a bear in its lair, but the storm was heavy with thunder and vivid with lightning. The lightning was uncommonly bright. Frequently the wet boughs and trees stood out in the glare like so much carving, and Henry was forced to shut his dazzled eyes. But he was neither lonely nor afraid. He recognized the tremendous power of nature, but it seemed to him that he had his part here, and the whole was to him a majestic and beautiful panorama.

Henry remembered the fight that he and his comrades had had at the deserted village, and he found some similarity in his present situation, but he did not anticipate the coming of another enemy, and, secure in the belief, he slept while the storm still blew. When morning came, the rain had ceased. He replenished his food supplies with a deer that he had shot by the way and he cooked a little on one of the heaps of stones that the Indians had used for the same purpose. When he had eaten he glanced at the other bark shelters and he saw the name of Braxton Wyatt cut on one of them. Henry shuddered with aversion. He had seen so much of death and torture done on the border that he could not understand how Simon Girty, Braxton Wyatt and their like could do such deeds upon their own countrymen. But he felt that the day was coming fast when many of them would be punished.

He began the great trail anew upon turf, now soft and springy from the rain, and, refreshed by the long night's sleep in the bark shelter, he went rapidly. Eight or ten miles beyond the camp the trail made an abrupt curve to the eastward. Perhaps they were coming to some large river of which the Indian scouts knew and the turn was made in order to reach a ford, but he followed it another hour and there was no river. The nature of the country also indicated that no great stream could be at hand, and Henry believed that it signified a change of plan, a belief strengthened by a continuation of the trail toward the east as he followed it hour by hour. What did it mean? Undoubtedly it was something of great significance to his enterprise, but now he grew more wary. Since the course of the army was changed bands of Indians might be loitering behind, and he must take every precaution lest he run into one of them. He noticed from time to time small trails coming into the larger one, and he inferred that they were hunting parties sent off from the main body and now returning.

The trail maintained the change and still bore toward the east. It had been obliterated to some extent by the rains, but it was as wide as ever, and Henry knew that no division had taken place. But he was yet convinced that some subject of great importance had been debated at the place of the long camp. On the following day he saw two warriors, and he lay in the bush while they passed only twenty yards away, close enough for him to see that they were Miamis. They were proceeding leisurely, perhaps on a hunting expedition, and it was well for them that they did not search at this point for any enemy. The most formidable figure on all the border lay in the thicket with both rifle and pistol ready. Henry heard them talking, but he had no wish for an encounter even with the advantage of ambush and surprise on his side. He was concerned with far more important business.

The two Indians looked at the broad trail, but evidently they knew all about it, as it did not claim more than a half minute's attention. Then they went northward, and when Henry was sure that they were a mile or two away, he resumed his pursuit, a single man following an army. Now all his wonderful skill and knowledge and developed power of intuition came into play. Soon he passed the point where the trail had been made fainter by the latest rains, and now it became to his eyes broad and deep. He came to a place where many fires had been built obviously for cooking, and the ashes of the largest fires were near the center of the camp. A half circle of unburned logs lay around these ashes. As the logs were not sunk in the ground at all they had evidently been drawn there recently, and Henry, sitting down on one of them, began to study the problem.

On the other side of the ashes where no logs lay were slight traces in the earth. It seemed to him that they had been made by heels, and he also saw at one place a pinch of brown ashes unlike the white ashes left by the fire. He went over, knelt down and smelled of the brown pinch. The odor was faint, very faint, but it was enough to tell him that it had been made by tobacco. A pipe had been smoked here, not to soothe the mind or body, but for a political purpose. At once his knowledge and vivid imagination reconstructed the whole scene. An important council had been held. The logs had been drawn up as seats for the British and Tory officers. Opposite them on the bare ground the chiefs, after their custom, had sat in Turkish fashion, and the pipe had been passed from one to another until the circle was complete. It must have been a most vital question or they would not have smoked the pipe. He came back to the logs and found in one of them a cut recently made. Someone had been indulging in the western custom of whittling with a strong clasp knife and he had no doubt that it was Braxton Wyatt who had cut his name with the same knife on the bark shelter. It would take one whittling casually a long time to make so deep a cut. Then they had debated there for two or three hours. This meant that the leaders were in doubt. Perhaps Timmendiquas and Caldwell had disagreed. If it could only be true! Then the little stations would have time to renew their breath and strength before another great attack could be made.

He sat on the log and concentrated his mind with great intensity upon the problem. He believed that the master mind in the council had been that of Timmendiquas. He also had inspired the change of route and perhaps Caldwell, Girty and Wyatt had tried to turn him back. Doubtless the course of Timmendiquas had been inspired by news from the South. Would the trail turn again?

He renewed the eager pursuit. He followed for a full day, but it still ran toward the east, and was growing fresher much faster than before. He argued from this fact that the speed of the army had slackened greatly. On the day after that, although the course of the main body was unchanged he saw where a considerable band had left it and gone northward. What did this mean? The band could not have numbered less than fifty. It must be making for some one of the great Indian towns, Chillicothe or Piqua. Once more the reader of the wilderness page translated. They had received news from the South, and it was not such as they wished. The Indian towns had been threatened by something, and the band had gone to protect or help them.

Shortly before nightfall he noticed another trail made by perhaps twenty warriors coming from the south and joining that of the main body. The briers and grass were tangled considerably, and, as he looked closely, his eyes caught a tint of red on the earth. It was only a spot, and once more the wilderness reader read what was printed in his book. This band had brought wounded men with it, and the tribes were not fighting among themselves. They had encountered the Kentuckians, hunters perhaps, or a larger force maybe, and they had not escaped without damage. Henry exulted, not because blood had been shed, but because some prowling band intent upon scalps had met a check.

He followed the ruddy trail until it emerged into the broader one and then to a point beside it, where a cluster of huge oaks flung a pleasant shade. Here the wounds of the warriors had been bandaged, as fragments of deerskin lay about. One of them had certainly suffered a broken arm or leg, because pieces of stout twigs with which they had made splints lay under one of the trees.

The next day he turned another page in his book, and read about the great feast the army had held. He reached one of the little prairies so common in that region. Not many days before it had been a great berry field, but now it was trampled, and stripped. Seven or eight hundred warriors had eaten of the berries and they had also eaten of much solid food. At the far edge of the prairie just within the shade of the forest he found the skeletons of three buffaloes and several deer, probably shot by the hunters on that very prairie. A brook of fine clear water flowed by, and both banks were lined with footsteps. Here the warriors after eating heavily had come to drink. Many of the trees near by contained the marks of hatchet strokes, and Henry read easily that the warriors had practiced there with their tomahawks, perhaps for prizes offered by their white leaders. Cut in the soft bark of a beech he read the words "Braxton Wyatt." So he had been at work with the clasp knife again, and Henry inferred that the young renegade was worried and nervous or he would not have such uneasy hands.

Most of the heavier footprints, those that turned out, were on one side of the camp and Henry read from this the fact that the English and Tories had drawn somewhat apart, and that the differences between them and the Indians had become greater. He concentrated his mind again upon the problem, and at length drew his conclusion from what he had read.

The doubts of Timmendiquas concerning his allies were growing stronger, so Henry construed. The great Wyandot chief had been induced with difficulty to believe that the soldiers of the British king would repay their red allies, and would defend the Indian villages if a large force from Kentucky were sent against them. The indications that such a force was moving or would move must be growing stronger. Doubtless the original turn to the eastward had been in order to deflect the attack against the settlements on the upper Ohio, most probably against Fort Henry. Now it was likely that the second plan had been abandoned for a third. What would that third be?

He slept that night in a dense covert about half a mile from the camp, and he was awakened once by the howling of wolves. He knew that they were prowling about the deserted camp in search of remnants of food, and he felt sure that others also were following close behind the Indian army, in order to obtain what they might leave at future camps. Perhaps they might trail him too, but he had his rifle and pistol and, unafraid, he went to sleep again.

The broad trail led the next day to a river which Henry reached about noon. It was fordable, but the army had not crossed. It had stopped abruptly at the brink and then had marched almost due north. Henry read this chapter easily and he read it joyfully. The dissatisfaction among the Indian chiefs had reached a climax, and the river, no real obstacle in itself, had served as the straw to turn them into a new course. Timmendiquas had boldly led the way northward and from Kentucky. He, Red Eagle, Yellow Panther and the rest were going to the Indian villages, and Caldwell and the other white men were forced either to go with them or return to Detroit. He followed the trail for a day and a half, saw it swing in toward the west, and theory became certainty. The army was marching toward Chillicothe and Piqua.

After this last great turn Henry studied the trail with the utmost care. He had read much there, but he intended to read every word that it said. He noticed that the division, the British and Tories on one side and the Indians on the other, continued, and he was quite sure now that he would soon come upon some important development.

He found the next day that for which he was looking. The army had camped in another of the little prairies, and the Indians had held a great dance. The earth, trampled heavily over a regulated space, showed it clearly. Most of the white men had stayed in one group on the right. Here were the deep traces of military boot heels such as the officers might wear.

Again his vivid imagination and power of mental projection into the dark reconstructed the whole scene. The Indians, Wyandots, Shawnees, Miamis and the others, had danced wildly, whirling their tomahawks about their heads, their naked bodies painted in many colors, their eyes glaring with the intoxication of the dance. Timmendiquas and the other chiefs had stood here looking on; over there, on the right, Caldwell and his officers had stood, and few words had passed between officers and chiefs.

"Now the division will become more complete," said Henry to himself, as he followed the trail anew into the forest, and he was so sure of it that he felt no surprise when, within a mile, it split abruptly. The greater trail continued to the west, the smaller turned abruptly to the north, and this was the one that contained the imprints of the military boot heels. Once more he read his text with ease. Timmendiquas and Caldwell had parted company. The English and Tories were returning to Detroit. Timmendiquas, hot with wrath because his white allies would not help him, was going on with the warriors to the defense of their villages.

Without beholding with his own eyes a single act of this army he had watched the growth of the quarrel between red and white and he had been a witness to its culmination. But all these movements had been influenced by some power of which he knew nothing. It was his business to discover the nature of this power, and he would follow the Indian trail a little while longer.

Henry had not suffered for food. Despite the passage of the Indian army the country was so full of game that he was able to shoot what he wished almost when he wished, but he felt that he was now coming so near to the main body that he could not risk a shot which might be heard by outlying hunters or skirmishers. He also redoubled his care and rarely showed himself on the main trail, keeping to the woods at the side, where he would be hidden, an easy matter, as except for the little prairies the country was covered with exceedingly heavy forest.

The second day after the parting of the two forces he saw smoke ahead, and he believed that it was made by the rear guard. It was a thin column rising above the trees, but the foliage was so heavy and the underbrush so dense that he was compelled to approach very close before he saw that the fire was not made by Indians, but by a group of white men, Simon Girty, Blackstaffe, Quarles, Braxton Wyatt and others, about a dozen in all. They had cooked their noonday meal at a small fire and were eating it apparently in perfect confidence of security. The renegades sat in the dense forest. Underbrush grew thickly to the very logs on which they were sitting, and, as Henry heard the continuous murmur of their voices, he resolved to learn what they were saying. He might discover then the nature of the menace that had broken up or deferred the great invasion. He knew well the great danger of such an attempt but he was fully resolved to make it.

Lying down in the bushes and grass he drew himself slowly forward. His approach was like that of a wild animal stalking its prey. He lay very close to the earth and made no sound that was audible a yard away, pulling himself on, foot by foot. Yet his patience conquered, and presently he lay in the thickest of the undergrowth not far from the renegades, and he could hear everything they said. Girty was speaking, and his words soon showed that he was in no pleasant mood.

"Caldwell and the other English were too stiff," he said. "I don't like Timmendiquas because he doesn't like me, but the English oughtn't to forget that an alliance is for the sake of the two parties to it. They should have come with Timmendiquas and his friends to their villages to help them."

"And all our pretty plans are broken up," said Braxton Wyatt viciously. "If we had only gone on and struck before they could recover from Bird's blows we might have swept Kentucky clean of every station."

"Timmendiquas was right," said Girty. "We have to beware of that fellow at the Falls. He's dangerous. His is a great name. The Kentucky riflemen will come to the call of the man who took Kaskaskia and Vincennes."

The prone figure in the bushes started. He was reading further into this most interesting of all volumes. What could the "Falls" mean but the Falls of the Ohio at the brand new settlement of Louisville, and the victor of Vincennes and Kaskaskia was none other than the great George Rogers Clark, the sword of the border. He understood. Clark's name was the menace that had turned back Timmendiquas. Undoubtedly the hero was gathering a new force and would give back Bird's blows. Timmendiquas wished to protect his own, but the English had returned to Detroit. The prone figure in the bushes rejoiced without noise.

"What will be the result of it all?" asked Blackstaffe, his tone showing anxiety.

Girty—most detested name in American history, next to that of Benedict Arnold—considered. The side of his face was turned to Henry, and the bold youth wished that they were standing in the open, face to face, arms in hand. But he was compelled to lie still and wait. Nor could he foresee that Girty, although he was not destined to fall in battle, should lose everything, become an exile, go blind and that no man should know when he met death or where his body lay. The renegade at length replied:

"It means that we cannot now destroy Kentucky without a supreme effort. Despite all that we do, despite all our sieges and ambuscades, new men continually come over the mountains. Every month makes them stronger, and yet only this man Clark and a few like him have saved them so far. If Caldwell and a British force would make a campaign with us, we might yet crush Clark and whatever army he may gather. We may even do it without Caldwell. In this vast wilderness which the Indians know so well it is almost impossible for a white army to escape ambush. I am, for that reason, in favor of going on and joining Timmendiquas. I want a share in the victory that our side will win at the Indian towns. I am sure that the triumph will be ours."

"It seems the best policy to me," said Braxton Wyatt. "Timmendiquas does not like me any more than he does you, but the Indians appreciate our help. I suppose we'd better follow at once."

"Take it easy," said Girty. "There's no hurry. We can overtake Timmendiquas in a day, and we are quite sure that there are no Kentuckians in the woods. Besides, it will take Clark a considerable time to assemble a large force at the Falls, and weeks more to march through the forest. You will have a good chance then, Braxton, to show your skill as a forest leader. With a dozen good men hanging on his flank you ought to cause Mr. Clark much vexation."

"It could be done," replied Wyatt, "but there are not many white men out here fighting on our side. In the East the Tories are numerous, and I had a fine band there, but it was destroyed in that last fight at the big Indian town."

"Your old playmate, Henry Ware, had something to do with that, did he not?" asked Girty, not without a touch of sarcasm.

"He did," replied Wyatt venomously, "and it's a good thing that he's now a prisoner at Detroit. He and those friends of his could be both the eyes and ears of Clark. It would have been better if Timmendiquas had let the Indians make an end to him. Only in that manner could we be sure that he would always be out of the way."

"I guess you're right," said Girty.

The prone figure in the bushes laughed silently, a laugh that did not cause the movement of a single muscle, but which nevertheless was full of heartfelt enjoyment. What would Wyatt and Girty have thought if they had known that the one of whom they were talking, whom they deemed a prisoner held securely at Detroit, was lying within ten feet of them, as free as air and with weapons of power?

Henry had heard enough and he began to creep away, merely reversing the process by which he had come. It was a harder task than the first, but he achieved it deftly, and after thirty yards he rose to his feet, screening himself behind the trunk of an oak. He could still see the renegades, and the faint murmur of their voices yet reached him. That old temptation to rid the earth of one of these men who did so much harm came back to him, but knowing that he had other work to do he resisted it, and, passing in a wide circle about them, followed swiftly on the trail of Timmendiquas.

He saw the Indian camp that night, pitched in a valley. Numerous fires were burning and discipline was relaxed somewhat, but so many warriors were about that there was no opportunity to come near. He did not wish, however, to make any further examination. Merely to satisfy himself that the army had made no further change in its course was enough. After lingering a half hour or so he turned to the north and traveled rapidly a long time, having now effected a complete circuit since he left his comrades. It was his purpose now to rejoin them, which he did not believe would prove a very difficult task. Shif'less Sol, the leader in his absence, was to come with the party down the bank of the Scioto, unless they found Indians in the way. Their speed would be that of the slowest of their number, Mr. Pennypacker, and he calculated that he would meet them in about three days.

Bearing in toward the right he soon struck the banks of the Scioto and followed the stream northward all the next day. He saw several Indian canoes upon the river, but he was so completely hidden by the dense foliage on the bank that he was safe from observation. It was not a war party, the Indians were merely fishing. Some of the occupants of the boats were squaws. It was a pleasant and peaceful occupation, and for a few moments Henry envied them, but quickly dismissing such thoughts he proceeded northward again at the old running walk.

On the afternoon of the second day Henry lay in the bushes and uttered their old signal, the cry of the wolf repeated with certain variations, and as unmistakable as are the telegrapher's dots and dashes of to-day. There was no answer. He had expected none. It was yet too soon, according to his calculations, but he would not risk their passing him through an unexpected burst of speed. All that afternoon and the next morning he repeated the signal at every half hour. Still the same silence. Nothing stirred in the great woods, but the leaves and bushes swaying before the wind. Several times he examined the Scioto, but he saw no more Indians.

About noon of the third day when he uttered the signal an answer, very faint, came from a point far to the west. At first he was not sure of the variations, the sound had traveled such a great distance, but having gone in that direction a quarter of a mile, he repeated it. Then it came back, clear and unmistakable. Once more he read his book with ease. Shif'less Sol and the others were near by and they would await him. His pulse leaped with delight. He would be with these brave comrades again and he would bring them good news.

He advanced another two or three hundred yards and repeated the cry. The answer instantly came from a point very near at hand. Then he pressed boldly through the bushes and Shif'less Sol walked forward to meet him followed by the others, all gaunt with travel, but strong and well.

CHAPTER XVI. THE RIVER FIGHT

Henry shook hands with them all in turn and they sat down under the shade of an oak. Mr. Pennypacker looked him over slowly and rather quizzically.

"Henry," he said, "I scarcely realize that you were a pupil of mine. Here in the wilderness I see that you are the teacher and that I am a pretty poor and limping sort of pupil."

"You can teach us all many and useful things," said Henry modestly.

"What did you learn, Henry?" asked Paul.

Henry told the tale in brief, concise words, and the others expressed pleasure at his news.

"And so Clark is coming," said the schoolmaster thoughtfully. "It is wonderful what the energy and directing mind of one man can do. That name alone is enough to change the nature of a whole campaign. 'Tis lucky that we have this Cæsar of the backwoods to defend us. What is your plan now, Henry?"

Mr. Pennypacker, like the others, instinctively looked upon Henry as the leader.

"We'll go straight to the Falls of the Ohio," replied Henry. "It will take us two or three weeks to get there, and we'll have to live mostly on our rifles, but that's where we're needed. Clark will want all the men he can get."

"I am old," said the schoolmaster, "and it has not been my business hitherto to fight, but in this great crisis of Kentucky I shall try to do my part. I too shall offer my services to George Rogers Clark."

"He'll be glad to get you," said Tom Ross.

After the brief rest they began the long journey from what is now the middle part of the state of Ohio to the Falls of the Ohio and the new settlement of Louisville there. It was an arduous undertaking, particularly for the schoolmaster, as it led all the way through woods frequented by alert Indians, and, besides deep rivers there were innumerable creeks, which they could cross only by swimming. Bearing this in mind Henry's thoughts returned to the first boat which they had hidden in the bushes lining the banks of one of the Ohio's tributaries. As the whole country was now swarming with the warriors the passage down the Ohio would undoubtedly be more dangerous than the path through the woods, but the boat and the river would save a vast expenditure of strength. Henry laid the two plans before the others.

"What do you say, Sol?" he asked.

"I'm fur the boat an' the river," replied the shiftless one. "I'd rather be rowed by Jim Hart than walk five hundred miles."

"And you, Paul?"

"I say take to the boat. We may have to fight. We've held them off on the water before and I'm sure we can do it again."

"And you, Tom?"

"The boat."

"And you, Jim?"

"The boat, an' make Sol thar do his share uv the work."

"What do you say, Mr. Pennypacker?"

"I'm not a forester, and as all of you are for the boat, so am I."

"That seems to make it unanimous, and in an hour we'll start for our hidden navy. It's at the edge of the next big river east of the Scioto and we ought to steer a pretty straight course for it."

They traveled at a good pace. Mr. Pennypacker, while not a woodsman, was a good walker, and, despite his age, proved himself tough and enduring. They crossed Indian trails several times, but did not come into contact with any of the warriors. They swam three or four deep creeks, but in four days they came to the river not many miles above the place at which they had hidden the boat. Then they descended the stream and approached the point with some anxiety.

"Suppose the boat isn't there," said Paul; "suppose the Indians have found it."

"We ain't supposing'," said Shif'less Sol. "We're shore it's thar."

They waded among the bushes growing at the water's edge and the shiftless one, who was in advance, uttered a suppressed cry of pleasure.

"Here it is, jest ez we left it," he said.

The boat had been untouched, but Henry knew all the time the chances were in favor of their finding it so. With the keenest delight, they pulled it out into the stream and looked it over. They had made of it a cache and they had left in it many valuable articles which they would need. Among these were four extra rifles, two fine fowling pieces, a large supply of powder and lead, axes and hatchets, and extra clothing and blankets. They had stocked the boat well on leaving Pittsburgh, and now it was like retaking a great treasure. Shif'less Sol climbed aboard and with a deep sigh of pleasure reclined against the side.

"Now, Saplin'," he said, "I'll go to sleep while you row me down to Louisville."

"We'll do most of our traveling by night," said Henry, "and as we'll have the current with us I don't think that you or Jim, Sol, will have to work yourselves to death."

After their examination of the boat to see that everything was all right, they pulled it back into the bushes, not intending to start until the dark set in. There was a considerable supply of salted food, coffee and tea on board, but Henry and Sol killed two deer farther up the river bank which they quickly cleaned and dressed. They now thought themselves provisioned for the trip to the Falls of the Ohio, and they carried, in addition, fishing tackle which they could use at any time.

They pulled clear of the bushes about 8 o'clock in the evening and rowed down the river. But as the stream was bank full and running fast, they did not have to make any great effort. Toward midnight when they reached some of the wider parts of the river they set the sail and went ahead at a swifter pace. Henry calculated that they could reach the Ohio slightly after dawn, but as the night was uncommonly clear, with the promise of a very brilliant day to follow, they furled their sails at least two hours before sunrise, and, finding another shallow cove, drew their boat into it among the bushes.

"Now for a sleep," said Henry. "Tom and I will keep watch until noon and then Sol and Paul will take our places. At night we will start again."

"And where does my watch come, pray?" asked Mr. Pennypacker.

"We want you to help us to-night," replied Henry. "We'll need your knowledge of the sail and the oars."

"Very well," replied the unsuspicious schoolmaster. "It is understood that I do extra work to-night, because I do not watch to-day."

Henry, when he turned his face away, smiled a little. It was understood among them all that they were to spare the schoolmaster as much as possible, and to do so, they used various little devices. Theirs was a good roomy boat and those who were to sleep first disposed themselves comfortably, while Henry sat in the prow and Tom in the stern, both silent and apparently listless, but watching with eyes and ears alike. The dawn came, and, as they had foreseen, it was a bright, hot day. It was so close among the bushes that the sleepers stirred restlessly and beads of perspiration stood on the faces of the watchers. Not a breath of air stirred either in the woods or on the river. Henry was glad when it was their turn to sleep, and when he awoke, night had come with its cool shadows and a wind also that dispelled the breathless heat.

Then they pulled out of the bushes and floated again with the stream, but they did not hoist their sail. The air after the close heat of the day was charged with electricity, and they looked for a storm. It came about 11 o'clock, chiefly as a display of thunder and lightning. The flashes of electricity dazzled them and continued without a break for almost an hour. The roar of the thunder was like the unbroken discharges of great batteries, but both wind and rain were light. Several times the lightning struck with a tremendous crash in the woods about them, but the boat glided on untouched. About midnight they came out into the flood of the Ohio, and, setting their sail, they steered down the center of the stream.

All of them felt great relief, now that they were on the wide Ohio. On the narrower tributary they might have been fired upon from either shore, but the Ohio was a half mile and sometimes a full mile from bank to bank. As long as they kept in the middle of the stream they were practically safe from the bullets of ambushed Indians.

They took turns at sleeping, but it was not necessary now to use the oars. The wind was still strong, and the sail carried them at great speed down the river. They felt safe and comfortable, but it was a wild and weird scene upon which they looked. The banks of the Ohio here were high and clothed in dense forest which, in the glare ofthe lightning, looked like gigantic black walls on either shore. The surface of the river itself was tinted under the blaze as if with fire, and often it ran in red waves before the wind. The darkness was intense, but the flashes of lightning were so vivid that they easily saw their way.

"We're going back on our old path now, Paul," said Henry. "You remember how we came up the river with Adam Colfax, fought the fleet of Timmendiquas, and helped save the fort?"

"I couldn't well forget it," replied Paul. "Why, I can see it all again, just as if it happened only yesterday, but I'm mighty glad that Timmendiquas is not here now with a fleet."

"Will we tie up to the bank by day as we did on the other river?" asked Mr. Pennypacker.

"Not on the Ohio," replied Henry. "As white immigrants are now coming down it, Indians infest both shores, so we'll keep straight ahead in the middle of the stream. We may be attacked there, but perhaps we can either whip or get away from anything that the Indians now have on the river."

While they talked Shif'less Sol looked carefully to their armament. He saw that all the extra rifles and pistols were loaded and that they lay handy. But he had little to say and the others, after the plan had been arranged, were silent. The wind became irregular. Now and then gusts of it lashed the surface of the giant stream, but toward morning it settled into a fair breeze. The thunder and lightning ceased by that time, and there was promise of a good day.

The promise was fulfilled and they floated peacefully on until afternoon. Then shots were fired at them from the northern bank, but the bullets spattered the water a full fifty yards short. Henry and Sol, who had the keenest eyes, could make out the outlines of Indians on the shore, but they were not troubled.

"I'm sure it's just a small hunting party," said Henry, "and they can do us no harm. Their bullets can't reach us, and you can't run along the banks of a great river and keep up with a boat in the stream."

"That's true," said Shif'less Sol, "an' I think I'll tell 'em so. I always like to hurt the feelin's of a bloodthirsty savage that's lookin' fur my scalp."

He opened his mouth to its widest extent and gave utterance to a most extraordinary cry, the like of which had perhaps never before been heard in those woods. It rose in a series of curves and undulations. It had in it something of the howl of the wolf and also the human note. It was essentially challenging and contemptuous. Anybody who heard it was bound to take it as a personal insult, and it became most effective when it died away in a growling, spitting noise, like the defiance of an angry cat. Henry fairly jumped in his seat when he heard it.

"Sol," he exclaimed, "what under the sun do you mean?"

The mouth of the shiftless one opened again, but this time in a wide grin of delight.

"I wuz jest tellin' them Injuns that I didn't like 'em," he replied. "Do you reckon they understood?"

"I think they did," replied Henry with emphasis.

"That bein' so, I'll tell 'em ag'in. Look out, here she comes!"

Again the mouth of Shif'less Sol swung wide, and again he uttered that fearful yell of defiance, abuse, contempt and loathing, a yell so powerful that it came back in repeated echoes without any loss of character. The Indians on the bank, stung by it, uttered a fierce shout and fired another volley, but the bullets fell further short than ever. Shif'less Sol smiled in deep content.

"See how I'm makin' 'em waste good ammunition," he said. "I learned that trick from Paul's tales o' them old Greeks an' Trojans. As fur ez I could make out when a Greek an' Trojan come out to fight one another, each feller would try to talk the other into throwin' his spear fust, an' afore he wuz close enough to take good aim. All them old heroes done a heap o' talkin' an' gen'ally they expected to get somethin' out o' it."

"Undoubtedly the Greeks and Trojans had thrilling war cries," said Mr. Pennypacker, "but I doubt, Mr. Hyde, whether they ever had any as weird as yours."

"Which shows that I'm jest a leetle ahead o' any o' them old fellers," said Shif'less Sol in tones of deep satisfaction.

The boat, moving swiftly before the wind, soon left the Indians on the northern bank far behind, and once more they were at peace with the wilderness. The river was now very beautiful. It had not yet taken on the muddy tint characteristic of its lower reaches, the high and sloping banks were covered with beautiful forest, and coming from north and south they saw the mouths of creeks and rivers pouring the waters of great regions into the vast main stream. Henry, as captain of the boat, regarded these mouths with a particularly wary and suspicious eye. Such as they formed the best ambush for Indian canoes watching to pounce upon the immigrant boats coming down the Ohio. Whenever he saw the entrance of a tributary he always had the boat steered in toward the opposite shore, while all except the steersman sat with their rifles across their knees until the dangerous locality was passed safely.

They anchored a little after nightfall. The current was very gentle and fortunately their anchor would hold near the middle of the stream. Henry wished to give rest to a part of his crew and he knew also that in the night they would pass the mouth of the Licking, opposite the site of Cincinnati, a favorite place of ambush for the Indian boats. All the indications pointed to some dark hours ahead, and that was just the kind they needed for running such a gauntlet.

This time it was he and Tom Ross who watched while the others slept, and some hours after dark they saw fitful lights on the northern shore, appearing and reappearing at three or four points. They believed them to be signals, but they could not read them.

"Of course there are warriors in those woods," said Henry. "Timmendiquas, knowing that Clark has gathered or is gathering his forces at the Falls, will send his best scouts to watch him. They may have seen us, and they may be telling their friends on the south side of the river that we are here."

"Mebbe so," said Tom Ross.

Changing their plans they took up the anchor and the boat, driven by wind and current, moved on at good speed. Tom steered and Henry sat near him, watching both shores. The others, stowed here and there, slept soundly. The lights flickered on the northern shore for a few minutes, and then a curve of the stream shut them out. The night itself was bright, a full moon and many stars turning the whole broad surface of the river to silver, and making distinct any object that might appear upon it. Henry would have preferred a dark and cloudy night for the passage by the mouth of the Licking, but since they did not have it they must go on anyhow.

They sailed quietly with the current for several hours, and the night showed no signs of darkening. Once Henry thought he saw a light on the southern shore, but it was gone so quickly that keen-eyed as he was he could not tell whether it was reality or merely fancy.

"Did you see it, Tom?" he asked.

"I did, or at least I thought I did."

"Then, since we both saw it, it must have been reality, and it indicates to my mind that Indians are on the south as well as on the north bank. Maybe they have seen us here."

"Mebbe."

"Which renders it more likely that they may be on watch at the mouth of the Licking for anything that passes."

"Mebbe."

"According to my calculation we'll be there in another hour. What do you think?"

"I say one hour, too."

"And we'll let the boys sleep on until we see danger, if danger comes."

"That's what I'd do," replied Tom, casting a glance at the sleeping figures.

No word was spoken again for a long time, but, as they approached the dangerous mouth, Tom steered the boat further and further toward the northern bank. Both remembered the shores here from their passage up the Ohio, and Henry knew that the gap in the wall of trees on the south betokened the mouth of the Licking. Tom steadily bore in toward the northern bank until he was not more than thirty yards from the trees. The moon and the stars meanwhile, instead of favoring them, seemed to grow brighter. The river was a great moving sheet of silver, and the boat stood out upon it black and upright.

Henry, with his eyes upon the black wall, saw two dots appear there and then two more, and he knew at once their full significance. The ambush had been laid, not for them in particular, but for any boat that might pass.

"Tom," he said, "the Indian canoes are coming. Keep straight on down the river. I'll wake the others."

The remaining four aroused, took their rifles and gazed at the black dots which had now increased from four to six, and which were taking the shape of long canoes with at least half a dozen paddlers in every one. Two of the canoes carried sails which indicated to Henry the presence of renegades.

"In a fight at close quarters they'd be too strong for us," said Henry. "That force must include at least forty warriors, but we can run our boat against the northern shore and escape into the woods. Are you in favor of our doing that?"

"No," they answered with one accord.

Henry laughed.

"I knew your answer before I asked the question," he said, "and as we are not going to escape into the woods we must prepare for a river race and a battle. I think we could leave them behind without much trouble, if it were not for those two boats with the sails."

"Let 'em come," said Shif'less Sol. "We've got plenty of rifles an' we can hit at longer range than they can."

"Still, it's our business to avoid a fight if possible," said Henry. "George Rogers Clark wants whole men to fight, not patients to nurse. Tom, you keep on steering and all the rest of us will take a hand at the oars."

The boat shot forward under the new impetus, but behind them the six canoes, particularly the two on which sails had been fitted, were coming fast. The night was so bright that they could see the warriors painted and naked to the waist sending their paddles in great sweeps through the water. It was evident also that they had enough extra men to work in relays, which gave them a great advantage.

"It's to be a long chase," said Henry, "but I'm thinking that they'll overtake us unless we interfere with them in some rude manner."

"Meaning these?" said Shif'less Sol, patting one of the rifles.

"Meaning those," said Henry; "and it's lucky that we're so well provided. Those boats are not led by ordinary warriors. See how they're using every advantage. They're spreading out exactly as Indian pursuers do on land, in order that some portion of their force may profit by any turn or twist of ours."

It was so. The pursuing fleet was spreading out like a fan, two boats following near the northern shore, two near the southern and two in the center. Evidently they intended neglecting no precaution to secure what many of them must already have regarded as a certain prize. Mr. Pennypacker regarded them with dilated eyes.

"A formidable force," he said, "and I judge by their actions that they will prove tenacious."

"Shorely," said Shif'less Sol, as he tapped the rifle again, "but you must rec'lect, Mr. Pennypacker, that we've oncommon good rifles an' some o' us are oncommon good shots. It might prove better fur 'em ef they didn't come so fast. Henry, kin you make out any white faces in them two boats in the center?"

"It's pretty far to tell color, but a figure in the right-hand boat, sitting close to the mast, looks to me mightily like that of Braxton Wyatt."

"I had just formed the same notion. That's the reason I asked, an' ef I ain't mistook, Simon Girty's in the other boat. Oh, Henry, do you think I kin git a shot at him?"

"I doubt it," replied Henry. "Girty is cunning and rarely exposes himself. There, they are firing, but it's too soon."

Several shots were discharged from the leading boats, but they fell far short. Evidently they were intended as threats, but, besides Henry's comment, the pursued took no notice of them. Then the savages, for the first time, uttered their war cry, but the fugitives did not answer.

"Ef they mean by that yell that they've got us," said Shif'less Sol, "then they might ez well yell ag'in."

"Still, I think they're gaining upon us somewhat," said Henry, "and it may be necessary before long to give them a hint or two."

Now it was his turn to tap the rifle significantly, and Henry with a calculating eye measured the distance between their own and the leading boat. He saw that the warriors were gaining. It was a slow gain, but in time it would bring them within easy rifle shot. The fleeing boat carried many supplies which weighed her down to a certain extent, but the pursuing boats carried nothing except the pursuers themselves. Henry raised his rifle a little and looked again at the distance.

"A little too fur yet, Henry," said Shif'less Sol.

"I think so, too," said Henry. "We'd best wait until we're absolutely sure."

A cry broke from Paul.

"Look ahead!" he cried. "We've enemies on both sides!"

The alarming news was true. Two large boats loaded with warriors had shot out from the northern bank four or five hundred yards ahead, and were coming directly into the path of the fugitives. A yell full of malice and triumph burst from the savages in the pursuing canoes, and those in the canoes ahead answered it with equal malice and triumph. The fate of the fugitives seemed to be sealed, but the five had been in many a close place before, and no thought of despair entered their minds. Henry at once formed the plan and as usual they acted with swift decision and boldness. Tom was now steering and Henry cried to him:

"Shelter yourself and go straight ahead. Lie low, the rest of you fire at those before us!"

Their boat went swiftly on. The two ahead of them drew directly into their path, but veered a little to one side, when they saw with what speed the other boat was approaching. They also began to fire, but the six, sheltered well, heard the bullets patter upon the wooden sides and they bided their time. Henry, peeping over, marked the boat on the right and saw a face which he knew to be that of a white man. In an instant he recognized the renegade Quarles and rage rose within him. Without the aid of the renegades, more ruthless than the red men themselves, the Indians could never have accomplished so much on the border. He raised his rifle a little and now he cocked it. Shif'less Sol glanced up and saw the red fire in his eye.

"What is it, Henry?" he asked.

"The renegade Quarles is in the boat on the right. As we have to run a gauntlet here, and there will be some shooting, I mean that one of the renegades shall never trouble us any more."

"I'm sorry it's not Girty or Wyatt," said the shiftless one, "but since it ain't either o' them it might ez well be Quarles. He might be missed, but he wouldn't be mourned."

The boat, with Tom Ross steering, kept straight ahead with undiminished speed, the wind filling out the sail. The Indians in the two boats before them fired again, but the bullets as before thudded upon the wooden sides.

But Henry, crouching now with his cocked rifle, saw his opportunity. Quarles, raising himself up in the canoe, had fired and he was just taking his rifle from his shoulder. Henry fired directly at the tanned forehead of this wicked man, who had so often shed the blood of his own people, and the bullet crashed through the brain. The renegade half rose, and then fell from the boat into the stream, which hid his body forever. A cry of rage and fear came from the Indians and the next moment four other marksmen, two from the right and two from the left, fired into the opposing canoes. The schoolmaster also fired, although he was not sure that he hit any foe; but it was a terrible volley nevertheless. The two Indian boats contained both dead and wounded. Paddles were dropped into the water and floated out of reach. Moreover, Tom Ross, when his cunning eye saw the confusion, steered his own boat in such a manner that it struck the canoe on the right a glancing blow, sideswiping it, as it were.

Tom and his comrades were staggered by the impact, but their boat, uninjured, quickly righted itself and went on. The Indian canoe was smashed in and sank, leaving its living occupants struggling in the water, while the other canoe was compelled to turn and pick them up.

"Well done, Mr. Ross!" called Mr. Pennypacker. "That was a happy thought. You struck them as the old Roman galleys with their beaks struck their antagonists, and you have swept them from our path."

"That's true, Mr. Pennypacker," said Shif'less Sol, "but don't you go to stickin' your head up too much. Thar, didn't I tell you! Ef many more bullets like that come, you'd git a nice hair cut an' no charge."

A bullet had clipped a gray lock from the top of the schoolmaster's head, but flattening himself on the bottom of the boat he did not give the Indians a second shot. Meanwhile Henry and the others were sending bullets into the crews of the boats behind them. They did not get a chance at Girty and Wyatt, who were evidently concealing themselves from these foes, whom they knew to be such deadly sharpshooters, but they were making havoc among the warriors. It was a fire so deadly that all the canoes stopped and let the boat pass out of range. The little band sent back their own shout, taunting and triumphant, and then, laying aside their rifles, they took up the oars again. They sped forward and as the night darkened the Indian canoes sank quickly out of sight.

"I think we'll have the right of way now to the Falls," said Henry.

CHAPTER XVII
THE ROAD TO WAREVILLE

Henry made no mistake when he predicted that they would have the right of way to the Falls. Days passed and the broad river bore them peacefully onward, the wind blowing into ripples its yellow surface which the sunshine turned into deep gold. The woods still formed a solid bank of dark green on either shore, and they knew that warriors might be lurking in them, but they kept to the middle of the current, and the Ohio was so wide that they were fairly safe from sharpshooters. In addition to the caution, habitual to borderers, they usually kept pretty well sheltered behind the stout sides of their boat.

"Tain't no use takin' foolish risks," said Shif'less Sol wisely. "A bullet that you ain't lookin' fur will hurt jest ez bad ez one that you're expectin', an' the surprise gives a lot o' pain, too."

Hence they always anchored at night, far out in the water, put out all lights, and never failed to keep watch. Several times they detected signs of their wary enemy. Once they saw flames twinkling on the northern shore, and twice they heard signal cries in the southern woods. But the warriors did not make any nearer demonstration, and they went on, content to leave alone when they were left alone.

All were eager to see the new settlement at the Falls, of which reports had come to them through the woods, and they were particularly anxious to find it a tower of strength against the fresh Indian invasion. Their news concerning it was not yet definite, but they heard that the first blockhouse was built on an island. Hence every heart beat a little faster when they saw the low outline of a wooden island rising from the bosom of the Ohio.

"According to all we've heard," said Henry, "that should be the place."

"It shorely is," said Shif'less Sol, "an' besides I see smoke risin' among them trees."

"Yes, and I see smoke rising on the southern shore also," said Henry.

"Which may mean that they've made a second settlement, one on the mainland," said Paul.

As they drew nearer Henry sent a long quavering cry, the halloo of the woodsman, across the waters, and an answering cry came from the edge of the island. Then a boat containing two white men, clad in deerskin, put out and approached the five cautiously. Henry and Paul stood up to show that they were white and friends, and the boat then came swiftly.

"Who are you?" called one of the men.

Henry replied, giving their identity briefly, and the man said:

"My name is Charles Curd, and this is Henry Palmer. We live at Louisville and we are on the watch for friends and enemies alike. We're glad to know that you're the former."

They escorted the five back to the island, and curious people came down to the beach to see the forest runners land. Henry and his comrades for their part were no less curious and soon they were inspecting this little settlement which for protection had been cast in a spot surrounded by the waters of the Ohio. They saw Corn Island, a low stretch of soil, somewhat sandy but originally covered with heavy forest, now partly cleared away. Yet the ax had left sycamores ten feet through and one hundred feet high.

The whole area of the island was only forty-three acres, but it already contained several fields in which fine corn and pumpkins were raised. On a slight rise was built the blockhouse in the form of an Egyptian cross, the blockhouse proper forming the body of the cross, while the cabins of the settlers constituted the arms. In addition to the sycamores, great cottonwoods had grown here, but nearly all of them had been cut down, and then had been split into rails and boards. Back of the field and at the western edge of the river, was a magnificent growth of cane, rising to a height of more than twenty feet.

This little settlement, destined to be one of the great cities of the West, had been founded by George Rogers Clark only two or three years before, and he had founded it in spite of himself. Starting from Redstone on the Monongahela with one hundred and fifty militia for the conquest of the Illinois country he had been accompanied by twenty pioneer families who absolutely refused to be turned back. Finding that they were bound to go with him Clark gave them his protection, but they stopped at Corn Island in the Ohio and there built their blockhouse. Now it was a most important frontier post, a stronghold against the Indians.

Before they ate of the food offered to them Henry looked inquiringly at the smoke on the southern shore. Curd said with some pride:

"We're growing here. We spread to the mainland in a year. Part of our people have moved over there, and some new ones have come from Virginia. On the island and the mainland together, we've now got pretty nearly two hundred people and we've named our town Louisville in honor of King Louis of France who is helping us in the East. We've got history, too, or rather it was made before we came here. An old chief, whom the whites called Tobacco, told George Rogers Clark that the Alligewi, which is their name for the Mound Builders, made their last stand here against the Shawnees, Miamis and other Indians who now roam in this region. A great battle occurred on an island at the Falls and the Mound Builders were exterminated. As for myself, I know nothing about it, but it's what Tobacco said."

Paul's curiosity was aroused instantly and he made a mental note to investigate the story, when he found an opportunity, but he was never able to get any further than the Indian legend which most likely had a basis of truth. For the present, he and his comrades were content with the welcome which the people on Corn Island gave them, a welcome full of warmth and good cheer. Their hosts put before them water cooled in gourds, cakes of Indian meal, pies of pumpkin, all kinds of game, and beef and pork besides. While they ate and drank Henry, who as usual was spokesman, told what had occurred at Detroit, further details of the successful advance of the Indians and English under Bird, of which they had already heard, and the much greater but postponed scheme of destruction planned by Timmendiquas, de Peyster, Girty and their associates. Curd, Palmer and the others paled a little under their tan as they listened, but their courage came back swiftly.

"At any rate," said Curd, "we've got a man to lead us against them, a man who strikes fast, sure and hard, George Rogers Clark, the hero of Vincennes and Kaskaskia, the greatest leader in all the West."

"Why, is he here?" exclaimed Henry in surprise. "I thought he was farther East."

"You'll see him inside of half an hour. He was at the other blockhouse on the southern shore, and we sent up a signal that strangers were here. There he comes now."

A boat had put out from the southern bank. It contained three men, two of whom were rowing, while the third sat upright in a military fashion. All his body beneath his shoulders was hidden by the boat's sides, but his coat was of the Continental buff and blue, while a border cap of raccoon skin crowned his round head. Such incongruous attire detracted nothing from the man's dignity and presence. Henry saw that his face was open, his gaze direct, and that he was quite young. He was looking straight toward the five who had come with their new friends down to the river's edge, and, when he sprang lightly upon the sand, he gave them a military salute. They returned it in like manner, while they looked with intense curiosity at the famous leader of the border forces. Clark turned to Henry, whose figure and bearing indicated the chief.

"You come from the North, from the depths of the Indian country, I take it," he said.

"From the very heart of it," replied the youth. "I was a prisoner at Detroit, and my comrades were near by outside the walls. We have also seen Bird returning from his raid with his prisoners and we know that Timmendiquas, de Peyster, Girty, Caldwell, and the others are going to make a supreme effort to destroy every settlement west of the Alleghanies. A great force under Timmendiquas, Caldwell and Girty came part of the way but turned back, partly, I think, because of divisions among themselves and partly because they heard of your projected advance. But it will come again."

The shoulders in the military coat seemed to stiffen and the eyes under the raccoon skin cap flashed.

"I did want to go back to Virginia," said Clark, "but I'm glad that I'm here. Mr. Ware, young as you are, you've seen a lot of forest work, I take it, and so I ask you what is the best way to meet an attack?"

"To attack first."

"Good! good! That was my plan! Report spoke true! We'll strike first. We'll show these officers and chiefs that we're not the men to sit idly and wait for our foe. We'll go to meet him. Nay more, we'll find him in his home and destroy him. Doesn't that appeal to you, my lads?"

"It does," said five voices, emphatic and all together, and then Henry added, speaking he knew for his comrades as well as himself:

"Colonel Clark, we wish to volunteer for the campaign that we know you have planned. Besides the work that we have done here in the West, we have seen service in the East. We were at Wyoming when the terrible massacre occurred, and we were with General Sullivan when he destroyed the Iroquois power. But, sir, I wish to say that we do best in an independent capacity, as scouts, skirmishers, in fact as a sort of vanguard."

Clark laughed and clapped a sinewy hand upon Henry's shoulder.

"I see," he said. "You wish to go with me to war, but you wish at the same time to be your own masters. It might be an unreasonable request from some people, but, judging from what I see of you and what I have heard of you and your comrades, it is just the thing. You are to watch as well as fight for me. Were you not the eyes of the fleet that Adam Colfax brought up the Ohio?"

Henry blushed and hesitated, but Clark exclaimed heartily:

"Nay, do not be too modest, my lad! We are far apart here in the woods, but news spreads, nevertheless, and I remember sitting one afternoon and listening to an old friend, Major George Augustus Braithwaite, tell a tale of gallant deeds by river and forest, and how a fort and fleet were saved largely through the efforts of five forest runners, two of whom were yet boys. Major Braithwaite gave me detailed descriptions of the five, and they answer so exactly to the appearance of you and your comrades that I am convinced you are the same. Since you are so modest, I will tell you to your face that I'd rather have you five than fifty ordinary men. Now, young sir, blush again and make the most of it!"

Henry did blush, and said that the Colonel gave them far too much credit, but at heart he, like the other four, felt a great swell of pride. Their deeds in behalf of the border were recognized by the great leader, and surely it was legitimate to feel that one had not toiled and fought in vain for one's people.

A few minutes later they sat down with Clark and some of the others under the boughs of the big sycamore, and gave a detailed account of their adventures, including all that they had seen from the time they had left for New Orleans until the present moment.

"A great tale! a great tale!" said Clark, meditatively, "and I wish to add, Mr. Ware, an illuminating one also. It throws light upon forest councils and forest plans. Besides your service in battle, you bring us news that shows us how to meet our enemy and nothing could be of greater value. Now, I wish to say to you that it will take us many weeks to collect the needful force, and that will give you two lads ample time, if you wish, to visit your home in Wareville, taking with you the worthy schoolmaster whom you have rescued so happily."

Henry and Paul decided at once to accept the suggestion. Both felt the great pulses leap at mention of Wareville and home. They had not seen their people for nearly two years, although they had sent word several times that they were well. Now they felt an overwhelming desire to see once again their parents and the neat little village by the river, enclosed within its strong palisades. Yet they delayed a few days longer to attend to necessary preliminaries of the coming campaign. Among other things they went the following morning to see the overflow settlement on the south shore, now but a year old.

This seed of a great city was yet faint and small. The previous winter had been a terrible one for the immigrants. The Ohio had been covered with thick ice from shore to shore. Most of their horses and cattle had frozen to death. Nevertheless they had no thought of going away, and there were many things to encourage the brave. They had a good harbor on the river at the mouth of a fine creek, that they named Beargrass, and back of them was a magnificent forest of gum, buckeye, cherry, sycamore, maple and giant poplars. It had been proved that the soil was extremely fertile, and they were too staunch to give up so fair a place. They also had a strong fort overlooking the river, and, with Clark among them, they were ready to defy any Indian force that might come.

But the time passed quickly, and Henry and Paul and the schoolmaster were ready for the last stage of their journey, deciding, in order that they might save their strength, to risk once more the dangers of the water passage. They would go in a canoe until they came to the mouth of the river that flowed by Wareville and then row up the current of the latter until they reached home. Shif'less Sol, Jim and Tom were going to remain with Clark until their return. But these three gave them hand-clasps of steel when they departed.

"Don't you get trapped by wanderin' Indians, Henry," said the shiftless one. "We couldn't get along very well without you fellers. Do most o' your rowin' at night an' lay by under overhangin' boughs in the day. You know more'n I do, Henry, but I'm so anxious about you I can't keep from givin' advice."

"Don't any of you do too much talkin'," said Silent Tom. "Injuns hear pow'ful well, an' many a feller hez been caught in an ambush, an' hez lost his scalp jest 'cause he would go along sayin' idle words that told the Injuns whar he wuz, when he might hev walked away safe without thar ever knowin' he wuz within a thousand miles uv them."

"An' be mighty particular about your cookin'," said Long Jim. "Many a good man hez fell sick an' died, jest 'cause his grub wuzn't fixed eggzackly right. An' when you light your fires fur ven'son an' buffalo steaks be shore thar ain't too much smoke. More than once smoke hez brought the savages down on people. Cookin' here in the woods is not cookin' only, it's also a delicate an' bee-yu-ti-ful art that saves men's lives when it's done right, by not leadin' Shawnees, Wyandots an' other ferocious warriors down upon 'em."

Henry promised every one of the three to follow his advice religiously, and there was moisture in his and Paul's eyes when they caught the last view of them standing upon the bank and waving farewell. The next instant they were hidden by a curve of the shore, and then Henry said:

"It's almost like losing one's right arm to leave those three behind. I don't feel complete without them."

"Nor do I," said Paul. "I believe they were giving us all that advice partly to hide their emotion."

"Undoubtedly they were," said Mr. Pennypacker in a judicial tone, "and I wish to add that I do not know three finer characters, somewhat eccentric perhaps, but with hearts in the right place, and with sound heads on strong shoulders. They are like some ancient classic figures of whom I have read, and they are fortunate, too, to live in the right time and right place for them."

They made a safe passage over a stretch of the Ohio and then turned up the tributary river, rowing mostly, as Shif'less Sol had suggested, by night, and hiding their canoe and themselves by day. It was not difficult to find a covert as the banks along the smaller river were nearly always overhung by dense foliage, and often thick cane and bushes grew well into the water's edge. Here they would stop when the sun was brightest, and sometimes the heat was so great that not refuge from danger alone made them glad to lie by when the golden rays came vertically. Then they would make themselves as comfortable as possible in the boat and bearing Silent Tom's injunction in mind, talk in very low tones, if they talked at all. But oftenest two of them slept while the third watched.

They had been three days upon the tributary when it was Henry who happened to be watching. Both Paul and the teacher slumbered very soundly. Paul lay at the stern of the boat and Mr. Pennypacker in the middle. Henry was in the prow, sitting at ease with his rifle across his knees. The boat was amid a tall growth of canes, the stalks and blades rising a full ten feet above their heads, and hiding them completely. Henry had been watching the surface of the river, but at last the action grew wholly mechanical. Had anything appeared there he would have seen it, but his thoughts were elsewhere. His whole life, since he had arrived, a boy of fifteen, in the Kentucky wilderness, was passing before him in a series of pictures, vivid and wonderful, standing out like reality itself. He was in a sort of twilight midway between the daylight and a dream, and it seemed to him once more that Providence had kept a special watch over his comrades and himself. How else could they have escaped so many dangers? How else could fortune have turned to their side, when the last chance seemed gone? No skill, even when it seemed almost superhuman, could have dragged them back from the pit of death. He felt with all the power of conviction that a great mission had been given to them, and that they had been spared again and again that they might complete it.

While he yet watched and saw, he visited a misty world. The wind had risen and out of the dense foliage above him came its song upon the stalks and blades of the cane. A low note at first, it swelled into triumph, and it sounded clearly in his ear, bar on bar. He did not have the power to move, as he listened then to the hidden voice. His blood leaped and a deep sense of awe, and of the power of the unknown swept over him. But he was not afraid. Rather he shared in the triumph that was expressed so clearly in the mystic song.

The note swelled, touched upon its highest note and then died slowly away in fall after fall, until it came in a soft echo and then the echo itself was still. Henry returned to the world of reality with every sense vivid and alert. He heard the wind blowing in the cane and nothing more. The surface of the river rippled lightly in the breeze, but neither friend nor enemy passed there. The stream was as lonely and desolate as if man had never come. He shook himself a little, but the spiritual exaltation, born of the song and the misty region that he had visited, remained.

"A sign, a prophecy!" he murmured. His heart swelled. The new task would be achieved as the others had been. It did not matter whether he had heard or had dreamed. His confidence in the result was absolute. He sat a long time looking out upon the water, but never moving. Anyone observing him would have concluded after a while that he was no human being, merely an image. It would not have seemed possible that any living organism could have remained as still as a stone so many hours.

When the sun showed that it was well past noon, Paul awoke. He glanced at Henry, who nodded. The nod meant that all was well. By and by Mr. Pennypacker, also, awoke and then Henry in his turn went to sleep so easily and readily that it seemed a mere matter of will. The schoolmaster glanced at him and whispered to Paul:

"A great youth, Paul! Truly a great youth! It is far from old Greece to this forest of Kaintuckee, but he makes me think of the mighty heroes who are enshrined in the ancient legends and stories."

"That thought has come to me, too," Paul whispered back. "I like to picture him as Hector, but Hector with a better fate. I don't think Henry was born for any untimely end."

"No, that could not be," said the schoolmaster with conviction.

Then they relapsed into silence and just about the time the first shadow betokened the coming twilight Paul heard a faint gurgling sound which he was sure was made by oars. He touched the schoolmaster and whispered to him to listen. Then he pulled Henry's shoulder slightly, and instantly the great youth sat up, wide awake.

"Someone is near," whispered Paul. "Listen!"

Henry bent his head close to the water and distinctly heard the swishing of paddles, coming in the direction that they had followed in the night. It was a deliberate sound and Henry inferred at once that those who approached were in no hurry and feared no enemy. Then he drew the second inference that it was Indians. White men would know that danger was always about them in these woods.

"We have nothing to do but lie here and see them as they pass," he whispered to his companions. "We are really as safe among these dense canes as if we were a hundred miles away, provided we make no noise."

There was no danger that any of them would make a noise. They lay so still that their boat never moved a hair and not even the wariest savage on the river would have thought that one of their most formidable enemies and two of his friends lay hidden in the canes so near.

"Look!" whispered Henry. "There is Braxton Wyatt!"

Henry and Paul were eager enough to see but the schoolmaster was perhaps the most eager of all. This was something new in his experience. He had heard much of Braxton Wyatt, the renegade, once a pupil of his, and he did not understand how one of white blood and training could turn aside to join the Indians, and to become a more ruthless enemy of his own people than the savages themselves. Yet there could be no doubt of its truth, and now that he saw Wyatt he understood. Evil passions make an evil face. Braxton Wyatt's jaw was now heavy and projecting, his eyes were dark and lowering, and his cheek bones seemed to have become high like those of the warriors with whom he lived. The good Mr. Pennypacker shuddered. He had lived long and he could read the hearts of men. He knew now that Braxton Wyatt, despite his youth, was lost beyond redemption to honor and truth. The schoolmaster shuddered again.

The boat—a large one—contained besides Wyatt a white man, obviously a renegade, and six sturdy Shawnee warriors who were wielding the paddles. The warriors were quite naked, save for the breechcloth, and their broad shoulders and chests were painted with many hideous decorations. Their rifles lay beside them. Braxton Wyatt's manner showed that he was the leader and Henry had no doubt that this was a party of scouts come to spy upon Wareville. It was wholly likely that Braxton Wyatt, who knew the place so thoroughly, should undertake such an errand.

Henry was right. Timmendiquas, de Peyster and Girty as leaders of the allied forces preparing for invasion in case Clark could not gather a sufficient force for attack, were neglecting no precaution. They had sent forth small parties to examine into the condition of every station in Kentucky. These parties were not to make any demonstration, lest the settlers be put on their guard, but, after obtaining their information, were to retire as silently as they had come. Braxton Wyatt had promptly secured command of the little force sent toward Wareville, taking with him as lieutenant a young renegade, a kindred spirit named Early.

Strange emotions agitated Wyatt when he started. He had a desire to see once more the place where he had been a boy with other boys of his own white race, and where he might yet have been with his own kind, if a soul naturally turning to malice had not sent him off to the savages. Because he was now an outcast, although of his own making, he hated his earlier associates all the more. He sought somehow to blame them for it. They had never appreciated him enough. Had they put him forward and given him his due, he would not now be making war upon them. Foolish and blind, they must suffer the consequences of their own stupidity. When Wareville was taken, he might induce the Indians to spare a few, but there were certainly some who should not be spared. His brow was black and his thoughts were blacker. It may be that Henry read them, because his hand slid gently forward to the hammer of his rifle. But his will checked the hand before it could cock the weapon, and he shook his head impatiently.

"Not now," he said in the softest of whispers, "but we must follow that boat. It is going toward Wareville and that is our way. Since we have seen him it is for us to deal with Wyatt before he can do more mischief."

Paul nodded, and even the soul of the good schoolmaster stirred with warlike ardor. He was not a child of the forest. He knew little of ambush and the trail, but he was ready to spend his strength and blood for the good of his own people. So he too nodded, and then waited for their young leader to act.

Braxton Wyatt passed on southward and up the stream of the river. There was no song among the leaves for him, but his heart was still full of cruel passions. He did not dream that a boat containing the one whom he hated most had lain in the cane within twenty yards of him. He was thinking instead of Wareville and of the way in which he would spy out every weak place there. He and Early had become great friends, and now he told his second much about the village.

"Wareville is strong," he said, "and they have many excellent riflemen. We were repulsed there once, when we made an attack in force, and we must take it by surprise. Once we are inside the palisade everything will soon be over. I hope that we will catch Ware and his comrades there when we catch the others."

"He seems hard to hold," said Early. "That escape of his from Detroit was a daring and skillful thing. I could hardly believe it when we heard of it at the Ohio. You're bound to admit that, Braxton."

"I admit it readily enough," said Wyatt. "Oh, he's brave and cunning and strong. He would not be so much worth taking if he were not all those things!"

Early glanced at the face of his leader.

"You do dislike him, that's sure!" he said.

"You make no mistake when you say so," replied Wyatt. "There are not many of us here in the woods, and somehow he and I seem to have been always in opposition in the last two or three years. I think, however, that a new campaign will end in overwhelming victory for us, and Kaintuckee will become a complete wilderness again."

The stalwart Shawnees paddled on all that afternoon without stopping or complaining once. It was a brilliant day in early summer, all golden sunshine, but not too warm. The river flowed in curve after curve, and its surface was always illumined by the bright rays save where the unbroken forest hung in a green shadow over either edge. Scarlet tanagers darted like flashes of flame from tree to tree, and from low boughs a bird now and then poured forth a full measure of song. Braxton Wyatt had never looked upon a more peaceful wilderness, but before the sun began to set he was afflicted with a strange disquiet. An expert woodsman with an instinct for the sounds and stirrings of the forest, he began to have a belief that they were not alone on the river. He heard nothing and saw nothing, yet he felt in a vague, misty way that they were followed. He tried to put aside the thought as foolish, but it became so strong that at last he gave a signal to stop.

"What is it?" asked Early, as the paddles ceased to sigh through the water.

"I thought I heard something behind us," replied Wyatt, although he had heard nothing, "and you know we cannot afford to be seen here by any white scout or hunter."

The Indians listened intently with their trained ears and then shook their heads. There was no sound behind them, save the soft flowing of the river, as it lapped against either bank.

415

"I hear nothing," said Early.

"Nor do I," admitted Wyatt, "yet I could have sworn a few minutes ago that we were being followed. Instinct is sometimes a good guide in the forest."

"Then I suggest," said Early, "that we turn back for a few miles. We can float with the current close up to the bank under the overhanging boughs, and, if hunters or scouts are following us, they'll soon wish they were somewhere else."

He laughed and Braxton Wyatt joined him in his savage mirth.

"Your idea is a good one," said Wyatt, "and we may catch a mouse or two in our trap."

He gave another signal and the Shawnees turned the boat about, permitting it to float back with the stream, but as Early had suggested, keeping it in the shadow. Despite his experience and the lack of proof that anyone else was near, Wyatt's heart began to beat fast. Suppose the game was really there, and it should prove to be of the kind that he wanted most to take! This would be indeed a triumph worth while, and he would neglect no precaution to achieve it. They had gone back about a mile now, and he signaled to the warriors to swing the boat yet a little closer to the bank. He still heard no sound, but the belief was once more strong upon him that the quarry was there. They drifted slowly and yet there was nothing. His eye alighted upon a great mass of bushes growing in the shallow water at the edge of the river. He told the paddlers to push the boat among them until it should be completely hidden and then he waited.

But time passed and nothing came. The sun dropped lower. The yellow light on the water turned to red, and the forest flamed under the setting sun. A light breeze sprang up and the foliage rustled under its touch. Braxton Wyatt, from his covert among the bushes, watched with anger gnawing at his heart. He had been wrong or whoever it was that followed had been too wary. He was crafty and had laid his trap well, but others were crafty, too, and would turn from the door of an open trap.

The sun sank further. The red in the west deepened but gray shadows were creeping over the east and the surface of the river began to darken. Nothing had come. Nothing was coming. Braxton Wyatt said reluctantly to himself that his instinct had been wrong. He gave the word to pull the boat from the canes, and to proceed up the stream again. He was annoyed. He had laid a useless trap and he had made himself look cheap before the Indians. So he said nothing for a long time, but allowed his anger to simmer. When it was fully dark they tied up the boat and camped on shore, in the bushes near the water.

Wyatt was too cautious to permit a fire, and they ate cold food in the darkness. After a while, all slept but two of the Shawnees who kept watch. Wyatt's slumbers were uneasy. About midnight he awoke, and he was oppressed by the same presentiment that had made him turn back the boat. He heard nothing and saw nothing save his own men, but his instinct was at work once more, and it told him that his party was watched. He lay in dark woods in a vast wilderness, but he felt in every bone that near them was an alien presence.

Wyatt raised himself upon his arm and looked at the two red sentinels. Not a muscle of either had stirred. They were so much carven bronze. Their rifles lay across their knees and they stared fixedly at the forest. But he knew that their eyes and ears were of the keenest and that but little could escape their attention. Yet they had not discovered the presence. He rose finally to his feet. The Indians heard the faint noise that he made and glanced at him. But he was their commander and they said nothing, resuming in an instant their watch of the forest.

Wyatt did not take his rifle. Instead, he kept his hand on the hilt of a fine double-barreled pistol in his belt. After some hesitation he walked to the river and looked at the boat. It was still there, tied securely. No one had meddled with it. The moon was obscured and the surface of the river looked black. No object upon it could be seen far away. He listened attentively and heard nothing. But he could not rid himself of the belief that they had been followed, that even now a foe was near. He walked back to the little camp and looked at Early who was sleeping soundly. He was impatient with himself because he could not do likewise, and then, shrugging his shoulders, he went further into the forest.

The trees grew closely where Wyatt stood and there were bushes everywhere. His concealment was good and he leaned against the trunk of a huge oak to listen. He could not see fifteen feet away, but he did not believe that any human being could pass near and escape his hearing. He stood thus in the darkness for a full ten minutes, and then he was quite sure that he did hear a sound as of a heavy body moving slightly. It was not instinct or prescience, the product of a vivid fancy, but a reality. He had been too long in the woods to mistake the fact. Something was stalking something else and undoubtedly the stalker was a man.

What was the unknown stalking? Suddenly a cold sweat broke out on Braxton Wyatt's face. It was he who was being stalked and he was now

417

beyond the sight of his own sentinels. He was, for the moment, alone in the midnight woods, and he was afraid. Braxton Wyatt was not naturally a coward, and he had been hardened in the school of forest warfare, but superstitious terrors assailed him now. He was sorry that he had left the camp. His curiosity had been too great. If he wished to explore the woods, why had he not brought some of the Indians with him?

He called upon his courage, a courage that had seldom failed him, but it would not come now. He heard the stalker moving again in the bushes, not fifteen yards away, and the hand on the pistol belt became wet. He glanced up but there was no moon and clouds hid the sky. Only ear could tell when the danger was about to fall, and then it would be too late.

He made a supreme effort, put his will in control of his paralyzed limbs, and wrenched himself away. He almost ran to the camp. Then bringing his pride to his aid he dropped to a walk, and stepped back into the circle of the camp. But he was barely able to restrain a cry of relief as the chill passed from his backbone. Angry and humiliated, he awakened four of the Shawnees and sent them into the woods in search of a foe. Early was aroused by the voices and sat up, rubbing his eyes.

"What is it, Braxton?" he asked. "Are we about to be attacked?"

"No," replied Wyatt, calming himself with a violent effort, "but I am convinced that there is someone in the bushes watching us. I know that I heard the noise of footsteps and I only hope that our Shawnees will run afoul of him."

"If he's there they'll get him," said Early confidently.

"I don't know," said Braxton Wyatt.

The Indians came back presently, and one of them spoke to Wyatt, who went with them into the bushes. The moon had come out a little and, by its faint light, they showed him traces of footsteps. The imprints were ever so light, but experienced trailers could not doubt that human beings had passed. The renegade felt at the same time a certain relief and a certain alarm, relief to know that he had not been a mere prey to foolish fears, and alarm because they had been stalked by some spy so skillful and wary that they could not follow him. The Indians had endeavored to pursue the trail, but after a rod or so it was lost among the bushes.

Wyatt, apprehensive lest his mission should fail, doubled the watch and then sought sleep. He did not find it for a long time, but toward morning he fell into a troubled slumber from which he was awakened by Early about an hour after the sun had appeared above the eastern forest.

"We must be moving," said Early, "if we're going to spy out that Wareville of yours and tell our people how to get in."

"You're right," said Wyatt, "but we must watch behind us now as well as before. It is certain that we are followed and I'm afraid that we're followed by an enemy most dangerous."

Neglecting no precaution, he ordered a warrior to follow along the bank about two miles in the rear. An Indian in the deep brush could not be seen and the renegade's savage heart thrilled at the thought that after all he might be setting a trap into which his enemy would walk. Then his boat moved forward, more slowly now, and hugging the bank more closely than ever. Wyatt knew the way well. He had been several times along this river, a fine broad stream. He meant to leave the boat and take to the forest when within twenty miles of Wareville, but, before doing so, he hoped to achieve a victory which would console him for many defeats.

The warrior left behind for purposes of ambush was to rejoin them at noon, but at the appointed hour he did not come. Nor did he come at one o'clock or at two. He never came, and after Wyatt had raged with disappointment and apprehension until the middle of the afternoon he sent back a second warrior to see what had become of him. The second warrior was the best trailer and scout in the band, a Shawnee with a great reputation among his fellows, but when the night arrived neither he nor the other warrior arrived with it. They waited long for both. Three of the Indians in a group went back, but they discovered no sign. They returned full of superstitious terror which quickly communicated itself to the others and Wyatt and Early, despite their white blood, felt it also.

A most vigilant watch was kept that night. No fire was lighted and nobody slept. The renegade still hoped that the two missing warriors would return, but they did not do so. The other Indians began to believe that the evil spirit had taken them, and they were sorry that they had come upon such an errand. They wished to go back down the stream and beyond the Ohio. Near morning a warrior saw something moving in the bushes and fired at it. The shot was returned quick as a flash, and the warrior, who would fire no more, fell at the feet of the others and lay still. Wyatt and his men threw themselves upon their faces, and, after a long wait, searched the bushes, but found nothing.

Now the Indians approached the point of rebellion. It was against the will of Manitou that they should prosper on their errand. The loss of three comrades was the gravest of warnings and they should turn back. But Wyatt rebuked them angrily. He did not mean to be beaten in such a way by an enemy who remained in hiding. The bullet had shown that it was an earthly foe, and, as far as Manitou was concerned, he always awarded the victory to courage, skill and luck. The Indians went forward reluctantly.

The next night they tied up again by the wooded bank. Wyatt wanted two of the warriors to remain in the boat, but they refused absolutely to do so. Despite all that he could say their superstitious fears were strong upon them, and they meant to stay close to their comrades upon the solid earth. Dreading too severe a test of his authority the renegade consented, and all of them, except the guards, lay down among the bushes near the shore. It was a fine summer night, not very dark, and Wyatt did not believe a foe could come near them without being seen. He felt more confidence, but again he was sleepless. He closed his eyes and sought slumber by every device that he knew, but it would not come. At last he made a circuit with Early and two of the Indians in the forest about the camp, but saw and heard nothing. Returning, he lay down on his blanket and once more wooed sleep with shut eyes.

Sleep still refused obstinately to come, and in ten minutes the renegade reopened his eyes. His glance wandered idly over the recumbent Indians who were sound asleep, and then to those who watched. It passed from them to the river and the black blur of the boat lying upon the water about twenty yards away. Then it passed on and after a while came back again to the boat.

Braxton Wyatt knew that optical illusions were common, especially in the obscurity of night. One could look so long at a motionless object that it seemed to move. That was why the boat, tied securely to low boughs, did that curious trick of apparently gliding over the surface of the river. Wyatt laughed at himself. In the faint light, brain was superior to eye. He would not allow himself to be deceived, and the quality of mind that saved him from delusions gave him pride. He did not have a very good view of the boat from the point where he lay, but he saw enough of it to know that when he looked again it would be lying exactly where it had been all the time, despite that illusory trick of movement. So, to show the superiority of will over fancy, he kept his eyes shut a longer time than usual, and when he opened them once more he looked directly at the boat. Surely the shifting light was playing him new tricks. Apparently it was much farther out in the stream and was drifting with the current.

Wyatt reproved himself as an unsteady fool. His nerves were shaken, and in order to restore his calmness he closed his eyes once more. But the eyes would not stay shut. Will was compelled to yield at last to impulse and the lids came apart. He was somewhat angry at himself. He did not wish to look at the boat again, and repeat those foolish illusions, but he did so nevertheless.

Braxton Wyatt sprang to his feet with a cry of alarm and warning. It was no trick of fancy. He saw with eyes that did not lie a boat out in the middle of the stream and every moment going faster with the current. The power that propelled it was unseen, but Wyatt knew it to be there.

"Fire! Fire!" he shouted to his men. "Somebody is carrying off our boat!"

Rifles flashed and bullets made the water spout. Two struck the boat itself, but it moved on with increasing swiftness. Wyatt, Early and the Indians dashed to the water's edge, but a sharp crack came from the further shore, and Early fell forward directly into the river. Wyatt and the Indians shrank back into the bushes where they lay hidden. But the renegade, with a sort of frightened fascination, watched the water pulling at the body of his slain comrade, until it was carried away by the current and floated out of sight. The boat, meanwhile, moved on until it, too, passed a curve, and was lost from view.

Wyatt recovered his courage and presence of mind, but he sought in vain to urge the Shawnees in pursuit. Superstition held them in a firm grasp. It was true that Early had been slain by a bullet, but a mystic power was taking the boat away. The hand of Manitou was against them and they would return to the country north of the Ohio. They started at once, and Wyatt, raging, was compelled to go with them, since he did not dare to go southward alone.

CHAPTER XVIII. THE SHADOWY FIGURE

After Braxton Wyatt and the Indians had fled, their canoe proceeded steadily up the stream. Henry Ware, with his head only projecting, and sheltered fully by the boat, swam on. He heard neither shots nor the sound of men running through the bushes along the bank in pursuit. Nor did he expect to hear either. He had calculated well the power of hidden danger and superstition, and, confident of complete victory, he finally steered the boat toward the farther shore, bringing it under the overhanging boughs, about a mile from the point where Braxton Wyatt's canoe had been. As the prow struck the soft soil and he rose from the water, Paul came forward to meet him. Paul carried in his hands a rifle that he had just reloaded.

"It was a success, Henry, more thorough even than we had hoped," Paul said.

"Yes," replied Henry as he stood up, a dripping water god. "Fortune was surely good to us. I have not been pursued, and I know it is because the Indians did not dare to follow. They will certainly flee as fast as they can to their own country, and meanwhile we are the gainer by one fine big boat, which I think is not empty."

"No, it is not," said Mr. Pennypacker, appearing from the bushes, "but I will never again enter into such another enterprise. It may suit young foresters like you two, but it is not for me, an old man and a schoolmaster."

"Still, we have turned back a scouting party which might have carried dangerous information," said Henry, "and I propose that we now look and see what is in our new boat."

The spoils were richer than they had expected. They found two extra rifles of good make, a large quantity of powder and bullets, some blankets and much food.

"We can use all these things," said Henry, "and we'll go to Wareville in this big canoe, tying our own little one behind. When we get there we'll contribute the rifles and other things to the general store."

"Where they may be welcome enough," said Mr. Pennypacker. "Well, you lads achieved this deed, while I filled the rôle of spectator and well-wisher. I am very glad, however, that you have secured this boat. It is a great improvement upon our own small one."

The schoolmaster was a fine paddler, and he insisted that Henry and Paul rest, while he showed his skill. He was anxious, he said, to do his own part in the return, and this offered him the only chance. Henry and Paul acquiesced and he paddled stoutly on for a long time. But before morning he gave in, and the lads relieved him. Paul had slept for an hour or two, but Henry had remained wide awake.

The river now flowed very slowly, and with but little opposition from the current, they were able to make good time. Both were full of eager anticipation. By the following night they ought to reach Wareville, the snug home of theirs that they had not seen in so long a time.

"I wonder if they will know us," said Henry.

"Not at first sight. Of that I am sure," replied Paul. "It seems to me, Henry, that you have grown at least six inches since we were last at Wareville."

"You haven't been any sluggard yourself, Paul, so far as growth is concerned. They may or may not know us, but I feel quite certain that they won't believe everythingwe tell them, although every word will be gospel truth."

"No, it's not likely, and yet sooner or later we can bring the witnesses. I suppose they'll find it hardest to believe about Wyoming. I wish myself that it wasn't true."

Paul shuddered at the black memory.

"But we've already struck back for it," said Henry. "It caused the destruction of the Iroquois power."

Then both were silent. The schoolmaster, lying on a roll of the captured blankets, slept soundly. His breathing was steady and rhythmic, and the two youths glanced at him.

"At any rate we're bringing him back," said Paul. "They'll be glad to see him at Wareville. I've no doubt they gave him up for dead long ago."

The day came with a splendid sun shining on the green world. The spring had been very rainy, and the summer thus far had rejoiced in frequent showers. Hence no brown had yet appeared in the foliage, and the world looked fresh and young. Although they were now approaching Wareville the forest was unbroken, and no sound of civilization came to their ears. Henry told Paul, who was very tired, to go to sleep as he could paddle the boat alone. Paul lay down on the blankets beside the schoolmaster, and in a couple of minutes was off to slumberland.

Henry paddled on. Before him was a long reach of the river almost without current and the prow cut the still water, leaving behind it a long trailing wake of liquid gold. Henry had never seen a finer sun. Beneath it forest and river were vivid and intense. Birds of many kinds chattered and sang in the boughs. Battle and danger seemed far away. Peace and beauty were to attend their coming home and he was glad. His strong arms swept the paddle through the water for a long time. The action was purely mechanical. His muscles were so thoroughly trained and hardened that he was not conscious of action. He was watching instead for the first sign of Wareville's presence, and a little before noon he saw it, a thin spire of smoke rising high, until it stopped like the point of a spearhead against the sky. He knew at once that it hung over Wareville, and his heart throbbed. He loved the great wilderness with an intensity that few men felt for their own acres, but he had been away a long time, a time, moreover, so crowded with events that it seemed far greater than reality.

He did not yet awaken Paul and the schoolmaster, but, putting more power in his arms, he sent the boat on more swiftly. When he turned a point where a little peninsula, covered with forest, jutted into the river, he let the paddle swing idly for a minute or two and listened. A steady thudding sound, as regular as the beat of a drum, though slower, came to his ears. It was the woodsman's ax, and, for a moment, Henry flinched as if he himself lay beneath the blade. That ax was eating into his beloved forest, and a hundred more axes were doing the same. Then he recovered himself. The hundred axes might eat on, the hundred might become a thousand, and the thousand ten thousand, but they could eat only the edge of his wilderness which stretched away thousands of miles in every direction. The trees, and with them the deer and the bear, would be there long beyond his time, though he might live to be a hundred, and beyond that of the generation after. He took comfort in the thought, and once more felt deep content.

It was not solely as a hunter and scout that Henry loved the wilderness. Forest and river and lake touched far deeper springs in his nature. They were for him full of beauty and majesty. Green forest in spring and red forest in autumn alike appealed to him. Brooks, rivers and lakes were alive. When duty did not call he could sitperfectly motionless for hours, happy to see the wilderness and to feel that it was all about him.

He swung the paddle again, and the boat moved leisurely forward. The ring of the ax grew louder, and he heard others to the right and to the left. Presently something struck with a crash and, in spite of all his reasoning with himself, Henry sighed. A great tree cut through by the ax had fallen. Many others had gone in the same way, and many more would follow. The spire of smoke was attended now by smaller spires and Wareville could not be more than three miles away. He awakened Paul and the schoolmaster.

"We shall be at home in less than an hour," he said. "Listen to the axes!"

Paul glanced quickly at him. His fine and sensitive mind understood at once the inflection in Henry's voice, and he sympathized.

"But they are our own people," he said, "and they are making homes which we must help to defend."

"A stronghold in the wilderness, where man, woman and child may be safe from wild beast and savage," said the schoolmaster oracularly. "Ah, boys—boys! how much do I owe you! Truly I thought I should never see this comfortable little village again, and here I am, sound and whole, returning in triumph upon a captured vessel."

They saw at the right a cleared field, in which the young corn was growing amid the stumps, and on the left was the sheen of wheat also amid the stumps. Mr. Pennypacker rubbed his hands delightedly, but Henry was silent. Yet the feeling was brief with the youth. Thoughts of his people quickly crowded it out, and he swung the paddle more swiftly. The other two, who were now helping him, did likewise, and the boat doubled its pace. Through the thinned forest appeared the brown walls of a palisade, and Henry, putting a hand in the shape of a trumpet to his lips, uttered a long, mellow cry that the forest gave back in many echoes. Faces appeared on the palisade and three or four men, rifle on shoulder, approached the bank of the river. They did not know either Henry or Paul, but one of them exclaimed:

"Ef that ain't Mr. Pennypacker riz right up from the dead then I'm a ghost myself!"

"It is Mr. Pennypacker," said the schoolmaster joyfully, "and I'm no more of a ghost than you are. I've come back from captivity, bringing with me two of those who saved me, young citizens of this village, Henry Ware and Paul Cotter."

They turned the head of the boat to the bank and the whole population poured forth to meet them. Henry and Paul were greeted half with laughter and half with tears by their parents—border stoicism was compelled to melt away at this moment—and then they blushed at the words that were said about them. Their stature and strength attracted the attention of everybody. The borderers could not fail to note the ease and grace of their movements, the lightness with which they walked, and the dexterity with which they pulled the big boat upon the bank. It was evident that these two youths were far above the average of their kind, that naturally of a high quality they had been trained in a school that brought forth every merit. Henry towered above his own father, who no longer looked upon him as one to whom he should give tasks and reproofs. And the admiration with which they were regarded increased when the schoolmaster told how he had been rescued by them and their comrades.

Henry sat that night in his father's house, and told long and true tales of their great wanderings and of danger and escape on land and water. He and Paul had eaten hugely, there was no escape, and he felt that he must sit quiet for a while. He was loth to talk of himself, but there was no escape from that either, and his story was so vivid, so full that it fairly told itself. As he spoke of the great journey and its myriad events between New Orleans and the Great Lakes, the crowd in the big room thickened. No one was willing to lose a word of the magic tale, and it was past midnight when he lay down on the blankets and sought sleep.

The next day and the next were passed in further welcome, but when Henry sought the blankets the third night he became conscious that the first flush of the return was over. The weather had turned very hot—it was now July—and the walls and ceiling of the room seemed to press upon him and suffocate him. He drew deep and long breaths, but there was not air enough to fill a chest that had long been used to the illimitable outside. It was very still in the room. He longed to hear the boughs of trees waving over him. He felt that only such a sound or the trickle of running water could soothe him to sleep. Yet he would make another effort. He closed his eyes and for a half hour lay motionless. Then, angry, he opened them again, as wide awake as ever. He listened, but he could hear no sound in either the house or the village.

Henry Ware rose to his feet, slipped on his clothing, and went to the window. He looked forth upon a sleeping village. The houses, built of solid logs, stood in ordered rows, gray and silent. Nothing stirred anywhere. He took his rifle from the hooks, and leaped lightly out of the window. Then he slipped cautiously among the houses, scaled the palisade and darted into the forest.

He lay down by the side of a cold spring about a mile from the village. The bank of turf was soft and cool, and the little stream ran over the pebbles with a faint sighing sound. The thick leaves that hung overhead rustled beneath the south wind, and played a pleasant tune. Henry felt a great throb of joy. His chest expanded and the blood leaped in every vein. He threw himself down upon the bank and grasped the turf with both hands. It seemed to him that like Antæus of old he felt strength flowing back into his body through every finger tip. He could breathe here easily and naturally. What a wonderful thing the forest was! How its beauty shone in the moonlight! The trees silvered with mist stood in long rows, and the friendly boughs and leaves, moving before the wind, never ceased to sing their friendly song to him.

Deep peace came over him. Lying on his side and soothed by the forest and flowing water his eyelids drooped of their own accord. Presently he slept, breathing deeply and regularly, and drawing the fresh air into his veins. But he awoke before daylight and reëntered the village and his father's house without being seen by anyone. To the questions of his parents he said that he had slept well, and he ate his breakfast with an appetite that he had not known since he came within the palisade.

The news that Henry and Paul had brought of the great invasion threatened by an allied Indian and British force disturbed Wareville. Yet the settlers felt much safer when they learned that the redoubtable George Rogers Clark intended a counterstroke. More than twenty of the most stalwart colonists volunteered to go to Louisville and join Clark for the blow. Henry told his father that he and Paul would return with them.

"I suppose it is your nature," said Mr. Ware, "but do you not think, Henry, that you have already suffered enough hardship and danger for the sake of the border?"

"No, Father, I do not," replied Henry. "Not as long as hardship and danger are to be suffered. And I know, too, that it is my nature. I shall live all my life in the forest."

Mr. Ware said nothing more. He knew that words were useless. That question had been threshed out between them long ago. But he gave him an affectionate farewell, and, a week after their arrival in Wareville, Henry and Paul departed again for the North, the whole population of Wareville waving them good-by as they embarked upon the river.

But the two youths were far from being alone. A score of strong men, mostly young, were with them in four boats, and they carried an ample supply of arms and ammunition. Mr. Pennypacker wanted to go back with them, but he was dissuaded from undertaking the task.

"Perhaps it is best that I stay in Wareville," he said regretfully. "I am really a man of peace and not of war, although war has looked for me more than once."

Their boats now had oars instead of paddles, and with the current in their favor they moved rapidly toward the north. They also had a favoring breeze behind them and Henry and Paul, who were in the first boat, felt their hearts swell with the prospect of action. They were so habituated now to an eventful life that a week of rest seemed a long time to them. Already they were pining to be with George Rogers Clark on the great expedition.

"How many men do you think Colonel Clark will be able to gather?" asked Ethan Burke, one of the stoutest of the Wareville contingent.

"I don't know, but his name is something to conjure with," replied Henry. "He ought to get together six or seven hundred at least, and that many men, experienced in the woods, will make a formidable force."

They rowed down the river for three or four days, stopping at intervals to beat up the woods for marauding Indian bands. They found no traces of an enemy. Henry surmised that the experience of Braxton Wyatt's party had been a warning, and that possibly also the chiefs had learned of Clark's plan. The news that he was comingwould alone suffice to put an end for the time to the Indian raids.

The voyage continued in unbroken peace until they entered the Ohio. Here they were assailed by a summer storm of great severity and one of the boats, struck by lightning, narrowly escaped sinking. A rower was knocked senseless, but nobody was seriously injured, and by great efforts, they got the boat into condition to resume the journey.

The little fleet came to the Falls, and turned in to the southern shore, where the main settlement of Louisville now stood. Several spires of smoke rose, and they knew that no Indian disaster had befallen. As they drew nearer they saw many boats along the bank, far more than the inhabitants of a little village could use.

"A big force has gathered already," said Henry. "Ah, see there!"

A boat shot out from the mass and came rapidly toward them.

"Don't you know them?" said Henry to Paul.

"My eyes may be dim from old age," replied Paul, "and perhaps I only guess, but I should say that the one nearest us is a shiftless character whom I used to know in my youth, a man who, despite his general worthlessness and incapacity, had a certain humorous and attractive quality of mind that endeared him to his friends."

"I am of the opinion that you are right," said Henry, looking under his hand, "and the second, I think, is a voluble person named Thomas Ross, who has talked a wide circle of acquaintances nearly to death."

"Even so, and the third is a long thin fellow, one James Hart, noted for his aversion to the delicacies of the table and his dismissal of cookery as a triviality unworthy of the consideration of a serious man. Am I right, Mr. Ware?"

"You are right, Mr. Cotter. Hey you, Sol, how have you been?"

His voice rose in a mellow peal across the waters, and three shouts simultaneous and joyous came back.

"Hey, Henry!" cried Shif'less Sol in a voice that could have been heard a mile. "We're mighty glad to see you, an' we're mighty glad that you've brought such good company with you."

In a few more moments their boat was alongside and there was a mighty shaking of hands. The three knew all the Wareville men and Shif'less Sol said the reënforcement would be very welcome.

"But we've got an army already," he said. "You just come and see it."

As they tied their boats to the bank Henry noticed many tents along the sloping shore. One larger than the rest was surmounted by the new flag of the United States.

"That's Colonel Clark's tent," said Shif'less Sol, noticing the direction of his eyes, "but the Colonel won't sleep in a tent many more nights. We start soon up the Ohio and all these are to be left behind."

Henry was received that very day in the Colonel's tent. Clark, apt to grow sluggish and careless in idleness, was now all energy and keenness. The confidence of the borderer in him was not misplaced. Henry left his comrades behind when he was summoned to the Colonel's presence, but when he entered the big tent he saw others there whom he knew. A tall man, much bronzed by weather, blue of eyes and gentle of manner, greeted him warmly.

"It's pleasant to see you again, young Mr. Ware," he said, "an' it's still more pleasant to know that we're to serve together under Colonel Clark."

Daniel Boone, as gentle of speech as a woman, held out his hand and Henry fairly blushed with pride as he grasped it. Another man, darkened by weather like Boone, was Abe Thomas, also a celebrated scout, and there were yet others whose names were household words all along the border.

"Sit down, Mr. Ware, sit down," said Colonel Clark genially. "We're to hold a council of war, and we felt that it would not be complete without you."

Henry experienced another throb of gratified pride, but as he was much the youngest present he spoke only when he was addressed directly. The debate was long and earnest. Colonel Clark had assembled between six and seven hundred good men, and he intended to go with this force up the Ohio to the mouth of the Licking. There they would be joined by another force under Colonel Benjamin Logan coming down the Licking. The united army after camping on the north shore of the Ohio, on the site of the present city of Cincinnati, would march straight for the Indian country. Boone, Henry Ware and other accomplished scouts would go ahead and guard against ambush. It was dark when the council ended, and when they prepared to leave, Clark said in his most sanguine tones:

"If we do not strike a blow that will pay back Bird's and with interest then I'm not fit to lead. Our Indian friends will find that though they may destroy a village or two of ours their own villages will have to pay for it. And this great invasion that they've been planning will have to wait for another time."

"We'll strike, and you're the man to lead us," said the others.

It was night now and they stepped forth into the darkness. Henry passed among the tents toward the edge of the woods where his comrades were camped, and he saw a tall figure moving in the shadow of the trees.

429

He would not have looked twice at the figure had not something familiar about it attracted his attention. It was the height, the breadth of the shoulders, and a certain haughty poise of the head that struck him all at once with the intensity of conviction. His friends had left him, going their respective ways, but Henry immediately darted toward the shadow.

The tall and dusky figure melted away immediately among the trees, but the young forest runner pursued at his utmost speed. He did not doubt. It was no figment of fancy. It was the great chief himself spying with incredible daring upon his enemies. If he were permitted to escape, the advance of Clark would be surrounded with numberless dangers. The fertile brain and the invincible spirit of the great Wyandot would plant an ambush at every turn. The thought made Henry increase his speed.

The figure flitted away among the oaks and beeches. Henry might have called for help earlier, but he was now too far away for anyone to hear, and, confident in his own strength and skill, he pressed on. The shadow was running eastward, and the way grew rough. Yet he did not lose sight of it flitting there among the trees. There was no swifter runner than he, but the distance between them did not decrease. It seemed to him that it remained always the same.

"Stop or I shoot," he cried.

The shadow did not stop and, raising his rifle, he fired. The figure never wavered for an instant, but continued its rapid and even flight, until it reached the crest of a little hill. There it suddenly turned about, leveled a rifle and fired in its turn. The bullet burned Henry's cheek and for a moment he hesitated, but only for a moment. Reloading his own rifle he continued the pursuit, the figure running steadily eastward, the gap between them remaining the same.

The fugitive reached Beargrass Creek, darted swiftly through the water, climbed the opposite bank and was again among the trees. Henry crossed also and hung on with tenacity. He knew that Timmendiquas had probably reloaded also, but in the excitement and rush of the moment, he did not think of another return bullet. When he did recall the fact, as the chase lengthened, he felt sure that the chief would not stop to fight at close quarters. He could not afford to risk his life in an encounter with a single person, when he was the very keystone of the great Indian campaign.

The chase still led northward through the deep woods that ran down to the shore of the Ohio. Strive as he would Henry could not gain. He did not forget that Timmendiquas had twice saved his life, but he in return had spared that of Timmendiquas, and now greater things were at stake than the feeling that one brave soul has for another. The light grew worse in the shadow of the giant trees and only at times could he see the flitting figure distinctly. At last was he able to secure what he considered a good aim, and he pulled the trigger a second time.

Henry was an unerring marksman, perhaps the finest on all the border. The target at that moment was good, a shaft of clear moonlight falling directly upon the broad chest, and yet the bullet clipped a bush three feet away. Henry was conscious that, at the supreme instant when his finger pressed the trigger, he had been shaken by a sudden emotion. The muzzle of the rifle which bore directly upon the body of the chief had shifted just a little, and he was not surprised when the bullet went wide.

Timmendiquas stopped, raised his own rifle, but fired straight up into the air. Then uttering a long whoop which the night gave back in clear echoes, he rushed directly to the river, and sprang far out into the dark waters. Henry was too astonished to move for a few moments. Then he, too, ran to the bank. He saw far out a dark head moving swiftly toward the northern shore. He might have reloaded, and even yet he might have taken a third shot with tolerable accuracy, but he made no effort to do so. He stood there, silent and motionless, watching the black head grow smaller and smaller until at last it was lost in the darkness that hung over the northern bank. But though hidden now he knew that the great chief had reached the far shore. In fancy he could see him as he walked into the woods, the glistening drops falling from his tall figure. Timmendiquas and he must fight on opposing sides, but real enemies they could never be. He felt that they were sure to meet again in conflict, and this would be the great decisive struggle. Timmendiquas himself knew that it was so, or he would not have come to look with his own eyes upon the force of Clark.

Henry walked slowly back toward the little settlement. He waded the waters of Beargrass Creek, and soon saw the log cabins again. He and his comrades, when the ground was not wet, slept in neither a cabin nor a tent, but spread their blankets on the turf under a mighty beech. The four were already waiting for him there, and, in the darkness, they did not notice any unusual expression on Henry's face. He sat down beside them and said quietly:

"I have just seen Timmendiquas."

"What!" exclaimed four voices together.

"I have just seen Timmendiquas. Moreover, I fired twice at him and he fired once at me. All three bullets missed."

Then Shif'less Sol, experienced and wise, raised himself up on his blanket, looked at Henry, and said in a tone of conviction:

"Henry Ware, you an' Timmendiquas together might miss with one bullet, but miss with three is impossible. I believe that you've seen him ez you say so, but I don't believe that you two missed three times."

"We fired three times, as I said, and I should add that Timmendiquas fired a fourth time also, but he must have been aiming at a star, as he pointed his rifle straight upward."

"Ah!" said four voices together again, but now the four understood.

"I think," said Henry, "that he came to see for himself what Colonel Clark is doing. Now he is gone with the facts. I came here merely to tell you first, and I leave at once to tell the Colonel next."

He found Colonel Clark still in the council tent, but alone and poring over a rude map. A burning wick in a basin of tallow scarcely dispelled the darkness, but Henry could see that the commander's face was knit and anxious. He turned expectantly to the youth.

"You have some news of importance or you would not come back at this hour," he said.

"I have," replied Henry. "When I left this tent I passed through the edge of the woods and I saw a figure there. It was that of an Indian, a chief whom I have seen before. It was Timmendiquas, the great Wyandot, the bravest, wisest and most daring of all the Western chiefs. I pursued him, fired at him, but missed. It was evidently not his object to fight anyone here. He sprang into the Ohio, swam to the northern shore, and no doubt is now on his way to his own people."

Colonel Clark gazed thoughtfully at the flickering candle and did not speak for a long time.

"I am glad you saw him," he said finally. "We know now that the allied tribes will be on their guard. They may meet us in force many days before we reach the Indian towns. Timmendiquas is a born leader, energetic and wary. Well, well hasten our own departure, and try to strike before they're ready. What do you say to that, my lad?"

"My opinion is worth little, but I would say that we ought to strike as soon as we can."

"I don't think a man among us will take any other view. We can leave with seven hundred men now, and we'll meet Logan with three hundred more at the mouth of the Licking. Then we shall have the largest white force ever gathered in the West, and it will be strange if we do not pay some of the debt we owe to the Indians and their allies. I wish, Mr. Ware, that you and your friends would march with Boone on the southern bank of the river. It is only a wish, however, as I have agreed that you should choose your own method of helping us."

"It is just what we should wish most to do," said Henry, "and we shall be with Mr. Boone when he crosses to the other side."

Henry walked back to the big beech and found his comrades yet wide awake and glad to hear that they would march in thirty-six hours.

"We'll be back in the thick of it," said Shif'less Sol, "an' I'm thinkin', Henry, that we'll have all we kin do."

"No doubt," said Henry.

CHAPTER XIX. A HERALD BY WATER

The start from Louisville was made and the great expedition began among the cheers of the women and children of the little place and from the men who were left behind. Most of the army were in boats which also carried great quantities of arms, ammunition and food. All of the little settlements buried in the deep woods of Kentucky, though exposed at any time to sudden and terrible raids, had sent volunteers. They took the risk nevertheless, and dispatched their best to the redoubtable hero, George Rogers Clark. Few people have ever given more supreme examples of dauntless courage and self-sacrifice than these borderers. Tiny outposts only, they never failed to respond to the cry for help. There was scarcely a family which did not lose someone under the Indian tomahawk, but their courage never faltered, though for nearly twenty years no man was safe a single hour from savage ambush. They stood fast and endured everything.

Henry, Paul and their comrades were not in the boats, but were with Daniel Boone who led a party of the best scouts on the southern shore. It was not only their business to find their enemy if he should be there, but to clear him out, unless he were in too great force, and it was a task that required supreme skill and caution. Throughout its whole course dense forests grew along the Ohio, and an ambush might be planted anywhere. The foliage was still thick and heavy on the trees, as it wasnot yet August, and one seldom saw more than a hundred yards ahead.

The boats, keeping near the southern shore where their flank was protected by Boone's scouts, started, the sunlight streaming down upon them and the water flashing from their oars. The scouts had already gone on ahead, and the five were among the foremost. In a few minutes the last sign of the new settlement disappeared and they were in the wilderness. At Boone's orders the scouts formed in small bodies, covering at least two miles from the river. The five formed one of these little groups, and they began their work with zeal and skill. No enemy in the underbrush could have escaped their notice, but the whole day passed without a sign of a foe. When night came on they saw the boats draw into a cove on the southern bank, and, after a conference with Boone, they spread their blankets again under the trees, the watch not falling to their share until the following night. Having eaten from the food which they carried in knapsacks they looked contentedly at the river.

"Well, this will be twice that we have gone up the Ohio, once on the water, and once on the shore," said Paul. "But as before we have Timmendiquas to face."

"That's so," said Shif'less Sol, "but I'm thinkin' that nothin' much will happen, until we get up toward the mouth of the Lickin'. It's been only two nights since Timmendiquas hisself was spyin' us out, an' afore he strikes he's got to go back to his main force."

"Mebbe so an' mebbe not," said Tom Ross. "My eyes ain't so bad and this bein' a good place to look from I think I see a canoe over thar right under the fur shore uv the Ohio. Jest look along thar, Henry, whar the bank kinder rises up."

The point that Tom indicated was at least a mile away, but Henry agreed with him that a shape resembling a canoe lay close to the bank. Shif'less Sol and the others inclined to the same belief.

"If so, it's a scout boat watching us," said Paul, "and Timmendiquas himself may be in it."

Henry shook his head.

"It isn't likely," he said. "Timmendiquas knows all that he wants to know, and is now going northeastward as fast as he can. But his warriors are there. Look! You can see beyond a doubt now that it is a canoe, and it's going up the river at full speed."

The canoe shot from the shadow of the bank. Apparently it contained three or four Indians, and they had strong arms. So it sped over the water and against the current at a great rate.

"They've seen all they want to see to-night," said Henry, "but that canoe and maybe others will be watching us all the way."

A half hour later a light appeared in the northern woods and then another much further on. Doubtless the chain was continued by more, too far away for them to see. The men in the main camp saw them also, and understood. Every foot of their advance would be watched until the Indian army grew strong enough, when it would be attacked. Yet their zeal and courage rose the higher. They begged Clark to start again at dawn that no time might be lost. Boone joined the five under the tree.

"You saw the lights, didn't you, boys?" he said.

"We saw them," replied Henry, "and we know what they mean. Don't you think, Mr. Boone, that for a while the most dangerous part of the work will fall on you?"

"Upon those with me an' myself," replied Boone in his gentle manner, "but all of us are used to it."

For two successive nights they saw the fiery signals on the northern shore, carrying the news into the deep woods that the Kentucky army was advancing. But they werenot molested by any skirmishers. Not a single shot was fired. The fact was contrary to the custom of Indian warfare, and Henry saw in it the wisdom and restraint of Timmendiquas. Indians generally attack on impulse and without system, but now they were wasting nothing in useless skirmishing. Not until all the warriors were gathered, and the time was ripe would Timmendiquas attempt the blow.

It gave the little white army a peculiar feeling. The men knew all the time that they were being watched, yet they saw no human being save themselves. Boone's scouts found the trail of Indians several times, but never an Indian himself. Yet they continued their patient scouting. They did not intend that the army should fall into an ambush through any fault of theirs. Thus they proceeded day after day, slowly up the river, replenishing their supplies with game which was abundant everywhere.

They came to the wide and deep mouth of the Kentucky, a splendid stream flowing from the Alleghany Mountains, and thence across the heart of Kentucky into the Ohio. Henry thought that its passage might be disputed, and the five, Boone, Thomas and some others crossed cautiously in one of the larger boats. They watched to see anything unusual stir in the thickets on the farther shore of the Kentucky, but no warrior was there. Timmendiquas was not yet ready, and now the land portion of the army was also on the further shore, and the march still went on uninterrupted. Paul began to believe that Timmendiquas was not able to bring the warriors to the Ohio; that they would stand on the defensive at their own villages. But Henry was of another opinion, and he soon told it.

"Timmendiquas would never have come down to Louisville to look us over," he said, "if he meant merely to act on the defensive at places two or three hundred miles away. No, Paul, we'll hear from him while we're still on the river, and I think it will be before Logan will join us."

Boone and Thomas took the same view, and now the scouting party doubled its vigilance.

"To-morrow morning," said Boone, "we'll come to the Licking. There are always more Indians along that river than any other in Kentucky and I wish Logan and his men were already with us."

The face of the great frontiersman clouded.

"The Indians have been too peaceful an' easy," he resumed. "Not a shot has been fired since we left Louisville an' now we're nearly to Tuentahahewaghta (the site of Cincinnati, that is, the landing or place where the road leads to the river). It means that Timmendiquas has been massing his warriors for a great stroke."

Reasoning from the circumstances and his knowledge of Indian nature, Henry believed that Daniel Boone was right, yet he had confidence in the result. Seven hundred trained borderers were not easily beaten, even if Logan and the other three hundred should not come. Yet he and Boone and all the band knew that the watch that night must miss nothing. The boats, as usual, were drawn up on the southern shore, too far away to be reached by rifle shots from the northern banks. The men were camped on a low wooded hill within a ring of at least fifty sentinels. The Licking, a narrow but deep stream, was not more than five miles ahead. Clark would have gone on to its mouth, had he not deemed it unwise to march at night in such a dangerous country. The night itself was black with heavy, low clouds, and the need to lie still in a strong position was obvious.

Boone spread out his scouts in advance. The five, staying together as usual, and now acting independently, advanced through the woods near the Ohio. It was one of the hottest of July nights, and nature was restless and uneasy. The low clouds increased in number, and continually grew larger until they fused into one, and covered the heavens with a black blanket from horizon to horizon. From a point far off in the southwest came the low but menacing mutter of thunder. At distant intervals, lightning would cut the sky in a swift, vivid stroke. The black woods would stand out in every detail for a moment, and they would catch glimpses of the river's surface turned to fiery red. Then the night closed down again, thicker and darker than ever, and any object twenty yards before them would become only a part of the black blur. A light wind moaned among the trees, weirdly and without stopping.

"It's a bad night for Colonel Clark's army," said Shif'less Sol. "Thar ain't any use o' our tryin' to hide the fact from one another, 'cause we all know it."

"That's so, Sol," said Long Jim Hart, "but we've got to watch all the better 'cause of it. I've knowed you a long time, Solomon Hyde, an' you're a lazy, shiftless, ornery, contrary critter, but somehow or other the bigger the danger the better you be, an' I think that's what's happenin' now."

If it had not been so dark Long Jim would have seen Shif'less Sol's pleased grin. Moreover the words of Jim Hart were true. The spirit of the shiftless one, great borderer that he was, rose to the crisis, but he said nothing. The little group continued to advance, keeping a couple of hundred yards or so from the bank of the Ohio, and stopping every ten or twelve minutes to listen. On such a night ears were of more use than eyes.

The forest grew more dense as they advanced. It consisted chiefly of heavy beech and oak, with scattered underbrush of spice wood and pawpaw. It was the underbrush particularly that annoyed, since it offered the best hiding for a foe in ambush. Henry prayed for the moon and the stars, but both moon and stars remained on the other side of impenetrable clouds. It was only by the occasional flashes of lightning that they saw clearly and then it was but a fleeting glimpse. But it was uncommonly vivid lightning. They noticed that it always touched both forest and river with red fire, and the weird moaning of the wind, crying like a dirge, never ceased. It greatly affected the nerves of Paul, the most sensitive of the five, but the others, too, were affected by it.

Henry turned his attention for a while from the forest to the river. He sought to see by the flashes of lightning if anything moved there, and, when they were about half way to the mouth of the Licking, he believed that he caught sight of something in the shape of a canoe, hovering near the farther shore. He asked them all to watch at the point he indicated until the next flash of lightning came. It was a full minute until the electric blade cut the heavens once more, but they were all watching and there was the dark shape. When the five compared opinions they were sure that it was moving slowly northward.

"It's significant," said Henry. "Daniel Boone isn't often mistaken, and the warriors are drawing in. We'll be fighting before dawn, boys."

"An' it's for us to find out when an' whar the attack will come," said Shif'less Sol.

"We're certainly going to try," said Henry. "Hark! What was that?"

"Injuns walkin' an' talkin'," said Tom Ross.

Henry listened, and he felt sure that Ross was right. Under his leadership they darted into a dense clump of pawpaws and lay motionless, thankful that such good shelter was close at hand. The footsteps, light, but now heard distinctly, drew nearer.

Henry had a sure instinct about those who were coming. He saw Braxton Wyatt, Blackstaffe, and at least twenty warriors emerge into view. The night was still as dark as ever, but the band was so near that the hidden five could see the features of every man. Henry knew by their paint that the warriors belonged to different tribes. Wyandots, Miamis, Shawnees, and Delawares were represented. Wyatt and Blackstaffe were talking. Henry gathered from the scattered words he heard that Blackstaffe doubted the wisdom of an attack, but Wyatt was eager for it.

"I was at Wyoming," said the younger renegade with a vicious snap of his teeth, "and it was the rush there that did it. We enveloped them on both front and flank and rushed in with such force that we beat them down in a few minutes. Nor did many have a chance to escape."

"But they were mostly old men and boys," said Blackstaffe, "and they had little experience in fighting the tribes. Clark has a bigger force here, and they are all borderers. You know how these Kentuckians can use the rifle."

Wyatt made a reply, but Henry could not hear it as the two renegades and the warriors passed on in the underbrush. But he did hear the click of a gun lock and he quickly pushed down the hand of Shif'less Sol.

"Not now! not now, Sol!" he whispered. "Wyatt and Blackstaffe deserve death many times over, but if you fire they'd all be on us in a whoop, and then we'd be of no further use."

"You're right, Henry," said the shiftless one, "but my blood was mighty hot for a minute."

The band disappeared, turning off toward the south, and the five, feeling that they had now gone far enough, returned to the camp. On the way they met Boone and the remainder of the scouts. Henry told what they had seen and heard and the great frontiersman agreed with them that the attack was at hand.

"You saw the war paint of four nations," he said, "an' that proves that a great force is here. I tell you I wish I knew about Logan, an' the men that are comin' down the Lickin'."

It was now nearly midnight and they found Colonel Clark sitting under a tree at the eastern edge of the camp. He listened with the greatest attention to every detail that they could give him, and then his jaw seemed to stiffen.

"You have done well, lads," he said. "There is nothing more dangerous than the calling of a scout in the Indian wars, but not one of you has ever shirked it. You have warned us and now we are willing for Timmendiquas and Girty to attack whenever they choose."

Many of the men were asleep, but Clark did not awaken them. He knew fully the value of rest, and they were borderers who would spring to their feet at the first alarm, alive in every sense and muscle. But at least a third of his force was on guard. No attack was feared on the water. Nevertheless many of the men were there with the boats. It was, however, the semicircle through the forest about the camp that was made thick and strong. Throughout its whole course the frontiersmen stood close together and keen eyes and trained ears noted everything that passed in the forest.

Henry and his four comrades were at the point of the segment nearest to the confluence of the Ohio and the Licking. Here they sat upon the ground in a close group in the underbrush, speaking but rarely, while time passed slowly. The character of the night had not changed. The solemn wind never ceased to moan among the trees, and far off in the west the thunder yet muttered. The strokes of lightning were far between, but as before they cast a blood red tinge over forest and river. The five were some hundreds of yards beyond the camp, and they could see nothing then, although they heard now and then the rattle of arms and a word or two from the officers. Once they heard the sound of heavy wheels, and they knew that the cannon had been wheeled into position. Clark had even been able to secure light artillery for his great expedition.

"Do you think them big guns will be of any use?" asked Shif'less Sol.

"Not at night," replied Henry, "but in the daytime if we come to close quarters they'll certainly say something worth hearing."

It was now nearly half way between midnight and morning when the vitality is lowest. Paul, as he lay among the pawpaws, was growing very sleepy. He had not moved for so long a time and the night was so warm that his eyes had an almost invincible tendency to close, but his will did not permit it. Despite the long silence he had no doubt that the attack would come. So he looked eagerly into the forest every time the lightning flashed, and always he strained his ears that he might hear, if anything was to be heard.

The melancholy wind died, and the air became close, hot and heavy. The leaves ceased to move, and there was no stir in the bushes, but Henry thought that he heard a faint sound. He made a warning gesture to his companions, and they, too, seemed to hear the same noise. All of Paul's sleepiness disappeared. He sat up, every nerve and muscle attuned for the crisis. Henry and he, at almost the same moment, saw the bushes move in front of them. Then they saw the bronze faces with the scalp lock above them, peering forth. The five sat perfectly silent for a few moments and more bronze faces appeared. The gaze of one of the Indians wandered toward the clump of pawpaws, and he saw there one of the five who had now risen a little higher than the rest to look. He knew that it was a white face, and, firing instantly at it, he uttered the long and thrilling war whoop. It was the opening cry of the battle.

The five at once returned the fire and with deadly effect. Two of the warriors fell, and the rest leaped back, still shouting their war cry, which was taken up and repeated in volume at a hundred points. Far above the forest it swelled, a terrible wolfish cry, fiercest of all on its dying note. From river and deep woods came the echo, and the warriors in multitudes rushed forward upon the camp.

Henry and his comrades when they discharged their rifles ran back toward the main force, reloading as they ran. The air was filled with terrible cries and behind them dark forms swarmed forward, running and bounding. From trees and underbrush came a hail of rifle bullets that whistled around the five, but which luckily did nothing save to clip their clothing and to sing an unpleasant song in their ears. Yet they had never run faster, not from fear, but because it was the proper thing to do. They had uncovered the enemy and their work as scouts was over.

They were back on the camp and among the frontiersmen, in less than a minute. Now they wheeled about, and, with rifles loaded freshly, faced the foe who pressed forward in a great horde, yelling and firing. Well it was for the white army that it was composed of veteran borderers. The sight was appalling to the last degree. The defenders were ringed around by flashes of fire, and hundreds of hideous forms leaped as if in the war dance, brandishing their tomahawks. But Colonel Clark was everywhere among his men, shouting to them to stand fast, not to be frightened by the war whoop, and that now was the time to win a victory. Boone, Abe Thomas and the five gave him great help.

The riflemen stood firm in their semicircle, each end of it resting upon the river. Most of them threw themselves upon the ground, and, while the bullets whistled over their heads, poured forth an answering fire that sent many a warrior to explore the great hereafter. Yet the tribes pressed in with uncommon courage, charging like white men, while their great chiefs

Timmendiquas, Red Eagle, Black Panther, Moluntha, Captain Pipe and the others led them on. They rushed directly into the faces of the borderers, leaping forward in hundreds, shouting the war whoop and now and then cutting down a foe. The darkness was still heavy and close, but it was lit up by the incessant flashes of the rifles. The smoke from the firing, with no breeze to drive it away, hung low in a dense bank that stung the mouths and nostrils of the combatants.

"Keep low, Paul! Keep low!" cried Henry, dragging his young comrade down among some spicewood bushes. "If you are bound to stick your head up like that it will be stopping a tomahawk soon."

Paul did not have to wait for the truth of Henry's words, as a shining blade whizzed directly where his head had been, and, passing on, imbedded itself in the trunk of a mighty beech. Paul shuddered. It seemed to him that he felt a hot wind from the tomahawk as it flew by. In his zeal and excitement he had forgotten the danger for a moment or two, and once more Henry had saved his life.

"I wish it would grow lighter," muttered Shif'less Sol. "It's hard to tell your friends from your enemies on a black night like this, and we'll be all mixed up soon."

"We five at least must keep close together," said Henry.

A fierce yell of victory came from the southern side of the camp, a yell that was poured from Indian throats, and every one of the five felt apprehension. Could their line be driven in? Driven in it was! Fifty Wyandots and as many Shawnees under Moluntha, the most daring of their war chiefs, crashed suddenly against the weakest part of the half circle. Firing a heavy volley they had rushed in with the tomahawk, and the defenders, meeting them with clubbed rifles, were driven back by the fury of the attack and the weight of numbers. There was a confused and terrible medley of shouts and cries, of thudding tomahawks and rifle butts, of crashing brushwood and falling bodies. It was all in the hot dark, until the lightning suddenly flared with terrifying brightness. Then it disclosed the strained faces of white and red, the sweat standing out on tanned brows, and the bushes torn and trampled in the wild struggle. The red blaze passed and the night shot down in its place as thick and dark as ever. Neither red men nor white were able to drive back the others. In this bank of darkness the cries increased, and the cloud of smoke grew steadily.

It was not only well that these men were tried woodsmen, but it was equally well that they were led by a great wilderness chief. George Rogers Clark saw at once the point of extreme danger, and, summoning his best men, he rushed to the rescue. The five heard the call. Knowing its urgency, they left the spicewood and swept down with the helping band. Another flash of lightning showed where friends and foe fought face to face with tomahawk and clubbed rifle, and then Clark and the new force were upon the warriors. Paul, carried away by excitement, was shouting:

"Give it to 'em! Give it to 'em! Drive 'em back!"

But he did not know that he was uttering a word. He saw the high cheek bones and close-set eyes, and then he felt the shock as they struck the hostile line. Steel and clubbed rifle only were used first. They did not dare fire at such close quarters as friend and foe were mingled closely, but the warriors were pushed back by the new weight hurled upon them, and then the woodsmen, waiting until the next flash of lightning, sent in a volley that drove the Indians to the cover of the forest. The attack at that point had failed, and the white line was yet complete.

Once more the five threw themselves down gasping among the bushes, reloaded their rifles and waited. In front of them was silence. The enemy there had melted away without a sound, and he too lay hidden, but from left and right the firing and the shouting came with undiminished violence. Henry, also, at the same time heard in all the terrible uproar the distant and low muttering of the thunder, like a menacing under-note, more awful than the firing itself. The smoke reached them where they lay. It was floating now all through the forest, and not only stung the nostrils of the defenders, but heated their brains and made them more anxious for the combat.

"We were just in time," said Shif'less Sol. "Ef Colonel Clark hadn't led a hundred or so o' us on the run to this place the warriors would hev been right in the middle o' the camp, smashin' us to pieces. How they fight!"

"Their chiefs think this army must be destroyed and they're risking everything," said Henry. "Girty must be here, too, urging them on, although he's not likely to expose his own body much."

"But he's a real gen'ral an' a pow'ful help to the Injuns," said Tom Ross.

Clark's summons came again. The sound on the flank indicated that the line was being driven in at another point to the eastward, and the "chosen hundred," as the shiftless one called them, were hurled against the assailants, who were here mostly Miamis and Delawares. The Indians were driven back in turn, and the circle again curved over the ground that the defenders had held in the beginning. Jim Hart and Tom Ross were wounded slightly, but they hid their scratches from the rest, and went on with their part. A third attack in force at a third point was repulsed in the same manner, but only after the most desperate fighting. Each side suffered a heavy loss, but the Indians, nevertheless, were repulsed and the defenders once again lay down among the bushes, their pulses beating fast.

Then ensued the fiery ring. The white circle was complete, but the Indians formed another and greater one facing it. The warriors no longer tried to rush the camp, but flat on their stomachs among the bushes they crept silently forward, and fired at every white man who exposed a head or an arm or a hand.

They seemed to have eyes that pierced the dark, and, knowing where the target lay, they had an advantage over the defenders who could not tell from what point the next shot would come.

It was a sort of warfare, annoying and dangerous in the extreme, and Clark became alarmed. It got upon the nerves of the men. They were compelled to lie there and await this foe who stung and stung. He sought eagerly by the flashes of lightning to discover where they clustered in the greatest numbers, but they hugged the earth so close that he saw nothing, even when the lightning was so vivid that it cast a blood red tinge over both trees and bushes. He called Boone, Henry, Thomas and others, the best of the scouts, to him.

"We must clear those Indians out of the woods," he said, "or they will pick away at us until nothing is left to pick at. A charge with our best men will drive them off. What do you say, Mr. Boone?"

Daniel Boone shook his head, and his face expressed strong disapproval.

"We'd lose too many men, Colonel," he replied. "They're in greater numbers than we are, an' we drove them back when they charged. Now if we charged they'd shoot us to pieces before we got where we wanted to go."

"I suppose you're right," said Clark. "In fact, I know you are. Yes, we have to wait, but it's hard. Many of our men have been hit, and they can't stand this sort of thing forever."

"Suppose you send forward a hundred of the best woodsmen and sharpshooters," said Boone. "They can creep among the bushes an' maybe they can worry the Indians as much as the Indians are worrying us."

Colonel Clark considered. They were standing then near the center of the camp, and, from that point they could see through the foliage the dusky surface of the water, and when they looked in the other direction they saw puffs of fire as the rifles were discharged in the undergrowth.

"It's risky," he said at last, "but I don't see anything else for us to do. Be sure that you choose the best men, Mr. Boone."

Daniel Boone rapidly told off a hundred, all great marksmen and cautious woodsmen. Henry, Paul, Shif'less Sol, Long Jim and Tom Ross were among the first whom he chose. Then while the defenders increased their fire on the eastern side, he and his hundred, hugging the ground, began to creep toward the south. It was slow work for so large a body, and they had to be exceedingly careful. Boone wished to effect a surprise and to strike the foe so hard that he would be thrown into a panic. But Henry and Paul were glad to be moving. They had something now to which they could look forward. The two kept side by side, paying little attention to the firing which went on in unbroken volume on their left.

Boone moved toward a slight elevation about a hundred yards away. He believed that it was occupied by a small Indian force which his gallant hundred could easily brush aside, if they ever came into close contact. Amid so much confusion and darkness he could reach the desired place unless they were revealed by the lightning. There was not another flash until they were more than half way and then the hundred lay so low among the bushes that they remained hidden.

"We're beatin' the savages at their own game," said Shif'less Sol. "They are always bent on stalkin' us, but they don't 'pear to know now that we're stalkin' them. Keep your eye skinned, Henry; we don't want to run into 'em afore we expect it."

"I'm watching," replied Henry in the same tone, "but I don't think I'll have to watch much longer. In two or three minutes more they'll see us or we'll see them."

Fifty yards more and another red flash of lightning came. Henry saw a feathered head projecting over a log. At the same time the owner of the feathered head saw him, fired and leaped to his feet. Henry fired in return, and the next instant he and his comrades were upon the skirmishers, clearing them out of the bushes and sending them in headlong flight. They had been so long in the darkness now that their eyes had grown used to it, and they could see the fleeing forms. They sent a decimating volley after them, and then dropped down on the ridge that they had won. They meant to hold it, and they were fortunate enough to find there many fallen trees swept down by a tornado.

"We've cut their line," said Boone, "an' we must keep it cut. I've sent a messenger to tell Colonel Clark that we've taken the place, an' since we've broke their front they'll be mighty good men, Indians and renegades, if they're ever able to join it together again."

The warriors returned in great force to the attack. They appreciated the value of the position, but the sharpshooters fired from the shelter of the logs.

The five, following their long custom, kept close together, and when they threw themselves down behind the logs they took a rapid accounting. Paul was the only one who had escaped unhurt. A tomahawk, thrown at short range, had struck Henry on the side of the head, but only with the flat of the blade. His fur cap and thick hair saved him, but the force of the blow had made him reel for a minute, and a whole constellation of stars had danced before his eyes. Now his head still rung a little, but the pain was passing, and all his faculties were perfectly clear and keen. A bullet had nicked Tom Ross's wrist, but, cutting a piece of buckskin from his shirt, he tied it up well and gave it no further attention. Jim Hart and Shif'less Sol had received new scratches, but they were not advertising them.

They lay panting for a few minutes among the fallen trees, and all around them they heard the low words of the gallant hundred; though there were not really a hundred now. Boone was so near that Henry could see the outline of the great forest-fighter's figure.

"Well, we succeeded, did we not, Colonel Boone?" he said, giving him a title that had been conferred upon him a year or two before.

"We have so far," replied Boone, guardedly, "and this is a strong position. We couldn't have taken it if we hadn't been helped by surprise. I believe they'll make an effort to drive us out of this place. Timmendiquas and Girty know the need of it. Come with me, Mr. Ware, and see that all our men are ready."

Henry, very proud to serve as the lieutenant of such a man, rose from his log and the two went among the men. Everyone was ready with loaded weapons. Many had wounds, but they had tied them up, and, rejoicing now in their log fortifications, they waited with impatience the Indian onset. Henry returned to his place. A red flare of lightning showed his eager comrades all about him, their tanned faces, set and lean, every man watching the forest. But after the lightning, the night, heavy with clouds, swept down again, and it seemed to Henry that it was darker than ever. He longed for the dawn. With the daylight disclosing the enemy, and helping their own aim, their log fortress would be impregnable. Elsewhere the battle seemed to be dying. The shots came in irregular clusters, and the war whoop was heard only at intervals. Directly in front of them the silence was absolute and Henry's rapid mind divined the reason for all these things. Girty and Timmendiquas were assembling their main force there and they, too, would rely upon surprise and the irresistible rush of a great mass. He crawled over to Boone and told him his belief. Boone nodded.

"I think you are right," he said, "an' right now I'll send a messenger back to Colonel Clark to be ready with help. The attack will come soon, because inside of an hour you'll see dawn peeping over the eastern trees."

Henry crawled back to his comrades and lay down with them, waiting through that terrible period of suspense. Strain their ears as they would, they could hear nothing in front. If Timmendiquas and Girty were gathering their men there, they were doing it with the utmost skill and secrecy. Yet the watch was never relaxed for an instant. Every finger remained on the trigger and every figure was taut for instant action.

A half hour had passed. In another half hour the day would come, and they must fight when eyes could see. The lightning had ceased, but the wind was moaning its dirge among the leaves, and then to Henry's ears came the sound of a soft tread, of moccasined feet touching the earth ever so lightly.

"They are coming! They are coming!" he cried in a sharp, intense whisper, and the next instant the terrible war whoop, the fiercest of all human sounds, was poured from the hundreds of throats, and dusky figures seemed to rise from the earth directly in front of them, rushing upon them, seeking to close with the tomahawk before they could take aim with their rifles in the darkness. But these were chosen men, ready and wonderfully quick. Their rifles leaped to their shoulders and then they flashed all together, so close that few could miss. The front of the Indian mass was blown away, but the others were carried on by the impetus of their charge, and a confused, deadly struggle took place once more, now among the logs. Henry, wielding his clubbed rifle again, was sure that he heard the powerful voice of Timmendiquas urging on the warriors, but he was not able to see the tall figure of the great Wyandot chieftain.

"Why don't the help from Colonel Clark come?" panted Shif'less Sol. "If you don't get help when you want it, it needn't come at all."

But help was near. With a great shout more than two hundred men rushed to the rescue. Yet it was hard in the darkness to tell friend from enemy, and, taking advantage of it, the warriors yet held a place among the fallen trees. Now, as if by mutual consent, there was a lull in the battle, and there occurred something that both had forgotten in the fierce passions of the struggle. The dawn came. The sharp rays of the sun pierced the clouds of darkness and smoke, and disclosed the face of the combatants to one another.

Then the battle swelled afresh, and as the light swung higher and higher, showing all the forest, the Indian horde was driven back, giving ground at first slowly. Suddenly a powerful voice shouted a command and all the warriors who yet stood, disappeared among the trees, melting away as if they had been ghosts. They sent back no war cry, not another shot was fired, and the rising sun looked down upon a battlefield that was still, absolutely still. The wounded, stoics, both red and white, suppressed their groans, and Henry, looking from the shelter of the fallen tree, was awed as he had never been before by Indian combat.

The day was of uncommon splendor. The sun shot down sheaves of red gold, and lighted up all the forest, disclosing the dead, lying often in singular positions, and the wounded, seeking in silence to bind their wounds. The smoke, drifting about in coils and eddies, rose slowly above the trees and over everything was that menacing silence.

"If it were not for those men out there," said Paul, "it would all be like a dream, a nightmare, driven away by the day."

"It's no dream," said Henry; "we've repulsed the Indians twice, but they're going to try to hold us here. They'll surround us with hundreds of sharpshooters, and every man who tries to go a hundred yards from the rest of us will get a bullet. I wish I knew where Logan's force is or what has become of it."

"That's a mighty important thing to us," said Boone, "an' it'll grow more important every hour. I guess Logan has been attacked too, but he and Clark have got to unite or this campaign can't go on."

Henry said nothing but he was very thoughtful. A plan was forming already in his mind. Yet it was one that compelled waiting. The day deepened and the Indian force was silent and invisible. The inexperienced would have thought that it was gone, but these borderers knew well enough that it was lying there in the deep woods not a quarter of a mile away, and as eager as ever for their destruction. Colonel Clark reënforced the detachment among the fallen trees, recognizing the great strength of the position, and he spoke many words of praise.

"I'll send food to you," he said, "and meat and drink in plenty. After a night such as we have had refresh yourselves as much as you can."

They had an abundance of stores in the boats, and the men were not stinted. Nor did they confine themselves to cold food. Fires were lighted in the woods nearest to the river, and they cooked beef, venison, pork and buffalo meat. Coffee was boiled in great cans of sheet iron, and breakfast was served first to the gallant hundred.

Shif'less Sol, as he lay behind his tree, murmured words of great content. "It's a black night that don't end," he said, "an' I like fur mine to end jest this way. Provided I don't get hurt bad I'm willin' to fight my way to hot coffee an' rich buff'ler steak. This coffee makes me feel good right down to my toes, though I will say that there is a long-legged ornery creatur that kin make it even better than this. Hey, thar, Saplin'!"

Long Jim Hart's mouth opened in a chasm of a grin.

"I confess," he said, "I'm a purty good cook, ef I do tell it myself. But what are we goin' to do now, Henry?"

"That's for Colonel Clark to say, and I don't think he'll say anything just yet."

"Nice day," said Tom Ross, looking about approvingly.

All the others laughed, yet Tom told the truth. The clouds were gone and the air had turned cooler. The forest looked splendid in its foliage, and off to the south they could see wild flowers.

"Nothin' goin' to happen for some time," said Shif'less Sol, "an' me bein' a lazy man an' proud o' the fact, I think I'll go to sleep."

Nobody said anything against it, and stretching himself out among the bushes which shaded his face, he was sleeping peacefully in a few minutes. Paul looked at him, and the impression which the slumbering man made upon him was so strong that his own eyelids drooped.

"You go to sleep, too," said Henry. "You'll have nothing to do for hours, and sleep will bring back your strength."

Paul had eaten a heavy breakfast, and he needed nothing more than Henry's words. He lay down by the side of his comrade, and soon he too was slumbering as soundly as Shif'less Sol. Several hours passed. The sun moved on in its regular course toward the zenith. Paul and the shiftless one still slept. Toward the eastern end of the camp someone ventured a little distance from the others, and received a bullet in his shoulder. A scout fired at the figure of an Indian that he saw for a moment leaping from one tree to another, but he could not tell whether he hit anything. At the other end of the camp there were occasional shots, but Paul and the shiftless one slept on.

Henry glanced at the sleepers now and then and was pleased to see that they rested so well. He suggested to Jim Hart that he join them, and Jim promptly traveled to the same blissful country. Henry himself did not care to go to sleep. He was still meditating. All this sharpshooting by the two sides meant nothing. It was more an expression of restlessness than of any serious purpose, and he paid it no attention. Silent Tom noticed the corrugation of his brow, and he said:

"Thinkin' hard, Henry?"

"Yes; that is, I'm trying," replied Henry.

Tom, his curiosity satisfied, relapsed into silence. He, too, cared little for the casual shots, but he was convinced that Henry had a plan which he would reveal in good time.

The sniping went on all day long. Not a great deal of damage was done but it was sufficient to show to Colonel Clark that his men must lie close in camp. If the white army assumed the offensive, the great Indian force from the shelter of trees and bushes would annihilate it. And throughout the day he was tormented by fears about Logan. That leader was coming up the Licking with only three or four hundred men, and already they might have been destroyed. If so, he must forego the expedition against Chillicothe and the other Indian towns. It was a terrible dilemma, and the heart of the stout leader sank. Now and then he went along the semicircle, but he found that the Indians were always on watch. If a head were exposed, somebody sent a bullet at it. More than once he considered the need of a charge, but the deep woods forbade it. He was a man of great courage and many resources, but as he sat under the beech tree he could think of nothing to do.

The day—one of many alarms and scattered firing—drew to its close. The setting sun tinted river and woods with red, and Colonel Clark, still sitting under his tree and ransacking every corner of his brain, could not yet see a way. While he sat there, Henry Ware came to him, and taking off his hat, announced that he wished to make a proposition.

"Well, Henry, my lad," said the Colonel, kindly, "what is it that you have to say? As for me, I confess I don't know what to do."

"Somebody must go down the Licking and communicate with Colonel Logan," replied the youth. "I feel sure that he has not come up yet, and that he has not been in contact with the Indians. If his force could break through and join us, we could drive the Indians out of our path."

"Your argument is good as far as it goes," said Colonel Clark somewhat sadly, "but how are we to communicate with Logan? We are surrounded by a ring of fire. Not a man of ours dare go a hundred yards from camp. What way is there to reach Logan?"

"By water."

"By water? What do you mean?"

"Down the Ohio and up the Licking."

Colonel Clark stared at Henry.

"That's an easy thing to talk about," he said, "but who's going down the Ohio and then up the Licking for Logan?"

"I—with your permission."

Colonel Clark stared still harder, and his eyes widened a little with appreciation, but he shook his head.

"It's a patriotic and daring thing for you to propose, my boy," he said, "but it is impossible. You could never reach the mouth of the Licking even, and yours is too valuable a life to be thrown away in a wild attempt."

But Henry was not daunted. He had thought over his plan long and well, and he believed that he could succeed.

"I have been along the Ohio before, and I have also been down the Licking," he said. "The night promises to be cloudy and dark like last night and I feel sure that I can get through. I have thought out everything, and I wish to try. Say that you are willing for me to go, Colonel."

Colonel Clark hesitated. He had formed a strong liking for the tall youth before him, and he did not wish to see his life wasted, but the great earnestness of Henry's manner impressed him. The youth's quiet tone expressed conviction, and expressed it so strongly that Colonel Clark, in his turn, felt it.

"What is your plan?" he asked.

"When the night reaches its darkest I will start with a little raft, only four or five planks fastened together. I do not want a canoe. I want something that blends with the surface of the water. I'll swim, pushing it before me until I am tired, and then I'll rest upon it. Then I'll swim again."

"Do you really think you can get through?" asked the Colonel.

"I'm sure of it."

Colonel Clark paced back and forth for a minute or two.

"It looks terribly dangerous," he said at last, "but from all I have heard you've done some wonderful things, and if you can reach Logan in time, it will relieve us from this coil."

"I can do it! I can do it!" said Henry eagerly.

Colonel Clark looked at him long and scrutinizingly. He noted his height, his powerful figure, the wonderful elasticity that showed with every step he took, and his firm and resourceful gaze.

"Well, go," he said, "and God be with you."

"I shall start the moment full darkness comes," said Henry.

"But we must arrange a signal in case you get through to Logan," said Colonel Clark. "He has a twelve pound bronze gun. I know positively that he left Lexington with it. Now if he approaches, have him fire a shot. We will reply with two shots from our guns, you answer with another from yours, and the signal will be complete. Then Logan is to attack the Indian ring from the outside with all his might, and, at the same moment and at the same point, we will attack from the inside with all of ours. Then, in truth, it will be strange if we do not win the victory."

Henry returned to his comrades and told them the plan. They were loth to see him go, but they knew that attempts to dissuade him would be useless. Nevertheless, Shif'less Sol had an amendment.

"Let me go with you, Henry," he said. "Two are better than one."

"No," replied Henry, "I must go alone, Sol. In this case the smaller the party the less likely it is to be seen. I'll try, and then if I fail, it will be your time."

The night, as Henry had foreseen, was cloudy and dark. The moon and stars were hidden again, and two hundred yards from shore the surface of the river blended into the general blur. His little raft was made all ready. Four broad planks from the wagons had been nailed securely together with cross-strips. Upon them he laid his rifle and pistols—all in holsters—ammunition secured from the wet, and food and his clothing in tight bundles. He himself was bare, save for a waist cloth and belt, but in the belt he carried a hatchet and his long hunting knife.

Only his four comrades, Colonel Clark and Boone were present when he started. Every one of the six in turn, wrung his hand. But the four who had known him longest and best were the most confident that he would reach Logan and achieve his task.

Henry slipped silently into the water, and, pushing his raft before him, was gone like a wraith. He did not look back, knowing that for the present he must watch in front if he made the perilous passage. The boats belonging to the army were ranged toward the shore, but he was soon beyond them. Then he turned toward the bank, intending to keep deep in its shadows, and also in the shade of the overhanging boughs.

The Indians had no fleet, but beyond a doubt they were well provided with canoes which would cruise on both rivers beyond the range of rifle shot, and keep a vigilant watch for messengers from either Clark or Logan. Hence Henry moved very slowly for a while, eagerly searching the darkness for any sign of his vigilant foe. He rested one arm upon his little raft, and with the other he wielded a small paddle which sent him along easily.

As it nears Cincinnati the Ohio narrows and deepens, and the banks rise more abruptly. Henry kept close to the southern shore, his body often touching the soft earth. Fortunately the bushes grew thickly, even on the steep cliff, to the water's edge. When he had gone three or four hundred yards he pulled in among them and lay still awhile. He heard the sound of distant shots and he knew that the Indians were still sniping the camp. The curve of the Ohio hid the boats of his friends, and before him the river seemed to be deserted. Yet he was sure that the Indian canoes were on watch. They might be hovering within fifty yards of him.

He listened for the noise of paddles, but no such sound came, and pushing his tiny craft from the coil of bushes, he set out once more upon the Ohio. Still hearing and seeing nothing, he went a little faster. Henry was a powerful swimmer, and the raft, small as it was, gave him ample support. Meanwhile, he sought sedulously to avoid any noise, knowing that only an incautious splash made by his paddle would almost certainly be heard by an Indian ear.

Presently he saw on the northern bank a light, and then another light farther up the stream. Probably the Indians were signaling to one another, but it did not matter to him, and he swam on towards the mouth of the Licking, now about a half mile away. Another hundred yards and he quickly and silently drew in to the bank again, pushing the raft far back, until it, as well as himself, was hidden wholly. He had heard the distant sounds of paddles coming in his direction, and soon two Indian canoes in file came in sight. Each canoe contained two warriors. Henry inferred from the way in which they scrutinized the river and the bank, that they were sentinels. Well for him that the bushes grew thick and high. The penetrating Indian eyes passed unsuspecting over his hiding place, and went on, dropping slowly down the river to a point where they could watch the white boats. A hundred yards in that darkness was sufficient to put them out of sight, and Henry again pushed boldly into the stream.

The young blockade runner now had a theory that the sentinel boats of the Indians would keep close in to the shore. That would be their natural procedure, and to avoid them he swam boldly far out into the river. Near the middle of the current he paddled once more up stream. Only his head showed above the surface and the raft was so low that no one was likely to notice it. The wisdom of his movement soon showed as he made out three more canoes near the Kentucky shore, obviously on watch. Toward the north, at a point not more than seventy or eighty yards away he saw another canoe containing three warriors and apparently stationary. Others might be further ahead, but the darkness was too great for him to tell. Clearly, there was no passage except in the middle of the stream, the very point that he had chosen.

Many a stout heart would have turned back, but pride commanded Henry to go on. Fortunately, the water lying long under the summer heat was very warm, and one could stay in it indefinitely, without fear of chill. While he deliberated a little, he sank down until he could breathe only through his nostrils, keeping one hand upon the raft. Then he began to swim slowly with his feet and the other hand and all the while he kept his eyes upon the stationary boat containing the three warriors. By dint of staring at them so long they began to appear clear and sharp in the darkness. Two were middle-aged, and one young. He judged them to be Wyandots, and they had an anchor as they did not use the paddles to offset the current. Undoubtedly they were sentinels, as their gaze made a continuous circle about them. Henry knew, too, that they were using ears as well as eyes and that nobody could hear better than the Wyandots.

He decreased his pace, merely creeping through the water, and at the same time he swung back a little toward the southern shore and away from the Wyandots in the canoe. But the movement was a brief one. To the right of him he saw two more canoes and he knew that they formed a part of the chain of sentinels stretched by Timmendiquas across the river. It was obvious to Henry that the Wyandot leader was fully aware of the advance of Logan, and was resolved to prevent the passage of any messenger between him and Clark.

Henry paused again, still clinging to his little raft, and holding his place in the current with a slight motion of his feet. Then he advanced more slowly than ever, choosing a point which he thought was exactly half way between the Wyandots and the other canoes, but he feared the Wyandots most. Twenty yards, and he stopped. One of the Wyandot warriors seemed to have seen something. He was looking fixedly in Henry's direction. Boughs and stumps of every sort often floated down the Ohio. He might have caught a glimpse of Henry's head. He would take it for a small stump, but he would not stop to surmise.

Holding the planks with but one hand, Henry dived about two feet beneath the surface and swam silently but powerfully up the stream. He swam until his head seemed to swell and the water roared in his ears. He swam until his heart pounded from exhaustion and then he rose slowly to the surface, not knowing whether or not he would rise among his enemies.

No one greeted him with a shot or blow as he came up, and, when his eyes cleared themselves of water, he saw the Wyandot canoe cruising about sixty or seventy yards down the stream, obviously looking for the dark spot that one of them had seen upon the surface of the river. They might look in his direction, but he believed that he was too far away to be noticed. Still, he could not tell, and one with less command of himself would have swam desperately away. Henry, instead, remained perfectly still, sunk in the water up to his nostrils, one hand only yet clinging to the raft. The Wyandots turned southward, joined their brethren from the Kentucky shore and talked earnestly with them. Henry used the opportunity to swim about a hundred yards further up the stream, and then, when the canoes separated, he remained perfectly still again. In the foggy darkness he feared most the Indian ear which could detect at once any sound out of the common. But the Wyandot canoe returned to its old place and remained stationary there. Evidently the warriors were convinced that they had seen only a stump.

Henry now swam boldly and swiftly, still remaining in the middle of the stream. He saw several lights in the woods on the southern shore, not those of signals, but probably the luminous glow from camp fires as they burned with a steady blaze. The Indians were on watch, and the faint sound of two or three rifle shots showed that the night did not keep them from buzzing and stinging about Colonel Clark's force. Yet Henry's pulse leaped in throat and temple. He had passed one formidable obstacle and it was a good omen. The stars in their courses were fighting for him, and he would triumph over the others as they came.

But he checked his speed, thinking that the Indian canoes would be thick around the mouth of the Licking, and presently he became conscious of a great weariness. He had been in the water a long time and one could not dive and swim forever. His arms and legs ached and he felt a soreness in his chest. It was too dangerous to pull in to the bank at that point, and he tried a delicate experiment. He sought to crawl upon his little raft and lie there flat upon his back, a task demanding the skill of an acrobat.

Three or four times Henry was within an inch of overturning his frail craft with the precious freight, but he persisted, and by skillfully balancing himself and the raft too he succeeded at last. Then he was compelled to lie perfectly still, with his arms outstretched and his feet in the water. He was flat upon his back and he could look at only the heavens, which offered to his view nothing—no bright stars and shining moon, only lowering clouds. If an enemy appeared, he must depend upon his ear to give warning. But the physical difficulty of his position did not keep him from feeling a delightful sense of rest. The soreness left his chest, the ache disappeared from his arms and legs, and he drew the fresh air into his lungs in deep and easy breaths. An occasional kick of his feet kept the raft from floating down stream, and, for a while, he lay there, studying the clouds, and wondering how long it would be until the twinkle of a star would break through them. He heard the sound of both paddles and oars, the first to the north and the other to the south. But his experienced ear told him that each was at least two hundred yards away, which was too far for anyone to see him stretched out upon his boards. So he rested on and waited for his ears to tell him whether the sounds were coming any nearer. The boat with the oars passed out of hearing and the sound of the oars became fainter and fainter. Henry's heart ticked a note of thankfulness. He would not be disturbed for the present, and he continued his study of the low clouds, while the strength flowed back into every part of his body.

It occurred to him presently that he could steer as well as propel his float with his feet. So he set to work, threshing the water very slowly and carefully, and turning his head towards the mouth of the Licking. Occasionally he heard the sounds of both oars and paddles, but he judged very accurately that those who wielded them were not near enough to see him. He was thankful that the night was not broken like the one before with flashes of lightning which would infallibly have disclosed him to the enemy.

After a half hour of this work, he felt a strange current of water against his feet, and at first he was puzzled, but the solution came in a few minutes. He was opposite the mouth of the Licking, and he had come into contact with the stream before it was fully merged into the Ohio. What should he do next? The cordon across the Licking, a much narrower river, would be harder to pass than that on the Ohio.

But he was rested fully now, and, sliding off his boards into the water, he took a long survey of his situation. No break had yet occurred in the clouds, and this was a supreme good fortune. To the east, he dimly saw two boats, and to the south, the high black bank. No lights were visible there, but he saw them further down the shore, where it was likely that the majority of the warriors were gathered. Henry resolved to make directly for the angle of land between the mouth of the Licking and the Ohio, and he swam toward it with swift, powerful strokes, pushing his raft before him.

He calculated that at this angle of land he would be between the two Indian cordons, and there, if anywhere, he could find the way to Logan. He reached the point, found it well covered with bushes, and drew the little raft into concealment. Then he climbed cautiously to the top and looked long in every direction, seeking to trace the precise alignment of the Indian force. He saw lights in the woods directly to the south and along the shore of the Licking. The way there was closed and he knew that the watch would be all the more vigilant in order to intercept the coming of Logan. He could not pass on land. Hence, he must pass on water.

There were yet many long hours before daylight, and he did not hasten. Although the water was warm he had been in it a long time and he took every precaution to maintain his physical powers. He did not dress, but he rubbed thoroughly every part of his body that he could reach. Then he flexed and tensed his muscles until he had thrown off every chance of chill, after which he lowered himself into the water, and pushed out with his raft once more.

He turned the angle of land and entered the Licking, a narrow, deep, and muddy stream, lined there, like all the other rivers of that region, with high and thick forests. Ahead of him, he saw in the stream a half dozen boats with warriors, yet he continued his course towards the cordon, keeping his float very close to the western banks. It is said that fortune favors the daring, and Henry had often proved the truth of it. Once more the saying held good. Clouds heavier and thicker than any of the others floated up and plunged river and shores into deeper obscurity. Henry believed that if he could avoid all noise, he might, by hugging the bank, get by.

He went in so close to the shore that he could wade, but finding that he was likely to become tangled among bushes and vines, thus making sounds which the warriors would not fail to hear, he returned to deeper water. Now the most critical moment of the river gauntlet was approaching. He saw about one hundred yards before him, and directly across his course, a boat containing two warriors. The space between this boat and the western shore was not more than thirty yards. Could he pass them, unseen? The chances were against it, but he resolved to try.

Swimming silently, he approached the opening. He had sunk deep in the water again, with only one hand on the float, and there was yet nothing from the boat to indicate that the two warriors had either seen or heard him. Despite all his experience, his heart beat very fast, and his hand on the float trembled. But he had no thought of going back. Now he was almost parallel with the boat. Now, he was parallel, and the watchful eye of one of the warriors caught a glimpse of the darker object on the surface of the dark water. He stared a moment in surprise, and then with a yell of warning to his comrade, raised his rifle and fired at the swimming head.

Henry had seen the upraised rifle, and diving instantly, he swam with all his might up stream. As he went down, he heard the bullet go zip upon the water. Knowing that he could not save his little craft, he had loosed his hold upon it and swam under water as long as he could. Yet those boards and the packages upon them saved his life. They were the only things that the warriors now saw, and all rowed straight towards the raft. Meanwhile, Henry rose in the bushes at the edge of the bank and took long and deep breaths, while they examined his rifle and clothing. Before they had finished, he dived into the deep water once more, and was again swimming swiftly against the current of the Licking.

CHAPTER XX. THE COUNTER-STROKE

Colonel Benjamin Logan was standing in a small opening near the banks of the Licking about five miles south of its junction with the Ohio. Dawn had just come but it had been a troubled night. The country around him was beautiful, a primeval wilderness with deep fertile soil and splendid forest. His company, too, was good—several hundred stalwart men from Lexington, Boonesborough, Harrod's Station and several other settlements in the country, destined to become so famous as the Bluegrass region of Kentucky. Yet, as has been said, the night was uneasy and he saw no decrease of worry.

Colonel Logan was a man of stout nerves, seldom troubled by insomnia, but he had not slept. His scouts had told him that there were Indians in the forest ahead. One or two incautious explorers had been wounded by bullets fired from hidden places. He and the best men with him had felt that they were surrounded by an invisible enemy, and just at the time that he needed knowledge, it was hardest to achieve it. It was important for him to move on, highly important because he wanted to effect a junction for a great purpose with George Rogers Clark, a very famous border leader. Yet he could learn nothing of Clark. He did not receive any news from him, nor could he send any to him. Every scout who tried it was driven back, and after suffering agonies of doubt through that long and ominous night, the brave leader and skillful borderer had concluded that the most powerful Indian force ever sent to Kentucky was in front of him. His men had brought rumors that it was led by the renowned Wyandot chief, Timmendiquas, with Red Eagle, Black Panther, Moluntha, Captain Pipe and the renegade Girty as his lieutenants.

Colonel Logan, brave man that he was, was justified when he felt many fears. His force was not great, and, surrounded, it might be overwhelmed and cut off. For the border to lose three or four hundred of its best men would be fatal. Either he must retreat or he must effect a junction with Clark of whose location he knew nothing. A more terrible choice has seldom been presented to a man. Harrod, Kenton and other famous scouts stood with him and shared his perplexity.

"What shall we do, gentlemen?" he asked.

There was no answer save the sound of a rifle shot from the woods in front of them.

"I don't blame you for not answering," said the Colonel moodily, "because I don't know of anything you can say. Listen to those shots! We may be fighting for our lives before noon, but, by all the powers, I won't go back. We can't do it! Now in the name of all that's wonderful what is that?"

Every pair of eyes was turned toward the muddy surface of the Licking, where a white body floated easily. As they looked the body came to the bank, raised itself up in the shape of a human being and stepped ashore, leaving a trail of water on the turf. It was the figure of a youth, tall and powerful beyond his kind and bare to the waist. He came straight toward Logan.

"Now, who under the sun are you and what do you want!" exclaimed the startled Colonel.

"My name is Henry Ware," replied the youth in a pleasant voice, "and what I want is first a blanket and after that some clothes, but meanwhile I tell you that I am a messenger from Colonel Clark whom you wish to join."

"A messenger from Colonel Clark?" exclaimed Logan. "How do we know this?"

"Simon Kenton there knows me well and he can vouch for me; can't you Simon?" continued the youth in the same pleasant voice.

"And so I can!" exclaimed Kenton, springing forward and warmly grasping the outstretched hand. "I didn't know you at first, Henry, which is natural, because it ain't your habit to wander around in the daytime with nothing on but a waist band."

"But how is it that you came up the Licking," persisted Colonel Logan, still suspicious. "Is Colonel Clark in the habit of sending unclothed messengers up rivers?"

"I came that way," replied Henry, "because all the others are closed. I've been swimming nearly all night or rather floating, because I had a little raft to help me. I came up the Ohio and then up the Licking. I ran the Indian gauntlet on both rivers. At the gauntlet on the Licking I lost my raft which carried my rifle, clothes and ammunition. However here I am pretty wet and somewhat tired, but as far as I know, sound."

"You can rely on every word he says, Colonel," exclaimed Simon Kenton.

"I do believe him absolutely," said Colonel Logan, "and here, Mr. Ware, is my blanket. Wear it until we get your clothes. And now what of Clark?"

"He is only about six miles away with seven hundred veterans. He was attacked night before last by Timmendiquas, Girty and all the power of the allied tribes, but we drove them off. Colonel Clark and his men are in an impregnable position, and they await only your coming to beat the whole Indian force. He has sent me to tell you so."

Colonel Logan fairly sprang up in his joy.

"Only six miles away!" he exclaimed. "Then we'll soon be with him. Young sir, you shall have the best clothes and the best rifle the camp can furnish, for yours has been a daring mission and a successful one. How on earth did you ever do it?"

"I think luck helped me," replied Henry modestly.

"Luck? Nonsense! Luck can't carry a man through such an ordeal as that. No, sir; it was skill and courage and strength. Now here is breakfast, and while you eat, your new clothes and your new rifle shall be brought to you."

Colonel Logan was as good as his word. When Henry finished his breakfast and discarded the blanket he arrayed himself in a beautifully tanned and fringed suit of deerskin, and ran his hand lovingly along the long slender barrel of a silver-mounted rifle, the handsomest weapon he had ever seen.

"It is yours," said Colonel Logan, "in place of the one that you have lost, and you shall have also double-barreled pistols. And now as we are about to advance, we shall have to call upon you to be our guide."

Henry responded willingly. He was fully rested, and at such a moment he had not thought of sleep. Preceded by scouts, Logan's force advanced cautiously through the woods near the Licking. About a score of shots were fired at them, but, after the shots, the Indian skirmishers fell back on their main force. When they had gone about two miles Logan stopped his men, and ordered a twelve-pound cannon of which they were very proud to be brought forward.

It was rolled into a little open space, loaded only with blank cartridges and fired. Doubtless many of the men wondered why it was discharged seemingly at random into the forest, because Colonel Logan had talked only with Henry Ware, Simon Kenton and a few others. But the sound of the shot rolled in a deep boom through the woods.

"Will he hear?" asked Colonel Logan.

"He'll hear," replied Simon Kenton with confidence. "The sound will travel far through this still air. It will reach him."

They waited with the most intense anxiety one minute, two minutes, and out of the woods in the north came the rolling report in reply. A half minute more and then came the second sound just like the first.

"The signal! They answer! They answer!" exclaimed Colonel Logan joyously. "Now to make it complete."

When the last echo of the second shot in the north had died, the twelve-pounder was fired again. Then it was reloaded, but not with blank cartridges, and the word to advance was given. Now the men pressed forward with increased eagerness, but they still took wilderness precaution. Trees and hillocks were used for shelter, and from the trees and hillocks in front of them the Indian skirmishers poured a heavy fire. Logan's men replied and the forest was alive with the sounds of battle. Bullets cut twigs and bushes, and the white man's shout replied to the red man's war whoop. The cannon was brought up, and fired cartridges and then grape shot at the point where the enemy's force seemed to be thickest. The Indians gave way before this terrifying fire, and Logan's men followed them. But the Colonel always kept a heavy force on either flank to guard against ambush, and Henry was continually by his side to guide. They went a full mile and then Henry, who was listening, exclaimed joyfully:

"They're coming to meet us! Don't you hear their fire?"

Above the crash of his own combat Colonel Logan heard the distant thudding of cannon, and, as he listened, that thudding came nearer. These were certainly the guns of Clark, and he was as joyous as Henry. Their coöperation was now complete, and the courage and daring of one youth had made it possible. His own force pushed forward faster, and soon they could hear the rifles of the heavier battle in the north.

"We've got 'em! We've got 'em!" shouted Simon Kenton. "They are caught between the two jaws of a vice, and the bravest Indians that ever lived can never stand that."

Logan ordered his men to spread out in a longer and thinner line, although he kept at least fifty of his best about the cannon to prevent any attempt at capture. The twelve-pounder may not have done much execution upon an enemy who fought chiefly from shelter, but he knew that its effect was terrifying, and he did not mean to lose the gun. His precaution was taken well, as a picked band of Wyandots, Shawnees and Miamis, springing suddenly from the undergrowth, made a determined charge to the very muzzle of the cannon. There was close fighting, hand to hand, the shock of white bodies against red, the flash of exploding powder and the glitter of steel, but the red band was at last driven back, although not without loss to the defenders. The struggle had been so desperate that Colonel Logan drew more men about the cannon, and then pressed on again. The firing to the north was growing louder, indicating that Clark, too, was pushing his way through the forest. The two forces were now not much more than a mile apart, and Simon Kenton shouted that the battle would cease inside of five minutes.

Kenton was a prophet. Almost at the very moment predicted by him the Indian fire stopped with a suddenness that seemed miraculous. Every dusky flitting form vanished. No more jets of flame arose, the smoke floated idly about as if it had been made by bush fires, and Logan's men found that nobody was before them. There was something weird and uncanny about it. The sudden disappearance of so strong and numerous an enemy seemed to partake of magic. But Henry understood well. Always a shrewd general, Timmendiquas, seeing that the battle was lost, and that he might soon be caught in an unescapable trap, had ordered the warriors to give up the fight, and slip away through the woods.

Pressing forward with fiery zeal and energy, Clark and Logan met in the forest and grasped hands. The two forces fused at the same time and raised a tremendous cheer. They had beaten the allied tribes once more, and had formed the union which they believed would make them invincible. A thousand foresters, skilled in every wile and strategy of Indian war were indeed a formidable force, and they had a thorough right to rejoice, as they stood there in the wilderness greeting one another after a signal triumph. Save for the fallen, there was no longer a sign of the warriors. All their wounded had been taken away with them.

"I heard your cannon shot, just when I was beginning to give up hope," said Colonel Clark to Colonel Logan.

"And you don't know how welcome your reply was," replied Logan, "but it was all due to a great boy named Henry Ware."

"So he got through?"

"Yes, he did. He arrived clothed only in a waist band, and the first we saw of him was his head emerging from the muddy waters of the Licking. He swam, floated and dived all night long until he got to us. He was chased by canoes, and shot at by warriors, but nothing could stop him, and without him we couldn't have done anything, because there was no other way for us to hear a word from you."

"Ah, there he is now. But I see that he is clothed and armed."

Henry had appeared just then with his comrades, looking among the bushes to see if any savage yet lay there in ambush, and the two Colonels seized upon him. They could not call him by complimentary names enough, and they told him that he alone had made the victory possible. Henry, blushing, got away from them as quickly as he could, and rejoined his friends.

"That shorely was a great swim of yours, Henry," said Shif'less Sol, "an' you're pow'ful lucky that the water was warm."

"My little raft helped me a lot," rejoined Henry, "and I'm mighty sorry I lost it, although Colonel Logan has given me the best rifle I ever saw. I wonder what will be our next movement."

Colonel Clark, who was now in command of the whole force, the other officers coöperating with him and obeying him loyally, deemed it wise to spend the day in rest. The men had gone through long hours of waiting, watching and fighting and their strength must be restored. Scouts reported that the Indians had crossed the Licking and then the Ohio, and were retreating apparently toward Chillicothe, their greatest town. Some wanted Colonel Clark to follow them at once and strike another blow, but he was too wise. The Indian facility for retreat was always great. They could scatter in the forest in such a way that it was impossible to find them, but if rashly followed they could unite as readily and draw their foe into a deadly ambush. Clark, a master of border warfare, who was never tricked by them, let them go and bided his time. He ordered many fires to be lighted and food in abundance to be served. The spirits of the men rose to the highest pitch. Even the wounded rejoiced.

After eating, Henry found that he needed sleep. He did not feel the strain and anxiety of the long night and of the morning battle, until it was all over. Then his whole system relaxed, and, throwing himself down on the turf, he went sound asleep. When he awoke the twilight was coming and Paul and Shif'less Sol sat near him.

"We had to guard you most of the time, Henry," said Shif'less Sol, "'cause you're a sort of curiosity. Fellers hev kep' comin' here to see the lad what swam the hull len'th o' the Ohio an' then the hull len'th o' the Lickin', most o' the time with his head under water, an' we had to keep 'em from wakin' you. We'd let 'em look at you, but we wouldn't let 'em speak or breathe loud. You wuz sleepin' so purty that we could not bear to hev you waked up."

Henry laughed.

"Quit making fun of me, Sol," he said, "and tell me what's happened since I've been asleep."

"Nothin' much. The Indians are still retreatin' through the woods across the Ohio an' Colonel Clark shows his good hoss sense by not follerin' 'em, ez some o' our hot heads want him to do. Wouldn't Timmendiquas like to draw us into an ambush,—say in some valley in the thick o' the forest with a couple o' thousand warriors behind the trees an' on the ridges all aroun' us. Oh, wouldn't he? An' what would be left of us after it wuz all over? I ask you that, Henry."

"Mighty little, I'm afraid."

"Next to nothin', I know. I tell you Henry our Colonel Clark is a real gin'ral. He's the kind I like to foller, an' we ain't goin' to see no sich sight ez the one we saw at Wyomin'."

"I'm sure we won't," said Henry. "Now have any of you slept to-day?"

"All o' us hev took naps, not long but mighty deep an' comfortin'. So we're ready fur anythin' from a fight to a foot race, whichever 'pears to be the better fur us."

"Where are Paul and Tom and Jim?"

"Cruisin' about in their restless, foolish way. I told 'em to sit right down on the groun' and keep still an' enjoy theirselves while they could, but my wise words wuz wasted. Henry, sometimes I think that only lazy men like me hev good sense."

The missing three appeared a minute or two later and were received by the shiftless one with the objurgations due to what he considered misspent energy.

"I'm for a scout to-night," said Henry. "Are all of you with me?"

Three answered at once:

"Of course."

But Shif'less Sol groaned.

"Think o' going out after dark when you might lay here an' snooze comf'ably," he said; "but sence you fellers are so foolish an' headstrong you'll need some good sens'ble man to take keer o' you."

"Thank you, Sol," said Henry, with much gravity. "Now that we have your reluctant consent we need only to ask Colonel Clark."

Colonel Clark had no objection. In fact, he would not question any act of the five, whom he knew to be free lances of incomparable skill and knowledge in the wilderness.

"You know better than I what to do," he said, smiling, "and as for you, Mr. Ware, you have already done more than your share in this campaign."

They left shortly after dark. The united camp was pitched at the junction of the Ohio and Licking, but along the bank of the larger river. Most of the boats were tied to the shore, and they had a heavy guard. There was also a strong patrol across the mouth of the Licking, and all the way to the northern bank of the Ohio.

The five embarked in a large boat with four oarsmen and they lay at ease while they were pulled across the broad stream. Behind them they saw the numerous lights of the camp, twinkling in the woods. Clark meant that his men should be cheerful, and light ministers to good spirits. Ahead of him there was no break in the dark line of forest, but they approached it without apprehension, assured by other scouts that the Indian retreat had not ceased.

They were landed on the northern bank and stating to the boatmen that they would be back in the morning, they plunged into the woods. There was some moonlight, and in a short time they picked up the trail of the main Indian force. They followed it until midnight and found that it maintained a steady course toward Chillicothe. Henry was satisfied that Timmendiquas meant to fall back on the town, and make a stand there where he could hope for victory, but he was not sure that smaller bands would not lurk in Clark's path, and try to cut up and weaken his force as it advanced. Hence, he left the great trail and turned to the right. In a mile or so they heard sounds and peering through the woods saw Braxton Wyatt, Blackstaffe and about a dozen Shawnee warriors sitting about a small fire. Paul incautiously stepped upon a dead bough which cracked beneath his weight, and the Indians at once leaped up, rifle in hand. They fired several shots into the bushes whence the sound had come, but the five had already taken shelter, and they sent bullets in return. Rifles cracked sharply and jets of smoke arose.

A combat did not enter into Henry's calculation. It was one thing that he wished especially to avoid, but neither he nor any other of the five could bear to make a hasty retreat before Braxton Wyatt. They held their ground, and sent in a fire so rapid and accurate that Wyatt and Blackstaffe thought they were attacked by a force larger than their own, and, fearing to be trapped, finally retreated. The result appealed irresistibly to Shif'less Sol's sense of humor.

"Ef they hadn't run, we would," he said. "Jest think how often that's the case. Many a feller gits beat 'cause he don't wait for the other to beat hisself."

They were all buoyant over the affair, and they followed some distance, until they saw that Wyatt and Blackstaffe had changed their course in order to join the main band, when they started back to Clark, having seen all they wished. They arrived at the river about daylight, and were ordered to the southern shore where they made a report that was greatly satisfactory to the commander. Clark passed his whole force over the Ohio the next day and then built a small fort on the site of Cincinnati, placing in it all the surplus stores and ammunition.

Several days were spent here, and, throughout that time, Henry and his comrades scouted far and wide, going as far as thirty miles beyond the fort. But the woods were bare of Indians, and Henry was confirmed in his belief that Timmendiquas, after the failure at the mouth of the Licking, was concentrating everything on Chillicothe, expecting to resist to the utmost.

"Thar's bound to be a pow'ful big battle at that town," said Shif'less Sol.

"I think so, too," said Henry, "and we've got to guard against walking into any trap. I wish I knew what thought is lying just now in the back of the head of Timmendiquas."

"We'll soon know, 'cause it won't take us many days to git to Chillicothe," said Tom Ross.

The army took up its march the next day, going straight toward Chillicothe. It was the most formidable white force that had yet appeared in the western woods, and every man in it was full of confidence. It was not only an army, but it marched in the shape and fashion of one. The borderers, used to their own way, yielded readily to the tact and great name of Clark. The first division under Clark's own command, with the artillery, military stores and baggage in the center, led; Logan, who ranked next to Clark, commanded the rear.

The men walked in four lines, with a space of forty yards between every two lines. On each flank was a band of veteran scouts and skirmishers. In front of the white army, but never out of sight, marched a strong detachment of skilled woodsmen and marksmen. In the rear and at a similar distance, came another such band.

Clark also took further precautions against surprise and confusion. He issued an order that in case of attack in front the vanguard was to stand fast while the two lines on the right of the artillery were to wheel to the right, and the two on the left were to wheel to the left. Then the cannon and the whole line were to advance at the double quick to the support of the vanguard. If they were attacked from behind, the vanguard was to stand fast, and the whole proceeding was to be reversed. If they were attacked on either flank, the two lines on that flank and the artillery were to stand where they were, while the other two lines wheeled and formed, one on the van and the other on the rear. The men had been drilled repeatedly in their movements, and they executed them with skill. It now remained to be seen whether they would do as much under the influence of surprise and a heavy fire. Everyone believed they would stand against any form of attack.

The commanders seemed to think of all things, and the training of the army excited the admiration of Henry and his comrades. They felt that it would be very hard to catch such a force in a trap, or, if it should be caught, there was nothing in the wilderness to hold it there. The five were not in the line. In fact, they kept ahead of the vanguard itself, but they often came back to make their reports to Clark. It was now the beginning of August, and the heat was great in the woods. The men were compelled to rest in the middle of the day and they drank thirstily from every brook they passed.

Clark expected that they would be annoyed by the Indian skirmishers, but the first day passed, and then the second and not a shot was fired. The five and the other scouts assured him that no warriors were near, but he did not like the silence. Bowman and a strong force had attacked Chillicothe the year before, but had been repulsed. Undoubtedly it would now have a still stronger defense and he wondered what could be the plan of Timmendiquas. A border leader, in a land covered with great forests was compelled to guard every moment against the cunning and stratagem of a foe who lived by cunning and stratagem.

The second night a council was held, and Henry and all his comrades were summoned to it. Would or would not the Indians fight before the white force reached Chillicothe? The country was rough and presented many good places for defense. Colonel Clark asked the question, and he looked anxiously around at the little group. Daniel Boone spoke first. He believed that no resistance would be offered until they reached Chillicothe. Simon Kenton and Abe Thomas shared his opinion. Henry stood modestly in the background and waited until Colonel Clark put the question. Then he replied with a proposition:

"I think that Colonel Boone is right," he said, "but I and four others have been associated a long time in work of this kind. We are used to the forest, and we can move faster in it. Let us go ahead. We will see what is being prepared at Chillicothe, and we will report to you."

"But the risk to you five?"

"We're ready to take it. Everybody in the army is taking it."

Henry's plan was so promising that he soon had his way. He and the others were to start immediately.

"Go, my boy, and God bless you," said Colonel Clark. "We want all the information you can bring, but don't take excessive risks."

Henry gave his promise, left the council, and in five minutes he and his comrades were deep in the forest, and beyond the sight of their own camp fires. The weather was now clear and there was a good moon and many stars. Far to the right of them rose the hoot of an owl, but it was a real owl and they paid no attention to it.

"Jest what are you figurin' on, Henry?" asked Shif'less Sol.

"I think that if we travel hard all of to-night," replied Henry, "and then take it easy to-morrow that we can reach Chillicothe early to-morrow night. We ought to learn there in a few hours all that we want to know, and we can be back with the army on the following day."

None of the five had ever been at Chillicothe, but all of them knew very well its location. It was the largest Indian village in the Ohio River Valley, and many a foray had gone from it. They knew that the forest ran continuously from where they were almost to its edge, and they believed that they could approach without great difficulty. After a consultation they settled upon the exact point toward which they would go, and then, Henry leading the way, they sped onward in a silent file. Hour after hour they traveled without speaking. The moon was out, but they kept to the deepest parts of the forest and its rays rarely reached them. They used the long running walk of the frontiersman and their toughened muscles seemed never to tire. Every one of them breathed regularly and easily, but the miles dropped fast behind them. They leaped little brooks, and twice they waded creeks, in one of which the water went far past their knees, but their buckskin trousers dried upon them as they ran on. The moon went behind floating clouds, and then came back again but it made no difference to them. They went on at the same swift, even pace, and it was nearly morning when Henry gave the signal to stop.

He saw a place that he thought would suit them for their informal camp, a dense thicket of bushes and vines on a hill, a thicket that even in the daylight would be impervious to the keenest eyes.

"Suppose we crawl in here and rest awhile," he said. "We mustn't break ourselves down."

"Looks all right," said Tom Ross.

They crept into the dense covert, and all went to sleep except Henry and Ross who lay down without closing their eyes, theirs being the turn to watch. Henry saw the sun rise and gild the forest that seemed to be without human being save themselves. Beyond the thicket in which they lay there was not much underbrush and as Henry watched on all sides for a long time he was sure that no Indian had come near. He was confirmed in this opinion by two deer that appeared amid the oak openings and nibbled at the turf. They were a fine sight, a stag and doe each of splendid size, and they moved fearlessly about among the trees. Henry admired them and he had no desire whatever to harm them. Instead, they were now friends of his, telling him by their presence that the savages were absent.

Henry judged that they were now about two-thirds of the way to Chillicothe, and, shortly before noon, he and Tom awakened the others and resumed their journey, but in the brilliant light of the afternoon they advanced much more slowly. Theirs was a mission of great importance and discovery alone would ruin it. They kept to the thicket, and the stony places where they would leave no trail, and once, when a brook flowed in their direction, they waded in its watery bed for two or three miles. But the intensity of their purpose and the concentration of their faculties upon it did not keep them from noticing the magnificence of the country. Everywhere the soil was deep and dark, and, springing from it, was the noblest of forests. It was well watered, too, with an abundance of creeks and brooks, and now and then a little lake. Further on were large rivers. Henry did not wonder that the Indians fought so bitterly against trespassers upon their ancient hunting grounds.

The twilight of the second night came, and, lying in the thicket, the five ate and drank a little, while the twilight turned into dark. Then they prepared their plans. They did not believe that Chillicothe was more than three miles ahead, and the Indians, knowing that the army could not come up for two days yet, were not likely to be keeping a very strict watch. They meant to penetrate to the town in the night. But they waited a long time, until they believed most of the children and squaws would be asleep, and then they advanced again.

Their surmise was correct. In a half hour they were on the outskirts of Chillicothe, the great Indian town. It was surrounded by fields of maize and pumpkin, but it seemed to the five to consist of several hundred lodges and modern houses. As they made this reckoning they stood at the edge of a large corn field that stretched between them and the town. The stalks of corn were higher than a man's head, and the leaves had begun to turn brown under the August sun.

"We must go nearer," said Henry, "and it seems to me that this corn field offers a way of approach. The corn will hide us until we come to the very edge of the town."

The others agreed, and they set off across the field. After they entered it they could see nothing but the corn itself. The dying stalks rustled mournfully above their heads, as they advanced between the rows, but no sounds came from the town. It was about three hundred yards across the field, and when they reached its far edge they saw several lights which came from Chillicothe itself. They paused, while still in the corn, and, lying upon the ground, they got a good view of the big village.

Chillicothe seemed to run a long distance from north to south, but Henry at once noticed among the buildings, obviously of a permanent character, many tepees such as the Indians erect only for a night or two. His logical mind immediately drew the inference. Chillicothe was full of strange warriors. The Wyandots, Shawnees, Miamis, Delawares, Ottawas, Illinois, all were there and the circumstance indicated that they would not try to lay an ambush for Clark, but would await him at Chillicothe. He whispered to his comrades and they agreed with him.

"Can you see how far this corn field runs down to the right?" he asked Tom Ross.

"'Bout two hundred yards, I reckon."

"Then let's drop down its edge and see if the new tepees are scattered everywhere through the town."

The trip revealed an abundance of the temporary lodges and farther down they saw signs of an embankment freshly made. But this breastwork of earth did not extend far. Evidently it had been left incomplete.

"What do you make of that, Henry?" asked Ross.

"That the Indians are in a state of indecision," replied Henry promptly. "They intended to fortify and fight us here, and now they are thinking that maybe they won't. If they had made up their minds thoroughly they would have gone on with the earthwork."

"That certainly sounds reasonable," said Paul, "but if they don't fight here where will they fight? I can't believe that Timmendiquas will abandon the Indian towns without resistance and flee to the woods."

"They have another big town farther on—Piqua they call it. It may be more defensible than Chillicothe, and, if so, they might decide to concentrate there. But we can be sure of one thing. They have not yet left Chillicothe. It is for us to discover within the next few hours just what they mean to do."

At the lower end of the corn field they found a garden of tall pea and bean vines which they entered. This field projected into the village and when they reached its end they saw a great increase of lights and heard the hum of voices. Peeping from their precarious covert they beheld the dusky figures of warriors in large numbers, and they surmised that some sort of a council was in progress.

Henry was eager to know what was being said at this council, but for a long time he could think of no way. At last he noticed a small wooden building adjoining the garden, the door of which stood half open, revealing ears of corn from the preceding season lying in a heap upon the floor. He resolved to enter this rude corncrib knowing it would contain many apertures, and see and hear what was being done. He told the others his plan. They tried to dissuade him from it but he persisted, being sure that he would succeed.

"I'm bound to take the risk," he said. "We must find out what the Indians intend to do."

"Then if you're bent on throwin' away your life," said Shif'less Sol, "I'm goin' in with you."

"No," said Henry firmly. "One is enough, and it is enough to risk one. But if you fellows wish, lie here behind the vines, and, if I have to make a run for it, you can cover me with your fire."

The four at last agreed to this compromise, although they were loth to see Henry go. Every one of them made up his mind to stand by their leader to the last. Henry left the shelter of the vines, but he lay down almost flat, and crept across the narrow open space to the corncrib. When he saw that no one was looking he darted inside, and cautiously pushed the door shut.

As he expected, there were plenty of cracks between the timbers and also a small open window at one end. The ears of corn were heaped high at the window, and, pushing himself down among them until he was hidden to the shoulders, he looked out.

CHAPTER XXI. THE BATTLE OF PIQUA

The window, doubtless intended merely for letting in air, was very small, but Henry had a fine view of a wide open space, evidently the central court of the village. It was grassy and shady, with large oak and beech trees. About fifteen yards from the corncrib burned a fire, meant for light rather than heat, as the night was warm. Around it were gathered about fifty men, of whom six or seven were white, although they were tanned by exposure almost to the darkness of Indians.

Henry knew a number of them well. Upon a slightly raised seat sat Timmendiquas, the famous White Lightning of the Wyandots. He wore only the waist cloth, and the great muscles of his chest and arms were revealed by the firelight. His head was thrown back as if in defiance, and above it rose a single red feather twined in the scalp lock. Just beyond Timmendiquas sat Moluntha, the Shawnee; Captain Pipe and Captain White Eyes, the Delawares; Yellow Panther, the Miami, and Red Eagle, the Shawnee. Beyond them were Simon Girty, Braxton Wyatt, Moses Blackstaffe and the other renegades. There was also a Mohawk chief at the head of a small detachment sent by Thayendanegea. All the chiefs were in war paint tattooed to the last note of Indian art.

Henry knew from the number of chiefs present and the gravity of their faces that this was a council of great importance. He heard at first only the rumble of their voices, but when he had become used to the place, and had listened attentively he was able to discern the words. Timmendiquas, true to his brave and fierce nature, was urging the allied chiefs to stay and fight Clark for Chillicothe. In the East before the battle on the Chemung, he had been in a sense a visitor, and he had deferred to the great Iroquois, Thayendanegea, but here he was first, the natural leader, and he spoke with impassioned fervor. As Henry looked he rose, and swinging a great tomahawk to give emphasis to his words, he said:

"The one who retreats does not find favor with Manitou. It is he who stays and fights. It is true that we were defeated in the battle across from Tuentahahewaghta (the site of Cincinnati), but with great warriors a defeat is merely the beginning of the way that leads to victory in the end. This is the greatest town of our race in all the valley of Ohezuhyeandawa (the Ohio), and shall we give it up, merely because Clark comes against it with a thousand men? Bowman came last year, but you beat him off and killed many of his men. The soldiers of the king have failed us as we feared. The promises of de Peyster and Caldwell have not been kept, but we can win without them!"

He paused and swung the great war tomahawk. The firelight tinted red the glittering blade, and it made a circle of light as he whirled it about his head. A murmur ran around the circle, and swelled into a chorus of approval. These were the words that appealed to the hearts of the warlike tribes, but Simon Girty, crafty, politic and far-seeing, arose.

"Your words are those of a brave man and a great leader, Timmendiquas," he said, speaking in Shawnee, "but there are many things that the chiefs must consider. When the white men are slain, others come from the East to take their places; when our warriors fall their lodges stay empty and we are always fewer than before. You were across the mountains, Timmendiquas, with the chief of the Iroquois, Thayendanegea, and so was my friend who sits here by my side. The Iroquois fought there on the Chemung River, and brave though they were, they could not stand against the Yengees and their cannon. They were scattered and their country was destroyed. It would have been better had they fallen back, fighting wherever they could lay a good ambush.

"Now Kentucky comes against us in great force. It is not such an army as that which Bowman led. They are all trained, even as our own, to the forest and its ways. This army, as it marches, looks before and behind, and to right and to left. It will not stick its head in a trap, and when its cannon thunder against your Chillicothe, smashing down your houses and your lodges, what will you do? Clark, who leads the men from Kentucky, has beaten our allies, the British, at Vincennes and Kaskaskia. Hamilton, the governor at Detroit before de Peyster, was captured by him, and the Yengees held him a prisoner in Virginia. This Clark is cunning like the fox, and has teeth like the wolf. He is the winner of victories, and the men from Kentucky are ready to fight around him to the last."

Another murmur came from the circle and it also indicated approval of Girty's words. Always greatly influenced by oratory, the opinion of the chiefs now swung to the latest speaker. Timmendiquas flashed a look of scorn at Girty and at some of the chiefs near him.

"I know that Girty thinks much and is wise," he said. "He is faithful to us, too, because he dare not go back to his own white people, who would tear him to pieces."

Timmendiquas paused a moment for his taunt to take effect, and looked directly at the renegade. Girty winced, but he had great self-control, and he replied calmly:

"What you say is true, Timmendiquas, and no one knows it better than I. The whites would surely tear me in pieces if they could catch me, because my deeds in behalf of the Indians, whom I have chosen to be my brethren, are known to all men."

Girty had replied well, and the older and more cautious chiefs gave him another murmur of approval. Timmendiquas flashed him a second glance of contempt and hate, but the renegade endured it firmly.

"What, then, do you say for us to do, Girty?" asked the Wyandot chief.

"As the enemy comes near Chillicothe fall back to Piqua. It is only twelve miles away, yet not all the warriors of Piqua are here ready to help us. But they will wait for us if we come to them, and then we shall be in stronger force to fight Clark. And Piqua is better suited to defense than Chillicothe. The enemy cannot come upon the town without receiving from us a hidden fire."

Girty spoke on, and to the listening youth he seemed to speak plausibly. Certainly many of the chiefs thought so, as more than once they nodded and murmured their approval. Timmendiquas replied, and several of the younger chiefs supported him, but Henry believed that the burden of opinion was shifting the other way. The tribes were probably shaken by the defeat at the mouth of the Licking, and the name of Clark was dreaded most of all.

Indians love to talk, and the debate went on for a long time, but at last it was decided, much against the will of Timmendiquas, that if they could not catch Clark in an ambush they would abandon Chillicothe and retreat toward Piqua. The decisive argument was the fact that they could gather at Piqua a much larger force than at Chillicothe. The advance of Clark had been more rapid than was expected. They would not only have all the Piqua men with them, but many more warriors from distant villages who had not yet arrived.

The fire was now permitted to die down, the crowd broke up and the chiefs walked away to their lodgings. Henry left the little place from which he had been peeping, drew himself from the corn and prepared to open the door. Before he had pulled it back more than an inch he stopped and remained perfectly still. Two warriors were standing outside within three feet of him. They were Miamis, and they were talking in low tones which he could not understand. He waited patiently for them to pass on, but presently one of them glanced at the door. He may have been the owner of the crib, and he noticed that the door was shut or nearly shut, when it had been left open. He stepped forward and gave it a push, sending it against the youth who stood on the other side.

The Miami uttered an exclamation, but Henry acted promptly. He did not wish to fire a shot and bring hundreds of warriors down upon himself and his friends, but he sprang out of the door with such violence that he struck the first Miami with his shoulder and knocked him senseless. The second warrior, startled by this terrifying apparition, was about to utter a cry of alarm, but Henry seized him by the throat with both hands, compressed it and threw him from him as far as he could. Then he sprang among the vines, where he was joined by his comrades, and, bending low, they rushed for the corn field and its protection.

The second Miami was the first to recover. He sprang to his feet and opened his mouth to let forth the war cry. It did not come. Instead an acute pain shot along his throat. He did not know how powerful were the hands that had constricted him there. Nevertheless he persisted and at the fourth trial the war cry came, sending its signal of alarm all through the village. Warriors poured out of the dark, and led by the Miamis they dashed through the garden in eager pursuit.

The five were already in the field, running down among the corn rows. Over them waved the highest blades of the corn, still rustling dryly in the wind.

"We are as good runners ez they are," said Shif'less Sol. "An' they can't see us here in the corn, but ain't that a pack o' them on our heels. Listen to that yelp."

The war cry came from hundreds of throats, and behind them they heard the patter of many feet on the soft earth of the field, but they were not in despair. Not far beyond lay the woods, and they had full faith that they would reach their cover in time. The rows of corn guided them in a perfectly straight line, and the number of their pursuers were of no avail. They reached the woods in a few minutes, and, although the warriors then caught dim glimpses of them, and fired a few shots, no bullets struck near, and they were soon hidden among the trees and thickets. But they were too wise to stop merely because they were out of sight. They continued at good speed for a long time on the return journey to Clark.

Henry's comrades asked him no questions, knowing that when they stopped he would tell them everything, unasked. But they saw that he was in an excellent humor, and so they inferred that he brought valuable information from Chillicothe.

"I call it luck," said Shif'less Sol, "that when you have to run for your life you can at the same time run the way you want to go."

"Yes, it's our lucky night," said Henry.

Stopping occasionally to listen for pursuit, they ran about four hours, and then took a long rest by the side of a cool little brook from which they drank deeply. Then Henry told what he had heard.

"It's not their intention to fight at Chillicothe," he said. "Timmendiquas, of course, wanted to make a stand, but Girty and the older chiefs prevented him and decided on Piqua. It's likely, I think, that the authority of White Lightning has been weakened by their defeat at the mouth of the Licking."

Then he related every word that he had been able to catch.

"This is mighty important," said Paul, "and Colonel Clark will surely be glad to hear your news."

After a rest of one hour they pushed on at great speed and they did not stop the next day until they saw Colonel Clark's vanguard. Clark himself was at the front and with him were Boone, Kenton and Thomas. The face of the Colonel became eager when he saw the five emerge from the undergrowth.

"Anything to tell?" he asked briefly.

When Henry related what he had heard from the window of the corncrib, the Colonel uttered short but earnest words of thanks, and put his hand upon the lad's shoulder.

"Once more we are in great debt to you, young sir," he said. "You brought our forces together at the Licking, and now you guide our main campaign. This news that the savages will not defend Chillicothe will give our men great encouragement. Already they will see the enemy fleeing before them."

Colonel Clark was a good prophet. The men cheered when they heard that the Indian force was likely to abandon Chillicothe and they were anxious to press forward at increased speed, but the leader would not permit, nor would he allow them to disarrange their marching order in the slightest. He had never been defeated by the Indians, because he had never given them a chance to trap and surprise him, and he did not mean to do so now.

"Plenty of time, boys—plenty of time," he said, soothingly. "Before we finish this campaign you'll get all the fighting you want. Don't forget that."

That night, which was to be the last before reaching Chillicothe, he doubled the guard. Except the five, who had fully earned the right to sleep, the very best of the scouts and sharpshooters were on watch. Skirmishers were thrown far out among the bushes, and no matter how dark the night might be, no considerable Indian force could ever get near enough for surprise. Boone, Kenton, Thomas and others heard signals, the hoots of owls and the howls of wolves, but they continued their watch undisturbed. So long as a thousand good men were there in the wilderness in a heavy square, bristling with rifles and artillery, they did not care how many signals the savages made to one another.

Morning came, bright and hot. It was the sixth of August, the month when the great heats that sometimes hang over the Ohio River Valley usually reach their uttermost.

This promised to be such a day. After the bright dawn the atmosphere became thick and heavy. Sweat stood on every face. Exertion was an effort. Yet the men felt no abatement of zeal. In three or four hours more, they would reach Chillicothe unless the enemy gave battle first. Nevertheless little was said. The veteran frontiersmen knew the valor of their enemy, and his wonderful skill as a forest fighter. This was no festival to which they were going. Many of them would never return to Kentucky.

They marched about three miles. It was noon now, and the sun from its vantage point in the center of the heavens poured down a flood of burning rays upon them. Colonel Clark, with his usual patience, made the men halt for a few minutes and take food. Their formation had never been broken for a moment. No matter from what side the attack came the whole army could face it inside of two minutes.

The five with Boone, Kenton and Thomas were just ahead of the vanguard, and Colonel Clark who was now on horseback rode up to them.

"How far would you say it is to Chillicothe?" he asked Henry.

"We should be there in an hour."

Colonel Clark looked at his watch.

"One o'clock in the afternoon," he said. "That will give us plenty of time for a battle, if they choose to offer it to us, but it looks as if we would receive no such offer. All that you have said, young sir, is coming to pass."

They were following the broad trail left by the Indian army on its retreat, but not a single warrior appeared to oppose them. There were no sounds in the woods save those made by themselves. No bark of dog or signal of savage came from the village which was now just beyond a thin veil of forest.

Colonel Clark's iron self-control yielded a little. He allowed the men to hasten somewhat, and they came all at once into the corn field which Henry and his friends had entered. They saw, beyond, the walls and roofs of

Chillicothe. Colonel Clark instantly ordered a halt. A field of waving corn could hold a thousand hidden warriors, but Boone, Henry and the others were already in the corn and announced that nobody was there. Then the army with a great shout advanced on the run, the wheels of the cannon grinding down the corn.

In five minutes they were at Chillicothe, and then they saw flames leaping from the highest houses. The town was on fire and all its people had fled. The broad trail, littered with fragments, showed that they had gone towards Piqua. But the army, still kept in battle order, did not follow yet. It watched the burning of Chillicothe and helped it along. The soldiers, with the cannon in the center, were drawn up just on the outside of the town, and, under order of the officers, many of them seized torches and lighted tepee and wigwam. The dry corn in the fields and everything else that would burn was set on fire. What would not burn was trampled to a pulp beneath the feet of men and horses.

Meanwhile the flames spread to every part of the village, united and fused into one vast conflagration. The sight thrilled and awed even Henry, Paul, and the others who had seen similar things in the Iroquois country. But there were not many in that army of white men who felt pity. This was Chillicothe, the greatest of the Western Indian towns. Some of them had been held prisoners there. Others had seen their friends tortured to death at this very place. The wives and children of many had been taken away to Chillicothe and no one had ever seen or heard of them again. Here the great Indian forays started and the very name of Chillicothe was hateful to the white men who had come from beyond the Ohio to destroy it and the warriors who lived there. They were glad to see it burning. They rejoiced when wigwams and Council House crashed down in blazing timbers. It pleased them to see the corn and beans and all the Indian stores destroyed, because then the warriors must hunt in the forest for food, and would have no time to hunt in the Kentucky woods for white scalps.

The five stayed on the side of the town somewhat away from the conflagration. The heat was tremendous. It was a big town and the flames rose in an enormous red tower waving under the wind, and roaring as they ate into fresh food. Light tepees were licked up in an instant. Sparks flew in myriads and red coals were carried by the wind. Orchards and fields were swept away with the rest by the fiery blast. A great pall of ashes began to settle over the country surrounding the town.

"I've never seen anything before on the same scale," said Paul, "and it will certainly be a terrible blow to the Indians."

"But it will not break either their spirit or their power," said Henry. "To do that we've got to beat them in battle, and they'll be waiting for us at Piqua."

The fire burned all the afternoon, but when the twilight came the town was wholly consumed. Not a house or tepee was left standing. Over a wide area there was nothing but a mass of burning coals, which glowed and cast a bright light against the coming dark. Clouds of smoke gathered, but the wind blew them off to the eastward and the site of Chillicothe was yet almost as light as day. On the outward edges of this mass of coals the men cooked their suppers.

The night advanced. Again it was very hot and close, with but little wind stirring. All about them it was still as light as day. For more than a mile the embers, yet red and glowing, lay, and in the orchards tree trunks smoldered casting out alternate flame and smoke. Save for those melancholy ruins everything was swept bare. At the edge of the woods an Indian dog poked his nose at the sky and howled dismally. It affected the nerves of Henry and Paul, who walked across the corn fields and chased him away with stones.

"I'm sorry," said Paul, looking back at the wide range of ruin, "that these things have to be done, even in war."

"So am I, Paul," said Henry, "but think how many bands have gone forth from this place to do destruction upon our people. We have to fight such a foe with the weapons that we can use."

They did not stay long at the edge of the woods, knowing that Indian sharpshooters might be lurking there, but went back to their friends and the army. The men having eaten amply and having looked upon the destruction of Chillicothe were in joyous mood, but their leader did not permit them to relax caution a particle. Too often the borderers, thinking victory won, permitted themselves to fall into disorder, when their victory was turned into defeat by the shrewd foe. Now the men spread their blankets far enough away from the woods to be safe from sharpshooters hidden there. The guard was made of unusual strength, and gunners were always at the cannon in case of a night attack.

The five were not on duty that night, in view of what they had done already, and they spread their blankets near the edge of the corn field, across which they had run at such good speed. The coals still glowed. Far off they heard the howling of wolves.

"Is there any danger of a night attack?" asked Paul.

"I don't think so," replied Henry. "Of course the Indians have spies in the woods and they will report that it is impossible to surprise us."

It was a long time before Henry could go to sleep. The great events through which he had been crowded upon his mind. He had seen the Iroquois win and then he had seen them destroyed. The western tribes had won victories too and now a great commander was striking at their very heart. Their capital lay in ruins, and, unless Timmendiquas could defeat the white men in battle, when they marched on Piqua, then the western tribes also would receive a blow from which they could never recover. Despite himself, he was sorry for Timmendiquas. Nevertheless he was loyal in every fiber to his own people.

The howling of the wolves came nearer. They would find little for their teeth among these ruins, but they knew somehow that destruction had been done, and instinct called them to the place. It was an unpleasant sound and it made Henry shiver a little. It made him think of what was to come for the Indians. Even savages, in the fierce winters of the North, would suffer for lost Chillicothe. Wooden houses and lodges could not be replaced in a day. While the great beds of coals were still glowing he fell asleep, but he was up with the others at dawn.

It was one of the most somber days that Henry had ever seen. The heat, close, heavy and thick, like a mist, endured, but the sun did not shine. The whole circle of the sky was covered with gray clouds. Everything was sullen and ugly. Some timbers in the vast ruin of Chillicothe yet burned and showed red edges, but it would be impossible to conceive of a more desolate heap. Piles of ashes and dead coals were everywhere. The fires that were soon lighted served the double purpose of cooking and of making cheer. But while they ate, the skies grew perceptibly darker. No ray of the sun broke anywhere through the steel-colored atmosphere.

Colonel Clark became anxious. He had intended to start early for Piqua, but storms in the woods must be reckoned with, as one reckons with an enemy. He delayed and sent forward a scouting party of fifteen men under Boone, who, of course, included the five in the fifteen. Boone, owing to his captivity among the Indians, knew something about the country, and he led them straight toward Piqua. As Piqua and Chillicothe, two large Indian towns, were only twelve miles apart, there was an Indian road or broad trail between them, and they followed it for some distance.

The road showed the haste with which the inhabitants of Chillicothe had fled. Here and there were feathers which had fallen from the scalp locks of the men or the braids of the women. Now they came to a gourd, or a rude iron skillet bought at a British post.

After four or five miles Boone deemed it wiser to turn into the thick woods. The Indians with such a formidable force only twelve miles away would certainly have out sentries and skirmishers, and his cautious movement was just in time, as less than three hundred yards further on they were fired upon from the bushes. They replied with a few shots, but it was not Boone's intention to precipitate a real skirmish. He merely wished to know if the Indians were on guard, and, in a few minutes, he drew off his men and retired.

They were followed by derisive yells which said plainly enough that, in the opinion of the Indians, they were afraid. Some of the younger men wanted to go back, but Boone remained firm in purpose and tranquil in mind.

"Let 'em yell at us all they want to," he said in his peculiarly gentle voice. "We can stand it, and we'll see how they can stand the battle to-day or to-morrow when the army comes up."

They were back at the camp about two hours after noon, and reported that the Indians had sentinels and skirmishers on the way to Piqua. But Clark thought they could be brushed aside, and as the clouds had lightened somewhat, they started at four o'clock. Good humor was restored at once to the men. They were moving now and in a few hours they might bring the campaign to a head, if the Indians only stood. Some believed that they would not stand even at Piqua.

The order of march that had been preserved all the way from the mouth of the Licking remained unbroken. Colonel Clark led, Colonel Logan commanded the rear guard, the soldiers were in four lines, ready to wheel in any direction, and the cannon were in the center. They followed the Indian road, but ahead of all were Henry and his comrades, always searching the woods for a sight of some flitting Indian figure. Henry did not believe there would be any skirmishes before they reached Piqua, but he was not among those who did not think the Indians would make a stand there. He knew Timmendiquas too well. The Wyandot leader had yielded, when the majority of the chiefs favored Piqua instead of Chillicothe, but now he would certainly hold them to the agreement. The trail led on unceasingly, but the brightening of the skies was deceptive. The clouds soon closed in again, heavier and blacker than ever. Although it was only mid-afternoon it became almost as dark as night. Then the lightning began to play in swift flashes, so bright that the men were dazzled, and the thunder cracked and roared in tremendous volume.

"If I live through the campaign," said Paul, "I shall certainly remember it by this storm, if by nothing else."

The thunder was so great that he was compelled fairly to shriek out his words. Save when the lightning flashed he could see only the head of the army. Presently both thunder and lightning ceased, the wind set up a vast moaning and then the rain came. Colonel Clark and his officers were already at work, instructing the men to put up as many tents as possible, and, under any circumstances to keep their arms and powder dry. Here again discipline and experience told, as the orders were obeyed to the last detail.

The five sheltered themselves as well as they could under the trees and they felt that Paul's words about the storm were true. Certainly they could never forget it. The bottom had dropped out of the clouds, and all the rain, stowed for months, was pouring down in a few hours. They soon abandoned any attempt to protect themselves, and devoted all their care to their ammunition.

For more than two hours the rain fell in seemingly solid sheets. Then it ceased abruptly, and the late afternoon sun broke out, tingeing the forest with gold. Yet every bush and tree still ran water. Pools and often little lakes stood in the valleys. The earth was soaked deep. The precious ammunition and most of the stores were dry, but every man whether in a tent or not was wet to the skin.

It was obvious that they could not go on and attack Piqua at once, as they would arrive far in the night, and the most skilled of the borderers were ordered to try their cunning at lighting fires. Patience and persistence had their reward. The bark was stripped from fallen trees, and dry splinters were cut from it. When these were lighted with flint and steel the problem was solved. Heat triumphed over wet, and soon twenty glorious fires were blazing in the forest. The men were allowed to dry their clothes in relays, each relay baring itself and holding its clothes before the fire until the last touch of damp was gone.

All the time a vigilant watch was kept in the woods. Indians might attack when their enemy was depressed by storm and wet, but nothing to disturb the peace of the drying army occurred. Wolves howled again far away but they were still prowling among the ruins of Chillicothe, seeking unburned portions of venison or other meat. After the storm the close oppressive heat disappeared. A fresh and cool wind blew. Out came the

481

moon and stars and they shone in a silky blue. The leaves and grass began to dry. The five lay down within range of the fires. Shif'less Sol made himself very comfortable on his blanket.

"I don't want anybody to bother me now," he said, "'cause I'm goin' to sleep all through the night. No Injuns will be roun' here disturbin' me, an' I don't want no white man to try it either."

The shiftless one knew what he was talking about, as there was no alarm in the night and early the next morning the army began its march again. But Henry was sure there would be a fierce fight at Piqua.

They still followed the Indian road, and now went a little faster, although never breaking their old formation for a single instant. Yet every heart throbbed. They would soon be at Piqua, face to face with the allied forces led by their best chiefs. It was likely that their fire would burst from their undergrowth at any moment. But the scouts still reported nothing. Most of the morning was gone and they came to a broad but shallow stream. It was Mad River, and Piqua was not more than a mile up its stream.

"Surely they will fight us here," was the thought of Clark. He halted his army and the scouts crossed the stream at many points. They beat up the woods and found no enemy, although Piqua was so near. Then the order to march was given again, and the whole army plunged into the stream. The heavy wheels of the cannon grated on the bottom, but they were still kept in the very center of the force. Clark never abated his resolve to protect these guns at all hazards from capture. But the cannon passed safely, and then came Logan with the rear guard. It, too, crossed and the commander drew a mighty breath of relief.

"How far away is Piqua now?" he asked of a man who had once been a prisoner there.

"Not more than a mile," he replied. "Soon you can see the smoke from it rising above the trees."

"Ah, I see it now. Then they have not set their town on fire, and they are not running away. We shall have a battle."

The news was quickly passed throughout the army, and eagerness began to show. The men wanted to be led on at once. It was nearly noon, and grass and foliage were dry again. There was not a cloud in the heavens, and the sun was a golden circle in a solid blue dome.

"Finest day for a fight I ever saw," said Tom Ross.

Paul laughed but it was a nervous laugh, coming from high tension. He was not afraid, but he knew they were going into battle. They passed into the forest and beyond in an open space they saw the houses, wigwams and tepees of Piqua scattered along Mad River. Just before them was a sort of prairie covered with weeds as high as a man's head. Henry threw himself flat upon the ground and peered in among the weeds.

"Back! back!" he cried in a tremendous voice. "The warriors are here!"

His sharp eyes had caught glimpses of hundreds of forms lying among the weeds. The whole army recoiled, and then a sheet of flame burst from the field, followed by the fierce war whoop of the Indians. The bullets sung in swarms like bees over his head, but knowing that all would fire at once after the Indian custom, he leaped to his feet, and ran to the shelter of the forest before they could reload and deliver the second volley.

"Here's a tree, Henry," said Shif'less Sol; "a lot of officers wanted it, but I've saved it for you."

But it was good-natured banter. There was not a sign of panic in the army. The men at once formed themselves into line of battle, according to their instructions, and opened a terrible fire upon the weeds in which the warriors lay concealed. Hundreds of bullets swept every part of the cover, and then the cannon sent in round shot and grape, cutting down weeds and warriors together, and driving the savage force in flight to shelter.

But Timmendiquas, who had chosen the position, had reckoned well. The field was not only covered with high weeds, but the portion near the town was intersected with deep gullies. The warriors fell back in good order and sought refuge in these gullies which would hold hundreds. Here bullets, cannon balls and grape shot alike passed over their heads, and suffering but little loss, they sent back a storm of their own bullets.

The army advanced to the edge of the woods, and was ready to charge across them but Colonel Clark hesitated. Before they could reach the gullies his men might be cut in pieces by a protected foe. The five, Boone, and many other of the best frontiersmen had already sought the shelter of stones or little hillocks, and were firing at every head that appeared above the edge of the gullies. Before the smoke became too dense Henry saw beyond the gullies that Piqua was a large town, larger than they had supposed. It would perhaps be impossible for the army to envelop it. In fact, it was built in the French-Canadian style and ran three miles up and down Mad River.

Henry heard the fierce war whoop rising again and again above the firing which was now an unbroken crash. He also heard another and shriller note, and he knew it was the shouting that came from the vast swarm of squaws and children in Piqua. The yell of the Indians also took on a triumphant tone. It seemed that the beginning of the battle was in their front, and the ambushed warriors in the gullies were strengthened by other forces on their right and left that crept forward and opened a heavy fire from cover. Along a range of more than a mile there was a steady flash of firing, and it seemed impossible for any force to advance into it and live.

Fortunate, again fortunate, and thrice fortunate were the frontiersmen who were veterans, also! The cannon were sheltered in the wood and the men were made to lie down. The great guns still thundered across the field, but the riflemen held their fire, while the Indian shout of triumph swelled higher and higher. In this terrible moment when many another commander would have lost his head, the staunch heart of Clark never faltered. He hastily called his leading officers and scouts, and while the battle flamed before them, he gave his orders behind a screen of bushes. He bade Colonel Logan, assisted by Colonel Floyd and Colonel Harrod, to take four hundred men, circle to the east of the town as quickly as he could, and attack with all his might. After giving a little time for the circuit, Clark, with the artillery, would march straight across the field in the face of the main Indian force. He gave Henry and his comrades their choice as to which body with which they would march.

"We go with you and the artillery across the field," replied Henry at once.

"I thought so," said Clark with a smile.

The five lay down at the edge of the forest. Full of experience, they knew that it was not worth while now to be sending bullets toward the gullies. They knew, also, that the charge in which they were about to take part would offer as much danger as anything they had ever met. It is likely that every one of them thought of Wareville, and their kin, but they said nothing.

A few men in front maintained the fire in order to keep the Indians across the field busy, but the great majority, lying quiet, waited to hear the rifles of Logan and the four hundred. Meanwhile this flanking force emerged from the woods, and having now become the left wing of the American army, sought to rush the town. It was immediately assailed by a powerful Indian force, and a furious battle followed. One side of it was exposed to another field from which Indians sent in bullets in showers. Nevertheless the men, encouraged by Logan, Floyd, and Harrod, drove straight toward Piqua. The Indians in front of them were led by Girty,

Braxton Wyatt, Blackstaffe and Moluntha, the Shawnee, and they fought alike from open and covert, offering the most desperate resistance. The four hundred were compelled now and then to yield a few yards, but always they gained it back, and more. Slowly the town came nearer, and now Logan's men heard to their right a welcome crash that told them Clark was advancing.

As soon as Clark heard the sound of Logan's battle, he gave the signal to his men to attack. In front of them, much of the smoke had lifted, and they could see the field now, with most of its weeds cut away. Beyond was a strip of woods, and on the other side of the woods but already visible through the bushes, lay the long town.

"Now for it!" cried Henry to his comrades who were close about him.

"Forward!" shouted Clark, and with a tremendous shout the men charged into the field, the artillery drawn as always in the center and blazing the way. From the gullies came the answering fire in shower after shower of bullets. Henry heard them thudding upon human bodies, and he heard the low cries of men as they fell, but the smoke and the odor of gunpowder were in his nostrils, and his head was hot. Everything was red before him, and he had a furious desire to reach the gullies and rush in among the Indians. It was only two hundred yards across the field, but already the smoke was gathering in dense clouds, split apart now and then by the discharges of the cannon. Behind them the charging men left a trail of dead and dying. Henry took a hasty look to see if his comrades were still upon their feet. Two were on one side of him and two on the other. There was a patch of red on Jim Hart's shoulder and another on Tom Ross's, but they did not seem to amount to anything.

Half way across the field the column staggered for a moment under the heavy fire which never slackened for an instant, but it recovered itself quickly and went on. The smoke lifted and Henry saw Timmendiquas at the edge of the nearest gully, a splendid figure stalking up and down, obviously giving orders. He had expected to find him there. He knew that wherever the battle was thickest Timmendiquas would be. Then the smoke drifted down again, and his head grew hotter than ever. The firing increased in rapidity and volume, both before them and on their left. The crash of the second battle moved on with them. Even in those rushing moments Henry knew that the left flank under Logan was forcing its way forward, and his heart gave a leap of joy. If the two commands ever united in the village they might crush everything. So eager did he become that he began to shout: "On! On!" without knowing it.

They were nearing the gullies now and once more Henry saw Timmendiquas who seemed to be shouting to his men. It was a fleeting glimpse but so vivid and intense that Henry never forgot it. The great Wyandot chief was a very war god. His eyes flamed and fiercely brandishing his great tomahawk, he shouted to the warriors to stand.

The left flank under Logan and the larger force under Clark were now almost in touch. The American line of battle was a mile long and everywhere they were faced by a foe superior in numbers. Despite the cannon, always terrifying to them, the Indians stood firm, and behind them thousands of women and children urged them on to the conflict. They knew, too, the greatness of the crisis. The war that they had carried so often to the white settlements in Kentucky was now brought to them. One of their great towns, Chillicothe, was already destroyed. Should Piqua, the other, share the same fate? Timmendiquas, the greatest of the leaders, the bravest of men said no, and they sought to equal his courage. No Indian chief that day shirked anything; yet the white foe always advanced, and the boom of the cannon sounded in their ears like the crack of doom. Some of the balls now passed over the fields through the strip of woods and smashed into the houses of the town. The shouting of the women became shriller.

Nearer and nearer came the white enemy. The great barrels and wheels of the cannon loomed terribly through the smoke. The blasts of fire from their muzzles were like strokes of lightning. The Indians in the first gully began to leap out and dart back. Henry saw the dusky figures giving way and he shouted, still unconsciously,—"On! On! They're running! They're running!" Others had seen the same movement, and a roar of triumph passed up and down the white line, thinned now by the rifle fire, but no longer in doubt of victory.

They rushed upon the gullies, they cleaned out the first and second and third and all; they helped the cannon across, and now the contact between the two forces wasperfect. They bore down upon the town, but they encountered a new obstacle. Rallied by Timmendiquas and others the warriors filled the strip of woods between the fields and Piqua. They lay down in the undergrowth, they hid behind every tree, and shouting their war cries, they refused to give another step. But Clark, the astute, would not permit any diminution in the zeal of his men, now carried to the highest pitch by seeming victory. He knew the danger of allowing the fire of battle to grow cold.

He ordered a rifle fire of unparalleled rapidity to be poured into the wood, and then the cannon were loaded and discharged at the same spot as fast as possible. Not an Indian could show his head. Boughs and twigs rattled down upon them. Saplings cut through at the base by cannon shot fell with a crash. Although Timmendiquas, Moluntha, Captain Pipe and others raged up and down, the warriors began to lose spirit. It was soon told among them that Girty and all the other renegades had ceased fighting and had retired to the town. Girty was a white man but he was wise; he was faithful to the Indians; he had proved it many times, and if he gave up the battle it must be lost. Never had the Indians fought better than they had fought that day but it seemed to them that the face of Manitou was turned from them.

While they doubted, while the moment of gloom was present, Clark with his whole united force rushed into the wood, drove every warrior before him, followed them into Piqua, and the Indian host was beaten.

CHAPTER XXII. THE LAST STAND

Every one of the five felt an immense exhilaration as they drove the Indians back into the town. They were not cruel. They did not wish to exult over a defeated enemy, but they had witnessed the terrible suffering of the border, and they knew from the testimony of their own eyes what awful cruelties a savage enemy in triumph could inflict. Now Clark and the Kentuckians had struck directly at the heart of the Indian power in the West. Chillicothe was destroyed and Piqua was taken. The arms and ammunition sent to them by the power, seated in Canada, had not availed them.

Henry did not know until much later that it was the cunning and crafty Girty who had given up first. He had suddenly announced to those near him that Piqua could not be defended against the American army. Then he had precipitately retreated to the other side of the town followed by Braxton Wyatt, Blackstaffe and all the renegades. The Indians were shaken by this retreat because they had great confidence in Girty. The Delawares gave up, then the Ottawas and Illinois, the Wyandots, Shawnees, Miamis and the little detachment of Mohawks, as usual, stood to the bitter last. At the very edge of the village the great war chiefs, Yellow Panther, the Miami, and Red Eagle, the Shawnee, fell almost side by side, and went to the happy hunting grounds together. Moluntha, the other famous Shawnee chief, received two wounds, but lived to secure a momentary revenge at the great Indian victory of the Blue Licks, two years later. Timmendiquas would have died in the defense, but a half dozen of his faithful warriors fairly dragged him beyond the range of the Kentucky rifles.

Yet Timmendiquas, although the Kentuckians were in the town, did not cease to fight. He and a hundred of the warriors threw themselves into the strongest of the houses, those built of timber, and opened a dangerous fire from doors and windows. The woodsmen were ordered to charge and to take every house by assault, no matter what the loss, but Clark, always resourceful, sternly ordered a halt.

"You forget our cannon," he said. "Logan, do you, Floyd and Harrod keep the riflemen back, and we'll drive the enemy out of these houses without losing a single man on our side."

"Thar speaks wisdom," said Shif'less Sol to the other. "Now in all the excitement I had clean forgot that we could blow them houses to pieces, but the Colonel didn't forget it."

"No, he didn't," replied Henry. "Stand back and we'll see the fun. A lot of destruction will be done soon."

The twilight had not yet come, although the sun was slowly dimming in the East. A great cloud of smoke from the firing hung over Piqua and the bordering fields that had witnessed so fierce a combat. The smoke and the burned gunpowder made a bitter odor. Flashes of firing from the strong houses, and from ambushed Indians here and there pierced the smoke. Then came a tremendous report and a twelve-pound cannon ball smashed through a wooden house. Another and another and it was demolished. The defenders fled for their lives. Every other house that could be used for shelter was served in the same way. The last ambushed foe was swept from his covert, and when the twilight fell Piqua, throughout its whole length of three miles along Mad River, was held by the Kentuckians.

The Indian women and children had fled already to the forest, and there they were slowly followed by the warriors, their hearts filled with rage and despair. Beaten on ground of their own choosing, and not even able to bring away their dead, they saw their power crumbling. Fierce words passed between Timmendiquas and Simon Girty. The Wyandot chieftain upbraided the renegade. He charged him with giving up too soon, but Girty, suave and diplomatic, said, after his first wrath was over, that he had not yielded until it was obvious that they were beaten. Instead of a fruitless defense it was better to save their warriors for another campaign. They could yet regain all that they had lost. There was some truth in Girty's words. Blue Lick and St. Clair's terrible defeat were yet to come, but Clark's blow had destroyed the very nerve-center of the Indian confederacy. The Kentuckians had shown that not only could they fight successfully on the defensive, but they could also cross the Ohio and shatter the Indian power on its own chosen ground. Neither the valor of the warriors, nor the great aid that they received from their white allies could save them from ultimate defeat.

Henry, Paul, the officers, and many others felt these things as the night came down, and as they roamed through Piqua, now deserted by the enemy. Paul and Jim Hart went in one direction to look at the big Council House, but Henry, the shiftless one, and Tom Ross remained with Colonel Clark.

"We've won a great victory, though we've lost many good men," said the Colonel, "and now we must consign Piqua to the fate that Chillicothe has just suffered. It's a pity, but if we leave this nest, the hornets will be back in it as soon as we leave it, snug and warm, and with a convenient base for raiding across the Ohio."

"We'll have to give it to the flames," said Colonel Logan.

The other Colonels nodded. First they gathered up all the dead, whether red or white and buried them. At Henry's instance the two old chiefs, Yellow Panther, the Miami, and Red Eagle, the Shawnee, were laid side by side in the same grave. Then he fixed a board at their head upon which he cut this inscription:

In this grave LieYellow Panther, the Miami,And Red Eagle, the Shawnee;They were great Chiefs,And died fightingFor Their People.

Not a white man disturbed the epitaph. But as soon as the last of the fallen were buried, and the soldiers had eaten and refreshed themselves, the torch was set to Piqua, even as it had been set to Chillicothe. In an hour the town was a huge mass of flames, three miles long, and lighting up the neighboring forest for many miles. The Indian refugees, thousands of them, from both towns saw it, and they knew to the full how terrible was the blow that had been inflicted upon them. Timmendiquas sought to rally the warriors for a daring attack upon an enemy who, flushed with victory, might not be very cautious, but they would not make the attempt. Timmendiquas then saw that it would take time to restore their shaken courage and he desisted.

Henry, Shif'less Sol and Tom Ross watched the fire for a long time, while the soldiers destroyed all the orchards, gardens and crops. They saw the flames reach their highest until the country around them was as bright as day, and then they saw them sink until nothing was left but darkness made luminous by the coals. The great village was gone.

"I think we'd better get Paul and Jim and go to sleep," said Henry.

"So do I," said Shif'less Sol, and they looked around for the two. But they were not found easily.

"Ought to have stayed with us," said Tom Ross.

"An' they'd have saved a lazy man a lot of trouble, lookin' through this big place fur 'em," said Shif'less Sol.

Tom and Jim became still harder to find. The three hunted everywhere. They hunted an hour. They hunted two hours, and there was not a sign of their two comrades. They asked many about them and nobody could tell a word. It was nearly midnight when they stopped and looked at one another in dismay.

"They are not in the camp—that is sure," said Henry.

"And they've got too much sense to go out in the woods," said Sol.

"Which means that they've been took," said Tom Ross.

Tom's words carried conviction, sudden and appalling, to all three. Paul and Jim Hart, going about the burning town, had been seized by some lurking party and carried off, or—they would not admit to themselves the dreadful alternative—but they hoped they had been merely taken away, which they deemed likely, as hostages would be of great value to the Indians now. The three sat down on a log at the northern edge of the town. They saw little now but the river, and the clouds of smoke rising from it.

"We'll never desert Paul and Jim," said Shif'less Sol. "Now what is the fust thing fur us to do?"

"We've got to find this trail, and the trail of those who took them," replied Henry. "The army, of course, cannot follow all through the northern woods in order to rescue two persons, and it's not fitted for such a task anyhow. We three will do it, won't we?"

"Ez shore ez the sun rises an' sets," said Shif'less Sol.

"I reckon we will," said Tom Ross.

"And we must start upon the road this minute," said Henry. "Come, we'll see Colonel Clark and tell him that we have to go."

They found the commander about a mile away, encamped as near the burned town as the heat would allow. Logan, Floyd, Harrod, Boone, Thomas, and others were with him. They were talking together earnestly, but when Henry approached and saluted, Colonel Clark greeted him pleasantly.

"Why, it's young Mr. Ware!" he exclaimed, "the lad to whom we owe so much. And I see two of your comrades with you. Where are the other two?"

"That is why we have come, Colonel Clark," Henry replied. "We do not know where the other two are, but we fear that they have been taken by the retreating Indians. The campaign, I suppose, is over. We wish therefore to resign from the army, follow and rescue our comrades if we can."

Colonel Clark sprang to his feet.

"Two of your friends taken, and we to desert you after what you have done for us!" he exclaimed. "That cannot be. The army must march to their rescue!"

The other officers raised their voices in affirmation. Henry and his friends bowed. All three were affected deeply. But Henry said:

"Colonel Clark, you can't know how much we thank you for such an offer, but we three must go alone. If the army followed into the woods, and pressed the Indians closely, they would put their prisoners to death the very first thing. They always do it. In a case like this, only silence and speed can succeed. We must follow alone."

Daniel Boone spoke up in his gentle, but singularly impressive tones.

"The boy is right, Colonel Clark," he said. "If the job can be done it is these three alone who can do it."

"I suppose you are right," said Colonel Clark regretfully, "but it does hurt me to see you leave us, unhelped. When do you wish to go?"

"Now," replied Henry.

Colonel Clark held out his hand. There were actual tears in his eyes. He shook hands with the three, one by one, and all the others did the same. Boone and Kenton went with them a little distance into the woods.

"Now, lads," said Boone, "don't ever forget to be careful. You got to get your friends back by stealth and cunnin'. Keep out of a fight unless the time comes when everything depends on it. Then if you've got to fight, fight with all your might."

The three thanked him. Last hand-clasps were given and then Boone and Kenton heard for a brief second or two only faint and dying footfalls in the forest. They went back quietly to camp ready for the return with the army to Kentucky, but the three were already deep in the forest, and far beyond the area of light.

"I'm thinkin'," said Sol, "that the Indians hev crossed the river. It's likely that they'd want to keep the water between themselves an' us."

"Looks like good argument to me," said Tom Ross.

Henry being of the same opinion, they decided to cross Mad River also, and approach as nearly as they could to the chief body of the Indians. It was probable that many bands were wandering about and they would be in great danger from them, but it was their business to follow the advice of Daniel Boone and avoid them. They exercised now their greatest skill and patience. At a distance of eight or ten miles from Piqua they found two Indian camps, but, after a thorough examination, they became satisfied that Paul and Jim were not in either of them. Just before daylight they found a valley in which a great mass of warriors, women and children were huddled. Evidently this was the chief point of retreat, and creeping as near as they could, they saw Timmendiquas, Moluntha, Girty and Braxton Wyatt passing about the camp.

The three lay close in the bushes and they observed Wyatt intently. Two or three times he passed between them and a camp fire, and they studied his face.

"Doesn't look like that of one who has lost," whispered Henry.

"No, it don't," said Shif'less Sol. "O' course he don't mourn much about the Indians, an' I reckon he's got somethin' to make him happy."

"And what he's got is Paul an' Jim," said Tom Ross.

"No doubt you're right," said Henry. "I think it likely that they were trapped by a band under Braxton Wyatt, and that they are his especial prisoners. Look! There they are now, by the tree!"

Some shifting of the Indians gave a distant view of the two prisoners bound securely and leaning against a tree. Wyatt passed by, and looked upon them with an air of possession. They were sure now that it was he who had taken them, and, drawing further back into the forest, they waited patiently for the next move in the great game of life and death.

Indian scouts several times passed within a few yards of them, but they knew that the minds of these men were upon the army not upon them. They were scouting to see whether Clark would follow them into the forest and, when they became certain about noon that he would not do so, they gathered their own numbers together and started northward to the villages of their brethren.

Henry, Shif'less Sol and Tom Ross followed closely enough to know what was going on, but not so closely that they would walk into a trap. Fortunately the country was heavily wooded with evergreen and there was still an abundance of leaves on the trees. Fortified by such a long experience as theirs it was not difficult to keep under cover, and when the tribes went into camp that night, the three pursuers were not a quarter of a mile away.

The three hung around the camp half the night, but they saw no chance to rescue their comrades. The crowd about them was too great. They followed in the same way the next day, and continued thus a week. Henry began to feel sure now that Paul and Jim were in no immediate danger of death, and he ascribed the fact to the influence of Timmendiquas. Even if they were Wyatt's own prisoners, he would not dare to go directly contrary to the wishes of the great Wyandot chieftain.

Now a change occurred, the motive of which baffled the three for a while. Timmendiquas, Braxton Wyatt, about twenty warriors, and the two prisoners, leaving the main body of the Indians, turned toward the Northwest, following a course which would lead them around the lower curve of Lake Michigan. The three sitting among the bushes debated it a long time.

"I think," said Henry, "that Timmendiquas is making a last desperate effort to lead a great force against us. He is going into the far Northwest to see if he can bring down the Sacs and Foxes, and even the Ojibways, Chippewas, and Sioux to help against us."

"Then why do they take Paul and Jim along?" asked the shiftless one.

"As trophies to impress the distant Indians or maybe as a sacrifice. Braxton Wyatt goes, too, because they are his prisoners."

"It may be so," said Tom Ross. "The more I think about it, the more I think you're right. Anyhow it'll give us a better chance to get at Jim and Paul."

"But we've got to play the Injuns' own game," said Shif'less Sol. "We must follow them a long time without lettin' them know we're on their track. Then they'll begin to go easy and won't keep much guard."

Shif'less Sol was undoubtedly right, and for many days they followed this band deep into the Northwestern woods. August passed, September came. Whenever the wind blew, the dead leaves fell fast, and there was a crisp touch in the air. The nights became so cool that they were compelled to sleep between the two blankets that everyone carried at his back. They were thoroughly convinced now that Timmendiquas was in search of help in the far Northwest, and that Paul and Jim would be offered as trophies or bribes. Several times the Indians stopped at small villages, and, after a brief and hospitable stay, passed on. It became evident, too, that neither Timmendiquas nor Wyatt thought any longer of possible pursuit. Both knew how the five would stand by one another but it had been so long since the battle at Piqua, and they had traveled so many hundreds of miles from the burned town that pursuit now seemed out of the question. So they traveled at ease, through an extremely fertile and beautiful region, onward and onward until they began to near the shores of the greatest of all lakes, Superior.

The cold in the air increased but the three pursuers did not mind it. They were inured to every hardship of the wilderness, and the colder it grew the more pleasant was the fresh air to the lungs. They felt strong enough for any task. Now that the guard was relaxed somewhat they hoped for a chance to save Paul and Jim, but none came. Three separate nights they went near enough to see them by the camp fire, but they could not approach any closer. Henry surmised that they would soon reach a large village of the Chippewas, and then their chances would decrease again. The attempt must be made soon.

It was now late October and all the forests were dyed the varied and beautiful colors of an American autumn. The camp of Timmendiquas was pitched on a beautiful stream that ran a few miles further on into an equally beautiful little lake. Food had become scarce and that morning he had sent most of the warriors on a hunting expedition. He sat with Braxton Wyatt and only two warriors by the side of the small camp fire. The two prisoners were there also, their arms bound, but not in a manner to hurt. Motives of policy had compelled Timmendiquas and Wyatt to be seeming friends, but the heart of the great chief was full of bitterness. He had not wanted to bring Wyatt with him and yet it had been necessary to do so. Wyatt had taken the two prisoners who were intended as offerings to the Northwestern tribes, and, under tribal law, they belonged to him, until they were willingly given to others. His presence would also convince the Ojibways, Chippewas and others that white men, too, were on their side. Yet nothing could make Timmendiquas like Wyatt. It seemed unnatural to him for a man to fight against his own race, and he knew the young renegade to be treacherous and cruel.

They were sitting in silence. Wyatt spoke once or twice to Timmendiquas, but the chieftain made no reply. Timmendiquas stared into the fire, and planned how he would bring down the Northwestern tribes. The two warriors were as still as statues. Paul and Long Jim were leaning against the fallen tree, and Braxton Wyatt's eyes wandered over them. He sneered at Paul, but the boy took no notice. Wyatt had often tried to annoy the two prisoners on the march, but he was afraid to go very far because of Timmendiquas. Yet he remembered with great satisfaction how he had trapped them that night after the battle of Piqua, when they wandered too near the edge of the forest.

His eyes passed from them, wandering around the circle, and came back to them again. Did he see Long Jim start? Did he see a flash of intelligence appear in the eyes of the hunter? Could he have heard something? He looked again. Long Jim Hart's face expressed nothing. Braxton Wyatt felt that he was growing nervous, and the next instant he sprang to his feet with a shout of alarm. Three figures sprang from the undergrowth and, with leveled weapons, commanded the four unbound men who sat by the fire to throw up their hands. Up went the hands of the four, and Timmendiquas smiled sadly.

"Your patience has been greater than ours," he said, "and the reward that you are about to take belongs to you."

"We could fire upon you, Timmendiquas," said Henry, "and for the moment the advantage is ours, but even if we should win the victory, in the end some of us would fall. Those who are bound, and for whom we have come, would surely be slain. Then, I say to you, mighty chief, give us our friends, promise that you will forbid pursuit, and we go."

Timmendiquas stood up and his face bore a singular look of dignity and kindness.

"You speak fairly," he said, "and I wish, Ware, that we could be friends in peace. Cut the bonds of the prisoners."

He spoke to the two warriors, but at that moment some demon leaped up in the soul of Braxton Wyatt. "I will do it," he said. But his rage and disappointment were so great that they nearly blinded him. He snatched out his knife and rushed at Paul Cotter, but the blade was turned toward the bound boy's throat, and not toward the thongs.

Henry uttered a cry and sprang forward, but the great war tomahawk of Timmendiquas left his hand, and flew through the air so swiftly that the eye saw only a flash. The glittering edge struck the head of Braxton Wyatt, and he fell, cloven to the chin. He was dead before he touched the ground.

"We keep faith," said Timmendiquas.

The five bade the great Wyandot chieftain farewell and ten minutes later were on their return journey. They knew that they were safe from any pursuit by the band of Timmendiquas. They returned to Wareville and they fought always with distinction throughout the border wars. They were at the Blue Licks that dreadful day when Timmendiquas and Moluntha, Caldwell and Girty, who finally came, with the Wyandots and Shawnees destroyed more than half of the Kentucky force. Strangely enough they went with Clark from the mouth of the Licking just two years after the first expedition, again with a thousand riflemen against Piqua which had been rebuilt, and they destroyed it, as before, in revenge for Blue Licks.

Years later they were in the terrible slaughter of St. Clair's army, and they were with Wayne when he inflicted the crushing and final defeat upon the allied tribes at the Fallen Timbers. After the peace all the five, every one of whom lived to a very great age, became the fast friends of Timmendiquas, famous war chief of the Wyandots, the nation that knew no fear.

THE END

Made in the USA
Monee, IL
22 October 2020